The Electrician

From Altar Boy to Addict:
Growing Up Irish Catholic
in 1970s Blue-Collar Boston

By **Andrew Winslow**
and Jeff Muir

"The Electrician"

ISBN (Print): 978-1-54394-913-1
ISBN (eBook): 978-1-54394-468-6

"We say to all men in all professions,
and all walks of life, from the statesman to him who wields a hoe:
If you would know your universe of motion, your relation to it
and your control over it, first thoroughly know just one cycle of an
electric current and the still fulcrum from which it has its being."

- Walter Russell, "Atomic Suicide"

"Get the Lead Out!"

I heard my father bark these words from the second-floor window. A snowstorm had just done its business all over my suburban Boston neighborhood. This was Massachusetts and we were Catholics. That being the case, the drill was to suit up, show up, and shovel. Despite the fatherly barking and the shoveling, I enjoyed the New England winters and the snow because it also meant snow forts, snowmen, and flexible fliers. I looked up and down my street and saw families gathered with their shovels in their driveways. However, it was very rare to see my hard-working father doing any yard work.

"That's why you'se have children," was his explanation.

My father drank this hot black stuff called "coffee." I would watch him while he drank it and noticed that shortly after a few gulps, he underwent a change. His appearance became simultaneously more rigid and more hyperbolic. Post-coffee, sitting at the table or on the couch, his legs seemed to become autonomous, tapping, twitching and crossing.

It was winter, so today we were outside, assigned to remove the snow. If it had been autumn, the chore would have been leaves. The routine was largely the same. My father would be in the house drinking his hot black liquid, making periodic visits to different windows on the second floor, barking out orders.

"Get the lead out!"

"Look alive!"

"Take it a level at a time, you'se will eventually see the driveway."

"Use that shovel like it's your spoon!"

He had very large arms. No matter how cold it was, he would hang one out the window while he gave orders. The black cat tattoo on his arm seemed to be glad it was inside with him. He wasn't yelling the orders at me, for the most part, as I was a wee lad and had the smallest shovel. It was plastic. His attention was typically focused on my brother Jeff. I shared a bunk-bed with Jeff.

During one of my father's periodic visits to the window, he noticed something about Jeff that caused his complexion to redden. I took a quick glance up to the window, to the man with the tattoo of big black cat, a ruddy, intense coffee-induced visage framed by gray hair. He and my brother Jeff began to discuss shoveling. Apparently, Jeff wasn't "getting the lead out." My father mentioned that and gave him one last warning.

"Don't make me tell you'se again: get the frigging lead out of your ass!"

My father was a devout Catholic and wouldn't swear. Instead, he used poetic fake-curses like "frigging," "flipping," and "effing."

I asked myself, "What is this dangerous 'lead' substance?" Did it travel through the snow and up a leg, clinging to a person's ass if they weren't moving fast enough? Or, did lead form on the ass while one was sleeping? I didn't know the answer, but it worried me. Apparently, however, only by moving aggressively could this lead be eradicated. I moved my little plastic shovel as fast as possible, in mortal fear of the lead. As time wore on that morning, Jeff seemed to slow down and began to complain about his situation. Obviously, these were symptoms of lead on his ass.

A few minutes later, the second-floor window of my sister's room flew open. My father yelled out the name of the God we worshipped on Sundays: "Jesus H. Christ!" Proclaiming this incantation must have given him even more energy than the black beverage. His face rapidly progressed from a shade of blush pink to rose and then scarlet and was now a crimson red. While this demi-God named "Father" was hanging out of a window in suburban Boston, the real God was hanging on the side of a cloud, no doubt looking down on his children, concerned about the state of lead on their asses.

The window slammed shut and he disappeared. Seconds later he reappeared in front of me, much like Jesus H. Christ probably could. He was running directly at Jeff, who he summarily tackled, rolling in the snow. My father brushed himself off and proceeded to demonstrate the proper way to remove snow. He then pointed down at my brother and said, "Now, start shoveling!"

Apparently, the tackle worked, removing the lead-like substance from my brother's ass, for he was now shoveling rapidly. The neighbors across the street and to either side of us watched passively and then went back to their own shoveling. I wondered why they didn't use the same "yell and tackle" method to increase the rate and volume of snow removal for their households.

After that day, my brother's name morphed from "Jeff" to "Lead," which it has remained ever since.

Lead finished removing his allotted portion of snow a few hours later and went his separate way. I was left alone with my plastic shovel, trying to finish the little path I had been assigned to clear. I now had a new fear: the fear of lead (not my brother, but the substance that had been attached to his ass, slowing him down, and requiring a swift blind-side tackle to remove).

Did this lead slither up from the ground, through the snow, and then up one's snowsuit, clinging to one's buttocks? I knew that once it attached itself to the ass it slowed one's production down and could even result in getting fired from a job later in life ... but I couldn't figure out how it worked. Nonetheless, it made an impression on me and I vowed then and there to keep busy the rest of my life.

As my father was Jesus H. Christ's demi-God representative in our home, responsible for dispensing wisdom to me, I learned the important lessons in life from his proclamations and anecdotes, which I took as Gospel. He dispensed one of these to me one day which instilled in me another fear regarding a mortal danger that loomed under the snow. This one was potentially worse than lead.

A child will see defects in people and wonder, occasionally even innocently asking about them. One day I asked my father why his jaw was crooked. He was the type of man who usually just gave one-word answers to even the most complex questions. However, on that day, he went into slightly more detail to answer my query.

"I'ze was sledding somewhere as a kid in Boston, on a toboggan with my friends..." his story began.

Unbeknownst to them, a group of "hooligans" had gathered at the bottom of a hill. When he and his friends arrived at the bottom of the hill, they spotted the hooligans and immediately ran away in terror. My father couldn't run fast enough, so the hooligans caught him and gave him a severe beating, breaking his jaw, which never went back in place.

I shivered in terror. I had never seen a hooligan or even heard of such a species. I imagined 4-foot-tall furry creatures, traveling silently and invisibly in packs under the snow. Maybe these wild hooligans were the parents of the cute, small furry creatures that lived in tiny cages in my pre-school? Perhaps they were so fierce and angry because their children had been captured and forced to live in these small metal boxes, fated to suffer lifetimes of poking, prodding, and torment at the hands of young humans?

Would I be singled out by a wild band of these angry beasts, in retribution for the torment I meted out daily to their caged children at school? Was it my fate to be captured and beaten to the point of a broken jaw, as my father had been? The thought haunted me.

From then on, I kept a wary eye out in every direction as I attended to my shoveling duties throughout the long New England winters. With every gust of wind, my head darted around, looking for lurking hooligans, or a lump of snow heading my way that contained the lead trying to attach itself to my ass. At the sound of every falling icicle, I froze, peering around defensively for the packs of angry, furry hooligan beasties (which I assumed were related to the flying monkeys from Oz). Surely, these dangers were hiding in the trees or in the shrubs, ready to pounce.

When I finished clearing my assigned portion of snow, my father said, "Good job, Joe." Naming conventions in Catholic Boston could be complex. In reality, my name was Andrew; I was named after a priest, but my father called me Joe. I liked to be called Joe. The nice guy that paved our driveway was named Joe. My father always said he was a hard worker and a "good egg." Joe was better than my given name because there was a girl named Andrea in my class at school and I feared that the common association would precipitate a case of the cooties.

With my father's approval in-hand, I was finally free to meet up with friends and play … in the snow. We gathered our flexible fliers and drank our own dark, warm beverage, a sweet concoction prepared in a faraway land by a happy looking lady named Swiss Miss.

No hooligans or lead got to me that afternoon. But from then on, I slept a little uneasy each night, worried about the lead and its tendency to cling to people and slow them down; anxious about the hooligans and their desire to break my jaw; scared of their kin the flying monkeys. As long as I kept busy and moved quickly, I should be fine. I woke up the next morning, seemingly free from a broken jaw, a leaden ass, or monkey bites and went off to worship the God whose name my father yelled out the window: Jesus H. Christ.

GONE

My grandmother lived with us. When I wasn't in that program where you are dropped off, played chase, drew with crayons, drank Zarex, and then teased furry live animals, I was with my grandmother. She always joined me, G.I. Joe and my three-legged dog in watching Sesame Street. I don't know if she liked the program as much as I did, but I let her in on everything that was going on down there with the kids and monsters.

Sometimes she would wince over in pain. I would hold her hand, and she would say, "It's fine, honey." After Sesame Street, my grandmother would lie down to rest. Once each day's Sesame Street ended, a guy named Jack LaLane would come on, and my mother would follow whatever he did. He jumped, she jumped. He bent, she bent. Jack looked pretty happy. Obviously, he had no lead on his ass.

My grandmother went to stay in the hospital to have something "removed." After they removed it, she was left with a big scar on her stomach. From then on, I saw my grandmother less and less. She told me that she was watching Sesame Street on her TV at the hospital. I told her I would put my G.I. Joe doll in her spot on the couch until she came home. My parents saw me do this and told me that she would be out of the hospital and back with us soon. But the next day, when I put G.I. Joe on the couch in her spot and turned on the television, they sat down and told me she was gone. I was sad because she was my Sesame Street-watching partner. I still had G.I. Joe, but it wasn't the same. It made me sad that Grandmother was simply "gone."

BEE HIVES

Having successfully graduated from "pre-school," I was enrolled in a new school called "kindergarten." Here, too, there were opportunities to touch fury animals, play with crayons, and drink Zarex - the sickly-sweet beverage in a plastic bottle with a picture of a horse with the big grin. Only now, there was even *more* fun. Kindergarten would bring in "fun people" to do presentations on various topics, such as a guy named Aesop and his fables. The people putting on these presentations seemed very happy. They didn't move very fast, but it seemed to me they had no lead on their asses.

We also had puppet shows about positive things, like the golden goose and the message of trying not to rush a good thing. I now had to take a bus to school, but even that was pretty enjoyable. It was on the bus that I met the boys who would become my lifelong friends. There was Blumpkin with the red afro. There was Scott, who later was called Sully. There was Rich, who became known as Cashews. And there was Jeff.

They all seemed to possess the same energy and inquisitiveness that I did. Sometimes after school, we would visit each other's homes. Sometimes all of us would meet up together at one home. Sometimes we would all meet up at birthdays. We shared the same curiosity and fearlessness. No tree went unclimbed, no rock unflipped.

We had a collective fascination with snakes and would spend hours upon hours searching for them, grabbing them up, handling them with ease. Every day seemed to be about seeing and learning new things. Even school was about discovery. There were no grades or exams to worry about. Life was exploring and learning in both the great outdoors and the great indoors.

Summer was spent at a place called Hale Reservation, a park and nature reserve right in town. There we encountered all sorts of wildlife. The water snakes were a little more intimidating and larger than land snakes but they could still be caught. Many people looked at me with fear in their eyes when I would return from the "non-swimming area" swamps with a large black snake wrapped around my arm. But I was experienced in how to handle them and knew how to avoid getting bit.

The women at Hale Reservation had these funny hair designs that my mother called "beehives." They did indeed resemble the beehives we found draped from trees in the woods. Finding a beehive was a special accomplishment. A beehive was a rare find which conferred a temporary status of distinction upon the finder. Immediately upon discovery, each of us buzzed with excitement, knowing what was to come next: five boys flinging rocks skyward in a frenzied blur. Inevitably, a rock would find it's mark, damaging or knocking the beehive to the ground. At that point, five boys were running and screaming both in terror and sheer joy. The slowest guy, by virtue of being the slowest guy, inevitably and involuntarily performed an act of sacrifice on behalf of the rest of us, getting swarmed and stung mercilessly.

A lot of these women would go into the water but only up to their necks, thus keeping their beehive dry. They would wade around for a bit and then come out to towel off. I noticed that for some reason when a beehive woman exited the water, a lot of the men standing on dry land would turn and look. It must have been the hairdo and their own experiences with bees as kids, I surmised.

An observant boy, I noticed that one woman dried off, and then tried to apply lotion. Only, she couldn't reach one area on her back. Being a kind lad, I ran over and asked if I could help. She said, "Why, sure, young man, but first wash the sand off your hands." I ran into the water and then dried my hands off with her towel. Then she showed me the lotion-applying procedure: put a little in the palm, rub palms together, and then apply to the back. She laid down and I smeared the lotion. I rubbed on the spots that were dry. Her head was turned, and when I was finished, she said, "Good job, cutie pie."

Being a generous tyke, I did this as often as I could. I liked the compliments. To be even more helpful, sometimes I would dry off the beehive ladies before applying their lotion. After helping many beehive ladies, my mother told me that I should be polite and at least ask first. While applying lotion, I noticed that beehive ladies didn't have hair on their legs like men.

My father, having a rare day off, drove me to Hale Reservation. We didn't get there early because he stopped first at a place called Kentucky-something. A famous colonel apparently owned it and his happy face was on the box of chicken that my father acquired from one of this colonel's employees. That was a great day.

We ate the chicken, which was like nothing I had ever dreamed of before. Then I recognized some beehives coming out of the water, so I started performing my job. Sometimes, in appreciation for my efforts and deft expertise with the towel and lotion, I would get tipped with a slice of gum or some other snack. A lot of the beehive ladies knew me by then.

I would finish one beehive and then trot back to grab another bite of chicken. My father looked at me kind of funny; not angry, but quizically. Then he saw a woman coming out of the water and said, "What about this broad?" I said, "That is so-and-so and she is in college." I then went down to her, dried her off, and applied her lotion. I went back to the red and white box and grabbed another piece of chicken. My father then pointed to another beehive and said, "Well, what about 'dat number 'dere?" Some beehives were "broads," apparently, because of the width of their hair; some were "numbers," based on the height of the hair; some were "birds," presumably due to their ability to house certain avian species in their locks. I was beginning to understand the taxonomy.

One of the beehives even talked to my dad, remarking, "Your kid is a real professional, does he take after his father?" He had the ability to talk with food in his mouth and answered, a ball of coleslaw in his cheek, "Eh, yeah, I'ze taughts him everything." My father seemed very proud of me that day, much like the day I shoveled a small path through the snow in our walkway with my plastic shovel. I felt relieved, as this was an indication that there was no lead on my ass. When the day ended, my father rubbed my head and said, "Good job! Joe the Oiler."

Such was my life that summer after kindergarten: three square meals a day (some of which came in the red and white boxes from that nice colonel), almost everything seemed new and exciting, and people liked me. I checked the couch each day to see if my grandmother had returned from being "gone." But she never did reappear. Something called "first grade" was coming up, and my mother said we needed to get special "supplies" for it.

NOSEBLEEDS

First grade was very different from kindergarten. It was in a much bigger building with many more children and adults. To my surprise, it wasn't just first grade, but grades first through sixth. It was intimidating because not only were there more kids, but most of the other kids were a lot bigger than me.

The routine in my class seemed a lot more strict than kindergarten. We had to sit at "assigned desks" rather than sharing round tables. There was a chalkboard, and I began to hear the words, "pay attention," quite frequently. Sadly, this new first grade was also devoid of the school-supplied grape drink with the laughing horse. It seemed like play and fun were now very strictly limited to a thing called "recess."

It was at recess that I was finally able to meet again with my friends. After a momentary burst of exhilaration, we realized that recess was not all freedom and frivolity: for, it seemed that certain areas of the playground didn't belong to us and were strictly the domain of older kids. We were told menacingly by these older kids, "this is our spot." So, we had to vacate.

That first recess was a few moments of exhilaration, then our spirits falling upon learning that we were boys without a country in this territorially demarcated playground. We then discovered that, in the bat of an eye, recess was over. Even worse, recess was followed by a long afternoon of something called, "paying attention." Worse yet, at the end of the day, we were given something called "assignments." And I had to do these assignments as soon as I got home before I could go out and meet up with my friends.

As kindergarten progressed, I saw my friend Jeff less and less. He would be gone for days at a time and then reappear. He returned once, and his hair was gone. He said the doctors told him it would grow back. Something about his hair being gone meant he would randomly get nosebleeds. I would run to the nearest desk or office or bathroom to get him a tissue. Everyone assured me that, because they were praying, Jeff would get better soon, and everything would be okay. God would take care of him – because they were all praying for him.

Amazingly, Jeff never complained about having to go away for days at a time, the loss of his hair or his nose bleeds. Because Jeff was away more and more, I began to spend more time with the kid named Richie Cash. My father called him "Cashews" and soon so did everybody else. My father would complain about the time of day Cashews typically showed up. "Don't you'se friend Cashews knows what freakin' time it is?" he would ask. But my father liked Cashews.

My crew of fellow kindergarteners rapidly evolved from a state of awe and wonder to one of mastery and command of our surroundings, especially the suburban woods that lay adjacent to our neighborhood. Fall meant raking massive piles of leaves and jumping into them from tree branches. It meant gathering acorns in buckets, organizing opposing acorn armies, and doing battle with the small, hard, pointy nuts.

Autumn was fun, but Winter seemed to be the most entertaining season. We all eagerly welcomed the first snowfall. We would catch the snowflakes with our tongues. Sometimes the flakes would fall very slowly and were easy to catch. We could even see the design of the flakes. I figured that Jesus H. Christ made the flakes just for us, so he could see us laughing in wonder as they fell to the ground and accumulated. The buildup of snow meant sledding, snow angels, snowmen, snow caves, snowball fights – and of course the happy lady with pigtails named "Swiss Miss" and her sweet, warm concoction.

As first grade progressed, it became more and more common to see Cashews at the back door behind my parents' room. He was usually holding something in his hand or throwing something in the air, depending on the season. Winter meant sledding or hockey, with taped sticks and hand-me-down, ill-fitting skates. As far as I was concerned, the earlier the better. We could beat the highway department plowing our street and for a couple hours have the best sledding paths imaginable – and of course the best stories for the others who came out after the plow.

"You should have seen it: we were doing sixty!"

Next came the older kids, and things invariably got a bit rougher, as they challenged us to go down the most dangerous paths. Since avoiding the "chicken" label was utterly critical, we always did, and many cracked teeth and split eyebrows resulted. We were collectively becoming both more creative and bolder as we grew older and gained confidence in our surroundings. Rumor spread that if water was applied to the sledding paths it would freeze and increase exponentially the speed of our sleds.

The best sledding path in the neighborhood was on our street, but it never lasted long. We had to take full advantage before the plows came and decimated it. Occasionally an especially bad snowstorm meant that the man who plowed was too busy to make it to our street. But, even when he did plow, he left us with sharp and steep banks all through the cul-de-sac. These snowbanks reached several feet high and were packed hard, perfect for playing king of the hill, making snow forts, and constructing elaborate tunnels.

Best of all, when it snowed enough, school would be called off. Lead and I would sit in our bunks and listen to the radio for the closure announcements, which were given in alphabetical order. We lived in Westwood, so it was excruciating waiting through the entire alphabet to find out if we would have a glorious snow day off from school. When the radio did finally announce, "No school in Westwood," we cheered wildly. School was interesting, but play was better: no assignments, no sitting at a rigid desk, no "paying attention."

The day after a snow day, we usually did have school, but still enjoyed the snow on the playground even though we were restricted to our own small section. Our school was called Pond Plane. Supposedly airplanes used to land there. Later it was called Sheehan School, re-named after a police officer that was shot and killed in our town. It seemed odd to me that an act of violence would result in a school-naming because the teachers always told us how wrong violence was. For now, we enjoyed ourselves and the blessings and adventures brought about by New England's four seasons.

Getting ready for school was now mostly up to me. I had to wait in line for the one shower. There was another one, but it was strictly off limits and reserved for guests only. Sometimes I would watch my father get ready. He had to do a great deal more than me to prepare for his day. He had to "shave," which involved applying some sort of foam to his face, then scraping it off, then slapping on some smelly oily stuff called Old Spice. Then he would rub some other smelly thing under his arms.

Next, he put a cream called "VO5" on his head. It was a special cream just for electricians. Once applied to his hair and after a few florid strokes with his comb, my father's messy mane would suddenly have a design. Finally, he drank this stuff called Maalox, "For me ulcer," he would say.

When I was younger, hearing my father proclaim, "Oooh, me ulcer is back!" was a daily ritual that always startled me. I would look nervously out the window for what I imagined was a dog named Ulcer, returning to my father after what must have been a long adventure away from him. Maalox was a drink, and I wasn't sure what it had to do with getting the long-lost dog Ulcer to come home.

Then I figured it out. It didn't have anything to do with a lost dog. Apparently, my father had these tiny bird-like creatures that lived in his stomach. Maybe one of them was named Ulcer? The tiny birds survived by drinking this milkish liquid called Maalox. Cashews' father had the same condition, but he drank it by the spoon. My father just unscrewed the cap and swilled it from the bottle. I thought about ulcers and wondered whether they stayed in my father's stomach during the days, only to run out of his mouth at night to play, like the raccoons. I never saw a raccoon or an ulcer but I would hear about the overnight destruction they caused to our trash most mornings.

First grade ended. Summer came. One family on my street left, and a new family moved in. The new family had six children and another on the way. They were from Dorchester and, like us, they were Catholic. That summer I started hearing more strange expressions from my father, especially shouted at my older brother, who was in his teens now and seemed to be getting into more trouble.

Apparently, the lead on Lead's ass was becoming a serious condition. One night he came home late. My father ran downstairs in his underwear, grasping a belt, yelling, "Your goose is cooked, pal!" There followed a banging of doors and raised voices bordering on screaming. "You basstud," my father proclaimed. Then he returned upstairs.

Though I had never witnessed it, I intuitively understood the goose-cooking process. One reaches a certain age and is given a goose. The goose is kept at a semi-secret location. If you acted up or misbehaved or broke your curfew or had alcohol on your breath (as my brother had), the goose you were given was cooked as a ritual sacrifice to Jesus H. Christ. It would be a big ceremony. A man with a giant Mayoral top hat and fancy beard would stand at a podium and bang a hammer. He announced the crime in front of the town, stating, "Breaking the curfew and drinking alcohol," before slamming the mallet down on the podium. He would then declare, "Your goose is cooked, son."

The goose would be lead out from its holding cell by another man wearing a monocle, top hat and tuxedo. The goose would, of course, look nervously left and right, knowing he was going to be put into a large silver boiling pot.

The Lincoln-looking guy would then grab the goose, look at the accused with shameful disdain, and finally, ceremoniously, drop the goose into the boiling water. The townfolk would look at the accused in disgust before walking away, heads shaking in silent condemnation and scorn. That night, my father had decided that my brother's goose must be cooked for the honor of the family and in hopes that Jesus H. Christ would make my brother behave better in the future. So, tomorrow my father would have to tell the mayor to start planning for my brother's goose cooking.

My brother seemed to get in a lot of trouble that summer. Sometimes it wasn't "goose is cooked" trouble. Sometimes it was, "Your ass is in a sling!" trouble. This involved running downstairs with a belt, yelling, doors slamming before the sling of shame was finally attached to my brother's ass. The ass was the animal we learned about in school, the one that carried large quantities of supplies. Now my brother's goose was cooked *and* his ass was going to be in a sling. That couldn't be good.

There were other boys in the neighborhood that were either in their early or late teens. The Bullis brothers were a trio of teenagers. That summer their parents had gone away and they, too, seemed to be acting up or having fun, I wasn't sure which. Sometimes they were having fun and the police would have to put a stop to it. For instance, one time, one of them was caught riding naked up and down the street on a motorcycle – without a helmet.

On another occasion, an ambulance screamed onto our street, siren wailing and lights swirling. My father walked outside and asked a police officer what was going on. My father was very loud; although I was in bed, I heard him announce, "One of 'dem crazy Bullis brothers was on angel dust and tried flying off the roof!"

It seemed odd to me that they would try to practice flying at night. Was it the naked motorcycle rider again? Did he use two trash can lids as wings, running from one end of the roof to the next, flapping as hard as he could? And, what was this "angel dust?" Did it help with flight? Did you sprinkle the man trying to fly with this dust, and then start the trash can lid flapping procedures?

It all seemed strange and suspicious to me. I did like the Bullis brothers. But they were intimidating, with their shaggy hair, tattered denim jackets, and cigarettes. On the other hand, I respected that they seemed to enjoy themselves and weren't afraid to conquer their fears of flight or breaking records such as "the fastest man to ride naked on a motorcycle."

My senses seemed to be growing more acute. I was on the bottom bunk, below Jeff. There were noises and announcements coming from the rest of the house. My father seemed to step into the foyer no matter what time of night and make proclamations. Most of the time no one was there to hear him. He always seemed to have the same group of people after him.

"They tried to take me to the cleaners!" Or, "They tried to pull the wool over my eyes!" Or, "They left me with my ass on the line!"

On the Soul Train to the Creature Double Feature

Summer ended, and we were now in second grade. It became immediately apparent that second grade was going to be even more regimented than first grade. Crayons, paint brushes, and putting on smocks was out. We were no longer encouraged to "pay attention," we were now commanded to "pay attention," – and with greater frequency. Even worse, second grade also apparently required us to "sit still," and this was also a command, not a suggestion. Saturdays were still devoted to the cleanup of what New England delivered in the form of snow, leaves, or overgrown grass.

If for some reason there was no yard work, or I finished early, I immediately would head over to Cashews' house. I usually had Cashews tell his mother to call my mother for the invite. That way, I could get over there early and spend the entire day.

Cashews house was immaculate and specific procedures were required upon entering. First, you crossed into an area called "the breezeway," a small room between the garage and the actual entrance to the rest of the house. In the breezeway, you placed your shoes carefully adjacent to the other shoes in a neat row in a special shoe area. There would be an old newspaper placed on the floor with the shoes arranged on top. After the shoe deposit, I would knock on the door to be greeted by his mother. She was very kind and would bend down to meet me saying, "Head on downstairs, dear."

Cashews' father was different than my father. They were both intense, but my father was more shambolic, whereas Cashews' dad was neurotically particular about everything. He always seemed to be hurriedly walking from one room to another, checking things. To him, Cashews was "Dick." He would yell, "Dick, your friend is here!"

"Dick's downstairs!" he would snap at me. I would head downstairs to the basement, which itself was somewhat exotic.

My house was a split level, so we didn't have a basement and therefore I assumed they were somehow special. After all, we could close the door to the basement and be in our own world. It had its own unique temperature, atmosphere, and smell – not unpleasant, just distinctive. Cashews typically had everything set up by the time I got there: the TV was already tuned to its proper station for *Creature Double Feature* and the Ouija board was set up on the table.

Creature Double Feature was amazing because it was always something different. But, generally, no matter the film being shown, something would happen to the leading man. He might turn into a wolf-like creature and become all hairy when the moon was full and terrorize the town. He might be overtaken by a curse or spell and have to battle his way back to righteousness. Or, he might find himself in mysterious circumstances and have to struggle for the cause of all that is good and right.

The second "double" feature generally involved large monsters terrorizing cities that were far away from Boston. So, at least, we were safe for the time being. These creatures came from the faraway hills or the depths of some distant ocean and were therefore not imminent threats.

One especially horrifying creature rose out of some Oriental ocean. His name was Godzilla. As time went by, Saturday after Saturday, feature after feature, in Cashews' basement, Godzilla seemed to evolve and take on more subtle attributes. Godzilla even had a son at one point. In that *Creature Double Feature*, Godzilla taught his son how to go into battle and use his special talent for exhaling hot gas. In fact, eventually, Godzilla evolved from a purely destructive beast intent on tearing apart Tokyo to a demi-God with a conscience intent on defending this far-off city from other dangerous creatures – like giant moths, monstrous birds, and even man's own foibles.

While we were rapt with terror and excitement watching *Creature Double Feature*, Cashews' father would invariably fast-walk past us to the far corner of the basement, where his bar was located. Cashews' father would hurry by us, get to his area of the basement, and start making noise with ice cubes, mixing, and shaking. He would take a few sips of the drink he made, and then walk back by us. He would stop to look at the program we were watching, and then back at us, and then yell to his wife in a thick Boston accent: "Lou, they-uh watching mon-stahs again!" Then he would shake his head derisively and say, "This generation!" and walk upstairs, drink in hand. We would hear him upstairs, pacing back and forth in his slippers on the squeaky floor.

Cashews and I kept an intense focus on the far-off city getting ruined by a giant bird. We knew Godzilla would eventually come to the assistance of this city, but only after two very large animals fought each other in all the glory of 1960's stop-motion or costume-and-balsawood-city practical effects. It seemed that about every 15 minutes Cashews' father would make his way downstairs to "the bah."

Cashews' father seemed to become more intense each time he walked by. His complexion changed gradually from white to pink to an even more reddish purple. In my mind, I could picture his father wrestling with one of these monsters, if any of them ever dared to invade Boston. He would be called to assist the city's defenses by the police chief. Cashews' father would fast-walk out of the house with his glass in hand, ice cubes clinking, set his drink down on the curb, and start wrestling with the creature that was raising havoc. The final scene would be Mr. Cash removing one of his slippers and beating to a gory death the giant animal that was terrorizing our city.

Cashews' father made another drink and paused to glance at the TV. Cashews said, "Dad, that is Godzilla." His father rolled his eyes, walked up the stairs and yelled, "Lou the mon-stahs name is Gawd-ziller!" Followed by, "What the hell is it with this generation?"

No matter how loud we had the TV, we could always hear him upstairs, as his paces progressively became quicker. Next, we would hear him opening and shutting cabinets. He might sit down for a moment, but then the pacing would start again, followed by the cabinet door testing. Cashews seemed to be used to the routine, but it made me uneasy. Every time he came downstairs his complexion was more purple. His nose was almost magenta. His eyes became more and more like that of our hero, Godzilla … glowing. But maybe even more intense.

Creature Double Feature wrapped up, which meant we were now ready for *Soul Train*. Cashews and I would dance as soon as the songs came on, each introduced by the cool man with the deep voice and flashy suits. None of our fathers wore suits like that. The songs came on one after another and we danced, imitating the audience members with their smooth moves and funky coolness. Invariably, Cashews' father would make another trip past us on his way to the bar.

He would stop, mockingly glance at the TV, and then look at us contemptuously as we danced. He would make his special adult drink at the bar, then look once more at the TV before turning away and yelling, "Lou! Now they're watching some urban dance show!" Eventually, however, he would leave us to return up the steps to attend to a critical mission involving alphabetizing soup cans or triple-checking the torque on the cabinet door hinges.

We went back to dancing, thoroughly enjoying ourselves – but we had even more fun planned. We were soon about to know our future through the magic of the Ouija board. *Soul Train* ended, the host crooning to us his smooth farewell. We sat at the Ouija board. By simply placing our fingertips on a plastic device, we acquired the power necessary to discover our future, before it even happened. The box was opened up and we shared a moment of quiet solemnity and mild, excited dread. We asked the Universe the names of our future wives, whether or not we would be rich someday, and if we had a career in professional athletics.

Via the Ouija board, the Universe gave us answers in the affirmative to those important questions, though we quickly forgot the names of our future wives due to the thrilling knowledge that we would in a matter of mere years be wealthy professional athletes. The future looked bright for both Cashews and me. It would be smooth sailing from then out, according to the Universe.

As we geared up for round two, in which we would ask the Universe what kinds of luxury cars we would own and which professional sports teams we would play for, Cashews' father did his purple-faced quick-walking past us toward the bar. He paused. This was the first time he saw us with the Ouija board. His face grew even more purple and his yellow eyes bulged. His neck quivered. Cashews' father stammered, "Jesus H. Christ!"

"Lou!" he screamed, looking at us with a combination of shock and disgust. "Now they're practicing witchcraft!"

We stopped, frozen in place. Perhaps this was the Universe telling us we had gained enough knowledge about our future for one day. Cashews' father stomped over to his "adult drinks area" and began to mix another beverage. Mrs. Cashews cheerfully called down to us from the kitchen.

"Boys, time for lunch!"

She was a fabulous cook and put great care into her work. It being the 1970s in a working-class home, mothers of the era were required by both loving, maternal duty and necessity to master the art of actual cooking. Microwaves were non-existent in our homes, microwave food had not yet been invented, and TV dinners were reserved for "special" occasions. Mrs. Cashews meticulously laid everything out on the dining room table. To me, it appeared as if we would be having the President (or perhaps one of the Goose Cooking officials in their top hats) over for lunch. Mr. Cashews was assigned a seat at one end of the table while Mrs. Cashews presided at the other end; Dick and I sat opposite each other in the middle.

We were told to wait for Mr. Cashews to take his seat and bless the meal. He came up from downstairs with a look of churning rage on his face. After all, we were just found to have been practicing witchcraft. He sat down and looked at us both with fiery, disdainful eyes. He then said a quick blessing for the food we were about to eat, did the sign of the cross and, with a thick Boston accent concluded, "... in the name of the fah-thah, dah sun, and dah holy spare-et." Amen. He gave us one more look of pitiful disgust before we all started to eat our soups in advance of the main course.

Cashews and I would simply put the spoon in the soup, raise the soup-filled spoon to our lips, and empty the contents into our mouth ... down the hatch. Cashews' father, on the other hand, would stare intently into the bowl, as if trying to catch a fish with his eyes, then submerge the spoon into the bowl, extracting a thin layer of soup with it.

He would proceed to blow intently on the small amount of soup in his spoon, making a windy "whoooooo" sound. He would then empty the contents of the spoon into his mouth and conclude with a tiny "aaargh" sound. It was almost performance art. After about three cycles repeated in the same manner, Cashews and I began to look at each other. We simultaneously began to clench our stomachs in an effort to prevent a stray giggle from creeping out.

Mr. Cashews began to notice our smirks and the little snickers that escaped us. He surmised that we might, in fact, be laughing at him. His complexion began to change again, from a red hue to purple and back to red again. He continued to eat his soup in the same manner, but now when his neck went down to inspect the contents of his spoon he shot me and Cashews a side-eye.

Each time he dipped his spoon to the bowl, lifted the spoon to lips, blew on it with his windy "whooooooooo," and finished with his satisfied "aaargh," he shot us that threatening stare. By this time, we were unable to contain ourselves. Laughter spilled forth from us in waves. Mr. Cashews had enough. He pulled his napkin from his shirt dramatically, threw it on the table, rose and hurriedly placed the soup in the kitchen sink.

As he was leaving the kitchen he turned in the door frame and spun around. With an illuminated orchid-violet complexion, he pointed and said, "Here I am going to work everyday building ray-dah, to keep us safe from another Jap attack, and these kids watch mon-stahs, dance like Sammy Davis Jr., and practice witchcraft!"

He stormed off and we then heard a door slam. Mrs. Cashews said we shouldn't have laughed. But she then served us the main course. I noticed for the first time that day how much more frequently and in how many more situations we were being told that our laughter was inappropriate.

I gained a new fear that day. What was a Jap attack? What was a Jap? When would the attack happen? I imagined that Japs were sharp objects falling from the sky. I pictured Cashews' father in a one-seater airplane, holding his drink with ice in it to the side, fending off these Japs with his newly engineered ray-dah laser beam. Despite Mr. Cashews' inevitable technical prowess and determined defense of both us and the city, I nonetheless was frightened. Japs and hooligans?

The world was turning out to be a scary, un-fun place for a first-grader. Before embarking on my solitary walk home, I stood rail-still in Cashews' front yard. I looked up in the sky for any sign of falling sharp objects. I peered deep into the woods and behind all visible shrubs for 3-foot tall furry hooligans. Seeing there was no sign of either, I ran back home as fast as I could.

Once safely home, I settled in and was treated to what was a common meal for us on a Saturday night: hot dogs, baked beans, and brown bread. I especially liked the brown bread because it came in a can. It was moist and sweet, and my mother slathered butter on it. I finished supper, still worried about the dangers lurking all around us outside. I crept into bed wondering when and where this "Jap attack" would happen. I hoped that Mr. Cashews' lay-sah equipped ray-dah gun would detect and shoot these sharp objects out of space before they landed, impaling us, causing damage to our homes, perhaps even destroying our cans of brown bread in the process.

Razzles & Airplanes

I awoke to a Sunday morning and was happy to look outside and find an absence of destruction and mayhem. No sharp objects were sticking out of any roofs or freshly mowed lawns. My relief was quickly interrupted by the frenzied commotion which was normal for a Sunday in our home. After getting ready, we were all off to pile into the Country Squire station wagon and head to something called "mass."

We were Catholic. I didn't know exactly what that meant, but mentally I had it in the category of merely being Irish and from Boston. It was just something we were, something that made us favored and special. Being Catholic meant we worshiped Jesus H. Christ. This was the name of the God that both my father and Cashews' father would invoke when they needed an extra boost of energy or parental perception. Soon after the energy from Jesus H. Christ entered our fathers, their faces would become flush, and they became faster on their feet.

We were usually late for church, and my mother would be the one making us late. Her beehive hairdo always required extensive preparation and maintenance between the bathroom mirror and the Country Squire passenger seat. She typically had to literally trot from the house to the waiting automobile. My father would be fuming in the Country Squire, beet red, already having announced in his Boston accent that it was "hap passed the ow-wah!" He then violently jiggered the gear shift while stomping on a pedal. The tires spun. I rolled off the seat in the very back of the Country Squire.

On most Sundays, while driving to mass, my father would get into a coughing routine. Ultimately, he would eject something from his coughing fit. He would then say, "that's asbestos!" If I was lucky, this asbestos or ulcer that was ejected from my father's lungs would land on the side window. It looked like a thing called a slug we would find in the woods, yellow and brown, leaving a sticky trail. I wondered if maybe it was a baby or even adult ulcer that no longer wanted to live in my father's stomach. Perhaps he was giving it some kind of blessing before it left by saying, "that's asbestos." That must mean, "that's enough of you." We skidded into St. Margaret Mary's Catholic church, coming to an abrupt stop. I slid off the seat again. We hurried into mass to kneel, sit, stand, and maybe shake some hands.

The image of our God was very large and on the back of the altar. He had big brown eyes that always seemed to be looking at me, waiting for me to step out of line. If the sun hit this stained-glass figure of our God, his face would light up, like our parents when they were mad. If you were old enough, you were allowed to get a flat round biscuit. The largest biscuit was held up by the priest, and he would say, "this is the body of Christ." Apparently, the priest was allowed to shave off pieces of Jesus once a week, so we could all eat them.

I couldn't look at the image of our God that day, for I had been accused of witchcraft the day before. Surely the stained-glass image would shake his head and I, reading his lips, would understand him saying some things my father said, such as: "your goose is cooked," "your ass is in a sling," "your ass is mine," "you village idiot," or even "willy lump lump," or "Gunga Din."

I kept my mind focused on what was ahead after mass. We always visited a town called Norwood. It was pronounced "nah-wood." Unlike our town, Norwood seemed to have everything. Once in Norwood, we would be treated to Razzles, donuts, and airplanes. For the time being, that thought kept my mind calm. I looked down to the carpeted floor, never looking up at the image of our God. I didn't want my goose to be cooked and I didn't want my ass in a sling.

We finished mass, shook some hands, and jumped back into the Country Squire. We headed off to the Dunkin' Donuts in Norwood. Once there I would press my face against the glass to watch the donuts being made. When I was younger, I had always thought donuts grew from trees. I imagined the donut trees in rows right next to the apple and cherry trees.

But now I realized they weren't grown on trees. I marveled while watching the donut maker. He would nod his head when he saw me in a "what's up" gesture, and I would nod back in awe. This gesture was new to me, and I wasn't as good at it as he was. Surely the job of donut maker must be one requiring great technical skill and years of education, not unlike the ray-dah engineer.

He would grab the dough, roll it out, and take a metal object and press down on the dough. There was a newborn donut. They would disappear into a vat of bubbling oil and later reappear as adult donuts. Emerging from the oil, they were placed on a rack and sprinkled with white powder. Was this the angel dust that made the Bullis brothers drive naked on a motorcycle up and down our street? The very same that gave the power to fly off a roof? By this time, I could hear my father putting in his order for our donuts. "Ah, get me three of 'dem, two of 'doze, and four of dem udders." He then ordered coffee: "Lahge cream, nine sweet and lows."

The donut man packed up everything and placed it on the counter. My father said, "give me a hand Joe." I took the two boxes of donuts and headed to the car. He gave the kid outside some coins in exchange for a newspaper. Our mission accomplished, we loaded back into the station wagon and made our way to Norwood airport, a small set-up for light air-craft and private planes. We parked and waited for my father to begin the ritual. He grabbed the newspaper and put it on the dashboard in the sun.

He read the "funnies" and cackled to himself. Then he handed the funnies over to the oldest sibling. The Razzles were passed out, but we weren't allowed to eat them until we finished our donut. Only then could the Razzles be consumed, as these were intended to clean the donut debris from our teeth. So, we waited on the Razzles. Next, we each received our donut, however, two were always saved for my father. This was important.

These were the Boston cream donuts. We could not start eating our donuts until father performed his ceremony.

It was very similar to the ceremony witnessed an hour previously, with the priest holding up a round wafer claiming, "This is the body of Christ," then eating the wafer. My father held the Boston cream donut up to the rearview mirror, so we could all see, and stated, "Named aftah deh greatest city in the woild!" He then brought it to his open mouth and as the donut entered, proclaimed, "schaloompf." He then began to chew the Boston cream donut and shortly after made a gesture with his hand signaling the passing of the napkin. He tried to say "napkin" with half a Boston cream donut in his mouth, but it came out as, "sumbumbula." But I knew that sumbumbula meant "napkin." I handed him the sumbumbula.

We were now free to begin eating our donuts. Donut-eating noises filled the Country Squire. I saw his smiling face in the rearview and a half-eaten Boston cream in his mouth. I could tell that the donut brought about a change in his demeanor, but also noted that his Boston cream was absent the angel dust. He was smiling and seemed at ease.

Next, he dove into reading the newspaper, and his expression changed again. Every week the newspaper had a story about the same two guys, and these stories seemed to agitate my father. One was named "Pinko" and the other was named "Commie," and both had the same last name: "Bastuhd." My father said that they were both "going to hell in a handbasket."

Next, he would turn to the sports pages. The sports pages apparently had a lot of stories about the homeless. He would turn to me with donut still in his mouth and proclaim, "Dis' bum says he is in a slump! Can you imagine if I did nothing at work for two weeks and claimed I was in a slump?! They would can my ass!" I shook my head, imagining people from the sinister organization, T.H.E.Y, who were always after my father. They wanted to catch him and put his donkey in a can for a week because he was caught in something called a slump. Bastards!

As he finished each section of the newspaper he passed it back to the eldest. Having read up on that week's capers by Pinko and Commie and the Bums, he would pick up his binoculars and begin surveillance of the airplanes and the people getting into them. My father possessed an innate ability to determine who these people were and precisely where they were headed, simply by observing the airplane through his binoculars. Spotting one man, he would pronounce that he was "a hot-shot businessman."

Spying another, he announced it was a "fancy big-shot doctor." A beautiful new car pulled up to an airplane and from it emerged a man in a suit accompanied by a beautiful lady. They walked over to a very clean looking plane and shook the hands of a man in a white shirt with a black tie and a captain's hat. My father studied them intently. He then stated that man with the beautiful woman was "the cat's ass." I asked for the binoculars to see for myself what a "cat's ass" looked like.

I put the binoculars to my eyes and turned a knob to focus. The whole picture came in clearly. Everyone looked very happy. I looked at the rear-ends of the man and the beautiful woman to see this "cat's ass," but they looked the same as every other adult rear end that I could recall. We had a Siamese cat, and this man's behind didn't resemble that cat's ass – at least with pants on. But my father had eyes for that sort of thing, and I trusted his diagnoses. I handed back the binoculars. He kept looking.

I pondered the scene. I just saw happy-looking people, a shiny car, and a clean airplane. Recently, in school, we each got to pick what we wanted to be as adults. I chose fireman. Cashews chose policeman. Tomorrow, however, I would tell the teacher to officially revise my future career choice, because I now definitely wanted to be "the cat's ass" when I grew up.

The cat's ass got in his airplane with his beautiful lady friend and the plane revved up and took off. Another man emerged from the building and walked over to an airplane that looked very old and shabby. Smoke blew out of the engine as it lumbered away to take off. My father proclaimed that this man, "Is a regular guy, like us, probably getting away from his old lady for the day, flying around drunk in figure eights." That sounded fun, too.

Time passed, and the sun grew brighter as it climbed the sky. My father had finished his Boston cream donuts, his coffee, his funnies and reading about Pinko and Commie and the Bums; he had surveilled and diagnosed who everyone on the tarmac was, and where they were going. Finally, we could eat our Razzles. The day was a success. As we headed home I looked forward to a crackling fire, pizza, the *Wonderful World of Disney*, and finally that happy fellow Marlin Perkins and his *Mutual of Omaha's Wild Kingdom*. It occurred to me that Marlin Perkins resembled the Colonel guy on those boxes of chicken. Maybe Marlin and he were brothers, and Marlin captured chickens for his brother the Colonel. I liked Sundays and liked being a Catholic.

TOAST & GINGER ALE

School was now very regimented. Crayons were scarce. We needed things called "rulers," a Number 2 pencil (since this was 2nd grade, I surmised), and erasers. Our paper was no longer plain white or colored, meant for drawing or cutting; instead, it was now "ruled" with little blue lines. The teacher made a very big deal about "staying in the margins." It was a lot like sitting still, and I did not enjoy it. We had more assignments to take home. These second-grade assignments seemed to take much longer to complete and were commensurately more boring. All of this was cutting into my fun time. I now looked forward to the inevitable New England snowstorms and the possibility of a snow day with both gleeful anticipation and a whif of desperation.

A new neighbor had moved in and I started to see him more and more. The family name was Tibbals but he quickly became known as Tibbs. He never got up as early as Cashews. Dick and I were always up at the crack of dawn and had to wait around until noon before going over to his house, and he was usually still in bed. In addition to his unusual sleep habits, he also didn't get haircuts like us. We all had mushroom-style bowl haircuts. Except for Blumpkin, who had a red afro. But the new kid had a very different haircut and at the time "different" meant you were going to be ridiculed.

When the weather was warm his father would sit him in a chair on their porch and take an electric razor to his head. On haircut days my friends and I would all stand outside to watch this and laugh. The laughter didn't seem to bother his father, but it clearly bothered the new kid. After getting brushed off, he would be let loose. We stared at him with suspicion and awe because he was "different." But he was still an addition to our crew, on account of the fact that he lived on our cul-de-sac.

I received a phone call from my friend Jeff and my mother took me to see him. When I arrived, he was bald and seem very pale. He smiled and was happy to see me. His appearance worried me, but I told him that he would be fine because we were all praying for him. Our God would take care of him. He couldn't go outside and play because he was still too sick. So, we just sat on the couch and talked. I told him about everything we were doing in school, the assignments, and the new kid we had christened 'Tibbs.'

Jeff couldn't wait to get back to school and I couldn't wait to have him back as a regular participant in the crew and all our shenanigans. He told me he was going back to the hospital soon and wasn't sure how long he'd be there this time. Before I left his house that day, I took custody of Jeff's G.I. Joe. I told him that I would hold on to it until he got back. Jeff agreed that this would be a good plan. Soon we would be playing with G.I. Joe again, throwing him from trees into bushes, flying him around in circles.

It was a short visit. Jeff's mom said he had to sleep. I told his mom all the good news: We were praying for him, and everything would be fine. Her face got a funny look on it. She just rubbed my mushroom hair as I went out the door. When I got home I put Jeff's G.I. Joe in the shoe box under my bed.

Life continued to get worse at school. On the bright side, however, we had established control over our own parcel of land on the playground. Recess was brief, but we took advantage of it. Once back in the classroom, it was math, history, English, and fact-remembering, none of which was fun. It was hard to concentrate on math and all those numbers, then forget about the numbers and think of history and what someone said or thought 200 years before us.

During the winter lots of kids would be missing from school due to sickness. That year, as soon as the cold weather hit, Cashews went missing from school for a few days. I went to visit him and his mother said he had a cold, and not to get too close, so I just said hello from the door. He was bundled up like a newborn baby and all you could see was his face. His mother came in and took his temperature. I said goodbye and left.

When I got sick, or my mother suspected me of being sick, she would put her hand on my forehead and say, "You got the bug." I didn't know if that meant the flu or a cold, or how the bug got into me in the first place. My mother's method of getting the bug out of me involved opening the window, "letting the cold air in," and then make me eat toast and drink ginger ale. Since Lead was on the bunk above me, every time he was sick, I had to deal with the cold New England winter air. If I was sick, he had to deal with mother's methods of eliminating the bug as well. According to her, the same methods that cured the bug also conferred protective powers on the one of us who wasn't sick.

One day my mother's hand determined that the bug had entered my body. Maybe it got in there when I was laughing on the playground. In any event, I had "the bug," so the window was opened and I was told to eat the toast and drink the ginger ale. My mother stated that I would surely be fine by morning. I followed her instructions carefully.

It was hard to sleep with the window open and the frigid New England air blowing on me. As I lay there, I thought of the bug. Surely, he would crawl out of my mouth in an effort to escape the toast and ginger ale. And even if he decided to try and hide on my bedspread or in the shag carpeting, the cold air from the open window would definitely eliminate him. My brother and I were shivering. Our teeth chattered.

We stayed awake most of the night, shaking, but we knew it was the only method to freeze the bug to death or at least get him out of our room and back where he belonged in his own warm house. I was sure the bug would go home and announce to his friends and family, "I'm never going back to the Winslow house again! They tried to kill me!"

We eventually passed out from the cold and exhaustion. When we woke up for school, our lips were blue, and we were still trembling. My mother seemed unconcerned about the color of our lips. She placed her hand on my forehead and announced, "The bug's gone." She then adjusted the window, leaving it open a few inches. Frigid air streamed through the crack. Her remedy was remarkably effective, as neither my brother nor I nor any of the other Winslow children ever missed a day of school. After an hour or two in the classroom, I finally warmed up. Sadly, Cashews' bug was still in him; he was absent from school, so his mom's method of swaddling him in layers of quilts was obviously not working.

Soon thereafter, I was doing chores in the yard when my mother told me that my good friend Jeff was gone. This time, however, my mother didn't say "gone." Instead, she said, "I got news that Jeff has died." From my experience with my grandmother, I knew what "gone" meant and that it was permanent. But "died" seemed harsher. My G.I. Joe-playing partner with the lisp had been sick and suffered and the prayers to our God didn't work. He was taken away from me.

I looked up to the sky in anger. I ran upstairs and put away my children's Bible with the pictures in it. I lay in bed thinking of Jeff, the good times we had digging, fishing, playing with plastic soldiers; of putting his G.I. Joe in all sorts of dire circumstances and having my G.I. Joe come to the rescue.

I fell asleep.

The next morning, I got on the school bus. There was no yelling or screaming, no throwing gum and paper at the driver. Everyone seemed to know we just lost our friend. We got into our assigned rooms, and even the teachers looked upset. Time seemed to "take" people and I worried that others I cared for would soon be "gone." I scowled at the teacher, for she had been one of the adults that promised, "he will be fine because we are all praying." That day, her bottom lip was quivering, and she was trying to explain "life" and what had happened to Jeff.

She had been wrong about our prayers and God protecting Jeff. Was she lying on purpose? Or did she really believe that? Recess was announced, and my crew gathered near our spot under the trees. We didn't say much. A first grader crossed through a corner of our territory and we yelled at him. This was our tree, our shade, our grass. We were bitter and sad, but we had our own turf.

The day of the funeral finally arrived, and it was held at the same church we attended on Sundays. The only other time I had seen our church that crowded was on special and fun events called Christmas and Easter. I saw all my friends from school and their parents. The children looked curious, and the parents looked sad.

We all sat in our proper places, and then the priests and altar boys made their way down the center aisle and onto the altar. Men dressed in black, three on each side, carried a white box containing my friend. It was almost like a regular mass, with the sitting, kneeling, and standing. Then the priest gave a speech on why things like this happen. He told us that Jeff was gone from Earth, but we would see him again.

This gave some comfort to the word "gone." So, Jeff was "gone" from here but was actually in another place called Heaven where there was no more pain. I thought of the pain my friend had been going through, but he never complained about it, at least not in front of me. I remembered all the good times we had, the laughs and adventures. Maybe we would experience those again someday. I noticed many people crying but took comfort from the words of the priest; I pictured Jeff and I playing together again one day.

There was a special ceremony, where the priest walked around with some type of can that was smoking. He circled the white box that contained my friend. After that, the six guys rolled the white box past us. Everyone looked very sad. My classmates looked confused. I wiggled my way through the crowd and stood at the top step of the church and watched them put the white box into a big black car. I could see my own reflection in the big black car.

I waved the arm of the GI Joe at the big black car that took Jeff "away." For a brief moment, I felt a sense that everything was okay because we would meet again. There was one more ceremony outside, as the white box was driven away to a place where they put the "gone" and "away" people. The priest said a few final words, and then we all left.

When we got home I played outside at Jeff's favorite playing spot. I did the usual routine with Jeff's G.I. Joe, leaping from tree branches, running out from behind the tree, helping him try to fly. I thought about everything that just happened and it didn't make sense. Bitterness was gradually making its way into my world like the change of a New England season.

As I stood in our foyer I noticed that a group of neighborhood parents was mingling at my father's bar. I overheard one of them say, "The poor bass-tud was so young." The man who said that noticed me standing in the foyer and said, "Don't worry kid, you'se friend is in a bet-tah place." I walked upstairs to my room and pulled the shoebox out from underneath my bunk bed. I put the G.I. Joe away. It and the children's bible would remain untouched for a very long time.

The school year came to a close and, aside from the brief respites of art, recess, and gym, school was now something I decidedly did not enjoy. It came to my attention that, apparently, every so often, my parents would get these things called "report cards." These seemed to upset my father. As he read my report cards, he would pound the dinner table in disgust and then, once he was good and worked up, he would chase me around with a belt. So now school was not only boring – it was getting me in trouble.

THE RESERVATION

Summer finally arrived, the part of the year when I was normally able to spend considerably more time lolling around in our local woods, which is where I felt most at peace. However, my father announced that this summer would be different. This year we would be spending half of the summer at Hale Reservation and the other half at a place he called "the Irish Riviera," otherwise known as Marshfield, Massachusetts.

Hale Reservation was as wonderful as ever. Families got together with families for lunches, dinners, and activities. I spent more time fishing. That summer, I wasn't as interested in drying off and lotioning the bee-hives, because I wanted to spend all my time in nature. If I wasn't bobbing up and down with a diving mask in the swimming area, I was in the swamp trying to catch water snakes. I started to learn how to swim better, mastering serious strokes like "the crawl," "the backstroke," "the breaststroke," and the "butterfly."

Our summertime at Hale came and went quickly. Normally we would head home to spend the rest of the season in our own neighborhood. But this year, it was straight to "the Irish Riviera." I had been to the ocean before, but never for long enough to really understand it. This year we would spend an entire month seaside. After arriving, we unpacked and loaded the food and clothes into their proper places.

Then I went out and walked in the direction of the water. It all seemed wide open. The waves made a sound that invited me to jump in. We were in Bluefish Cove, which had jetties on both sides, where the boats would pass in and out. On one side was a massive rock formation and on it, I could see older kids jumping into the water. I heard my mother calling me, so I went back to the cottage, brimming with excitement for all the adventures I was sure this place had in store for me.

I could still hear the waves calling me as I lay in bed and fell asleep. Morning arrived, and after quickly slurping my breakfast I literally sprinted to the water. I threw my towel down on the beach and jumped into the surf. Immediately I understood what a sock in the dryer felt like, being tossed and turned and flipped around. I realized there was no use fighting against the raw power of the waves and relaxed. Once I let the waves have their way with me, I was quickly deposited back on the beach.

As time went on I got better at comprehending the rhythm of the surf and how to gain some measure of control simply by letting go and anticipating how the waves would act. But initially, the pounding surf merely tossed me around and spit me out when it was done with me. The ocean was so much bigger than Hale Reservation, it was difficult to comprehend. Here, I wasn't afraid to tread water and urinate.

It scared me to do this at Hale because it was so much smaller and more crowded. There, I always feared that somebody would feel the warmth of my urine on their ankles and notify my mother. But here, the massive ocean tossed and swirled constantly; I surmised therefore that it would be extremely difficult if not impossible for anybody detect the warmth of the Zarex leaving my body.

Playing in the ocean, surrounded by the massive power and sound of the waves and wind, made time disappear. I would have been completely oblivious to time passing except for one thing. As the day went on, something started to happen to the ocean. Barely detectable at first, this phenomenon initially caused me to wonder if I was losing my senses. But eventually, there was no mistaking it. It was the same phenomenon that I experienced in the bathtub when the drain plug was pulled. The water slowly left the tub.

But when that happened in the tub it was because my mother had pulled the plug. How could this be happening in the ocean? Was there a plug on the bottom of the ocean attached to a chain that ran under the beach, under the ground, and all the way back to our cabin? Had my mother pulled it because it was time for me to get out? Or, was there some maintenance man in a scuba suit somewhere way off in the distance? Did he do this because he had work to do? Or had my mother somehow signaled him?

As I stood there in the receding water an elderly woman said, "Here comes low tide." I instinctively looked around for whatever this "low tide" was – would it be a boat or airplane or a guy riding a water bicycle of some sort? The elderly lady seemed to be excited about whatever this low tide was. The older kids that had been jumping off the rocks had stopped and were walking away. The beach seemed to be getting longer.

I started making a sand castle and became intensely focused on my project. Soon I began to run out of the water needed to shape the large roofs. Then I noticed that the sand was cleaner, too. No duck dung that you might find at Hale. I was intent on building the largest sand castle ever. I looked up after some time and noticed the waves were crashing much further away from me. The elderly woman came walking toward me, grinning, holding a steel bucket.

She asked me if I wanted to go clamming. I didn't know what that meant, but she seemed to have the look of fun in her eyes, so I said yes. She said, "look for water squirting out from the sand, and then dig until you feel something hard, then dig more and pull it out." That sounded crazy. I just stared at her. But she quickly pointed to a stream of water shooting upward from the sand a few inches from my feet. I fell down to my knees and attacked the sand, digging as fast as I could. My fingers hit something hard, and then I dug faster. I grabbed what looked like a rock and held it up. The clam lady came over and I tossed the thing into her steel bucket.

She was wearing a special hat. A lot of people we studied in school wore special hats. Fireman had special hats, policemen had special hats. Nurses had special hats. This lady had a clamming hat. It was very tight and smooth and had two flowers on it. Probably her favorite flowers. She said she goes swimming after she clams and that the special cap would keep her hair dry. She pointed to another spout, and I immediately fell to my clamming position and went into action: kneel over squirting hole, dig aggressively around the shooting water, hit rock-like substance, dig around rock-like substance until loose, pull out the object and hold to the sky. After a few times, I really began to master the procedure and the clam lady seemed very pleased.

I repeated the procedure several times until I pulled out something different – it was skinny and long. I raised it into the air and the clam lady announced that I had found a razor clam. She stated that that was the meatiest type of clam and, giggling, that her husband now had something to shave with. I imagined her opening the clam and eating its insides, then handing the shell to her husband who would start scraping his face with it. It seemed like an odd series of things to do with the long, shiny object I was holding.

We continued to roam the beach hunting clams and I passed by a rocky formation that held lots of little pools of water. Looking around, I could see that after the water had receded off the beach, all of these rocky bath-tub-like things had emerged. I looked down inside one of the pools and saw a spider-like creature walking on the bottom. I grabbed him, and he grabbed my thumb. I yelled and tried to shake it off. Clam lady ran over and quickly extracted the hard-surfaced spider creature from my thumb. She then put it on the ground, and we watched it walk sideways back into the pool. I noticed its mean eyes. Its claws were open and pointing at me. He had the same eyes as my father when he scanned the report card, dart-ing side to side.

Clam lady said, "that's a crab." Then she did something extremely brave. She reached into the pool where the crab had just walked and grabbed it. Was she crazy? For some reason, it didn't bite her. She set it down on the sand and said, "Watch how to grab a crab." She again per-formed an act of extreme bravery and picked it up, and again it did not attack her. "Reach *behind* the claws," she said. She set it down again and as it tried to scurry away she once again reached down and grabbed it behind its claws, holding it up.

She put it down and said, "Now you try." I did not want to grab the crab, because I could tell he really did not like me. But I didn't want to upset the clam lady. I accepted that I was about to have my finger cut off violently by this armored spider of the sea ... and grabbed at it. I did as she said and picked him up behind his claws and saw how – even though he was staring at me with mean eyes and trying to slice off my fingers – he couldn't.

I nervously held the crab. A closer look revealed that he definitely did have my father's bad report card eyes. I didn't like the crab and the crab did not like me. We started at one another. Clam lady said I could put him back into his home and I very eagerly did so. She noticed I was bleeding from his initial assault and told me to rinse my hand off in the pool. She said saltwater was a great healer. The water stung a bit but in a way that felt kind of good.

We continued the clam search until most of her bucket was full and she had enough razor clams for her husband to shave. The valve in the bottom of the ocean must have gotten closed while we were clamming because the water started to rise again. She set the bucket down and told me to watch it. She jogged toward the waves and dove into the water with a loud "Whooh!" As she bobbed in the surf I could see her flowered clamming hat just above the surface. She bobbed around for a few minutes as I guarded our bucket of clams, then she came out of the water. As she dried herself off she said, "Thanks for the help, young man." She picked up the bucket and walked away.

I ran back to the cottage. Ignoring my mother, I grabbed a diving mask and ran back to the beach. I dove into the far end of the jetty. If something as amazing as the armored sea spider could be lurking in a pool up on the beach, then what, I wondered, could be hiding on the bottom of the actual ocean, under the waves? The jetty kept the waves from tossing me like a sock in a dryer, so I only had to get used to the sway and swell under the water.

I kicked my feet and looked around. As my eyes focused through the mask, I was amazed. It was as if I had literally dove into an entirely new world. There was planet earth above where humans lived, then there was this new ocean world that existed below the surface.

The rocks below looked like they were covered with crazy green hair and shell-like substances. Behind this flowing hair, I began to notice creatures. They appeared to be having fun, just swimming around in circles, rising and dropping with the swells of the water coming in and out. Some had very large teeth. Others seemed to have none but were faster. It seemed like the playground at school. The larger fish had their own areas and "turf." In the deeper water, the fish appeared larger and more menacing. Everything down there between the jetties was like a play. I was just floating there, an audience of one with my mask, taking it all in.

The creatures down there were incredible. One was snake-like and didn't swim around too much, it just seemed to wait, staring. It was obvious that he didn't want me too close. That guy clearly had no friends, but he definitely owned the whole playground. He wasn't the teacher's pet: he was clearly the principal, the teacher, and the custodian all-in-one. He ruled the school. Warily turning away from him, I gazed around at the rest of "seawater elementary." My stomach rumbled, so I kicked back to the surface and made my way to the cottage. My mother always seemed to have something cooked or pre-made and ready to eat.

I scarfed a PB and J as fast as I could. With every rushed chew all I could think of was that I was missing the action down under the waves. There was simply too much to see, so I had to eat as fast as possible and get back into the water. Indeed, Blue Fish Cove on The Irish Riviera had much more to offer than Hale Reservation. Still chewing, I ran back toward the beach past the large rock outcrop. The tide was once again high enough to allow a jump off of it, and I could see the larger kids scurrying around on it. The sheer height of it terrified me; it was obviously intended for teenagers. One of these bigger kids saw me watching from a distance, and shouted, "Hey kid, want to jump!?"

"No, just watching," I meekly replied. He seemed annoyed at my answer. "Just do it once, and you won't ever be afraid again," he explained. I sheepishly stepped to the top and looked down at the water, hundreds or possibly even thousands of feet below. My knees started to shake, and I felt dizzy. I pictured myself hitting a rock and being smashed to bits. I saw myself sinking into a deep hole, landing in the den of that snake-like creature that ran the show down there.

The teen pointed to a darker spot in the swelling water. "Aim for that or you'll smash-bottom and break your legs," he said, coolly. That didn't ease my nervousness. But he put his hand on my shoulder, nudging me forward, and said again, "Do it once, and you won't be afraid to do it again." I just stood there, kind of frozen. "Once you do it, it's all you will want to do," he said. I looked down, with shaking knees, and then back at the teens. They were smiling. They were mixed smiles, though, both happy and devious. In fact, they looked a bit like the snake creature between the rocks.

I stood at the very edge of the rock. My legs shook. I looked again at the teens. Their smiles were now leers. Some were missing important teeth. Some were even smoking. One had a tattoo. If I dove into that dark spot in the ocean, would these be the last faces I would see on Earth? The head of the pack said, "Just aim for the hole kid." Then he yelled, "Jump!" I closed my eyes and jumped. As I felt gravity yank me downward, I opened my eyes. I saw the horizon rushing toward me. I looked down at the hole in the swelling water. I tried to flap my arms. This must be how the Bullis brother felt as he flew off the edge of the roof under the power of Angel Dust and trash can lids. I hoped my landing wouldn't be as rough as his had been on the grass. Just before I hit the water I was overcome by exhilaration.

I finally landed. My entrance into the water hole created a loud crash. The sea water clapped my ears. I went under – down, down, down – and with terror, I waited to violently hit bottom. The bottom never came, and I feared ending up in the lair of the snake-like creature. Finally, I stopped my downward trajectory and the water held me. I looked up and paddled for the sun. As I broke the surface and took a desperate breath of air I heard the teens clapping and cheering. I grabbed onto the cliff edge, weak and wobbly. The swell of the water dragged me against the rocks. Sharp white things attached to the cliff scratched and scraped. The lead teen leaned down and said, "grab my hand."

My feet felt gravity holding me on the hard surface of the rocks. The bottom of my feet burned with pain. My arms were raw. I stumbled over to the group of teens and was met by high-fiving and pats on the head. One of them said, "Next time don't flap your arms, kid, it just makes landing more painful."

As the adrenaline receded, I felt amazing. The clam lady was a new friend, and now these teens had accepted me. I had faced numerous fears: the sea spider and his claws, heights, diving into the unknown. And, a fear of failing. The teens said goodbye, and I sat alone on the rock. It was a strange feeling. I craved the jump but was still terrified of jumping. I wanted to do it again, but now I was alone. Maybe I would be unable to climb back onto the rocks myself? I decided to jump again, even though no one was there to lend a hand to get me back up on the cliff.

This time I held my arms tight to my side, so my entry into the water was not painful. I swam to the rocks and struggled to climb back up without assistance. Waves pounded me and knocked me back into the water repeatedly. With each attempt, my arms and legs grew rawer from the scraping of the rocks. But I didn't give up and finally clawed my way onto land, exhausted.

I was covered with tiny scarlet cuts that bled. My arms and legs were limp. I lay down and felt the sun and wind sweep over me. I tried to understand how I could feel so much pain yet still feel so wonderful. I rose and ran to the edge of the cliff and jumped again. This time I made it back onto the rocks on my first attempt with fewer scrapes and scratches. I jumped and jumped and jumped as time disappeared.

From the cliff, I saw my father walk toward me holding a red and white box with the happy, white-bearded guy on the outside. I waved and yelled. He looked over at me from a distance. I felt powerful and proud as I ran to the end of the cliff and again jumped into the water. As I flew through the air and down toward the hole in the water I saw my father's face. It was a wide-eyed combination of astonishment and fear.

I scrambled back onto the rocks and joined him on the jetty. I told him all about my diving techniques. I told him about being like the Bullis brother on "angel dust." He said, "Well, you were jumping the smart way. That Bullis kid wasn't thinking." He noticed my legs covered in in bright red scrapes. He chuckled and said, "I see you rubbed up against the barnacles."

He opened the red and white box from Colonel-something and handed me a piece of chicken. The sun was getting closer to the horizon. Boats in all shapes and sizes were coming in for the day. I asked my father why we didn't have any boats, and when we would be getting one. He simply said, "Ah, we ain't boat people." I grabbed his binoculars and scanned the sea, looking at each water vessel. I studied the "boat people" to see what made them different from us.

Did they have fins? Scales? Why were we not boat people? Maybe it was a good thing that we weren't. Maybe they lived on the ocean and slept on their boats. Maybe they didn't have grass like me. I was still confused, but was grateful that I wasn't a "boat person." I couldn't imagine not having grass or trees or trails through the woods. I was grateful I didn't have to live on a boat, away from "land people."

I told my father about my new friends, "clam lady" and the "teens in cutoff jeans." I then told him about what I saw underwater and described the snake-like creature.

"That snake thing you saw is an eel," he said. "Better stay away from that guy, he'll tear your ass up."

I listened intently as my father explained the eel and its procedure for "tearing your ass up." I was impressed by his ability to provide such an extended explanation with such a large amount of chicken in his right cheek.

"That eel has a den; he sits there and waits for some clueless fish to swim by." He used his arm to illustrate the eel, and his fingers to illustrate the teeth in the eel's mouth. He used his other hand to illustrate a fish. "The clueless fish, he swims by the eel's house, and blam!" It looked pretty scary to me.

He then went on to explain that if I were to pass by or enter the eel's den, it would definitely tear my ass up. He now transitioned the hand that was the clueless fish into a ball and said, "This here's your ass." His other hand violently chomped on his balled-up fist. I imagined having my ass torn up by the eel and it terrified me. In my mind I could picture people running to the shoreline, gasping in horror upon seeing the back side of my bathing suit torn to pieces, the eel tearing and chomping. If that were to happen to me, I'd for sure be taken away, face down in an ambulance, and spend the rest of my summer on my stomach in a hospital bed. I determined with resolution that I would be extra cautious from now on. I would keep my distance from the eel's turf down under the jetty.

My father had one cheek full of chicken, and the cheek was grinning. "Quick, hand me the binocs," he said. He mumbled through his chewing: "Just look at this broad, taking a sunset swim." I asked to see, but he said: "Ah, you're too young." He scanned across the beach, still smiling and exposing a clump of chicken on one side of his mouth. He mumbled to himself, "Ah geez, just look at this bird," and, "Holy mackerel, take a gander at 'dat number." It made no sense to me. We watched the sun go down. As chicken filled my stomach and my hunger receded, the pain from the sunburn, jumping, and barnacles increased. But, that teen had been right. Now that I had successfully dove into the water, it was all I wanted to do.

The rest of the summer at the ocean seemed to fly by in a flash. There just wasn't enough time to explore everything that needed exploring. Each day I woke early and sprinted to the beach to jump the cliff or explore the undersea playground or help clam lady with her rounds. Each evening, after the sun had gone down, the sea fell back due to its plug being pulled. I now suspected that perhaps the boat people were responsible for this; after all, where were they going in their boats?

I limped home, sore, tired, happy. My thoughts raced to precisely what I would do the next morning when I returned. Despite my father's warnings, I regularly dipped down to the eel's turf to catch a glimpse of him and his leering glare. But I was careful not to get too close. I was determined to avoid getting my "ass torn up."

Each day brought new things into my realm of consciousness – strange rocks, cartoon-looking fish, and other sea creatures and plants that I couldn't even categorize. Clam lady would dutifully tell me the official name of whatever I had described. The underwater nooks and crannies and the small pools left behind by the low tide were filled with wonders. My father would also give the official name of whatever I might ask about, but his answers were always followed by some sort of story: "This one time, I saw a lobster the size of…"

The Irish Riviera was definitely both larger and wilder than Hale Reservation, and I had a lot more independence there. Although Hale was fun, the older I got the more the lifeguards blew their whistles at me. "Let go of that, stay away from that, put the snake down, stay away from the swamp." But at the Irish Riviera, I was totally free. No authority figures, no lifeguards. Just my ocean creature friends, clam lady, the still some-what-scary teens, and my father with his binoculars and fried chicken. The day came when my mother informed us it was Labor Day, which meant we had to leave. My stomach sank. School was right around the corner.

In the blink of an eye, I was back in the classroom, sitting uncom-fortably upright at a desk. I struggled each day, fighting against the sheer boredom of trying to absorb and remember figures, numbers, names, dates – for no other apparent purpose than regurgitating them back at some later date. I was also assigned a paper route, "for college," my father said. After delivering newspapers door to door each afternoon, I would try to study in my room. This proved to be nearly impossible. All I could seem to do would be look off into the distance, thinking of the Irish Riviera. Then I would watch the birds zooming around the yard. As the weeks passed, the days grew shorter and the air grew cooler. Fewer and fewer birds were zooming around.

What Kind of Vanilla
Do You Want?

As the days grew cold and short, life grew more rigid. On top of school and my paper route, I was responsible for certain chores. Every New England season required its own unique duties of me. Fall meant leaf cleanup and preparing the yard for Winter. It was also common to come home and find a massive pile of logs dumped at the top of the driveway; it was my job to stack them. Sometimes they were tree-type logs and sometimes they were factory-type logs, called railroad ties.

These were greasy but burned easy. It would be another year before I would be allowed to swing the ax. So, for now, my job was to make a neatly stacked pile of logs on the deck, and another one inside the house near the pot belly stove. Once this was done, in the last couple of hours of daylight, I would rake leaves. The next day it started all over again, with school, the paper route, chores, then trying to study and remember things I didn't care about.

Each day after school, I got a brief break from the drudgery on the bus ride home. But as soon as I arrived, I would see the stack of newspapers waiting for me. Dread. The only thing that helped ease the boredom was when Cashews would join me on the route. These were always animated bull sessions where we would speak in great detail about what we were going to do in life, and what kind of men we would grow to be.

I struggled to keep up with my homework. It seemed little things would distract me from studying. Especially the "blue-assed fly." My father frequently said about one knucklehead or another, "He is crazier than a blue-assed fly." When I was younger I always wondered where this particular fly was. That year, I found out. Each day as I tried to study and concentrate and remember, that blue-assed fly would buzz into my room and distract me. He would occasionally land near me, shake his head quickly, stare at me and rub his front hands together. What was he excited about? Was he planning to do someone evil – like urinate on my textbook?

This fly was on a daily mission to take my concentration off memorizing the boring facts about those important historical figures and what they did – throwing apples, tossing coins, charging up hills. This one particular figure cut down a cherry tree, and when his father questioned him, he told the truth. I usually got the fact that it was a tree, but it being a cherry tree didn't seem to register as anything of importance worthy of remembering. This resulted in a poor mark. I blamed it on the blue-assed fly distracting me.

If there was still some light out after the newspaper route, chores and studying, I got to go out and play. But Fall in New England meant the sun didn't shine as much. So, my weekdays and Saturdays were fun-limited. If my father wasn't working on Saturdays, the family usually went on some day trip. He would tell me on Friday, "Tomorrow we are going to get the best and longest hot dog in town!" At first, I was super excited about these bonus explorations. But I quickly realized that finding the best and longest hot dog in town always came after we visited his parents ... to shave his father.

Saturday came, and we took a ride. I noticed that when we arrived at his parent's neighborhood, there were fewer lawns, and the houses seemed to be stacked on top of each other. Sometimes three families lived in the same house. One family on the first floor, another on the second, and a third on the top. My grandparents' house had two levels and someone else lived on the bottom floor. My father would ring a bell and someone would shout, "Who is it?" Then he would yell, "It's Ed!" In a few years, this routine would be repeated without the grandparents or world's longest and best hot dog, and he would yell, "It's the Electrician!" But for today, it was just, "Ed!"

I would hear the door being unlocked from the inside, my father would turn the knob, and we would head upstairs. It was a very long wooden stairwell, and I looked up to the top. The door was open and there was my grandmother with her hands open, saying, "Well hello, pumpkin!" I stepped up those wooden stairs slower and slower because I knew what was to come. I was about to be kissed by my grandmother.

I didn't like to be kissed by her because it was wet and left a red mark from this stuff called lipstick. I reached the last step and she grabbed me tight and said, "Hi Pumpkin!" She then held me out to look at me more closely, then smashed me back into her and kissed me. My father once told me it was rude to rub off the red mark from a kiss when the kisser was witnessing it. So, I would announce after meeting everyone that I had to go to the bathroom … and rub it off there. My father pointed to another room, and commanded me, "Go say hello to your grandfather." He would be sitting in a leather chair, and in front of him was a thing called a "walker."

For birthdays, young boys got "Slinkies," "G.I. Joes,", or a "Barrel of Monkeys," and you would wear a paper coned hat, and sing happy birthday. When you get older you still had to wear the paper coned hat and sing happy birthday, but apparently, you got boring stuff like canes and walkers. He didn't have teeth, but I could see that he was happy to see me. He put his massive hand on mine, making it disappear into his. He then said something in old people language that sounded like, "hucks mucks stew." It must have meant, "How are you?" To be polite, I said, "hucks mucks stew" in reply.

My father then said, "Go see your grandmother's sister." Her name was Kay Foley. I was told her husband had been "gassed" in the war and had died. But my grandfather survived. There was a smell of boiling food in the kitchen that got more potent as I approached. The kitchen was very moist from all the boiling food. There were even teardrops of water on the ceiling. Kay saw me, and she got up and walked over and gave me a big hug, and then a kiss. Now I had two red stains on my face. She was doing this thing called the Rosary.

You grab a bead, say something, and then grab another bead, and say something else until all the beads are touched and something recited for each one. Her brown stockings were rolled down to her ankles, and it gave the impression that two brown snakes were taking a nap wrapped around her legs. She then looked at some of the pots boiling and stirred a little before sitting back down.

It was very hot and uncomfortable in that kitchen that smelled of boiling vegetables. There were two sinks. One was a normal sink, and the other was a utility sink. I noticed that right next to the stove on the counter sat my grandfather's teeth. They were laying in the bottom of a glass, almost laughing at me. I could hear my father talking to my grandfather. My grandfather was hard of hearing and my father, after telling him three times he was going to get a shave, finally yelled, "I'm going to shave you!"

Now all the neighbors knew about the shave.

My father came into the kitchen and I ran out to go the bathroom and wipe the red kiss marks from my cheek. As I returned my father was prepping my grandfather for "the shave." There were two clean towels, one laid out on the counter next to the sink, the other rolled up and resting atop the first. There was a mixing bowl, with a small mop-like thing in it. There was a bottle of liquid called "aftershave."

There was a razor that actually did look like one of the clams I dug out of the sand at the Irish Riviera. My father opened it up and put a brand-new razor into it, and set it down open, ready to shave. He poured some foamy substance into the bowl and started to turn it with the mop, and the foam grew to the top of the bowl. He then went to the room where my grandfather sat and said, "I'm ready for you." He said it again, louder. The third time he yelled, "I'm ready for you!"

Now all the neighbors knew we were ready.

My father assisted my grandfather out of his chair. I heard movement in the living room, and the sounds of, "Oooh," "Aaaaaaaahhhhhh," and then metal, and rubber hitting the wooden floors as he used his old person birthday present, "the walker." He would push it forward and it would go "click, click," then he would slide one of his laceless black shoes forward, making a "shish" sound against the wooden floor. Then he'd do the same with his right foot. Then he looked up briefly and I ducked into the kitchen. I peeked back out. He did this elderly dance until I saw him peak his turtle-like head and neck around the corner. He smiled as he started to enter the kitchen.

There were more "oooohhhhs" and "aaaaahhhhs" as my father assisted him into the chair against the sink. He then sat down in the chair with his head against the sink. My father put a towel around his neck and then took out an object from each of his ears. They must have been another present from one of his elderly friends. These, my father said, were called "hearing aids." My father whipped up the creamy substance in the bowl, and then applied the cream to my grandfather's face. Slowly he started to resemble Santa Claus, the guy that lands on your roof once a year, and leaves a Barrel of Monkeys, a G.I. Joe, Barbie dolls – or false teeth, walkers, and hearing aids, depending on your age, and sex.

My father would shave a patch, and then flick the cut whiskers and shaving cream into the trash bin. His technique was quite intense; he resembled an orchestra conductor and painter all at once. Little patches were shaved, the razor clam was flicked off, and then the next patch was shaved. My father took real pride in his work.

I recalled stories he had told me of his childhood, about his father losing his patience. Once he even smashed a violin over my father's back. Another time he pushed my father down the staircase. I always wondered if these incidents took place one after the other. I imagined my father scraping away at the violin, "do ray me fah bbzzzzzzzzzzzzzzzttt." Then I imagined the violin grabbed from him, smashed over his back, and him being thrown down the stairwell. What amazed me was the fact here he was with a large clam razor, in total control. He could easily say, "This is for the violin and stair incident," and start cutting my grandfather to pieces with the razor. Instead, he remained focused, never missing a spot.

I had to leave the room once in a while. The smell and moisture from the vegetables being boiled to death were so intense it made me nauseous. It didn't seem to disturb my grandmother's sister, Kay Foley. She continued to mumble things to herself, or to God, as she grabbed one of the spheres on the rosary. She would take a break once in a while to look at the boiling substances and stir. Then she would sit down and go back to God talk.

My father let the hot water run and then put a face cloth under the water, letting it sit for a short time. He then placed the towel on my grand-father's face and let it sit there for a minute. Then he took the towel off and announced with a grin, "The shave is done!" He then attempted to start a brief discussion with my grandfather. His hearing was much worse without the hearing aid.

"Do you want a trim?"

"Huh?"

"A trim!"

"Huh?"

"A hair trim?!!!"

"Gitty sly yah…" my grandfather would slur.

I couldn't understand my grandfather and his elderly talk. But my father obviously did, and looked at me, and said, "He wants a trim." I guessed that "gitty sly yah" meant "make my day." My father then disap-peared briefly and returned with an electric hair trimmer and some Q-Tips. My grandfather didn't have much hair left, but I did notice that what little hair he had was mostly in strange places, like a patch on his nose, or com-ing out of his ears.

My father began cutting the few hairs on his head and then the sides, which had more hair. He delicately cut the hairs on his nose, ears, and eyebrows. Then he took a brush and swished all the gray hair off. Then a Q-Tip was inserted into his ears, and what looked like a tiny crayon was extracted. My father held it up and said, "Look at this baby! No wonder the old man's deaf." He found another mini yellow crayon in his other ear, and shook his head in disbelief.

We had accomplished our goal of "the shave," and I thought we would leave. But there was one final step. He handed back my grandfather's hearing aids, and my grandfather placed them in his ears. Then my father brought the glass over with the teeth in them. My grandfather reached into the glass and inserted them. He looked younger now. I thought he would jump up and dance, but his body was still weak, and we had to assist him to the walker. We helped him to the dining room and got him seated.

My grandmother was busy setting up for what seemed like lunch for themselves. I was getting agitated thinking of the world's greatest foot-long hot dogs I had been promised. We moved into the dining room, and my grandfather was at the "head of the table." In our home, my father was the head of the table. I sat down on one side of my grandfather with my father on the other side. The Foley sisters were in the kitchen conversing in elderly talk while banging dishes and pans. Platters of food one by one came out, steaming. Everything appeared to be thoroughly boiled.

All the food was now in front of us on the dining room table. In the middle was a large chunk of meat called "corn beef," but I didn't see any corn on it. My father started to hack that up, placing a slice on everyone's plate. I noticed my grandfather looked a lot younger with his clean shaved face, trim, nose, ear and eyebrow hair reduction, and fake teeth. He smiled a lot more, and I could almost make out what he was saying. Now everyone had food in front of them, so "the head" of the table said a prayer and we all made a cross sign.

I took in what I had just experienced. The hairy-lipped mothball kiss of my grandmother, the brown snake stockings wrapped around Kay Foley's ankles. The heat and steam of the boiling kitchen. The false teeth in the glass. The hair protruding out of my grandfather's nose. The yellow crayon-like substances my father extracted out of his ears. The hearing aids. All these images circled through my mind, one by one, in color. The yellow wax, the white teeth smiling at me inside a glass full of water, the tan hearing aids. The brown, mushy food. I had difficulty eating what was in front of me. My father motioned with his hand on his chest and mentioned the importance of eating vegetables. Then he whispered, "Remember, it puts hair on your chest."

That made eating the steaming vegetables in front of me easier. I imagined the water that was in the glass with the false teeth had likely been thrown into the same pot as the boiling vegetables, as some elderly good luck ritual. I then thought of the fame and popularity I would certainly gain by eating my vegetables. At that time there was a television show called *Charlie's Angels* starring a lady named Farah. I ate the vegetables with ease, thinking of the clump of hair that would soon emerge on my chest, thus attracting Farah to me.

She would attend my birthday parties. My shirt would be buttoned down enough to expose my clump of hair. She would place her hand on my clump of hair after I had made my wish and blew out the candles on my cake. She would whisper, "Happy birthday, pumpkin," and kiss my cheek. But Farah didn't smell like mothballs or have a hairy lip. We would all be wearing coned paper hats. Farah's would be pink.

I ate more and more vegetables. Because of my new clump of hair, everything I did would almost certainly attract Farah. I would be sledding on my Flexible Flier with my snowsuit zipped down, exposing the clump of hair. She would be behind me, with one hand on my chest hair, and we would be sledding at high speeds to the roaring applause of my friends. Even the bullies that applied wedgies and noogies would applaud.

I was sure my clump of chest hair would look best during summer activities. Making sand castles, cliff diving, clamming. Farah probably had a special, small towel specifically designed to dry off the clump of hair each time I emerged from the ocean. I finished my vegetables and asked for more. My grandfather took notice and smiled with his false teeth and a lump of food in his mouth.

He said to my father, "He sum dum lum." My father replied, "Lebba leda bedda." This was special talk that was only performed by experts who could speak with food in their mouths. It took time and practice. All I knew is that they were both very pleased that I was asking for seconds. They didn't know it was it was because I wanted to hasten Farah's arrival, rather than out of enjoyment of the smelly, boiled plant matter. The corn beef was hard to eat, almost like rubber, but I managed. Everyone seemed to be making growling noises and talking in the special elderly food-chewing language.

We began wrapping up our meal, and my grandfather looked very content with his clean shave, haircut, and his perfect teeth. My father disappeared into the kitchen and I could hear the clinging, clanging, and mixing of something. My grandmother went into the kitchen briefly and reappeared with a cake and a knife. There were smaller plates already at the table for the dessert. My father returned with three small drinks, rattling with ice. "These are for adults," my father would say of the clinky ice cube drinks.

The drinks were placed in front of my grandfather, grandmother, and Kay Foley. Then the dessert was cut and placed on the dessert plates. The dessert was the only thing that wasn't boiled, and it tasted pretty good. I noticed that everyone had a funny way of drinking their adult drinks. My grandmother would sip and then raise her eyebrows, giggle, and look at her sister. Her sister would do the same thing. They started to smile more.

My grandfather would look into the glass and twirl the ice, then throw his head back, and say, "Aaahhh." He didn't sip and giggle. He held his glass up and my father took it from him, went into the kitchen. I heard more noises with glass, ice, and what sounded like shaking. He came back and gave another glass to my grandfather, who performed the same routine.

We finished everything and headed into the living room. My father made more adult drinks for everyone, and then he did the dishes. My grandmother sat at the piano and sang a song. Her sister sat down and sang along. My grandfather sat in his chair and lit a long brown object. The man had totally changed. From what looked like a sick turtle, using a walker, to this robust individual with smoke pouring out of his false teeth, looking down on his adult drink. He twirled the glass and watched the ice swirl around and then threw his head back, consuming the drink.

My father re-emerged from doing the dishes and grabbed everyone's empty glass, returning a few moments later with freshly-filled ones. My father didn't drink any. He said he was "on the wagon." He said when I was just about to be born a priest was giving him his "last rights" because of drinking too many adult drinks and developing a "bleedy ulcer." But now he was fine as long as he had his milky drink called Maalox. The Maalox kept the bleedy ulcers from bleeding.

My grandmother played one more song and then my father announced that we had to go. We all hugged and said goodbye, and they all seemed more lively after consuming their adult drinks. They all crowded at the top of the stairwell as we exited. I looked back about midway down, and there was the image of three happy Q-Tip looking individuals. My grandfather gave me one last word of advice, or perhaps it was a blessing, with his cigar: "Itchy sky ya." Followed by "Flibbity flew."

My grandmother blew me a kiss, and said, "Goodbye pumpkin." Kay Foley was holding her rosary, and she waved those. Soon one by one these happy, quirky people would be "gone," just like other decent people I knew and respected who had gone away. But the image of these three, at the top of the stairwell, would last a lifetime.

I had thoughts of heaven being this way. I would ring a bell, the doors of heaven would open, and I would be greeted by these three happy elderly people. "Come on in, pumpkin," my grandmother would say. "Hucks mucks stew," my grandfather would say. Kay Foley would shake her rosary beads.

After reaching the top step of the stairs to heaven I would enter a living room, and there would be the other people who had "gone." My friend Jeff would be there, and my mother's mother would be there. We would watch an episode of Sesame Street together and then play with the G.I. Joes. My grandmother would be playing the piano and all the adults would be enjoying their adult drinks.

I held onto that image as we headed to Simco's in Mattapan for the "best hot dog in town." Mattapan seemed to have a lot of energy. Mopeds would zoom past without using the proper turn signals. There were a lot of cool looking vans with moon-shaped windows and dragons painted on the side, all crazy colors.

My father then dispensed some advice that didn't really make sense to me. "We are the only white people here," he said. "So stay cool, and don't look at anyone." It was the mid-1970s in New England and I wasn't sure what was going on, and why I had to "stay cool, and not look at anyone."

We finally arrived at Simco's in Mattapan, and my father was right: we were the only white people. We got out of the car and walked to a very busy hot dog stand. One guy knew my father and said, "Hey Eddie, the usual?" My father nodded his head coolly and replied, "Ya, same for the kid too." We got our hot dogs and left.

We drove to a place called Dorchester to eat our hot dogs. It really *was* the best hot dog I ever had. My father did his usual food ritual and held up the hot dog before biting it, announcing, "I'm about to eat the best [insert food] in town." And then he would make a "harumph" sound while shoving it into his mouth. Immediately after the "harumph" I had to pass him a "sumbumbulah" (talking with food in your mouth language for 'napkin'). We finished the best hot dogs in Mattapan and/or Dorchester and then took a short ride to another part of town where my father announced, "I'm going to get you the best ice cream in town." He parked and said, "Stay cool, keep the doors locked, don't look at anyone." Before leaving me in the car he asked, "What kind of vanilla do you want?"

I looked around and could see that Dorchester was bustling with buses, fancy vans, mopeds, and busy people walking up and down the sidewalk. My father soon came back with his crooked jaw smiling and two ice creams. We then drove off, to a park in Milton, the next town over. The ice cream was in a dish, so it was somewhat safe to drive and eat. We parked and went to work in earnest on our vanilla ice creams. The day was a success. All parties were happy, fed and clean shaven (except my grandmother's lip). This would be the beginning for me of finding out what "the best in town" was for a variety of food item in a variety of local towns, as determined by Ed Winslow.

Altar Boys & the Path

There is a saying about birds of a feather flocking together. The birds in my flock were becoming less and less like inquisitive little starlings flitting about, discovering new things, and more and more like hawks, circling around the younger birds, taking their worms. My crew of friends all lived within walking distance of me and we all had the same bus route. It was interesting to me that, while each of my friends' families and homes had their own peculiarities, they all also shared many things that were very similar to my home and family.

For instance, all their parents had special places to mix and enjoy their "adult drinks." Cashews' father, of course, had his basement. My red-headed-afro friend Blumpkin's father frequented a place in Norwood called the Irish Heaven. Sully's father was apparently a nature lover, as he drank at a place called the Elk's Club. I imagined they felt a special need to protect the endangered elk by wearing fancy elk hats and coming up with plans to preserve elk habitat … over many adult drinks.

My closest friend at this time was Cashews. The one thing Cashews had going for him was his sharp memory, great vocabulary, and advanced ability to read. For now, the teachers loved him because of this. For now. When we were doing the newspapers, we would sometimes run into Blumpkin, whose own route covered most of Hartford street. I had to cross Hartford street to get to Kingfords street, where my route began. So, we would frequently cross paths with him.

Blumpkin had been doing his paper route for much longer than I had. During collection days, he would carry a sock in which he deposited his customers' payments. As an experienced paper route veteran, Blumpkin gave me advice on ascertaining which customers were cheap on tips or likely to be late on paying their bill. *The Daily Transcript* cost 85 cents a week. Blumpkin advised that, "If the customer doesn't give you at least a dollar tip, they are cheap."

He had a remedy for cheap customers: "Find a stick. Find some dog poo. Dip the end of the stick in the poo, then smear a tiny little bit on an inside page that they will read later." He recommended the sports page as a good one. "Then, put the newspaper back to its original state, and deliver as normal." I took his advice, and indeed, when I identified which customers were cheap or late on payments, I followed the Blumpkin technique.

The route was usually completed fairly quickly with Cashews assisting me. It went by even quicker, it seemed, because the entire time we were delivering papers, we would be discussing the world and what we would make of ourselves. Cashews had all sorts of dreams, ambitions, and goals that I hadn't even thought of at that time. I wondered why it was that he had thought so much about so many things that had never even crossed my mind.

We both had a fascination with sharks. We knew all the varieties and how to identify them by their size or markings or unusual features. A movie by the name of *Jaws* had been released that summer, and it both terrified us and inspired us. Cashews said that the only way to get close to these creatures and get paid was to become an oceanographer. That was a big word, but he explained that it was simply a person who studied the ocean and shared our attraction for sharks.

Cashews even had a timeline worked out on becoming an oceanographer. Once we graduated from high school, we would go to a specific type of ocean college. When we graduated from that college after studying oceanography, we would go to work in either in a lab studying marine life, in a cage in the ocean studying actual sharks, or outside the cage, studying more friendly creatures. My father had said the purpose of the paper route was saving up for college. So, we were on the route to our goals.

It seemed every customer we delivered to on the route had a different personality, just as their houses were shaped and painted differently. Some had pets, some were very loud homes, others were quiet. Some people talked a lot and were friendly, while others just seemed to want their paper and not to be bothered. Although a lot of the houses looked different, we were all in the same state, the same town, and we were all New Englanders. Yet … every person had their differences in mannerism. These were most markedly revealed when we were invited in on collection day.

I asked my father about some of the customers. Like, when ringing one particular doorbell more than once, the guy inside yelled at us. My father said, "Well, that guy, he was probably just getting off the sauce cold turkey." Images of that guy, with a "cold turkey" and a bowl of cold brown sauce, perhaps gravy, made me feel bad. Did the guy have to spend his nights in a cooler like the one our Thanksgiving turkeys were stored in? That would explain why he was miserable and mean when it became time to collect.

Another homeowner wore a sweater in a very special way, wrapped around his neck and tied in the center with the sleeves. It seemed odd to us that he would wear it that way because none of our fathers wore special sweaters tied around their necks by the sleeves. I was curious about this and asked my father about the sweater-wearing method. My father said, "Eh, I think that guy must be light in the loafers."

I told Cashews about this the next week while collecting. I had him look at the man's shoes and feet. Sure enough, the guy answered the door in socks, and we took note. He indeed had loafers, placed next to his other shoes off to the side. His loafers were indeed much larger than his feet. So, the extra air in his loafers truly did make them *lighter*.

My father had been correct.

There were two people on my route that would count out the 85 cents they owed me, and place the change in my palm. These tightwads counted each coin out loud, like, "twenty-five, fifty, seventy-five, and one dime makes 85 cents. There you go, young man."

"And there you go Mrs. Tightwad," I thought to myself.

"Dog feces on your sports page, coming right up."

Sometimes Cashews and I would smear the dog feces on the face of a picture of an athlete that had lost a game, or who happened to be in a slump. Since Blumpkin carried his collection money around in a sock, we started to do the same. One day a customer of mine, who my father referred to as "connected," noticed the sock. He looked at it curiously and then invited us in. He had a very thick Boston accent and was well dressed. His loafers did not appear to be light. He had a map of Italy on his wall that said, "the old country."

He was very nice and began to converse. He showed us his wallet, and I had never seen so much money. He said, "Aftah today, I want you'se to drop that sock and get a friggin' wallet." He then told me to dump the contents of the sock on the table. He organized the paper money and put it in piles, dollars, fives, and tens. Then he flashed his wallet again. He said, "You'se want it to be like this. You'se gotta organize your dough."

He even flattened the money, removing wrinkles and corner-folds from each bill. He knew the name of the white guys with bad haircuts on the currency and said, "This guy is first," (he called it a 'buck'). "Then the guy on fives," (he called it a 'fin')." Then, he said, "Next, the tens," (he called those 'sawbucks'). He then showed me how to organize and arrange them in the wallet he insisted I acquire.

This guy always tipped well and was immaculate. But my father would say, "Don't get too friendly with him, he's connected." My father never elaborated on exactly what that meant. I just figured it meant he was a good connection who paid on-time and tipped well. I told my father the connected guy had instructed me to buy a wallet. My father said, "Yeah, you should, but just watch: next week he'll want you to buy a Cadillac." Nevertheless, on my next collection day, my father presented me with a nice black leather wallet.

I felt better with the wallet. I mean, Blumpkin obviously knew what he was doing, but I had to part ways with him on the sock vs. wallet issue. Cashews and I went out collecting with a spring in our steps, and I made sure the connected guy was the last one we visited. I had done exactly what he said, flattening and organizing my bucks, fins, and sawbucks in the precise order he had advised. When he answered the door, I immediately flashed my wallet. He beamed from ear to ear, and said, "Good job kid." I felt a twinge of pride. We were now friends. I was "connected."

I inherited the *Boston Globe* route from my eldest brother, so I now had two routes, a morning one and an afternoon one. The *Globe* had to be done very early in the morning. Cashews couldn't join me that early, so it was just me and the family Labrador retriever, Ruby. Most people considered this dog to be strange because it ate leftover salad and didn't bark or jump on people. It had its own bed in the house and after being let outside to pee, she would politely and patiently paw the door to be let in and then go lie down on her bed. Her bond with me was very strong. She would follow me wherever I went and never tried to run away. I didn't like the idea of a second paper route at first, especially one that early in the morning. But soon I came to really love it.

Everything was still and quiet that early in the morning. There were very few cars out, no buses at all, and no lawnmowers going or people walking around. The only things out with me that early were a few creatures. Squirrels and crows seemed to be early risers and always busy. There was one particular crow with a white spot on its wing that lived on my street for years. With most people in my world, the crow had a bad rap, but I liked the crow. He cleaned up messes, like the neighbor's dead cat, Mittens, that got hit by a car. The crow looked extremely cool, all in black. He didn't fly south in the winter. And, he seemed really smart. He always gave a "caw caw caw," when he saw me.

While delivering, I would briefly read through the morning news and, aside from the sports section, it all seemed scary to me. A war had just ended. I delivered papers to people that had been in that war, or who had family members that didn't make it back from that war. At one of the homes I delivered to, if I rang the bell too much, the homeowner would yell. My father explained that this man had "shell shock" from the war and told me not to ring his bell more than once.

With homework, chores, and two paper routes, my opportunities for fun and play were now quite limited. Memories of training wheels and big wheels seemed very distant. In the free time we did have, my friends and I were now focused on making jumps on our bikes.

Soon we grew bored of simple wood "ramps" set-up on the sidewalk. It was time to build something bigger, in the woods, that provided greater opportunities for excitement and injury. Over many weekends, we expanded the narrow, overgrown walking trail in the woods adjacent to our neighborhood. Using hatchets and shovels borrowed from our fathers' garages, we cleared and engineered a path that twisted and turned through the woods. The purpose of this bike path was not "getting from here to there" smoothly. Rather, it was to provide opportunities for ghastly wipe-outs and wrecks.

Work on the bike path went on for many weeks, rain or shine. While the rest of us focused on relocating boulders or digging deep pits, Cashews wouldn't shut up about his future as an oceanographer. I liked Cashews, but he was what my father would call "an odd duck."

I never really agreed with my father's assessment until Cashews picked up a new obsession: after any kid fell on the playground, was hit with a dodgeball, or anything else that would cause a normal human being to cry, he would run over to the scene of the accident … not to help or render assistance, but to observe the details and ascertain as quickly as possible if the kid was going to burst into tears. If the kid did end up crying, Cashews mentally noted every aspect of the episode, so he could go into great detail about the incident later.

Of course, we were at the age and in a cultural space where crying, no matter how horrific the accident or injury, was a shameful, unforgivable sign of weakness. So, when Cashews wasn't talking about his future career as an oceanographer, he was recounting an incident where someone at school had cried. He would describe every aspect of the event. For instance: "He was pushed down the slide and fell over the edge. I ran over and could see that his bottom lip was quivering. His face was bright red and then a tear came down his cheek. It wasn't sweat; I checked. It was *definitely* a tear." Crying was already considered the worst thing a kid could do. But now that Cashews had become the chronicler of crying kids, we were even more afraid to break into tears.

Once Tibbs was hit with a baseball right in the eye. Cashews ran over, not to help, but to see if there were any tears. Sure enough, a tear ran down Tibbs' cheek. Cashews witnessed this, and turned around to clinically announce, "Tibbs is crying!" Seeking to avoid the stain of shame that this verdict would render on him for perpetuity, Tibbs objected strenuously.

"It's impossible to cry out of just one eye!" he explained.

But Cashews pushed back: "A tear is a tear."

Since his honor was at stake, Tibbs had no other choice but to smack Cashews upside the head, knocking him to the ground, where they proceeded to wrestle to a draw. The fact that he had been called out for crying had been mitigated by the fact that he defended his honor in this way.

The path was finally finished, and just as planned, it proved very dangerous. We ran through the path on our bikes, keeping a record of who was fastest. Sometimes when we got tired, we set our bikes aside and just walked the path, taking in and appreciating the degree of our accomplishment. Soon the path became a local talking point. One day I was collecting for the paper at the Ripley's house and Mrs. Ripley said she had heard about the path we built, had walked it, and proclaimed it to be "extraordinary."

Cashews and I, as the primary architects and builders of the path, felt very proud. A few days later, we were walking home after the paper route, and there in the middle of the street was one of the Bullis brothers. Bullis was Latin for 'bully,' I later discovered. I delivered the paper to his parents; now, seeing him standing there in the street, I was gripped with fear that he may have gotten one I smeared with dog poo.

I looked around for an escape route, but there was nowhere to run. Even if there had been, I knew that he could outrun us. There was nothing to do but keep walking toward him. With every step, we got closer to his mullet haircut, work boots, denim jeans, concert t-shirt, and leather jacket. Having mentally accepted that I was about to take a beating, I heard him say, "Did you'se build da path?" Now I wondered if in building the path, we had dug up a childhood pet he buried up there.

I asked "why," and he astonished us by saying, "I like it. I ride my mini-bike on 'dat path. It's wicked pissah." He didn't smile or shake our hands. He just walked away. Cashews and I looked at each other with a new prideful feeling knowing our work had been proclaimed "wicked pissah" by a Bullis.

Cashews and I seemed to be on our way to success and popularity. At school we were both considered "special" – Cashews because of his memory and vocabulary; me because I was labeled both "hyper" and "lazy." But outside of school, we were peas from a pod. We both loved to watch and play sports. We both loved to explore nature and engage in risky adventures. We both shared different but equally eccentric families that seemed to be the natural product of our Boston Irish Catholic world. In fact, we had recently been assigned the duties and responsibilities of being altar boys.

I enjoyed this assignment, and frequently Cashews and I were assigned to work together in altar boy duties. We did our jobs well, so we began to get assigned more frequent duties, not just on the weekend, but during the weekday evening special masses. One weekday evening our homes had received telephone calls stating that two altar boys were needed urgently. Moments later, Cashews and I met in the street and, like two firefighters, ran in a dead sprint the several blocks to the church. Bursting through the doors, we hurried to the back of the church and quickly donned our altar boy outfits.

Once we had the uniforms on, we lit all the massive candles, carefully poured wine into elaborate gold cups, arranged the circular crackers into their proper places, and then reverently waited for the priest to arrive. When he finally arrived, we realized that he wasn't from the same parish as our normal priest. He didn't seem too friendly like the priests that were normally assigned to our parish. But we were still excited that we possessed the power to make people rise and sit and rise again during mass. The priest got dressed, and we walked downstairs to take our positions at the back of the church.

Someone took notice that Cashews and I, the altar boys, had arrived in the room. People began to rustle in anticipation. And then everyone rose.

Men and women, adults and children, tradesmen, business owners, neighborhood slackers and old retired people. They all rose. We felt like kings during the 25-yard walk down the red carpet and onto the altar. When we finally arrived at the altar and sat, everyone else sat. I felt power. The mass soon got to its serious part, where Cashews and I had to be in sync with what the priest was doing. We had to ring bells on time and then perform a ceremony of washing the priest's sins away, with one of us pouring the water, and the other holding the basin and towel.

I was holding the towel on my forearm, and the small basin in my hands. Cashews poured the water over the priest's hands. The priest announced/requested that the "Lord wash away my iniquity and cleanse me from my sins." Cashews tilted the water jug, but ... nothing came out. Then he tilted it all the way and still ... nothing. Cashews' face grew bright red as he realized that he forgot to fill the water pot. The priest then grew bright red as well and glared at us with disgust. Nonetheless, he pretended to be washing his hands, and then he pretended to dry them as well. We took the dry towel and empty pot from him and returned to our seats. Everything probably would have been fine if not for what Cashews did next.

He leaned to me and whispered, "I guess his sins weren't cleansed." We both burst out laughing and couldn't stop. Momentarily, we figured that due to the priest's age he couldn't see us. Then we heard a voice coming from the sky, booming. It said, "Off the altar." We froze in terror and bewilderment. Was this voice coming from the stained-glass figure behind the altar? Was this God himself? Then the voice came again. "Off the altar." We looked up, and the priest was pointing to us. The voice was coming from the P.A. system.

I scurried to the sacristy, and as I exited, I took a look into the audience to see two red faces out of the hundreds of people. It was my father and Cashews' father. their complexions now illuminating St. Margaret Mary's parish in Westwood. Cashews and I sat there in the sacristy awaiting our fate. Finally, the priest came in. He gnashed his teeth and tore off his clergy outfit. "Never in my life have I seen..." he began.

"You are disgraces to the church..." he continued.

"I hope God forgives you..." he said, not sounding too forgiving.

As he was admonishing us, Father Coyle walked in. Father Coyle was our normal priest, and we all loved and respected him.

Father Coyle looked angry as well. He said, "What's going on here?" The other priest began describing the litany of our sins. Father Coyle finally cut him off, saying, "I'll straighten this out." Father Coyle was in charge, this was his building, so there was little the interloping priest could do. The mass had ended with the usual, "Let us go in peace and love and serve the Lord." People awkwardly exited the building until the only people left were our parents. Father Coyle then told the story of how, when he was an altar boy, his altar boy partner had tripped and fell and how they both laughed uncontrollably until told to leave.

Cashews and I looked at each other in relief. That should calm everyone's nerves, we thought. The visiting priest knew he had been defeated, but he got in the second-to-last word of the evening, saying that he still felt we had been a disgrace. We looked around the room, waiting for this to be over. The stained-glass image of our God still seemed angry. The complexion of our fathers hadn't changed. As we walked through the driveway to our car, my father got in the final last-word on the incident...

"Your ass is in a sling."

As soon as the door closed on the family station wagon, my father began yelling. He continued yelling all the way down Route 109. He continued yelling all the way home. He concluded his sermon as we pulled into our driveway with, "Nevah in da history of da church was anyone thrown off the altah!"

It was almost the same routine as getting report cards, but with the added shame of having embarrassed the family in front of the entire congregation. My mother wrung her hands, sitting on the couch, repeating her mantra of, "I just can't believe this ..." along with, "Oh, I'm so embarrassed." My father swilled his Maalox and with the chalky white substance foaming from his mouth he declared my sentence.

"Two weeks grounded."

Cashews and I conferred at school the next day, and he was grounded as well. That meant I didn't have a partner on the paper route for two weeks. We never served as altar boys together again. "What happened?" I wondered as I walked my paper route alone. One minute I was the number-two man, making an entire church congregation rise, basking in the prideful gaze of my parents and neighbors. And a few moments later, everything had flip-flopped.

THE WILDLIFE

So, I was grounded for being "the only person thrown off the altar in the history of the Catholic Church." My life now was a monotonous routine of sleep, school, the paper route, and yard work. I was, however, still allowed to join the family on an occasional trip.

One such trip was to acquire and consume, "the best onion rings in town," which according to my father, were located at Kelly's Roast Beef, in Revere. I thought we had pretty much surveyed and consumed all such "best foods" in the Greater Boston area. The "best hot dog in town" was in Mattapan. The "best pizza in town" was at Santarpio's in East Boston. The "best fish in town" was a no-name restaurant in downtown Boston. The "best vanilla ice cream in town" was in Dorchester at the Ice Cream Smith. Apparently, they only served vanilla, so I wondered how it was possible that they could actually be the best.

So, that day, we were going to get "the best onion rings in town." At each of these "bests," my father would perform the same ceremony with the food. Whether it was a folded pizza, a foot long, or a chunk of codfish, he would hold the food product up, eye-ball it with a mixture of maniacal desire and loving anticipation, and announce that it was, in fact, the best of that type of food product. Then his ulcers or some other body part would trigger the "guumpfh" just as it entered his mouth. This often caused embarrassment to his family. But that day, the day of the "best onion rings," we were going to eat our goodies in the Country Squire, thus sparing me the public embarrassment of his food rituals.

After I had finished my paper route, school work, and chores, we all headed out to Revere. I had learned about a guy named Revere in school. He had seen some people in funny-looking clothes and warned his friends. Shortly after, they named a town after him and put up a Kelly's Roast Beef stand in his honor. Getting there required that we traverse tunnels, bridges, and tolls. Along any road trip, my father would explain each landmark or structure as we passed by, around, under or through it.

"This tunnel was named aftah a guy that..."

Or, "this bridge was named aftah some crooked politician," followed by "... and some bastid 'trows 'imself off dis' here one a couple times a year."

He explained that in such instances, the Coast Guard would have to deploy to "hook the floaters out of the watah." I imagined that he should be wearing a safari hat and tan shorts to better match his persona of the tour guide.

"Ladies and gentlemen, welcome to the Callahan tunnel," he would say. "The tunnel, it's a mile long and just last week, some stupid bastud, on a moped, was zooming in out of da lanes, and he was run ovah by an 18 wheelah. They had to pressure wash and squeegee his remains off the road."

"Now ladies and gentlemen wee'ze are approaching the Tobin Bridge. Looks to you'se right, and you will see where a month ago anuddah stupid bastud bought it. He had just lost his job, and his old lady had under-cooked the meatloaf 'tree nights in a row. He couldn't take the pressure and snapped ovah it all."

"Now ladies in gentlemen, we are approaching Revere Beach Parkway where just last week..."

My father would always tell stories out loud but never directed to any-one in particular. That's why I thought he would make an excellent tour guide. If only he had the safari hat and tan shorts.

We reached Revere Beach, and I went with my father while he placed the order. "Eyez'll take 'tree of dem, 4 of 'doze, and a lahge one of 'dat." When the food arrived he would always say, "Tanks, take cay-ah."

We carried two massive bags of food to the station wagon. The items were all dispersed. One basket of onion rings was set aside, to be saved for "dah wildlife." When all the food had been disbursed, my father grabbed the onion rings and placed them on the hood of the car. Then he said, "Now, 'da wildlife." Returning to the station wagon, he cradled his basket of onion rings, tenderly picked up just one, and then performed his ritual. Holding up an onion ring like a priest holding up the "body of Christ," he announced, "The best onion rings in town … garuumph."

As my father was chewing, the "wildlife" showed up. They were gray and black, with smears of white. I had never seen this type of wildlife before and assumed they must be some exotic variety distinct to Revere. My father said they were pigeons. These pigeons were a lot different than the crows on my street. These things had a funny way of walking, and they didn't "caw" like the crows.

Rather, they made a ridiculous "boo booo boo" noise as they waddled around. They took two steps, bent their head back and forth, looked-over the onion rings, bent up again to look at us in the Country Squire, then bent down again to finally and very suspiciously take an onion ring. Once one pigeon had successfully acquired an onion ring, a whole gang of pigeons landed on the car, bobbed around, "boo booo booed," took up all the onion rings and flew off.

My father, being not only a tour guide but also a wildlife expert, described where they were going, if they were male or female, and what their intentions and motivations were. "Dat one is probably going to go back to her nest and feed the babies. Dat uddah one is going to just eat alone with his onion ring a park bench." It all seemed plausible to me.

I was enjoying the pigeon show. My father the tour guide and wildlife expert then spotted something through the window of the Country Squire. He stopped chewing and looked quite alarmed. "Here come the skysharks!" I then noticed big white birds that I had recognized from the Irish Riviera. Clam lady had called them seagulls, but to my father, they were "skysharks." It was obvious from the looks of the pigeons that they sensed trouble. Their heads bobbed feverishly, they looked left and right rapidly. They were obviously not friendly with the skysharks.

The skysharks dove just toward the hood of the station wagon, and without even landing, absconded with all the remaining onion rings. They didn't even touch the hood of the Country Squire. They just swooped down, hovered for an instant, grabbed their prize, and flew off skyward with the onion rings. Everything happened exactly like it did undersea when a shark would swim in, attack, and swim off with a chunk of meat. I knew this from my pre-college study of oceanography with Cashews. My father the wildlife expert was correct after all. These were indeed skysharks.

My father held his look of awe while chewing half a Kelly's Roast Beef sandwich in his cheek. He chewed a little, and said, "Well, dat's 'da wildlife." That afternoon, the hood of the Country Squire had been a stage, and the actors and actresses had been winged wildlife.

We drove home and my father the tour guide said we were going to deviate from the route we had driven on the way to Revere. He proclaimed we would be taking a shortcut called "da' pike." He gave a final tour guide tidbit as we drove. "Just last month 'dis tractah trailah drivah had been driving for 24 hours straight. 'Da headcase fell asleep at 'da wheel and jackknifed in the middle of 'da road. 'Dah moron backed up traffic for seven hours. Word is," he paused for dramatic effect. "… he'll nevah walk again." Thus ended my respite from being grounded and our trip to sample the "best onion rings in town."

WALKIE TALKIE

Sometimes, rather than taking a "road trip," the road trip came to our house. As faithful and observant Boston Irish Catholics, we had many religious holidays. And with my parents having five children, there were many birthdays on top of that.

I was still grounded, but I could tell something unusual was happening. My father returned from a store that supplied adult drinks, carrying cases and boxes. Some of the bottles were brown and some were clear. And there were stacks of cans that all had the same name on them. These were all put away behind the bar and in the garage refrigerator. That year, my mother decided we would celebrate my birthday early, so we could combine it with a religious holiday and have a "double whammy." My mother prepped both for my birthday and the religious celebration by taking things in and out of the oven, blending things, pouring things, and putting plates out – special ones for the adults and paper happy plates for the kids.

I assisted my father downstairs at the bar. There were things called "beer nuts" to pour into beer nut holders, pistachios to go in little dishes, chips piled on a special tray that had a dip holder on the side. Ashtrays had to be dispersed, ice buckets filled, the ice trays refilled with water and put back in the freezer. Adult glasses had to be placed on the bar, so they were ready to be prepped, poured, and served by me. My father had a silver shaker-mixer which was taken off the shelf and placed atop the bar.

My birthday was celebrated mostly with my friends outside. But I enjoyed being called in frequently to assist my father with the adult drinks. Screwing off the caps of the brown and clear bottles, I sniffed the contents and couldn't understand how people could drink that stuff. Whether it came from the brown bottle or clear bottle, it all smelled like the solution that was put on scrapes after very bad bicycle accidents. I would hear the call from my father: "Hey Joe!" I would run to the bar and get together the adult drinks and either hand them to the adults after they arrived or put them on a special adult drink circular thing called a "coaster."

One by one, the cars started to show up at our house. When the elderly arrived, we had to assist them. They all seemed to be from some sort of gang, as they all had the small statue on their automobile dashboards, and they all had the same walking devices and other elderly person apparatuses to assist them. The women all had hats with flowers, and all their clothing was a dull gray or black.

My father and I went outside to greet and assist each in getting to the house. My father had nicknames for all of them. One couple was dubbed, "Walkie Talkie," because the wife walked funny due to a bug named Polio that landed on her as a child, while the husband had to use a plastic device held to his throat to speak. After a few drinks, Talkie would let us play with it. Upon arriving, Walkie Talkie didn't seem to say much or look too happy. But I knew that as soon as they had consumed some magic adult drinks their attitudes would change.

The next car that pulled up with a statue on the dashboard was driven by James Moran. We just called him "Uncle James." He was with his wife Mildred, and they were originally from Dorchester. But now they lived in Falmouth. Uncle James' sister was Mary Fitzgerald, formerly Mary Moran, and she lived in Quincy. My father said she had a "lead foot" and would always hold the speed record from Quincy to Falmouth. She had developed something called a "stroke," which left one side of her paralyzed, so she had a cane, but for the most part, she could make her own way into the house. They weren't too talkative yet, either.

Pretty soon all the elderly had all arrived and were helped into the house and seated. One room needed to be set aside to pile up all their clothing, canes, hats, and walkers. My father started working the bar. He made Uncle James his special drink, mixed with ice and shaken up in the silver mixer. After consuming a few of those drinks, Uncle James started on the canned drinks called Miller. He must have been very thirsty, for he consumed all of his drinks *very* fast. The more he drank the nicer he got, and after a few he let me play with a lighter called Zippo; it was my job to light his cigarettes called Lucky Strikes. After taking him his drink or can and lighting his cigarette, I would trot back to the bar to assist my father.

"Joe," he would say. "These two go to Walkie-Talkie. The one on the left is for Walkie and the one on the right is for Talkie." I sniffed these disgusting drinks and all I could think of was the knee scrape medication that was put on a cotton ball and then applied to a wound. As I made the rounds with the drinks I started to see the ashtrays fill up with cigar butts and cigarettes, which meant I had to start emptying them. The men's cigarettes were short and stubby while the women's seemed to be narrow and long.

Shortly after the gang of elderly had arrived, had been helped in the house, were seated, and had consumed a few drinks, my friends started to show up one by one. They arrived with their presents and cards. Uncle James, who was now feeling quite happy, yelled that he was going to be in charge of the presents and cards. So, my friends had to hand the presents to him. He would look at one of them, shake their hand, take the present and card, and place it in a pile next to his chair. When all had been assembled, he picked up a card and read who it was from. The first was from Tibbs.

"Ah, you're John, what's your last name? Tibbs? What kind of a name is Tibbs?" And then, "Okay, Rich, what is your last name? Cash? Ah, a good Irish name!" My friend Jon Kent walked in. He handed the card to Uncle James. He looked at it and tried to read the name, which was written as "Jon K." My Uncle James then yelled, "Dis one's from 'Jonk' … hey, that's a Chinaman's name! Hey, Jonk, you even look like a Chinaman!"

My friend Jon just smiled awkwardly, but the nickname China had been proclaimed and it would stick. After all, the presents were received and recorded and all my friends had been embarrassed by my Uncle James, we left the adults to their drinks so we could go run around outside until it was time for dinner, followed by the opening of my presents. I still needed to run inside once in a while, to serve the drinks and clean the ashtrays. There were many silver Miller cans next to Uncle James now. He was yelling from the bottom floor, where the men were, up to the top floor, where the ladies were, about being out of Lucky Strikes. His sister Mary Fitzgerald yelled back that she only had Virginia Slims … and they were lady cigarettes. He finally said, "Ah, I don't care," and lurched and stumbled upstairs, coming back down with a lit cigarette. He looked funny with one of his massive hands holding the shiny Miller can and the other massive hand holding a very long, thin lady cigarette.

I went back outside and played with my friends until we got the call that it was dinner. There was one dining room table, a small circular table in the living room, a table in the main kitchen, and one outside on the porch. It was spring so me and my birthday guests would eat on the porch and then head back in for cake. When it was time to blow out my candles, I silently wished a very solemn wish: "May Farah Fawcett show up for my next birthday."

But first all the elderly, now very happy, males had to go from the downstairs to the upstairs. This meant a task that was performed for all celebrations at our house whether religious or not. This task was getting my massive grandfather from the bottom floor up to the top floor dinner table. It was always the same procedure. My grandfather would be sitting in a big black one-man chair downstairs. He would sometimes be in his own world, just staring with his piercing eyes across the room. My father said that his staring off into the distance was from "the war." Anyhow, my father had to interrupt his horizontal trance, and announce three times that it was "time for suppah!"

He smiled and then two men grabbed him, one on each arm. He was lifted up and then guided to the first set of stairs. Then my brother and I would stand behind him and push his bum, waiting for and responding to second-by-second guidance. It usually went something like, "Grab his friggin' ankle and put it on the friggin' step!" I was thus the "friggin' ankle grabber," responsible for guiding his massive ugly brown shoes up the stairs. It was only six steps to the foyer, and it took forever, but we finally made it. Next, it was six more steps to the second floor where his walker was.

We all took a breath and rested in the foyer. The two adults held my grandfather in place. Then after a moment, my father announced, "Okay boys, let's finish it." There was moaning from the two adults doing the pulling up front. I held his ankles and placed the giant ugly brown shoes on the next step. My father gave the command before each step: "Let's get the lead out, on three … one, two, three!" My grandfather was now smiling upon reaching the top and seeing his walker. He shuffled to the head of the table and waited. Then he was assisted into his chair and the walker was taken away.

The rest of the elderly then took their seats. It seemed their ailments had vanished due to the drinks, Virginia Slims and Lucky Strikes. "Gang Grey" settled in as fresh adult drinks were brought to them. Margaret Foley, my grandmother, arrived wearing huge sunglasses. My father said she had things called "cat racks" in her eyes. It was a religious holiday, so my grandmother said a prayer. She smiled when she prayed, and when she finished she mentioned three beings and then made a sign of a cross. All the other elderly did as well.

Soon we would be singing happy birthday, and it would be *my* happy birthday. We went outside and ate what we could and tried to save room for the cake. I was itching to put on my coned hat and silently proclaim my secret wish upon blowing out the candles. Finally, my mother made the announcement that it was time to sing happy birthday. The coned hats were brought out. The candles were lit and then the song 'Happy Birthday' was sung. There were three different choruses, and thus three different sounds. Some of the elderly had cigarettes dangling from their mouths which affected their singing; Talkie added another element with his electronic voice. The rest of us sang normally. People clapped. My grandmother then announced, "Happy birthday pumpkin," blew a kiss and did her trademark giggle. I made my wish for Farah and then blew out the candles. Everyone clapped and we started eating the cake.

My mother always made a mean cake. It was soft, chocolate, with thick frosting. This was the seventies and people were talking about Trans Ams, not "trans fats." Then the moment came to open the presents. Uncle James said he would assist me. He didn't ask me, he just stepped in. Everyone gathered in the living room next to the dining room and sat down. It was as if there was a fire in the house with all the cigars, Virginia Slims, and Lucky Strikes ignited.

I would reach for a card and sometimes a check for $3 or $5 dollars would pop out. A couple of birthdays ago my father had angrily instructed, "Don't complain about the $2 checks … that person was in the depression, and that is a lot of money for them." So, I would say "wow" to the $2 or $3 dollars when it popped out of the card.

Uncle James would pick up the card or present, look at it with a dangling Virginia Slim and announce, "It's from Rich." Then I would open the card, and read the greeting, and then open his gift. Then it was passed around and held up by each elderly person and they would make an announcement with their dangling cigarettes: "Wow, you can really use 'dis here 'ting," or "Hey, I never had fancy clothes like that, holy mackerel." The shirts and pants I received as birthday gifts were indeed very colorful compared to the black and gray uniformly worn by the elderly. Every piece of clothing was held up, examined and passed around by every member of Gang Grey, each with a dangling cigar or cigarette, and was ultimately folded back up "the right way" by my mother and placed into my room.

As the last gift was being passed around and commented on, guests began to gesture silently with their watches, swiveling their heads left and right, as a sign that it was time to get going. One by one the jackets, canes, hats (men's with feathers on one side, women's with flowers all the way around), galoshes and walkers were retrieved and handed out. The elderly were very happy now, having undergone a total metamorphosis from when they first arrived.

Now they were laughing and smiling and their collective 'art-ritis' and assorted stroke symptoms had miraculously disappeared. "Walkie" even had a little more bounce in her step. I attributed the transformation to the magic power in the adult drinks. One by one the elderly entered their cars and drove off waving, tooting the horn, and blowing kisses as they made their way back to Dorchester, Milton, and Quincy.

The last to leave were my father's parents, his aunt, and another lady named Anna Murphy. I was kissed by all the females and noted that they all smelled like bug spray or mothballs. Now it was time get my grandfather down the stairs. He still needed two adult males in front of him, but it was easier than the way up. He finally made it down the stairs and grabbed his walker. He shuffled out to his parking spot at the top of the driveway right next to the garage. I went out with my father, to wave goodbye to everybody.

My grandfather said something to my father and then stopped abruptly. He then hunched over his walker and vomited with the power of a firehose. Chunks of the chocolate cake, partially-chewed slabs of the religious ham, some liquid that practically glowed, and a foamy whipped substance completed the layers of barf that landed on the ground in front of him. It had begun with a booming "bloooohhhk" sound, followed by a clapping splash on the new tar driveway.

He paused for a breath and then one last lurch of a glowing green substance completed the process. Seeing the fluorescent green splatter, my father proclaimed, "that's the bile." I figured that was another word for "the end." I asked my father if grandfather was going to be okay, and he said, "Oh yeah, he's just flushing out his radiator." My father did not seem at all alarmed, so I felt relieved, and assumed this must have been a normal, healthy and common occurrence.

My father then guided him to the driver's seat of his car and assisted him in. Then he took the walker, popped the trunk, and placed it inside. He gave my grandfather the keys and the car was started. Everyone waved one last time. I looked at the patron saint statuette on the dashboard of his car. He put it in reverse and backed up rapidly, almost hitting the house, then he pulled forward a few feet.

He went forward and back a few times to get the car aimed at the driveway properly. I asked my father if he was sure they would get home, and if the statue on the dashboard would help. He said, "Sure … that's the patron saint of elderly drunk driving, they'll make it!" I felt comfort at this added benefit of our religion, all the automobile dashboard statuettes and the extra safety they provided.

Everybody seemed happy and satisfied. It had been a great birthday. I had new clothes (which I didn't get very often), had seen the magic effects of adult drinks on elderly people, and had even seen the power of our religious statues in action. And my friend Jon had been christened 'China' for perpetuity.

THE BLIZZARD OF '78

Residents of New England witnessed a historic blizzard that year. For decades hence, everybody remembered the Storm of '78. This blizzard would dump record inches of snow inland and tear homes off their foundations on the coast. Eventually, the snow melted, and the houses were repaired. But that winter a bitterness took root in me. Unlike the snow, it didn't melt away.

Even though I was a kid, life seemed to be a full-time job. School, two paper routes, homework, and yardwork seemed to constitute 90% of my waking hours. My father had been abstinent from alcohol for ten years. As he would say, he was "on the wagon." My mother seemed happy that he no longer drank adult drinks. I had very faint memories of a skinny guy that played guitar and laughed. Most of my life, though, he was ill-tempered, pudgy and gaining weight every year, and he never even looked at the guitar.

The temper came out more frequently the older I got, especially in association with my report cards. It was always the same routine of him taking out his glasses, looking intently at the report card, yelling "what's this," and then banging on the kitchen table. He would either chase me with his belt, or I would be grounded. In my mind, there was absolutely no hope of or path to getting better grades in school. *None*. That reality made me close up inside myself. I would see in the *Boston Globe* that the city was having a lot of problems. We lived only 7 miles away. There was a thing called "bussing," and people were going crazy over it. They were even fighting in the streets. I wondered why there was so much anger.

I started to feel uncomfortable in my own physical appearance. Other than the few new items of clothing I got on my birthdays, my wardrobe consisted of hand-me-downs, and I was the youngest – so by the time things got to me, they were quite worn and outdated. For that school year, I had plaid bell bottoms, platform shoes, and wide-collared shirts that my brother once owned. As I looked around, I noticed that nobody else was wearing clothing like this. I could even see some of the other students pointing and laughing.

One day, Cashews and I were exiting the playground and trying to avoid a group of older kids across the street. They spotted us, and it was obvious that we were going to get roughed up. The finger-pointing started, and they all began to ridicule my clothes. Cashews whispered that I better do something. I knew he was right. If you were teased once and let it go, it would continue forever. Plus, I knew that my John Travolta "Mr. Saturday Night" outfit wasn't going to change anytime soon.

One of the guys laughing at me stepped forward and said, "nice pants!" He slapped me upside the head. Before I knew what was happening, my right hand went into action, like the spring-action snake coming out of a can of fake peanuts. My right hand unleashed a barrage of punches to his face before he could even register what was happening. He had fallen on the ground, and his head lay near the curb.

I thought about kicking him in the head with my big platform shoes. But Cashews grabbed my arm and said, "It's all right man, calm down." The boy's face was white and his eyes wide as he looked up, blood starting to trickle from his nose. My homework was strewn all over the street. The crossing guard yelled at us and looked at me in disgust. That didn't make sense to me, because I was merely the one that had stood up for himself. All the other boys were silent as Cashews and I walked away.

I didn't even know what to think about what had happened. Just one season ago I had been relatively bright-eyed, excited about the world, and always looking forward to exploring and discovering new things around me. But in fact, I had been full of gunpowder all along and didn't even know it. I wondered why. I thought about the lies the world had told me, and how disappointing they were. The lie about prayers saving my friend. The lie about my grandmother coming home from the hospital. The lie that a kid's life should be fun.

Cashews and I walked home. Even he was stunned by my explosiveness. We delivered the paper together but didn't say a word to one another. My school paperwork was now probably blowing all over Route 109, but I didn't care. Later that night, I lay on my bunk bed looking up into nothing, anger my only emotion.

The next day, however, I discovered that something good had, in fact, come from my being teased. As Cashews and I arrived at school the next day, we immediately discovered that word had already spread about all the punches I landed on the bigger kid who had made the mistake of teasing me. The students were quiet as we had morning formation. Not one laughed or looked at my platform shoes and plaid bell bottoms. Nobody said anything, but we could both sense the aura of respect and awe coming at us from the other kids. We stood proudly at morning formation with our right hands on our chest pledging allegiance. That incident seemed to coincide with my entire group of friends becoming more aggressive.

We had our own spot on the school playground and those who crossed that spot were slapped upside the head. Soon, merely defending our spot and punishing actual trespassers was not enough. Our playground aggression was projected outward. I cannot recall what incident lead to the debut of the "slug train." This involved my crew lining up horizontally, putting our hands on each other's shoulders, repeating the words "slug-slug-slug-sluga-sluga-sluga" (it began as a whisper and grew into a war cry), all the while kicking the dirt like a cartoon bull.

Eventually, once a victim had been selected through some sort of hive-mind, telepathic communication, we began a slow trot in their direction. Once close to the victim, we separated before pouncing on him and throwing punches. The ritual ended with the victim's shoes being removed so he could be pummeled with them.

The first time we performed the slug train, kids and even teachers just stared, but then went back to their normal behavior. Perhaps they thought we were playing a friendly game and the victim was in on it. The next time we did it, we were all sentenced to stay in for recess the following day. We didn't learn our lesson and were soon back at it. By our third slug train, some of the girls on the playground, with their cute dresses and pigtails, seeing us in formation and hearing our chant growing, would begin to run and scream, "It's the slug train!" This was the signal for potential victims to scatter in all sorts of directions like a pack of gazelles. But we were the hyenas.

My life had changed from finger paints and *Sesame Street* to paper routes, chores, teachers that didn't like me because I struggled at school, and homework and report cards that I knew would disappoint. I noticed on the paper route, the conversations Cashews and I had also started to change. No more discussing dreams of being oceanographers riding on the back of dolphins and turtles, and getting as close as we could to the feared great white shark. Now we discussed plans for the next slug train and who would be our new victim.

I was constantly being scolded. Teachers seemed to be disgusted with me. Even the dentist seemed to have it out for me. He slapped me across the face for repeatedly having to ask me to open my mouth wider. I came out of his office holding my slapped cheek. My father queried what happened, and I told him. My father stormed into the exam room.

"You mothahfuggah!"

There was a lot of noise and things crashing, and the assistant was begging him to stop. When my father came back out he said we were never going back to that dentist. But then he yelled at me for not brushing my teeth well enough.

Halloween season arrived, and all our pumpkins had been carved and placed outside. My father heard suspicious activity in our yard, and shouted, "Hey, deys ah stealing ah pumpkins!" He bolted outside and I next heard the roar of the station wagon engine and the spinning of the tires. A bit later he returned and I overheard him describe the great pumpkin chase down Route 109.

"I got the pumpkins back, heh-heh!" he said.

I was not a smart kid and I knew it – at least not smart the way the world seemed to define it. But I took everything in. And increasingly, what I took in was being received with a negative cast to it. What would haunt me the rest of my life was taking my anger and frustration and dishing it back out on the innocent kids of our school playground via "the slug train."

In New England, winter pretty much starts the day after Halloween, and snow often precedes it. Snow meant the paper routes took longer and papers getting wet. I tried my best to deliver them promptly and keep them dry. But there was always someone that would complain. It appeared to me that those who were the cheapest, the ones who never tipped, were the ones who complained the most and would even shout. The shouting only made it worse for them as I could always find a fresh dog poo deposit in the snow to make my mark of punishment inside their newspaper.

I was watching the snow fall one day and noticed that the flakes were getting larger. They seemed heavy. Snowflakes were supposed to be delicate and dainty. But these were big, ugly, aggressive flakes. I could only think of the paper route that afternoon and how the snow would make it that much more difficult to deliver the newspapers. This snow indeed seemed very different. Not only was it fat and thick but it had started to blow very hard, hitting the windows with force and even sticking to the glass. I noticed the teacher looked startled and couldn't stay focused. It made some of the students nervous to see her nervous.

Then the principal came and spoke briefly with the teacher. The teacher with anxiety in her voice announced that a bad storm was found coming off the ocean and was meeting another storm that was coming in from the north, which would make for a great deal of snow. We were to be sent home.

Then came the announcement over the P.A. "Due to the change in the weather forecast, you will all be sent home early." I heard cheers from the other classrooms. The whole thing had a feel similar to that of our fire alarm drills. This, however, was no drill. I could sense some fear in the eyes of the teaching staff. Outside, we could barely see. I was walking home from school now, and it was as if the snow was being blown from Boston straight down Route 109, gusting horizontally. This excited my crew, and it brightened up my world. Ah, I thought, back to nature. We battled the storm all the way up Mill Street and onto Crystal Hill. China said he would meet me in the morning, to sled. We already knew that we wouldn't have to listen to the radio to find out if school was canceled.

That afternoon, we closed all the windows in the house, and my mother grabbed candles from the "hope" chest. Probably named after, "I hope the power doesn't go out." As the New England darkness fell upon us, the wind really picked up. My father called from his office in Jamaica Plain and said he wouldn't be coming home. Shortly after the call, we lost power.

We lit our candles and took in the noise of the wind shaking our windows as if to let in the horizontal snowfall. I wasn't afraid. I was amazed at the power of Mother Nature. Grown-ups went around all the time in the world they had created as if their systems and structures made them immune from nature. As if the world outside our homes and cars and stores was some museum exhibit. But this showed that wasn't the case. My Mom, in fact, said, "Mother nature must be pissed." Who pissed her off and how long was she going to be pissed, she didn't say. My mother was strange in a lot of ways.

When it came to being sick or losing power, she would simply say, "we'll be fine" and show no fear or emotion. Not like the teachers at our school that had panic in their eyes, which seemed to put panic in the eyes of the students. With the non-stop snow, my two brothers decided to jump off the roof of the house. This was a once in a lifetime thing, so they took advantage of it. We had a fire going in the porch stove, so my mom and I sat out there. I barely made out my brothers jumping from the roof onto the drifts that had formed below. They were experiencing two seconds of flight.

I was amazed at it all. It was one big art show put on by Mother Nature herself. Who or what "pissed" her off we didn't know. But she had decided to exhale her wrath all over Massachusetts. I was in a tank. Not able to leave; peering out each window in awe. Every window throughout the house showed a different scene. On one side, the stairwell leading outside was piled so high with snow that the door was no longer able to open. Directly behind us was a family of pine trees. The pines seemed to have the ability to sway more than the oaks in the storm. But it appeared they could hardly hold the weight of the snow and winds. I could hear branches snapping.

From the next set of windows, I could normally see Tibbs' house. Now there was nothing but snow being blown sideways. I thought of the bad storm in the *Wizard of Oz* and waited to see an ugly woman with a long nose ride by on a bicycle. Or possibly dead relatives and friends twisting by. The only fear I had was how long would it last. What if we were trapped there for life? I went to my room and lay down. But the noise wouldn't stop. It was as if the wind was beating on the windows, wanting to get in.

That night I stayed awake longer than ever before. The arms of the Mickey Mouse clock were past 12, a time I never witnessed. I had some joy through it all, as I knew we couldn't possibly have school, and the *Boston Globe* and *Daily Transcript* wouldn't be delivered. With those pleasant thoughts, I put my arms behind my head and fell asleep.

I awoke and it was as if nothing had happened ... and yet *everything* had happened. Our house was never this quiet. There was no power, no phones, no father announcing in the foyer that "they" were after him, or "they tried to take me to the cleaners!" My battery-operated Mickey Mouse clock seemed like the only thing that was ticking. My mother announced that Mother Nature was no longer "pissed," and she had stopped showing her fury. The sun was even peeking out. I looked outside in amazement. Cars were covered in snow, trees were down. Everything had stopped. There wasn't even a sign of the usual creatures I normally witnessed early mornings while delivering the paper. No squirrels. No crow.

I knew I could do whatever I wanted. It was as if I was back in kindergarten with no worries and only fun to look forward to. Tibbs didn't get up until noon on non-school days, even if it was 75 degrees and dry. So, I decided to walk to my friend's house who had recently been christened China. This was the 1970s, long before helicopter parents fretted and worried about every little possible danger their kids might encounter. So, despite the weather, my mother declared that going outside was "good for me" and to "go get some fresh air." Looking outside, it appeared that China and I were going to be the first ones out exploring.

I hadn't felt this sense of freedom in years. Everything recently had felt like being crushed between the margins that were placed on both sides of me. Homework, chores, and the paper routes on one side and school and teachers on the other. But that day I was free to do what I always liked: just explore. I carefully put on my snowsuit, boots, gloves, and hat, pulled the snowsuit hood over my head, and peered out the window.

There was snow piled over my head, so I wouldn't be able to open the doors. The blizzard had stacked snow about six feet high. I headed to the garage. It initially stuck, but with some effort, it finally opened. Before me was an amazing site, a world of white. Where before the streets and sidewalks and houses and telephone poles staked out a rigid world of routine and discipline, now I saw soft, bright, undulating shapes and forms everywhere.

I looked in all directions, to the towns of Dedham, Norwood, Dover, and Walpole. It was all white and lumpy. This must have been what the moon looked like. I walked a few feet and then had to act like a penguin, climbing up a drift of snow, sliding my way down, and waddling in the direction of China's house. The pent-up anger and resentment inside of me seemed to slip away with the light and cold and crunch of snow beneath my boots. Everybody else was upset with Mother Nature. But it felt to me like she was on my side. She wanted me to enjoy what she just dumped on us. After struggling for what seemed like an hour, I finally made it across the street to China's. His door was covered with snow, and I could only see my reflection in the glass storm door from the nose up. Indeed, in that snowsuit, I did look like a penguin.

I knocked on his door. Once I saw his face, it was obvious that he shared my joyful anticipation at the sight of what the blizzard had left. He changed in a flash, and his mom gave him the "be careful" and "be back before dark" routine. He opened his door and then leaped across the drift that had formed, sliding like an arctic otter down a marshmallow sculpture. The streets and sidewalks were covered up, so there was literally no direction to be had. It was just walk and explore aimlessly like we did

5 years before in kindergarten. I noticed again that there were no small creatures out. Looking at the houses along the street, I could see neighbors peeking out their windows and doors. Nobody had snow blowers back then, and I could tell that there wasn't going to be any shoveling that day.

Cashews wouldn't be joining us. Although he was adventurous, his mom was a forerunner of today's over-protective types, and she was very cautious with him. So, it was just me and China making the first steps out onto this moonlike surface, becoming the "the first to discover." This was our world and it would stay that way for at least a week.

The day finally ended. We had completed our exploration and reconnaissance mission out to the moonscape and had survived. It seemed like it was a big moment for us, "one small step for mankind, one giant step for the little people."

I noticed that even adults with the 1950's style haircuts, the ones who did the exact same mundane things every day, eventually seemed to enjoy what Mother Nature left. As if Mother Nature decided to say, "Hey, why doesn't everyone take a break from the hustle and bustle for a moment?" Take a break from rising at the same hour every day, with your toast lightly buttered, and your coffee with Half & Half stirred clockwise, checking your watch, getting a haircut every two weeks, and putting on your galoshes at exactly 6:15 every morning before driving the exact same route to work.

This storm must have felt uncomfortable, I pondered, for those people who iron their underwear and do certain things every day at the the same time. It must have been a shock to their system. Or maybe it was a wakeup call to enjoy life again.

The next day, China and I got up early again and were the first ones out of our spaceships and onto the moonscape. I noticed my friends the squirrel and the crow had somehow made it through the storm and were cautiously surveying things. With all the roads impassable, our street Crystal Hill became an Olympic-level sledding trail. The Flexible Flier was replaced with metal saucers and inner tubes, which were much faster and could cover any terrain.

Day by day, but slowly, more people took steps out of their homes and out into the white, powdery world. One who waited several days to emerge was Mr. Grimes, the accountant. He was a decent customer who always tipped, which I appreciated. He was pleasant enough, but he was the type that only existed within a set of iron-clad routines. His whole life seemed to run on a clock. He and his wife had no children, and their house was always immaculate. In the garage, everything was in order and neatly placed on a peg or organized on the workbench. Today, however, his routine had been interrupted. He wasn't going anywhere, and I could see his wife taking a picture of him next to a massive drift. It would be labeled, "Fred's wild years," I thought, and would commemorate the day Fred was forced to step out of his monotonous schedule.

China and I started to sled and we were soon joined by others. We didn't think of eating or drinking. We had to take advantage of this opportunity to sled down our street before it was plowed. Soon scores of kids of all ages joined in. Cashews even arrived. Mid-day came and Tibbs emerged. That day was for sledding. The next day we discovered snow forts. The day after that, we figured out how to connect the snow forts with snow tunnels. Since this snowfall had made history, we figured, anything we made from it, therefore, had to be historic. The paths for our sleds, the snowmen, the snow forts, the tunnels, the leaps we made from rock formations. Every day brought a new adventure.

One morning a massive piece of machinery came rumbling up Crystal Hill. It appeared as a metal T-Rex, like no other type of plow we had seen before. It was simply enormous. While impressed with the size of the lumbering beast, we watched with disgust as it removed the snow from Crystal Hill, thus eliminating our sledding path. However, China immediately realized the opportunity that came from this disaster. All the snow from the street was being pushed to the outer edge of the cul-de-sac circle. This created a massive bowl-like structure which soon became our fortress. It was quickly wormed out with tunnels. Snowball wars ensued.

Ah, we were kids again. We were notified that school would be opening in a few days, so we had to get our fun in. As the snow melted and was slowly removed, the regimented world of straight lines, borders, and margins began to reassert itself. After several days on hiatus, the daily stack of *Boston Globes* again began to be dumped on my porch. My father yelled, "Globe's here," which meant the fun ended and I needed to report for duty – not snowball war duty, but real-world duty. It took me three times as long to deliver the paper through the ice and slush and snow piles. I tried to make the best of it, exploring the remaining drifts along the way. A couple days later, the stack of *Daily Transcripts* arrived. I tried to deliver it as fast as I could to get back to my friends and our battle stations in the snow fortress. Fortunately, I already had created a path from delivering the morning *Globe*, so the afternoon paper delivery went a bit quicker.

I read the paper and could see the devastation on the coast as well as on the highways. Apparently, many people died of carbon monoxide poisoning by starting their cars to keep warm on the highway while stuck in the snow. So, the storm wasn't all that fun for some. The next day, school started back up. I almost couldn't believe that the glorious interruption to the real world of routine I was trapped in had ended. Sitting at my desk, I looked out the window often, thinking about what we could be doing outside.

So maybe Mother Nature hadn't been "mad" after all. Maybe she was disappointed, sad that society had neglected the everyday beauty she provided. Did she look down from above as people drove hurriedly past and through her beauty, as they ignored the foliage, the birds, the rising and falling of tides and the spring blooms? Had she sent the storm to slow us down, so we could take it all in again? She wasn't mad, I decided, as I looked out the window of my classroom. She simply wanted to slow us down. She probably felt bad that some died though, I thought.

When the roads were cleared my father insisted that we take a day trip to the Irish Riviera, to see the destruction the Atlantic caused to homes on the coast. Many had actually been lifted off their foundations and moved. They obviously didn't enjoy what Mother Nature brought them. My father the tour guide surveyed everything as we cruised the coastline in our American-made Country Squire.

"Dat poor bastard's going to be spending the rest of his life at a homeless shelter," he said.

"And 'dat poor bastard's probably bobbin' somewhere's out at sea!"

"'Dat guy's kitchen will float ashore in Portugal someday!"

We made our way back down to Bluefish Cove and to our astonishment the cottage we stayed in was still intact. We were all happy about that, as it meant we still had a place to go for the month of August. The house had been put up on cinder blocks many years ago, which probably saved it from floating away. But there was a great mass of wooden debris all around the place. We ventured out of the Country Squire and ran to the beach. When we got there we all said at once, "There's no beach!" It was as if Mr. Atlantic had vomited all over Bluefish Cove. Any unwanted material or marine life he felt wasn't "getting the lead out" he had hurled onto the beach. Lobster buoys, lobster pots, puffy fish, small fish with large teeth, lobsters, wood, and mounds and mounds of seaweed were strewn and piled everywhere.

There was no sign of the sand we had placed our towels on in the summer, but we now had Mr. Atlantic's vomit to play in. It was still very cold out, but once kids eye fun, they seem to become oblivious to the outside temperatures. Later, as adults, words like "nippy," "frigid," "clammy," or "stuffy" would be used, but as kids, we were immune to the fluctuations of weather.

In my mind, the lazy fish were now spilled out onto the beach. I held up one very bloated, funny-looking fish and my father gave it a name: "That's the friggin' puffah fish!" Long name, I thought. This went on until it got dark. My father, drinking his coffee on the seawall with his binoculars, yelling out names of objects when I held them up.

"That's a lobsterman's apron, the owner of it is probably at the bottom of the ocean right now!"

(Coffee Slurp).

"That's called a horseshoe crab, you step on one of those bastahds and you'll limp for two weeks!"

(Coffee Slurp).

"Eh, that there is a dogfish. It's like a baby shark, it'll tear your ass up!"

So it went, a school room amidst of the vomit of flotsam and jetsam from Mr. Atlantic, with my father the teacher identifying the dead marine life.

We drove home and images and impressions were implanted in my head of the bad side of Mother Nature and Mr. Atlantic. I was told close to 100 people had died. Then there were the people who had no friends, that were missing. Maybe they used the storm as an excuse to get away forever and were very happy somewhere, warm and safe, drinking adult drinks.

"Gone missing," I imagined.

"Ol' Chet was a quiet guy, who sat at the end of a bar, and is now missing."

A storm would be the best time to leave and go somewhere else. I thought it would be nice to convince China to just keep walking with me in the snow, far away from Crystal Hill.

THE SMOKE SHOW

Shortly after the Blizzard of '78, my grandfather became ill and quickly died. Or was he merely "gone"? He was a veteran of "the war" and I was told it was World War I. We studied World War II in school, so naturally I assumed World War III would be coming soon. I imagined that if war came, at least me and Cashews could get out of school, and do what we did best, which was running around in the woods and exploring. There was a special ceremony because of my grandfather's army service. My father said I was old enough to attend a thing called a "wake." This was a few days before the church service where the priest would circle the box the person is in with a lantern that smokes, after saying good things about him.

But for the wake, I was told I would get to "see" the person before they are put in that box. My grandfather never said much, but there were fond memories of seeing him without teeth, then putting the teeth in his mouth. Or the number of people it took to get him up the stairs at my parent's house to dinner. Or seeing him vomit outside, exhaling the particles of food from his stomach, starting with the last thing he ate, like my chocolate cake, to the first few beer nuts, then the fluorescent green stuff my father pointed out called bile. The bile was key, as it was a sign he was almost done vomiting and would soon be ready to get behind the wheel of the car and drive home.

Now I would see him in the "gone" state. He would be lying there, and I was told to say hi to everyone, and say sorry, then kneel by the box and say a prayer. What was I to say? "God, he was a good guy, you should let him in!"

There were many people there and even a couple young people from the military in uniform. I followed my mother in the line and saw my grandmother and a few other people next to the box. My mother shook everyone's hand and then knelt down. I did the same. My grandmother grabbed my face and said, "Thanks for coming pumpkin." And then it was my turn at the box. I got nervous but had rehearsed my prayer. "God, he is a good guy, let him in!" I took a quick glance at him, and he looked like they had painted his face.

I didn't see his false teeth. He had a great smile when they were in place, and I wondered why they weren't in now, smiling to let everyone know he was fine. I said my prayer, like a good Catholic, and walked away. It would have been nice if God could have made his left leg shake or something so I knew he received my prayers and that my grandfather was indeed a good guy and had been accepted into heaven. Instead, it was just another lousy feeling of someone being "gone."

There seemed to be two rooms. One room was for the women drinking coffee and nodding their heads, repeating, "Well, he's in a better place." Then there was another room, next to the kitchen, where the men were. They seemed to be all drinking those smelly adult drinks, smoking Lucky Strikes. It appeared they, in fact, knew he was in a better place, as they all seemed to be happy and showed no signs of sadness from somebody just dying. I just sat down and waited, and the noise got louder and louder from the men's area. A priest came in and we all gathered together. He said some special things out of a black book, which was nice, especially on top of the nice things I had said. Then we all left. The church ceremony with the smoking can would be the following day.

At home, I laid down on my bed, and the thoughts of witnessing someone in their "gone" state went through my head. Even though he couldn't walk well, it didn't seem fair to put him in such a small box. What if he decided to roam around later? Would it matter? Maybe heaven was like a conveyor belt, where the casket rolls in. God looks in says, "He's okay," and it rolls to the right and angels help you out of the box and "you're in." You're handed a harp and you play music that is pleasing to God's ear.

But if you're bad, the casket on the conveyor belt veers off to the left, where red-looking creatures pull you out and smile and say, "You're in!" Then you work in some boiler room yelling up to God, pleading your case. I prayed before I went to sleep with those scary thoughts. "Dear God, if I die before I wake, don't hand me a shovel or rake." I was in.

We went to Milton two days later, to a Catholic church. Right next to my cousin's house, the Murray's, where we would sometimes go for Thanksgiving. They literally lived right next to the Catholic church, which obviously had its pro's and cons. Weddings with the "ooh's and aah's" happened all the time in the spring and summer. And of course, the dark parades, the funerals, happened all year long, with the weeping, hugging, and old ladies nodding their heads so their turkey necks flapped as they all said, "Well, he's in a better place."

We filed in. My grandfather must have done something good for the Army because they sent those Army guys to put an American flag on his box. Then the members of the dark parade showed up. Six guys dressed in black with black cars, black shoes, black jackets and black ties. They rolled the box out of the black car, and the Army guys put the flag on top of it. Then we sat up front, and the priest for the parish came forward with the altar boys. We did the usual for our religion, which was stand, sit, and kneel, while repeating the prayers that the priest said.

The priest apparently knew my grandfather, and spoke many kind words, especially about his service in the war. He didn't mention him breaking the violin over my father's back or throwing him down a stairwell. Only the good stuff. Then there was the ritual. He brought out the smoking gold can. The priest said something else and circled the flag-draped box. He shook the can back and forth, the special smoke show.

Now death made more sense in my mind. You die, and the oldest female from Gang Grey goes into the room at the funeral parlor with the rest of the turkey necks. They drink coffee and eat S-shaped biscuits. The head elderly female says her prayers at the kneeler in front of the box. Words are exchanged between her and God, and then she comes into the room and, looking up at the ceiling with her turkey neck flab flapping says, "Well, he's in a better place." Then the others repeat these words with owl head movements. Then the men in the room next to the kitchen, having adult drinks and smoking Lucky Strikes in celebration of his being in a better place, raise their glasses and point skyward. Then the priest does his smoke show with the gold can.

The box is on wheels, which makes it easier for God's angels. They move the box to God's chair, and he kneels down, smells the smoke, and announces, "He's in! He's in a better place!" Then the box is moved one last time and another set of angels open the box, where my grandfather is told, "You're in." He wakes, steps out of the box, and then is handed golden false teeth, and a golden walker, and he gets his wings. But still needs the walker.

He flies like a pigeon, short distances, then needs the assistance of a walker for a few feet, then takes off again with his pigeon flying for a few more feet. With all that, it seemed strange that everyone looked so sad. After the priest's smoke show we went to a cemetery in Milton, where some more military personnel played a song with horns. The priest said a few more kind words out of the black book, and the box was then lowered into a shaft in the ground. I was sure that was where his box would get on the conveyor belt. When it was all over, I felt better about the expression "gone," because now I knew the true benefit of being Catholic and having the priest pour smoke over the box.

THE FONDUE STABBING

I was now counting the time before summer. School lasted a bit longer due to the blizzard of '78. I longed for the Irish Riviera and it's oceanside playground. For now, I had to sit upright in a chair, stare up at the blackboard, and look like I cared for four more months. As spring came, China announced that he would be moving to Maine. It was strange to think of him moving. I thought of who would be moving into our neighborhood to replace him. What age? What nickname did he have? What nickname would we give him?

The snow finally melted, and a massive cleanup was required to remove all the fallen trees and other debris. My father, who was rarely seen doing any type of yardwork, seemed to enjoy putting on massive ear muffs and safety glasses and working the chain saw. He cut large limbs into smaller pieces for me to stack for the next season or to throw into a pile to be burnt. He would give hand signals, or shout above the rumbling chain saw, barking his orders, letting everyone know to, "Stand back!" or, "This is a good log, save it!" or, "We'ze'll burn 'dis one today!"

Once the after-winter clean-up was finished, we looked forward to what spring would bring: baseball, street hockey, football, and a new activity called skateboarding. The street had to be swept for skateboarding, but there would be fun at the end of it, so we didn't look at it as labor; we went at the sweeping with joy and anticipation.

There were no elbow pads, knee pads, or helmets in those days. Crystal Hill became a haven for skateboarding and a new form of bicycling called "BMX-ing." Many kids took their bicycles and added a double fork to the wheels. There was one skateboarder who was especially talented. We called his mother "Russian Roulette" because, to us, she sounded like she was from Russia. Actually, she was from Germany. Her son taught us everything. Especially when we lost control and wiped out on the street.

He taught us to "walk it off," which meant after tumbling in all directions and losing one's skin to the streets, blood spurting, you were supposed to get up and walk around, usually in a wobbly, dazed figure eight. It really didn't ease the pain, but lying down and crying was forbidden. Plus, we all feared Cashews' ongoing obsession for peering into peoples' eyes after a fall or accident, to see if they were crying or likely to cry, then announcing his verdict dramatically to the entire crowd: "He cried!' or "He didn't cry."

One day I was riding on the back of my brother's banana seat bike with its double forks, to play a football game, and the double forks seemed to become unglued. They were wobbling uncontrollably, and my brother Lead couldn't control the handle bars. The additional pairs of forks gave way, and the tire fell off, and we tumbled. I lay bleeding, dizzy in pain. Apparently, the bloody scene was horrific enough that someone alerted the nearest neighbor to the crash scene. Her name was Mrs. Malarkey. I always figured that she must have come from a family of liars, because my father used to say, "You are full of malarkey," whenever he suspected me of lying.

She ran out of the house fast, and still had a lit cigarette dangling from her mouth. She looked down on my brother and me, and cried, "You poor things, I'll take care of you!" She reached down, grabbed my arm, and helped me into her house. She said she was a nurse, so we were in good hands. She had a little bar like my father's and made herself an adult drink, placing it on the round table next to me. She had what looked like a giant fishing tackle box. She smiled and said it was her repair kit.

She lit one cigarette with another. She put on her glasses and looked at us both with her cigarette dangling, ash dropping on us. She took a sip from her adult drink and said, "ahh." She seemed to know what she was doing as she opened bottles, gauzes, and bandages. She assured us that we would be fine, and we wouldn't have to go to the hospital.

Then I remembered her last name, "Malarkey." Could she be lying about our quick recovery? We had to be fixed, and I was in a great deal of pain, so I had to put that thought off to the side. She took a big swig out of her adult drink. She was skilled with the cigarette, for she could talk while it was still in her mouth.

She said I had several abrasions on my head and face. She took out a gauze and poured that familiar hydrogen something or other on it. Then she said, "close your eyes." I heard a sizzling noise as the gauze was padded down onto my wound. The solution dripped down on my face. She said that both of us would need butterfly stitches. Butterflies were very beautiful and seemed friendly, and on rare occasions would land on you. So, in my mind, a "butterfly stitch" couldn't possibly hurt. She left for a moment as thoughts of gentle butterflies fluttered around my mind, and then she came back with a fresh adult drink. She lit another cigarette as she prepared a butterfly stitch for the cut over my eyebrow. The aroma from her mouth smelled of the same solution she used on my cuts.

I must say, I had a growing respect for these adult drinks and the sense of calm they provided. It seemed inevitable that I, too, would someday imbibe in these drinks. But I didn't want to be like Cashews' father, who turned purple when he drank. Plus, his eyes seemed to bulge out a great deal. But the overall picture in my mind was that adult drinks were good for all types of afflictions and situations.

She said, "This will pinch a little." That cute butterfly bit like a bee. She did the same with my brother. All the bleeding did stop, and we sat in stunned silence for a moment. She seemed happy through all this. Happy that she was able to diagnose the situation and take the proper measures. Happy that she could stop the bleeding and send us on our way.

After a few minutes, we hobbled our way out the door, thanking her, and looked at the demolished bike. We picked it up and walked it back up Crystal Hill. Arriving home, sore, my brother and I headed to our bunks and "licked our wounds," as my father would say.

I lay in bed and looked out the window. I looked across the street and saw somebody with a fancy yellow jacket showing China's house to the possible new homeowners. It seemed strange that he would be leaving. But my father assured me that Maine wasn't too far, and I would be able to visit. We met a few days later and China said a doctor from India was buying the house.

Summer eventually came, which meant more fun. Once the *Boston Globe* was delivered in the morning, and the yard work was done, I had all day to be a kid. We were now playing football at full contact. Again, regardless of any pain, you had to simply, "walk it off," like the older kids and adults said. One day Tibbs came out to join in the game. He sat Indian style on a bunch of leaves and started to perform a rocking back and forth motion. Then it looked like he was whimpering. We all took notice and stopped the game. Cashews with his ostrich neck and eyes slowly and curiously approached Tibbs to see what was really going on.

He asked Tibbs a question, and Tibbs through his whimpering gave an answer. Cashews let out a loud, "What!?" He then turned to us and yelled, "His sistah told him if his muthah has to go upstairs one more time, to get his laundry, her leg will fall off, and that's why he is crying!"

This seemed to humor and upset Cashews at the same time. We then helped Tibbs out of his cross-legged position and got him in the game. I could see Cashews face, and that he was now infuriated with this sign of weakness out of Tibbs. Tibbs was on my team. I kept throwing the football to him, and each time Cashews would hit him at full speed. The whimpering finally stopped as Tibbs entered into manhood.

It seemed like every family in those days acquired this fancy new meat-cooking apparatus called a "fondue pot" that came with special forks. The pot held oil or cheese and sat over a flame, and you stuck meat in the pot on one of the long forks. The forks looked like miniature devil pitchforks. They were about 10 inches long with little wooden handles and two barbed tines on the end. One day a friendly fondue fork fight started between China and me, and I impaled him on the wrist. I turned around to face the rest of the crew, as the victor, and that is when he stabbed me in the back with his fondue fork. I fell to the ground, and someone announced

I had been stabbed. My mother rather nonchalantly came over, looked at me, and pulled it out of my back with a yank.

Later there was a summit meeting between parents, and the fondue fork impaling was proclaimed to be deep enough to be considered an actual stabbing. Nonetheless, I was told to shake hands with China and let bygones be bygones since I had initiated the incident by first sticking him in the wrist. Just a few days later China moved to Maine. I was glad we were still friends and that our parents told us to shake hands. I stood on the sidewalk in front of my house and watched China's family drive off in their station wagon. He gave a final look out the back window as they descended down Crystal Hill, waving to me. It occurred to me that we would probably never again sled down Crystal Hill together.

After China left, I went over to his old house and knocked on the door. The doctor from India answered and I asked if he wanted the newspapers delivered to his home. He only wanted the *Globe*, but it turned out that they were very nice people, and even tipped. So, they were spared dog poo smears on their sports page.

FRYING THE FUR

Changes were happening on Crystal Hill and perhaps the larger world outside. I began to notice that I no longer saw new station wagons appear in the driveways of Crystal Hill every year. Up until then, most families got a new one every two or three years. But starting that year, I saw that my father and other neighbors were repairing their old cars rather than getting new ones. It also seemed that the size of families was decreasing, or at least not getting larger. People were worried about money, but nobody would admit it. You could just feel it in the air. That frenetic childhood wonderlust that fueled our hearts and minds also seemed to be evaporating. There was even a sense of frustrated anger lurking in the adults. A kid could pick up a lot of this type of intel while performing two paper routes per day.

There are 168 hours in the week, and services at the Catholic Church only took up one of those hours. So, everyone seemed to try and look and act their best for that one special hour per week. But having the paper routes, I was able to glimpse and observe people during the hours they weren't in church. I picked up on the new, more aggressive vibe in the neighborhood. Perhaps it was also because I was no longer the cute little paperboy, so people were quicker to be short or nasty with me, say, if their paper was wet or crumpled.

Maybe I was no longer the cute paper boy. But it seemed to me that the early 1970's were a happier time in everyone's life. Now it was the mid to late 1970's and there were problems brewing everywhere, especially in

Boston. Being the paperboy in that pre-internet and pre-cable TV world, I always got first glance both at the news and peoples' reactions. I saw more and more of people hurting people and wondered why.

Somehow, the harsher and more frightful feelings out there in the world were permeating me, even though I didn't realize it right away. As the year wore on, I was becoming fearful and defensive. I knew the family trip to the Irish Riviera was just around the corner and hoped it would bring me back to my childhood, a sense of playfulness, and a fascination with nature. I longed for the month of August when I would have no responsibilities. No homework, no chores around the house, and no paper routes. Finally, August came and we began to prepare for the trip.

My mother surprised me with a new diving mask so I could better explore the underwater world. We packed the food and supplies into cardboard boxes and brown paper bags, along with towels, soap, my brother's newly repaired bike with its double forks, and many bottles of adult drinks such as wine and vodka.

My mother started the Country Squire and we headed off. As we traveled away from Crystal Hill, I noticed that there were fewer oak trees and more pine trees. I could always smell the salt of the ocean as we got closer to our destination. My mother would press the button for the electric car windows and command us to, "breathe in the fresh air!" For my mother, "fresh air" (along with ginger ale and toast) was not only the cure for virtually every illness – it was also a preventative health measure. If one didn't get enough "fresh air" one was probably doomed to getting sick eventually.

We approached the big green sign with white lettering that said, "Marshfield." Many winding roads later, after cutting through a trailer park, we arrived at Blue Fish Cove. I immediately ran out of the car and down to the beach to see if it looked the same. I suppose I was a little afraid that the increasing negativity out in the world might have somehow spoiled this patch of paradise. However, I was delighted to discover that this corner of the world remained unspoiled, at least upon first glance.

Seeing that all was well, I sprinted back to the Country Squire. I unpacked and changed into my Jacques Cousteau gear which consisted of garish 1970's swim trunks and my new diving mask. The waters of the Irish Riviera are always frigid, but to an excited kid, it made no difference. I sprinted back to the beach and threw myself into the icy waves and reacquainted myself with my underwater playground and undersea friends: the starfish, the mean looking eel, the rock perch with oversized teeth, they were all still there. Had they missed me as much as I had missed them?

I was literally in paradise and spent hours in the water, jumping off the rock formations, looking at the "boat people" as they were coming and going. I never wanted to leave. I did my best to get the most out of time, getting up at the same hours I would deliver the *Boston Globe*. I figured if one got the most out of work by working at it, then play should be the same: I needed to be diligent and work at. Each morning I would inhale my Lucky Charms and run to the beach as the sun rose up on the back of Mr. Atlantic.

Each morning I found the beach empty, except for Clam Lady. She recognized me and kindly exclaimed, "Well, good morning young man," and gave me a big smile. She said, "I see you've discovered that this is the best time of day. When it's quiet out here it is a good time to experience God." Experiencing God was not on my agenda, but I had to agree with her. At that moment, I really did feel God's presence, in a totally different way from what I experienced at church. I thought it was very nice of him to let me swim here in Mr. Atlantic's pool, and I surmised that Mr. Atlantic must be a relative of his, maybe his cousin even.

I smiled at her and said "hello" and immediately dove under water. I noticed that there were new morning fish that I didn't ever see during the day. Some of these morning fish were very large; they looked odd but interesting, like half smiling, half angry. The water was definitely colder in the morning than at midday, but it didn't bother me at all. As the sun rose higher and higher, the tide also rose, and I was able to leap off the rock formation without waiting in a line. As I fell I would flap my arms a few times, and then land with a crash. The exhilaration was worth the sting on the bottom of my feet. I climbed up several times and repeated the procedure. I thought it was funny that I had such tremendous fear my first time jumping off the rock formation, but now the feeling was the complete opposite.

Slowly people began to make their way down to the beach and set up their little camps. I watched as the wee little kids just stayed in one spot and picked up sand and rocks, and would just stare at the new discoveries in their hands for the longest time. I had my towel down, marking off my territory, and I sat for a moment and watched the sun, the ocean, the people and the birds. Life had gotten more difficult for me that past year, especially in school; they had eliminated art classes which took away the one actual class I enjoyed. But now here I was sitting on my towel at the Irish Riviera, assessing all of God's creations and thinking about their various assignments in life.

At school, they had started teaching us about something called "evolution" which apparently meant we all came from hairy creatures that walked funny. That sort of made sense, but sort of didn't. I surmised that more likely, we came from hairy, angry creatures that walked funny, but about every 100,000 years or so, God would send lightning down, frying the fur on those ape-like creatures, so slowly we began to look more and more like the men and women of today. Eventually, the ape creatures felt better about themselves due to all the fur being removed, became less angry, and started walking upright with a sense of happiness and pride.

I just sat there thinking about God and his creatures, not having a care. I eventually looked up and noticed some of the boats leaving the harbor, heading out to sea. They were mostly lobster boats, and I took a close look at the guys in them. They didn't look happy. But maybe that was because they were heading out, and hadn't caught anything yet. A lot of them just looked out to sea blankly, a cigarette dangling from their mouths, probably a Lucky Strike (which seemed to me would be a good name for a fishing vessel). I made a mental note to remember to look at them on their way back in to see if they had smiles from a fresh catch.

The beach became more and more crowded, and the water began to recede. This was another show performed by Mr. Atlantic. Allowing the tide to go out so I could explore between the rocks and tidal pools. Clam Lady eventually made her way out and I assisted her here and there in getting her catch. She always seemed happy, no matter how full or empty her bucket was. In between helping her I would pluck crusty little insect-like water creatures out of the tiny pools, and hold them up for inspection.

They seemed mad at first, but they would calm down once they saw my smile. Time flew by as I picked up creatures and helped Clam Lady. Before I knew it, I was witnessing the new tide coming in. I noticed that the adults didn't seem to enjoy the ocean as much as the kids did. They just put white stuff on their noses, planted their toes in the sand, and buried their noses in a book. I wondered why they didn't run and play and laugh and explore like us kids. Maybe they were out of fun? Perhaps they had experienced everything there was to experience at the beach when they were kids? Maybe they were just happy reading? But it still seemed odd and kind of sad that I never saw them laughing or just screaming with joy like all us kids. Would that happen to me, I wondered?

The new tide was coming in, and with it, more rock jumping. It would be nice to jump just before heading back to the cottage. I had a plan to jump, and then sit on the jetty, and watch the boat people and lobster-man return. The sandy beach began to evaporate in the tide. It was late afternoon, and people had started to leave. I could tell by the water level against the rock that it was now deep enough for jumping. Me and a few other brave souls, with the sun on our backs, began to jump. That was true freedom. Something about being in nature and being free gave me the energy and the ability to make those jumps over and over again, swimming back to the rock, climbing up and being scraped by barnacles, and not noticing or caring or getting even a little winded.

I now had some new rock jumping friends, and we made plans to meet again. I made my way over to the jetty and sat down to take in all the boats returning. My suspicion had been correct: the lobstermen looked a lot happier, and some even waved and smiled at as their Lucky Strikes dangled from their mouths. The boat people that could afford their own play boats seemed very happy as well. Some were even dancing on the back of their boats and waving. I wondered if that would ever be me someday. Would I ever be a boat person? Or did you have to get born into a special boat family to be one?

Sitting there, I didn't think about school or the paper routes or chores even once. It was my time to take in this world of art being performed by Mother Nature and Mr. Atlantic and their cousin God, for all to enjoy. The sun was disappearing, and I made my way back to the cottage. My mother introduced me to a man that was a year-round resident who had come over to visit. He was a lobsterman as well. He was, in fact, bright red, exactly like a cooked lobster, and introduced himself. He even gave us a few lobsters. My mother poured him an adult drink, vodka with a bit of cranberry juice. He smiled and said, "Ah, a Cape Cod!" He seemed happy already, but he became even happier after just a few sips.

My mom asked him to stay and enjoy another Cape Cod as thanks for the lobster. He said, "One more drink, and I have to go to bed. I gotta rise early." He mentioned that he needed a part-time helper, and would pay, so my mother volunteered my brother Lead. I noticed that Lead hadn't raised his hand, but rather, my mother just pushed him forward. Lead's eyes thinned and he sighed. A few days later I would see my brother Lead head out to sea in the lobster boat. He didn't have a dangling Lucky Strike, but he did smile and wave at me.

My mother announced that tomorrow we would go to the pier, to see all the tuna men, and lobstermen, and boat people. I lay down in my bed after a long day in the ocean and didn't remember falling asleep. I arose naturally early from all the early morning wake ups with the *Boston Globe*.

We spent some time at the beach and then went over to the pier with my brother and his two-forked chopper-style bike to take in the early morning preparations of those heading out to sea. I ran down to the water and dove in. The waves were my early morning shower. It was cold but felt good. It woke me up for the big day ahead. Me and Lead then headed out onto the pier on his chopper bike. There was a lot of commotion, but it seemed organized. The lobsterman had their boats on buoys and would row their small boats out to their lobster craft.

The "day boat" people drove in with their boats and then had to back up a trailer and down a ramp, and have one of their friends pull away once the boat was unhooked. There was another area for boat people that had really large boats. Some of those boat people either lived on these boats or pulled up with fancy cars and walked down to their floating castles. It seemed there was chaos with these people, both car and boat horns blowing, rope being tossed, smoke and bubbles coming out of the backs of the boats, and finally, everyone heading out and quiet.

With most of the lobstermen and boat people gone, we decided to make our way back to the beach. We passed over a small footbridge and heard some yelling underneath. Then one by one about six guys come out from under the bridge. They didn't look happy, and asked, "What are you'se doing on our bridge?" My brother Lead said, "I didn't see your name on it." This upset a couple of them, and out of nowhere, they started swinging. One guy ran at me, grabbed me and threw me down. There was a thud, and my head spun. I ran back to the house, and Lead followed.

We were both clearly shaken, and although I didn't realize it at the time, that incident marked the permanent takeover of a bitterness and defensiveness in me that would last a lifetime. I didn't make the connection that those guys did to us precisely what me and my crew did to kids on our school playground with the Slug Train.

I eventually made my way back down to the beach, but was very cautious, looking over my shoulder for those thugs. Once underwater, I feared coming up and seeing those six guys ready to pounce. I was no longer paying attention to beauty, and no longer thought of all the wonderful creations and activity coming from God. I thought of the fight I had after school for having plaid bellbottoms and platform shoes. Now instead of taking in the ocean and being at peace, my mind raced with fear and anger.

I took an old broomstick and tied a knife to it. No longer was I going underwater to view the fish on their stage. I would spear them and inflict injury. I didn't have good thoughts that night and felt guilty for spearing fish. I couldn't get the eyes of the fish that I killed out of my head. My paradise had become tainted.

Lead was going to work with the lobsterman again the next day. I would go to the beach, with less enthusiasm. I would be on guard for my own predators. The eels were now on the land, they hid under bridges, and I was the stray fish that had to be careful. Lead's lobster boat finally made its way out of the harbor.

I saw Lead and he waved from the bow and then got in back and seemed to be scurrying around. I went back to the beach, with my shoulders hunched. The tide went out, and I just looked around. I saw about 4 guys walking from the pier area to the new sand being revealed by the receding tide. It was those eel guys! I crouched down on the jetty and got ready to leave. Something had caught their eye on the other jetty and I was glad to see their focus was off of me. They pointed at two black guys sitting on the jetty.

They started yelling at the black guys, who didn't say anything back but eventually left. Now I saw them look around and I dove off the jetty like a harbor seal and swam underwater as far as I could. The eel guys never came back over, but they didn't have to, because I had a newfound fear, followed shortly by anger. This new feeling of anxiety and discomfort was on me like skin. Now I was having strange thoughts of even wishing summer would end. Is this how the victims of our slug trains felt? Instead of this being an eye-opener for me, the thought only made me angrier and want to dump that anger onto others.

My mother noticed the change and wondered why I no longer ran out the door of the cottage to the beach every morning. I stayed inside and watched the *Price is Right*, and only once in a while would I go to the beach. Finally, the summer on the ocean ended. The redness from the sun and ocean water disappeared, but my bitterness did not fade.

You Got Mooncai

Summer was now just about over, and so was my childlike love for the outdoors, nature, and my fellow man. I now started to see the world in a different light. People were dangerous and couldn't be trusted. We packed up everything in boxes and headed back to Crystal Hill. I still had a few days before school opened, and tried to get as much out of it as I could. The letter from school arrived that would tell me who my teacher was going to be for the new year. I called a few of the guys, and we agreed to all bring our unopened letters to the playground. We would open our letters in front of each other to see what teacher we had and how our crew would be divided up.

There were a few other kids there from our grade at the playground, some we called "Lakers" because they lived on Lake Shore Drive. I opened my letter first and it was quickly snatched from my hand and passed around. A kid named Sean Lapham, who was a Laker, burst into hysterics and yelled, "You got Mooncai!" It was as if I had some sort of rash in the shape of little crescent moons.

Everyone else started to laugh as well. She was the toughest teacher in Sheehan School. We all had heard the stories about kids getting slapped with yardsticks, about untidy desks being dumped out on the poor kid's lap, about her red pen that she used to write red goose eggs at the top of papers, marking them "zero." She demanded exact margins on all paperwork. Then there was "the fence." If you acted up in her classroom you had to stand straight and still along the chain link fence at the side of the playground. You had to stand with your hands by your side, and look up to her classroom window, where she would be peering down derisively.

I had seen this. If you misbehaved while standing at the fence, she would open the window, and just simply state, "One more day!" After all the Mooncai stories, the rest of the guys opened their letters. Cashews also got Mooncai. Cashews' brainy educational "special" would now blend in with my juvenile delinquent "special," slowly diluting his elite status with the teachers. All the letters were opened and we agreed we would get the best of Mooncai. We resolved to make her quit the teaching profession after a week with us.

We all went home and in a few days, it was back to school. We had a new principal; the last one had committed suicide that summer on a nearby forest path that my mother and I used to walk. Now with a head full of anger and resentment, two paper routes, and Saturdays reserved to yard work or assisting with my dad with minor electrical work, it seemed my only entertainment would be the classroom and recess. Of course, recess was again chasing new guys and "breaking them in" via the Slug Train.

School started, and it was off to Mooncai's classroom. Cashews and I immediately found seats in the back. Mrs. Mooncai had a stick she called "the pointer." She walked back and forth and up and down the aisles with it like an Army Colonel. She said we were to sit at a 90° angle with our hands on the desk at all times – unless we were writing or raising our hand. She marched up and down the aisles waving her pointer menacingly, her feet pointed outward like an angry penguin. Every few minutes she would throw me and Cashews a hairy eyeball.

She spent our first day together lecturing the class on the importance of obeying the rules. We may have gotten away with misbehavior previously, she said, but we would not do so in her class. She went into great detail about what would happen if we, "stepped out of the margins." If that occurred, we would be assigned the chain link fence. She went into more detail about the fence routine, describing precisely how we were to hold our hands by our sides while looking up into her window.

It was all rules and regulations. I wondered if she would demand that we all iron our underwear in a specific fashion. Crayons, finger painting, and Zarex breaks were officially a thing of the past. Finally, we broke for recess, the first of what would be very few recesses that year, at least for me and Cashews. My crew met under our tree, and two new guys were quickly spotted walking around cluelessly. As if on cue we immediately formed the Slug Train. "Slug-slug-sluga-sluga-sluga."

Then we sped up from a slow, menacing movement with our Chuck Taylors kicking a little dirt up, jogging in the direction of the new kids.

A cute girl in our class with a plaid skirt and two ponytails, who had witnessed several Slug Trains previously, turned to the new kids and shrieked, "Run! It's a Slug Train!" One kid was a survivor; he immediately perceived the threat and took off like a shot. That kid was very fast and got away. The other kid? He was the wounded baby gazelle, soon to be taken down by our pack of predators.

Gazelle Boy ran but looked back too much, which slowed him down. We were full speed ahead, running and still yelling, "sluga sluga sluga sluga..." Gazelle Boy then made the final mistake of taking one last look behind him only to realize that we would imminently be on top of him. We took our hands off each other's shoulders but kept chanting, "sluga sluga sluga," as we kicked and punched him. As a final display of dominance, we took off his shoes.

We later found out that Gazelle Boy was from Brockton. He couldn't fight well, but he had an amazing vocabulary. We were rough kids but still from the suburbs and all pretty much good Catholics and Protestants, so swearing was very rare for us. But this kid! It was all, "F*ck you," and, "You mother-f*ckers." He didn't cry at all (Cashews was inspecting him), and soon the teachers interrupted the Slug Train and pulled us off him.

One teacher tended to the new kid. Another teacher lined us up and asked our grade and what teacher we had. He then marched us up to the stand silently in the hallway and when recess was over our assigned teachers came out to convene on the situation. One teacher said we should write something one hundred times. Mooncai was livid. She literally goosestepped up and down before us, fuming, and then yelled, "Three days on the fence for all of them!" Mooncai yelled the loudest, so hers was the final decision. My entire crew was sentenced to the fence for three days.

The new kid from Brockton had earned his stripes. He took his beating like a champ, didn't cry, and to top it off, his vocabulary cemented his invitation to join our crew. The other new guy, the one who had escaped, was still on our radar. He would get his once our fence sentence was over. After three days on the fence, we spotted him. There were more teachers out on playground now, and they seemed to be eyeing us specifically. We milled about sizing up the situation. Cashews the cry cop eyed a girl that had just fallen off a slide, so he left the meeting to see if she was tearing up. Two teachers were attending her, but Cashews stuck his ostrich-like head in between and looked down on the girl. He came back to report the scene and confirm that crying imminent.

"Her bottom lip was quivering," he reported. "She is going to cry any second now."

We went back to our deep discussion of what to do with the new guy that was owed a beating. We had learned that he was from a town called Springfield. Recess ended before we could formulate and execute a plan, so we started to head upstairs to our assigned rooms. Upon entering the building, however, we noticed the new guy heading to the bathroom down the hallway. Like providence from heaven, our chance presented itself. However, the Slug Train wouldn't work in the building. We needed more room for that.

I had to think quickly. We followed him into the boy's room and he began to urinate. I looked under the stalls and didn't see any sneakers or shoes – so we knew no snitches were present. Almost preternaturally, my brain formulated the plan to perform the "spin around" maneuver on him. The "spin around" is a technique effective for inflicting deep and lasting humiliation and shame. You quickly grab the person urinating by the shoulders and spin them around. They usually can't stop urinating in time, and thus pee all over themselves to the laughter of others. I performed the maneuver, but despite flawless technique on my part, he only got a couple drops on him.

He quickly stepped back and zipped up, and I immediately realized that this guy didn't fear me. Not at all. He turned beet red and said, "What the f*ck?!" Surely, I thought, this guy would be going to hell with that type of language. He got in a funny stance with both arms up and his head tucked next to his left arm. He then said, "Let's go," and we circled each other. He threw a punch very fast that landed square on my head. I threw a punch back at him, but he quickly ducked and, like lightning, he hit me again. I then threw several in an overhand motion, but only hit him once. I was amazed at his stance and his ducking ability.

I lunged at him to get him in a headlock and succeeded but got hit a few more times. I was good at headlocks but felt pain from being hit about seven times and only connecting once in return. While I had him in a headlock, I gave him the rules. Who did he think he was just walking into Sheehan School like he owned the place? Then I heard Cashews yell, "Teacher!" It was a good thing because I was definitely afraid to let go of this guy and receive more punches. I knew I had lost the scrimmage. I let go, and he got back in his fighting stance. I said, "Hold up, teacher's coming!" It proved to be a false alarm, but the pause gave me a chance to ask him a question.

"Where do you learn to fight like that?"

He said his older brothers taught him how to box back in Springfield. I introduced myself and he reciprocated. I noticed as I walked out of the bathroom that I had several welts on my head and face. I walked outside, and announced to the crew, "He's in. He put up a good fight."

I got to Mooncai's and just sat upright per protocol. I had no wise-guy remarks once she turned her back. I had to "walk off" the pain mentally. I was just hit several times, and I could feel the soreness, the ringing in my ears, the thumping of the welts rising as blood seemed to rush to them. I didn't say anything. Cashews sat next to me looking at my eyes to see if they were watery, or if my bottom lip was quivering. He could sense pain a mile away. He said, "You're awfully quiet, what happened in there?" I simply said, "I tuned up the new guy. He took it well and he's one of us now."

Our first week with Mooncai finally drew to a close. We all had to acknowledge that she had won that week, but we weren't going to give up. She would eventually break down and pack her bags for retirement. We were committed.

The Helper

Adding to the degree to which my life was descending slowly into an un-fun ordeal to be endured, it became apparent that our family's fun little day trips on Saturdays had also ended. Now Saturdays were spent outside doing yard work or being an electrician's helper with my father. The electrician work began as performing favors for shirt-tail relatives. We would go to an area somewhere in Boston, ring a bell, and a voice out of metal hole would say, "Ehhh, who is it?" Then my father would shout, "The electrician!" – to which the tenant would invariably reply, "Who?!" My father would then scream, "It's ... the ... electrician!"

Once that had been finally established, we would be granted entry, and head up to work. I was usually escorted to the attic. There were all sorts of ways to get into an attic in these old Boston houses. There was the pull-down staircase. There was crawling through someone's bedroom closet and popping open the little access door. Some, but not many, even had a regular door I could just walk through. Once I had figured out how to shimmy into the attic, my father would point his flashlight and give me directions. "Take 'dis here wire, uncoil it, slide it under 'dose 'dere joists to 'dat far end of the attic. 'Den wait for my next instructions."

I would do this while he had coffee with what he called the Q-Tip, because of their white hair and blue skin. I would slide the white wire under the joists. There were always all sorts of different types of insulation. Some of it reminded me of Q-Tip hair, white like snow and crumply. I yelled down to my father to inquire about it and he said, "Ehh, 'dat's rock

117

wool, 'dey used to bring up a hose to the attic and blow that stuff right in. It's a pain," he said. "It'll take you longer to run the wire, cause it's like movin' snow outta the way." Rock wool was indeed not easy.

I finally made it to the other end of the house and yelled down to my father. He stuck his head through the attic enough to point to the next task. I was handed a drill, with what looked like a six-inch bit. I had drilled before, but my father showed me again anyway. "Yeah, hold it at a right angle, drill down like 'dis. Measure off that side of the wall about 7 feet, then drill down in the center of the wood, 'den shove 'dis snake down and I'll catch it." He gave one final warning: "Be careful or that drill will rip you'se arm off!"

I put the flashlight in my mouth, and headed to the far end of the attic with the gear. I measured and drilled. I could hear my father cutting a hole below. I sent the snake down, and he talked me through it. "Easy, easy," he said. Then I felt a little tug. "All right now, you'se are hooked, I'se pulling ya in!" I then tied the white wire down. He said, "All right, get outta 'dere."

I made my way back to the attic entrance and handed my father the gear. He told me to hold the flashlight, and he brought the white wire into a metal box and spliced it. He put the metal cover back on. He said, "We'se are outta here!" I felt a sense of accomplishment. But I also felt exasperation, like this was it for me: yard work and paper routes and electrical work and school.

There was a smidge of free time on Sundays but only after Mass for us Catholics and after "service" for the Protestants. After getting home from our religious obligations my crew would gather and burn off steam playing hard contact sports. Quickly, however, we entered into a new phase: the fire phase.

Long gone were the days of nature exploration. Gone were the days of lifting up rocks and holding hairy insects to the sky. Gone were the days of catching frogs, snakes, and turtles. Now, only fire entertained us. It began with small controlled fires surrounded by rocks. The sense of danger and rebelliousness was intoxicating for all of us. If a small controlled fire in a rock circle felt like that … what would a *real* fire feel like? We started throwing lit matches at each other. Inevitably, one of those lit matches missed the intended victim and caused an inferno. The first time an uncontrolled fire started we ran back to one of our homes and announce a lie.

"We witnessed a fire while walking in the woods!"

A phone call was made, and then the show began. Sirens, red lights, blue lights, questioning by police. The whole thing seemed like some sort of play, practiced and well-rehearsed, by the local police and fire department. The candy apple truck would roar up with about four guys, two in the front and two in the back. They all had their assignments. One would attach a hose to a fire hydrant, and they would head off into the woods, panting for breath, bouncing up and down in a forward motion.

In the beginning, the police believed our "witnessing a fire" story, and after questioning, we would head off to see them put out the fire. After a few of these fires, the only question they asked was, "Why did you'se light it?"

Sometimes, "we" the witnesses would guide them to the fire and then gaze upon the stage of their performance. They would first blast the fire with a hose. Then they would rake the dry oak leaves to reveal more smoke, then blast that. They, like us, seemed to be attracted by the fire.

The adults would always gather in the streets, sometimes with a look of horror on their faces, considering that they may have come close to losing their castles. I wondered how it went with the accountant guy down the street who lived the precisely regimented life. Was the fire truck commotion disturbing the hour he had scheduled for slurping his soup in his soup bib, facing the west window, looking out at the bird feeder?

So, although our play time had become severely restricted, we compensated by concentrating it into more and more dangerous and heart-pounding activities: hurting each other playing full contact sports or destroying acres of woodlands via the match.

No longer did I believe in the Tooth Fairy, the Easter Bunny, or Santa Claus, and I even had my doubts about God. We were now taught more and more about evolution. There were even maps and charts and everything describing how me, my family, friends and the people on my street had descended not just from hairy angry men that walked funny, but from monkeys like the ones at the zoo.

Despite the evidence and certainty and charts and graphs, evolution seemed a bit strange to me. It was like a lightning bolt had randomly struck a puddle, and out of the lightning and foam and bubbles, came the first life form. Then after more strikes and more time, finally emerged the son of an electrician. I looked at the charts. I wanted to be like the Cro Magnons, a wild fire-making, club-weilding beast. Cashews, who still retained some of his educational "specialness," studied the Cro Magnons, and came back with information. They were hunched over. They discovered fire. They used tools. That information improved the slug train. When the chase ended, and it came to the slugging part, we acted ape-like, with our shoulders hunched over, bouncing up and down and making grunting noises. This soon became the new name of our crew: The Cro Mags.

Whenever we got in trouble in Mooncai's class, I would use the evolution excuse: "It's just the monkey in me." Mooncai would simply reply, "Alright monkey, line up at the fence for recess."

THE IDIOT

The innocence of my childhood had evaporated and I could feel it. I felt it especially when it rained. I would remember times walking home with my dad from the barber shop after heavy rainfall and him taking a piece of gum out and making a tiny boat out of the aluminum foil wrapper and placing it into the stream of rainfall by the curb. "This'll be a life raft for the ants." I wondered what happened. Now there was no awe in the little things like a gum wrapper headed downstream to save a stranded ant.

I discovered my brother's record collection. My oldest brother had many albums, and they would be played downstairs on the record player each day until my mother or father would inevitably force him to turn it off. He had Jimi Hendrix, Iggy Pop, Led Zeppelin. I liked looking at the covers of these albums. The Iggy Pop album was called "The Idiot," and it had the lyrics on the back. Cashews and I would memorize these words, and even bring the album to school. We taught the rest of the crew these lyrics and would sing them behind Mooncai's back, tempting fate and the iron fence.

Our favorite song from that record was called "Funtime." When Mooncai would turn her back one of us would croon:

"Fun ... hey baby we like your lips ... fun ... hey baby we like your pants ... all aboard for funtime!"

Mooncai would say, "Okay, you want fun?!" and then yell our names, without even looking to see who had been singing, and say "Fence!" While at the fence, we would sing more Iggy Pop lyrics. Sometimes Mooncai wouldn't even have to look out her window to know we were not standing at attention, silently, hands by our sides, as the punishment demanded. She would simply hear us, twist her second-floor window open and yell, "All of you … three more days!"

We got caught once passing around the Iggy Pop idiot album. She confiscated it, and held it up, examining it as if it were some foul object of pagan worship. She eye-balled the photo of Iggy with dripping disgust and said, "Indeed … he *is* an idiot." I had to plead with her that it was my brother's and needed to be returned. She gave it back with the warning that if she saw it again, she would smash it to pieces.

At that time there was a book and movie out called *Helter Skelter*. For some reason, the Cro Mags formed a bond with the main character, Charles Manson. Cashews said that we may even be able to write to him in prison. Mooncai had us write stories about people we admired, and we figured it would be fun to write about Iggy and Manson. Mooncai found the book in Cashews' desk, along with the short stories we wrote about them. For whatever reason, *that* was the final straw. A meeting was to be held and it would include our parents, us students, Mooncai, and the principal. The new principal actually seemed pretty easy going, not like the one that committed suicide on the nature path.

The meeting convened. Mooncai was set up like a prosecuting attorney. She had dates, how many days I had spent on the fence, Iggy Pop's name, the book *Helter Skelter*, all organized in a cardboard box. She dumped it all on the table and started her case. She stated that (in addition to committing the crime of being 11-year-old boys) we had set a record in her teaching history for the amount of time sentenced to the fence, reiterating her point dramatically by emphasizing that it was still only Autumn. Then she went into a detailed accounting of my crimes that I didn't even *know* she knew.

Her first example was from music class. The music teacher would have us sing songs. Mooncai would walk up and down the aisle as we sang. Mostly, she eye-balled me and Cashews. There was a Cat Stevens song "I'm Being Followed by a Moon Shadow." We changed it to "I'm being followed by a Mooncai." There was the Irish song of the unicorn that went, "There were green alligators and long neck geese, humpty back camels and chimpanzees." Our version went: "There were green alligators and long neck Mooncais."

Her eyes were like flamethrowers and her mouth was like a machine gun. "*Never* in my teaching career..." Then, "Andrew and his friends are like a pack of hyenas; they form this type of train and ..." Finally, "His role models and short stories are written about a drug addict rock star named Iggy Pop and a mass murderer named Charles Manson."

My father went from his pasty, Vitamin D-deficient, New England complexion to a sun-burned boiling lava red as Mooncai presented her evidence. He then moved his lips, looking at me, silently mouthing the words, "Your ass is in a sling."

Soon we would be home. I would look up to the ceiling toward to the God we worshipped, Jesus H. Christ. My father would be yelling our Lord's name, which seemed to give him a jolt of energy, and then he would announce my sentence. Mentally, I scrolled through the possible options: a) I wouldn't see the light of day; b) I would be grounded until hell froze over; c) I would be on lock-down until the cows come home. For now, sitting in the classroom as Mooncai summed up her closing statement, he had to hold it in.

Every couple of minutes, he would look at me, his blue eyes glowing, surrounded by his crimson complexion. He didn't need to speak, because his eyes did a perfectly good job of conveying all of his famous lines, over and over, each with growing, silent, intensity. "Your ass is gonna to be in a sling! ... ... Your goose is cooked, buddy ... You ain't gonna to see the light of day!"

Once Mooncai finished, she looked at me with an evil, calm, satisfied stare of mastery. My father gave her his direct work phone number and said, "You just give me a call at my work whenever he acts up." He side-eyed me as he said this. The short ride home consisted of my father pounding on the dashboard every few moments. My mother did her usual routine of ringing her hands and repeating the same words over and over:

"Oh, I'm so embarrassed ... Oh, I'm just ... *so* embarrassed." That only served to drive my father even more nuts.

Surprisingly, he did not chase me around the house with his belt in one hand while holding up his pants up with the other. He did, however, say what I predicted: "You'se ain't gonna see the light of day! You ah' grounded right until hell freezes over!" He then goose-stepped just like Mooncai while pacing back and forth, pounding his fist against his hand.

"From now on, you will rise up and deliver the *Boston Globe.* You will go to school. You will do *exactly* what Mrs. Mooncai says. You will return from school. You will deliver the *Daily Transcript.* That will be immediately followed by you sitting at your desk and doing your homework." He didn't stop to breathe, but just continued: "I will then review your homework." He paused for dramatic effect. "And," he said ominously, "if you act up in class, I will hear about it via the phone." He glowered at me. My mother wrung her hands and said, "Oh, I'm *so* embarrassed." My father's eye twitched.

THE BLUE-ASSED FLY

The only light of day I would experience now would be during paper routes, recess, and the walk to and from school. I contemplated my near future of misery, which was decidedly more miserable than my newly miserable life already had become. The vise tightened around my mind. I was now *truly* trapped inside the margins. They were steel margins just like the fence we would have to line up at. I followed this routine for weeks on end. It was very difficult for me to settle in and study. I would notice a fly land next to me, and it would draw my attention away for a period of time, distracting me from memorizing facts about old guys in white wigs.

I looked at the fly and was amazed. He could swivel his head quickly. He would rub his front legs together menacingly as if he found something he liked or was about to do something evil. My father had an expression for describing some people's mental state. "He is as crazy as a blue-assed fly." Sure enough, this fly's ass did have a blue tinge. I imagined the fellow he was talking about performing the same type of behavior I saw in this fly: rubbing his hands, shaking his head, peering around ominously, running around a room with no apparent purpose.

I thought if there was a small fly, there must also be some monstrously huge fly, somewhere … perhaps lurking in the woods behind our home. I surmised that the monstrous boss fly was dispatching these little flies out to collect crumbs. It made sense that they would all assemble in the morning, pile up their crumbs, and then cower as the gigantic blue-assed fly gave out assignments, as well as the address and instructions to each house.

"Okay. I want you'se to go to the Winslow house, and case the joint. See if they leave crumbs around, and if they do, bring the crumbs back to me."

These thoughts crowded my mind as I tried to sit there studying. Time would go by very slowly, and then I would try to go back to studying the dead white guys with wigs, with their lousy black-buckled shoes, and remember something supposedly important they said or had done. Maybe I had "blue-assed fly syndrome," Whatever the case, it took me about 20 minutes to get the image of a giant blue-assed fly in the woods, giving directions to the little blue-assed flies, out of my head.

WALK IT OFF

Another New England season ended, and now winter was upon us. The good news was, the cold and snow would arrive shortly. That meant intense sledding and hockey. Gone were the days of the flexible flyer, and slow-moving sleds. Gone were the days of skating around in circles.

There were now very fast sleds, and they came in the form of rubber tubes. We would build sledding paths that became rites of passage into manhood. We would find the steepest incline on Crystal Hill; the newly formed snow would be packed with a shovel, a jump added to the slope, then water applied. After an overnight waiting period, the sledding path was ready to serve as a passage into manhood, due to the high likelihood it would cause injuries and (Cashews hoped) crying.

You simply couldn't decline a run. You absolutely could not say, "I'm scared" or show any fear or reluctance in front of the crew. Your only option was to just get on the inner tube – either by sitting, lying on your stomach, or like the luge on your back with head propped slightly forward – and barrel headlong into manhood. Predictably, more often than not, you would spin out of control at high speeds as you flew over the jump and, depending on how you were positioned on the tube, smash the back of your head on the iced slope or land hard on your face. Shortly after that, you would have an ostrich creature looking down on you to see if you showed any signs of crying.

We all eventually would wreck, and we all had our own ways of dealing with the excruciating pain. My method was to "walk it off," marching in tight circles, moaning. Others would simply lay where they landed, writhing and yelling. Others performed a combination of the two methods, taking a few limping steps, then flopping to the ground to squirm in pain, then getting up to walk it off for a few more steps. Being seasoned veterans, we all passed "the cry cop's" inspections.

What had previously been simply skating turned to full contact, intensely violent hockey. This quickly evolved into a new form of entertainment which we for some reason named after a photo one of us had shown around, of a Japanese guy smiling with the caption of "wok steki."

We were all avid fans of the Boston Bruins hockey team, and there were many guys on the Bruins that were our heroes, mostly because they fought all the time. One of them was Terry O'Reilly and the other was a very short, but powerful Native Indian from Canada named Stan Jonathan. There was always a joke about Terry O'Reilly's inability to skate; when taking the team photo the joke was to take it quick before he fell down.

I couldn't afford actual hockey skates so I had to use my sister's figure skates. We couldn't afford pads or anything either, so it was basically just ski hats, hockey sticks, and hand-me-down skates.

It seemed the aggression we all possessed was happily taken out on one another, or various, random, hapless kids we met on the pond. There were some older guys that usually showed up as well, some who even played organized hockey. These guys were very fast and, at first, made fun of our borrowed skates – especially my figure skates – and lack of proper equipment. But when it came to playing, our crew held its own. After one scrimmage, we were no longer being laughed at.

At least one fight was guaranteed each match. We tried to emulate O'Reilly and Jonathan by grabbing the opponent's shirt with one hand, pulling it over his face if possible, and throwing as many punches as we could at the guy's head. Once the fight went to the ground, being good Catholics and Protestants, it was broken up. I never feared being punched in the face several times, because it was just the inevitable outcome. But I did fear falling backward and landing on the back of my head.

Soon what had been somewhat organized hockey that loosely adhered to the actual rules of the game morphed into "wok steki." The new game was quite simple, but it took New England know-how to execute properly. We would stand on the thick white, safe ice, and slowly move to a spot where the pond was emptying out into a river; moving water meant it was difficult for ice to form to the appropriate thickness to support our weight. It was what we called "black ice." We would form somewhat of a line as if for a Slug Train, and the man in front was usually the luckiest because he would typically pass safely from the thick white ice, over the black ice, and then onto the land.

If everyone passed over to the land without falling in, we would then go from the land back over to the black ice, and then proceed in a line onto the white ice. Even if you didn't fall in, the fear of slipping and landing on the back of your head was ever-present. For our first run of wok steki we performed this ritual about three times when, finally, the new guy from Springfield fell through the black ice.

I raised my hands up yelling, "wok steki!" as the guy struggled to reach for thicker ice, kicking and flailing, making his passage into manhood. It took him a while to get to safety, and the rest of the crew began chanting, yelling "wok steki!" Finally, he made it to thick ice, panting and soaking wet. He had forever etched his place into our crew. It then as he was lying down on that cold New England ice that he became an official member of the Cro Mags. We didn't lend him a hand or a branch as he struggled in that ice, because as we saw it, that is life, just one big struggle. This was just preparatory work for what lay ahead.

The Cro Mags developed a new thing once Mooncai turned her back: it was called toilet mouth. We would fold up our tongues, and push our bottom lips out like frogs. It made no noise, but the challenge was not to laugh – and even some of the good students would get in on it. Mooncai would turn around, and see about ten people looking like frogs. After a few days, she caught on, and would even pretend to write before snapping around quickly to point out the three to four of us who had been caught in the act with the toilet mouth. "Fence!" she yelled.

Soon, phone calls were made, and my father announced that I would most likely be going to a special school for kids who could not behave. The threat of that didn't seem to improve my behavior.

Just to get a rise out of Mooncai, I would put just one letter, or even just a half of a letter of my homework, outside her beloved margins. She would mark her papers with a red pen. If there were a lot of errors she would turn it into what she called a "bloody paper," what she called "a red goose egg" – a big round red zero at the top. To further shame us, she would hold up both the perfect papers and the "goose eggs" and make a comparison about those that listened in life, and those that didn't.

ENTER THE DRAGON

Winter was still upon us, and to our astonishment, Mrs. Mooncai showed brief signs of levity. She spoke about her country of origin, and the Chinese New Year, and told us we would be celebrating this soon. She said we were going to build a Chinese dragon, and we, her students, would operate the dragon, with other students dressed up in traditional garb, dancing alongside. The whole thing sounded like one big art project. It was the first time she had ever mentioned anything at all about art. She bent down inches from my face and said, "Mr. Winslow, you'll like this, there will be no homework assignment for two weeks! You will all be working on the costumes, artwork, and dragon for this special presentation for your parents."

Cashews and a few other guys from my crew worked on the dragon with me. We would build the best Chinese dragon ever. It was always all or nothing with us. Mrs. Mooncai gave us photos of dragons, and all the supplies from what I figured must have been the Dragon Outlet store. For the first time that entire year, we all came into school with excitement and enthusiasm. We came in each day brimming with sheer delight to put on our art smocks and go to work like ants.

We put the picture of a real Chinese dragon on a table, studied it, and worked hard to create our own. We all had our own assignments, and everybody took it seriously. Cosgrove was assigned to be in charge of the scissors because he had a history with scissors and could be trusted. One day earlier in the year, I had one of the good students in the Winslow headlock. Cosgrove came over and started cutting the kid's hair with a pair of scissors, claiming with a smile, "I always wanted to be a barber." That was a major offense back in the 70's since we all had long hair. He was sent to the principal's office. That stunt got Cosgrove into the Cro Mags.

For those ten days, while building the dragon, I was never once assigned to the fence and my father was never called at his office. I never saw Mrs. Mooncai smile or laugh, but her expression did change, and she didn't do her back and forth goose-stepping routine. She actually stopped, picked up the picture of the dragon, looked at us, looked at the dragon we were constructing and called us, "Little Rembrandts." She patted me on the head. It felt odd not being hit by a yardstick or having my desk dumped.

I accepted this one-time kindness and went back to the dragon. I ran home and thought of the dragon non-stop as I ran around delivering the afternoon newspaper. I was happy for the first time since before the eel guys had assaulted me and my brother at the ocean that summer. I would put my arms behind my head and stare up at the plywood under my brother's bunk and think of the dragon and how it should look. (Lead's top half of our bunk bed would shake sometimes shortly after the lights went out. It must have been some type of sleep-shaking phase early teens go through.)

I ran to school and put on my art smock and told the dragon crew about my thoughts and we added more and more colors and shapes, and details. Mrs. Mooncai was impressed and even joked, "We should have made dragons all year, you would all receive A's." A few days before we would put on the "Chinese New Year Pageant," we had our first practice. That was mind-blowing. It was as if Mrs. Mooncai was literally a different person.

She was the director of this play that was about to take place in front of parents, and we were the actors. It was going to take place in the gym. Now, she actually danced and showed us how to dance while under the dragon. We looked at her in awe, as she taught us how to make the dragon look like it was alive. She ducked, rose up, ducked, sidestepped. We practiced and then delicately brought the dragon out and danced. She even clapped as we finished the routine. I loved school again! Other students had masks of butterflies, jesters, and other characters. But we were going to be the main attraction, the dragon!

We practiced with intensity. The day finally arrived and all the parents took their seats. Mrs. Mooncai went in first and made an announcement to the parents. She then put on the music and the actors and actresses began. Mrs. Mooncai signaled to us, and we got under the dragon and brought it to life. Cashews was working the head, Cosgrave the barber was in the middle and I was in the back. A few of the other students filled up the rest of "the best dragon ever," and we did our thing.

The parents stood up midway during the dance and clapped and cheered. We finished the routine, then took our bows as Mrs. Mooncai beamed at us with pride and approval. We exited the stage and headed out into the hallway. The new, kind, happy version of Mrs. Mooncai went back into applause and turned the music off. Parents came out and congratulated us and we bowed again. I was filled with happiness and couldn't believe how much fun I had at school those past two weeks.

We carefully placed the dragon upstairs in our classroom. Mrs. Mooncai was now full of life and congratulated us. She said we had done such a great job that, as a reward, as a class, we could keep the dragon and even take it out for recess. A part of me didn't want to damage it in the snow, but we were proud and wanted to show it off. The bell rang and we carefully brought the dragon outside where we again brought it to life to the amazement of all the other students. The rest of the Cro Mags got underneath and joined in. We were dancing inside the dragon when all of a sudden, Cashews yelled, "Slug Train!"

I couldn't see well since he was operating the head of the dragon, so I just tried to keep up as we went from walking and dancing to suddenly chanting, "slug-a slug sluga-sluga-sluga" and running full speed. The next thing I saw was another kid who seemed to be getting slugged underneath us. All of a sudden, it was as if a spell had overtaken us, or as if the beautiful art dragon we built had become possessed by an actual evil dragon. Our beautiful creation didn't last long and started immediately to disintegrate and come apart. After just a few moments, there was a kid on the ground bleeding and crying and our once colorful dragon was scattered, broken and muddy, strewn all over the cold New England snow.

The operators of the slug dragon were all escorted to Mrs. Mooncai's class. The very short-lived "nice," new, Mrs. Mooncai died instantly before our eyes as another teacher described the act. This was the maddest any of us had ever seen her. She lined us all against the wall outside her classroom. She went into her Chinese culture, how we ruined the good name of every Chinese person by using a Chinese dragon to pummel an innocent student.

She said we were like pigs: you can clean us and brush our teeth, but we will eventually jump into the mud. She had saliva dripping out of her mouth as she ranted, and I knew that wasn't good. My father would drool just like that when he was at his peak ranting phase. She walked up and down and back and forth as she worked herself up into a literal frenzy. I noticed that the other teachers had looks of fright on their faces as they eyed one another nervously.

We were instructed to go outside and pick up the dragon and dispose of its remains. Me, Cashews and Cosgrave went back to Mooncai's class after we had cleaned up. She looked very strange now, beet red with black and grayish hair frayed like a crazy person. We sat up straight and went back to work. The good students even gave us bad looks. At the recess bell, we heard the old term from her: "fence."

The next day all the Cro Mags were on the fence looking up at the second-floor window. We kept on our best behavior to let Mrs. Mooncai cool down a few days, but then we went right back to performing toilet jaws behind her back. My life was once again the paper route, homework, and fence. I remembered back to the day in summer when I opened the envelope to find out who I would have for a 5th-grade teacher and seeing the name "Mrs. Mooncai," and Lapham throwing his head back in laughter and pointing to me, saying, "You got Mooncai!" I remembered our plan to break her.

Now here we were, a permanent fixture of the fence, even on the last day of last day of 5th grade. Finally, Mrs. Mooncai opened the window and yelled down, "School's over, go home!"

Fifth grade ended and the score was:

Mooncai: 1

Winslow: Red Goose Egg

MONSTERS

Fifth grade was finally over, but oddly, I was no longer looking forward to our trip to the Irish Riviera, because I knew the eel guys had a slug train down there waiting for me. I was finally figuring out that what comes around goes around. I knew what it felt like to be a wounded gazelle out on the playground of Sheehan School, looking over my shoulders to see a pack of hyenas exiting a brick building for recess and thumping. I did go to the Riviera but was constantly looking over my shoulder.

I had lost that childhood wonder that always made being there so special. Summer came and went, and I got the letter informing me that my teacher for sixth grade would be a guy named Mr. Gibbons. He didn't have the mean reputation of Mrs. Mooncai, but he did have a reputation of being no-nonsense.

I would learn a valuable lesson that year, and it was a lesson about respect. There is respect out of fear, which makes a person push the boundaries of the person they fear. Then there is respect for someone that talks and treats *you* with respect and rewards or acknowledges you when you do the right thing ... the respect for a person who corrects you without being degrading or insulting when you are wrong.

School started, and there was a new "new kid," which meant he would be introduced to our school via a Slug Train. New kids usually roam the playground solo. They stand out, either by a different type of clothing or just being alone on the playground. This new kid ate alone, walked the halls alone, and went home alone. He would sometimes look our way, and the guy from Brockton, although he couldn't throw a punch, would throw f-bombs his way. The kid just turned back to his baloney sandwich.

The bell rang and us Cro Mags hit the recess field and immediately formed the Slug Train. The same girl with pigtails, cute freckles, plaid dress and an operatic voice looked at us, turned and screamed, "slug train!" We were sixth graders, and owned the playground now, so the sea of students parted, creating a path directly to the new guy. He obviously knew he was a target of something and ran. We were amazed at his speed and coordination: he ran around every obstacle on the playground.

We didn't have much time, once the girl yelled out "slug train!" A teacher would then send the alarm to other teachers. We split the train up and in good hyena fashion, cut him off, and one of us made the tackle, followed by the others. He was putting up a great fight, and that shocked us. Then we were grabbed by the hair and collars by some male teachers, one of which was my assigned teacher, Mr. Gibbons.

He dragged me into a supply closet, and kept repeating, "You think ya' tough!? You think ya' tough!?" There was a gym teacher there too, an ex-marine recently returned from Vietnam. He kept repeating the same thing. I was told that I would be assigned a thing next recess called "monsters," without much additional explanation.

The next day arrived, and I was brought outside to the basketball court, and Mr. G. Showed me what a monster was. It was touching the first line, then running across the court to the opposite line, touching it, and then back to the first line, then and back to the original. He had me do this ten times, and I felt like vomiting. I went back to class soaking wet and on the verge of puking. Mr. G. simply said, "Are you done with your slug train?" I replied, "Yes, sir!" and that was that.

After feeling on the verge of vomiting, I all of a sudden was overtaken by a tranquil feeling. I felt less irritable and restless. I was walking home and noticed the new guy. A sort of spiritual thing came over me, like the time I was going to kick the guy I was fighting who made fun of my bell-bottoms and platform shoes and an angel or something said, "Don't do it." I followed the kid down Route 109 to his house and waited until he got inside. Then walked up to the door and knocked, and he answered, and I said I was sorry.

His father obviously knew that his kid was being harassed. He stood up and was very intimidating. He had a grayish/black afro, an adult drink in his hand, and a cigarette dangling from his mouth. He said it was a miracle that I came over, as my entire crew was a few days away from an ass whopping. He shook my hand for coming down and apologizing, and then I left. I don't know what compelled me to do that. Maybe there was a God, and every so often I would hear the small inner voice from Him telling me not to commit an act of violence. I felt better walking away and hoped maybe that was the new me. Maybe I would be a priest; after all, they had a free car, free shoes, and free adult drinks. I was a new man.

The next day, the Cro Mags sat for lunch. The new guy walked into the slop line, disappeared for a few moments behind the wall, came out, and paid. The other fellows didn't know I had gotten a little soft and had gone to his house to apologize. He paid for his lunch, gave us all a quick look, but before he could turn away, I waved him over. Cashews the cry cop and second in command said, "What's this?"

"He's in," I said, shooting Cashews a stern look … and that was that. There was no vote, no special ceremony. He was just in. He sat down and one of the Cro Mags said, "So where you from?"

"Marshfield," he said.

Cashews and I just looked at each other. Indeed, he was in: he was from the Riviera. It was his first day with us, so we walked him around the playground we had inherited by virtue of being sixth graders. The new guy shared his Riviera stories, and we were taking it all in. He invited me home, and it turned out his mother was a saleswoman for Cadbury, which would soon introduce the best sweet of all time, the Cadbury Cream Egg. They had a whole box of them, and we got wired downing them before he showed me something he learned from back home.

He brought out an empty bottle of what looked like one of the adult beverages his father would drink. He lead me out back to where his lawnmowers and chore equipment was stored. There, he filled up the bottle with gasoline, poured a small amount of gas on a rag, and stuffed most of the rag into the bottle. He said with a smile, "This is a Molotov cocktail." I figured it must have been named for the one and only Russian guy that lived in the Riviera. We then went to the large body of water behind his house, Buckmaster Pond, the designated hangout of the older kids known as Leatherheads. They had named it "The Rez." We had to look around quietly to see if there were any Leatherheads hiding behind trees. When it was all safe, we entered.

The Rez carried a scary connotation even for us Cro Mags, almost as if it were haunted. The Leatherheads would drink and party here, smoking a smelly substance and getting in fights. It seemed like at least once a year, some poor Leatherhead would be pulled out of The Rez' swimming hole, dead. That day, there were none there, so it was our laboratory. I was going to witness Mr. Molotov's cocktail in action. The new guy found a very large rock, the size of an automobile, and told me to back away. He lit the cloth wick.

He held it up to what I believe was the same God we all worshipped and yelled with power, "the Molotov cocktail!" He threw it with brute force. I could tell he had some anger in him, which made me like him even more. Maybe he understood what I was going through.

The cocktail smashed against the rock and literally exploded. In the dusk light, the explosion seemed even more intense. I ran up to him and vigorously shook his hand, mentally thanking Mr. Molotov for this incredible invention. We had a new weapon in our war against society. The Molotov cocktail. This new Russian weapon would keep our fire department on their toes and keep us occupied until we discovered our next new vice.

We didn't act up in Mr. G's class because he didn't stand for it and we respected how he conducted things. But outside of school, we returned to our Cro Mag state of mind. We also began to call ourselves "ments," short for "mental." We burned everything in sight, and when winter came, we would introduce the new guy to wok steki.

One day, we stumbled upon a flower when out looking for fresh foliage to burn. None of us had ever seen anything like it. It seemed like it didn't belong in our neck of the woods. It was pink and very odd shaped. It almost looked like an alien. Or, something that had dropped out of God's hands by accident for some reason. Maybe to slow us down, to take in his creation. Cashews, who was a walking encyclopedia, bent down with his ostrich neck and studied the flower. He then rose up and announced the type of flower it was. He said it was a Lady Slipper and that it was very rare in this neck of the woods, and it was even a crime to pick it. We all looked at the flower.

Cashews bent over, clearing the pine needles and twigs away from the Lady Slipper, making her even more precious. We stood looking down at her a little longer. It was almost a spiritual experience. We then walked away with our Molotov cocktails. We ended up in a place named "Pete's Rock." I never met Pete, but for whatever reason, he had a rock the size of a garage in the shape of a highway cone named after him. We sat at the base of Pete's Rock talking about our first sighting of a Lady Slipper. We were all in awe. Maybe there was a God.

We did have the Molotov cocktails, and couldn't waste them, so we broke out of the spiritual moment, and got to work tossing the gas-filled glass bottles onto Pete's Rock. F*ck Pete. Eventually, the fire got out of hand and shortly thereafter came the blue and red lights. We watched from behind oak and pine trees as the flames were doused and the firemen shook their heads. The good news was, it didn't spread to the Lady Slipper. She remained unharmed.

I liked school again mostly because I respected the teacher. That didn't mean that I never got out of line, but I knew when I did get out of line, Mr. G. would assign me to a rigorous exercise routine that would calm me. He even allowed me to write outside the margins. He would simply say, "I'm more concerned with your ideas and *what* you write than I am with your penmanship." I never once got a red goose egg in his class.

Mr. G. would even read to us, and for the very first time, books and reading became fun for me, especially fiction. No longer was it about memorizing facts, but rather, hearing words and understanding new ideas. He would read for about 45 minutes every day, and we all sat in awe and listened. Then we discussed what he had read. It seemed odd for Mr. G. to be reading with enthusiasm and dramatic flair – because he seemed more like a professional wrestler or football player. Nobody ever questioned *his* manhood, but in our neck of the woods, the men of our father's generation wouldn't be caught dead doing a dramatic reading – for fear of being called a hairdresser or having the lightness of their loafers questioned. But Mr. G pulled it off. It was quite a lesson for us Cro Mags to sit and see his massive hands holding a novel and reading it to 6th graders.

Once in a while, I would see Mooncai goose-stepping down the hallway. She never missed an opportunity to throw me a hairy eyeball. I even imagined hearing a snake-like hissing noise from her whenever we passed.

Winter came and the new guy had acquired his Cro Mag name. His last name was Simonon. It organically morphed into "Simma." We introduced him to wok steki, and he handled himself very well. When he broke through the ice he did initially have a look of panic on his face. But it also seemed he had done this before, as his method of kicking to safe ice and twisting his body while getting out seemed practiced. As he emerged from the ice after his first breakthrough we all raised our hands, yelling "wok steki." Simma told us stories of the hijinks he and his old pals had gotten up to in his old town on the Riviera, which included games similar to wok steki. He fit right in.

Winter was still fun at this age, and very challenging. Full contact skating. Maniacal sledding that resulted from finding the steepest paths in the woods, icing them down and then trying to maneuver through at high speeds without hitting the unmovable oaks. Of course, if one struck an oak, the usual remedy was applied: "walk it off" without crying, otherwise Cashews would be there to document the shame. Sixth grade flew by and life was settling in for me.

OLD TURKEY VODKA

As sixth grade ended we all had a combined sense of exhilaration and dread, knowing that next year we'd be stepping up to Thurston Junior High – probably named for some guy who wore a wig like Washington and ugly black buckled shoes like the pilgrims. On the one hand, we were moving up and getting away from the little kid stuff at elementary school. But, on the other hand, we were now going to be the low men on the totem pole.

For many, going from 6th to 7th grade and from elementary to middle school marks the shift from childhood into young adulthood, and it did for me. I pondered what I thought I knew in life up to that point. I had thus far learned many lessons on Crystal Hill. Most of these had made me bitter and caused me great guilt later on down the road.

What I thought I knew then consisted of the following: People in your life come and go. Where they go to once they are "gone" is "the better place," but only if you were good in life. But, if you weren't so good in life? Then you probably wake up in Mooncai's class every day without end for eternity, getting red goose eggs, hairy eyeballs, and smacks on the back of the neck with a yardstick.

It seemed elementary school was a time when deep opinions are formed of the world and your surroundings. That world seemed violent to me, and the Cro Mags, of which I was the leader, in turn, spewed acts of violence back out into the world. Heading into middle school, it seemed the core of me had changed; I was defensive and had begun to keep somewhat of a distance from others. I felt if I became too close, they could end up in that "gone" category. On the other hand, my views about school softened a bit, temporarily, from having a teacher I respected for sixth grade. But the defensive shell had been formed and would only thicken.

Cashews father had inherited a beach house down the cape in a town called Eastham. Now that he and his sister were older, the parents trusted the eldest sister to watch over the house and Cashews while they spent the weekend at the cape. His sister would stay upstairs or go out with her friends. She let us have our own area, which was the basement. One Saturday, when his parents were gone, I happened to have a rare day off after the *Boston Globe* had been delivered. For some reason, that day, there was no yard work to be done and no assisting my father doing electrical work in someone's attic in the city.

Cashews invited me over to watch *Creature Double Feature* and *Soul Train*. That day would be different because we wouldn't have his father running down the stairs to his bar, looking at the TV with his beet red complexion, and yelling up to his wife, "Lou! They're watching Soul Train!" We had it all to ourselves. The only thing I would miss was Mrs. Cashews' cooking. We turned on the tube and sat back. Then Cashews said, "Hey, let's take a look at the bar!" The bar was always off limits, so naturally, there was an attraction to us.

The bar appeared as if it belonged in some tropical island. It had bamboo, wood trim and even a tropical island painting in back. We turned the overhead lights on, and the bar came to life. Our eyes dazzled. We looked at all the glasses. Then the bottles ... brown ones, clear ones, green ones, small ones, some even figure-eight shaped. Then we examined the specific names on each bottle, which we assumed were related to the bottle's purpose.

Old Grand Dad ... that was obviously reserved for adult males or Cashews' father's father. Wild Turkey ... surely something consumed before heading out in a red plaid flannel shirt for a turkey hunt. Johnny Walker and Jack Daniels ... no doubt famous men that Mrs. Mooncai never mentioned in history class. Then there was a drink made for those of us with some Irish ancestry, called "Bailey's Irish Cream." Cashews and

I stood there like scientists pondering this new laboratory. We looked at each other. Then, naturally, we decided to try our first drink.

I knew a little bit about prepping drinks from watching my father at family functions at our house and working the bar. There was a metal mixer, and I said we should take a little bit of each drink, and pour it into this metal mixer. We took a little bit of the Wild Turkey, Vodka, and Old Grand Dad and poured it all into the metal mixer. I then put a cap on it and held it over my shoulder like my father did and shook the contents. It was now our drink which we dubbed, "Old Turkey Vodka." We took the drinks and sat at the bar like adults. We raised our glasses and drank. We noted our observations, like scientists.

"It burns!"

"It's hot!"

We winced as the liquid went down … but we finished our first drink.

I wondered how anyone could drink that awful-tasting stuff. We then went to the couch and turned on the TV and watched a giant bird by the name of Rodan fight an upright lizard named Godzilla on some island named Japan. A strange sensation began to come over me. I felt warm and even started to sweat for no reason. Then a newfound mental state came over me. It was a feeling of euphoria. It was as if all my fears had vanished, fear of the unknown, fear of death, fear of people.

I even began to grin a childhood grin. I looked at Cashews, and he seemed to be experiencing the same effects. We simultaneously said, "whoa!" My constant fidgetiness was gone. We sat there for a moment. As a pair of good scientists, we concluded that if one drink resulted in us feeling this good, another good-sized glass of Old Turkey Vodka would be even better. We went back to the bar, and like an experienced bartender, I mixed the Old Turkey Vodka over my shoulder and poured. We raised our glasses again, this time to God, and drank.

It didn't seem to burn this time, so we drank it even faster. We returned to the TV and our friend, the host of *Soul Train*, greeted us. We danced like we never had before. Cashews' sister Patty came down and stared, then burst out laughing at our dancing … not knowing we had just visited the tropical island adult bar in the corner of the house. She got laundry and headed upstairs. We seemed to dance for the whole show. Then we went back to the bar. I stumbled a bit. We made one last Old Turkey Vodka and this time added a lot more of the ingredients, which required getting larger glasses.

We drank it down like two people that just came from a long hike. I guess it had been a long hike, a long hike through elementary school and childhood. Now the hike was over. We headed out to the backyard, to discuss our wide-open futures. As I walked down the long corridor, I noticed that I wobbled and bumped into the wall. It didn't faze me. Rather, I merely noted the effects as part of the science experiment.

We finally made it out to the lawn where the grass was still bright green. Since I couldn't stand very well, I decided to lay down. Cashews the walking encyclopedia began talking about our inevitable future as oceanographers. "It's like being a scientist," he explained. "Except the laboratory is the entire ocean." Shockingly, Cashews seemed to talk even more and even faster than usual under the influence of these adult drinks.

I laid down, looking up at the sky, looking to my left, and then to my right. Taking in the beautiful scenes of the beginning of a New England summer. All the birds were back from Florida, everything was bright green. Cashews was laying out our future in detail, from the beginning, where we entered the ocean backwards off a boat, taking our underwater biological discoveries to the laboratory and then looking at our discoveries under a microscope. He said we would be surrounded by water most of the day. That made me feel even more comfortable, being back in my saltwater playground.

I felt like a kid again, and all it took was the magic in the adult drinks. Now I finally knew why the adults drank. It gave them power over whatever ailed them: the art-ritis, the cat-racks, the strokes ... and, in the end, it allowed you to "clear out your radiator," as my grandfather did, vomiting up any undesirable food. It seemed like a miracle substance.

My arms were behind my head, and I was thinking big. All was possible, and all the world was just waiting to be discovered. I lay there until the sun began going down and the birds grew quiet. I got up, but stumbled, and shook Cashews' hand. We were both smiling. He said, "I will tell the others about our discovery." As I recalled, all of the other Cro Mags had either a bar or a special "liquor cabinet" somewhere in their homes. This was going to be great!

That summer, one by one, in different pairs of two's and three's, we *all* made the "adult drink" discovery. This was good news for homeowners, firefighters, police officers – not to mention the trees, shrubbery, and wild-life – as the fires in the woods stopped abruptly.

Cashews' parents returned a few days later, and his father suspected something was missing, or out of place. Good luck for us, however, as he suspected Cashews' sister and her friends. After all, in his parent's eyes, Cashews was still in the "special" category, with his high IQ. So, it couldn't possibly have been him.

THE CAPTAIN

I wasn't as thrilled to go to the Irish Riviera that summer, because I knew I had a slug train to avoid while down there. But then I remembered that my mother had vodka there, so that made up for my lack of enthusiasm. I was a little sad realizing that the novelty of the Atlantic and Blue Fish Cove had worn off. But there were other day trips I would discover that summer, one of which was with a new friend a grade below me. Despite his tender age, he had already earned the reputation of "ment." His name was Mike B. and his father was going to take us to a place that I would fall in love with. It was called Nauset beach, and it was located on Cape Cod.

His father seemed to be very easy going, which Mike took full advantage of in everything he did. We had to leave early due to the location of this beach, being near the far end of Cape Cod. I noticed his father dressed just like mine when he was at the beach: plaid shorts, black socks, leather shoes, and sunglasses. I helped pack the car with an ugly grey blanket and a cooler full of baloney sandwiches. His father was a chain smoker and he loaded the glove box with a few packs for the ride.

We piled in and headed for this Nauset beach. His father lit his first of several dozen cigarettes which seemed to ignite a smile as well. We headed off and his father turned on a jazz station and we listened to that new music all the way down to the ocean. Along the way, he regaled us with stories of South Boston and what it was like growing up there. His father traveled at great speeds, and when we finally arrived, he said he cut the time by 20 minutes by way of judicious navigation. He certainly gained my respect by getting us there earlier.

We pulled up to the gate and Mr. B., with a big grin and cigarette dangling, greeted the attendant with, "Good morning young man," and paid for parking. We then unloaded the trunk, the blanket and two small coolers. One contained our baloney sandwiches on white bread. The other Mr. B. grabbed and held onto like it was a sick puppy. We spread the blanket, and I looked out at the massive beach and the enormous waves crashing in. It didn't have all the rock formations of Blue Fish Cove, but the mammoth waves made up for it. Mike and I ran into the surf and were immediately and violently thrown to the bottom. It didn't bother us, and we leaped up and then swam out to where the waves were actually swelling up. Mike had some experience riding waves, so I followed his lead. We bobbed up and down and waited for a big one. I took a look at the beach and saw Mr. B. making a drink for himself while keeping one eye on us.

Mike said, "Let's go," and displayed a natural ability to swim *with* the wave. The swell carried us up high where I could see even more of the beach. We glided in, on a free ride from the wave. Then I began to lose control as it curved, and I was smashed to the bottom, tossed and turned and crushed into the sand.

I finally emerged, and Mike gave me more instructions. Before we headed out again, I took a look at Mike's dad. He had a glass in his hand with ice, and what looked like an adult drink inside, and a cigarette in his mouth. He just smiled. Before, I would wonder what parents were smiling at in moments like this, but I now knew, as I looked at him, exactly what the feeling he had was, for I had tasted the forbidden adult drink and understood its calming effect.

We made it out to the magic spot where the waves somehow created themselves, seemingly out of nothing. We would tread water, waiting for the biggest hump of water, and then ride the wave. This was the scariest part for me, the waiting. The movie "Jaws" had been released not too long before, and I knew our white legs fluttering back and forth would make a great snack for some relative of the shark that was blown up in the movie. I felt safe in the wave though, because the shark wouldn't be stupid enough to ride a wave into the beach and then be beaten down to the sand like us. Only us stupid humans would do that.

Mr. B. had a small radio and just kept looking out to the Atlantic, grinning. He did mutter, "Ay-yo, the Sox are winning!" There was a bottle called Captain Morgan partially covered beside him. He made a quick drink, put some ice in the glass, and said, "Ahhhhhh … Cape Cod."

The beach soon became more crowded, and we even heard different languages. Mike said these people were French Canadian. The men had very small bathing suits, and the women's exposed a great deal of their bums. They must not have been decent devout Catholics like we were, with long bathing suits or long plaid shorts like Mr. B.

It seemed as the day went on, the waves only intensified. While treading water, if I wasn't thinking of losing both my legs by shark bite, my mind would look out into the ocean, wondering what was out there on the other side. What were those people like on those distant shores? I would look at Mr. B. Grinning as he indulged in that wonderful magic drink.

We made friends with these French kids, and we couldn't even speak each other's language. The day flew by and we shook hands with our new paks. They said, "Bonjour," and we said, "Later." The beach was clearing, but Mr. B, made no sign of leaving; he just kept looking out into the Atlantic, smiling with his cigarette dangling and his ice clanking. We had the waves to ourselves, and they were monstrous now, no longer in their fun stage, but a new fight-for-your-life stage.

Mike and I decided to accept the challenge. We found the massive water hump, swam with it, and no matter what we did, in the end, it slammed us to the bottom. I now knew what it may have felt like to be the victim of a slug train. Helpless, at the bottom of the Atlantic as the waves kicked me all over the sand. The sea bottom was like sandpaper on my skin, and I was raw and red. But we wouldn't let the waves win. I looked at Mike as we rode our last wave, his body being thrown feet first into the air. Shortly after, it was my turn. I was a sock in a dryer. Helpless. We crawled out of the Atlantic, having faced our fears, but in the end, the Atlantic won. It was a successful day.

I looked around and there was just a guy with a metal detector and Mike's father left on the beach. We got back to the blanket and he said, "Well, looks like we all got our money's worth." Mike said we should go. His father said, "I guess you're right." We packed everything up and headed to the car. Mike's dad walked a few steps and fell, covering himself with sand. He announced, "Eh, too much sand." We walked some more and he stumbled again, but was able to catch himself with one arm and said, "Effing sand." We finally made it to the car and he fumbled for his keys, and then opened the trunk. He made a small drink, announcing, "This is for the road." And with that, the Captain Morgan's was finally empty.

We drove for about 30 minutes and then hit major traffic. We were hardly moving when Mike said, "Dad, do what you always do." Mr. B responded, "Great idea Mike!" Mike explained, "This is the breakdown lane." No one else was driving in it. Mike's dad must have had some special pass in order to drive in this lane. Or maybe if he was pulled over, he would say, "Captain Morgan," and the police would let him go, being a close friend and all of Captain Morgan.

As we drove by the traffic at high speeds, it seemed other people didn't like our special driving privileges, as they gave us bad looks, beeped their horns, and even did very un-Catholic things like put out their middle fingers.

Mike and I were altar boys and had seen Mike's father bring up the water or wine at church on an occasional Sunday; sometimes he even worked the collection basket. I couldn't believe the behavior of these other people, especially giving the middle finger to two altar boys and a parent. Mike's father said they were just jealous, and not to pay attention. I figured his father worked hard for these breakdown lane privileges.

We made it home and beat all the traffic. My father was there as we pulled up. He looked in the car and asked Mr. B how the day went. He simply said, "Smooth sailing!" and roared with laughter. That must be what you say after drinking Captain Morgan, I thought: "smooth sailing." My mother had our traditional Saturday night meal ready, which was hot dogs, beans, and brown bread. I was told by my father at dinner to never, *ever*, get in the car with Mr. B. again. I thought that night of Captain Morgan.

The drink must be for ex-sailors, or exclusively a beach drink since every adult drink seemingly had a name, a purpose, and a specific place appropriate for indulging.

Despite my fears, I accompanied the family to the Irish Riviera that summer. Sure enough, my mother had lots of vodka there. She never paid much attention to those bottles, since we were there infrequently, as were other guests. The bar was sort of a liquor library, it's inventory always changing. The booze gave me the bravery to walk to the beach each day, despite my fears of the eel boys.

I never did see them that summer, but their specter still sullied the old, good memories of the place. The vodka gave me the ability to swim out further and with less worry of the sharks or being carried off to a foreign country by the tides. We came back home a few days before school was to open, and I found out that Cashews and the crew had been conducting experiments with alcohol more and more frequently.

MISS TROPICAL ISLAND

If there is a time in life where the first, most dramatic changes happen, it has to be 7th grade. No discussions or pamphlets are handed out ahead of time to discuss what the male teen's body goes through, such as acne, aggressive behavior, noticing girls. You go from not wanting to square dance with a girl in fourth grade, to all of a sudden wanting to do so *very badly* in 7th grade. If I was to ask my father, it would be the usual quick answer: "Keep it in your pants." I had previously been told that I needed to eat my vegetables to "put hair on your chest." I noticed towards the end of 6th grade, the hair had begun to arrive, but in the wrong places. Had I somehow chewed the vegetables incorrectly?

Little red dots were forming on my face as well, but there was medication for this in the medicine cabinet. I just brushed it off and thought of school and seeing the kids from the other five or six other elementary schools from our town that would come together as one in a building called Thurston Junior High.

My mother announced that she that had splurged, and bought me a brand new, unused, pair of Chuck Taylor Converse basketball sneakers. This was one of the first non-hand-me-down pieces of clothing I had ever gotten. My pants *were* still hand-me-down plaid bell bottoms, and my shirts were all still 1970's style wide brimmed collar types, but I was very happy to get rid of the used sneakers, and of course, the platform shoes.

The day came, and I was ready. I was still nervous about arriving at school as the "young kid" at the bottom of the totem pole, but I also knew that my newly discovered alcohol drink would calm me down in times of stress. The bus picked up the Cro Mags of Crystal Hill and took us to school. There was an imposing figure waiting at the front door, a man who looked like Darth Vader with a pasty white complexion. I was very soon to find out who he was.

Each bus seemed to contain a different group of students, all of whom wore the same style clothes. On one bus, the males wore colored shirts, most of them with the collar raised; on their shirt was some sort of small figure, either an alligator or a guy on a horse with a golf club. Their pants were Chinos, which people in my world only wore at special functions. They even had these belts that had whales on them. None of them wore sneakers. Instead, they wore a shoe that I had seen people wearing at the Riviera, particularly the boat people. These were called Docksiders. As these kids came off the bus, they seemed to shine. We, of course, made fun of them and even yelled, "Hey, nice shirt, nice shoes!"

The next bus carried kids wearing a completely different uniform. These kids we occasionally saw in the woods or milling around one of the local convenient marts, the Leatherheads. They had flannel shirts, or concert t-shirts, denim jeans, and work boots. Then it was our turn. We jumped, pushed, and shoved, and made our way into the school. We were greeted by Darth Hanley, the junior high vice principal.

Darth Hanley was an angry, God-like figure, with a dull black suit, polished black shoes, and a trench coat. He must have seen us pushing and shoving our way in, and immediately pulled us aside. Looking at us sternly, one by one, he said to us, "The buck stops here!" His lips and eyes were mere inches from our faces, and his breath smelled like coffee and mints.

He then yelled, "Now! In the auditorium!" My brother had fore-warned me about Darth Hanley and all the teachers to be careful of. He said Hanley was a veteran of World War II and had a metal plate in his head. We filed into the auditorium and it was almost full. About ten seats in the back seemed to be reserved for us Cro Mags. We sat and waited for more instructions.

It was very noisy with laughing, joking and near pandemonium. Then a man in all black with slicked back, oily hair came in and walked to the middle of the floor. He screamed, "Silence!" The room immediately went silent. He paced back and forth without a microphone and gave us all the do's and dont's of his school. It was apparent from the discussion that we had more dont's than do's. When it ended, he looked up at us specifically and threw a series of especially hairy, hairy eyeballs. Then he stormed out. We went down to a table in the hallway and found the number of our homerooms. I wandered off to find mine and noticed the place looked more like an old hospital than a school. It was not bright and colorful like Sheehan. There were no cut out butterflies or leaves on the billboards.

I was given a piece of paper with the number to an assigned locker, and a list of the classes I had. We all walked to each class like robots, taking quick lefts or rights through the hallway. I found the doorway with the right number on it, walked in, and sat down. Each teacher explained his or her specific areas of study, and then their expectations of us. As the day was nearing an end, I loped to my last class. It was Spanish and apparently, I was going to learn a new language. We all went into the classroom and sat down. There was no teacher at first.

I looked around and didn't recognize anyone. My crew was scattered around the school. I took in the outfits and the new faces. No one said anything, but it was obvious we were getting fidgety. Then I heard the recognizable, fast-paced click-clack, click-clack of a women's shoe on linoleum. It got closer and closer, then, "Buenos dias mi amigas y amigos!" This lady was no Darth Vader! She was hopping joyfully as she entered. In dress alone, she appeared different than all the other teachers. Her attire was all very colorful, and even her complexion was olive-like, not pasty white like the other teachers.

She smiled the whole time and wasn't there to pounce on us if we got out of line. She said she was from what sounded like, "Sud America." Then she pointed to a map of South America. I noticed that there was something happening to my body, especially below my belt. I didn't give this area of my body any command or signal to act. It was doing it on its own. Then there was a small drum beating sensation pulsating out rhythms in my neck and face. I kept looking at this happy, beautiful, olive-skinned teacher from Sud America, as she went on describing her class. But I had become lost. The sound of her voice was gone. I could see her lips moving, but couldn't make out her words. The sensation below my belt was intense. I noticed my pants began to rise. What was going on!?

Mentally, I was envisioning her and me on some tropical island. She was walking toward me from a bamboo-roofed bar, colorful tropical adult drinks with umbrella's in them waiting for us. I had on a straw hat, and she handed me a drink and said, "Mi amiga, Andy!" I made a toast to my Spanish teacher and we sipped from the straws. We drank from our adult drinks and decided to be kids once again.

We built sandcastles. I dove for shells. I carried her out to sea, piggy-back. My pants got tighter. I then came back to reality, and she was still smiling and almost dancing as she went up and down the aisles. We were going to learn it all, she said, beginning with the alphabet, then numbers, and then sentences. By the end, we would know the Spanish basics. The class ended, and I had to put my three-ring spiral notebook over my belt in order to hide this new strange phenomenon.

The Cro Mags seemed to have been purposely separated by some government plot. But for lunch, it was easy to pick them out. Blumpkin with his red afro, Cashews with his bleach blonde hair and ostrich neck. Once I found those two, the rest of the tribe were not far behind.

We all sat together and spoke about our new school, new faces, and classes. Maybe we would all change for the better? We now had a clean slate, a wide-open future. We looked around the lunchroom at all the different "crowds." They all seemed to possess a lot more color than our crew. Their Chinos looked clean, bright, and ironed. Their collars were popped. Even the shoes called Docksiders looked polished. There was even a new sneaker that a couple of them wore called Nike. It was all white, only went up to the lower ankle and had some silly red wave like symbol on it.

We ate our lunch and began to disperse to our remaining classes. We passed by a lone alligator shirt kid in the auditorium. What happened next was merely a knee-jerk reaction. One of the Cro Mags said, "We can't afford fancy clothes like that." Cashews eye-balled the kid's watch, grabbed his wrist and said, "My, what a nifty watch you have there, kid!"

Then someone made the initial move and tugged at his shirt, and we were all on top of him. We acted quickly, and his docksiders were taken off and thrown down the hallway. It happened very fast but with purpose, and then we were gone. I looked back and saw the kid brushing himself off. I felt justified in the heat of the action since he was part of the boat people tribe, people that had more than me.

It seemed in this school, there was a class for every subject known to man. Everything but oceanographer. I did pay particular attention to the chemistry classes. The teacher mentioned we were going to work with fire, which ignited my interest. We would mix chemicals and record their reactions.

School ended with a bell, and we got onto the yellow caterpillar-like vehicles and headed home. We were officially institutionalized by bells and assigned rooms with numbers, but there was still that free-spirited Spanish teacher – and the chemical fire experiments – that held out some promise of perhaps enjoying the school year.

I took care of my paper routes and thought of all the classes we had and all the different subjects. How was I going to handle chemistry in 50 minutes and then jump to another class like history with a mind full of chemistry? Tomorrow there would be a few more classes to be introduced, too. At least there was an easy A in both gym and art. Then again, I thought, my brother had warned me about both of *those* teachers.

Mr. Crowe was the gym teacher, an ex-marine from the Korean conflict, and Wolverton, the art teacher, a Vietnam vet. Based on the vets I met on the paper route, the Vietnam guys seemed to be the most intimidating. They had very long hair and possessed the stare my grandfather had. There was one guy we labeled Manson. He used to sit on a stoop on Route 109 and just look across the street. If we passed by, he would just stare at us, not say anything … just stare.

At home, I organized my institutional three-ring binder and got into my mental "blue-assessed fly" zone. I took in all the tough birds outside my window. These were the birds that wouldn't take off when Mr. New England blew in his first stiff cold breeze. My favorite was the crow. The garbage man of the bird world, he seemed to wear a big black leather jacket. He had a bad rap, but I considered him my friend. It was getting dark, and he made a yawning gesture with his wing, waved me goodbye, and took off into the sky.

My oldest brother had moved on to college, so Lead took his room, and the bunk bed was dismantled. I now had the room to myself. I was older, a middle schooler now, but I still liked the Star Wars character bed sheets and pillowcases. I fell asleep in my usual position, hands behind my head, taking it all in. I thought of the angry vice principal in his black clothes and black shoes, pants, dark shirt, and slicked back hair.

Then I thought of that Spanish teacher. She epitomized freedom to me. She liked her job ... she had almost danced into my classroom. Then I remembered what happened in my pants. I felt it wasn't something I should inquire to my father about. He was the king of the wise-ass, not especially relevant answers. If he came back with a new haircut, I would say, "Did you get a haircut?" and he would say, "No, I got my ears lowered."

So, I decided to just brush it off and not say anything. I fell asleep after saying the scary prayer of, "If I die before I wake, I pray the Lord my soul to keep." Ah, Catholicism. Like a good Catholic, I went to sleep with my last thoughts on dying before I should wake. I went into a dream shortly after. I was on the small rubber raft with plastic oars my father gave me to maneuver around the roaring Riviera. I was blown way offshore and awoke and the only thing I knew to do was paddle. I noticed the water was a different, clear blue, color. I looked around and noticed I wasn't on the Riviera. I saw land and rowed to a tropical island.

As I came ashore I recognized a woman in a long colorful dress. She was writing something in the sand. She pointed to her work in the sand and it read, "Hola, Andy." We both laughed and I hugged Miss Tropical Island. Then she said, "Do you want to go swimming?" She took off her dress and had on a very nice bikini. We ran into the blue ocean splashing and laughing. We came back and started on a sand castle.

I awoke remembering my prayer, "If I die before I wake." Well, I was awake and still alive, but there was something wrong with my Star Wars sheets. I finally got up and out and did my usual chore of delivering the paper, and then headed off to the institution.

Just the jostling of the bus ride caused the swelling in my pants. The three-ring binder came in handy. I noticed the vice principal, again standing outside the door to greet us. Why, I wondered, was he still there on the second day of school? As we disembarked the bus and headed in, he pulled each one of us aside. It was apparent from the salted-cod color of his skin that he hadn't spent much of his summer outside. We followed his dark trench coat into an office. The secretary looked nervous. We stood in a row. He paced back and forth, then yelled, "Congratulations, it only took you screwballs 24 hours to make it here!"

He came inches from each of our faces. His teeth were as bad as his breath, like he couldn't sit still in the dentist's office and a simple cleaning resulted in cracked and crooked teeth. He stated that we had bullied someone, and then asked if we wanted to dance with him. I let out a small laugh thinking of elementary school and square dancing, picturing me and Darth Vader dancing around while a small record player spun out lousy music. He sentenced us to two days of clean up. We would be cleaning the school after hours. He said there was a late bus for clowns like us. Then he said, "Get outta here." We scattered.

I walked all the way down to the end of the hallway, and there stood Charles Manson's twin, except hairier. He looked like he was the chief honcho of all Leatherheads, but with a little bit of a twist. His attire was a green army jacket, a button-down shirt, and a stained tie. His hair wasn't regulation. It flowed wildly, and he had a very long beard. Word was, he had served in Vietnam.

He followed me with those, "I've seen a monster," eyes into the classroom and we all sat down. He took off his jacket and hung it up. He then looked around and pointed at me said, "You! Step in here!" He held the door open to a room with art supplies. I thought it was kind of him to open the door for me. He then hit the light switch and slammed the door. He got millimeters from my face. I could see scars under his beard.

His eyes looked right through me, piercing down on me. He said, "If I get wind of you bullying someone, I will rearrange your face." I thought of poor Mr. Potato Head and how he ended up sometimes, with an ear placed where his nose should be. I looked at the art supplies, and back into his eyes and simply said, "Yes sir." I thought of collecting money on my paper route, with a rearranged face. The wives would say, "You poor thing," and the men would say, "You'se probably deserved it."

He politely opened the door and I sat back at the art tables. He went back up front and explained his class, and I could now see a lighter side of him. He stood next to the door of the other art teachers' room and loudly said, "We will *not* be making papier-mâché Easter bunnies or clay ashtrays in *my* classroom!"

He then held up some previous artwork, done by past students, and I was in awe. There were drawings of objects in the background, and on the surface was a geometric shape. Mostly squares. "Everybody in this class is going to make something like this," he said. The project would take many weeks, but once done, it would be a masterpiece. He asked all of us to start thinking about what we wanted to draw. I remembered visiting Logan airport as a kid and getting a tour of a plane. I told my mother I wanted to be a pilot, and ever since had a fascination with planes. We were handed a large piece of special art paper and went to work on the object that would be in the background. He went to each student and had a small discussion. It was my turn, and I told him my idea.

"Cool, I'll give you a hand on the outline," he said.

He drew lightly with a pencil and sketched an outline. I was amazed at the preciseness and speed at which he sketched an airplane.

Moments before, I was about to get my face rearranged, but now my idea was "cool." He met with each student, and then went to a stereo in the back and turned on the music. The radio played a song and he said, "This is Tommy James and Shondells singing Crimson and Clover." He had a smile that was pleasant but a bit psychotic. I respected this man immediately, especially his threatening me but then giving me a chance. We drew for the remaining time and placed our work in a special drawer to await us for the next class. I treated mine with tender care. It was time to leave his class, to step out of the art world ... and back into the institution.

THE PHANTOM

The next class was physical education. Like my fifth-grade teacher, Mrs. Mooncai, I had been forewarned about this teacher: "Beware of Crowe!" He was an ex-marine, a Korean war vet. We entered the gymnasium, and he stood at center court. We paid little attention and just shot the breeze. All in our little circles identified by clothing. Then there was a deafening announcement.

I knew it wasn't from the speaker system because there was no static crackle and the speakers would have fallen off due to the number of decibels. It came from center court. "Line up against the blue line!" We found the blue line on the basketball court and lined up. He paced up and down like a grizzled crow, and we were the dead carcasses he was examining. He was even dressed like a crow: black sneakers/shoes, dark socks, black athletic shorts, black shirt with a pocket, black whistle, shaved head on the sides, with black shoe polish dyed hair on top.

He paced up and down the line, barking out instructions. "You will not be playing volleyball, dodgeball or grab ass in here! You will be doing pushups, sit ups, pull ups!" Someone had their foot over the line, and he growled, "Stay over *your* side of the line!" He detailed what our outfits needed to consist of the following week. Sneakers, white tube socks, shorts, and a white t-shirt with our last name stenciled on the back in 2-inch lettering. He even mentioned where we could get that made at the local sporting goods store. He went into how we would address him by sir in the beginning and sir at the end. So, it was no longer "yeah" or "yes" – it was going to be, "Sir, yes sir!"

We then took a tour of the locker room, where we would change out of our school clothes and into our gym clothes. He said, "When I'm done with you, you will be covered in sweat." He gave us a look into the shower and said he wanted it spotless when we were done.

"That's it, ladies, see you in a couple days!"

He didn't seem that bad, aside from shouting at the top of his lungs for a guy stepping over the line. I couldn't make up my mind about the guy, so I figured I would need to push the envelope with him, like I did with Mrs. Mooncai, and see how he handled it.

I went home from my second day of school feeling some hope, especially with the introduction to the art class. I was busy with the paper route, and attempted to do some homework, but couldn't shake the blue-assed fly syndrome and my new feelings for the Spanish teacher. I looked beyond the pine trees and oak trees into the home of the Spanish teacher on her native tropical island.

I returned to the dream I had of us making sand castles, diving for crabs and having conversations in Spanish. I noticed the now uncontrollable half of my body below my belt was again acting up. I looked down and my bargain basement plaid bellbottoms were disfigured. What was going on? Time passed by and the homework I was supposed to complete got lost at the beach with me and the Spanish teacher.

I didn't have much time to go down to the local sporting goods store to get my name stenciled on by some machine with rigid two-inch lettering. Instead, I took out an old Catholic Youth Organization shirt, figuring Mr. Crowe may be Catholic, and therefore would not be too upset. I crossed out "CYO Basketball" on the front with a marker, and wrote "Winslow, A." on the back. Mr. Crowe was even more intense the second day of class. He walked quickly around the gym and, one by one looked at the sneakers, socks, and shirts on everyone. He finally made his way to me. He sneered at me as if I had some sort of poisonous insect crawling on my t-shirt.

It turned out that he *was* Catholic, which I could tell because he yelled, "Jesus H. Christ!"

He laid into me. I remembered quickly how I was supposed to answer as he screamed.

"Are you special!?"

"Sir, no sir!"

"How could you desecrate a CYO shirt?! You're seriously telling me you can't afford a shirt in *this* zip code!" On he went inches from my face.

"Give me 30!"

"Sir, 30 what, sir?"

"Thirty push-ups you pond scum!" he screamed. His veins were bulging and his eyes were red like ketchup.

I did the push-ups very fast like Mr. G. had taught me, and the teacher seemed to relax. He told me to pick up his clipboard and whistle that he had thrown on the basketball court. Then we all counted off by threes. There were three stations: one for push-ups, one for sit-ups, and one for pull-ups. We rotated through the stations for the remainder of the class.

He was right, we were dripping in sweat. The exercise felt good, and he didn't mention the shirt fiasco to me again. However, I walked down to the sporting goods store the next day and acquired regulation gear out of respect for him. Again, I noticed that I felt better having just performed rigorous exercise. It was almost the same sensation as having my first adult drink. A calming sensation.

Crowe yelled, "Remember ladies, one minute in the shower!" We showered in fast-motion and I started dressing. Then I heard, "Jesus H. Christ!"

Then there was another shout, almost painful.

"Which one of you *animals* defecated in my shower!?"

He screamed for us to line up facing each other. He ran over to the toilet area and got a bunch of brown paper towels, cursing as he walked by. Then we heard him mutter in astonishment, "What sort of sick son of a bitch?" He reappeared with a brown 8-inch object nestled in the paper towel. He was now the purple complexion of a birthday balloon.

Carrying the turd like it could bite, he continued to curse as he held it at maximum arm's length. "Never in my *entire* career!"

I noticed the look of disgust on the faces of the other kids. One student strangely did *not* appear repulsed. In fact, he even looked happy, as if Crowe was a doctor carrying his newborn son. Crowe passed by with this brown, smoking turd. Now he was alive, full of hate, and revenge. His body even became contorted. He was yelling and bouncing on one foot. "Next class," he said, "You're all going to exercise until you puke!"

The institutional bell rang, and he screamed, "Dismissed!" As we passed by Crowe, he looked at each of us intently. He was looking for any sign of guilt or complicity. We made it out with no suspects being identified. But in a few days, we would all pay the penalty for one demented human. We made our way to the hallway and I asked the guy who had been standing across from me smiling if it was his turd. He merely stared at me, put his finger to his lips, and continued walking down the hallway. That was my introduction to the infamous "Phantom Shitter."

A few days later we returned to gym class. There was an initial bark from Crowe, but then he just stood at one end of the gym as we circled around doing monsters on the basketball court, then push-ups, then pull-ups, over and over until a few minutes before the bell. He was right, when we were done, I was at the toilet dry heaving. I had never done such physical exercise in my life. There were no feces left on the tiled floor of the gang shower that day, and it obviously taught us all a lesson ... except for the Phantom Shitter.

My body started to grow dramatically. I developed something in my knee from growing too fast that the doctor called Osgood-Schlatter. Like most diseases, they were named either by some fancy Latin words or by some guy that wore a wig like George Washington. I grew like a weed and developed a body like that of that of an octopus. Large head, long legs and long arms. This was bad news and ruled me out of most sports that required coordination. But it was a perfect body for swimming.

Time went on, and the Cro Mags slowly got mixed up into all the different crowds. Cashews was hanging around more and more with the Leatherheads. Blumpkin took on the Spanish name of Esteban and was hanging around with a small group we called "army heads." They favored wearing army fatigues around school. Sully always excelled in math and was with people we called "computer heads."

The guy from Marshfield was still in my category, a "ment." I made friends with the Phantom Shitter out of pure curiosity. He never admitted to it, but he had that smile like when we would torch the woods and hide behind trees and watch the faces of the homeowners and fire department personnel. You broke a rule, but you had some pride in your technique and hardness under pressure.

This new friend was from an area called Martha Jones. He and his crew were pyros as well, so we hit it off. They weren't wearing alligator shirts, but they didn't wear hand-me-downs either. He even had a few friends from an area called Cloverland. This was a place where a lot of people migrated from parts of the city like South Boston and Dorchester. Many of the parents were divorced, and it was a well-known pocket of the Leatherheads.

He showed me a way to get to his house via Cloverland. I was amazed by all this guy's clever and ambitious shortcuts, both through the woods and on the streets. He even boasted about it, saying those secret routes were the reason he'd never been caught from all the fires *he* lit. As we passed through Cloverland to get to his house, I warily looked to my left and right; Cloverland was a leatherhead stronghold. I had to be ready to do the manly thing … and run.

The Leatherheads were obviously still sleeping. I noticed in this neighborhood, the paint was peeling off the houses, the grass was over-grown in almost every lawn, and there were even shattered windows on many garage doors. It was obvious that the fathers here were more lenient than the fathers in the "Hill" areas where my crew was from … Green Hill and Crystal Hill. The paths were crooked and even had a few fallen trees along the way. He pointed out that these obstacles assisted him in his getaways. The fallen tree, combined with a quick hairpin turn, could leave the pursuer moaning in the background.

We finally made it to that area of woods where he built fires and experiment with alcohol. I felt like one caveman talking to another, about our outdoor fireplaces. He had nicely formed rocks surrounding his pit, and it seemed more organized than our forest area. We then meandered around more pines, oaks, wild grass, and made our way to his home. His house was like none I had ever seen. He told me his father was from Europe and designed the house to look like some Swiss chalet.

It was totally different from our home, with the fact that it was sealed tight. A door unlocked, and then we had to take our shoes off in the foyer. Our house was wide open, and aside from goulashes, everyone ran up or down the stairs with their shoes on. There was no dog smell either. He introduced me to his parents. His father, having only been in the United States for 25 years, still had a very thick accent.

He asked, "What duz za fah-ter do?"

I said, "He is an electrician."

He said, "Is he union?"

I said, "Yes."

He smiled and said, "Ah, a good union bruza."

He insisted I tell my father that he was a union tile setter. We went downstairs, and it was then that I noticed all the tile work. It was beautiful. A true craftsman. We went into another room, and there was a bar. My new caveman friend said this is where he steals *his* alcohol. His said his father wasn't too strict, for, in his European culture, teens were *allowed* to drink. The bar even had a Bavarian theme and design. His father was proud of where he came from, and yet also proud to be an American. So, he had built a bar to fit into the new land, surrounded by pictures of the alps from his old country.

I was amazed at how quiet and orderly the house was, even with both his parents there. It contrasted from my house, where my father would be trying to talk from one floor to another, or through the walls. Dogs would be scratching at the door, either to be let in or out. Someone would always be screaming, "Let the dogs in!" Or, "Let the dogs out!"

He walked me back home all through the twisting and turning paths and the obstacles that he knew like the back of his hand. He seemed like a more organized caveman compared to us Cro Mags from "The Hill" regions, just a mile away. All of a sudden, a pack of Leatherheads emerged, a gaggle of black leather jackets, pale complexions, and wild eyes. At the last second my new friend said, "Crap, it's Runci!"

Runci was a name that sent shivers down everyone's spine. My brother Lead told me a story of Runci fighting another guy and how he repeatedly beat him, even after the guy cried uncle, naming uncles on both his mother *and* father's sides of the family. That, in our neck of the woods, was going beyond the pale. We were monsters and degenerates, but we even *we* had a code. Runci was the acknowledged CEO of the Leatherheads and was now looking directly at us. Could *he* run? Should *we* run? Would I remember the carefully laid out paths through the woods? We just kept walking.

Now the Leatherheads circled us. There was a ring of them surrounding us. Runci approached me and asked my name. I tried to think as quickly as I could. Should I tell him I was named after a priest at St. Margaret Mary's Catholic church? Maybe he was Catholic and would spare me a beating and the ritual of having to name all my uncles. Or maybe I should just say, "MacDonald," the side of my family that came over on the Mayflower. Maybe there was a Captain Runci and we could talk about that? I came back to reality, and just said, "Andy." He yelled, "You dumb bastard, your last name!"

We were now nose to nose. His eyes were red, and he stunk of adult drinks and a certain smoke. I then said, "Winslow." He leaned back and grinned. Was this him coiling like a snake before the strike? He then bounced back and we were nose to nose once more. This time, with a psychotic grin he said, "Do you have a brother ... Jeff?" I said yes.

He said "Aw. Okay. He's a funny bastard." All the Leatherheads simultaneously melted invisibly into the woods, and me and my friend stood there alone, breathing heavily. We looked at each other. I mentally thanked my brother for being a funny bastard.

We still had to make it through another area where there was a rumor of a different species of ruffians called Punk Rockers. These kids dressed differently and were into a new music scene that was rumored to have been spawned by Mrs. Mooncai's nemesis, Iggy Pop. They listened to the Sex Pistols, The Clash, Black Flag, and the Dead Kennedys. We were about to go up Burgess Ave., which had a steep hill. As we made it up the incline and it leveled off, we could see what appeared to be some punk rockers emerging from the shadows.

I recognized one guy with a shaved head, rumored to have a safety pin through his cheek. He had the same reputation as Runci for administering relentless beatings. It was still early in the night, so they weren't too drunk yet. They just looked at us with disgust and allowed us to walk by.

The rest of the way home we only encountered angry dogs, and a few old people that couldn't yell anymore. I made it to my house and was amazed at how close we were to this whole other world j ust across the woods, not a mile away. I was nervous about the Phantom Shitter's ability to make it home safely through the Punk Rockers and Runci's crew. But he assured me that he would use all his football training and run all the way home.

WOK STEKI

Seventh grade went on, and I even managed to make friends with a few of the alligator and polo shirt people. They weren't bad guys. They all had parents who kept some sort of a bar in the basement, so they, too, had started taking their first drinks.

As winter arrived a standing hockey game became the norm. I was amazed at all the ponds in our town, each one being claimed as the property of the crew from a certain neighborhood. Our pond was named Mitchell's, after the Mitchell family that lived nearby and their deceased son who died on Route 128.

The other kids lived beyond walking distance, so their older brothers or mothers dropped them off. We watched as all these new shiny cars arrived. Many of them had these big black bags that contained "Little Johnny's hockey gear." They took their seats on the frozen New England ground. They had everything in that bag. Hooks that tightened their skates, tape, special socks, even special hockey pants, and gloves. Then there were the skates themselves. Special hockey skates, skates we only saw on TV on the Bruins players. We looked at each other and what we had for gear: taped, broken sticks, borrowed or hand-me-down skates (in my case, my sister's figure skates), and an endless supply of Scotch electrical tape from my electrician father ... for in-game repairs. Our gloves consisted of old leather driving gloves, oversized, mothball smelling mittens ... and, in my case, rubber, high-voltage electrical work gloves.

Before each game, we taped everything back together. Today we were finally ready to take on these shiny looking kids with the fancy cars and expensive equipment. A pair of Converse sneakers marked our goal, and two white sneakers with a red stripe called Nike marked the other goal. We assisted Tibbs to the net, holding our stick out for him to grasp since he couldn't skate very well. That's why he was the goalie.

The puck was placed in the middle of our manmade rink. It was Electrical Tapes versus the shiny Nike kids. There was a countdown from 10 to 1, and we all raced for the puck. It was obvious very early that we would lose, and lose hard. The puck was swept up by one of the Nike people. Tibbs was like a cow on skates. The puck was easily flicked past him and the Nike team cheered. Tibbs "skated" in small circles in disgust with his head down. He did manage to stay on his skates out of spite and pride, so that was progress.

The puck was again placed at center ice, and once again, the countdown from ten commenced. We raced and were again beaten. The Nike team skated around us, passed to each other effortlessly, and once again Tibbs was beaten. This same scene was repeated over and over and went on for about an hour. By the end of it all, the Electrical Tapes had been checked, pushed, shoved, and scored upon mercilessly by the Nike kids. We escorted Tibbs off the ice. He was holding Esteban's stick and gliding back with us to our spot on the cold New England soil, losers.

The shiny new vehicles started to arrive to pick up the Nike kids. There was one straggler that put his gear away in its proper bag and came over with us. It was about to be this lad's first lesson in wok steki. We had to act fast, as his mom would be arriving any second. We walked over to the black ice where the river met the pond. We formed the line and made sure he was last. All the Cro Mags passed, which made the ice weak. The Nike kid passed without falling through. *Try and try again* the motto goes.

On the second pass, I could feel the ice sway; it was ready to go. This kid with the fancy sneakers screamed as he fell through, his weight plummeting into the icy water. We then cheered and raised our hands and chanted, "Wok steki! wok steki! wok steki!" We yelled as the Nike kid struggled, shocked, frantically trying to make it to safety. He had a look of panic, especially when he saw we weren't going to lend a helping hand or even a branch. After all, we couldn't break the wok steki rules just because he had fancy hockey equipment and wore Nikes.

He finally made it to thick ice, panting and sporting a look of shock. What he didn't realize was that he had just crossed over that mysterious teenage line that separates an enemy from friend.

His mother pulled up as this just happened and had a look of horror as her son lay there soaking wet. We were still chanting "wok steki." He got himself up and walked over to the car. His mother met him at the shoreline, and then threw us a fancy, shiny, designer hairy eyeball and assisted her soaking wet son to her gleaming new car.

The day ended, and the loss of the hockey game didn't feel so bad now. We just trained someone in the art of wok steki, and I got a feeling of payback for my anger at not being a boat person, seeing his Nike sneakers submerged under the ice. But, we also had gained a new friend through the fragile ying-yang art of humiliation and respect.

Cashews was becoming closer with the Leatherheads and a big follower of their music. Rush, Led Zeppelin, Black Sabbath, etc. He had bought his first leather jacket and was wearing denim jeans and work boots. There was even word in the neighborhood that he was "experimenting" with … marijuana. Esteban was still with the soldier of fortune types, a small crew of guys he met in the boy scouts. They wore army fatigues for pants and were into building traps, fishing, hunting – and showering infrequently.

I was now with my friend the Phantom Shitter and the guy from the Irish Riviera, Simma. His house was very laid back, a lot quieter than my home. His parents were gone quite frequently, and he would let us make use of the mini bar, where we got accustomed to having nice long relaxing drinks. His father worked as a mechanic at MIT and he seemed to fit the part: an almost completely gray afro, front pocket full of pens and pencils, and the laboratory stare. It was as if he carried around with him the weighty knowledge that something he just discovered could kill every form of life on earth if it were to be unsealed.

If I stayed a little late or if it was a Saturday, I could catch Simma's father drinking something called Dewar's. This was the drink, apparently, of the laboratory worker. He would sometimes catch us watching TV, or sitting around the kitchen table, and after a few of these special lab drinks, he would corner us and begin his "life graph lecture." He would never look us in the eye; he was always off out to the horizon.

This was a look I most preferred, as his direct stare made me wonder if he indeed had some secret planet-killing discovery just in the other room. Plus, he appeared otherworldly-wise when looking out into the distance with that stare ... as if he was looking to past ancestors or past historical figures. He paused at random times and just sat there silently, before proceeding. Then, as if on cue, after a brief moment of looking out on the horizon, he got the nod to proceed from his ancestors. The lecture included his drawing pictures of us as stick figures, on a graph, showing where we were in life at the present moment, and where we should end up.

The scene was made even eerier and more significant due to his massive afro, his wild blue eyes, his Dewar's drink in one hand, and a lucky strike burning away in the other. He would be holding up a picture of us, as stick figures and our fantastic futures – *if* we followed his directions. If we had a few adult drinks in us, we were all on the same page, and he would be speaking our language. We would indeed end up at the top of the graph in twenty years. All would be well. Cashews house had been my second home throughout elementary school, but Simma's house became my new second home in my teen years.

Sully was the trailblazer in our group when it came to girls. He was the first one with an official girlfriend. Then one day he said they had broken up. This was a complex ritual which meant progressing from having your initials written on your three-ring spiral notebook with a plus symbol in between, to blotting out those symbols in an angry scrawl. I spotted his now ex-girlfriend one day and noticed that she was taller than most girls and very athletic. She was olive skinned and had an Italian last name. I inquired with Sully if it was *truly* over. Emotionless, he showed me his notebook: her initials were indeed scratched out.

That was a green light for me. I put the word out. Word out for what? That I wanted her initials on my three-ring spiral. We passed by in the hallway, she giggled, and I smiled. This happened a few times. Then came the big day when I finally screwed up the nerve to say, "Will you go out with me?" I was terrified ... but determined.

I remembered that the recipe for my anxieties was alternatively adult drinks and rigorous exercises. I disappeared into an area that had little traffic and did pushups until my arms were shaking. This relieved some pressure, and then I headed over to her metal institutional locker, shaking from the pushups, but less anxious, and said, "Will you go out with me?" She said "Yes!"

The anxiety was coming back. But I was resolute. My next move in this ritual would be to ask for her number. I skipped class and did more pushups. Then I searched for her. I saw her and asked, "Can I have your number?" She wrote it down, both of us smiling. I scampered away.

I did more push-ups out of excitement. I found that I had a little more bounce in my step. I felt sure that I would succeed on that life graph written by Simma's father. There was a dance coming up called "Night Under the Cold Miserable New England Skies," or something close to that. There were rumors that people were not only experimenting with marijuana, which I was convinced had to be a sin. But now I heard people were *kissing* too. Was that also a sin? I knew drinking wasn't a sin, because the priests drank. Plenty.

But kissing? Was it saved for marriage? It was about ten days before the big "Night Under the Frigid Depressing New England Skies," dance. I thought at night about my Spanish teacher and this girl with the olive skin. I had great dreams, and woke up with my Star Wars sheet pitched like a tent. I did twenty push-ups to alleviate the malady and prepped for school. I got to school and asked a few other Catholic boys if they ever kissed. One of the alligator shirts had, and I was told it wasn't a sin, and even how to practice using my forearm.

I went to my classes and passed by the girl that gave me her number. She said, "Call me tonight." I smiled and said, "Okay," and mentally planned how I would ask her to the dance on the phone later that day. I did the afternoon paper route and practiced kissing my forearm once the paper bag was empty.

I wanted to perform the first kiss well and was excited to know it wasn't a sin from the other Catholic boys. I did some push-ups to calm me down before the phone call. Her father answered and asked who I was and what I wanted. I wanted to give him my full name and mention the fact that everything was cool because I was named after a priest. But instead, I just said, "Uh, it's Andy."

He then yelled my name to his daughter, and she picked up the phone. I was very nervous again. I immediately asked her to the dance, and she said yes. I became too nervous and said that I had to go because my father had to use the phone. I told her we would meet at school. She said, "Okay," and we hung up. I did more pushups out of joy. I stayed up most of the night thinking of what could happen while kissing. I thought of the scary movie, *The Exorcist*, where green slime came out of the mouth of the young girl. I remembered the same type of green substance that was projected out of my grandfather onto the driveway after a religious celebration. I spent hours in private on my forearm.

The dance night arrived, and I decided to walk with my crew. It was a very long walk, but that would calm me down a bit. I was walking near the school and saw a row of vehicles emptying out the dance attendees. Inside, the lights dimmed, and music started to play. Some danced, or, more realistically, jumped up and down. I broke from my circle and greeted my date. We spoke a little bit and then decided to sit and talk in the auditorium section. We sat next to each other, and asked and answered those all-important mating ritual questions, like, "What is your favorite pizza?" I noticed other kids had already started to kiss.

I became very anxious and wanted somewhere to do calming pushups, or find an adult drink. My mind raced. Would I try to kiss, and the ex-marine gym teacher with his militant haircut pop out with his cop-like flashlight and then say, "Give me fifty!" Or, would it be a cardinal or bishop in their full religious outfit?

Or, would it be the green bile? Would it just start uncontrollably and cover both of us, resulting in a parent-to-parent discussion about me ruining their daughter's sweater with green slime? Then I thought of the Irish Riviera. Leaping from the rocks and feeling victorious after flying from those heights. I had put a lot of kissing practice into my forearm, after all. I was due.

We looked at each other and smiled. I inched closer, still smiling. We then were inches away from each other and finally kissed. I noticed she had closed her eyes. I kept one eye open, vigilant for the marine gym teacher or the Catholic cardinal and, of course, my father. I finally closed my eyes too, and all was safe. I resurfaced after a few moments of the kiss and looked around. No authority figures, or green bile. We both smiled, and drew closer, and kissed more. Time flew, and we held each other.

I quickly remembered that she had an Italian last name, and images of the *Godfather* went through my head. She couldn't be late greeting her parent's car. I didn't want a horse's head cut off, and inserted under my blankets. I wrapped my jacket over my swollen pants. I walked her to the entrance of the school and we hugged. Cashews' father picked us up, and it was obvious that he had been drinking. He was beet red and was driving erratically. But, he had a lot of practice driving in that state, so we felt safe. Cashews had even acquired himself a Leatherhead girl, and they had kissed that night as well. I was dropped off and proceeded to do happy push-ups.

I called my first-kiss girl the next day and asked for permission to put my initials, a plus sign, then her initials, on the back of my three-ring binder. She agreed. Now we were *really* an item. I went to school on Monday and showed her the notebook. She covered her mouth and giggled, and I smiled with pride.

MANISCHEWITZ

I made a new friend whose father was a dentist. His attire from head to toe showed that they would spare no expense to get him in the finest clothing. He was Jewish, which I wasn't too sure about, merely from lack of ever having known any Jewish people. He invited me to something called a Bar Mitzvah. It was a big, very fancy ceremony, my mom said, and she put together the best-looking discount clothing ensemble she could find from a place called "Building 19," so I would look nice. I knew I would be dapper from a distance, but my past experiences with clothes from the discount store proved that every single item always had *some* flaw, like a quarter-sized burn mark somewhere, or holes in both pockets.

I tried the stuff on, and indeed looked sharp … but immediately discovered that the right pant leg was longer than the left. I thanked my mom and set about figuring out a way to hide the extra four inches of pant leg. Solution: I would reach into my right-hand pocket, and tug on that side of the pants whenever I stood still.

You couldn't notice the flaw when I was walking, and I mitigated that more by taking longer strides. But, when standing still, I would have my right hand in my pocket, tugging on the pants. I made it to the only Temple in our town and was shocked at all the shiny new cars I saw parked or pulling in. Cars with names I didn't even recognize. My father always bought Fords, but here were names like Mercedes, BMW, Cadillac, and Porche.

Everyone was dressed impeccably. We entered the temple, and there was hugging, kissing, and warm greetings. I now had my right hand in my right pocket, pulling upward to hide the excess right leg fabric. Everybody I met seemed to want to hug me or shake my hand for some reason, so I had to pull my hand out of my pocket as quickly as possible, and then shove it back in to even out the pants and avoid looking ridiculous. We filed into the temple and sat down, so I felt momentarily safe, not having to be pulling on my pant leg.

I noticed some differences between the ceremonies at the Catholic church and this temple. There was still an altar and a shrine-like area for the important religious articles. There was less stained glass and fewer statues, I noticed. The service began, and I could tell what they were saying was important, because it was in a different language. I guessed it was Hebrew. When we had important services in *my* church, they were in Latin.

The next thing I noticed was, we didn't have to sit, stand, and kneel all the time like in a Catholic mass. My religious leaders' hats were high and pointy. This guy's religious hat was small, and only took up a tiny section of his head. He also wore a lovely table cloth-like garment with many tassels, strapped over his shoulders.

My new alligator shirt friend joined the religious leader on the altar and recited, in a different language, some important message. I had learned in my thirteen years on Earth that God speaks many different languages. The ceremony ended, and we then went to a banquet over in Norwood. Everybody filed into the banquet hall and found a nice spread waiting for us.

I was amazed at how organized and pretty everything was. We all sat down, and a meal was placed at our tables. There was a blessing, and we all ate. Everything looked very expensive and as if it took a lot of time to prepare. After we ate, there was music and traditional dancing. A massive cake was brought out and, one by one, candles were lit as the music played.

Everyone seemed happy, loving, and free from life's everyday worries and cares. There was a big difference in my family's religious festivities and my new friend's. I only saw a little bit of wine consumption, and the bar wasn't even open. I found that rather shocking. There was no Schlitz, no Budweiser, no bartender ... not even a drunk cousin pouring out adult drinks. There wasn't the drunken uncle gathering all the cards that were brought and announcing what they gave or what that person's nationality was or what he thought they looked like. After the banquet, we headed back to the celebrant's house, and the adults gathered around in the back-yard. The kids all gathered in the basement.

In the basement, there *was* a bar, and we eventually weaseled our way into making drinks. I couldn't wait for the feeling I would get from my first few drinks. I had already come to love the magic of the first few drinks. However, we weren't drinking the strong-stench stuff that was our usual fare. Instead, we were drinking wine made by some cousin of Jack Daniels by the name of Manichevitz. I needed a few more than usual to get the magic feeling, but it eventually came, and I felt happy. My habitual fidgetiness was gone, and I was no longer concerned about the red dots on my face.

We went out to the backyard, where there was more celebration and clapping and dancing. I definitely *was* feeling God's presence at that point, with the four glasses of wine in my system. All was well. My friend had entered into a state of manhood, and I would be next, soon, by way of a ceremony called "confirmation."

Seventh grade went on, and I have to say, life seemed pretty good. I had a girlfriend, was doing well in Spanish and art, and whenever I felt anxious or upset there were the adult drinks and the euphoric effect they brought. I was frequenting my father's bar more often, but my folks never suspected me, due to my age, and having two older brothers.

THE STEAMING SUB

I was actually looking forward to 8th grade, as we would no longer be the lowest ranking kids in school. We all entered 8th grade with a little more bounce in our step, and in my case, a little hairier. The bonus of eating vegetables was finally starting to pay off. The hair still didn't end up on my chest, but it was something.

We weren't performing Slug Trains, but we *were* performing a stunt where we would grab some poor 7th grader from the front of the bus, drag him to the back, and take out our aggression on him ... elbowing, kicking, pulling hair. Then, when we were done, he was handed over to a guy named Polumbo, who had grown to massive proportions, and was, in fact, being honed into a muscle-bound behemoth by the football team's special diet and heavy lifting.

This guy had earned the king's seat on the back of the bus near the emergency exit. It was reserved only for the biggest and baddest. When we were done with the pulling of hair, kicking, and elbowing, the new meat was handed over to Polumbo, and from there, he was put into a headlock and forced to recite his "uncles" on both sides of the family. Then he was released to pick up his books and lunch box and stumble back to his seat. Fortunately, our alcoholic bus driver was too busy trying to stay in his own lane to see anything, and the rest of the students were too scared to say anything.

When my brother Lead returned home from school one day he informed me that, apparently, we had messed with the wrong kid during one of our school bus assaults. The kid's older brother, in fact, was a member of both the high school varsity hockey *and* football teams ... and was known for his hard hits. To avoid a beating at the hands of the kid's older brother and his goon friends, there had been a sit-down. Fortunately, Lead, with his massive glasses and sense of humor, straightened it all out. We only got a warning. We were after that very selective in who we grabbed and dragged to the back of the bus.

One big change in eighth grade was that the gym teacher, Mr. Crowe, had left. It was immediately clear that the new gym teacher was not quite up to the task. He gave us an inch, and we took a mile. He came out with a mesh bag full of balls, and we instantly proceeded to throw them at each other, at the lights, the walls, everything. He just stood to the side in horror for forty-five minutes of chaos, with balls being thrown violently in every direction.

My old art teacher had also left. My heart sank as the new art teacher described her class. "We'll be doing clay ornaments for each holiday," she informed us. "Porcelain pumpkins, turkeys, leprechauns, and Easter bunnies." It was as if the art program was now on some institutional color-by-numbers plan of precisely what to make and when to make it.

I met up with my girl and we both smiled. She got braces over the summer, but she was still cute as a button. "Good to see you again," she said. I stammered and clutched my three-ring binder, and we went our separate ways. All was well.

Fortunately, I had the same Spanish teacher, and she seemed her normal self. She even touched my hand and said, "Welcome back, amigo!" Seeing my girl and having the Spanish teacher touch my hand made me feel wanted. I was fortunate enough to be near a chair and sat down. I had new techniques to fight this inflation in my pants. I thought of things I didn't enjoy, like raking leaves, seeing dead relatives in pine boxes, seeing the snow plow coming up Crystal Hill, ruining our sledding path.

When school ended for the day I went home and delivered the *Daily Transcript*. Cashews was no longer a big part of my life, as he was hanging around more and more with the Leatherheads. He was even taking on their attire of work boots and t-shirts, and growing his blonde hair out. We were becoming more and more separate, but I knew that we would one day again be close friends, as oceanographers diving off backward into the sea, grinning through the masks … because we had those plans already made on the life graph. We still attended mass on Sundays, but for some reason, we usually zipped right home. There were no more Razzles, donuts, and airplanes after mass. My father seemed to always have to rush off to work.

I was still afraid of God, even though at times I felt him in peaceful ways out in nature or with my friends. But not so much at mass. The stained-glass window image of him, where he always seemed to be looking at me with anger and disappointment, made mass ominous and unpleasant. If the sun hit the glass just right, which it always did, his face would glow red. I wondered if he was thinking, "Jesus H. Christ!"

I didn't get mass. I didn't understand what all the sitting, kneeling, bowing, dumping money in a basket, and eating a round wafer had to do with God. I was still an altar boy but was getting a bit old for it. I was no longer the cute little tyke on my Big Wheel, except maybe in my girl's eye or, maybe, for Miss Tropical Island. Most of my friends were Catholic, so even though some of us were drifting apart at school, I would see them briefly at church each week. We all had the same traditions of bars in the basement, worried mothers, and no eating meat on Fridays.

One Friday a bunch of us skipped class and met at Soko's, the local pizza shop. I wanted to test God that day, so I announced that I would try eating meat. For Catholics, this is tantamount to killing a puppy or knocking down an old lady – maybe worse. Someone called my dare and said that they would even buy a steak and cheese sub, just to see what would happen to me for eating meat on Friday. The order was placed, and the Greek guy that owned Soko's – who knew we were all Catholic – looked very nervous handing over the meat. I waited anxiously and wondered, what was I about to do?

I had heard about the "cardinal" sins but, like much else in my religion, I never got any sort of detailed or age-appropriate explanation as to what these were. Was this it? The cardinal sin? With my friends staring at me, I was now in too deep. Turning back now would be just like walking away from a fight. Even if you get your head beat in, walking away is worse, because it meant a lifetime of ridicule.

The sub came out on a tray, steaming. I sat down as my fellow altar boys gathered around and watched. Thoughts raced through my head. When would I be punished? Would it be public humiliation, after word spread through the church, from Norwood all the way to Rome, with the top religious men ultimately convening and announcing my sentence? I could already see my mother ringing her hands, crying, and repeating, "Oh, I'm so embarrassed," while my father alternated between turning purple, rolling his eyes at my mother, and silently mouthing the words to me, "Your goose is cooked."

Or, would God himself make a piece of the steak swell up inside my throat, and leave me choking on the floor? I looked at all my Catholic friends as the smoking steak and cheese was placed in front of me. Some had a look of worry, others a look of morbid anticipation for what God would do to me for this cardinal sin. I hesitated, and the crowd sensed fear. Good Catholics or not, they were more concerned with the show than my eternal salvation.

"He ain't gonna do it ... look at him, he's scared!"

My manhood was being called out. I shoved the thing in my mouth with my eyes closed, trembling. Which bite would make my head explode? Was there a priest lurking with binoculars somewhere? Then again, maybe God wasn't awake yet, or was busy punishing some poor sap in New Jersey or something, and would never find out?

I continued to chew but didn't swallow. Maybe that would buy me more time. Then someone noticed, and said, "Ahhhh, go on! You're just chewing. Swallow it!" I was now out of options so I swallowed ... and nothing happened. I took another bite, more confident, and quickly masticated and swallowed that one. Still, no exploding head or S.W.A.T-style takedown by a lurking team of priest commandos.

I continued to eat as fast as I could, and finally, it was gone. There was a collective look of unbelief and shock on the faces of my friends. Nobody spoke. I was feeling good – and it was pretty a damn tasty sub – but I think my crew was waiting for lightning to strike. I got up and we started walking. Curiously, some of the kids, especially the ones who had been goading me to go ahead and eat, now seemed insulted, like I had disrespected our religion. Others had a look of pure joy on their faces as if my act of defiance had set them free ... free to eat meat on Friday ... and heck, who knew what else, right?

We walked home, my friends cautiously following a safe distance out of fear of the wrath of God from the sky or maybe even being infected by my meat cooties. I made it to the bottom of my driveway and my friends waved goodbye like it could be the last time they would ever see me. I delivered the papers as fast as I could, running through the trees and paths, dodging possible lightning bolts from God.

I made it home, and then in the safety of my room, panic hit me. I repeatedly prayed my Catholic prayers, "Hail Mary, Full of Grace," and even added a few little twists, "Sorry about the meat on Friday." I used to run to the cover of my grandmother when I was in trouble, but now, thanks to the fact that I was Catholic, Mary, the mother of Jesus, could go to bat for me. I tried to sleep but kept looking around for the images of God, Jesus, and the Holy Ghost. I looked out the window, then under my Star Wars sheets. I got very little sleep and woke to deliver the *Globe* as rapidly as I could, all the while, dodging God's lightning strikes under trees, and between bushes and cars.

I got on the bus, and some of my crew smiled, shocked to see me alive and not injured or malformed. I made it to school and there were looks from other Catholic boys: some seemed happy to know they were free to enjoy meat Friday. Others distanced themselves out of fear to be too close to a guy that just crossed the line. Weeks passed and it was obvious that Mary, the mother of Jesus, had pleaded my case to God, Jesus H. Christ, and the Holy Ghost.

THE BREAK-UP

There was a dance at the high school, and I happened to have that Saturday off from chores, so I got to go. We had typical teen-aged fun, yelled and screamed, and played grab-ass. I saw my girl but she seemed to be avoiding me, and when we finally met face to face, she said she wanted to talk to me. Most people had left, and she and I walked to the high school football field. Then came those words: she wanted to "be friends." I thought, "What a great idea!" Not only would we be friends, but we would be dating too! A double whammy. What a lucky guy I was. But then she said, "No, I mean we won't date anymore, I *just* want to be friends." It registered. I was in dumb-founded shock. We shook hands and I walked away. It may have been puppy love, but this puppy was sad.

I walked back to the school and met up with the crew. We began to walk home. Someone mentioned that we should take a few drinks. My parents were out, so that is exactly what I did. I made a few strong adult drinks and threw them back. Even though it was a lot tougher to stomach, the strong adult drinks had a quicker effect than beers. I was drinking vodka. I mixed it with cranberry juice, and within a few moments, that warm fuzzy feeling came over me, and all seemed well again. Getting dumped didn't hurt so much. I even forgave the girl for dumping me and would move on. But I would distance myself from the possibility of getting hurt again. I crossed her initials off the back of my three-ring binder.

I crawled under my Star Wars sheets, sweating, which was now common for me after a number of drinks. I looked up to the patterns on the ceiling and saw some faces of dead relatives, past presidents, and previously undiscovered sea creatures. I fell asleep and woke in what seemed like minutes to see it was morning. Dragging myself out of bed I set out to deliver the *Globe*. Maybe, I thought, the breakup was my punishment for eating the steak and cheese on Friday? It was a bad punishment, but at least I knew God could have done a lot worse.

TUCE

Eighth grade was about to end and I now had more hair on my body and more bitterness implanted on my mind. I felt unwanted as a result of the break-up, but I had the adult drinks to take the edge off. We started calling it "the sauce" after hearing an older kid refer to it like that. This sauce wasn't meant to be slathered on hot dogs or steak; it was spread over one's mind to alleviate the pain of war, lost pets, dead relatives, physical ailments and, in my case, a break-up.

The hard liquor had the fastest effect, so I would drink that as quick as I could before the parents got home. I even started to sneak the sauce before doing the afternoon paper route. This made me feel like a child again, and I took in the trees, the grass, birds, everything. Ah, the magic of the sauce. Bitterness always returned, but I simply had to apply more sauce, and it was soon gone.

I now just was a few weeks away from leaving 8th grade. I could speak some Spanish and had a remedy for my woes. That was all I needed to move on. I still played hard contact sports with the Cro Mags, sometimes after school. We all happened to be there one day, and I paused and took in everyone's new identity.

Cashews was now in denim jeans, work boots, and a leather jacket. Esteban Blumpkin had on army fatigues. Simma from the Riviera had on Levi's, Converse sneakers, and a t-shirt. Sully was trying to dress like the Nike kids and had somehow managed to get an Alligator shirt. Dressed differently or not, when we were in our neighborhood playing sports, we were still the same guys. We played a mean game of hard contact football, and then sat back and discussed how things would be after 8th grade. Tibbs was going to Xavierian, an all-boys Catholic school. The rest of us were heading to high school.

Cashews pulled out a brochure that said there was some sort of fitness program over the summer. There wasn't much detail. Would it be like our present gym class where the instructor would dump a mesh net of volleyballs onto the ground and we would whip them at each other? Then I saw it mentioned the fitness instructor's name: Mr. Paul Tuccelli. He had a reputation that preceded him, just like Mooncai and Crowe. Some stories had to have been exaggerated, but then again, none of us were on his football team, so maybe the course was just a babysitting service for adolescents. It wasn't that expensive, and I decided to use some money from the paper route to sign up.

We all split up, and I went home for my traditional Friday American Catholic meal: fish, potato, and macaroni preceded by a blessing. I asked Lead, who just finished high school, if he knew anything about this Mr. Tuccelli. Lead smiled, and said, "You mean Tuce?" He then went on with Tuce stories: He was the gym teacher at Westwood High School, and the defensive coach at Walpole High School, then the number one high school football team in our region.

Then Lead went on about his legendary gym classes: people vomiting and passing out from over-exercising was a normal occurrence. Complaints from parents about "Little Johnny" coming home holding his stomach in agony from excess sit-ups was the norm. None of this mattered to Tuce. Like Crowe, he taught physical education with an emphasis on "physical."

He did mention that, unlike Crowe, with Tuce, if you pushed yourself, you would be rewarded. It wouldn't be all just yelling and popping veins. My father chimed in, with the usually large lump of food in his cheek, "It'll be good for you'se. Maybe it'll even straighten yer ass out!"

The day arrived, and we assembled into the gym where the brochure stated to meet. There were many other kids there as well. There were some high fives, pushing, and shoving. Then there was a whistle, and we all stopped the pushing and shoving. A massive figure approached us from the other end of the gym. Just from his physique, it was obvious that he didn't play chess, yoga, or volleyball, and we weren't about to either.

"Listen up, ladies!"

The room snapped into silence. Like a drill sergeant, Tuce described his class, and my suspicion was right: we weren't going to be balancing bean bags on our heads or walking in figure eights, or square dancing. He described the course, his expectations, and the goals we would all accomplish by the end of the course. He had a thick Boston accent and pronounced words like some of my older relatives. "My goal is to turn you yoo-mans into at-letes," he growled.

We were then told to go out to the high school track. The whistle was the only similarity he had with Crowe. We didn't have to march in single file or buy matching shirts with our names on the back. I would find out real soon, however, what turning a yoo-man body into an at-lete really entailed. We gathered at the track.

"Eye'z am going to time you'se on the 12-minute run." He said, "Run until I tell you to stop."

He blew the whistle and we circled the track. You could hear Tuce no matter where you were on the track.

"Step it up a notch!" he yelled. "Move it!" As I circled past him, it became obvious that he grew up in my father's neighborhood.

"Get the lead out!" he screamed.

It seemed like the running would never end. I passed him again, and this time was praised with a "That's it! Keep it going!" I noticed Esteban, who's moniker had recently morphed into Wild Blumpkin, across the track, sucking wind, his big red afro bobbing in last place. It was obvious he had hit the sauce the night before. Me? I felt better the more I ran. Then I heard the whistle. The 12-minute run was over. We were dying, hands-on wobbly knees, and he screamed for us to "hustle" back. We all limped back to Tuce. He then pointed to me, Cashews, Sully and Wild Blumpkin.

"Oh, I've heard about you'se guys!" He said, scowling, "And believe you me, I will get that gah-bage out of you'se systems!"

There was no question, he knew we were into the sauce. With Tuce, there was no, "I will show you a film on drinking with a swollen liver in a metal pan." Instead, it was a nice, cold New England, "I will get deh gahbage out of you'se systems!" I gained immediate respect for Tuce. One, he didn't belittle us, and two, we weren't lectured like little boys or morons. Next, we went into stretching. We did things with our bodies that I thought weren't possible. Bending in all sorts of directions.

"One, two, three … one thousand!"

Sweat was pouring out. Then I noticed something astonishing: I was feeling the very same sensations that a few stiff drinks brought about. I felt calmer.

Tuce said, "Take a knee, girls." Followed by, "Enjoy it, ladies, because 'dis is the easiest day for you'se all." Then he described what we would be doing. Strength training, balance and coordination, endurance. We next had to run up the grandstands of the football field. Up, turn, back down, up again, like one giant snake.

The course for the day finally ended. Tuce even said, "Good job stepping it up out 'dere." There was no handshake, hug, or rubbing my back. Just a "good job" on getting the lead out. He was speaking my language. It was the first time in many years I could remember that someone had given me a compliment of any sort. I walked home with my old crew. We were together again, exhausted, and soaking wet from Tuce's course.

I made it home, and I felt great. Whatever toxins alcohol had put in me, they now seemed to be pouring out of my skin. I now had two releases from bitterness and anxiety: alcohol and rigorous exercise. Exercise put me on the brink of vomiting with the world spinning. But then, shortly after the pain, something happened to my mind. There was some sort of release. There was peace. Being a bright fellow, I did the math, and figured, "Why not add alcohol to the mix?"

I felt great as I delivered the papers, and then a thought came to mind: Tuce promised that he was going to get that garbage out of our systems. I made a decision: that would be my last drink for a while. I finished the route and made my way home, to a traditional meal of spaghetti and potatoes and boiled vegetables. We talked of Tuce, and my father, with a wad of food and a smile, said, "I told you it would be good for you'se!"

I crashed hard from it all that night, but it was a good crash. I crashed from what was described by Tuce as the *easiest* day of his course. Then in an instant, I woke, eager to go back for more. I could only imagine how much more calm and peaceful I would feel after today if yesterday was the *easiest* day. And I thought, "Isn't that life? Yesterday is the easiest day."

We arrived at the gymnasium and did a Tuce warm up. This was different than warming up like the rest of the world, turning the dial on the thermostat, putting on a scarf, or ear muffs. This warm-up was doing monsters up and down the basketball court until we yoo-mans, soon to be at-letes, were "warmed up." We were huffing and puffing and the sweat valve started to open and flow. We then started stretching, putting our bodies in positions that seemed wholly unnatural but that in fact felt good. Then it was jogging out to the football field where my girlfriend had dumped me.

There were cones and dumbbells on the field. Tuce bellowed, without a bullhorn but still loud enough for our town and the three surrounding towns to hear. There would be the "duck walk," where you grabbed a set of dumbbells, squatted and walked like a duck. He demonstrated this and he looked rather funny imitating a duck and circling the cones, but nobody laughed. Then he announced, "Another set of you'se will be going up and down the grandstands and once you have done three sets, go to the duck walk." Then the last set was a strange run. You ran sideways, hands spread from side to side, and then feet crossing. Tuce demonstrated.

We were all split up evenly and then given the order, and the warning, "Don't you'se dare cheat cuz I'ze got eyes in the back of my head." Then the whistle. The lines started moving. I saw as everyone started to perform for the first time, jogging sideways and duck walking. It was my turn to jog sideways. It was all new, and my growth spurt, and Osgood-Schlatter, and my octopus body couldn't pull it off. I fell, but Tuce just said, "Brush it off." I got back up and finished.

I finished jogging sideways and then went to the duck walk. I was given dumbbells and then acted like a duck, crouching and walking around the cones. I thought of ducks and how they always seemed to be happy, walking in a perfect row. This didn't seem like the happy ducks crossing the streets in a row. The whistle blew, and Tuce yelled, "Change it up!"

I ran over to the grandstands and stood in line. Without getting a rest, Tuce blew his whistle again. We would run up the left side of the steps of the grandstand, descend on the right side of the stairwell, avoiding the future "yoo-man at-letes" that were ascending, and then to the next set of stairs.

I noticed I that had very few thoughts while doing rigorous exercise. Finally, the whistle blew. "All of you'se gather 'round! Good job, out 'dere … now we'ze are gonna stretch it out!" We jogged over to the gym, and he stood in the center. He announced, "Now you'se are gonna start weight training. Weight training will help you'se in all fields of at-letics. I will record how much you do today, and in 8 weeks, you should be above and beyond what eye'ze record today."

We then went to the weight room, and he explained what each exercise was called. The names didn't sound too friendly: the deadlift, the squat, the military press, the bench press, the clean and jerk. He went through all the routines with a few reps on each, and then we were assigned, three to four to a station. Tuce told us to start out with light weights, and we lined up into small groups behind each unfriendly sounding station.

Tuce then walked around with a clipboard, making notes next to each one of our names. He wasn't using his whistle, but just monitored every-one's lift. If he felt you could do more, he would tell the next guy in line to increase the weight. "Trow on anudder 10 pounds on each side." When a kid struggled, Tuce would yell, "Push it! Push it! Push it!" And the kid would get in one or two more reps.

Returning from the exercise it appeared the kid "pushing it" had pushed all the blood back to his heart, for his face was white. I saw one kid return from the deadlift, walk over to the trash barrel, and dry heave. Tuce, in fact, congratulated him on that: "Good job! Dat means you'se are *trying*." It was my turn at this thing called squats. You put this bar on your back and looked forward. You pushed the bar with your shoulders and raised it up off the holders. Then, as Tuce said, you pretended you were sitting down, all the while looking forward.

I did ten and then heard his voice, "Add anudder 25 pounds on each side." I went down and squatted fairly easily. Coming back up was a struggle, then down, and the second time up I was shaking. The third time, I couldn't make it half way when Tuce stepped in: "Push it! Push it! Push it!" I finally made it up.

"Again!" he shouted.

I went back down, but could barely move up at all. But I pushed, and with a struggle, made it. Tuce slapped my back said, "Atta boy!" I caught a quick glimpse in the mirror, and I was white as a ghost and felt like vomiting. I got to the next station, which was deadlifts. Named after someone that took Tuce's class, I thought. This didn't seem as bad as the squat until Tuce came over to our station. We were only halfway through, and I was whipped. I stood at the back of our small line and had a thought of Tuce and what type of childhood this guy must have had.

His full name was Paul Tuccelli. I pictured his father yelling, "Paul, I want you'se to take out the trash! I left dumbbells at the bottom of the driveway, and I want you'se to grab them when the trash is taken out completely, and duckwalk back to the garage."

What was Christmas like at the Tuccelli home? A stocking full of tiny dumbbells, jump rope, and a hand-held whistle? Did he have to run with his feet in front and then in back around the Christmas tree for 12 minutes before opening his presents?

We finally all finished and Tuce announced, "I have all you'se performances on dis' heeya clipboard. A few weeks from now, you'se should be 50 percent stronger." Then he looked at us Cro Mags. "That is if you'se don't put any more of dat gah-bage into you'se systems."

The summer fitness program continued and the amount of weight, repetitions, and times walking like certain animals increased as well. At the end of the course that summer, just as he had promised, we all had become stronger. Before we left his last class, he gave us a regime to follow. He shook all of our hands and then gave a mini-speech to the Cro Mags. "You'se can all be good at-letes, if you'se put the garbage down."

The garbage was alcohol, we knew ... and more recently marijuana with a few of the Cro Mags.

My father didn't say much but I could tell he was proud of me because he picked up a brand-new set of weights. It was a very rare instance of getting something new out of the box, as opposed to a hand-me-down, reject store item or some treasure from the curbside. He said, "Those there weights put me back a ways, but it'll do you'se some good."

I continued the weight training but picked up where I left off with the sauce, which I hadn't done at all since the first day of Tuce's class.

MY VISIT TO CHINA

Out of the blue, I got an invite to visit my old friend China, who had moved up to Maine. The plan was to stay up there for a week. I packed the summer usuals. Underwear, socks, swim trunks, shorts, and t-shirts. My father drove me to a Greyhound bus stop in Boston. I boarded the bus and was off. As the bus drove north, I noticed that the scenery became greener and greener. The houses became further apart from each other. I was able to crack the window a bit, and it even smelled fresher and freer.

We stopped a few times, letting some people off while others got on. We continued to drive and finally made it to my stop. I walked down the steps, and there was my old buddy China. We were happy to see each other, and we jumped into his father's car. Here we were, kids of the first two families to arrive at Crystal Hill, reunited again. We then had to drive further, to an area called the Sebago Long Lakes region. We came over a small hill, and down into an area with two big bodies of water and a bridge in between. China pointed out that Long Lake was on the right and Sebago was on the left.

We continued on "the causeway," as my friend pointed out all the pizza shops, arcades, candy stores, and characters that every town seemed to have. China said that his new town, even all the way up there in Maine, had its own Leatherheads.

These Maine Leatherheads had the same outfits as ours, but they were all on motorcycles. One character stood out. He had red hair, cut as a mohawk. As we passed, China's father cautioned not to look at them. The causeway was slow moving, and it wouldn't have been a good idea to stare. But like everything thus far in my life, if I was told, "don't touch" or "don't look" or "keep out," it was inevitable that I was going to disobey. I just *had* to look at that guy with the mohawk. Sure enough, he saw me giving him the eyeball. Crystal Hill had our Runci, Maine had this guy with the red mohawk.

His crew was a sea of work boots, denims, and leather. He was at the end, staring directly at me, with his eyes saying, "This is *my* lake region, so watch your back." I turned around after seeing his pale complexion and piercing eyes. I made a mental note to lock the window before going to bed that night. I asked, "Who was that?" China's dad told us the stories. "He's been in and out of jail for beating people within inches of their lives. Definitely walk on the other side of the causeway if you see them."

We finally arrived at China's new house, and I was very impressed. His mother sold antiques and "trinkets," of which my father would say, "Ah, 'dose are 'da little ornaments, usually porcelain, that ladies buy and put all over the house." Trinkets were the natural enemy of the electrician because they were always in your way when you went to work in someone's house. It added an extra hour of work to most jobs because you would have to move them, placing them as far away as possible from the work location.

You never wanted to start a job off by destroying somebody's heirloom, irreplaceable 3-inch porcelain giraffe. That would entail not only having to delay the job while trying to glue the thing back together, but also enduring the inevitable explanation of how Great Aunt Martha was given the 3-inch porcelain giraffe by Napoleon's third cousin in 1824, how she smuggled it in her pantaloons on the dangerous voyage across the Atlantic to America, and how it had survived the Civil War, the Great Depression, and countless other electricians up to that point.

Well, China's mom seemed to be doing very well in her antique and trinket shop. We walked into the house itself and went upstairs. I placed my gear down, and we went right to work. My Blizzard of '78 fellow explorer took out the list of activities we were going to perform for the week, and we went over the list. Every day, he had something mapped out for us to do. Starting right away. We were about to leave, and China had to go to the bathroom. While he was out of the room, I thought of Mohawk man and proceeded to close and lock all the windows. He could sneak in at any time, after all, and hide under my bed or in the closet.

China emerged, and we headed out. Even at a young age, China always had his act together. We were both into model boats, planes, tanks, and antique cars, the kind of models you assemble with glue that made you feel dizzy and giggly if sniffed. China took this type of activity very seriously, whereas my procedure might have been a bit more haphazard. He would lay out aluminum foil, pour a little bit of glue on the aluminum foil, and with a toothpick, follow the directions of the model maker down to every last detail. With precision, he dipped the toothpick into the small pile of glue and then dabbed it on the model he was making.

I would just pour the glue onto the model, and so, in the end, mine looked like quite different than his. This bothered China, so he took it upon himself to train me up in proper model-making techniques, which resulted in my models looking like they rolled off an assembly line. This required X-acto knives, aluminum foil, toothpicks and, most important, *following the directions*. That was China.

Now here he was, with this list. Timetables, locations, directions … we would have to stay on a precise schedule, rain or shine. He showed me the plan where we were going to ride on a speedboat, then a river cruise then hit the arcades, etc. He even had a little league game planned, and his coach was going to let me sit on the bench to watch. The schedule said it was time to play, so we headed to his backyard. This was no normal, suburban Boston backyard – this was land that stretched to the horizon. We played until dark, exploring everything, then headed home for dinner.

China's mom seemed happy and stated she had a good day of sales. She asked about the old neighborhood. I told her a doctor from India had moved into her house, and he was very kind. Tomorrow was the riverboat cruise, and in the early evening was his little league game. We went to sleep and I felt safe with the windows locked. We woke, ate Lucky Charms, and his father drove us to the docks. He paid our way, and we boarded.

There weren't many people, so we could sit anywhere we liked. We headed off and sat back to take in the scenes. I was amazed how open everything was; we didn't even see any homes. It was all green trees and vegetation. Then there was a small clearing and I noticed a rope. China pointed out that there was a rope swing that we would visit as well because it was on his schedule of events. I was in a new world, the world of Maine, with slow talking and slow moving, and generally happy folk ... except for mohawk man.

The cruise finished and we docked and headed back. He had to get dressed for his game. For an early teen, he had his act together. I was sort of happy to hear that he hadn't experimented with the sauce. Up there, I felt there was no need for the sauce either. There was no hustle and bustle. Worry seemed far off, very distant. Anxiety and fear were somewhere else.

China finally was suited up in his baseball uniform. He played many sports but was always great at baseball. We headed to the ballpark. As we sat in the back seat of the family station wagon, he brought up his nickname on Crystal Hill. He said, "Whatever you do, don't let anyone know my nickname was China." I didn't promise, but I nodded. We got out and I was allowed to sit on the bench. I was introduced to everyone on the team.

They warmed up and then with a big Maine hoo-rah the ump said, "Play ball!" The good news was my friend's team was first up at bat, and he was third at-bat. The first kid went up to bat, and pop-flied; the next kid hit a screaming grounder and got to first base. Then China hit a single. Now there were two men on base. His closest friend who sat next to me said, "He is a great ball player." I said, "Yeah, China was always great at baseball."

"What?!" he said.

"China's best sport was always baseball," I said. Then I realized ... I had let it slip.

Without delay, the guy started yelling, "Hey, nice hit China!" The next kid hit a double, and China slid into third base face first, safe. The bench stood up and applauded. Then two more guys yelled, "Nice running, China!" I got a glare from him. Another base hit followed, and he ran home. He glared at me, but the game went on. The yelling of his nickname must have helped, for he had the best game of his life both offensively and defensively. Both teams shook hands, and we headed off to the cars. You could hear a pin drop on the ride home. We headed to bed, and he simply said, "I'm ruined."

We woke up and followed his schedule. After a few hours, we began to talk again. We did everything on the list that week, and Maine was a success. China and his father dropped me off at the bus station, and we waved goodbye. As I drove south to Boston, the houses became closer together, and people seemed to be in a rush. I could feel the world crowding in on me. I felt a little more anxious with every mile, which was normal, knowing I would be around my father shortly, who always seemed to be in a rush or upset with someone or something.

China and I kept in touch, and he told me that I wouldn't have to worry about mohawk man for a while – he robbed a bank, wearing a bandana over his face. I wondered how far he got in his getaway, with a description of a man with a red mohawk, driving at high speeds on a Harley in Maine.

DICK GOES FOR A RIDE

I settled back in from my trip to Maine. I got home and saw a few of the fellows from the Hill. Tibbs was up so I knew it wasn't before noon time. He was vacuuming his father's car out sitting Indian style. He mentioned again that he was going to an all-boys Catholic school called Xavierian. He didn't look too pleased, but his father said it would straighten him out. I then figured I'd walk through the thirty yards or so of brush that separated Crystal Hill from Cashews' house on Green Hill.

I walked over to the front of the house and saw his father with his purple complexion and a cigarette dangling from his mouth ... which meant he had been drinking. He was carrying luggage and seemed to be in a rush. He looked at me, huffing and puffing and blowing smoke in my face and said, "Dick is going for a ride!" I had never seen Mr. Cashews smile or laugh, he just yelled. But today, he seemed to crack a smile in the same corner of his mouth that held the cigarette. He seemed pretty pleased about this "ride" his son was going on.

The luggage was packed and I saw Dick in the back. He didn't look too happy. We glimpsed each other. There was the guy I'd known since I was 3 years old, going away, somewhere. For how long, who knew? In any event, I knew that in a few years we would be graduates of one of the best oceanography schools in the United States, swimming with the sharks.

Well, it seemed little by little the Cro Mags of Sheehan School were being dismantled. I was starting my freshman year of high school and had 4 years to prove my intelligence so I could get into a decent college, get decent grades there, get a job, get assigned a cubicle, marry the girl in the cubicle next to mine, come home every night, put on my button-down sweater, iron my underwear, and read the newspaper with a pipe in my mouth.

My mother must have hit the lottery because she came home with a twelve-inch shoe box that said "Docksiders." I was shocked. Now, here I was about to enter the world of the "boat people" wearing a shoe named distinctly for walking down those docks to their boats. Surely my luck would change for the better, once I started wearing those shoes.

My mother, being Scottish and having a very strong "thrifty" gene, explained that there was a going-out-of-business sale; she pointed out that there was a small tear on the shoe that one could only find using a high-powered microscope. Plus, she had haggled with the cashier. I awoke for the first day of High School and slipped on my new Docksiders, ready for my new life.

Soon, if I kept on the life graph, I would be walking proudly down those docks to my massive yacht. For now, I walked proudly down Crystal Hill with my head in the sky. Images of fame and fortune slid through my mind. I waited for the bus on cloud nine. The bus stopped, and a very short bus driver got out and up into my face and said with a thick Boston accent: "Okay Winslow! I ain't puttin' up with any of you'se shenanigans. You, sit up front!" I boarded the bus and in front was Wild Blumpkin, and Sully, both looking sheepish. We made one more stop where Simma boarded, and he got the same treatment.

There would be no more sitting in back, writing graffiti, cutting up the seats, or grabbing smaller kids and pummeling them before handing him over to Polumbo for the headlock. This Boston "lady" was going to rule her bus with an iron fist. I took a quick glance behind me and noticed there were lots of very large guys staring at us. These were high school football players, products of *years* with Tuce.

We made our way to Westwood High School, and I noticed some students had driven their own cars to school. There seemed to be separate parking for the boat people with their fancy cars, and then another area for people from my part of town, with their 20-year-old beaters. We walked into the front entrance, and the freshmen were ordered into the auditorium. It was another giant institutional bee-hive, and we all disappeared into the brick catacombs of public education. Who was the king bee here, I wondered? Would he be like the Darth Vader principal from middle school?

Turns out that the king bee of Westwood High School was named Phil Flaherty and his Lieutenant enforcer bee was Charles Flahive. I wondered whether they were veterans of World War II, Korea, or Vietnam? We all assembled, and king bee Flaherty walked up and down the aisle. Immediately we picked up on his slurring speech, and his spitting whenever he said a word that contained an "s" in it. His grey institutional pants were several inches above his ankles, giving him a ridiculous look. And then there was his neck flab, which overhung his shirt, which was too tight on the neck but still buttoned all the way up. A dingy, stained tie completed the ensemble.

His face was the color of red licorice as he sounded off the instructions and behavior he expected while we were in his beehive. The collective mind of the Cro Mags immediately and silently began formulating a plan for Phil Flaherty Day, when we would button up our shirts to the top, wear our fathers' ugly gray polyester pants, pulled up too high. While passing each other in the hallway, we would slur our speech and try to have spittle come out. The do's and don'ts finally ended, and we were given maps to find our way around the brick hive, along with class schedules.

I noticed immediately that the upperclassmen were very large. There were even rumors about a drug called steroids. Tuce gave us a briefing on this drug and said, "Itta' make you'se nuts tiny and shrink you'se manhood and den you'se forehead will grow too big and youse'll look like a caveman." But these guys were big and intimidating, so I just looked straight ahead or at the wall when walking around.

We passed by the upper courtyard, which looked like a glass tank that held the brains and jocks of the school. Then we passed the lower courtyard, the smoking courtyard, that housed the Leatherheads as well as a related crowd called Gearheads, guys that worked on cars – and their girlfriends. I followed the map and was about to make it to my first class, when I heard, "Freshman!" I felt a slap and all the books I was carrying scattered on the floor.

I turned quick, to put this guy in the famous Winslow headlock. However, one look at the guy, and I could see his forehead and chin were freakishly larger than normal. We eyeballed each other, and he walked away. I picked up my books as the reality of being a freshman was sinking in. The day ended, and we took our bus ride home, sitting up front. I now knew that the Docksiders wouldn't work magic on their own, so I would have to step it up. I wouldn't let the proud Docksider corporation down. I would succeed and someday wear their loafers on the yacht docks.

I managed to make it through the week without getting beaten up or getting in trouble. Friday arrived, and we were told there was a pep rally for the football team. We were to assemble in the gymnasium. Everyone finally made their way into the stands. Then cheerleaders gathered and lined up across from each other shaking their pompoms. My pants grew tight.

The P.A. guy announced, "Now, ladies and gentlemen, can we have a big round of applause for the football team." The cheerleaders went crazy. I had thoughts of the swim team that I had signed up for. Would there be a pep rally for the swim team? Would the cheerleaders be jumping and jiggling for us like this? Of *course*, they would. We would have our own manager, who took care of the suits, cleaning the goggles, and maintaining the chlorine level.

He would announce, "Now ladies and gentlemen, please stand and give a round of applause for the Westwood High School swim team." I would run out with my speedo swimsuit, bathing cap, goggles, and kickboard placed out in front. I would even run as if I was swimming. Each cheerleader would look at me longingly as they jumped and jiggled with joy. I couldn't *wait* for that moment.

High school was so much bigger than middle school, with so many more students, which meant a lot of shenanigans could go down. There was just no way the teachers could keep on top of everything. One guy earned my deepest respect early on. He was called Skinny for obvious reasons. Skinny somehow found out that there was a pig fetus in one of the laboratories. He stole the fetus and threw it off the mezzanine, onto the floor of the cafeteria below. The timing was perfect, as there was a tour of the school being held with a few local muckety-mucks. The faculty was probably pointing out the high percentages of students who went on to college after leaving this facility.

My future friend Skinny used a bowling bowl ball technique with the fetus. He lobbed it perfectly, and it landed on the floor with a sickening smack just feet from the tour, then slid across the tiles, oozing guts.

"Pay no attention to that sliding pig fetus. I merely forgot that the science department was conducting the pig fetus slide test today. Did I mention that 98% of our students go on to college?"

I really tried to stay firmly on the docks, sticking closely to the life graph, inspired by my docksiders. Due to high school being more rigorous and me being on the swim team, I had been allowed to retire from the paper route, so I now had a few hours after school to study or explore the "other sides" of my town. My world was getting bigger. Long ago the town fathers had decreed that Westwood would be a "dry" community, and no alcohol was allowed to be sold within the town limits.

By all appearances, that plan had backfired. Loads of people in high school were drinking heavy, even on weekdays. In my after-school explorations, I became acquainted with all the different groups' "spots," each based on the location of their neighborhoods. Each spot was guarded and maintained by a certain crew.

The spots included The Lot, The Sunoco, Pigeon City, Pete's Rock (our turf), Martha Jones, Roach Brothers, The Rez, and The Shack. These were all hangouts, and each associated crew had their own special means of obtaining the forbidden fruit, alcohol, as well as their own local custom for consuming the sauce, which had been laughingly "forbidden" by the white wigs of days gone by.

I managed to mingle with the heads of each of these locations and drink from their forbidden fruit. I started out at The Lot. This crew had gone to the Deerfield Elementary school. It was co-captained by a guy with a long Italian last name that couldn't be pronounced but that began with an O. His first name was Joe, thus he was known merely as Joe O.

His father was a bartender in Norwood. His lieutenant was another ex-altar boy that I had served masses with. His nickname was "River," due to being found half dead in the Charles River in Dedham; he had survived both oxygen deprivation *and* hypothermia.

I made my way over to The Lot, which was across from a convenient store. My first night there, I listened to instructions. There were to be *no* fires. I was given escape routes and told to put my empty beer cans in a certain location, later to be picked up. The Lot's crew contained some good sized "New England potatoes," as my father would call them. These were the large, half-submerged rocks that dotted the New England landscape, ranging in size from a television to a refrigerator to a Volkswagon Beatle.

These made great tripping hazards, my new friends pointed out, especially if you didn't know the ins and outs of their escape routes. We then drank, without the fire, and blended into the darkness as we watched the cars go by. I felt the calmness as a few drinks come over me. I had to watch myself, for we were devout Catholics, and prayer and dinner were at a specific time. If we were lucky back then, someone would have a watch set to the right time.

That night nobody did, so I left when it felt like it was getting close to dinner time. I passed by the office where my father beat the dentist who slapped me. Then I passed St. Margaret Mary's, where I had been baptized, named after the priest, and then became an altar boy. I took a fork and headed down Pond Street.

I passed by my friend Danny's synagogue, where he celebrated his bar mitzvah and had entered manhood. I loved the feeling alcohol had on me, it made all these things beautiful. I got home, and we said a prayer at the dinner table and ate. I went to my room to "study." All I could manage was to flip through all the books and just look at the pictures. Faraway places, chemicals, math problems that needed to be solved, Greeks and their myths of ladies with snakes for hair. I looked down on my Docksiders. They were dirty and scuffed.

Another favorite hangout was Sunoco. It had many escapes routes, and you could light a fire. There, however, you had to bring your own brew or had to pay a fee to drink on their keg. There were two circles. One for the grade above us, and the other for us. We could see the grade above us pounding beers around the fire, listening to Grandmaster Flash and the Furious Five.

"Don't push me, 'cause I'm close to the edge."

The fire illuminated the whole crew. They looked as if they all had dressed each other or called each other up, and agreed on matching attire. Their jackets were Barracuda brand, zipped up tight. The pants were designer and rolled up to expose converse sneakers – not the canvas type, but leather high tops. I grabbed my beer and backed up to the cold outer circle. I swilled my brew and reached for another. I continued to drink as fast and as much as I could. I looked at these guys and had a feeling they were all headed for trouble, unlike me, who had the protection of the Docksiders, the Virgin Mary, and the life graph.

There was also the birthplace and breeding ground of the Leatherheads, or "Islington Burners," – Islington, a small section of town that was triangular shaped. Here "the Burners" would take off their leathers and play street hockey on the tennis courts, and then smoke marijuana to relax. They had a little get together one night near the commuter rail tracks and supermarket. They drank hard liquor and passed a marijuana pipe. It came to me and I smiled and said, "Eh, first time." A very polite Islington Burner took me under his wing. He lit the pipe and took a big hit. He said, "Inhale, hold it, and then blow out." He passed it to me without wiping it down with an alcohol wet nap.

The nice Burner guided me now and even lit it. "Okay, breathe in, hold it, now let it out. Eyyy, that was a good hit!" The smoke was sweet and sour and went into my lungs with a sting. I held it and exhaled. My plastic cup was filled with more adult drink, and the pipe continued to be passed to me.

I was becoming a better smoker as it went around. I smiled for no reason. It was time to go, but I didn't feel the need to run home ... I walked, dreamily, instead. I laughed at nothing and everything. What was this drug that seemed to mix in so well with the adult drinks? I always walked briskly and even half jogged when under the influence of alcohol. But now, in this weed haze, I just took everything in with a mellow, relaxed ease.

I finally made it home and was starving. We blessed the meal, and I made a cross symbol. I kept piling on food I normally wouldn't eat. My father took notice and inquired. I said swim season was coming up, and I needed to get fit. He grunted and nodded with a golf ball sized clump of cauliflower in his cheek.

I began to notice things I hadn't noticed before, like all the trinkets my mother collected, not only in the kitchen but throughout the house. Crucifixes, clocks that didn't work, vases, baskets, pictures of relatives, colorful drapes. Why had I never noticed all this cool stuff before?

I made it to my room to "study" and just looked around. I looked outside. I looked at my feet. I still had my Docksiders on. They were dirty and scuffed.

I had a few more weeks before swim team, and most of the fall preparations for winter were done, such as cutting wood and removing the last remaining leaves on the grass. This allowed me to set foot in a few more places, two in particular. These areas were in the same vicinity and were frequented by the same crews. Their parents had money, but their outfits were worn carelessly like they really didn't want to wear them. The clothes were forced on them. They even owned mini bikes. Next to this area was a massive sand pit and transmission lines. This provided a great area to drink in, with many escape routes. However, these guys didn't seem to care about that, because they had dirt bikes.

There was a massive liquor distributor up the road, and this crew had recently heisted cases and cases of what looked like a mini trash can type of beer called Foster's. They seemed to have an endless supply. After drinking I don't know how many, the crew decided we needed to remove ourselves to the adjacent spot, which required a short dirt bike ride. I hopped onto the back of a dirt bike, and we headed for a place called The Shack, an oversized tool shed.

I inquired whose tool shed it was. What escape route did they have? I felt trapped indoors. There was no answer. I was probably geographically at the furthest point away from my residence, but still in my town. We swilled a few more Foster's and then I was glad to get out of there. One of the dirt bike guys offered to give me a ride to the furthest point he could go legally with his bike. It was a hellish ride, especially with my oversized head catching all the wind. I had to duck branches and guy wires and hold on for my life.

BLUE-COLLAR MISFITS

The day arrived where I was finally on an organized athletic team, the swim team. We wouldn't be swimming that first day, as it was simply an introduction. We were told to meet in the bleachers behind the shallow end of the pool. I arrived and watched others lope in. Surprisingly, there were a few dudes that looked like they belonged on the football team. I recognized one in particular and knew about his reputation as a menace on the football field. Apparently, he never touched weights, but just swam to keep in shape.

We sat there and another imposing figure entered from a small office. He was intense, almost Tuce-like. He paced back and forth and said, "I'se here because I like swimming, but not half-ass swimming. I'se'll fine tune 'ya techniques. Owah strategy is to practice more 'den the guys on 'de uddah teams."

"Deyah ain't much in 'da budget fors us, but I'se'll make use of what we do have," he continued. "And 'dis'll will be the easiest day you have in quite a while."

I got home and the one thing we always had in our house were goggles and swimsuits since we all swam due to our shared Octopi-like bodies.

I went to school and sat through the institutional facts and figures, but I was thinking of swimming. The brick beehive bell rang, and we headed down to the pool. We were briefed. "Get changed into you'se suits, shower off any pond scum you'se got on you'se, and meet back here in ten."

We came back wet from the shower, all in different outfits and goggles. The coach announced, "We'se'll warm up with 40 laps, and 'den get into 'da timed swims." There was a massive clock on wheels that didn't tell local time; it was a giant stopwatch. Then there was a chalkboard. It had our swim instructions. First warm-ups, then 5x100 (that was 4 lengths of the pool with rest in between). The faster you go the more rest you get. However, the faster you go, the more you are out of breath. Then it was kickboards. Then a million other routines. He blew the whistle to start warming up. We swam warm-up style, which usually put me in a fantasy land. I would drift off someplace. Someplace where I was famous, or just an important person telling jokes at a yacht club, wearing my special Docksiders, canary yellow pants, and a sweater tied around my neck.

Coach then directed our attention to the giant portable stopwatch, and how to read it. He said it was now time for practice. All sets had to be done under a certain time. We were to do one set, look at the time and go right into the next set. Each lane had about three guys in it and we simply followed the lead, snaking our way back and forth. Coach started the clock and blew his whistle. We were off. I heard coach yelling and encouraging. "Dat's it move, move, move!" I pushed off again and noticed it was no more fantasy-land thinking. It was rigorous swimming, and gasping for air.

As my head bobbed out at the end, I heard more yelling. "Move it, move it, move it!!" I pushed off again and again. It was a blur of bubbles, blue lines on the bottom, the clock, and a red-faced guy pacing up and down on the pool deck. We finished, and I was gasping for air. I vowed to myself to never eat bad food again; from now on I would only eat broccoli and bananas. I felt the need to vomit.

It finally ended, and Coach gained my respect simply by saying "good job!" We were then singled out for what our individual strong points were and how we could best contribute to the team. Some were long-distance swimmers, some butterfly, some breaststroke; I was going to be a short distance specialist and backstroke. It was two hours of torture, but good torture. We showered and dressed. My father picked me up, and with his trademark handful of pistachios in his cheeks, he looked at me and said, "I knew it'd be good for ya."

I concentrated on eating only vegetables at dinner. I needed to get every type of junk out of my "yoo-man digestivez sytemz," as Tuce would say. I wanted to minimize that dry heaving. I didn't think much that night. The saying "crawled into bed" definitely applied to me.

Next day's swim practice was the same. During warm-ups I was in fantasy-land, imagining myself in Docksiders, famous, on the cover of magazines, being quoted. Then fantasy-land went out the window as the real practice started and we were timed. Afterward, I was informed that I would not only swim backstroke individually but also in a medley. That was a combination of swimmers in a relay, each performing his own specialty, finishing his race and touching the wall to release the next swimmer. All had to perform as a team. It was swimming and athletics at their best: not letting others down.

Our first swim meet finally arrived. It was held in a real boat people type of town. Right away one could tell by the shiny new cars, and lack of graffiti. All the lane markers on the streets were clean, straight, and freshly painted. Before we filed off of the bus, the coach said, "Men, 'dis is what you prepped for!" We filed in, showered and headed out with our half-assed towels, borrowed bathing suits, and grimy goggles.

We were literally laughed at. The other team was huddled together as we took our seats and everything they possessed matched. Their school obviously had deep pockets, and it showed. They all seemed to be the same height, weight, and build. All clones, now looking at us and laughing. Members of my team all had different shapes. The secret weapon on our team was a junior, the fastest at his event by far.

He didn't look the part, as he was tubby and had a major pot belly. He was built like a killer whale. The flab on his stomach protruded downward, over his small speedo suit, giving the impression he was naked, which obviously caused laughter. We were allowed a little bit of practice. After that, they seemed to stop laughing as they witnessed us swimming, as opposed to focusing on our sub-par gear or lack of athleticism.

It was showtime. Everyone took their assigned seats. The meet was on. I was up, and it was the "fifty freestyle." It was me, the obese guy, and some kid that is now a doctor. "Swimmers take your mark!" Bang. We were off. I didn't think, I just swam out of respect for my teammates and coach and for fear of coming in last. We finished one, two, three. The obese orca-like creature and future chef came in first, the yoo-man octopus and future electrician came in second, and the tiny future doctor came in third. We emerged from the pool, the misfits, all in different swimming trunks.

The coach ran over and got inches from our faces. He screamed, "Great job!" I dry heaved in the gutter and emerged to glance over at the clones, who stared at us in silent shame. We rested, and the other misfits on our team went out and did their thing, with great success. The meet had one final event, the medley – and we were again victorious. Everything paid off.

Blue Collar Misfits: 1

Suburban Clones: 0

I got home, and my father warmed up my meal. I told him about our success and, with succinct wit, he congratulated me with the name I was given after the guy that tarred our driveway: "Good job, Joe." He continued chewing. I slipped downstairs to the bar. I deserved "a stiff one" since I had worked so hard and succeeded. I mixed it and raised the drink and said, "Hula-boom!" – a local word for chopping wood, shoveling, working on cars and just getting it done. I drank it down and took a seat. The vodka did its magic, and I looked up at the plaster and thought of the life graph. I was surely heading to the top of that graph.

The season went on, and we continued to win. We never got the rally the football team got, but each week at home meets, more and more people filled the small stands we had. Having proved ourselves, about midway through the season, we got matching trunks. We were now in uniform. We still had blue-collar family towels with skid mark stains. But now when we lined up on the starting blocks our bathing suits matched. We performed well enough, and many of us made it to the state finals. The swim year ended with success. I was in the best shape of my life. My back was widening, and so was my neck. I pledged to try and watch my eating habits during the off-season and to *only* drink vodka straight, with no filthy, sugary additives. I would keep myself tight at all times. Maybe there *was* magic in those Docksiders.

A DISTINGUISHED GENTLEMAN

Ninth grade ended, and the good news was, I was no longer a freshman. My books getting dumped or an occasional slap on the back of the head wouldn't happen as often. I kept myself clean and attended the various drinking spots "only" two days a week. Sully and Blumpkin had migrated to their own neighborhood hangouts, Tibbs had disappeared into the Catholic school system, and Cashews had gone for "the ride," so I was spending more time with Simma and Mike B., whose father had taken us to Nauset Beach.

It was Columbus Day, and even though he didn't discover America, a day off is a day off, and Mike B. had smuggled a bottle from his house in celebration. It wasn't that difficult to accomplish, as his father seemed to always have a glass full of ice and adult drink in his hand. He was usually distracted, playing at the piano or making sales calls. We hit the contents of this new bottle, and right away it hit back. It wasn't the smooth, comfortable taste of vodka I had grown used to. I squinted during the first few gulps, and then the magic of alcohol began to spread through me and I was grateful to Columbus.

Evil Knievel was no longer jumping, but we were kids of the 70's, and would still perform tricks in his honor. After a few more slugs, we were thoroughly lit up, so it only made sense to break out our bikes and attempt to perform some stunts like Mr. Knievel. He surely must have had a few stiff drinks before performing his death-defying jumps. The driveways and embankments on Crystal Hill enabled us to attain great speeds and acceleration on our bikes. The jumps usually began with a small board placed atop a brick, but soon graduated to a full sheet of plywood leaned up against several cinder blocks.

That day I found a very strong wooden door and four cinder blocks. After some initial engineering, it was positioned at the perfect angle to line up with the banking I was going to land on. A few younger kids had gathered as I was about to take off. I pedaled up our neighbor's driveway, looked down on the crowd, waved like Evel Knievel, and began downhill. I had to remember to pull the handlebars back just before exiting the ramp. I pedaled down the driveway and banking and hit the pavement at high speed. I hit the ramp and pulled the handlebars back right on cue. I went airborne and then landed perfectly – but couldn't control the front wheel. The last thing I remember was wobbling violently out of control, being flung over a 10-foot ledge and finally flipping over the handlebars. Everything went dark.

I woke up to the smell of alcohol and pipe tobacco. The alcohol scent came from Mike's mouth; he was leaning over me. "Hey man, you went 12 feet in the air!" The pipe tobacco was coming from Mr. Viola's pipe. He was the neighbor who rescued me. He, too, was leaning over me and stated, "Can ya feel ya legs?" I moved my legs and said, "Yes sir." The only other thing I felt was pain on the top of my head and fire between my shoulder and neck. For some reason, I got up and ran. I was dizzy and noticed my right arm dragging. I made it into my house, hobbling. My sister's boyfriend looked at my misshapen arm and, after a short diagnosis, stated that I had *definitely* broken *something*.

I needed to go to the hospital. But my mother had just cooked a meal, which couldn't be interrupted.

"Eat some food, dear, it'll make you feel better," she said, as I veered in and out of consciousness, trying to chew.

The meal seemed to take forever, and once we were finished I was brought to the hospital in the Country Squire. The nurse assisted me to the x-ray room. A few minutes later a doctor came in with the x-rays. He said, "Well, there's no physical signs of damage to your skull, except for the fact that you've been drinking."

"And," he said, "you have a broken collarbone." I looked at him with pleading eyes. "Doc, *please*, don't tell my father about the drinking."

"Sure, kid," he said, winking, "as long as you don't tell him about mine. I'll give you a pill for the pain, and write a prescription."

My father came in and the doctor explained everything: how long it would take to heal, how long I had to refrain from all activities, and how to administer the pills for the pain. There was no mention of my drinking. *Whew*. I scarfed the pill, and a brace was put over my shoulders. I had to wear it for *six* weeks. We left the hospital, and I went straight to bed. I awoke, and the pain was back in full force.

My mother did the usual, with a twist. She opened the window a little more, to "kill the bug," and brought me a small plate of toast, some ginger ale, and one of the doctor's pills. I drank the ale, ate the toast, and followed with the pill. I could barely lift my head up without feeling excruciating pain. The pills were left on my nightstand. I couldn't go back to sleep because of the searing pain, so I just looked up at the plaster. About 40 minutes later, I noticed there was less pain. Was it the window being cracked open, the cold air "killing the bug"? Maybe it was the ginger in ginger ale. Maybe the toast had medicinal effects.

More time went by, and not only was the pain gone, but I began to experience a familiar feeling. The magic of the first drink, now found in a *pill*. Ah, euphoria. I was sure that, just like the Six Million Dollar Man, after this accident, I would be "faster, better, stronger." I rose out of bed, with no pain, and was able to use the bathroom. I looked in the mirror and even repeated, "faster, better, stronger."

I decided to experiment to see what was making me feel better – the ginger ale, the toast, the window being open, or the pain pills. I took one more pill. Moments later, a swell of euphoria swept over me. Okay, so I knew then it was the pain pills. I looked at the bottle and noticed the label had a little picture of a face with its eyes half-closed. I was feeling it: eyes half-closed to stress, to anxiety, to fear, to doubt, to insecurity and, oh yeah … to pain.

I looked at my Star Wars bed sheets. R2D2, C3PO, Chewy and everybody else looked happy. I stared up at the plaster ceiling. Faces and figures stared back at me from the patterns in the light. There were dead relatives, who seemed happy to see me like they were enjoying their stay in heaven. There were animals I had seen on visits to Benson's wild animal farm petting zoo. They seemed happy. I remembered one visit when I saw two turtles having sex, and the one on top was thrusting. My father told me they were playing hopscotch.

Getting up to pee, I walked to the bathroom and noticed the shag carpet and all the colors on it. Then I took in the kaleidoscope of colors on the fabric of the toilet seat lid. The feeling of carpet between my toes was like pudding. Who had the brilliant idea of designing a toilet seat lid made out of carpet, I wondered? How long did society suffer before the carpeted toilet seat lid had been created? And why were no schools or bridges or big New England rocks named after *that* person?

Peering around the bathroom, it seemed like all the trinkets began to look back at me. I had never really appreciated those things previously.

"Bathroom trinkets, Mrs. Winslow, aisle five, next to the 'going out of style' aisle where you buy your son's clothes."

There I was, gazing intently at bathroom trinkets. My Lord, we even had "show soap." Show soap was presumably real soap, but it was under no circumstances to be touched or used.

I wondered why it was even made of soap if it couldn't be used. Why not just make fake show soap out of plastic? After all, it was merely soap that other women who also bought trinkets could hold up and say, "Heavens to Betsy, Mrs. Winslow, where on Earth did you get this incredible shell-shaped, coral-colored soap? It's fabulous!" But then, being in on the whole show soap concept, they would place it back down in its soft and fluffy soap crib, the idea of using it to wash their hands never even entering their bee-hived brains.

I made my way out of the lovely blue bathroom, back to my cozy Star Wars sheets. I just stared straight up. I noticed one last fly, that must have been on one last crumb-acquiring or reconnaissance mission for the giant Chief blue-assed fly back at fly headquarters in the woods behind my house. He did his usual routine. Buzz. Stop. Look around. Buzz. Stop. Play with his hands. He flew around in a circle and then landed on the end of my nose. I had no desire to swat him.

I did consider telling him that it was his fault I wasn't on the honor roll, due to all the times he ruined my concentration while studying. There he was; we were face to face. I felt sympathy for him. People used him as an example of mental illness, like my father pointing to somebody who had just done something stupid or who had major problems in life, and saying they were "crazier than a blue-assed fly."

But there he was, on the end of my nose. Head swiveling like he was having a seizure. It appeared he had several eyes within his two main eyes. He rubbed his hands together like he had just come up with a brilliant idea. Maybe carpeted toilet seat covers for the little fly toilettes back at fly headquarters. I looked at his ass. It was, in fact, blue. Just like my eldest brother's Camaro Z-28 after a fresh wax. It was, actually, a beautiful fly ass. I made a buzzing sound as best as I could but slurred it. He spun his head counter clockwise a bit. I grinned. A bond was formed. I must have wished him to stay warm that winter because he became emotional. He must have shed a little fly tear because his front hands rubbed his many fly eyes. Then he was off and flew out the window.

Okay, now I believed in God again. Surely God was real. After all, how else did the blue-assed fly come into existence? We were Catholics and were supposed to believe in the Trinity. The father, the son, and the holy spirit. I imagined God at the top of the conveyer belt to heaven, announcing the creation of the blue-assed fly.

"He will be this big, he will have this many eyes, he will bother people at picnics. However, someday the almost-lost son of an electrician will see my infinite love and creativity in this fly, and he will come back to his childhood awe of all my work."

Then he started the conveyer belt, and the fly went down the belt, had his ass painted a lovely blue by God's son, and then he was given life by the holy spirit, before finally rolling down the conveyer belt to earth.

I was becoming emotional. Deep in my subconscious, I feared that the cry-cop Cashews was lurking. I knew he could emerge any second, returned from his "ride," and appear in my bedroom. If he witnessed even a tear or two he would run out of my house yelling, "Winslow is crying!" Biting my lip, I fought off the tears that were welling due to the joy of rediscovering God. Hmmm. Now I wanted to know God even more closely, to understand his mysteries even better. So, I decided to take another pill. I propped my head up and put the beautiful pill in my mouth and put my head back on my Star Wars pillowcase.

I laid back and waited for the magic of those laboratory ingredients to take effect. I fell deeper and deeper into a wide-awake dream. Now, I didn't even *want* to get out of bed. The deep thoughts were coming heavy, holding me down due to their ... deepness. I couldn't physically move. My body seemed cut off from my brain. My thoughts were so lovely they wouldn't fit into words. I drifted on clouds and sunsets until the face of Mr. Pill Popper popped into my mind.

Mr. Pill Popper wore a huge black hat, sported a Lincoln-like beard, and wore an impeccable black suit with tails. He carried a black, folded umbrella, and was always ready to pull it out to shield an elderly woman from the weather.

I was Mr. Pill Popper. I would walk the streets, and every once in a while, reach into my pocket to grab the prescription bottle, open my mouth, remove my big black hat and snap my head back, popping a pill.

Then I would walk around town, assisting people with all their needs. Saving children from car accidents. Preventing pets from running across busy streets. Walking by a playground, I would say, "Ma'am, you're pushing that swing way too fast for Little Johnny."

"Why, thank you ever so much, Mr. Pill Popper," she would say.

I would tip my hat a little in recognition. Then head off to dispense more advice and prevent any other accidents or near-misses. Clouds would form, and I would be there just in time to expand my umbrella over an elderly woman before she was pelted by rain. She would look up at me and say, "Oh, thank you, Mr. Pill Popper!"

"My pleasure, Mrs. Snodgrass," I would reply. "I'm ever so glad to be of assistance." I would tip my hat and nod.

Then my mother, who was physically incapable of walking into a room to announce a visitor, yelled from three rooms away: "Andy! Your friend Mike is here!"

I heard my friend Mike's footsteps coming up the stairs, and then coming down the hall. He peeked his head into my room. "Hey man! You alright?" he asked? He pulled up a chair. Mike was a natural chatterbox. Nowhere near the almost psychotic-level of jabber displayed by Cashews, but a chatterbox nonetheless. He described my record-breaking jump and subsequent epic wipe-out in clinical detail.

"Man, you were going about 60 when you hit that ramp. When you went over that ledge, you did a full summersault and your feet were like six feet in the air."

I was proud of having had my feet six feet in the air. He then said, "Man, you don't look so good. You're sweating and white as a ghost." I tried to speak but apparently could only talk in some sort of hybrid, half-fly, half-human dialect.

"Bzzzzzzzzz. Take a pill. Bzzzzzzzz," I said.

"What?!" asked Mike.

My brain finally connected to my body, and my left hand was able to grab the pill bottle.

"Bzzzzzzz," I said. "Bzzzzzz... take one."

He must have been served Flintstone vitamins as a kid because he was a real natural pill-popper. He threw his head back like a proper pill-popper and swallowed a pill. Then he ate my last piece of toast.

He asked, "So, what's it do?" I could only mutter, "Bzztt ... trust me."

He was still excited about my record-breaking bike jump, and said, "Man, you *are* the next Evel Knievel." He got up to leave, and said, "Okay, see ya around in a couple of weeks."

I lay there all warm and fuzzy. This was the way one should go through life, I thought. Then I thought of the Six Million Dollar Man and his recovery plan: faster, better, stronger. I had images of myself in the pool at a swim meet. Faster, better, stronger. Huge crowds, immense fame, a gigantic pep rally. Andrew Winslow was representing the United States in the Olympics. The school was sending me off to capture multiple Gold Medals. The yellow school bus pulled away. It had red, white and blue bunting on the sides and flags attached to the mirrors. In it were just me, the coach, and the bus driver.

Each town I passed through had its best cheerleaders assembled, jiggling and shaking their pom-poms. The cheerleaders formed a "W" for Winslow, one final gesture in recognition of me, their hero. Arriving at Logan airport, I walked onto my own special plane. The pilot announced, "We will be in Olympic Village in about 8 hours, Mr. Winslow. Just relax, and good luck." The stewardess wrapped me in my Star Wars sheets and kissed my cheek. I made a cute sound, like the Pillsbury Dough Boy.

I awoke to the phone ringing and then my mother yelling, "Pick up the phone!"

It was Mike B. Now he was talking the fly talk.

"Bzzzzzzzz. These pills are wicked pissah, man. Bbbbbbzzzzztttttt."

"Yeah," I replied. "Bbbbbbzzzzttt."

He hung up.

Night came, and my father returned home. "You'se hangin' in there, Joe?" he asked.

I nodded.

"I see 'dem pills got a refill on 'em," he said. "Eyez'll get more before ya runz out."

My mother left a fresh mound of toast and a full glass of ginger ale on the nightstand. I drifted off to sleep.

I awoke about six hours later and felt like I had just been whacked by a bat on the shoulder. It was a dull, throbbing, fiery pain. What was this? Moments earlier all was well and I was on a Lear jet heading to the Olympics. Now there was only one thought, and it was pain. I reached for my pills. I popped one, followed by some toast and ginger ale. How long would this take? I lay back down and waited, and sure enough, the pain started to drift away. Shortly thereafter, images of me being faster, stronger, and better returned, and I drifted off to sleep.

I awoke to my mother's voice.

"Wow, Mike, that was nice of you to come over before school."

This couldn't be the same Mike, I thought. He said he wouldn't return for two weeks.

"Andy! Mike is here!"

"What? Mike?" I thought.

Then, sticking his head around the corner, I saw that it was indeed Mike. Why, how nice, I thought, of him to check up on me. He pulled the chair up, and whispered, "What's in those things, man? I need a few more."

I nodded as he put two in his pocket and a third in his mouth. He snapped his head back, popped the pill, and then wolfed down a piece of toast. He disappeared. I was now minus a piece of toast and three pills. I got up to go to the bathroom. I took everything in again, the warm and fuzzy feeling of the carpet, the blue hues of the bathroom, the trinkets, the "show soap" sitting in its own basket, like Baby Jesus in a manger scene.

I used the toilette and closed the beautiful rug-covered lid that matched the blue rug on the floor. I washed my hands with the regular soap, all the while looking at the Baby Soap Jesus lying in its own soap crib. I looked in the mirror. There I was, half-closed eyes, just like the little face on the prescription bottle. I grinned. This was the way to go through life, I thought, with half-closed eyes, and zero pain.

I got back to my room, and it was all good thoughts. I could spend the rest of my life in that room. I lay down and felt a twinge of a throb of pain. For some reason, I held off taking another pill. I was curious how much pain I would otherwise be in from my horrific injury. That experiment didn't last long, as the hurt came back like a tidal wave.

All wonderful thoughts vanished, and now it hurt just to move in bed. I needed to avoid pain by all means. I grabbed for the pills. Now I was shaking and sweating with pain. The only thing I didn't like about the pills was, they took too long to kick in. Vodka, on the other hand, seemed to work much quicker. Then it dawned on me: "What if I was to mix the two?"

I grabbed the pill bottle and saw that it said something about not mixing with alcohol. But, surely, they must be talking about Schlitz or Captain Morgan, whereas I drank vodka. They couldn't be talking about my transparent liquid lady from Russia. Those Russians put a lot of thought into this, surely. I hobbled downstairs and passed by my mother, who spent most of her time outdoors. She was heading out with bulbs to plant before winter.

"My oh my," she said, "you're sure making a quick recovery!" She was confident in her ginger ale, toast, and fresh air remedy.

She headed out to plant bulbs. It was as if the Earth and my mother were spiritually connected. My father was the opposite. He hated anything to do with gardening. He said if he was single, he would pave all around the house and just paint it green. Once my mother went outside, she would disappear into her gardening world, and only reappear for a "slicker" if it started raining. It wasn't raining or about to rain, so I was safe going to the bar. I poured the clear liquid lady into a glass, held it up, and announced, "Hula-boom." I swilled it. I deserved it, having just set a record for the most amazing bike jump in the history of Crystal Hill. I cleaned the glass and headed upstairs. I looked at the first set of steps and remembered the days when we had to get my grandfather up the stairs to the second floor for meals. All the effort it took four men. People would be huffing and puffing.

I was now huffing and puffing. The alcohol was already doing its magic. The pain was leaving my body. Moments later, I was comfortably numb under my sheets. I drifted off into a pain pill and alcohol euphoria. I decided I would forever stay in this tiny room. Dieting on toast, ginger ale, vodka, and pain pills. I would write music, poems, novels, paint, and slide these major artistic works under the door. My agents would return with fat checks. I would sign them, they would be cashed, and I would have an endless supply of toast, ginger ale, vodka and pain pills.

Years later, after my death, not only would this house on Crystal Hill be famous, but there would be tours. "Now, ladies and gentlemen, we are about the enter Andrew R. Winslow room. He was a noted author, painter, and philosopher." Then they would discuss my diet of ginger ale, toast, and always keeping the window cracked to "kill the bug." The tour guide would leave out my diet of pain pills and vodka.

I heard my mother talking. "That's nice of you to keep checking up on him, Mike." It was my "friend" back to check up on me. He usually was pretty swift walking up the steps, but now, it sounded like the ghost of my grandfather wearing his massive brown shoes. Slow and calculated. He was even slow coming down the hallway. Then he stuck half his head in.

I saw his hair, forehead, and the trademark half-closed eye. Then more of his face, and that new pill-induced smile. He then politely said, "mind if come in?" Not being able to say much, I just made a gesture with my index finger. My "friend" proceeded to eat my last piece of toast and said, "Man, these things are awesome." He wasn't talking about the toast.

I signaled with my index finger to come closer. I slurred, "Try it with alcohol." He took a couple more bites of my toast and tip-toed his way out.

It became dark, so my mother wrapped up her gardening and started whipping up dinner. She made me another batch of toast and poured a fresh glass of ginger ale. She dropped that off, and with her man-sized hands touched my forehead. She cracked the window a little bit more. Tomorrow I would start my recovery exercises to become faster, better, and stronger. I had a brochure. I looked at the pictures.

I heard my father make his common entry announcement. "I'ze home!" He went into the kitchen and grabbed his usual can of Tab cola. He then headed for my room and asked, "You'se alright, Joe?" I pointed to the pills. "Ah, you need a refill!" he said. I nodded. "Okay, Joe, but just be careful not to take too many o'dem. I'm goin' to the drug store for you'se refill." He left, and the phone rang. My mother yelled, "Andy! It's your friend Mike!" I picked up the phone and heard Mike, but could only make out that he had a few drinks with the pills.

"I tooooooooook demmmmmm wit al-keeee haaaaah," he said and hung up. I understood the language. "He took them with alcohol."

I crashed and dreamt of everything being made of the same substance as the Nerf football. Bullets and bombs just bounced off their targets. There was no longer a hard landing on any surface. No more stitches, abrasions or broken bones. I came out of Nerf-world to some throbbing pain on my right shoulder. I had a fresh bottle of pills. I opened the bottle, tossed a few back, followed by some ginger ale and toast. I noticed my mother outside with her gardening bag and crept downstairs for a nice tall glass of vodka. It was time to perform the recommended stretches and exercises on the brochure for recovering from a broken collarbone. Faster, better, and stronger.

I was sweating profusely doing these exercises. Pain, the coward that it is, crept back into his corner, as the combination of vodka and pills took over. I glimpsed at my mother as she trenched, dug, and planted. I knew when spring came, her hard work would be seen popping its head out of the cold mother earth. All different shapes, colors, and sizes. With all sorts of different fancy Latin names. I drifted. Time flew by, and I was soon drenched in sweat. I took a well-deserved shower and climbed into bed. This routine went on for about a week, and then I returned to school.

No one could see the brace under the shirt I wore for the collarbone break, and we were still at the pushing and shoving stage. So, I had to tell the crew not to hit me from behind or slap me on the back. I was a bit nervous since the pills were running low. I needed them to concentrate in the brick institution. I was the model student on these pills, neither looking left nor right. They were like the sauce, but on these, I didn't feel like acting up or getting in a fight. I didn't feel much. That was the way I wanted it. But the beautiful bottle that contained these magic pills was running dangerously low.

I put the word out to the various neighborhood crews, and in less than 24 hours, received notice that a meet-up had been arranged. I was clandestinely introduced to a guy from the lower courtyard. It was funny, we went to the same elementary school, and were even in the same grade. He had in fact been an occasional victim of the slug train. But he didn't seem to have harbored any ill-will. In fact, I think he knew the rough treatment we had given him only made him stronger. Indeed, he now had a reputation for brawling.

He was a Leatherhead now and was known to go to the surrounding towns of Dedham and Norwood and return with a black eye or a fat lip. But word was, he would never back down from a fight. He never *won* a fight, but he never backed down, which in our world was equivalent to winning the fight. I attributed that to the slug train. He would get thrown down on his back and punched several times, but he never cried uncle.

I was told to meet him in the lower courtyard. Glass surrounded this courtyard. I peered around and spotted him. I walked out there with my high society docksiders. At the time most of the other kids were wearing Members Only or Barracuda jackets. In stark juxtaposition to my authentic Docksiders, I wore the discount aisle version of the Member's Only jacket, called "Numbers Only." I walked out to the courtyard with my maroon Numbers Only jacket, and contrasting Docksiders, to meet my former victim, now a known tough, wearing a leather jacket and work boots. Immediately, the Leatherheads were eye-balling my shoes. My contact looked at me from my feet up to the top of my head. He smiled and put his hand out.

"Long time, no see."

He didn't mention the slug train. I told him about my accident and the pain pills. He smiled and said to meet him at the pool exit at the closing bell. When we met, he said, "I live in the Maze." The Maze was a collection of homes that were built after World War II, and they all looked the same. Every single home and every single lot was utterly identical, except for the paint and landscaping. The Maze was a nest of Leatherheads. We went to his house. It was full of cats and a stench that 10 years of scrubbing with Pine Sol could never eradicate. He said his mother was divorced and always came home late, so: "Everything is cool."

I told him again about my dilemma, having just filled the script bottle, but running dangerously low. He said, "Yeah, that's a scary feeling man. I know that feeling." He then told me the good news.

"We are at an age," he said, "where more and more kids are getting their wisdom teeth pulled. Take notice, and gather that information."

Hmmmm, I thought. I never realized that this guy was such a tactician.

"If they are computer heads," he continued, "threaten them with violence if they don't bring a few pills in for you. Then there are the athletes and all their recent injuries. Don't threaten them, obviously."

I was catching on.

"Next," he said, "if you happen to have access to your neighbors' homes, check their medicine cabinets for any bottles with half-closed eyes."

He said he had a friend that worked at an elderly housing complex, and he was able to gain access to the medicine cabinets of the Q-tips, thus resulting in a fairly steady flow of pain pills and other sedatives. I was then instructed to "always share the wealth if you score." He said all this work and collective effort kept the pills rolling in. He then told me to relax, and walked away, returning momentarily with some paraphernalia.

He had a pill, and said it belonged to a "family." I wondered why he cared which family it was stolen from. Then he explained that the different pills belonged to different classifications based on the effect they produced, i.e., their "family." The pill he held out, he explained, was from the same family as the ones I was running low on. He then pulled out something he called a "bong," and a rumpled plastic bag. That was, he said, "Humboldt County sensimelia."

I was nervous, not only because of my low pill supply but because, after all, this was his mother's house. I said, "Eh, what if your mother comes home?" He chuckled and replied, "No biggie. She smokes too."

He prepped bong as I scarfed the pill. I pulled the lever to the couch and my legs flung up, exposing my docksiders. He smiled and said, "That's it, chill out man. You're going to be fine."

I was given bong instructions. I did exactly what he said, and he congratulated me with a laugh, exclaiming, "that's it, man."

Someone walked in another Leatherhead from the neighborhood. He nodded and took a quick glance at my shoes. The host mentioned my new itch for a particular pill family, and the other guy nodded. "All right man," he said. He shook my hand.

After that most mellow of rituals, we were of the same world. The product from California was working, and my responses to everything became delayed. Cartoons were put on, and the entire room filled with smoke. I had to be home by 6:00 p.m. sharp for the traditional Catholic meal. I looked at the clock. We continued to laugh at the cartoons. Popeye got power from spinach. We got power from another green, leafy substance from California. My eyes again found the clock on the wall, and it was time to go.

I went to get up, but felt light-headed, and remembered that I had taken some sort of pill. The host and his friend laughed a bit as I stumbled, but we were friends now, with a common bond, so it was friendly laughter. I shook hands and was off. Although I was only about a mile from home as the crow flies, every house looked the same, and all the streets were identical. I walked very slow, having no sense of direction. I noticed more Leatherheads walking around. I asked one, and it was obvious he was high as well. He looked at my shoes, and then at me. He must have seen my pink, pinpoint eyes, the universal secret handshake that we were in the same world.

I asked him where Pond Street was and listened intently to instructions on how to get out of the Maze. I finally made it home and noticed I still had a foul stench on my Numbers Only jacket. I left that in the boiler room, as very soon the smell of the oil burner that never worked correctly would wipe out the smell of burnt Humboldt County California sensimilla.

I was just in time for dinner and washed up. I looked at the "show soap" and then myself in the mirror. I was indeed pink-eyed but didn't blink. I got to the table, and it was, "our father, who art...." I ate a great deal, but my father knew it was for swim training and injury recuperation purposes, so he didn't make any wisecracks. I hit the rack. I was exhausted.

I would miss most of the swimming season, and it would be a while before I would realize my mission of becoming better, faster, and stronger. However, I proved fairly successful at "gathering worms and bringing them to the nest." The pill acquisition techniques my friend told me about worked like a charm. Working almost every Saturday in Boston neighborhoods as my father's electrical helper meant I gained access to a lot of medicine cabinets of the elderly. I was told as long as I "scored" some sort of half-closed eye pill bottle, the Maze scientists would use it.

We continued to gather these pills, and I was impressed not only by the strategy but also the information-gathering and distribution networks. Word went out quick about who had recent sports injuries, wisdom teeth extractions or stupidity-related injuries (such as my bike accident). We would then flock over to that person and demand, nicely, if they were an athlete, menacingly, if they were not, to hand over a few. If it was a computer head, they would have to fork over the entire bottle, and were suggested to go on aspirin, or tell their mother they lost it.

I felt kind of bad muscling a kid who recently had his wisdom teeth pulled. The surgery didn't go well, and his cheeks were black and blue. But I did the math like a greedy pill popper, which meant more pills for us.

He couldn't talk well, still having a great deal of gauze in his mouth. But word is, if you lose one of your senses, the other senses become stronger. So, he seemed to listen intently as I said, "We want some of your pills. Nod your head if you understand." He nodded, and then generously dumped half his bottle into a little sandwich baggy I had.

My collarbone eventually healed, but there remained a tenderness in my shoulder. I tried to rehab as best I could, and was able to catch the tail end of the swimming season. However, I wasn't the same swimmer, not by a long shot, and that affected me mentally. Coach still respected me, and put my poor performance on my injury. But I knew a lot of it was from my new-found fixation with pills. Anyway, he said, "Keep your chin up, there's still next year."

Now, I was getting frustrated with the pill phase, and constantly needing to be on the hunt "to score." It was a rush at first but was becoming a chore. Also, it seemed there was what the Leatherheads called a "jones" from this pill. I was told a "jones" or "jonesing'" was a reaction the body goes through after a drug or even lengthy alcohol use was leaving the body. It can cause fidgetiness, physical and mental pain. Exactly the things I was taking the pills to *avoid*.

I had been popping pills for some time by then, taking gradually more and more. The effect wasn't as strong and didn't last as long, so the "jones" came on more and more rapidly. I seemed to sweat, and my whole body felt like it had been beaten by a bat. The images of me being a respected man walking the streets with a black hat, Lincoln-like beard, and carrying an umbrella by my side – known, greeted, and respected by the townsfolk as Mr. Pill Popper – was gone. I felt every cracked tooth, every old wound from wok steki, every bang-up from pond hockey and backyard football, every sucker punch, kick and slap I received in my entire life. I decided to stop taking the pills.

Next, the physical pain was accompanied by a feeling of being nauseous. I got through initially with a few drinks, and the pill phase was over. I began to train with the weights my father had purchased and got myself back into the pool. Faster, better, stronger. The six-million-dollar swimmer. I even kept the drinking "down" to a few days a week. I was a lifeguard and would swim after hours, plus there were morning swim clubs as well. I was getting back in the groove. But the thought of the wonderful effects of popping pills would never leave my mind.

I made a few more new friends with the Leatherheads and lower courtyard crew, and we would now nod as we passed by each other. My Docksiders, lack of pills, and training and swimming would surely lead me back to the docks of high society. I had just experienced one of the "hiccups" or "speed bumps" in life, that was all. Just a slight deviation from Mr. Simonon's life graph. I had survived the hiccup, and was heading upward and onward again.

A Cute Fuzzy Baby Squirrel

I passed the test that life had thrown my way. A broken bone. A mad, crazy, torrid love affair with pills, which, like my short-lived first romance that ended abruptly one night on the football field, was now over. But, like the memories of my pretty first girlfriend, the thought of the pain pills and their euphoric feelings would forever be etched in my mind. Oh, it had been dreamy ...

Having the last fly of the season land on my nose, with its beautiful blue ass, and seeing him rub his hands together in deep thought. Seeing God's infinite intelligence in this fly. My revelations about the toilette seat cover.

Why did I not take in God's beauty on a daily basis? When I wasn't drunk or high? I missed the deep thoughts, but the recent jonesing scared me. The only thing comparable to coming off of the pain pills was the flu. But the jones was worse.

I would stick to the day-after sickness that alcohol brought. It lasted only a few hours, and could even be remedied after a few quick belts in the morning. Plus, there were many commercials on TV advertising alcohol, with pretty horses trotting down the road, guys catching fish and then having a few drinks, volleyball on the beach with jiggly, pretty girls, everyone laughing and sipping beers. So, I knew the sauce wasn't "bad."

The pills, however, were a bit sinister. They were hidden ... hidden in medicine cabinets, hidden in socks and lockers. Only whispered about. Also, you don't invite someone over for a few pills, after work. Or say,

"Son, go downstairs and get a few pills for these guys." I was done with it. With that determined thought, I felt the bounce in my Docksiders again.

Mike and I were walking to his house, and we noticed a rustling in the dead brown oak leaves. It wasn't just a wayward breeze: there was something under there. Cautious, we removed some of the leaves and found a cute, fuzzy, baby squirrel trying to climb up the embankment. He even turned to look at us and didn't seem frightened. He must have fallen out of a tree and was performing a squirrel limp up this embankment. My father had warned me about picking up wounded animals, as "Dey's can turn on you'se in a heartbeat and 'den tear 'ya ass up." I had seen a safety show about calling an animal control officer if you see an animal acting suspicious, like foaming at the mouth, or running around in circles.

I thought about picking it up but then thought about what a bite from a wounded animal would mean: having my ass torn up, and having to endure my father repeatedly saying, "I'se told ya so!" as he visited my torn-up ass in the hospital. So, I told my friend Mike to pick it up.

He was hesitant, but I pointed out that it was indeed cute, fuzzy, and a baby, and therefore posed no threat. I convinced him, and he placed his hands under the squirrel, like the good Catholic that he was, as if about to receive the holy wafer at communion. He bent down and came back up with the cute, fuzzy creature cupped in his hands. The squirrel looked somewhat relaxed, as if on a hammock. A hammock now made of Mike's devout Catholic hands, the same hands that received the body of Christ every Sunday from the priest.

We looked at it, and it appeared relatively calm. We didn't see any blood. We would do the right thing and call some animal rescue personnel. Maybe even push it around for a few weeks in a squirrel baby carriage we would build, feeding it ground-up acorns. It would be our squirrel, and we would have a name for it as well. Happy thoughts raced through my head, and I decided to pet its cute fuzzy head. He allowed me to pet it, and it even began to smile.

The smile grew and it exposed its squirrel teeth. They were massive. I guess they had to be in order to pick up those huge New England acorns. It started making a noise. Mike, obviously having more squirrel knowledge than me, said, "That's just how squirrels laugh." So now we were all laughing. Our laughter must have made the squirrel laugh even louder, for his noises became high-pitched.

I recalled this noise coming from squirrels behind our house. Now the "hands-on test" was certain: squirrels did indeed laugh. It was cute. The squirrel must have thought we were laughing at him, and not with him. His head looked quickly at me, then at Mike. His eyes bulged, and with the last quick turn of his head, he sunk his huge, overgrown, brown, acorn-eating teeth into Mike's thumb.

Mike was no longer laughing. He started running back and forth on historic Crystal Hill, all the while, with the cute, fuzzy baby squirrel clamped down on his thumb. I tried to remove the squirrel, but I couldn't keep up with Mike's erratic movements. He was trying desperately to shake the fuzzy baby squirrel. Finally, the thing realized that he wasn't chewing on an acorn, but rather a human thumb, and let go. It ran into the woods as Mike kept running in circles. I ran after Mike.

Being a lifeguard, I had to take a CPR and first aid class. I had passed with honors. Mike didn't appear to be having a heart attack, but he was bleeding. He needed a tourniquet, I thought. By this time, Mike had taken off, but he left behind him a pretty impressive blood trail. Man, I thought, that's a lot of blood coming from a wound produced by such a small, tender, cute, fuzzy little baby squirrel. I trotted ahead, following the blood.

It lead to his house. I burst through the door. His father was playing the piano with his adult drink and cigarette burning. Mike was still hopping around erratically, so I told his father to get a towel and get him to the hospital. He grabbed his drink from the piano, and with a cigarette dangling from his mouth, fetched a towel. Mike yelled, "Get me to the friggin' hospital!"

I looked at his father and said, "Glover in Needham ... not Norwood!" Norwood was known for amputating the wrong legs and other mishaps. Mike's father threw the towel to his son. They both sped off, Mike holding the towel, and Mr. B holding his adult drink in one hand, his still-burning cigarette resting between his lips.

Cashews would have been impressed, because Mike didn't shed a single tear. Nor did his lip quiver even once. I called a few hours later. His mother said, "Mike can't talk, he is sedated. What was he thinking picking up a wounded animal?!"

"I don't know what your son with thinking Mrs. B.," I said. "By the time I got there, it was too late to warn him about wounded animals."

"Well, we're waiting for the blood work to see if he has rabies, so let's pray he doesn't!"

I heard the word sedatives, and the pinball machine in my head came to life. I would now become a "friend" and show up with comic books and tootsie rolls for the same "friend" that visited me after my collarbone break ... knowing that I would get some pills.

Dinner that night was traditional. We blessed ourselves, and I spoke of the incident. My father then asked, "Didn't ya warn him about wounded animals? How they act when approached.?"

"Well, by the time I got there to warn him about those hazards, it was too late," I said.

My father, the electrician-slash-medical advisor said, with a lump of food in his cheek, "Dat bastud knows better now! If he's got da' rabies, dere is close to a hundred shots ya take right in 'da breadbasket!"

Then, of course, I had to hear for the hundredth time one of the stories of my father's childhood and his experience with rabies or close calls. The story was always the same, but the size of the animal or person he was fighting changed with each telling. So, "the rabid raccoon in Mattapan" stayed the same, except for its size.

"Eyez was walking to my friend's house as a kid in Mattapan. The trash was out and eyez noticed this black and white creature standing next to deez metal trash barrels. It den regis-ta'd to me dat it was daylights and deez bastuds shouldn't be outa da woods. So, it was obvious to meez dey was rabid. My friend came out, and I yelled, 'get a bat!' He came back out of da house with a bat and fearing for some elderly woman getting bit, I went after it. It stood upright and started walking towards me. I swung like Ted Williams and got a single. It shook its head and came after me again.

Dat time I hit a triple. It snarled and ran into the woods. I had tah swing upward to reach its noggin, so dat monstah had to be a five or six-footer!"

He repeated, "Never approach friggin' wounded animals," shaking his head, and looking at me, chewing his food.

I pretended to do homework but was thinking of what Mrs. B. had said. "Mike can't talk, he's heavily sedated." I grabbed a few comic books and some candy. I ran down to Mike's house and was greeted by Mrs. B. I acted real Eddie Haskell-like, just returning the favor to Mike. I said, "Hi Mrs. B., I would like to check on Mike, and give him a few treats."

She said, "He's downstairs, recovering." I went downstairs, and it was obvious he was on the pills. He was just staring at the cartoons playing on the TV. His baby squirrel-bitten hand was soaking in a solution. He motioned to the coffee table, and there were the pills. There was no communication, just grunts. Like a proper pill popper, I snapped my neck back, and let the pill roll down my gullet. Fearing Mike may have rabies, I didn't drink from his glass, but took a belt from one of his Father's brown adult drink bottles. I placed the few tootsie rolls and comic books next to Mike.

"We got refills!" he said with a smile.

It was time to get to school, so I ran to the bus stop. What was previously hairy eyeballs between me and the bus driver was different that day. I felt love for her. "Good morning bus driver," I said. She smiled. "Good morning to you too." She did look startled. I sat in my assigned seat up front. I sat upright, Docksiders pointing forward, not like a slacker all akimbo. I soon noticed that this was indeed a pain pill, but a lot more potent than any I had ever taken. We pulled up to the brick beehive, and I went to get up … but it was as if everything turned into Nerf-world, all squishy and soft.

School was different that day. I would become institutionalized. Sitting upright, watching the board, never looking left or right at females. Docksiders facing forward, I walked the hallways, and the ground was spongy. The day went by, and aside from the common side effect of sweating profusely, there was no telling I was under the influence. I made it back home and walked to Mike's house to "check up on my friend"

"That's so nice of you to be checking up on him all the time." Mrs. B said.

I went downstairs, and his hand was wrapped. He was still staring at the TV. He looked very content. He muttered something and I got closer.

"I doooon't .... Haavvvve ... ray beeeeees."

"Oh, you don't have rabies?" I said. He nodded. That was good I thought, but then ... What if rabies provided a year of pain pill supply? Maybe it wasn't good not to have rabies. I grabbed a couple of his pills. He was able to give me thumbs-up with his good thumb. I walked home on the soft, cushioned pavement. I finally arrived, and my mom was prepping the outside for some celebration. Witches and ghosts for Halloween, a turkey with corn in his mouth for Thanksgiving. She was sprucing up some seasonal ornament and asked how Mike was. I gave her the thumbs-up and announced, "He doesn't have rabies!" She said, "Well, heavens to Betsy, thank Goodness!"

Her ornament-sprucing would give me time to pour a stiff one. I crept downstairs and poured the transparent Russian elixir into a glass, placed a pill on my tongue, raised the glass, and toasted, "Hula-boom." I sat down on the couch. The plaster was different. I saw faces I missed. Dead relatives appeared. They were all okay and I knew that, as the eldest woman at a funeral parlor said, "They're in a better place."

I heard my father yell, "I'm home!" and I knew I would be eating soon. I heard them both prepping the meal and then holler, "It's ready." I went to the bathroom and looked at the show soap. I thought of the baby squirrel that could have been our pet, nestled in a soft comfortable bed, lying on a nice soft piece of trinket cloth. I got to the dinner table and we prayed. I mentioned that Mike didn't have rabies. My father then went into a long story about, "... a kid I knew growin' up." He never remembered the kid's name, but could explain in detail what happened.

Soon Mike and I had devoured even the refilled bottle. We both jonesed from the pills, but alcohol made it less painful.

THE COMBAT ZONE

The pill phase ended again, or at least the ample supply ended. Mike and I turned back to alcohol, which was in abundance. Besides the bars in every home of people we knew, there were many other avenues available to acquire this "forbidden" yet socially acceptable substance. I became reacquainted with the Phantom Shitter, who was an expert at alcohol acquisition.

There was a liquor store "in town," which meant in Boston. It was in Chinatown to be exact, and would sell liquor to anyone. We could easily get liquor from the older crowd in our town, but there was a decided thrill of going "in town." The Phantom told me it was like the *Warriors* movie: there were all different groups of people and all different neighborhoods, and we had to go through their turf and make it back alive to our zip code. Me, Phantom, and Polumbo became the Chinatown booze-getting crew. We soon got our routine down pat.

We boarded a bus in Islington, with those two wearing legitimate Members Only jackets, and me the fake knock-off. Same maroon color, just a different name. But still, it was obvious. The bus took us through Dedham, Roslindale and then finally Jamaica Plain. The homes there were much closer together, and if they had any land, it was minuscule. It was all much more congested. People were literally on top of one another.

We boarded the raised Orange Line and rode that for many stops. I was told by the Phantom not to look anyone in the eye, as it could cause a beef.

"Just look at the floor," he said. We got off that train and boarded another one, headed for the North End. I knew the North End for its pizza; there was a restaurant there where my father would hold up a slice and say, "Ah, dis is the best pizza in town."

But as we entered the North End from the subway, I didn't recognize it. We disembarked and I followed the Phantom. Then I saw it, like Nirvana glowing in the distance: a massive liquor store. I grew excited, but the Phantom said, "That ain't it." He pointed to an ugly, dirty tunnel, and said, "First, we gotta get the entertainment." We walked in the direction of the tunnel. There was then an alley just before the tunnel. We turned to walk down the alley. We came to an opening, and there was a very large man at the entrance.

"What do you'se want?" he asked, menacingly.

The Phantom, being experienced, gave him an order for fireworks. This many Roman candles, this many cherry bombs, this bottle rockets. The Phantom handed over the money. The big guy actually congratulated us and said, "Good. You'se guys came prepared." He then whistled, and another guy appeared. He handed him a slip of paper with our order on it. The big guy didn't say anything else, he just kept looking left and right.

I noticed under his big black leather jacket was a crucifix and gold necklace in the shape of Jesus, the son of God. I had mine on, too, but I didn't wear it like him, outside my shirt. I figured we were both Catholics, so I thought I would strike up a nice Catholic conversation. What was the name of his parish? Was he an altar boy? And oh, by the way, I was named after a priest. He didn't seem to be in the mood for talking. He just kept looking left and right.

Then the fireworks appeared in a brown bag. It was given to the big guy, who peered inside and then handed it to us. The Phantom looked inside to quickly count the order. That seemed to piss off the one-time altar boy, who said, "What? You'se don't trust us!?"

The big leather-clad altar boy then gave us the warning. "Listen, if you'se blow ya fingers off, don't come crying to me." I knew from my first aid and CPR background that in the event of fingers being blown off, I would put them on ice in a cooler and head to Glover Hospital in Needham to get them reattached. We left, and just before going into the narrow alley, I gave one last glimpse to my fellow Catholic. He was still looking left and right. We passed by another group but kept our eyes down, so we weren't jumped.

We got back on a train, and headed to Chinatown, which also bordered an area known as "the combat zone" or simply, "the zone." We got off the train, walked up the platform stairs, and entered the zone. Right away it reminded me of a circus. All sorts of entertainment. Even in broad daylight, there were pimps, prostitutes, bums, peep shows, strip joints, liquor stores. This particular liquor store would do business with anyone. The Phantom told us to wait near the back door, and he would be out soon. As we waited, I surveyed the human traffic.

Unlike a real circus, these people didn't look like they laughed or wanted to make people laugh. They all seemed to be walking away from, or toward, problems. I noticed a guy next to me that was staring off into the distance, to ancestors, or images from his past, I assumed. He was even screaming, but no one around cared or gave it any concern. They just walked by like he was a common fixture. A black guy walked by and must have noticed that we were waiting outside for our bottle.

"Be careful of the liquor, man," he said to me. "That is what will happen to you. He's got the wet brain."

"Wet brain," I thought. What the heck is wet brain? The Phantom reappeared and we now had two brown bags. We headed back on the Orange line, and by then, it was dark. We finally landed back in the Phantom's stomping ground, Martha Jones. We cracked open the vodka and pulled out the fireworks. The phantom lit a cigar and quoted the leader of the A-Team:

"I like when a plan comes together."

He flashed his trademark evil grin. I drank, but couldn't lose the images of that drunk talking to himself, and being told he had the wet brain. Could that happen to me? Nah, I wouldn't let it. This was just a phase in my life. Perfectly normal.

Men of Responsibility

I had all these years been attending a thing called CCD, which was a Catholic educational program. The good news about taking these classes was it was held in the early evening, not right after school. This allowed me to take my now customary afternoon drink. All the while, parents were thinking we were still in school, doing our homework. Yet there I was, at one of my favorite drinking spots, "The Lot," a few hundred yards from St. Margaret Mary's. After years of CCD and being an altar boy, confirmation was fast approaching. Confirmation was something about accepting responsibility for one's faith and decisions.

I was usually drunk at most of my CCD classes, so I really didn't pay too much attention to what was being said. I know it had something to do with a new faith and making responsible decisions. I pondered these thoughts as I stood at The Lot. Faith and responsibility. The vodka was working, and I was indeed having deep, responsible thoughts. I watched as the fancy cars returned from the city. One could see the changes happening in our town right from The Lot. There were fewer and fewer vans and pickup trucks coming home from a hard day's work. Now, I witnessed the shiny new foreign-named cars coming and going. The new people were all wearing Docksiders, I figured. I would become one of them someday. Cruising back into the town where I grew up in some fancy foreign car. Probably wearing an authentic Member's Only jacket.

Those thoughts were fleeting. I thought about what I had witnessed in The Zone. A man, that was once a boy. A boy, like us, who had probably raised his hand in second grade when the teacher asked, "what do you want to be when you grow up?" He proudly raised his hand in the air, and said, "I want to be a doctor." What happened, between that time, and "wet brain"? Was it the horrors of war? His upbringing? A series of wrong decisions? Years later, there he stood. A spectacle to us, who didn't have guys in our zip code standing and staring off into the distance, yelling at things we couldn't see. I thought of the guy and looked briefly at the bottle I was drinking. It was time for CCD.

We all met in the basement of St. Margaret Mary's and listened to the priest tell us what confirmation was, how to prepare, what we will become, and how to act after being confirmed. It was going to be held on the 16th of March. St. Patrick's Day was the 17th, the celebration of some Irish guy named Patrick that hated snakes. We usually had a big family dinner on that day, but this year the celebration would happen on the 16th after I was confirmed.

We then were informed that we would be going upstairs to the church itself to rehearse for this confirmation ritual that would take me into adulthood. As I went to stand, I was hit with the "vodka bat." It's a phenomenon that happens after slamming large quantities of vodka in a short period of time. Unlike beer, where the feeling comes on gradually, the vodka seems to swing a rubber bat at your head, the room spins, and your language is all of a sudden slurred.

I had definitely been hit with the vodka bat but was able to catch myself. Sully guided me to the steps. We made it up to the church and all its beautiful stained glass and stations of the cross, and I saw the angry image of our Lord and Savior Jesus Christ. The good news was, it was pitch black, so the sun wasn't shining through his head, reflecting his angry eyes through the stained glass down on me. I turned away from the image so he wouldn't see that I was drunk.

The priest mentioned all the important higher-ups in the hierarchy of the Catholic church that would be attending this ceremony. We would practice more during the week, but for that night we were dismissed. I got home, was feeling better, and my father mentioned what would take place at our house after the church ceremony. There would be a large spread and then, being half Irish and in consideration of St. Patrick, I would be given a Claddagh ring, which represents love, loyalty, and friendship.

I was now more focused on the party we had planned at The Shack. I didn't exactly like The Shack, because there were no escape routes. However, I knew some of the guys on the police force, from my father performing electrical installations, and they had Irish names. I figured they wouldn't be out patrolling since it was St. Patrick's Day and would be inside the station house enjoying their traditional boiled vegetables and corned beef.

Confirmation day arrived. We were about to become more responsible. We arrived early, and put on our red outfits and performed last-minute rehearsals. We would become adults and enter another spiritual dimension. I looked up at the stained glass image of our Lord and savior. All the lights were on, and it illuminated his face. Our eyes locked, and his eyes said, "I know you are going to the shack tomorrow." I quickly turned away. He knew. After all, he was all-knowing.

The church began to fill: aunts, uncles, grandparents, parents, brothers, sisters, wheelchairs, walkers, canes, hearing aids, dentures, children's diapers, adult diapers – all to witness me enter another level of spirituality and responsibility. We prepped, pushing and shoving. Knowing that in 24 hours we would be drunk as monkeys. As everyone took their seats, the local hierarchy of Catholicism walked out. They were dressed in the finest linen, wearing all different types of hats. The guy with the highest pointy hat was obviously the most important, and he had a big golden staff. He didn't look that happy for being the holiest of them all.

We filed in by twos. Girls on the left and boys on the right. Everyone stood up for us. Then the guy with the tallest hat handed it to an altar boy, and the hat disappeared. He motioned for everyone to sit and they all sat. Some took longer than others. Then he went into discussing what we were all gathered for. This is when the blue-assed fly syndrome entered and I drifted off, all the while trying to avoid eye contact with the highest-ranking priest, and the stained-glass image of Jesus.

I thought of the life graph, me heading in the right direction, celebrating tonight's big achievement ... but being at The Shack tomorrow. I thought of St. Patrick and his accomplishments of clearing snakes out of Ireland. We did the standing, sitting, kneeling thing, received the Eucharist, and then shook hands. After all that, the highest ranking spiritual leader came over and said a very special prayer in Latin, and touched our foreheads.

We were now responsible.

We all filed out and everyone stood up for us. We took off the robes, and I was greeted by my family. We headed home, and before dinner, there was the special ceremony for me where I was handed a box with the lid opened to the sparkle of a gold Claddagh ring. My grandmother Gertrude Foley gave me a big smile. I was still her "pumpkin," and she let me know by placing her hands on my cheeks and saying, "Congratulations, pumpkin."

I was a happy pumpkin. I was being rewarded for my hard work thus far. There were too many people, and too much attention on me, and my gnawing anxieties returned. I needed a drink, to quell this uncomfortable feeling. All the guests were on the bottom floor, surrounding the bar. I needed a drink. I knew there were always bottles of wine on the back deck, chilling. I wasn't a wine drinker, but ...

I excused my newly spiritual self and headed upstairs. I went out into the back deck where several bottles of wine stood on the wooden table. One was cracked open, and I nervously turned the cork and said, "hula-boom," before drinking the whole thing in a swig. The wine took effect immediately, and I could tell it contained some sort of a giggly ingredient. No wonder, I thought, that the people of the Evil Empire in Russia never laughed. Vodka was missing this giggly ingredient.

I mingled. A mellow guy that reminded me of Howard Cosell started talking about sports. He would say something like, "Pass the pineapple dish." Then, "Oh, this reminds me, I was watching the Bruins play the St. Louis Blues, and...." Or, "Yeah, it was the Foreman-Frasier fight, and I was eating pineapple at..." I fit right in and shared my best swimming anecdotes. I told him about my injury and missing most of the season. He encouraged me, saying, "Ah, you'll be better next year."

I felt comfortable. Thank you, alcohol. We were all happy. We ate and had a few more drinks before getting everyone back into their cars. They were protected by Jesus and would get home safely, for they all had the Patron Saint of elderly drunk driving on their dashboards.

The Lights Were Getting Closer

I told my parents that a buddy of mine from the other side of town was having a traditional Irish meal and celebration and that I was invited. They thought it was a good idea to celebrate my Irish ancestry with a traditional boiled meal, and let the leash go a bit since I was now confirmed and responsible. I was picked up by the Phantom's sister, and we drove what seemed to be about fifteen minutes, then the Phantom yelled, "Here!" He then yelled, "Run!" and took off like a shot. I followed him, but he was a land athlete, very fast in football and stealing bases in baseball.

He ran way ahead of me and disappeared into the Shack. I saw a brief light and heard a noise as the door opened. I headed for the light, running so the neighbors wouldn't see us. I got to the Shack, panting, and politely knocked. The door opened. The historic barn was wall to wall with Irish American revelers. Many were dressed in green and there was a big green ornament in celebration of St. Patrick. There was also a big bag of green grass, from the lovely hills of Humboldt County, California.

The product was being rolled and packed. I paid for the vodka that my friend from the Irish Riviera bought, and drank heavily – but now responsibly – being recently confirmed and having entered manhood. Some of the green product was packed into a bowl. Marijuana cigarettes and pipes went in every direction. Maybe some were for right-handed people and the others were for left-handed people. I took in the other crews from all over town. I noticed a few Islington Burners. Guys that were probably never *not* stoned. I noticed when the bowl hit their mouths, they looked like

243

naturals, and could make it glow from their powerful inhales. Also, they never coughed or sputtered.

Simma motioned to me to pass him the bottle. I nodded and passed it. I guess I was having fun. How is fun measured? Can it be measured? There was the Mood Ring of the 1970's. It changed colors, supposedly based on the mood of the wearer, but more likely based on the temperature of the finger it was on. Why wasn't there a Fun Bracelet? It could show you if you were having fun or not. I could invent that, and make millions, I thought.

Irish Americans and actual Irish people and wannabe Irish people were buzzing around me, "celebrating" St. Patrick – but I drifted off into my dream world where I was the inventor of the Fun Bracelet. Not only would it tell you if you were having fun, but it would record the time you had fun and for how long. Say you had a blackout the night before ... the Fun Bracelet would remind you the next day how much fun you had. My fantasy was interrupted when someone yelled the word, "Cops!" Every pink-eyed sheep in that pen became instantly silent. There was only one way in and out of The Shack, and everybody was now crowding to get to it.

They were all worried about escaping, but I yelled to Simma to grab the bottle. The police were getting out of their cruisers. We made it out the door and in a mad dash, I followed the people in front of me through some trees and bushes. We ended up in a small field. I saw the police flashlights head towards The Shack. It was a strange scene in my vodka and marijuana and adrenaline-enhanced state. I couldn't see the actual police, just the beams of light from their flashlights undulating through the woods. They looked like aliens. Then the aliens shined their lights toward us. Immediately, insults started to fly.

"Hey, you fat basstuds!"

"Hey, you donut-eating son of a whore!"

"Hey, Piggy! Oink, oink!"

Instantly, a wave of rocks and sticks and more insults crashed down on the other-worldly police aliens as they made their way closer. People were pushing and shoving in the dark and I decided it would be an excellent time to back away quietly and let the rock-throwing revelers and the light-beam police have fun together without me. I began to attempt to walk home, however, the journey was a jumble of scratching tree branches, stumbly rocks, spongy sidewalks, car headlights, and parking lot security lights. I just kept walking.

After a few blocks or miles, I noticed there were people walking with me, fellow evacuees from The Shack. Then the flashlights reappeared and everybody scattered. The alien flashlight spoke to me and said, "Freeze!" I remembered the safety tips from Mutual of Omaha's Wild Kingdom, especially the ones about being stalked by alligators. They can only run straight, so if being chased by an alligator, the thing to do is run in zig-zag formation. Or, push the guy next to you into the gator's mouth, and at the funeral parlor tell the mother of the victim that her son was very brave and fought the alligator to the death so that I could live.

"Well, Mrs. Snodgrass, at least your son in a better place."

I had experience with zig-zag running from Tuce's summer program. I would make Tuce proud and at the same time lose this alien alligator with its light beam on my tail. I was awful with land sports and immediately saw my friends pass me by. First, it was the Phantom. He disappeared in a flash. Then the adopted black kid from Puerto Rico zoomed by. He ran track and passed me like a shot.

I heard jingling. The lights were getting closer. The light could now talk. "Stop running," the light said. However, Tuce taught us to never stop, to never give up. So, I wasn't going to stop now. I would make Tuce proud. I rounded one more imaginary orange highway cone and felt a metal thud on the back of my head. Then the alligator was on me. I knew I had to wrestle with this gator before it went into its death roll. I would fight it to the end so the Phantom and the adopted black Puerto Rican guy could get away, and they could tell my mother how brave I had been sacrificing myself so they could escape and live on.

Maybe it was the metal smack on my head that snapped me back to reality. But as I prepared to wrestle the alligator, I noticed it was, in fact, a police officer from the local station. He didn't look like he was in the St.

Patrick's Day spirit. Then I felt a brand-new shoe kicking me from above, and metal, non-fun bracelets were wrapped around my wrists.

I was escorted by both cops to their car and roughly tossed in the back. The fat cop helped me get in the car more quickly by kicking me as I leaned in. I looked out the window and saw neighbors shaking their heads and looking at me with a mixture of condescension and horror. We cruised away and within a couple of blocks, I saw a shabby looking guy jogging down the sidewalk. It was Sully. The police slowed down to where we were driving alongside Sully. They rolled down the window and motioned for him to pull over, even though he was literally jogging. He looked at me in the back seat and stopped running.

"And just where was you tonight?" asked the first cop.

"Yeah," chimed the second cop. "And why are you covered in mud."

"I was sledding," said Sully, panting, hands on his knees. Seeing how it was March and there was no snow on the ground, that was the wrong answer. Like two fat alligators attacking a hapless baby gazelle as it gently sipped water from the edge of a pond, the two police officers immediately and in unison took Sully down, one knee in his back and another on his neck, and handcuffed him. They flung him around a bit and then tossed him in the backseat next to me.

"You'se kids are in BIG trouble," the one cop said.

"BIG trouble!" added the other one. I wondered which of these two could eat more donuts in an hour, and figured it would be a close call.

"Throwing rocks at the police? Calling us fat bas-tuhds? Making us chase you'se 'trew the woods … when we should be back at the station celebrating St. Patty's?"

By now the vodka and marijuana fog had almost completely lifted. It dawned on me that I was probably in trouble. BIG trouble. We got to the station, and the police relived us of our belts, shoelaces, wallets, keys, and jewelry. A mere twenty-four hours after my Claddagh ring had been placed on my hand by Grandmother Gertrude Foley, it was now placed in a plastic police property confiscation box. I sat on a bench in the waiting area by the night desk, wondering what was next when … literally out of nowhere my father appeared.

"Why, you bastahd!" I heard him yell … right before he tackled me and wrestled me to the ground. The police joined in the pile to "get him off" me but I'm pretty sure they landed a couple of courtesy blows in the process. He was finally pulled off me. I was tossed back on the bench. My father processed me out, and I could feel his raging, silent scorn from across the room.

He drove at record-breaking speeds all the way home. Not a word was said. When I got home, there was my mother, wringing her hands and crying, "Oh, I'm so embarrassed, I'm SO embarrassed…" That was too much for my father. He made another goal-line tackle right there in the kitchen after yelling, "You basstud!"

My brother Lead came up, and thankfully put some distance between us. The night went on like this for quite a while … my mother wringing her hands, exclaiming that she was quite embarrassed, that driving my father nuts, and him diving at me while calling me a bastard. Finally, because of his age, he ran out of breath. I went to bed. As I drifted off, for the briefest, most wonderful of moments, I really, really, thought it was all a bad dream. Alcohol was my friend; this couldn't happen on alcohol.

Then I woke and my head was throbbing. It was covered by lumps, an especially large one behind my right ear.

"Get up, you bum!"

My father had stuck his head in my room.

"We will talk later! Oh yes we will," he muttered as he walked away.

I hobbled out of bed and wobbled off to school.

The day flew by, and I was thinking about alcohol and the life graph. This was merely a small hurdle, or hiccup. "Repent and don't do it again," I told myself. I got home and was told to sit in a chair. I sat. My father was now foaming at the mouth as he read out my sentence: grounded until further notice, ass in a sling, goose cooked, etc., etc.

We had a court appointment on Monday. I would get back on track again shortly, I assured myself. One thing was for certain: I wouldn't drink at The Shack again. That was the real problem here, the lack of appropriate entrances and exits at that place. The other lesson, I thought, was to always, always address police officers beginning with sir and ending with sir.

Hey, lessons learned!

I awoke Monday to the yelling of, "Get your best suit on, wee'ze got to take your sorry ass to court!" It seemed the only time I put on a tie was a death, a special religious event, or a happy wedding. Now this. We got to court and the place was literally packed with people whose St. Patrick's Day celebration had gone wobbly. Today's appearance was apparently just a "hearing." Later, there would be a "sentencing." Sully arrived with his parents and we all sat on a bench. The cop that represented the town showed up and spoke with my father. I heard mention of rocks, sticks, insults being thrown at his boys.

"Eh, I can't believe all this stuff 'day was being 'trown at us," he said, as if we had perpetrated the crime of the century.

There must have been thirty kids at the party, but only me and Sully were being held responsible for all of their actions. And I had neither thrown any object toward the police nor hurled any insults.

As we were sitting on the bench. I heard chains and foul language. Then three of the scariest looking dudes I had ever seen in my life walked toward me. They were going to a place for bad adults. This was another case where I shouldn't have made eye contact. These guys were not only handcuffed but were also chained together at the waist and the ankles. They wore scrubby, ill-fitting orange jumpsuits. Most had bruises on their faces, and tattoos covered every inch of visible skin. I accidentally locked eyes with the tallest guy. He glared at me, with a little twinge of a smile in the corner of his lips.

"I'll be waiting for you'se, princess!" he said, in a very thick Boston accent. I did the manly thing and looked away, trying not to pee my pants. My father was beet red. Then the shorter guy on the chain gang looked at the cop, and said, "Seriously? You'se guys got nothing better to do but arrest a few kids drinking!? Big bust, huh? You all getting' commendations for bravery?" Then he started to cackle, along with the fellow chain gang associates.

The cop looked humiliated and then a very large prison official dragged the three of them into the hallway, as they were still laughing. We were called into a room and the cop representing our town described to the judge in great, dramatic detail exactly what had gone down at the Great St. Patrick's Day Riot. I giggled a bit at the sheer ridiculousness of the tale he was weaving, and the fact that I was being held responsible for a mob action.

"Oh, you think this is funny?" said the judge.

"No 'ya hona," I said sheepishly. "It's just that, I didn't throw anything. I was just trying to get away."

I then remembered that I may have in fact shouted, "donut eating bastards."

The judge, in what seemed to me like highly un-sound legal reasoning, said, "Well, you were with those that did, so you are just as guilty!" I was about to engage in some spirited legal debate when I felt my father's breath behind my neck. I felt his foaming, purple stare pierce a hole through the back of my skull.

Sentencing commenced and resulted in probation by the Dedham district court, and "not seeing the light of day" until further notice by my father. The only light I was going to see was the New England sun – which didn't seem to be that warm – from behind the windows of my room, the school bus, and classrooms at the brick beehive. My father dropped me off to school with a "rolling stop." The truck was still moving when he shoved me out the door. I rolled to the ground and my nice suit was ruined.

The year of tenth grade wasn't a good year. But, hey, I took my licks and learned about a few things. The half-closed eye pills. Jonesing. Never to drink at The Shack. Always address police officers with a "sir" in the beginning and a "sir" at the end. I now had a deep, fearful respect for the power of the police. I didn't, however, respect them chasing and beating kids that were just having a few brews. But boy, I was glad when the year ended. I chalked everything up as merely a phase. A pill phase. An arrest phase. Probation phase. Just minor deviations on Mr. Simonon's life graph.

MARIO FRIGGIN' ANDRETTI

I visited the bone specialist one more time. He took the x-ray and showed me how my collarbone had healed.

"The part that broke off ended up resting on the other part," he said. "There will be a bump there, and the length from your shoulder to your neck will be shorter than on your left side. No one will notice ... and, hey, you weren't going to be a model anyway!" It was the same doctor that told me he wouldn't tell about my drinking if I didn't tell about his. We both laughed.

I recovered fully, minus the lump and the fact that my two shoulders would no longer be symmetrical. Any future modeling career was ruined. I set out once again to become faster, stronger, better. The six-million-dollar 11th-grade swimmer. I watched what I ate, and didn't put any filthy additives in my vodka. It was pure vodka only for me, the health nut. Pure clear vodka from the clean mountain streams and fields somewhere in Russia. No more pills – and no more smoke, I resolved – would enter my asymmetrical body.

I swam all summer between 10th and 11th grades. I swam as a lifeguard at Houghton's Pond in Milton. I swam at the Irish Riviera. In between swimming, I did push-ups, sit-ups and hit the weights. Junior year finally arrived, and I was ready to go upward and onward on my life graph. Some guys were getting drivers licenses, and I was old enough. I took the courses in an official school driver's ed car. There was a pedal on the passenger side, so if the lady felt I was out of control, she could slam on the brake.

As soon as I got in the car, I noticed that she stunk of liquor. "Ah," I thought. "This will go well because we have the saucer's bond." She would doze off every few moments and then awake shouting, "slow down!" or, "watch out!" Test day came and the driver's ed lady sat in the back. A real straight-laced officer got in the passenger's seat. Not a wrinkle on his outfit. This was a guy who surely ironed his underwear. He said nothing, and just scribbled words on some form.

No opportunity for bonding with this guy.

No, "What does your father do?"

"He's a union electrician."

"Oh, my father's a union plumber."

None of that. He just scribbled on his clipboard said, "Pull out."

I looked in the rearview and started pulling out. Then the passenger brake slammed down, and he said, "Get out ... you failed."

I had heard of one girl from the Izod part of our town salvaging her driving career in this exact scenario by merely crying – but I didn't know how to cry. Even if I did, I still feared running into Cashews and having him spot a quivering lip or tear in the corner of my eye and yelling, "He's crying!" I went back into the registry and set up another appointment. At that night's traditional Catholic dinner, I announced my failure.

My father said, "You and me Joe, we'll go through a driving boot camp. By the time I'm done with you'se you will be Mario friggin' Andretti." I didn't know who that was and assumed it was one of the guys that tarred our driveway in the early 1970's.

So, I now had driving practice every day. Two days a week with the lady that smelled of the sauce and every other day of the week with my father. My father would grab a cup of coffee, and then we were off. After a few loud gulps of coffee, which made his complexion more red, and his eyes protrude out more than normal, we were off. It was two hours of, "slow down!" and "look out!" and "you'se gonna get us both killed!" and "holy mackerel!"

We went to the high school parking lot, thank God during early hours when no one could see us. He would get out and with his trademark Dunkin' Donuts coffee and red complexion, I would have to drive around him, stop at his shins, and do three-point turns. In the beginning, there was a lot of screaming, but as time went on I got better and better. Soon it went from, "Holy mackerel!" to "That's it, that's the ticket!" Finally, we were ready for the re-test.

My father was there that time, and I think with his significant broken jaw, coffee induced red face, and bulging eyes, the mean, underwear-ironing testing guy seemed a little less intimidating. I did everything he said: parallel parked, three-point turns, backed up straight (and did it with my head turned around this time). After each exercise, my father would say, "That's it, Joe, just like I showed ya!" I think the testing guy was just happy to get away from all my father's commentary and cheerleading and coffee-induced fidgetiness.

"Okay, kid, you passed," he said.

Then I drove home. My father always had pistachios with him. No matter where we were he always managed to pull out some pistachios like he was performing a magic trick. He sure wasn't one to give hugs or even high fives. But, I could tell what kind of mood he was in by the way he ate his pistachios. If he fidgeted with the shells one at a time, he was not happy.

If he threw a handful into his mouth and then somehow skillfully kept a wad in his cheek while continuously adding 5-6 new ones every few minutes while talking – he was happy. On the way home, he did just that. He threw about thirty into his mouth, pushed about twenty-six into his cheeks, and skillfully chewed four at the same time while proudly saying, "Winslow's never fail!"

Thank God, I thought, he wasn't eating them one at a time. That was, "gonna break someone's ass" pistachio mode, for when someone owed him money, when somebody was driving poorly and slowing him down, or when I had done something wrong. In those cases, he would eat the pistachios one by one, chewing them very slowly, staring beet red at me or off to the distance at the mental image of the person he was resentful at. He would put a few in his hands, grab one, chew it very slowly, and mutter about the resentment and what he was going to do to the person he was resentful at.

Despite my success, I was rarely allowed to drive. It was usually just to pick up groceries, a can of pistachios and a six pack of Tab for my father, or on our sojourns into the city to do weekend electrical work for distant relatives. Sully had recently gotten his license, followed shortly thereafter by Simma.

So now it was no more bus rides, sitting straight and quiet behind the bus driver. We were now men. We drove everywhere. Usually, Sully drove to school. He earned the nickname of "gas/brake" because he always had one foot on the gas and the other on the brake. We were typically nauseous after a few miles, and someone would have to tell Sully to pull over, so one of us could drive.

Simma's father was a mechanic at MIT who took apart and rebuilt machinery for the nerds. As a result, Simma usually spent Saturdays working on cars with his father. He did this every Saturday without fail, through all sorts of weather, in either the unheated garage if it was raining, or outside if there was no precipitation. His father was showing him the ropes of auto mechanics.

Simma would typically drive up in a different 1970's used car every time we saw him. He would mention that they had put some special part in the vehicle, usually from MIT, and then with pride would rev the engine. His hands were cut up from wrenches slipping, but it was all worth it. We would break records getting to school or on "road trips" to far-off lands 30 or 60 miles west of us.

I was deathly afraid of drinking and driving and was limited with my car use anyway. The funny thing was, Simma would actually drive *slower* under the influence. We taught Sully how to drink and drive, which seemed to improve his performance as well. When he was drunk, we convinced him to put his left foot under the seat and to rarely use the brake. But once he was sober, it was back to gas/brake.

The Oceanographer Sighting

I was allowed to take the car for errands, and one time my father said, "Gets some gas at Mike's and 'den go to 'da Dean Street cah warsh in Nahwood and get it warshed." Mike's was the Sunoco diagonally across from Simma's and just a few hundred yards behind it was the watering hole for the class above me. Mike Lally, the owner, was from the old school.

His parents couldn't afford a polio shot, or he skipped school that day and missed the vaccine, so he got bit by the polio bug. Thus, he had a severe limp. Sometimes he would lose control and regain his balance by grasping onto your vehicle. He had the ability to smoke while pumping gas, somehow not causing an enormous explosion.

He always had a friendly New England greeting with the dangling cigarette, popping his head in your car.

"How'z ya faddah?"

"Good."

"Good tah he-yah. Tells 'em Mike sez halo."

Then he would give a special window wash, and a final blessing of, "You'se can see clearly now."

Then he'd hobble away after tapping the roof.

I made my way to the Dean Street car wash and remembered my father saying something about getting the Super Deluxe and giving me an extra buck to "duke" the towel man. I waited in line and finally got to the front.

"Super Deluxe," I said.

"Right on man, that's the way to go," said the attendant. I pulled in, put it in neutral, and put the Country Squire's seat down a bit while the automation took over.

Soon, I couldn't see anything. Everything was covered with soap, then the black rubber hula skirts and brushes went into motion. When my view opened again, I could make out a very tall figure standing with a towel at the exit of the car wash. The figure became clearer as the vacuum machine sucked the water off the car. The guy had long blonde hair, was wearing a poncho, and stood very tall. He was a bit damp from working in and around a car wash and had some soap bubbles hanging off his poncho.

He was fully smiling now as I hit the button and the window rolled down. He leaned over and said, "I know that license plate, man!" I absolutely did not recognize this tall, blonde, damp, soapy figure in a poncho. Then he said, "Hey I'll towel your car, then we'll talk, man." The guy had real long arms, making him the perfect towel man. Shortly, the Country Squire was all dry, from the two-towel technique application by this dude. He yelled in the direction of the entrance and said, "I'm takin' five, man!"

He looked at me, and said, "Pull over here!" I pulled off and got out. Then this damp figure said, "It's me man, Cashews!" I was six-foot-two. When last I saw him he was a scrawny, Ostrich-necked kid not more than five-foot-nine. Now, here he was standing at least six-foot-five with shoulder length blonde hair.

We just looked at each other. He mentioned that I had filled out and my head no longer appeared so large. I was kind of stunned still, so just listened to him. He said he followed "the dead," and then explained, "... the Grateful Dead."

Then someone yelled, "Hey Cash, break's over!"

We shook hands and he said, "Hey, I'll see you around." I looked in the rearview as my fellow future oceanographer toweled off another car. As kids, we were obsessed with sea creatures and becoming oceanographers. Now, here we were in our mid-teens. Cashews was drying off cars and I was in the grips of alcohol.

PIGEON CITY

There were now infinitely more transportation options available to get to and from parties. Woods parties were becoming less and less frequent. I still liked bending the elbow outdoors. There had been another heist at one of the local liquor distributors, which meant cases and cases of those giant cans of Foster's were readily available and in high circulation. I wasn't a big fan of Foster's – or any type of beer for that matter. However, it had that "heist discount," so the price was right. I went to a small get-together with my friends Beanz and Seanzo, and the Foster's was flowing.

Both guys were from the Pigeon City area, located in a part of our town that was surrounded by the high-speed commuter rail, Route 128, East Street, and Route 1. They were both Gearheads with tendencies in the Armyhead direction. They took everything apart and reassembled it for fun – lawnmowers, dishwashers, electric fans – and now they were building their own cars. Gearheads. They had the latest crossbows, pellet guns, traps, and survivalist gear. Beanz had stacks of magazines like *Field & Stream* and *Soldier of Fortune*. Armyheads.

I got the invite to Pigeon City shortly after the Foster's heist; Beanz had bought a major quantity on deep discount. I felt safer at Pigeon City than drinking in the woods. I liked the outdoors and bonfires, but now was extremely anxious about the constant threat of a nightstick or 20-inch metal flashlight full of D batteries. Plus, if there was a foreign invasion, being in the company of Seanzo and Beanz would be the safest spot. We stood on the middle of the inbound tracks of the Massachusetts Bay Transportation

Authority ... A.K.A. the MBTA, where my father had worked for nearly three decades.

Being a good host of his establishment, Beanz briefed me on the escape routes. The police could only enter from one direction, the Dedham side of the tracks. He had cut holes in the train fences by the railroad company markers. Once you saw the markers, you quickly counted your steps, and either took a sharp left or a right. I remembered that I still had a little probation time left, so I listened to the instruction intently. Once you took the sharp left you dove on your belly, and slid under a guy wire from the utility pole and right into Beanz' yard. Then you ran into an area called Underwood, where the corporate office for the company that made Spam was located. Then you just hid behind the vegetation and waited until all was clear.

Beanz was like the Phantom with his turf traps and escape routes, both natural or man-made. He had the stash of Foster's hidden in a freshly dug hole. Plastic lined the hole and it was packed with ice. A board was placed over it and covered with brush. A handy lesson learned from *Soldier of Fortune*, I guessed.

The New England darkness came upon us a little later now, as spring was turning into summer, but we had to wait for the full darkness so we could drink under cover. Finally, after a few beers, Beanz looked at his survivalist watch and said it was time to light a fire.

The pile of wood had previously been soaked in gas, so it was ready to instantly turn red, yellow, and orange. Beanz lit the gas-saturated wood and all of a sudden, we were cavemen, getting warm by the fire. The blaze illuminated everything around us, and I could see all the pigeons flying back and forth, dropping feathers and dung, some brave ones even coming close to us to take in the fire. I felt bad that I couldn't feed them onion rings like my father did at Revere Beach.

Beanz and Seanzo talked about carburetors, radiators, and generators, and I just drank by the warm fire. It had been a long time since I drank beer. Beer and wine had the same effect. The "everything is going to be alright" feeling comes on gradually, you smile more, but have to urinate more as well. Vodka was quick and to the point. Less of a giggly stage. But with vodka, you were put into a new dimension and could see your bright future at the yacht club.

Time went on, and I noticed Beanz check his watch. He said the outbound was coming in about 30 minutes. I noticed with the traffic of Route 128 above us, and Route 1 not far off, we seemed to be shouting in order to have a conversation. Soon, Beanz pointed to the headlight of the train. He then motioned to get up on the cement ramp under the highway. The fire was raging and it was bright all around us. Beanz said the train was slowing down which wasn't normal. We spotted the conductor as they passed. He threw us a hairy eyeball and then seemed to grab his radio.

I saw the rail passengers, the sheeple going from one pen to another and now returning to their home pen. That wouldn't happen to me. I didn't belong on a daily commuter rail. I could make my image out somewhat in the reflection of the train and could see the fire, pigeon feathers falling, my sooty face, holding a very large blue Australian beer can.

Being an eye reader, I noticed the expressions of the passengers as they passed by. The men's eyes just said, "You friggin' bums!" The women's eyes were different; they basically all said the same thing: "What if my Little Johnny ends up like that, covered in pigeon feathers and soot, drinking, with no hopes, goals, or dreams."

Were any of *them* eye readers? Could they tell what I was thinking? Because I was looking at them thinking, "Oh my God, what if I end up like *those* poor saps, having three outfits, entering the same metal box, at the same train stop, every day, sitting next to the same guy, every day. Going to and from the same pen, every day." I wouldn't let it happen. I wouldn't waste away like that.

Meanwhile, my eye reading told me that the two Gearheads were thinking, "How many ponies (horsepower) is in that engine?" I think Beanz might have had one additional thought: Who was the engineer on the radio with? The metal sheeple pen crawled by and then sped up to match everyone's synchronized watches on board, getting back on schedule for their synchronized lives.

It wasn't as loud now, and Beanz and Seanzo got back to their shop talk. I stared off into the distance. I fretted about being sentenced to the life I just saw go by on the train. I wouldn't let it happen. I would be fine. I got back to my Foster's-induced giddiness. I pounded the next one in a gulp to put me further into the happy state. I finished the can and saw a one-eyed alien to my left. The one-eyed metal alien. I looked again, and another one appeared.

I motioned to Beanz and he didn't give it any thought, he just said, "Follow me." I followed the path that was mapped out earlier. I took a quick look behind me, and the one-eyed aliens were gaining. I passed by the marker, saw Beanz and Seanzo jump, counted roughly ten strides, and leaped in the air.

I landed hard, crawled about four feet under the utility pole guy wire, got up and began to run through Beanz' yard to the Spam meat headquarters. Just as I got up to run, one of the alien eyes briefly shined on the left side of my face and yelled, "There they are!" Then I heard what sounded like someone falling, and then someone hitting metal. Then I heard groaning and, "Aggghhhhgggg .... I got clotheslined!"

I gave a quick glance behind, and the eyes of the aliens were pointing in lost directions. They had fallen. I could see the shadows of the guys ahead and followed them, running as fast as an out-of-water octopus with asymmetrical arms can run. Then from behind the tall corporate shrubbery, I heard Beanz yell, "Over here." I ran behind the bushes and was told to crouch. He pointed to the direction of his house, and there we saw the flashlights finally emerge from the darkness. They seemed to be brushing one another off and turning the lights on each other.

One of the aliens looked very dirty in the face. Beanz was smiling now as I looked at him. All the *Soldier of Fortune* and Boy Scout training had paid off. The traps and planning had worked. The aliens shined their lights in circles and up in the trees, but we were nowhere to be found. In bruised, dusty defeat, they went back onto the tracks.

We eventually went back to Beanz' house and entered through the basement. We sat down and relaxed. We had expended a lot of energy. Reflections of blue lights then appeared. A first reaction to blue lights is to run. But that only makes one suspect. Beanz said to just sit there and chill. There was a knock on the door above, and Beanz' mother, a city girl with flaming red hair, answered the door. We took in the whole conversation.

"Hi Miss, we are looking for three men that ran by your house."

She said, "What were they suspected of doing?"

"Ma'am, they had lit a fire near the tracks, and were drinking as well."

She said, "Don't you'se have anything better to do than chase a few guys having a beer, like rescuing a cat up a tree?" She then slammed the door. The blue lights went off, and we waited a little more. Beanz' mother must have known we were downstairs, and said, "Boys! You'se can leave now, it's safe!"

Seanzo lived nearby and walked away. Beanz had some souped-up early 1970s Camaro. The body was beat up, but the engine was very powerful because he worked night and day on it. He even worked as a dishwasher to pay for the parts. We got in the car and sped away. He had strange controls installed in the Camaro. The more levers he pulled and knobs he twisted, the faster we went. I made it home for my curfew with time to spare and without questioning. Mentally, I thanked the utility pole guy wire for saving me from breaking my probation. I climbed under my Star Wars sheets and drifted to sleep to the sound of pigeons and trains and that Camaro engine.

I still had to report to the brick beehive every day. However, I was taught by a few upperclassmen how to make my own hive, *within* the hive. You had to know what classes to take, which teachers were easy, and which classes you could cheat in. There were still some classes you *had* to take. But for the most part, I was able to pick ones that I could easily pass with little to no effort. This kept everyone at probation happy and the parental units off my case.

By now the realization hit me that I could excel in swimming, but that academics, which required a different sort of concentration and effort, were simply not my calling. I could put all of my innate effort into academics, but I'd never, ever produce the type of results that the system said was acceptable. The real smart kids – or the kids who were "smart" in the way the brick beehive and the metal sheeple train had been designed for – they could keep their letters inside the margins; they could keep their after-school activities inside the margins. They were in their own hive, which included the best teachers, the biggest textbooks, and the thickest glasses.

The hive was full of "AP" (advanced placement) people classes going to AP classes. These were people whose brains innately understood and performed according to the brick beehive specs. Paying attention, remembering, written and verbal expression – they were not only capable of these things, but these things seemed intuitive and innate to them, and things they even enjoyed. I simply had not been built that way.

I imagined myself on some factory floor covered in industrial soot, with these people looking down on me barking orders through a PA system: "Pick up your mess, Winslow! Hurry up with that baloney sandwich Winslow, break's over!" Alas, that was only *potentially* in the future and, for now, I had freedom. My friends and I had drivers licenses for "road trips," and classes that we could pass just by showing up. We were occasionally tested on our overall progress, but Simma had taught me how to take and pass those tests as well. It was called "taking the cab."

All you had to do was color the oval with your institutional #2 pencil, repeatedly coloring in the answer to the multiple-choice questions, starting with "c," then an "a," then a "b." Then you repeat it again, "c," "a," "b," …

"You do that all the way to the end, and you'll get enough answers right to pass," he assured me.

He was correct. For the more difficult classes that were required, the Phantom had a guy on payroll doing the homework for him. He would then pass the papers to me, and I would copy the answers and hand them in. Some of the teachers for these fancy classes were more concerned with their own professional assessments than they were about what we learned – so a few of them might give us a passing grade if we came remotely close. That way, *they* looked better – no students failing their classes! My, weren't they good teachers, who deserved a raise? I had stopped caring academically; I would have to make it to the yacht club on just my swimming ability.

For tests, we would get into a "cheat circle." The Phantom was not only known for his terroristic fecal deposits; he could also get information. He had many talents, including unscrewing the wheels on teachers' swivel chairs, or putting liquid soap in the filter of the biology class fish tank. Now, we were having our homework done for us. More freedom!

The Phantom and I decided it was time to take out the kid that was doing our homework, for "a beer." The kid accepted, but said, "Look, fellas, I do have to be home at a certain time." With an evil grin, the Phantom said, "Oh we'll get you back in time, don't worry about that."

We went to Martha Jones with the crew of guys called "Oakers" and a few guys from Cloverland, and the Phantom gave me a tour of the drinking cave and its surroundings. He had escape routes, logs for tripping hazards (for the pursuing flashlights), and he knew precisely what time the flashlights would be there. He even had decoys.

Word was that the State Police had helicopters that would circle our town to spot fires, then call in the coordinates to the locals. Flashlights would show up and make the "big bust." So, the Phantom had a decoy. He would set up a mock fire a couple of miles away, and either light it himself, or have someone else light it. That way, the local police would get the big signal from the helicopter people, the ones who were picked last for gym class, and they would spend time putting out that fire and looking for the big bust.

Then, the Phantom would light the real fire, and begin the festival at his cave. The cavemen in this area were now drinking this thing called "Matt's Beerball." It was a golden plastic dome full of beer. Cheap, easy to carry, and when it was empty, you played a game called "Matt's beer ball soccer." You broke the drunks into even teams and kicked this empty golden dome back and forth. He dug a hole into which he placed ice and the beer ball, then covered it with a downed New England pine bough. It would rest there until later that evening, and was then was served chilled.

The only down-side to this whole thing, as he pointed out, was, "Matt's gives you the splats." A side effect of this beerball was that the next day one would have the splats, the trots, the runs – or in proper Latin (Greek?)

terminology: diarrhea. You had to be near a toilet at all times the following day. No trips with the family or to sporting events.

The day arrived for our date with the kid who did our homework. The Phantom picked me up, and we headed to the other side of town. This certain neighborhood had a reputation for Italian contractors that did very well. Most of the homes were brick and had all sorts of statues on the lawn. The Phantom mumbled the number of the house, and we arrived and tooted. The guy that did our homework emerged from this beautiful home. He was dressed like he was about to take the exam of his life.

He got in back, and I thanked him for joining us and for doing our homework. He smiled and said, "No problem, glad to assist." I noticed he had pens and pencils in his front pocket.

"What are you doing with those?" I asked?

"Uh … I always carry them with me." He said. "Just in case."

The phantom was known for his lead foot, and we made it to the vicinity in record time. We parked the car in a safe location, and then followed the Phantom. The new guy was wearing shoes that were designed for admissions interviews to a prestigious college. This guy's shoes didn't belong in the woods and neither did his pens and pencils. The Phantom had a couple of guys prepping the scene.

"Drinks are on us," we said to the new guy. I had my pint of vodka handed to me, and put my few dollars in the hat for that and the beer ball. There was a saying, "Liquor before beer, never fear, beer before liquor, makes you sicker." So, drink your liquor first, then the beer, and you won't get sick. The beer ball was tapped, and the guys that had been waiting were eager. There were certain rules and they abided by them closely. But having a chilled beer ball in the ground and not being able to indulge in it, was difficult.

The guys that had the pre-alcoholic jitters were served first. They had that first-drink smile, followed by, "ahh." Then we asked the new guy, how much he had been drinking up to this point. He said, "This is my first time." We were astonished. Most of us were going on 5 or 6 years. This was a historic moment. A man's first drink! The Phantom repeated what the new guy said and looked at us: "The *first* drink."

The new guy was handed a plastic red cup. We gathered around with a mini flashlight. This was a big event. The Phantom instructed him to tilt the plastic cup, so there wasn't too much foam. The red plastic cup was slowly filled, and as it was, he was instructed to slowly bend it back to its upward position. Now the new guy had a full cup of Matt's Golden Dome Beer Ball beer. We all stood in silence, watching this new guy, reminiscing about our first drink and its euphoric results. We gave our local salutation, which was, "Hula-boom!" The new guy said something in Italian: "Salu!"

He drank it somewhat slow, but the Phantom caught him and instructed him to take it in a few gulps. The new guy did, and his first beer was soon gone. I thought of my first drink with Cashews, and laying on his freshly mowed lawn, which then became wavy.

I thought about our dream of being oceanographers and experiencing a moment with zero fear or anxiety for the first time in my entire life. The sauce still worked, but I would never again grasp that feeling of the *first* drink. Now I watched the guy who did my homework taking *his* first drink. The Phantom saw he had emptied his cup, and said, "Good job." He quickly poured the guy another drink.

He drank the second one faster, and a broader smile emerged. Then the Phantom said to turn the flashlight off, and he looked at his glow-in-the-dark watch. Sure enough, a cruiser circled by on the street out beyond the woods. He drove slowly, shining his light all over the school, and briefly into the woods. The Phantom had instructed someone else to light the decoy fire at that precise moment, just a mile or two away. The Phantom, again looked at his watch, snapped his fingers, and, like clockwork, we heard sirens in the distance. Now we were safe to light *our* fire.

The Phantom lit his cheap cigar and again quoted the head of the A-Team: "I like it when a plan comes together." We were all standing in the glow of the fire now, and I could see the alcohol induced-smiles on everyone ... that Gerber baby smile ... that Mona Lisa smile. The new guy put his hand out indicating that he was ready for another one. He was fitting right in. He didn't need to be told to "drink up," he was ready to drink more once the previous cup was gone. The shy guy with pencils in his pocket and college interview shoes was now in the buzzy giggly stage of inebriation.

He was laughing and even got into "his story." I was fascinated. He said his parents were both from Italy and came to America with just the shirts on their backs, worked hard, put money away and now – Voilà – were in this zip code in a nice brick house. His father was an accountant, loved gardening, and even made his own wine. His mother was an avid gardener as well. In the summer, most of their vegetables came from her garden. Here he was, center stage behind Martha Jones elementary school, and the fire provided the spotlight. A once-shy guy was now very talkative, and the Phantom refilled his cup every time it got low.

We finally finished the beer ball and began to play "beer ball soccer." We split the crew up and took our sides. The beer ball was placed in the center of our caveman area, and someone yelled, "Go!" One side eventually won, and the Phantom checked his watch. It was time to get the guy who did our homework back home. The Phantom was proud of his cave, so we had to tidy the place up and extinguish the fire with urine and rocks. He even had a small bag to put the cups in.

We all congratulated the new guy on his first drink, and for drinking both appropriately fast and frequently. We finally made it out of the woods, and we assisted the new guy into the car. I buckled him up just in case. He was staring up at the roof, grinning.

He slurred, "I'm Stewed."

We dropped the "ed" and his nickname became "Stew." I looked at the Phantom and saw his sick, perverted, Grinch-like grin. That grin usually meant he was about to do something evil, or had just done it. Then he yelled, "Mom I'm home!" We accelerated to a very high speed, as beautiful brick homes whizzed by. I screamed, "What, are you nuts!?" But this only made the Phantom smile more. Then another evil yell, "Mom, we're home!"

He slammed on the brakes and we skidded for what seemed like forever, miraculously coming to a halt precisely in front of Stew's house.

Lights came on inside the house, followed by the outside lanterns. The phantom, now laughing, yelled, "Get him out!" I unbuckled Stew, and got him to the walkway in a sort of full-nelson slash Heimlich maneuver hold, and let him go. He started to perform the "Little Johnny's first steps" routine, wobbling back and forth like a baby learning to walk.

His mother was on the stoop yelling to her baby boy in Italian. She looked at me and gave me a hand-flick-under-the-chin gesture and screamed. The Phantom then beeped the horn and yelled, "Goodnight, ma'am!" I jumped back in as Stew was being assisted by his mother on the walkway. She turned to us one more time and gave a banshee Italian yell that contained lots of vowels and emphasis. The Phantom let the tires spin on his powerful American-made Buick.

Monday came and we all greeted Stew, congratulating him on his first drink. Of course, he had been sentenced to never see the light of day again, and was repeatedly lectured about how hard his parents had worked to make it in America and how he should never have gone out with the sons of Irish tile setters and electricians.

FOX HOLE DAVIS

One of the classes we voluntarily picked was U.S. History with Mr. Davis, aka "Fox Hole Davis." You would not only learn history but, word was, you would also learn the life experiences he had during World War II. At the first class, we all took our seats and waited rapturously. He started by telling us who he was, how long he had been teaching, where he grew up, the fact that he was a World War II veteran – and then he looked at someone and told them to take their hat off in his class.

We were then told to stand up and, one by one, recite our names. He looked out the window into the upper courtyard. In nice weather, the football heroes would lounge out there with their girlfriends. But today, the weather was foul, and it must have reminded Fox Hole Davis of something. He saw something we didn't see. We continued to uncomfortably stand up and recite our first and last names, as the teacher looked out the window. The Phantom stood up; he had very significant German first and last names. His father was from Europe and was proud of his heritage, and gave him a Bavarian first name to match his last name.

The teacher snapped his neck around and said, "Please recite your name again." The Phantom complied. Fox Hole Davis said, "Is that German?"

"Yes," said the Phantom.

"I fought the Germans in World War II, but I won't hold that against you."

"Thank you," the Phantom said, sitting down.

Mr. Davis turned back to the window, looking at something only he could see. The students finally finished reciting their first and last names. Mr. Davis mumbled something to the window, and then turned around and went into what time periods of U.S. history we were going to study. It wasn't going to be today, for he briefly went into his mental "foxhole" and looked out the window. It was late fall, still early in the morning, and the grass seemed to be exhaling, letting out vapor. He said that reminded him of some of the days in Germany during the war.

"It was quiet, winter was coming. The ground was damp, and a mist was rising from the soil, just like now. You were scared, you didn't know what the Gerry's were thinking. Would they suddenly appear above you with their bayonets? Were they reloading? That was the scariest time. You always had to be ready ... second place was the first to die."

Shortly after this description, a very pretty girl walked in and said, "Sorry, I'm late. I was in the office." She handed him a note. He looked at it and crumpled it in his hand and whipped in the trash barrel.

"In the army, it was sick call, not referral!" he said.

"Sick call was for those that couldn't hack it in the army. They always tried to get out of duty by going to sick call! But once you were on the battlefield, there was no sick call!"

He then paced back and forth from the window to the wall.

"You have the luxury of being late now, young lady," he said. "But let me tell you: if you were late getting into your foxhole, you would be filled with lead!" He then turned to the window, grabbed an imaginary gun, and made the sounds of automatic weapon fire.

"Dat dat dat dat dat....!"

The phantom and I looked at each other, astonished, even a little nervous. Then he yelled, "That's what would happen to you if you were late in *my* world!"

Then he went from the trenches and foxholes of Germany to the trials of growing up in Dedham.

"We never had the luxury of flushing toilets like you do today! I had to go out with an ice pick and hack the lid of the seat just so I could take a crap!"

Then he brought up television. "We never had any TV's. Today, I get home, and my daughter doesn't even acknowledge me. She's too busy watching Luke and Laura on General Hospital! Today it's baby-town USA!"

With that, the bell rang, and he said, "Tomorrow, we start with the civil war!"

We left looking at each other with dismay, knowing now why they called him Fox Hole Davis. I knew I would learn a great deal because I was a visual guy. Mr. Davis was very descriptive and spoke a language I could understand.

MADE BY A MACHINE IN MILWAUKIE

Swim team started, and I was prepared and fully healed from the previous year's collarbone injury. I still enjoyed the warm-up most, when I would mentally drift off as we were doing 40 lengths. I imagined my future self: successful, speaking a foreign language, living in a foreign land. Then we got into the big red hands on the clock, the whistle, gasping for air, and dizziness. It was somewhat like alcohol. The first few drinks go down rough, but the pay-off was euphoria. You swam hard, and then by the time you hit the hot showers, the happy people in your skull danced around, emitting a pleasant feeling, like a vapor.

My fellow Cro Mag from elementary school, Wild Blumpkin, had joined the team. I hadn't seen him in quite some time. He excelled in school and was hanging around with the thick-glasses during the day, and the Armyheads on weekends. He mentioned teaching the guys with thick glasses how to drink like us; he was successful, and now they were even holding things called "idiot fests."

It went like this: They all had parents that both worked. Said hard-working parents would leave the house; now that some kids had access to cars, they would show up at the home just after the homeowners had left. Once there, the drinking began, normally at around 7:30 a.m. This was done on certain holidays or an occasional skip-school day. I got an invite to the next one.

"Just bring a few bucks' entrance fee."

"Will do," I said.

The morning arrived and I knew to show up at a given address, and at a certain time. I was a little leery about drinking before noon. Wasn't that a sign that you may have a problem? Or was it prohibited or frowned upon by my religion? I didn't have a drinking problem. I went to church every Sunday, so I was covered there. At the given address at the certain time, the diverse crews showed up. Many would be future scientists, engineers, politicians, lawyers, and doctors. Then my crew showed ... future painters, electricians, and carpenters.

Money was exchanged and we were lead to the idiot juice. There was a keg, and vodka, both well-prepped and cold. We stood in our separate areas at first, arranged by collars – ours blue and theirs white. As time went on and the alcohol worked its magic, we started to mingle with the other collars. Some of these guys were even from the AP crowd. They took foreign languages and voluntarily enrolled in math classes that I couldn't even pronounce the name of, like *geocalculometry*.

It would be nice, I thought, to remain in touch with these guys through life. If I ever had a question regarding how long Johnny's shadow was if he is 5'5" tall, and the sun was at mid-day in October, on the 45th parallel, and the train was heading east at 47 miles per hour – I would have somebody to call. Now that alcohol was taking its effect, I imagined myself drinking in my bathrobe, wearing carpet slippers, on my yacht.

Wild Blumpkin had taught the thick-glasses set well ... to have plenty and drink fast and drink plenty. I liked that morning drink ... it seemed to get me in a great mood to conquer the day. Probably like coffee did for those that drank that awful smelling stuff. Our new friend Stew was there; he was still grounded, but as far as his folks figured, he was at school.

I decided to switch my attention to the keg after a few slugs of vodka. It tasted a lot better once the numbness of the hard sauce took its effect. Then you could really appreciate and savor the taste of the lovely hops and wheat and mountain glacier spring water – or whatever – they advertise on TV to sell their beer. Yeah right. I knew it all came from a factory in St. Louis or Milwaukie, made in a machine by some drunk wearing sweatpants, stirring a giant metal pot with a ridiculously large spoon.

There weren't too many of us there for the head bee back at the brick hive to notice anything, but if they suspected any "shenanigans" it would for sure be the blue-collar kids that would be washing the school after hours. The jocks and the AP kids seemed to get special privileges, like "second chances" and "alternative" punishments. After all, why besmirch the permanent academic record of a future scientist, thus harming his chances of gaining entry to Hah-vahd, just because of a little youthful indiscretion? Us blue collar kids, though? We were headed in the wrong direction, and only a stiff punishment would teach us the life lessons we needed to stay out of jail and excel at that factory job that was surely in our future.

The day went on and by noon some of the kids were vomiting and stumbling around, but it was fine. Vomiting was just a sign that the stomach was making room for more booze. Time flew by and eventually, the host of the idiot fest announced that we had to clean up and vacate. After doing my part, I headed to school. I respected my swimming coach, so I decided to go to swim practice ... drunk. Wild Blumpkin said I was crazy, but I had to show respect for the coach.

I performed the warm ups and felt ok. But then we went into the sprints. I lasted two sets and then immediately vomited into the gutter. I showered and headed home, and felt a little better after the puke and the exercise. I thought of that morning drink. I made a vow not to drink alone before noon. Maybe that was the trick: don't drink alone before noon.

THE CUSTODIANS

My schedule now was full. Attendance at school, lifeguarding, swim team and keeping up with all the drinking events. There was never a dull moment. My friend the Phantom was now leaving his kamikaze fecal deposits in specified locations around the school. They were well-concealed locations, but a few moments after he dropped one, his signature stench would creep out aggressively in every direction. After laying one at the base of some remote stairwell, that entire section of the building would fill with his foul funk. He would also conduct other pranks, like loosening screws on the hinges of especially large and heavy doors.

Wild Blumpkin's father drank at a bar in Norwood called the Irish Heaven. It was a real big hangout for the older blue-collar crowd. These were the guys that would shake their heads and fists at "this generation." The custodians at our school apparently frequented this bar. They discussed the situation at our school and mentioned to all the patrons that they had a "serial crapper," a "phantom shitter," on the loose. They had a meeting about how to catch this sick culprit. They made threats: "If I'ze got to put on another rubber glove and fetch one more steaming poo from another stairwell, I quit!"

"If I'ze find that phantom, I'z'll stick his head in it!"

That was the talk one night at the Irish Heaven. Wild Blumpkin's father discussed the news at the dinner table and bemoaned the "sick generation" that was out there. Wild Blumpkin then relayed the message to the Phantom the next day.

Challenge accepted.

The Grinch-like grin grew wider and more sinister. His output and artistry increased dramatically in the following weeks.

There were a few teachers that, although I respected, I could not imagine living the lives they lived. They were completely institutionalized. Just by looking at them, I knew they got up at the same time every day, wore the same outfit on designated days, ate the same food prepared the same way on a schedule. I wondered what the Phantom and his deposits did to their routine?

I imagined the guy who lives his life on a schedule, who has his toast and coffee set at the same time and location in the kitchen table every morning; he gets into the same car, parks in the same parking spot, walks to the same desk; then the same items in his lunch pail are eaten at the same time every day; he goes home at the same time, to the usual meal served on that day of the week. He's trying to keep on schedule, goes into the bathroom for his 2:15 p.m. urination break and – BAM! – sees a big steaming dump clogging the standing urinal.

Maybe that was a *good* thing? A public service, even? Maybe it is so odd that it breaks his routine. Maybe it is so unusual, that it tears the fabric of his mundane world, causing him to say to his wife, "Honey, we are going out to eat tonight."

A high school custodian has seen everything – dirty notes, filthy toilets, vomit, condoms, cigarettes. Even to him, the steaming dump in the urinal is a bit of a challenge. But to a teacher that has been living the same routine for 20 or 30 years, it had to have some sort of existential effect. The Phantom snuck into one of the science classes before the teacher arrived. He was one of those robotic, green sweater-on-Thursday, pee-stained Sansabelt slacks on Monday kind of teachers.

The Phantom had written, "Mr. Snodgrass Loves Penis," on the chalkboard, and then pulled the projector screen down in front of it. There was always a short break before classes, and I imagine this particular teacher was smoking a pipe in the teacher's lounge – worrying whether his wife remembered to pick up the flank steak because for the love of God in Heaven it was Thursday, and on Thursday, by Jove, they ate flank steak.

The teacher arrived for class and was very disturbed to see the projector screen down. It baffled him. It had never happened in his 30 years of teaching. Then, with a practiced pull at the bottom of the screen, it rolled itself up with a snap, revealing a detailed drawing of him, with his pants down, and the words, "Mr. Snoddgrass Loves Penis."

He stood there speechless. This wasn't supposed to happen, it hadn't happened in his entire career. What was this that was breaking his routine? Of course, we all burst out in laughter. He didn't seem upset at the artwork or the suggestion that he loved penis. He merely seemed disturbed that his routine had broken. His scheduled Thursday night dinner of flank steak at exactly 6:00 p.m. would not be the same. Does he tell his wife? Will that break *her* routine?

Oh, my.

I would find out certain teachers loves or pet peeves, and report that to the Phantom for exploitation. There was one of my teachers that just loved the big institutional clock. He would smile at the clock as the bell rang, perfectly synchronized. This bell/clock synchronization seemed to give him an almost erotic satisfaction. I reported this to the Phantom, and he snuck in and adjusted the clock a few minutes ahead. At the end of class, the bell rang, but it was not synchronized with the clock! He looked utterly befuddled. According to his routine, now he couldn't even give us our homework assignment. He went over to the clock and just stared at it. He looked at his watch, confused. Meanwhile, we walked out.

Another class was located directly above the men's urinals. The teacher was aloof, but a decent guy. We called him Doc Baker. He saw what we saw. He even said, "This place is a nut house." The Phantom would urinate out the second-floor window of the men's room, and if our class on the first floor had its window open, Phantom pee would splatter on the window. Doc Baker would just announce, "The patients are at it again," and look up at the ceiling. He said when he was new to the school he would run upstairs and chase the culprit. Now, he would just say, "The patients are at it again," and look up at the ceiling before going back to the chalkboard.

They couldn't get the Phantom, because he fit in with everyone else. He was average height, average build. Plus, he was an athlete, so he wasn't the type they would normally suspect. Also, he knew that as a result of being an athlete, he would get off if caught – which only gave him additional confidence, which inevitably decreased his chances of raising suspicion. I was suspected and accused of being the Phantom Shitter many times, but this was before DNA and security cameras, so without catching me in the act, they couldn't actually punish me.

One day some of the fellas took a road trip to the Cape. They returned to the school parking lot just as we were exiting for the day, and seemed very happy, hugging, high fiving ... and then gave us the news. The Phantom had struck the Kennedy compound in Hyannisport. It was the Phantom's greatest achievement. We were all proud of him. This family, that had grown rich and powerful by supposedly working for working families, had been shat upon by the son of a tile setter.

Highbrows: 0

The Phantom: 1

It's Crampless

I had always been surrounded by music. My father played guitar when we were young. Songs were sung at family gatherings. There was a guy that was spotted on a TV show called Austin City Limits in Texas named Stevie Ray Vaughn. I made a round of phone calls to the crew, advising them to tune in and see this guy. They switched it on and called me back with their approval. We determined to get tickets if and when he ever came to town. Shortly after this, we heard of his coming to Boston and got the tickets. Now, all we needed was vodka.

An acquaintance of ours was back in town and was going to join us. He went by "NM" and was a few years older. He had gone to school with us, and would even occasionally join us, youngsters, while we drank. He was a natural athlete and was then the starting center for one of the best football teams in Massachusetts. He was a junior, and in those days, to start as a junior was a real accomplishment. Now, he was frequenting our town more and more. He kept track of the idiot fests, and other special religious or historical occasions.

My father was all for me seeing a musician. He said, "Pahk at Rivah-side, and take the green line into this station, then get ahff at this station, then you'se will see a monument; the ass of the monument is facing east, so cross the street and then take a left; dat 'dere is the Orpheum theater."

The day was upon us to see this amazing guitarist from Texas. It would be Sully, Simma, NM, and myself. There wasn't a "bag job" (electrical work for a relative in Boston) that Saturday, so I was swinging an ax, splitting railroad ties that had been previously cut into small squares and dumped at our house. Now I was cutting them into smaller squares. Then I was cutting the ones that still had metal hooks embedded in the base. It didn't bother me, because I knew that after about 7 hours of that, I would be closer to the drink. It seemed that I craved the drink more and more now. The diabetic needed his insulin to function, and I was licking my lips for my shot of booze every day.

Simma, after weeks of working in the cold with his father, emerged from their garage with an early 1970s Pontiac Le Mans. Special parts had been installed, of course, provided by the Massachusetts Institute of Technology. The good thing about Sunoco Mike across the street was, if you bought gas from him, you could usually get an emissions sticker without the inspection. So, the retro-fitted Le Mans passed with flying colors.

I finished my chopping. I scrubbed all the creosote from my hands and face. The early darkness arrived. My father was partially deaf from being around the subway and other loud machinery like generators his whole life. So, I was able to sneak a drink, his partial deafness along with the growing darkness aiding my stealth. I snuck it on the dark front porch; we never had the porch lights on. My mother hated to have too many lights on, because, after all, she was Scottish and besides, "We don't own Edison." I heard a rumbling outside, and it was Simma in his rebuilt Le Mans. It was showtime.

Sunoco Mike had clearly not inspected this vehicle, as the muffler was either falling off or had as many holes as a flute – or both. It resulted in a rumbling, ominous bass sound. Simma revved the engine with pride, and I gave him the thumbs up. He even had a tape deck prepped with Stevie Ray Vaughn that we blasted as we picked up Sully. Then we had to go to Walpole and pick up the center of the football team, NM. Tuce was the defensive coordinator of that team, and the head coach was a guy they named General Lee. NM was in the driveway, smoking a cigarette. We drove off to Riverside Station, the last stop on the Green Line.

We pulled up to the station, and the attendant seemed to be starting to drink as well. We paid him with a few crumpled up dollars and then found a parking spot away from everyone else. He popped the trunk, and there were bottles of the cheap Russian vodka staring at us. We worked on our first bottle. After a few stiff ones, a voice from the heavens came over the P.A. and announced, "Do yah drinking somewheres else!" I pointed to my chest, and then the Godlike voice said, "Yah, you'se." We disappeared into the darkness. We were natural naturalists and so could always find some brush to hide behind. We drank excitedly. We downed the first bottle, and someone with a 90-cent watch said it was time to go.

We decided to head for the green caterpillar, trying to conceal our magic sauce in a brown bag. It arrived in a whirl, swallowed us up, and headed "in town." There was a map on the wall, and we had several stops before we evacuated the caterpillar. It rode above ground and then disappeared underneath. I thought of the men, years ago, that had to dig this hole for us to be able to see this concert. We rode in darkness. Then there was light at a station; people came on board, and we were off for more darkness. Finally, we arrived at the Boston Commons.

We headed for the cover of a few trees off to the side. There we pulled the bottle out of its brown bag and got back to business. I didn't want the feeling to wear off. We drank and took in our surroundings. There were beautiful brown stone buildings around us. NM started giving us a history lesson. "The British soldiers once walked around this area, then some of the non-British threw snowballs at the soldiers and then they started shooting ... that was the start of the Revolutionary War..."

I heard the familiar sound of a Harley Davidson. It came from nowhere. The headlight startled me. Then the frightening image of a man in long leather boots going up to his knees, black pants, black leather jacket, and black gloves and helmet. It was a Boston motorcycle cop. I feared a beat down and didn't feel drunk anymore. He said, "What are you'se doin?" Instinctively, I said, "Sir! We are waiting for the Stevie Ray Vaughn show to begin, sir!"

"Ah right," he said. "Put the bottle in the bag, and enjoy the show."

"Sir! Yes sir!" I said.

He got back on the Harley and putted away. We all looked at each other. What was this, no chase, no beat down, no giant metal flashlight across the back of the head? Simply put the bottle in a bag, and even "enjoy the show"? These Boston police were real pro's. They were too busy with actual crime to worry about a few Cro Mags with a bottle. We polished off the bottle. I forgot the directions my father gave me about taking a left at the ass of some statue, so we just followed the crowd.

We got near the entrance of the Orpheum, and there was brick on the left and right of us. We were surrounded by Leatherheads. We were the only ones wearing a combination of Members Only and Barracuda – or in my case Numbers Only –jackets. We stuck out, but no one seemed to care. They hadn't opened the doors yet, so people just stood outside. The Leatherheads were always a tough crowd, so you didn't see anyone complaining about the bitter cold. A guy with a leather, Indiana Jones type of hat, along with a denim jacket, leather vest, jeans and black boots approached us.

Was there going to be a fight? Leather jackets versus one Members Only, two Barracudas, and one Numbers Only? He walked up and smiled, and stuck out his hand. I think he said his real name, and that his friends called him Chains. It didn't sound Catholic, but he was still nice. He said, "I got two hits of acid left."

Then he said it was three dollars each, and that he could guarantee that his acid contained no strychnine, "So you won't get cramps." It must have been organic.

I was learning a valuable lesson, about not judging a book by its cover. This guy who at first appeared as a gunslinger on some old Western was now offering acid that had no filthy additives or preservatives, and thus no cramps. And he only had two left! It was obvious he was a generous guy because, even though he only had two hits left, he would sell them at a discounted price. My mother loved discounts and would have really liked this man.

I was interested how these two hits of acid were going to be applied. Would he dab a cloth with a bottle of acid? Would we raise the bangs of hair on our foreheads, so he could wrap the cloth over his fist and dab us with it, like my father did with hydrogen peroxide to wounds? We accepted his once in a lifetime, discounted crampless acid. He reached into his jacket and pulled out aluminum foil. There were two tiny pieces of paper. We grabbed our crumpled-up dollars. He straightened them out and smiled.

I had to be in church in the morning. Sully was leaning up against the wall, incoherent. So, it was going to go be Simma and NM who were lucky enough to get the crampless acid. The nice Leatherhead then split the two pieces of paper in half. Like a priest, he told them to open their mouths. NM, being Catholic, put his head back and stuck out his tongue. Simma followed suit. Then the nice Leatherhead said, "Just let it rest on your tongue." They followed his instructions, and he smiled reassuringly at their obedience.

We talked for a while, and then the doors to the concert hall finally opened. Sully was still leaning against the brick wall, looking up at nothing. Having had first aid training, I assisted him into the Orpheum. He was like a large ventriloquist dummy now –smiling and floppy and passive, me trying to make him look and act like a real, living human being. We fooled the ushers and made it to our seats. Sully then slumped in his seat, staring at nothing. I waited for the show to start. Simma and NM sat down. The lights dimmed, and everyone stood up, except Sully, who stayed limply in his seat, staring up at the ceiling.

All of a sudden, I was hit hard with the vodka bat; all the clear Russian elixir I had consumed to that point hit me at once. I had to put one hand on the seat in front of me to maintain balance. I noticed NM and Simma beginning to behave abnormally. They were pointing at stage lights, smiling like crazy people. They were making hand gestures to each other. They seemed to be communicating in some sort of otherworldly sign language. Sully merely stood stationary, yelling repeatedly, "You muthah fuggah!"

The concert finally ended, and I could see that Simma and NM were still entranced with something they alone were experiencing. I grabbed Sully and assisted him all the way back to the train station, with NM and Simma following blindly, still pointing at shapes and lights as if they were divine signs of Nirvana from another dimension. The caterpillar swallowed us up, and we took the ride back to Riverside. We got to the car, and

Simma looked into the abyss and smiled as he prepared to turn the key. I asked, "Are you sure you should be driving?" He just shot me a look of utter, wild insanity and turned the ignition.

We drove off very slowly. The driver's seat had a glitch. It rested all the way back, almost horizontally. On the drive to the show, Simma compensated by merely sitting up ramrod straight, not leaning on the seat back. Now, however, he drove in a reclined position, leaning all the way back. I had no idea how he could even see over the wheel, not to mention steer. Somehow, he made it work. We dropped off Sully, and I assisted him to his door. He opened it and stepped in. Simma then headed in the direction of my house to drop me off. I asked NM what the acid was like. He just smiled and said, "No cramps, man." I was dropped off and stumbled into the house.

I awoke to a loud shout of, "Get ready for mass! It's already happassed!" My ears were ringing from my first concert. I now knew what my father must have felt like after a life of being around extremely loud electrical generators and trains. I felt ill, in the way only large amounts of vodka can make you feel the next morning. I avoided eye contact with the stained-glass image of Jesus. I remembered the feeling of the morning drink, and couldn't wait to sneak one soon to set things right. Fortunately, by the time mass was over, it would be past noon. After all, drinking alone before noon meant you might have a problem with alcohol.

I hula-boomed a glass of vodka as my family prepared the traditional Sunday meal. The near-deafness of my father, coupled with the clanging of glasses and porcelain by my mother, allowed me to hula-boom a toast to Stevie Ray Vaughn and the nice crampless acid man in solitude.

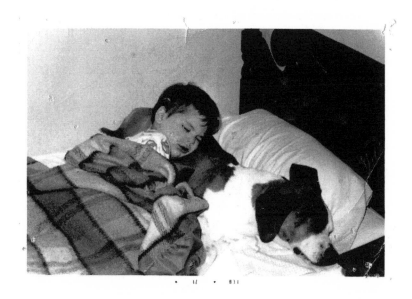

Using a three-legged dog as a pillow.

The family's beloved three-legged dog.

When life was good.

My father and his coffee eyes.

My father Ed Winslow Jr. in Navy uniform
with my grandfather Ed Winslow Sr.

My brothers Lead and E.J. on mandatory snow-removal duty.

Mowing New England.

My uncle James Moran and his beloved Miller beer
on birthday present distribution duty.

Altar boy duty at St. Margaret Mary's in Westwood, Massachusetts.

*With my cousins and siblings and
Uncle James Moran near Pete's Rock.*

Age six, wearing an Evel Knievel Halloween costume.

*My brother Ed J. Winslow III, a.k.a, E.J. on
enforcer duty at Mitchell's Pond.*

*My great aunt Kay Foley (left) and my mother Carole (right)
at a "he's in a better place" gathering.*

My grandparents, Mr. and Mrs. Edward Winslow Sr.

Age five enjoying my first cigarette, pretending to be Evel Knievel.

Whether it was a family birthday or religious holiday, I was put on party assistant duty from the time I could walk.

My brother Lead with his souped-up bike before the horrific crash.

Wee-Wee Wuvwee Cuwuz

Swimming was going well, and despite the regular vodka consumption, my body seemed to be at its physical peak. Academically, I had pretty much accepted the fact that I would never be the guy in the factory office looking down on the workers. Rather, I would be the worker. But, for the time being, I could enjoy my youth. I frequently cruised by the lower courtyard at school. I noticed a few new faces, and one, in particular, was a very attractive female. She was tall, had long, silky brown hair that flowed down to her lower back, wore a leather jacket and tight, designer denim jeans.

We made eye contact a few times through the glass of the lower courtyard. The first time, she just exhaled smoke and glared at me. The second time, she betrayed a bit of a grin between the small puffs of smoke coming from the side of her mouth. I asked a few of my friends about her. They said she was from Norwood and was a new student. They even set up an intro and soon I wandered into the forbidden lower courtyard. It was a sea of leather jackets and denim. It had the feel of a biker rally. In walks me, with docksiders and a ridiculous Numbers Only jacket. You could hear a pin drop as I made my way in.

I was escorted by a couple of my Leatherhead friends from the Maze, so I wasn't hassled, despite my attire. I was brought directly to this tall female Leatherhead. I sheepishly put my hand out and introduced myself, and she politely exhaled her cigarette smoke at me and told me her name:

Magenta. After an awkward few seconds, everybody went back to their own business, and I was able to ask for her number. She complied, saying nothing. As soon as she gave it to me, I did a nervous about-face followed by an awkward half-jog, half-walk out of the courtyard.

I turned around before exiting and we both waved; I put an imaginary phone to my head. She nodded, and her look was a bit sinister. With her height, designer leather jacket (complete with tassels), and tight jeans, she could have been the leader of a female biker gang. Maybe one called the "Queen Bees." Or, the "Bloody Mary's." I called her that night, and she sounded funny. "Must be a bad connection on the phone," I thought. We set a date, for my favorite Chinese restaurant, The Kahana on Route 1A in Walpole. The Kahana was fancy, I thought, because it featured a row of booths, and each booth had its own tropical fish tank.

Fish swimming around in a tank always seemed to relax me. The owner knew my father and I knew he would set me up with one of the fish tank booths. I picked her up at one of the few "triple deckers" in our town. These are three family homes, one stacked on top of another. It was located in Islington. She told me to just beep once when I got to the address. I thought it was a bit classless to beep, but she said, "It'll save you from running up three flights of stairs."

I got there and hesitated to beep, still wondering if the gentlemanly thing to do would be to climb the steps and greet her in person. She must have heard the car or seen the lights, because while I was still pondering, she ran down, opened the door, and hopped in.

She said she liked the Kahana – they even let her drink at the bar there – so the night was off to a good start. We entered, and I eye-balled the owner. I pointed to myself, and said, "Son of Ed." He smiled and said, "Ah yeah! Et's gud!" I asked for a "fish view," and he obligingly sat us down next to a tank with an assortment of truly magnificent fish.

I was very nervous and really would have liked a drink to calm myself. However, I was petrified of drinking and driving. I knew watching the fish would help ease my anxiety. The fish looked like my crew: flat heads, big heads, round heads … and some that even swam like Sully drove: forward, stop, forward, stop.

I didn't want to order any fish from the menu, being right next to the fish tank. I feared they would all be gathered at the edge of the tank, leering at me as I consumed one of their relatives. Magenta lit a cigarette. This put me more at ease, especially since she didn't ask if I minded. Then she started talking. She looked at the fish and said, "They are wee-wee wuv-wee cuwuz."

"Yes, they are lovely colors," I said.

We both smiled. We ordered the same food. At the Kahana, the food always came fast, plus there was the water guy who always kept your glasses full. I already knew a great deal about her town of Norwood. It had many bars, lots of liquor stores, numerous fast food restaurants, copious convenient stores, and a bowling alley that was known for the frequent fights in its parking lot.

I said, "Do you miss Norwood?"

She said she did, but it was only a couple bus stops away, so she was still able to see her old friends. There was no talk of sports, but she told me an acid story. She said she and her friend took acid once right before going to school. Her friend ended up "freaking out" and was taken away to Norwood hospital in an ambulance. Magenta said she had managed to "hode it too-gever."

"The way-dee-ay-tows (radiators) seemed like they were bweeving (breathing)," she said. "But, I knew dey wee-wee wuh-wunt."

I was more relaxed now, having one eye on the fish, and one eye on this girl talking like Barbara Walters about acid. Magenta had a healthy appetite and we hula-boomed everything. There was none of the cute first date chatter, like what is your favorite color or flavor of ice cream. Instead, it went right into "bweeving way-dee-ay-tows." I was still a bit nervous. Was there something in this girl's eyes saying that I should just call it off mid-way through this first date? Before there was any attraction? Should I save myself the inevitable romantic beat-down from this leader of the Queen Bees bike gang?

The pineapple and fortune cookies showed up. I was totally counting on some really sound advice from the cookie, like, "Make this your last date." Or, "By the way, you are going to be living in your mother's basements into your mid-forties." Instead, it simply said:

I did notice that Magenta "sniffed" a great deal, and had to constantly use a napkin because her nose was always running. But it was the dark season of New England, so I figured she just had a little cold. We finished the meal and took one last glimpse at the brightly-colored fish swimming around like they had been fed crushed pain pills. Slow, easy, small circles. I thanked the owner and the water boy, and we departed. We got back into the family station wagon. Magenta turned the radio on to a rock and roll station and lit a cigarette – without asking if it was okay. Apparently, she was unaware that this vehicle transported good Catholics to and from church each Sunday.

We arrived at her triple-decker in Islington and she invited me up. As we walked up the stairs, I noticed a familiar stench – marijuana. We entered and, although it was clean, I knew my clothes were going to smell like weed. Dangit! I was going to have to open the windows to the Country Squire to even potentially eradicate the smell of Magenta's cigarette and now this marijuana. That was going to be a cold ride home.

We entered the domicile and I was introduced to her father. He was still in his work clothes and work jacket. She whispered in her father's ear, "Dad, 'diff-iv Andwoow." He reached out his hand slowly, as if trying to grab a falling feather. He looked forward with half-closed eyes. Magenta said, "He've on pain pi-wuhs fo-wah his back, so he've quiet now."

With *that* info, I *knew* this wouldn't be my last date with Magenta. The fortune cookie was correct: I was hungry, and I was right not to have bolted from the Kahana between the main course and the pineapple. Oh, joy! "Pain pills" were now in the picture again. I looked over to where the smoke was coming from. There was her mother, puffing away on a pipe. She seemed very happy; her hands and mouth were covered with orange Dorito powder. I leaned over and shook her hand. She lit her bowl and offered it to me. I wanted to say, "Aw, geez, ma'am, it's just our first date, and I hold deep religious convictions," but instead I just said, "No thank you Mrs. McGillicutty." She laughed in a way reminiscent of a *Creature Feature* witch.

"Ah! Finally! A polite one!" she cackled.

She even had long black hair. She was now laughing with her head on the couch, looking up at the ceiling. I was nervous and signaled to Magenta that we should go to another room. We got up to walk away, and Mrs. McGillicutty waved and said, "You'se is a nice boy!" Followed by an evil laugh.

We went to another room. I figured since she had been up-front about ingesting acid before school, it would be okay to talk about her father's back and the medication they gave him for his pain. She smiled and said, "Why? You want some?"

I said, "Well, now that you mention it, sure. Just a few ... my back's been acting up." She left quickly and returned fast with the largest prescription pill bottle I had ever seen. It was the size of a Big Gulp. She said she wasn't into downers, but that I was welcome. She poured a pile into my hands.

No, *indeed.* This *wasn't* going to be our last date. We talked awhile, and then it was time to go. She walked me down to the Country Squire and we kissed. Opening my eyes mid-kiss, I noticed how pretty she was; just a bit rough, but a biker's dream girl. I got into the station wagon and put all the windows down. Mass was in 12 hours, and I still had to get the smoke smell off of me and out of the Squire.

As I pulled away and turned the corner I noticed a guy smoking a cigarette in a parked muscle car. He looked very angry and glared at me. Maybe he just hated the Ford Motor Company, I thought, for laying off his cousin, or something. I drove away, focused on airing out the family's religious transport vehicle.

The Unpardonable Sin

The fish-viewing date with Magenta at the Kahana had been a success. There were a few odd things I recalled, like her lighting a cigarette in the car without asking, her telling stories of taking acid before school, her mother's weed smoking and long black witch-like hair and orange Dorito-powdered hands, her father still in his work clothes and unable to remove himself from the couch – not to mention the menacing biker-looking guy leering at me from inside the parked muscle car.

Other than those few minor things, we had a good time. Plus, I now had access to the largest bottle of pain pills I had ever seen. Each day, I would pass by Magenta in the lower courtyard. She would blow smoke, smile, and wave. There was something about her that made me nervous. Like, I might eventually have to leave town if I ever decided to break up with her. She came up to the glass window that separated the lower court-yard from the hallway.

It was the same glass that separated my Docksiders from their work boots; that separated my Numbers Only from their leather jackets. With her Barbara Walters accent, she said, "I got a hand-fuw ub pee-uws." We both smiled. She came outside and gave me a baggie of them. Magenta said that her father's back condition was permanent, and he got unlimited refills.

I saw my friend Mike B., who had fully recovered, physically at least, from the squirrel attack; psychologically, however, he would never be the same. He remained forever fearful of the sound of leaves rustling under oak trees, and the sight of acorns sometimes made his eye twitch. I showed him the baggie. His natural Catholic reaction was to open his mouth and throw his head back. We both hula-boomed a couple of pills, thinking they would provide the same pharmacological effects as the batch from the killer baby squirrel attack. The pills weren't that much bigger, so I figured, no worry. I recalled something about MG's (milligrams) from science class, but gave it no heed when I took the pill.

After about 30 minutes, things slowed down considerably. By necessity, my walk became very calculated. I had regained that beautiful half-closed eye-sight. The brick beehive didn't seem so institutional. The bricks and cinder blocks felt soft to the touch. Everything belonged exactly where it was. I felt great peace at the fact that the bricks, lights, floorboards and acoustical ceiling tiles had all been carefully placed with love.

I remembered that I had one more class, but it seemed the signal from my brain to my legs was diffused or diluted or simply ignoring me. It was now an effort to make my legs move. After what seemed like a ten-year walk across 1,000 miles of light, I finally made it to my next class. I didn't so much sit down as float down into my chair, like an autumn leaf drifting to earth on a puffy breeze. I looked around and sat up straight. I put my head upright, my legs straight, feet pointing forward, my hands flat on the desk. Just like Mrs. Mooncai had always wanted me to do back in fifth grade. I was now the picture-perfect student.

Someone could have taken my picture at that moment and captioned it: "Ninety-nine percent of our students go on to college! In fact, our students sit at the perfect 90° angle, facing the chalkboard with their hands on their desk and their feet pointed straight."

Swim team was next. There was an hour before practice. I was in super slow-mo. I passed by Magenta, and she just said, "Dem piwls awuh powafoo, ha?" I touched Magenta's face. She was beautiful. The daughter of an ironworker on pain pills; the daughter of a weed smoking witch mother; a smoker; an acid taker. Not the type of girl I ever pictured myself with … me of the Docksiders and Numbers Only jacket. But now, here I was in the brick beehive. Faculty, football heroes, and AP kids that I was destined to someday work for were walking by, staring. I didn't care, I just wanted to caress Magenta's face. She didn't care either. She was the toughest girl in the school.

She smiled and mentioned that the pain pills were great because they contained so many "miwagwams" each. I headed down to the pool. I got there early, which was good, because it took me a long time to get out of my clothes and into my speedo. I decided to float around in the pool. I knew the custodian that was just in charge of the pool. He kept it looking tropical, but the temperature was always frigid, like the Irish Riviera.

I dove in and just floated around. I loved the water. I was always told never to fight the water. It can be like a boa constrictor. If it senses you are nervous or panicked, it will strike. So, when in a riptide or strong current, it'd always better to just enjoy the ride; let the liquid that is surrounding you take you where it will.

I dove down to the bottom of the pool and floated. I looked up and exhaled, so I wouldn't be so buoyant. The light was beaming down on me. I seemed to be able to hold my breath an incredibly long time on these pain pills. I noticed a human figure looking down at me. Was that a dead relative? The figure put his face closer to the surface of the water. I decided to float up and talk to this dead relative. As I surfaced, I recognized the confused face of the coach.

"What are you doing down there?" he asked.

"Pre-warmups," I stammered.

Other kids filed in and jumped into the pool, and the real practice started. All I saw was blue tile and that massive clock. I felt no pain during the practice, but my time was down significantly. I told coach I had the flu, and I was let off the hook that day. But I made a mental note: don't take the pills that close to practice.

The next day I felt a residual calmness. I was more alert. I didn't even take a pill. I wondered if the normal state of man was like this, on pills ... or was the normal state of man nervous and irritable? I went to my Fox Hole Davis class. At least two days a week, some question or something he would see would set him off, and it was back to World War II. A beautiful girl would walk by, and he would say, "You couldn't walk around like that where I was! Her beautiful long legs would be *full* of lead!"

Magenta passed me in the hall, smiling. She said she wanted to talk to me. We ducked into an alcove. She mentioned we had been dating awhile.

"I'm on the pee-uw, you know," she said, and left.

Being a devout Catholic, I had no idea what she was talking about. I figured she popped a pain pill and was excited to tell me about it. But then I remembered, she said she didn't like downers. Hmmmmm.

I decided to seek counsel from the Phantom. He punched me in the arm and gave me his trademark evil grin.

"Dumbass," he said. "She is talking about sex. Dude, you are right around the corner from getting completely naked with her!"

Oh, my. I was a Catholic. Yes, I had eaten a steak and cheese sub on a Friday. God seemed to let that go. Hmmmm. The Phantom was a good Catholic. I knew he was having sex. He could see the wheels turning and stepped in.

"If God wanted you to wait for marriage to have sex, your Johnson wouldn't get hard until your honeymoon," he said. I was glad I had such wise and thoughtful friends.

We had a mutual friend who was frequently seen singing songs to himself in the hallway. When asked, he always replied the same thing: A song from Dark Side of the Moon. His first name was Dan. People began calling him "Dark," due to his obsession with that record. In the greater Boston area, most people don't pronounce their "R's" too well, i.e., "I'm going to pahk the cah." So, Dan soon became Dak.

His mother was a successful real estate agent, but also a woman of the sixties. She wasn't worried about the small stuff. So Dak lived two lives. On weekends and summers, he was with the high society crowd in his high society outfits, at country clubs or down Cape Cod. He would never, ever, set foot on the low-brow, working-class Irish Riviera or at Hale. It was either luxurious pools or the sugar sand beaches of Cape Cod for him. He also swam. During the week, however, he was always in the lower courtyard with the Leatherheads and after school, he would be found in

Islington at the tennis courts with the Burners. He wore the Leatherhead outfit during the day. But on weekends he was at the yacht docks or golf clubs, where it was Docksiders, chino's and polo shirts, with the collar turned up.

School faculty absolutely loathed a guy like that, because he was also a genius. He could show up late for tests and then get 100 percent. He scored in the 99th percentile on his sophomore year SAT. The school officials accused him of cheating. After all, only a very small handful of kids per year in the entire State of Massachusetts scored above the 99th percentile on the SAT – and they weren't Burners or Leatherheads. They had last names like Chang or Greenstein. Dak just said, "I'd be happy to take it again, and if I don't do better, you can let the lower of the two scores stand."

He took it again … and got a *perfect* score.

Faculty doesn't like students who dress and hang with the "derelicts," and then ace tests. This type of anomaly is a living case study that their simplistic life lessons and threats are bullshit. They also feared a guy who could put on a button-down cardigan sweater and hold conversations with lawyers and doctors pool-side at golf clubs. You could hang out with him one night and not see him for a week or two. That was Dak. He was always on the move.

The Phantom organized everything for a double date with him and some girl and me and Magenta. Dak was kind enough to make his house available to us on a night when his mother was going to be out.

I was excited, but petrified. I knew that my tinklebutton was only meant for urinating or marriage. And I knew that neither urination nor marriage were on the agenda for the double date. So, this could only mean one thing: sin. The worst of sins. The "cardinal sin" they talked about in church. Time seemed to fly by as the date approached. I had the itch, but the fear outweighed the itch. This was no steak and cheese sub on a Friday. The night before I was planning to commit the unpardonable sin, I was tossing and turning.

I imagined my father with the same high priest that had put some sort of oil on my head confirmation night. I imagined this very important Catholic figure with his golden staff, long pointed red hat, jewelry, and the smoking can. The can they use when someone dies, and they circle the casket to perform a final smoke show. This high priest and my father were in his electrical bucket truck. Just as I was in the middle of having sex, my father would extend the beam of the bucket truck and smash through the second-floor window of Dak's house, and see me having sex. My father would say, "Holy mackerel! Young lady, put on your knickers, for the love of Pete!"

The priest would then announce that I had committed the "cardinal sin." He would get out of the bucket and perform a religious ceremony, removing my tinklebutton, placing it in a shoe box, light the smoking lantern, and circle the box. It would then be placed in some sex sin cemetery. But, I had the itch, so I played Devil's advocate with myself. After all, the meat on Friday experiment had gone well. Plus, I had been named after a priest, and was an altar boy. Maybe it would be okay.

The sun rose on the day that my first sexual experience had been scheduled. I hadn't really slept. I went to work as an electrical helper with my father. Everything reminded me of sex. The drill going into the wood. The snaking of wires and my father yelling, "Feed it to me!" Would Magenta be saying that? Panic was rising in me. I was surprisingly fast at work, trying to fight the nervous energy. My father noticed I was tweaky and on the ride home and just said, "Hey Fred Astaire, shut your leg off!" I had no idea what this meant. Was Fred Astaire the first one to have his tinklebutton cut off and placed in the sex sin cemetery?

The hands-on all the clocks spun too fast. The time was nigh. I needed a few drinks. I ran downstairs, shaking. I toasted anyway in a traditional, "hula-boom." It calmed me a bit. The Phantom showed up ... the chain-smoking athlete, grinning from ear to ear.

"It's *your* turn!" he said.

Indeed, it seemed that the Phantom had been spared any consequences from committing the cardinal sin. We headed towards Dak's house. On the way, I devised a plan: I would get Magenta alone and tell her to lie about it; she could just tell everybody that we had sex, even though we wouldn't do it. My mind now went into overdrive as we headed across town to Islington. How would I do this? Was it like swimming? I turned to the Phantom, and he just said, "Relax. She'll know what she's doing."

We picked up our dates and then headed for Dak's. Dak was his usual self, "It's all cool, I'm heading out." Dak left and we had this very nice house to ourselves. The Phantom pointed to a room to the left of the top stairwell and said, "That's yours." We walked upstairs, my legs trembling with fear. Every tendon in my leg was trying to signal that I was walking toward the unpardonable sin.

We entered the room and Magenta started to undress, smiling. Did Eve smile when she was having the conversation with the snake about the red apple? I said I needed to go to the bathroom. She said, "I'll be waiting!" I was planning to jump out the window. Then I remembered Tuce and his "motel exercises."

"If you'se can't find a gym, you can do the following motel exercises." One was deep knee bends. I started doing those and threw in a few preliminary Catholic prayers, "Hail Mary full of grace."

Magenta yelled "You ok?

"Er ... fine," I said.

I headed to the room to describe the plan I had devised. I noticed her clothes next to the bed, her long black hair all over her shoulders, her fully exposed shoulders and arms. Then nature took over. I was losing control of logic and reason and started to disrobe. I was now naked but still had some nervousness and some fear of my father's bucket truck with the high priest, so I put the shades down and locked the windows.

I made one last attempt to get out of this den of iniquity and said, "Look, Magenta, why don't we..." But she started to kiss. And then she grabbed my bum. It was the first time a woman had grabbed my bum like that. I was going in. My natural octopus ability to swim now became a natural ability to have sex. But all the while I was looking at the windows and waiting for a guy – zoomed up on coffee, yellow-stained teeth, along with a Catholic religious figure – to bash through the windows.

Magenta said, "Wook at me." I looked at her and thought of poor Adam in the garden of Eden. Minding his own business. Happily raking leaves, naked, and having a good relationship with God. Then Eve comes around and hands him an apple. Here I was, an innocent ex-altar boy, and the son of an electrician. She was a sinful girl living in the only triple-decker in Westwood. Now she was trying to make me perform the cardinal sin. But while I was thinking this, my body was doing its own thing.

Then a feeling came over me, like all my birthdays wrapped up in one. Boom. I laid back, waiting for the lightning bolt to strike me, or for the house to start sinking into to ground. I imagined the Phantom somehow escaping and looking down at me as I descended to hell, with his evil grin, yelling, "You screwed up! You trusted me!"

Magenta just giggled and said what I thought was, "I'm in wuv," and then excused herself. She went to the bathroom, and I peeked out the shades to see if I could spot a bucket truck or any sort of headlights. I said a quick Hail Mary and then Magenta was back. I had some fear of God calling to me, like he called Adam: "Andrew ... Andrew ... where are you?" ... only to find me hiding under the sheets with a girl from Norwood. I would at least tell Him of the courageous fight I put up. Maybe God was like my grandfather, too slow to catch me? Or maybe you could hear him coming down the hallway with his walker clicking on the wooden floors? That way, I could escape before he could point his arthritic, crooked finger at me and say, "Go to hell!"

We got dressed, and I unlocked the windows and put the shades up like they had been. I made the bed. I headed to the bathroom and did a few more "motel exercises" and then headed downstairs. The Phantom was working on his drink and started clapping, smiling, cigarette in mouth. He stood up and shook my hand. Magenta was smiling as well and giggled with the other girl at the end of the table. I poured a stiff one, and we saluted, "hula-boom." Guilt was sinking in. But the drink would help with that. The Phantom and I then had a serious nose-to-nose chat about having just committed the unpardonable sin.

He smiled and blew a smoke ring out into the room. It drifted over my head like a halo hovering over me. He said, "Hey, don't sweat it.

We're Catholics! You just gotta tell a priest in confession. He'll say a few prayers, give *you* a few prayers to say, and then all will be forgiven." I let that sink in. He was right! Confession! Boy, was I glad to be a Catholic at that moment. I leaned back and sighed. I had a free pass! I could confess, and be wiped clean of sin.

We all left and I was full of relief. I slept pretty darned good that night, trying not to look R2D2 and C3PO in the eyes, and woke to Sunday morning and the impending mass. I didn't look at the stained-glass image of our Lord and Savior; I knew his eyes were on me though. The next week I went to the confessional. I tried to talk out the side of my mouth, like my father, so I wouldn't be recognized by the priest. He just listened, and then assigned me a few prayers as my penance; I stepped outside … a free man.

Looking around, I noticed that I was surrounded by mostly elderly women. What could *they* have possibly done to be there at confession, I wondered? I cringed at the thought. Maybe they had enough of their husbands and were spiking the morning coffee with Ex-Lax to keep Old Fred in the bathroom all day?

I saw Dak and thanked him. He said, "Sure thing, man," but then relayed that his place was only for really special occasions; it wasn't a place I could frequent in the normal course of business. However, I soon perfected a little trick in the Country Squire: The passenger seat could go all the way down to a totally horizontal position. I picked up the Phantom and told him to try out this new portable love nest, thanks to the Ford Motor Company and their team of engineers. The Phantom sat in the passenger seat, where my mother would stare in the visor mirror and put on her finishing touches of makeup before church. He put the seat all the way back and then gave his trademark evil smile.

Seat Adjustments

Performing the cardinal sin was almost as addictive as drinking and pill popping. I had some guilt, but on the other hand, the cardinal sin had the same effects as rigorous exercise: it released tension. Besides, the Phantom may have been right: If God didn't want you to have sex, he wouldn't have designed our organs to work before marriage and the honeymoon. Plus, there was the free pass we got from being Catholic.

Not wanting to take any more chances than absolutely necessary, I made sure to hit confession as often as possible. I started using the four Catholic churches that surrounded me so the priests wouldn't catch on. There were two in my town, and two in Norwood. "I tried to fight it, but she insisted," was my line. It was an Adam and Eve story, so what could they say? Just put the blame on the one that handed me the apple. I would even duck down in the confessional and speak upward, just in case the priest could see my oversized octopus head and recognize it from the round of confessing a few weeks previous.

When the Phantom and I did double dates, we would pull the Country Squire into the woods and shut the lights off. Magenta and I would take a walk in the woods, and then when the Phantom and his date had finished their cardinal sin, he would either beep the horn or flash the lights. Then they would take a walk, and I would use Ford Motor Company's portable love nest.

I would drop everyone off, and then have to search the car. Being friends with the Phantom didn't make me immune from his sick pranks. My worst fear was failing to find a used condom, nestled in the visors, alongside my father's sunglasses, or in the glove compartment. The Phantom was already suspected of sending pornographic magazines to my house with my name on it, so it wouldn't surprise me to find a condom in the first aid kit, or nestled in a highway map.

NECK BEARD

Soon I started to see significant changes in Magenta. Her clothes weren't ironed as much, her hair wasn't as neatly combed, and she seemed to be always in the lower courtyard smoking. Then there was the constant sniffling. She finally offered me this product that made her sniffle. Coke, she said. Yea-yo, or "the cheese." I knew it was taboo, not from some film in health class, but from the movie *Scarface*. I pictured myself as Tony Montana, rising up the ranks and then finally going down in a gun battle on the top of my mother's staircase. I wouldn't have it.

This was the mid-1980s, however, and it seemed to be everywhere. Most everyone was sniffling, except the AP kids. Then there was that Dave character, the guy leering at me from inside his muscle car the night of our first date. Of course, he was Magenta's psycho ex. One day, after visiting Magenta at her triple-decker in Westwood, I spotted this character leaning against his muscle car across the street. He flagged me down. I knew there would be a beef.

Beefs in the daylight are safer, I thought. Someone will tend to break it up which is good if you were losing. In that neighborhood, some elderly woman was likely to come out of nowhere with an umbrella and beat the guy causing the fracas, just like the cartoon with Tweety Bird and Sylvester. But there we were, at night. He approached and took a swing at me. He was bigger than me, but I had had enough. I quickly put him into my patented octopus arm triple headlock and pounded him. He stopped swinging and whimpered, "But, I had been with Magenta for 5 years." I gave him an incredulous Cashews cry cop look and said, "Man, are you are crying?"

I laughed, released him, and walked away. Trying to regain some credibility, he threatened, "Just wait, man, I'll be back with my crew!" But he had lost, and he had whimpered. He had no credibility. Driving home, I imagined my crew on the swim team and the eventual rumble. We would disembark the yellow swim team bus with goggles, speedos, kick boards, lane markers, and the big clock on wheels. They would have their biker boots, denim, leather jackets, helmets, ax handles, and metal bicycle chains. I would announce, "We will win this fight in one minute," and point to the portable clock.

There would be kickboards flying, bicycle chains being swung, and lane markers landing hay-makers. We would win the brawl, due to our training and clean lungs, and then get back on the yellow bus, victorious. I thought about the whole scene, this guy yelling outside the window, seeing him whimper. What was that emotion? Cashews in the 1970's had eradicated the expression of sadness or pain from our emotional landscape; it was unthinkable.

I thought of Magenta and me. But with this guy Dave in the picture, her now obvious cocaine problem, and her incessant hanging out with the heaviest of hitters in a small circle of reprobate Leatherheads ... it was time to move on. I wanted to go back to a life of less hassle. The days of eating right, rigorous exercise, and straight vodka. Separating from Magenta would get me away from the pain pills too.

It was hard to catch Magenta alone because she was always hanging around one of two people. One was a girl from Dedham. Her nickname was "Sick Lisa." She had probably been attractive once, but now she was skinny with long brown scraggly hair and that Keith Richards loping walk, where her legs always seemed to be one step ahead of the rest of her body.

Then there was a guy we called "Neck Beard." He must have had a genetic defect of some sort because he couldn't grow a beard on his face. The hair only grew on his neck. He had a girlfriend that was very unkept and they would argue almost every day, and then Neck Beard would start yelling and screaming through the hallways, slamming doors. Everyone kept out of his way.

I didn't fear him, or many people, for that matter. I just didn't want the hassle of breaking up with Magenta and seeing the reaction of Sick Lisa and Neck Beard and his gross Janis Joplin-looking girlfriend. So, I called magenta, and told her about the beef with her ex, mentioned her worsening nasal problem and its source (but withheld saying anything about her witch-like mother with her creepy hair and laugh, always covered in orange Dorito dust, surrounded by marijuana fumes). No wonder her father was on the most powerful pain pills.

Magenta, said, "Hey, the guy hass-aw-wing you is about to be taken cay-uh of by my muvvah's bwuv-ah."

I said that was nice, but there was still the matter of her coke problem. She assured me it was down to a few days a week. I congratulated her. But I was determined. I told her so, and she went ballistic.

"But I wuv yoow!" she said.

"Dats a tewa-bull ting to doow!"

"You'se are gowig to pay fuw dis!"

She hung up.

I didn't fear men too much, but Magenta, in my mind, had the capability to do something crazy. At least I had never introduced her to my parents! Now I needed to calm down, and think clearly. I poured a stiff one, quickly said "hula-boom," and decided I needed to talk to my father, just in case she somehow remembered my last name through her cocaine-induced stupor and decided to pay us a visit.

He was working on the Country Squire, and I told him I had been seeing a girl and didn't think she was stable; I had just broken up with her. He went over to his truck, reached under his seat, and held up a pistol. He then said, "Let her bring it on! I'm *always* packing heat!" He put it back under the seat and went back to fiddling with the Country Squire.

I went to school and announced to the Phantom that I needed his stealthy, sneaky-bastard, athletic skills. I told him about the break up with

Magenta and he said, "You better watch your ass!" I employed him now, to walk in front of me with his stealthy skills. Magenta and her small crew were all in a "special" class. So, they were always together in the same room all day. The phantom walked a funny walk, half jogging, half strolling. He peeked through small windows and doors and then signaled me to come forward.

He was a good friend and enabled me to see Magenta from distances, so I successfully avoided her entirely for two weeks. After about six days, the phone threats stopped, and we both went our separate ways. My goal was to return to what I considered to be a normal existence. That would still include heavily drinking ... but never alone in the morning, and only after rigorous exercise.

WHITE CHICKENS FLY AT YOUR FACE

Spring arrived and with it, the New England darkness started to disappear. There was more light at the end of the commuter tunnels – or whatever tunnel the white wigs referred to when they said, "There's a light at the end of the tunnel." The leaves were even starting to bloom, but not yet enough to provide drinking cover from the stormtroopers. I had my best year swimming, and aside from the deformity of having one shoulder shorter than the other, was fully recovered. I was a full-time member of the "idiot fests" and even had friends that were part of the AP crowd. One of them was always a phone call away for math questions.

There were definitely more drugs on the scene, but I stuck for the most part to that pure Slavic dew of the Gods that was … vodka. If I stumbled upon a pain pill while working in someone's home, I would thoughtfully take a few, just to spare that homeowner from the horrors of addiction.

A more frequent hang-out for me became Simma's place. His mother, the saleswoman for the Cadbury candy company, always had sweets on hand in mass quantities. I knew it was springtime because there were boxes of delicious Cadbury Cream Eggs on a platter in the entryway. I would gobble up a couple on my way in, put the wrapper in my pocket, knock on the door, and then innocently say, "Oh, do you mind if I have a couple?"

"Oh yeah sure," she would say. "That's what they're there for!"

Simma's house had a historic plaque affixed to the exterior, as it had been built by the old white wigs. His room, in fact, was historic; it featured a secret compartment that once probably contained the original Constitution or the first printing of the English Bible. Only now, that secret compartment held vodka, Jim Beam, Jack Daniels and Mr. Simonon's favorite, Dewar's.

I sat down and Simma looked a bit suspicious. It was obvious that we were about to have a historic meeting. He reached into his pocket and emerged with a bunch of aluminum foil. He opened the foil and there were tiny pieces of paper.

"It's acid," he said.

He wrapped it back up, and I thought about the nice guy outside the Orpheum and his guarantee, "You won't get cramps." I mentioned this to Simma, and he said, "Yeah, no cramps, its clean." I didn't want cramps. I imagined my father trying to apply Ben Gay on my stomach as I lay in pain at 3:00 a.m. on the kitchen floor. Then I thought back to the 1970's and the acid and angel dust events that happened at the Bullis house. That poor kid thinking he could fly, and that man with no clothes racing up and down the street on a motorcycle.

"Will I do and see weird things?" I asked.

"Well, you're not going to see white chickens fly at your face," he replied.

That was good enough for me. With the guarantee of no cramps, and no white chickens flying at my face, it seemed like a no-brainer. I would "experiment" with some lysergic acid diethylamide. I really wasn't afraid of white chickens, anyway. But as I slowly unraveled the Cadbury Cream Egg I had pocketed in the entryway, I thought of birds ... all sorts of birds, and them flying at me. At the last second, each bird resembled my father's face, or the face of a high-ranking priest; If I took this acid, would I freak out and have to "go for a ride," like Cashews?

We both ingested our individual portions of lysergic acid diethylamide. It was a nice sunny spring day and we went outdoors. I said, "Let's do it at Pete's Rock. We know the area, and it has lots of escape routes. We'll be safe there." Simma consented.

We finished our lysergic acid diethylamide and our Cadbury Creme Eggs. We were boarding the A-train ... the Acid Express. Mr. Simonon came in with an empty glass full of fresh ice. He poured the Dewar's. Apparently, it was time for a historical discussion. He looked off into the horizon and must have envisioned the white wig ancestors that had once occupied this house. He began to talk. We were in the middle of the life graph, he said, and were doing a good job thus far. He mentioned that we were still heading upward, but our mechanical ability would see us through to the end. He noted how much money skilled laborers were paid, and gave his blessing. Then the salt and pepper afro dad disappeared ... along with the spectral forefathers he could see on the horizon.

Simma said it would take about 20 to 30 minutes before this LSD A-train pulled up. We started to talk sports, car engines, girls. Time went by and we noticed we had stopped talking. We said nothing, and Simma walked into the woods. I decided to climb the 12-feet-above sea level boob-shaped boulder known as Pete's Rock. The boob. Until sex ed class, my friend Tibbs thought that the boob was where babies came from. In his mind, the doctor simply unscrewed the boob and a head emerged, and then the baby was pulled up and the nipple sewn back on.

Now here I was, hugging and crawling on this rocky boob-like formation. Why was I doing this? I climbed differently now, just like I learned from watching the inchworm as a kid, inching his way up the oak trees. It seemed to take forever using this method to climb Pete's Rock. I finally got to the top and gingerly laid down, my hands wrapped around the top of the boob. Gravity tried to pull me down. I found a small crevice, and put my foot down to counteract the force of gravity. The same thing that shattered my collarbone, and put a lump on my head. Gravity. I feared it now. I feared it pulling me into some massive pit. My obituary would say, "He died suddenly from gravity, the beloved son of Ed and Carole Winslow."

I planted my foot tightly and wrapped my octopus-arms around the boob-shaped rock. I looked around and saw Simma, who inherited the genes of his six-foot mother; he grew 10 inches over one summer and was now six-foot-four. But, unlike Cashews, who was still skinny and gangly and ostrich-like, Simma was big boned and had massively wide feet and hands. I looked over saw him wandering in the woods. A massive guy, with a gigantic head, tiptoeing in the spring daisies.

I was getting nervous. Surely, any moment now, some townsfolk would be up here with dogs, pitchforks, and torches chasing this monster Simma, clinging to the rock as they tried to grab my legs. I clung tighter to the petrified boob. I looked to the trees. Some of the birds were back from hanging out in Florida, and there was my buddy, the big black crow.

I had always admired his work while delivering the *Boston Globe* early in the morning. There he would be, dining on road pizzas, keeping a watch over everything. Even cars would swerve around him. He never complained, and never flew away to Florida like the other birds that couldn't hack the New England winters. My nervousness left. The crow would keep me safe from the attack of the angry villagers.

I looked into the trees. There was Old Man Oak. Now even he was springing to life, pulling nutrients to the end of his branches and producing little green buds. There was Lady Pine. The wind swept through her green hair; her tresses fluttered, and she was laughing. There was Brother Birch. His bark illuminated, glowing, he seemed to be plugged into some sort of power source – the Universe.

I looked at all three trees. Perhaps one of Lady Pine's cones had fallen next to one of Old Man Oak's acorns, and the Infinite Energy from the two trees produced an offspring, Brother Birch. I heard a noise in the woods ... it was the Frankenstein-like Simma, but he looked happy. He was covered in dirt and moss, and several rocks had been turned over. He was happily holding something. He turned to me and, not knowing the Latin term for it, held it up and said, "This is that 50-legged thing."

I turned back to the trees. There was a crew of birds that reminded me of our advanced placement students, all captains of the chess team. This was the type of bird that would report any misbehavior. They looked at us suspiciously and couldn't wait to fly into my father's room and announce that I had taken LSD. I started arguing with them.

I pointed out the fact that they never hung around New England for winter. They chirped something about my test grades and shook their heads at me in disgust. A cardinal flew by, bright red, happy. Now, *there* was a bird that spent its winters here. He was busy, and late for an appointment, and flew off. The others just hung around, laughing and shaking their heads.

Then two furry things appeared and started playing chase. Squirrels. That made me cling to the rock more. But their chasing seemed to scare off the advanced placement birds, which made me happy. The squirrels stopped their game of chase, took a look at me, and headed back down the tree. I watched intensely as they ran away. I turned back to Simma, who was now kneeling over, looking at something. He yelled, "It's Lady Slipper!"

"Don't touch it!" I shouted, "Or we'll be cursed!"

I remembered our destructive B.A. days (before alcohol). We would enter the woods with gas and matches and torch the place just to get the thrill of seeing all the red fire engines and firemen. I remembered when we were young, in the woods on an arson mission, and stumbled upon the Lady Slipper. We just took in her beauty, and even Cashews cleared an area for her, making her stand out more, then explaining with the encyclopedic mind of his how the Lady Slipper was special and endangered. He didn't even need to explain it … somehow all of us intuitively sensed it.

I heard a noise behind me and looked. It was a woman and a golden lab. This was not good. Was this the leader of the villagers that were here to take us away? I noticed she was walking on the very same path that Cashews and I had built while in elementary school. It was Mrs. Ripley. Like my mother, she spent her waking hours in the dirt, planting flowers or pulling weeds.

Her husband was a fulltime musician in the Boston Symphony Orchestra. I delivered their paper, and they tipped well. We were on good terms. She was a Christian Scientist. I never knew what that was, but always imagined people in white lab coats reading the bible and talking about Jesus. I got paranoid. Would she say, "In the name of Jesus and Science I condemn you for burning this forest!"

Instead, she smiled, and looked at me, and said, "I will never forget you and your friend building this beautiful path!" I was afraid to wave and have gravity swallow me. So, I said, "Er, glad you like it, Mrs. Ripley!"

"Hmmmm. It looks like you are in a precarious position!"

"Oh, uh, I'm just enjoying this lovely spring day and, uh, sunning myself like a reptile!"

She gave a cute laugh and covered her mouth primly.

Her yellow lab threw me a look that said, "I know you're on lysergic acid diethylamide. I can smell it in your blood and sweat." They trotted away.

The dog, the birds, the squirrel, and the 50-legged thing ... they all seemed to have a bond with us now that we were traveling at high speeds on the A-train. I took in the sun by squinting. Unlike feeling God's presence via the pain pills or vodka, the A-train came with a little paranoia. But the connection to God was stronger. I wanted to cry, it was all so beautiful – but feared Cashews perched on the top of some pine tree with binoculars, then flying away screeching, "Winslow cried, Winslow cried!" I held in the tear and bit my bottom lip to keep it from quivering. I wouldn't sin anymore after today. There *was* a God. Lysergic acid diethylamide had opened my eyes.

God was always all around us in nature, but we humans had become too busy to see it. I thought of all the biblical stories we read in church. Now, they all came to life. I thought of Noah's Ark. I could hear ducks in the pond. How had it happened? Years ago, they got a signal from God. They flew and landed and duck-walked over to where Noah was putting the finishing touches on the ark.

I didn't recall the bible mentioning the other workers on the ark. But surely Noah had helpers? They probably weren't all that bright. They probably didn't score too high on their school exams. But they could *work*. They were the ancestors of Simma, Sully, Wild Blumpkin, Cashews, and the Phantom. Their wives must have been the ancestors of Sick Lisa and Magenta. It made sense.

We could only be trusted with the manual labor. God still loved us, but certain things had to be left to the really smart people … or the people who were smart in different ways from us. We were smart, but somehow the world had been set up or changed so that only people with that kind of conceptual smarts would rise to the top. People with our kind of working smarts could only go so far.

We could only *see* so far … what was right in front of us. Had we been in charge, we would have bungled several important historical biblical events. Had one of us seen the burning bush, we would have turned it into "Sully's Burning Bush Bar & Grill." Had the phantom found the Ten Commandments, he would have packaged them up into a self-help program: "See the first five for free, but the next five will cost you a dollar."

But then I realized … none of God's wonders could be accomplished without us workers. The smart guys and ladies could think up all the fancy plans they wanted; they could get inspiration from God and put together strategies to carry out His works. But without us, they'd just be sitting around talking. Nothing would get done.

Simma emerged from the woods and had at some point decided to just wear his boxer shorts. We both looked skyward at the angle of the sun and decided it was time to take the A-train home. He put his pants back on and disappeared in one direction, and I disappeared in another. I ambled along in the light for a while and then recognized a rock formation … and then the tree fort that my father had built, suspended from cables in the air. I was home. Now I began to get more paranoid. Was that dog right? Does LSD have a stench? Do I smell like an old car battery? Or rotten eggs? Or rust? Maybe no one was home. I entered stealthily through the garage and walked real carefully into the house, fearing gravity.

I found my way to the downstairs bathroom. Looking in the mirror, I noticed that my eyes were massive. I would splash water on my face to get rid of any acid smell. I sprayed some of my brother's cologne all over me. Then I heard a God-like voice coming from above: "Hey Joe! Wash up! We'se are about to eat!" Uh-oh. People were home, and we were about to eat, but I was still on the A-train! Gah!

I made my way up the steps to the second floor, grasping the banister like my grandfather, fearing gravity with every step, fearing it would pull me down to become lost in space or purgatory where only years of prayer and penance would get me back to planet earth. After what seemed like eleven or twelve days, I made it to the top step. Breathe. My mind spun uncontrollably. Was my depth perception working? What if someone said, "Pass me a potato," and I threw it across the room thinking, "I was in left field and they were at home plate?"

Oh, shit: What if these weren't even my parents? What if I was chewing my steak and they suddenly peeled off their masks and revealed themselves to be aliens? I would have to take my chances. I lumbered to my seat, as if walking on a swaying ocean vessel, trying to keep my sea legs. It was time for grace. My father said, "Eh, Joe, why don't you'se say grace?" He wasn't asking. It was merely a rhetorical question, as in, a command. There was a brief hesitation and we looked at each other. Would I slip and mention acid?

"In the name of the Father, Son, and Holy Spirit, dear Lord thank you for this food we are about to receive, and the crampless acid I ingested today. Thank you for keeping the white chickens from flying at my face. Amen."

We looked at each other for what seemed like hours.

"Say grace," he finally said.

I did the symbol of the cross and thanked the lord for the food we were about to eat. I passed that test but now had to sit in this chair for approximately an hour. Fuuuuuuck. My mind was spinning, so I just focused on breathing. Everyone seemed to be in slow motion. My father resembled a salmon of some sort, a king salmon. A salmon that was swimming up-river all his life. He was banged up, had cracked teeth, and menacing eyes. He had a piece of potato that remained to the right side of his mouth; he didn't know it was there. He said when he was in the Navy they yanked a tooth but hit a nerve, so he couldn't feel that part of his face.

Then there was my mother. She drank a large glass of wine in two big gulps and my father poured her more. She had massive hands that she had inherited from her father, who died of a heart failure from drinking when she was just twelve. Now she was guzzling booze, grasping it with her father's gigantic hands. Then there was my youngest sister, like a breeze in the sun – carefree, always smiling, never in trouble. We ate and I somehow just knew not to talk. My father noticed I was extra quiet. He kept giving me the side-eye, as if waiting for something incredibly stupid to happen.

The meal took forever. But I endured to the end. When I was excused, I loped to my room, "to study." I hit the bed and just lay there as my thoughts seemed to be sucked out of me like a vacuum. The sun finally went down, and I climbed under the Star Wars sheets. Holding onto that boob rock must have taken quite a bit of energy, and I fell into a deep slumber.

I awoke and could immediately sense that I had become several notches dumber in my sleep. The only thought I could comprehend was that I was having very few thoughts. The LeMans showed up. I got in Simma's car and we just looked at each other. Maybe he had been stricken by this stupid-flu, like me. We both threw back a few beers back and headed to school.

We reported the LSD experiment to our crewmates. We both agreed that it had been significant and meaningful and successful – but we both noted that, in the immediate aftermath of exiting the A-train, any capacity for meaningful thinking was gone ... hopefully only temporarily. He dubbed this after-effect of lysergic acid diethylamide as "mind wipe."

SAUSAGE FINGERS AND THE CRYING ROOM

Life now seemed to get busier and busier. It was a good time. A time of handshakes that confirmed a deal, brief phone calls, face-to-face conversations. A stark contrast to today's world of smartphones, texts, Tweeting, Facebook … chaos. All noisy, irritating sounds to communicate with one another. Back then communication depended on a phone call or dropping by the neighborhood corner store (mine was very creatively named Convenient Mart) to get the latest information. There was a guy named Sausage Fingers.

He got this name, shockingly, due to the ridiculously large size of his digits. They were the size of a pale-colored bratwurst. In days gone by, his hands alone would have assured him a spot in a traveling circus. The strange thing was, the owner of Convenient Mart never seemed to care that Sausage Fingers just hung out in the front of his store, seemingly all day, every day. He just stood there, hour after hour, holding his giant plastic mug that was frequently refilled with some colored drink.

He was usually wearing his hockey jacket, standing with a leg bent and one foot placed on the brick curb. You would stop by, get something to eat or drink at Convenient Mart, and then ask him where the action was. It was either a woods party, a kegger behind Sunoco, stolen Foster's at The Rez, or a parental bar-raiding party at someone's house. Then that info was passed on at other hangouts, or by phone. It was our information super-highway.

The next thing you know, there would be a mob scene at the location given out by Sausage Fingers. Eventually, Sausage Fingers would make his appearance at the gig, and people would high-five him or shake his hand for relaying the message. He was proud of his job of getting the word out on the wire and took it seriously. He was never bothered by anyone for doing his job, because we all recognized it was important, and he was good at it.

Lately, a new method for acquiring controlled substances had emerged. There was this ex-altar boy I knew. When it was time for confession, he could always be seen in the crying room. At the front of the church was the stained-glass image of our Lord and Savior Jesus Christ. On the polar opposite end of the building was the crying room. I would confess my sins, give a quick glance above the altar, to the stained-glass image of Jesus, then genuflect, and turn around, and there would be another image through the glass-encased crying room.

The ex-altar boy always sported jet-black hair, slicked back, and all black clothing. Once your eyes met, he would give a demented grin, which meant he had something on him. Pain pills, LSD, or potent marijuana. It gave me an eerie feeling, seeing that guy in there. It was usually a pain pill or two for me, and then on my way out of the crying room.

Angry Tony

We now had a new early Saturday morning hang out: The Apollo, located in Norwood Center. The Apollo was the place to meet early on Saturday, have a very large breakfast, and then discuss the plans or information someone gathered the night before from Sausage Fingers. We would then go about our Saturday chores. For me, it was as my father's electrical helper, or swinging an ax, or pushing or pulling some sort of yard equipment. For Simma, it was working on a car.

The Apollo had various sections, each the home base for one crew or another. When you first walked in, to the left were the swivel stools owned by the boys in blue. They were mostly Norwood cops; arresting someone for drinking in their own town would be an embarrassment. So, they could eat there without any hard feelings from the locals. The Apollo served beer and it was common to hear the waitresses, even early in the morning, asking, "Do'se want some hair of the dog that bit you'se wit' yer eggs?" The waitresses didn't card people. As long as you were man-sized, they didn't care about your age – and neither did the Norwood cops.

My eyes would scan the diner. There were a couple of biker looking dudes, planning some gig, rumble, or heist. Whispering to each other. There was a young father, teaching his daughter how to use utensils. Then the older crowd, up near the entrance on the first five or six stools. They scared me. Not due to a threat of violence, but from my fear of ever adopting their lifestyle. These were the 1950's types. They were very patriotic, hard workers, clean shaven, well-mannered – but it was their routine that I despised and was determined to avoid at all costs.

Their same-time arrivals and departures, their galoshes and umbrellas put in the same spot in the closet, their same static-laden, dry AM radio host Paul Harvey, the same breakfast at the Apollo every Saturday at the exact same time: "The usual, hun," was all they had to say. And soon two eggs over easy and dry toast would be delivered. Bland and dry, matching their existence.

What do guys like that do after 30 or 40 years of the same routine? The same bus, train, or car ride to the same bland job wearing the same bland outfit. When someone says, "Fred, it's time for retirement," they were going to lose their minds. They would have more time on their hands than they knew what to do with. They would have to turn the cream and sugar in their coffee more than usual because they would have no place to go. I respected their work ethic. But they were not "human beings," they were human *doings*. They didn't know how to live, they just slid into a routine and "did" the routine, thoughtlessly. I couldn't become a "human doing."

In the row of booths on the other wall, there was the rougher crowd: more free-spirited, just 15 years out of 'Nam. They would dress in their green army jackets and give us a head nod as we took our seats. It was funny. Most of the 1950's types had served in a war – either World War II or Korea. After their service, it seemed that most of them just wanted that life of routine, of *doing*. They didn't seem too interested in "being" or experiencing. But the 'Nam guys? Most of them recoiled from the routine life expectations that supported the routine society the war they fought in served to maintain. They got it. They didn't want to be a part of that machine.

I feared war, but I got that sometimes it was necessary. Necessary so we could eat our omelets in Norwood, crack a brew, and not have to goose step for some chump with his picture sprawled all over the center of town. I understood that if it weren't for the 1950's types and their stopping Hitler and his minions, we wouldn't have the life and freedom we enjoyed. But Korea? Viet Nam? It wasn't as easy to make a connection between what we did in those countries and our way of life here in New England.

Once we finished our omelets it was off to work. If I had a little time to spare, I would head down the street to visit Angry Tony. I was introduced to Angry Tony by Joe O. Angry Tony was from Sicily. He was the neighborhood's old-school barber. His English wasn't that good, but he was a real pro. His place was immaculate, and you walked out looking like you just went through Paris Island. At least your head did. He had the full-length white barber's coat, and would even give you an old-school shave with the hot towels and the flipping blade that looked like the razor clams we pulled out of the Irish Riviera.

Every morning Angry Tony flipped the sign around stating that he was open and then turned on the red, white and blue spinning barber pole. In that neighborhood, the flat-top hair was always in style, and Angry Tony was the best. Joe O. took me there one day, and the angry little Italian guy in the white coat looked at me from my shoes up to the top of my head, side-eyed. He then asked Joe, "He 'ya friend?"

Joe said, "Yeah."

"Den he 'a my friend," said Angry Tony, shaking my hand.

He showed me all the beautiful pictures of Sicily on his wall and then cut Joe O's hair. I was next, and he proceeded with the flat top. I couldn't grow a beard, but I had patches of stubble. He brushed on lather like Michelangelo painting the Sistine Chapel and then snapped open the razor with a flick of his wrist. I was nervous and feared him saying, "Lock-a the door, dis a' bas-tad look-a like the same guy 'a drop-a my daughter off late." No Italian Neckties were administered, and when he brushed off my neck and wiped my face, I looked like a million bucks.

If we were ever attacked by a foreign invader, Tony was another guy I would want on my team. I could see him standing on the shores of Cape Cod, with his razor knife in one hand, his jaw jutting out to sea resolutely. I wondered what he would look like through binoculars of the captain who planned to invade.

Coating the Enzymes

It was the mid-eighties, and I noticed a great deal of cocaine busts in the news. People were getting pinched traveling from Miami to Boston with immense quantities of blow. Prosecution was swift, and you would most definitely "go for a ride," not to be seen for great lengths of time if large quantities of that substance were found in your possession. I saw what it did to Magenta, and that was before the wave of it came up north via Miami. It was a real Nor'easter, pounding us relentlessly with powdered snow.

Now it seemed more and more people I would pass in the hallway or even at the Convenient Mart had symptoms of being under the influence of this stuff. Their eyes were bulging, and their lower jaw seemed to be going back and forth, grinding their top teeth on their bottom teeth. Simma called one early evening and announced, "I got something new." I said I would be over in an hour, after my traditional Catholic meal of hot dogs, baked beans, and brown bread from a can. My mother loved that stuff.

I gobbled it up and walked down to Simma's historic house to see "something new." I noticed all the shades were down in this house. Maybe they found a historical treasure in the basement, and wanted to share it with me, and closed the shades, so the historical society wouldn't get their white-gloved hands on it and place it in some secure glass facility in a museum.

I noticed his parents' cars were gone. I grabbed a Cadbury cream egg, started munching on that, and knocked on the door. Simma answered, and wore a very intense look. He even shook my hand; there was most definitely some sort of discovered treasure involved here. I noticed sitting on the couch was the guy currently dating Simma's sister. A good guy, but he never talked much. Always seemed to be going somewhere in a hurry.

He was a car salesman, always dressed immaculately and always drove the newest model car. He was commonly seen exiting Convenient Mart with charcoal, chips, and a carton of cigarettes. He recognized me from Simma's house, and would just give me a head nod and exit the parking lot in his shiny new car. Now he was here in front of me, making drinks. He said, "What do you like?"

"Vodka and tonic," I replied.

"Good choice," he said, "Here, it's chilled. Go to the TV room."

I looked at Simma and he nodded. I was about to witness something historic with a chilled vodka and tonic in hand. We walked to the TV room. The car salesman finally finished mixing his adult drink and came walking in. He loosened his tie, and we all sat down. He had the same intense look that Simma had. They both sniffled. On the center of the coffee table was a box. It was fancy. It looked like the type of box that is handed to a little girl on her birthday, the kind that opens up and a ballerina starts spinning around to music.

More likely, I figured, it contained some sort of miniature alien or a baby cobra, and we would make money on breeding them and making anti-venom. He opened the box, and there was indeed a small white egg. Next to it, were baby white snakes, a razor blade, and a straw.

The car salesman said, "Watch," and put the straw in his nose, bent over and inhaled one of the three powered snakes. He then threw his head back and inhaled some more. He gave me a freshly cut straw and said, "Your turn." I wasn't that coordinated on land, and I was nervous about either getting the straw permanently stuck in my nose or falling on this table and spilling everything. He said, "Don't worry, I'll guide you through." My, he was caring, after all. I put the straw in my nose, closed the other nostril and followed the instructions to just inhale and move forward. I did it very quickly, and then he told me to put my head back. I put my head back and looked at the historic plaster on the ceiling. He said, "Good job."

I pulled the straw out and then put my head forward. Simma then said something like, "It coats the enzymes." So now there was another drug performance and quality measure. You wanted acid that didn't give you cramps. You wanted acid that didn't result in white chickens flying at your face. And you wanted cocaine that would "coat your enzymes."

Apparently, Simma knew that I had uncoated enzymes. What a nice guy. Now, my enzymes were happy, warm, and coated with this snake powder substance. If the police kicked the door down, I would simply relay the health benefits, and state, "I was merely coating my enzymes."

The wait for this product's effects was much shorter than acid or pain pills. It seemed to hit the brain rapidly. All of a sudden, I reached my arm out and shook everyone's hand. Hey! I wasn't the shy octopus any longer. The chilled vodka went down like water. The car salesman leaped up and made me another. Why yes, he certainly was a kind, generous, and caring man.

Grand ideas flooded my brain. We were still in the cold war, and the answer was simple: We would parachute this product from airplanes. We would drop it into any conflict zones with instructions and, of course, mini straws and razor blades. After a few toots, once everyone's enzymes were coated, hands would be shook and papers would be signed. Conflicts resolved! The euphoria was intense. The information from all the classes I had taken thus far in school downloaded into my brain in an instant. I was now an advanced placement student.

We talked about everything. The sad part was, we didn't write it down. That information was worth millions. We had the answers to all life's problems. This went on, and despite downing many drinks, I wasn't even hit with the vodka bat. All and still, it was time to crawl under the Star Wars sheets, so I shook everyone's hand (profusely) and went home. Strange thing, though, I couldn't sleep. My jaw became a typewriter. It would go as far as it could to one side, stop, grind, and then go as far as it could to the other side. All night.

My father yelled, "Joe! It's hap' passed and we'se are gonna be late for mass!"

I stumbled to the shower, my head pounding. I forgot how much I drank. What was this sickness? My eyes were beet red. I got to mass and just looked skyward so I could stay awake. I heard nothing and was losing balance with all the sitting and rising and kneeling and standing that were key aspects of our religion. I could barely open my mouth to get the Eucharist inside. The priest gave me a hairy eyeball. Finally, mass ended and when we got home I crashed into bed ... ah, sleep! But after just twenty sweet minutes of slumber, I was rudely reminded that I had to lifeguard.

"Joe! Wake up! You'se has to go lifeguard! What is wrong with ya's? Get the lead out!"

THE LADY SLIPPER

I was still drunk and high and I knew it. So, I said I didn't feel good and needed a ride. As my father put down his Sunday funnies and looked for his jacket, I ran downstairs to get the hair of the dog. I was drinking alone, but it was afternoon, not morning. In my frenzied state, I broke tradition by not holding the glass up and saying, "hula-boom." I was in too much of a hurry to worry about tradition, I just needed the bass drums in my head to stop pounding.

I prepped the pool and took out half the lane markers, then checked the chlorine level. I noticed someone new, and she just stuck her hand out and said her name. I couldn't even look in the mirror, never mind someone's eyes. She said she was the substitute. My head wasn't pounding, but I obviously had the effects of no sleep and an uncoated enzyme, so I paid little attention.

The pool opened and some of the usual people showed up: the 1950's guys did their usual bobbing up and down and talking politics in the shallow end. There were some people that swam and thought they were real athletes by merely doing what we considered "warm-ups." Once in a blue moon some man or woman would come in that had obviously done some competitive swimming. I just paced the deck to keep from passing out. Whatever I did the night before obviously resulted in a major low the next day. Maybe it was a bad Cadbury Cream Egg?

I paced the deck, looking at swimmers, looking at the ceiling, looking at the pool deck tile. No thoughts. Three hours dragged, and I must have logged several miles on the pool deck pacing back and forth. Finally, the last hour arrived, and it was adult swim. That usually meant another crew of 1950s guys bobbing up and down in the shallow end talking about world problems. I could relax. The crowd left and grabbed a chair to sit down. I looked up at the ceiling.

I looked over the six lanes of chlorinated water and the substitute was still standing. She asked with a smile, "Do you mind if I pull up a chair and study a bit."

"No, not at all," I said through my bloodshot eyes. "What school do you go to?"

"I go here," she said.

"Oh? What grade are you in?"

"Eleventh grade," she said.

"What?! We're in the same class?!" I said. "Funny, I never saw you before."

She said, "Yeah, funny I never saw you either."

She grabbed a chair and then opened a textbook that seemed about five inches thick. She loosened the fasteners in her hair. I whispered, "Oh, wow," to myself. She was very pretty. She then shook her hair a couple times in the sunlight. "Oh, my," I thought.

She looked at nothing but that textbook for the next 40 minutes and then, covering her mouth while laughing, looked at me and said, "I'm getting better at this calculus." Calculus? What was this 'calculus,' I wondered? The study of calcium and all its benefits? Why would you need 400 pages to learn about that?

Here we were the same age, the same class, and the same school. Only separated by six lanes of chlorine – but it might as well have been the Atlantic. We were on different continents as far as our interests and friends. It was time to start packing everything in. I rolled up the lane markers and blessed the pool with a little more chlorine. She seemed nervous and got up and asked what she could do to help. I told her to relax. I got to her side of the pool and said, "Eh, my name is Andrew." She said, "Andrew ... My name is Leiko." We both smiled. She had perfect teeth. Must have brushed them twice a day, probably even after lunch.

She stood up and her hair was down to her lower back, and clean. "Wish me luck on my exam tomorrow," she said. I hesitated, and she smiled.

"Is something wrong?" she asked.

Beauty was staring me in the eyes. I was having the Lady Slipper reaction: something beautiful and precious from heaven had been placed before me, and it clearly didn't belong here. All I could say was, "Leiko."

"Yes," she said. "My parents are from Japan. I'm a Japanese American."

I immediately forgave the Japanese for bombing Pearl Harbor and the Bataan death march. All their sins were forgiven.

"Eh ... okay. I wish you luck on your exam tomorrow, Leiko."

I let out a laugh. I've been told that I have a tendency to throw my head back and laugh up at the ceiling, looking a tad insane. She found it amusing and said, "Oh my, you have a robust laugh." She laughed at my laugh but felt the need to cover her mouth, and tilted her head to the side making her more beautiful. We shook hands and I closed the pool down. I noticed my father in the Country Squire with a cheek full of what was most likely pistachios, and a book. Her father picked her up and as she walked to the car, she spun around, and her long black hair twirled in the sunlight.

"It was nice meeting you Andrew!" she chirped.

Boom.

"Er, it was nice meeting you too, Leiko!" I stammered.

She disappeared.

I got in the Country Squire, and put the seat back a bit and muttered, "Leiko, Leiko, Leiko..." My father, with a mouthful of pistachios, said, "Watta ya's mutterin' to yah-self?" Once home, I literally crawled into bed and thought of Leiko.

I put on my "Leiko radar" at school but told no one. I saw her now and then, mostly buried in books, talking to another AP student about the exam that was about to be taken or had already been taken. I would call out her name, and she would then spring to life, and say "Oh hi, Andrew!" and even wave. Like the Lady Slipper, you could only look, and admire her beauty. A sight that didn't seem to belong in the harsh New England environment.

Eleventh grade was moving on. I mentally inventoried my extra-curricular activities. The A-train. The yea-yo. Merely experiments. The pain pills? Just phases. Marijuana? A happy substance that never hurt anyone. Alcohol had been around since man first crushed grapes, so there was no issue there. Hmmm. Life graph ...

COOKING STEW

The year finally came to an end. There was never a dull moment. It seemed I constantly had to be somewhere; mass, lifeguarding, swim team, swim clubs, and of course the idiot fests. The crew needed to take a road trip, having successfully completed another grade without quitting, being expelled, being sent "away" or dying. Well done, us. We were moving up on the life graph.

Stew had done us many good deeds. For all the classes that would have required critical thinking, he did our homework. So, it was only right that we took him on a proper road trip. This one was set a few days after our year was completely done. We would be free from the brick beehive: no mid-terms, no finals, no bells, no big clocks, no sitting upright, no facing forward, no schedules ... we would all be totally free for about a week ... before we all had to get summer jobs.

Nauset beach was known for its beautiful sand and big waves. I hadn't been there in years, in fact, not since Mike B. and I went there with his father.

This road trip was special, in honor of Stew. It was going to be *his* day! We packed the LeMans with beach supplies, vodka bottles, tonic water, big red plastic cups, ice, and the usual bag of 99 cent chips ... for food. We made our road trip drinks, raised our red plastic cups to the sky, and then saluted "hula-boom." It was our tradition to never cross the Sagamore or Bourne Bridges without having a good buzz going.

The LeMans rumbled up onto the driveway of Stew's house. His immigrant parents were doing some early morning gardening. His mother still had her hair in some sort of net, wires, and curlers. She looked at us with her hairy eyeballs and then yelled to his window in Italian. Stew came out beaming from eye to eye. It was obvious he hadn't been to the beach often, if ever. He had the same outfit my father and Mr. B would wear. Shoes, black socks, plaid shorts, and a nice short sleeve dress shirt with a pocket full of pencils – just in case he had to jot something down. Oh, and his massive glasses.

We pulled away, stopped out of sight about a block down the street, and handed Stew a red vodka-filled plastic cup. He smiled, itching for it. It was obvious to me he had a craving for the sauce. We all thanked him for his work that year and for helping us make it through. The teachers should have thanked him as well: without him, several guys would never graduate.

Like the blimp in Scarface advertised, "The world is yours" … it was wide open. Stew had mentioned that he had to be home at a certain time. Simma and I looked at each other. We just spent a year of our precious lives in a brick building. Raising our hands to urinate, bells telling us when to move, clocks telling us when to go to school, lines on the floor indicating the proper areas to assemble. Now Stew had mentioned that evil word, "time." My guess is, we were thinking the same thing, "This is *our* time, not our parent's."

"Time? Don't mention time," Simma said.

We pulled into town. We tried to follow the signs. We finally made it to the beach, and it was still very early. We paid the happy attendant, and she said, "Welcome to Nauset!" It wasn't an act, she *was* happy. Her parents had made her happy. She didn't cut railroad ties on the weekends, or crawl around attics, or repair old 1970's American cars. I needed a few drinks to smile now.

We stuffed everything into a giant cooler and argued about who would carry it. Simma couldn't because he drove "all the way down here." Yeah, but, I had "guided him." And besides, it was "Stew's day." So, Sully and Wild Blumpkin carried the cooler. We got to the beach and took a right.

We walked as far away as possible from the lifeguard stand. Away from the high tide and the families. We were classy, after all, and didn't want Little Johnny Suburb seeing us making the vodka and tonics, and our resultant behavior. We poured a few more, before testing the water. We had to have a toast. We raised our plastic glasses, "hula-boom," and drank them down. Then like free men, we ran into the frigid Atlantic.

We swam for a while, got out, and hit the vodka hard. As the sun climbed the sky, the vodka hit back. Once in a while, someone would take a long walk and see us. A long walk, like those advertised in the singles section of the newspaper: "likes long walks on the beach." They would see us, and do an about face and walk hurriedly away. Blumpkin with his red afro, me with my dickies cut off below the knees. Six-foot-four Simma, Sully buried up to his neck, being assisted by Stew, trying to drink. It was an odd scene and wasn't in the brochure for this national seashore.

The chips ran out fast, but they must have had some nutritional value because no one complained about being hungry. Stew was drinking fast and hard. He had crossed the line from social drinker, having the ability to not drink or stop once started, to not knowing when to stop and always craving more sauce. He said, "I shouldn't have anymore, I got to get home." Simma and I looked at each other. He mentioned a time *and* home. Two things that really should never be mentioned on this day.

"Shut up and drink," said Simma. He grabbed the plastic cup from Stew with his massive hands, and poured vodka into the cup, followed by a little tonic water. He forcefully handed it back and reiterated, "Shut up and drink." I couldn't talk, having been repeatedly smacked by the vodka bat, and just grunted in approval. I looked to my left, and people were now exiting the beach. We would be the last to leave. I couldn't walk well, so didn't join the others in riding the waves one last time. I just sat up and let the final swash of the wave, with its foam, wash over my legs.

We gathered the trash. We were blue collar and knew that some magic tidying elf wasn't going to come behind us and clean. We made our own beds in the morning, and were always told to "clean up after ourselves." The cups, chips, and scattered bags were all picked up and put in the cooler. The sun started to set.

It was dim now and we stumbled to the LeMans. We headed out of the lot, but the happy attendant had gone back to her happy home. We rumbled away. Unlike Mr. B., accelerating at high speeds in the breakdown lane, Simma drove very slow, leaning back in the LeMans. We arrived at Stew's. He had missed the wedding. He stumbled onto the walkway, and someone must have heard the rumbling of the LeMans muffler and turned on the light. It was Stew's day. Apparently, his parents weren't appreciative of his contributions to the youth of America; he spent most of his summer pulling weeds.

THE FINGER BALLET

Summer came and went. Houghton's Pond was its own little universe. It seemed there were more drownings than usual, especially at night when the lifeguards were off duty and someone tried to swim across. As we walked down to the pond, there would be frogmen, pulling the dead swimmer out. Lifeguarding wasn't easy.

There were those sweltering days when you couldn't count all the people there – it was elbow to elbow. The only thing you could look for was if somebody looked panicky. If they were wide-eyed, it was showtime. You ran in and swam around them, or under their feet, then got them in a lifeguard hold with an arm around their chest ... then swam back in to the point where they could stand.

The key was never to do a face-to-face rescue. You could swim a few feet before them, then dive down to their legs, spin them around, and come over the top of them, placing your arm over their chest, and swim in. Sometimes people could have stood up, but mentally, they thought they were in deep water and would get into a panic. Wasn't that a life lesson? Sometimes we aren't physically in over our heads, but we feel we are, mentally, and lose it.

Summer flew by, and when 12th grade began, we were the undisputed powerhouses of the school. We were seniors. Most of my classes were hand-picked, and they were all gravy. I was excited about one class, called marine biology. It was a fairly tough class, but I had an interest – it would bring me back to my childhood dreams with Cashews. I got to sit back and learn more about what lurked under the sea. The teacher wasn't just a "textbook teacher." He had the practical experience as well. He was a diver, had his own boats, and even a few lobster pots. I didn't seem to have my blue-assed fly syndrome in his class. I noticed a special needs student up front. He was quiet at first. Then after a few classes, he yelled as the teacher turned his back.

"What's up doc!"

At first, it was odd. Then, as it entered the funny stage, he would get a charge and would continue. It went from, "What's up doc!" to something from the Three Stooges: "Hey Moe!" One day, he turned around and made a hole with his fingers on one hand, and with his index finger of his other hand, pushed the finger in and out of the hole. A sexual gesture. All the women in the class told him to stop, but the men in the class burst out laughing.

This would cause this student to throw his head back in uncontrollable laughter. I'm a big fan of seeing people laugh, especially uncontrollable laughs. Laughs take one out of the boundaries that have been placed on us all our lives. There are many types of laughs, and my immediate friends all had their own. Wild Blumpkin just moved his shoulders up and down very fast and seemed to be gasping for air. Simma would throw his head back but keep his mouth closed and laugh out of his nostrils. Sully had a standard laugh, staring straight ahead. Cashews was the winner, with his ostrich head tilted all the way back, walking around in circles, a bird-like cackle spilling out of him for what seemed like minutes – especially if someone was crying.

But this special needs kid had them *all* beat. His head would be thrown back, looking up at the ceiling, with a giggle that seemed unstoppable. I don't think he was ever told, like we had all been, "no laughter." He had *no* restraints. If it got too bad, a call was made and he returned to the room he was assigned to with the other special needs students. He would return a week later and would behave for a few days, but then he would be right back at it once the teacher turned his back.

"What's up doc!?"

It was my favorite class, ever.

THEN I SAW LEATHER

There was a guy I got acquainted with that could get a ticket to almost any sporting event in the greater Boston area. We had access to games, and we especially liked the Patriots; we were true fans of a bad team, not like many of today's fans that are more interested in "fantasy" statistics or new jerseys or handsome quarterbacks. No cell phones, no websites, no apps or text messages, just go to a general geographical location somewhere near the stadium and find the ticket guy.

We would usually get someone's family church transportation vehicle, and that would be our ride to the game. For our first home game, we got lucky and found a lot and a spot all by ourselves. We got there at 8:00 in the morning for a 1 p.m. game and cracked open the keg. I spun the cap on my pint bottle of vodka counterclockwise and, in the traditional ritual of killing evil spirits, threw the cap over my shoulder. I wouldn't be needing that cap.

I now loved the morning drink. It made all the worries of the previous day and the future slip away. I hulla-boomed the tiny bottle of vodka like taking a breath of air and started working the keg with the rest of the fellas. I liked the keg idea: no messy cans all over the place to clean up. Just the red plastic cups, one for each drinker, filled repeatedly. There would be no handouts to the cheap, weasely guys looking to make new friends. Someone was always at the keg standing guard. We had a bag of chips. Someone had packed charcoal and a small hibachi grill. We lit the grill.

I wasn't concerned with food. But if there was a slab of meat leftover, I would chew it.

I was looking at the beautiful fall foliage. I would be taking my jacket off in about an hour, not embarrassed by the fuzzy bargain basement sweater my mother had bought for me for my birthday or a religious holiday. The day progressed and this dirt parking lot filled up. Winnebago's pulled in with the guys who had really high-end barbecues. They didn't mess around. They wore chef hats and laid out wine, cheese, and crackers.

We only bought a couple tickets, and the plan was to have a couple of us go in at a time, while the others guarded the keg. Back in those days, a ticket stub would get you in and out of the gates all game long, no problem. I was on the first shift. I worried about being without a drink for however long that would take, so I pounded several red cups of beer before departing. It was me, the guy that sold acid in the crying room of our church, and the adopted black Puerto Rican kid. He was now a card-carrying member of the Islington Burners. He went by the nickname of "Gear Jammer." Why, I have no idea.

We got past the Barney Fife, rent-a-cop security and stumbled around and were finally escorted to our seats. The escorts had funny looks and even a few gathered and pointed in the direction where we were seated. There was a massive camera behind us, but its lens was focused on the field.

Gear Jammer started rolling a joint without care. He was real fast, and it looked like a fat cigarette. Back then, holding a joint in public could get you in real trouble. He didn't seem the least bit concerned. Then it was time to stand for the national anthem. Gear Jammer and I stood up, true patriots, proud of our country. He even put his right hand on his chest, clutching the California sensimelia, and American made E-Z Wider rolling paper. The guy from the crying room, also known as River, was sitting with his head down as we sang the national anthem. He was probably too drunk to stand, but I took it as an insult. We were then seated, and the game started.

Gear Jammer lit the paper snake and we passed it around. The Pats were doing pretty good, so we stood up and yelled like everyone else. The smoke blew into the men behind us, and I figured they would be grateful for the free high. The tranquil feeling from the marijuana had not hit yet, and I got an angry thought about this guy not standing for the national anthem. I thought of all my ancestors fighting for America, and decided to call him a "commie." He didn't hear me at first, and then I said, "You friggin' commie! You didn't stand for the national anthem!" Without warning, he punched me in the face with his Patriots-emblem gloves.

He said his father worked for an engineering firm that built missiles to protect us from commies. I then hit *him* for hitting me. He hit *me* again and then I was grabbed by the back of my fluffy outdated sweater. It was one of the rent-a-cops, and more of them immediately descended on us. All three of us were grabbed. I figured it was to the Paddywagon for us. There was no wagon, just an exit. I was thrown to the ground. We headed for the parking lot to look for the woodchip pile. After stumbling around a bit, we found it. Gear Jammer said I had to watch out for River; when he had a few drinks, he tended to fight.

We found the others and they were the only ones in the lot now. I grabbed a red plastic cup and swilled a brew. I was a bit more sedated from the white paper stick. Someone said I had welts on my face so I looked at myself in the reflection of the car window. I finished my beer and calmly punched the commie in the face once more. He tried to fight back but we were immediately separated. The game ended, the Patriots won, and we continued to drink. Some skeevy looking guy approached us, and we went into defense mode, guarding the alcohol. He said, "I can't believe there are only six or seven of you guys on that keg." We circled our silver barrel, and he got the hint.

Waves of people were leaving the stadium. Then I saw leather. Leather boots, leather jackets, and big scary metal flashlights. I instinctively sobered up a few notches. These were the meanest of the mean, the baddest of the bad, the "elite" of the State Police Force.

"Staties."

They were known for wielding long clubs with short tempers. They were lined up about ten feet apart, moving like a wave in our direction. They were "clearing the lot," and approached our red family church transport vehicle. They had their giant metal lights pointed in our direction.

There was no, "Hey fellas, did you enjoy the game? After you finish your drinks, have a safe drive home." River was drinking beer out of a small glass fishbowl. A Statie yelled, "All of you'se, get out of here!" River stumbled for his keys and approached the driver's seat. Very skillfully, a Statie shined a light on the fishbowl, and with his other hand, grabbed his black wooden baton and smashed the bowl. My friend was covered with beer and glass and gave the Statie the same hateful look he gave me when I called him a commie.

The Statie must have recognized this look, as he raised the wooden stick. I jumped in with a barrage of "sirs."

"Sir, we will be on our way, sir. Sorry, sir."

The wooden baton went back into its holster.

He shined the light on me, and said, "Rough day."

"Sir, yes sir."

Then he showed us some kindness.

"Just get out of my sight."

"Yes sir," I said, and signaled our driver to get us out of here. We made it home and I stumbled down the hallway and climbed under Chewy, R2D2, and C3PO.

I woke to Simma honking and felt pain all over. We looked at each and just grunted. "Eh, the Pats won." That was all that mattered. He handed me a hair of the dog and we hulla-boomed.

I Don't Like the Floaters

Shockingly, the historically awful Pats were doing well. I was a true fan, and so committed to attending at least the parking lot scene of all the home games. I'd arrive around 8 a.m., and disappear around 10 p.m., just before the stormtroopers cleared the parking lot. I wasn't in the best shape, and there was a new coach for the swim team. I could tell he was soft. He spoke perfect English, with no Boston accent. He even said, "If you feel uncomfortable, just take a break or go to the fountain."

What?!

All that registered was "fountain" and "break." This was *never* allowed by the other coach. I lost all respect and decided to quit. However, I would leave slowly. During practice, I had the Phantom call up the pool phone, and play Grandmaster Flash:

"Broken glass everywhere, people pissing in the station, you know they just don't care."

I watched at the coach as he stared quizzically at the telephone receiver and then put it down, shaking his head. After a couple of weeks of this, I quit officially.

I had a steady stream of income now due to more nights as a lifeguard and working Saturdays "bagging" (doing residential electrical work) with my father. The money, shiny cars, and weekend trips that I remembered from the seventies were over. Now I had to maintain a work schedule, in addition to a drinking schedule.

Leiko was now a permanent lifeguard and we often worked together. I was nervous around her, but a few drinks would always help. I would say nothing during the first few hours, and just try to focus on the swimmers. I would look at Leiko from the Lady Slipper corner of my eye. I would pace the deck like Mrs. Mooncai did the classroom. She would stand on the other side of the pool and just look at the swimmers. Adult swim came; a few floaters wandered in and bobbed up and down, then left. I didn't like the floaters.

Either you are swimming vigorously and in an official "stroke" or you are doing nothing. That was my view of everything. If you claimed you were going skating, would you lace up the skates and just stand there? No, you either skated in great circles over and over and over, or you played hockey until bloodied and bruised.

I remember the 70's and the vicious hockey games down the street. Being pushed aside as two teens fought and then were broken up, or being hit by a puck and told to "skate it off." None of us stood still with the skates. Now here were these floaters, taking up my "Leiko study time," floating around and then later telling their wives they had swum "for an hour." Pah!

To me, there was no such thing as passive entertainment. I would even look at people that drank wine and shake my head. They sipped, pinky fingers raised outward, even leaving some of the wine behind. Either you drink or you don't drink. I would become furious with anyone that left behind a half-full drink at any party of mine. I would find the culprit, and they would be made to finish the dregs of their cup and would not be allowed over again.

My friends consisted of men that would do everything to the extreme or nothing at all. That was life. The floaters would wave to Leiko, but I would turn my back on these people because they annoyed me. Going through life, "floating around," driving the speed limits, being greeted by the same people, at the same time, at the same location – every day. That wouldn't be me.

The floaters left, and I shortly followed. Leiko went to get her study material, and I needed a drink of courage. I heard the floaters in the showers, yakking away about stuff they had no control over – taxes, government, the weather. They would float by it all, die and be called, "Fred, beloved husband of Martha," and that would be that.

I went to my special locker, took a few belts, and headed over to the other side of the pool. I started to roll up the lane markers and looked over as the Lady Slipper grabbed her massive book, highlighter, and notepad. Then she walked over to the chair on the deck. She put the dry-as-toast textbook, markers, and notebook on her lap.

Then came the slice of heaven. The blooming of the Lady Slipper orchid. I even noticed her upright position in the chair. She fiddled around with the back of her hair, releasing a long black mane of gorgeousness. A Japanese Rapunzel. And I wanted to climb her. This Irish/Anglo/Scot would eventually yell up to her second-floor window. She would let her hair down and I would climb up, enter her room, and ... study calculus?

She pulled the last of the tiny hair twisties out and her mane fell. I stopped rolling up the lane markers, as she then threw her hair back and opened the textbook all in one move. I did an almost Tourette's-like bark, like the special needs kid in biology class.

"What's up doc?!"

She turned to me smiling, and asked, "What's that?"

"Er, nothing," I said, and rolled up the other lane markers.

I cleaned the deck with the squeegee, took chlorine measurements, all the while, glancing over at her. She would only look up when she discovered the solution to some problem. She would cover her mouth as she giggled, and then go back to figuring out what makes ocean waves wave like they do. The few belts of vodka from my locker calmed me down. I was a meticulous pool guy, and the entire place was now immaculate. It was time to get ready to leave. We chatted briefly. I didn't mention any drinking or A-trains or "enzyme" treatments.

I talked about working on Saturdays, and then "rooting for the Patriots when they play at home" on Sundays. I suppose I was trying to create an image of me sitting there, well dressed, Docksiders and pink sweater tied around my neck, sitting in the stands saying, "Go team!"

She described her weekends.

"I spend most of my time studying, especially now that midterms are right around the corner. I take a few hours off on Saturday nights." She giggled upon saying that, like she was a delinquent. Then she caught me off guard and said, "You and I should go out one of these Saturday nights."

"Er, ya," I said.

She wrote her number down on her notepad and even drew a smiley face. We shut the lights off, and I entered the locker room. I needed a celebratory belt. I looked at the smiley face she had scrawled and let out a special needs-esque, "What's UP doc!?" I drained my flask of Godly transparent fluid from Russia.

"Hula-boom!"

We exited, and she went to her car, turned and said, "Have a good night Andrew!"

"Eh, you too Leiko."

Out of complete joy, I spurted, "What's up doc?!"

I entered the Squire, and my father said, "Eh, who's dat bird, Joe?"

I said, "Her name is Leiko. She is a Japanese American."

"Oh yeahz?" he asked. "And where was her father in December of 1942?"

He flipped a few pistachios in his mouth and slowly chewed.

I hid the piece of paper on which she had written her number and the smiley face. It belonged in a glass case at a museum, only to be touched by a curator. For now, it was mine, and I put in the "L" section of my Encyclopedia set, far away from my mother and her vacuum and her man-sized hands. I slept well thanking God for vodka and for Leiko.

The date was set for Saturday, and I decided I wouldn't drink anything at all in the 24 hours leading up to it. It seems time sails when you are dreading something like going to the dentist, or there is something exciting about to happen; in a strange sense, you want to pass this opportunity to someone else just so you won't have to deal with the stress and anxiety that precedes what you know will be the happy moments afterwards.

More and more the bar downstairs belonged to me. The parents weren't entertaining so much anymore now that we were all older. And, once my parents were in the porch, which was their usual evening routine, it meant my partially deaf father would be out of ear-shot and my mother, who got up at insane ours early in the morning, would be nodding out.

I was now thinking of our future together – me and Leiko. Her studying would pay off, and she would be very successful. Due to my blue-assed fly syndrome, and lack of concentration, and not caring too much about what textbooks have to say, I would end up working in a steel mill, just like in the movie *Deer Hunter*. I wasn't afraid of manual labor, and it would get me the deserved drink after work. Then I would return home, at the same time Leiko got home from the fancy lab she worked at.

Friday came, and it was time for my alcohol fast. The LeMans pulled up, and Simma handed me the normal morning beer. I said, "not today." He gave me a look of surprise and disgust. He then did the math, and it meant more for him and Sully, and he became less agitated. But he did ask, "You're not giving up on the sauce, are you?"

"What, are you nuts?" I asked. "Hell no, just for 24 hours."

I felt nervous and agitated all day. I even felt some physical pains. I didn't like this dry period. I tried to sleep that night, but only tossed and turned, annoying thoughts racing through my octopus mind. The next day meant an early trip to Norwood, first to the Apollo, then to Angry Tony's for a haircut. The fellas met me there, but when they all ordered hair of the dog, I passed. They gave me a look like I was about to be fired as a friend, or had insulted them. I just sighed and took off to Angry Tony's. I told him I wanted "the whole ball of wax," as he would say.

That meant the normal flat top and a shave. I sat down, and he did his thing. He even noticed that I was fidgety. He had to warn me that I would be cut to pieces if I didn't stop twitching around while he shaved. I was a new man in physical appearance, looking slick! I nervously headed out and soon got back to stock my father's truck. We drove off to someone's house in the city. I noticed that I lost focus of where we were. But the electrical work, with all its attic crawling, helped dissipate my nervous energy.

My father could always pick up on mannerisms, and as we drove home he noticed my legs moving back and forth.

"Hey Fred Astaire, shut your legs off!"

I mentioned my nervousness with having a date. He was a daily Maalox drinker and self-taught emergency room physician. He suggested I take a belt from his bottle in the glove compartment. I took a swig and he said, "It will free the butterflies in your stomach." That was good, butterflies were meant to fly freely. Not be trapped in my stomach. I said "hulla-boom" and took a huge swig. I showered and dressed, and noticed my nervousness was peaking; my hands were now even shaking. All over a date? I itched for a drink ... but had to stay on track.

Time went into fast mode. I drove over to the "other side" of town, where people had people working for them. I arrived at the address, and her father answered the door. He was dressed impeccably and looked at me from the shoes up. Then our eyes met. Having the natural gift of reading eyes, I could see exactly he was thinking, "Ah! I know you have taken the A-train, the half-closed eye pills, and coated your enzymes!" He turned after saying this silently with his eyes and pointed to an area of the foyer. He called Leiko, my precious Lady Slipper. I waited there and he gave me several hairy eyeballs, and then turned.

Leiko appeared and I let out a quiet and quick and now a natural, "What's up doc?" I led her to the Country Squire, the once portable love nest for me and the Phantom. But now, I was a straight-edge and had even been forgiven by God for all my sins, due to the many Hail Mary's assigned to me by the priests in the confessional.

We drove off, and our destination was the trusty Kahana in Walpole. The booth-side fish tanks would relax me. I noticed Leiko sitting upright. Just like the stem of the Lady Slipper. She was tall and proud and proper. We made it to the Kahana, and the owner recognized me; I pointed to the fish tank area. He said, "Sure, sure" and asked about my father. We were seated. She looked at the fish. I looked at her. Of course, she knew all the Latin names for every fish and began talking about their scientific and biological differences and peculiarities.

While she was doing that, I had a brief fear fantasy of seeing Magenta and her crazy drug addict biker ex-boyfriend sitting on the other side of the fish tank. They were feeding the fish, recognized me, and then ran at me with butcher knives. Leiko was discussing the genus and taxonomy of the fish. I snapped out of my Magenta murder fantasy and asked her how her day was. She gave me a detailed breakdown of what she had accomplished each hour and precisely what she had studied.

I watched her head as she drew with her finger some creature that can only be seen under a high-powered microscope, and described its purpose. Ah, the discipline that must be required to sit still in a chair and study microscopic things for hours. Clearly, Leiko didn't have the blue-assed fly syndrome. We ordered some sort of flaming platter and shared it. She even ate with discipline. First, she separated her portions into even smaller portions, organized by color or species. Then, she cut up these smaller portions into bite-sized portions.

I imaged the Cro Mags dining here – Wild Blumpkin, Sully, Simma, Cashews, and me. The fire on the flaming platter would trigger us to gorge like starving cavemen and put our hands through the flame, or break up the chopsticks and make a real fire at the table. I tried to control the Cro Mag in me and even tried to copy how Leiko ate. I cut everything up in small pieces, organized the pieces as best I could, cut up each piece into a smaller piece suitable for chewing, and placed each chewing-suitable piece carefully in my mouth; I chewed each piece exactly 9 times just like her, before swallowing. After each portion had been thusly chewed and swallowed, I dabbed the napkin daintily over my lips, just like her.

Then I noticed the umbrella drinks being carried out on small trays to practically every table … but mine. I needed one bad, to take me away from my anxiety. To make me more *me*, the relaxed me, the fun me. To help me enjoy this moment even more. I looked at the people enjoying their drinks. I looked at the colorful bar, the smoke, the pretty bottles, and heard the alcohol-induced laughter. I drifted away fantasizing about vodka. Leiko touched my hand and asked if I was alright.

I snapped back.

"Oh, I'm fine."

"You seemed to have gone off to another world," she said.

"Yeah, sorry," I stammered.

"Okay, well, are you back now?"

"Yes," I said, and pointed to the table. "I'm right back here."

She laughed and covered her mouth. I covered mine and said, "What's up doc?"

She giggled and asked what that was. I just said it was nervousness. She touched my hand and said, "You don't have to be nervous around me." We both smiled.

I tried not to look at the bar or the other booths with their colorful drinks. I looked only at the Lady Slipper in front of me. We finished eating and were served fortune cookies. We were in the giggly stage: young, minimal problems, able to laugh like kids. You can still gain the giggly stage as you get older, but you need to do what was going on around me: you needed umbrella drinks ... or vodka. We finished, chit-chatted, and I managed to get her home at the exact time her father had requested.

"Get her home early," he had said.

We walked to her front door, shook hands and hugged. I couldn't believe I was hugging the Lady Slipper. I got home and my father saw me and yelled, "Eh, how was the date, Joe?"

"It was actually great," I said, still kind of stunned that it had gone so well.

"Did the Maalox work?" He asked.

"Yeah, it did. All the butterflies flew away!" I said.

"I'se told you'se!" he replied.

That deep, meaningful father-son conversation about love and life ended there, and I went downstairs. I needed what those others were experiencing at the Kahana, after imbibing their fancy umbrella drinks with weird names like the Zombie, the Scorpion Bowl, the Mai Tai, etc. I shook a little as I poured the vodka.

"Hula-boom to Leiko!"

I drank like a thirsty man on a hot day. I would work at the steel mill, and she would be in the lab. We would forever be in the giggly stage.

Powdered Snakes

Simma picked me up on Monday and immediately gave me a suspicious look.

"You still on that crazy kick of not drinking?" he asked?

I reached for a brew from his mini cooler.

"Hell no!" I said as I pounded the morning drink in a single swig. Ah, the hair of the dog: the drink they tell you not to drink before noon. But we knew it was all a lie. The first-morning drink was the best drink of the day. It set the tone, put the mind right. The fear and anxiety scattered back into the hole it crawled out of.

Before we picked up Sully, Simma said, "Bring a couple of c-notes Friday night to my house, there's going to be a blizzard."

"A blizzard?" I thought. In southern New England? In early spring? It seemed odd.

We picked up Sully and headed to school. After a few more breakfast Budweisers, we were in the right dimension. Lunchtime would mean a few more to get us through the day.

There were still three convenient stores in our neck of the woods. One was across from Cloverland. Typically, there were always one or two guys from that neck of the woods hanging out front and yelling insults. Then there was the IGA, which you usually tried to avoid. It was a known Runci hangout. If my father or mother needed last minute items, I always went to Convenient Mart. The only guy there was usually Sausage Fingers, who was harmless.

I was picking up some last-minute items for my parents, and Sausage Fingers was there. He mentioned a possible woods party. Then I bumped into the car salesman. In elementary school, we were always told to look people in the eye, out of respect, a sign of being trustworthy. But the car salesman never looked anybody in the eye. He would look left and right, real shifty, and then get a little closer. That is exactly what he did this time and whispered, "There's going to be a blizzard this weekend at Simma's so bring a couple c-notes." Then he was off with his charcoal and a carton of cigarettes.

That party was very private, so Sausage Fingers didn't know about it. I got my items and drove by Simma's house. There would be a cloud over this yellowish historical house that weekend and it would produce a major blizzard, but only for the guests that were invited. Friday came and we had a traditional Catholic meal, no meat, just frozen fish sticks and tater tots. My father said, "Don't you'se clown around too much tonight. Hit the rack early, cuz we have a full day of electrical work ta-ma-rah."

I said I was just going to watch movies at Simma's. I excused myself and headed out. As I approached the house, I noticed all the shades were down, and most of the outside sconce lights were off. There was a small amount of light coming from the glassed-in family room. I walked to the now unlit side door area. I grabbed a Cadbury cream egg and started to unpeel it. Simma opened the door, and I walked down the short hallway into the kitchen. There were a few guys in ties, car salesmen who all looked fidgety.

I noticed another man wearing a tie over in the off-limits/only-for-show room. It was like my mother's decorative soap. It is in fact soap and would lather if wetted and rubbed in one's hands, but that wasn't its true purpose. Its true purpose was to lay there and look fancy. This off-limits/only-for-show room was the same. It consisted of actual walls, actual furniture that you could actually sit in, real art on the real walls, and a floor and ceiling that indeed functioned. However, the true purpose of the room was to ... lay there and look fancy.

I handed over my hard-earned lifeguarding money of $200 dollars. Simma gave it to the car salesman. He looked at me and said, "Okay. This will get ya through the weekend." Sort of like a weekend ski pass. The car salesman was working the ovens and one of his assistants was working the small bar. He asked what I wanted, and I said, "vodka and tonic." In a raspy, tweaky voice he said, "Good man."

There was another knock on the side door, and Sully walked in. He was given several car salesman head nods, and then handed a Budweiser.

"Okay, everyone's here," the car salesman said. He signaled to the guy in the don't-touch room. A big lid was lifted, and the very small crowd began, one-by-one, to enter this room. We took our seats, and I noticed an oversized golf ball on a mirror. It was missing a small notch. There were many white powdered snakes on the mirror. There seemed to be a mini straw cut for each of us. The other car dealers loosened their ties. The blizzard had begun. We all took turns, inhaling one by one. Shortly after, everyone loosened up, and the conversations started. I had to be cognizant of the time, for I had a "big day" ahead of me in the morning.

One of the salesmen, said, "So, what's your story?" Now, my enzymes had been coated. I just recently learned I had been accepted into the same college my brother and sister had attended, the Massachusetts Maritime Academy (thanks to Stew). I said, "I'm wrapping up my senior year, and headed for the Massachusetts Maritime Academy." He said, "That place will straighten your ass out, and you'se will come out clean cut."

Clean cut, I thought. Just like that clean-cut goose egg on the big mirror. Slowly this school would cut me down to expose the real me, the clean-cut, highly intelligent me. I pictured myself behind the wheel of a great big ship.

We were all off on our own mini conversations. The alcohol flowed down our gullets with ease. I took in the historical paintings that were on the walls. We were all now sitting in what I imagined to be large, fluffy, decorative soap dishes. It felt naughty.

I needed a refill and headed over to the same guy that gave me my first drink. I politely said, "Excuse me, Sir, may I have a refill?"

"Ah, another vodka drinker," he said.

He pointed to the bottle.

"This is top shelf, Stolichnaya."

Back in those days, Stoli actually was considered top shelf. Then he gave me a vodka lesson.

"Most are cheap and made out of potatoes, and just mass produced in factories," he said.

"This here Stoli is made by real craftsmen, from hand-picked wheat and rye, and fresh water from the Russian mountains. You'se gotta keep it chilled in the freezer."

"You'se don't even have to add a mixer," he continued. "You'se don't need no ice neither."

Well, bless you, Stoli, I thought. I hated ice in my vodka; there always seemed to be one cube that at the last minute would become un-lodged and push against my face and spill the drink all over my shirt. Plus, it just diluted the drink.

He poured me another drink, but with no ice and no mixer. We raised our glass to our new common bonds: vodka, the yea-yo, and being Americans.

"Hula-boom," I said.

He paused, eyeballed me, smiled, and then did a cheer of his own that I didn't recognize.

I reached into my pocket and said, "Here, let me pay for my drink."

"No way, brother. This is all paid for. This whole freezer full of Stoli. Included with your entrance fee."

Ah, all my lifeguarding had paid off, I thought.

I kept a laser-like focus on the time. My father, an avid listener of several police scanner channels, always said, "The real stupid action always starts at a certain time, especially in town, so be back before the real stupid action starts." I made sure I was always home before midnight because the real stupid action started at 12:01 a.m. precisely, according to my father.

My eyes seemed to control the clock. The more I looked, the more time I had. My new friend had to recoat his enzymes and signaled to the guy that was in charge of shaving the powdered egg to set him up with a white powdered snake. Then he said, "One for this guy too."

I put my drink down and inhaled. No drinks were allowed in the egg room, so I inhaled and then went back in the kitchen. I drank the Stolichnaya with ease; this clearly wasn't vodka-bat vodka. I just felt relaxed and filled with knowledge. I told tales to this guy about being an electrical helper. I pointed to receptacles, lights, and switches in the kitchen. I explained in great detail how to get the wire or pipe to those locations, and how some items, like the fridge, garbage disposal, and dishwasher, should be on their own circuit.

He said he was shocked once and as a result was afraid of electricity. I relayed a saying from my father:

"Don't be scared of it, respect it."

My new friend looked like I had just revealed one of the mysteries of the universe.

"I will," he said, mystically, "Oh, I *will*."

I had a few more vodkas and powdered snakes. I looked at my new friend, the clock, the drink, the clock, the guy cutting the powdered egg, the clock, another drink, the freezer, the oven clock, the historical ceiling, the microwave clock … and then it was time to go, before, "the real stupid action starts," and my father hears me on the police scanner.

I politely shook everyone's hand. The new friend looked at me intensely and asked if I was coming back. I assured him I was and he said, "Good, us vodka drinkers have to stick together."

I ran-walked home and took in the beauty along the way. I thought of the 1970's and delivering the newspaper. Of the people that were coming off something "cold turkey," and being yelled at for ringing their doorbells too much. Of the big tippers, and the cheap people. It was all gone now. Now the neighborhood was filled with small families, from where I didn't know. They all seemed to have plenty of money. Their houses and lawns were well-kept, but never by the children. Always by some hired hand.

I made it home and politely said good night. I lay down and thought of the Stolichnaya and the many health benefits of its wheat and rye and mountain spring water. Then I started biting my lip. Then I developed typewriter-jaw. I was wide awake. After some time, I needed to drain the pickle and tried to get out of bed. It was then that I discovered that I had, indeed, been hit with the vodka bat. That Stoli was sneaky!

I stumbled to the bathroom. I looked at the designer soap sleeping peacefully in its own blanket. I didn't want to look in the mirror. I stumbled back to my bed and didn't bother putting my sheets over me. I was grateful to have consumed a great deal of vodka, as that would help me sleep. One eye didn't seem to want to shut. I lay there wondering why, biting my lip, typing with my jaw, when the eye finally closed.

Mentally, I said to myself, "Ah, finally, sleep ..." I took a deep breath.

And then I heard, "Joe! Get yer ass out bed! It's hap-past!"

I tried to move but felt incapacitated. Was I dreaming? Didn't I just fall asleep?

"Get the lead out!"

I accepted the reality that it was half-past some hour, and I had to do electrical work.

I stumbled to the bathroom and felt I was on a ship rolling on the sea. I placed one hand on the tile to stand upright. This helped, and I dried off and started to put on my work pants. Then I heard the beeping and more shouts of, "It's hap-past! Get the lead out!"

"Everyone would be burnt dead if you'se was a firefighter," my father said, as I slid into the truck.

He spun the tires and we headed off. He calmed down after getting a coffee with ten sweet and lows, and a Boston cream donut. I didn't want anything but two days of sleep. Instead, I was up in an attic removing blown insulation. Then I was drilling, and shoving a snake down to my father. This snake wasn't powdery. While I was doing the bull work in the attic, my father usually spent this time talking to the homeowner, who was typically some distant relative of a distant relative that needed a favor. I could hear his usual loud talk. It was like a script:

"I looks to my right then I looks to my left, and I knew me shirt was ruined…"

I yelled, and he went over to the hole he cut in the wall. I pushed the snake downward and felt him grab it, the signal letting me know that he had gotten it. I then tied on the wire and he got that too. I pulled the snake back and cut the length of wire I figured I would need, and ran it over to a junction box. This same series of steps were repeated for the entire day, and then I spent the last hour cleaning. My head was pounding. It felt like it was filling with air and about to burst. I needed a hair of the dog – bad – and a few days of rest. But I wasn't going to get either. The day of pain finally ended. I stared up at the ceiling of the truck on the ride home. When we arrived, my mother had our Saturday night traditional meal all ready.

Brown bread from a can, baked beans, and hot dogs. I needed this food bad. I gobbled it up ravenously.

"Easy tiger, no one is gonna steal your plate!" said my father.

I refilled my water glass several times. I felt a little better and dismissed myself for Simma's. I ran to his house as if being chased by an albino tiger. I grabbed a Cadbury Cream Egg and knocked. Simma answered and it was obvious he hadn't slept one bit. Everyone was intense but still friendly. Ties were off, my new friend recognized me but didn't rush up from the table, he just pointed to the freezer. I quickly poured a drink and rudely drank without even saying hula-boom. I poured a few more quick ones and then the switch went off in my head. The game was on again. I was finally … myself.

I ran over to the enzyme table and the egg was now cut in half. My straw was still there and a white powdered snake was all ready. I inhaled it like air and was back on track. The others seemed a bit lethargic. There wasn't as much energy as the night before, but there were still big dreams being discussed and major life mysteries being solved. I was obviously the busiest bee in this hive and kept at the rounds. Just a few minutes before midnight I ran-walked home and got into bed. After maybe an hour of typewriter jaw and lip chewing, my one eye closed. Ah, sleep, I thought. About five minutes later I was woken up by a shout of, "Get the lead out Joe! You'se have guard duty!"

I packed all my orange guard gear and headed off. Arriving at the pool, I stumbled unseen down the hallway and stuck one hand out to the tile wall to keep myself balanced on the rolling ship. I got dressed and paced around the pool just to stay awake, and out of fear of falling in and drowning if I stood still for too long. It was adult swim, and thankfully no one showed. I sat down and pushed the chair all the way back to the wall, putting my head back and staring at the ceiling. My eyes kept closing and opening, seemingly having a will of their own.

Leiko was there, but I didn't even notice. She even said goodbye, and I think I just grunted. I drove home with one eye struggling to remain open; when we arrived I ran to bed, stating that I was ill. I must have slept for twelve hours. I felt better, but my head still pounded. I heard the rumbling of the LeMans. Monday morning had arrived. I quickly splashed water on my face and brushed my teeth and dressed. I jumped in the car and was handed a brew. I pounded that in a few fast gulps and then pounded a few more. Headache: gone! Simma, Sully and I said very little on the drive. It had been our first blizzard and we were *shot*. Like any blizzard, the snow coming down and the blowing wind is fascinating, but eventually, things get sloppy and there is a mess to clean up. That day, the mess was cleaned up with a hair of the dog.

A Sickening Loud Thud Sound

The Pats were, shockingly, having a good season, and there was an important game coming up. Like true fans, we would be there. This was before 9/11 security craziness and tickets with barcodes and scanners, and Sully knew a guy that worked the gates who never checked tickets. We would weasel our way in for free. We were experts at tailgating now, at least when it came to alcohol.

Massachusetts then had "blue laws," which meant no sales of alcohol on Sundays. So, we made sure to stock up on Saturday and to bring lots of extra, so there would be very little chance of running out and not being able to get more. That meant, in addition to the keg, several bottles of vodka. Only, not the hand-picked wheat and barley and mountain spring Stoli that required neither ice nor mixer. No, it meant good old American factory-made industrial vodka that came in plastic bottles.

There was the usual question on the ride to the stadium about food.

"Who brought food?"

This would be followed by short arguments and finger-pointing. Usually, someone brought a few cheap steaks or some scraggly hamburger meat, or at minimum a 99-cent bag of chips. But the important thing was we always had the right abundance of alcohol. And we always did.

The other important thing was guarding the alcohol. We were like squirrels, always looking left or right for someone trying to get cute and take a sip out of our giant metal acorn. Ah, the keg. We weren't big fighters, but when it came to preserving the booze, we were animals. Every few minutes our sensors would go off, and we would stop in whatever position we were in and surround the wise guy who was near our keg, posing a threat. Today was "special" because the Pats needed to win to make the playoffs, which only happened once every decade or so.

"The big game" made for a great all-around excuse for most males. It could be any "game," but every game was potentially somehow too important to miss. It went like this ...

"Honey, are you going to rake the leaves before the first snowfall?"

"Eh, I'm watching the big game. We have to win this one, so I can't miss it."

"That's what you said last weekend, dearest one."

"Well, if we hadn't won last weekend, then this game wouldn't mean anything. But we did win last weekend – thank God I watched it – so now we need to win today. Sorry smoochie bear."

"Okay, I suppose, darling. Just make sure you don't have some important game to watch next Sunday, because my mother is coming over for tea."

"Okay, pookie-heart. Hey, can you bring me those chips and freshen up my beer?"

For at least a decade into any marriage, this routine will work. It helps to get you out of Sunday tasks. You can even spring it on the Mrs., to catch her off guard. Just invite a friend, so he can knock on the door right before the love of your life approaches you with the honey-do list or a request to go to that romantic brunch. She'll answer the door, thinking it's flowers you ordered for her, but instead it will be your pal Philly, the one she hates because he "dated" her little sister that one time. He'll announce that he is there for "the big game."

Your wife may even get a phone call from the wife of the husband that was just raking leaves a few doors down.

"Martha, have you seen Fred?"

"Ugh, he's downstairs with Mike watching the big game. He said if you called to tell you to bring over that bag of chips on top of the fridge."

We arrived, and the New England sun had only been out for a short time. It was very cold, so we decided it would be a smart thing to drink the vodka, first to warm up. We would tap the keg, and let it "breathe." We would build a little fire as well. We made our tailgating preps, and cracked the vodka and poured it in our plastic cups. We raised our glasses to the important game, said "hula-boom" and the games began. Our games. The real game was hours away, but we would be prepared.

Like good Cro Mags, we started gathering wood and rocks to build our life-sustaining fire. It was like the whole parking lot was designed just for us. It was the "far off" lot, for people like us who had their priorities right. Most of us would get too sloshed to even enter the stadium. But we would tell our family and friends and significant others that we were at "the game."

We weren't like the people who painted their faces, had perfect and well-planned barbecues, and dressed in the team's attire ... they were somewhere else. They were in the *paying* parking lot. The lot where the camera crew could get their perfect shot of the well-mannered New England Patriots fan with his "World's Best Dad" coffee mug, wine, and fancy hours d-oeuvres.

We greeted the other Cro Mags from neighboring tribes with head nods. They came from Rhode Island, Maine, Vermont, Connecticut, New Hampshire. They, too, were New Englanders, here to the celebrate the important game of the New England Patriots. The Maine, New Hampshire and Vermont New Englanders were in my eyes the more rugged New Englanders. It was a tougher life in upper New England. They drove all the way down to here from the frozen wasteland just south of Canada. Like us, too, they would focus on getting hammered while simply turning on the car radio to listen to the game.

There would always be one guy in one car to the left or right of us that would sit in his vehicle, listening intently to the game. After any big play, or during time-outs, he would emerge excitedly with his drink, screaming updates to us, as if we hadn't been listening to ourselves. His screaming would reveal that dentists in upstate Maine are few and far between, as evidenced by the state of his teeth.

"Gwogan dust whipped wun to Mowgun en dey ah ad dah ten yahd nine."

Hours went by and the booze was beginning to wear me down. Then, the guy from upstate Maine emerged from his beat-up pickup and screamed, "Deh Pat's wun, deh Pat's wun!" The parking lot was screaming now! We were winners! I was in the vodka bat dimension and decided to congratulate the coach. I felt patriotic, though I couldn't walk very well. So, I sort of trotted, and half-skipped, toward the stadium. I got tired and decided to lay down by the side of the road to take a little rest when I saw a giant mob carrying the goal post toward me.

Being an electrician's helper, I saw the transmission lines above. I was just about to run over to let the mob know that if the metal goal post made contact with that transmission line, they would probably all die a hot and sizzly and painful death. I was thinking about doing that when I decided to take a real quick nap, to rest up so I could walk over there to alert them. One eye started to close, and then I heard a sickening loud thud sound, followed shortly by lights and sirens.

Eh, it looked like the authorities had everything under control, so I decided to go check on our keg. These mobs could get crazy, after all. I propped myself up and headed over to the lot. We had more drinking to do, since we were winners.

The next morning, I awoke and still felt like a winner. "We" won "the game" after all. My father was reading the paper.

"Jeez, looka 'dis ... buncha clowns tried to carry the goal post out and got whacked."

"Whacked" was not a mafia term for murder in our home. To a Boston electrician, "whacked" was a term used to describe the very foolish act of getting hit with electricity in a bad way. Getting "bit" meant you just felt a tingle; it could happen to anybody. But "getting whacked" was usually followed by a meat wagon, a priest giving you your last rights, and a wake where old ladies would tell the younger people that you were "in a better place." At the very least, if you were extremely lucky, "getting whacked" meant you'd be walking and talking funny for the rest of your life.

The only good news for the family of the victims was that they died doing what they loved, being at "the big game."

Many years later, I was having a discussion with a carpenter about the fact that I had been at that game. I derisively mentioned the clowns who carried the goal post down the street and got whacked.

"Yeah, I'se was one uh 'dem clowns." He raised his hand to reveal that it was grossly scarred and missing several fingers.

THE BULKHEAD DOOR

Because "we" won the big game, the Pats were headed to the Super Bowl. We were confident they would win, so we could feel like true winners. There was an important scheduled watching party at the house of a guy actually named Pat. His mother owned and operated a bar in Quincy, and they were fairly liberal about underage kids drinking in their home. The only rule was, once you were downstairs, you couldn't go upstairs. The good news was, there was always a better spread there than what we would normally have outside Sullivan Stadium, in the parking lot for misfits at the woodchip pile.

When I arrived, the basement was set up in a pretty nice fashion. There was one table for sandwiches and one keg that had been iced. Another table had a few bottles of vodka. We kept people from repeatedly opening and closing the bulkhead door to urinate, fight, or vomit. However, that meant the inevitable fight indoors, over who stepped on who's shoes, and then two guys rolling around like animals. It couldn't be prevented due to the circumstances.

We wouldn't turn on the TV until the actual kickoff. Who wanted to see steroid addicts pontificating? I had bought a cheap lab jacket at some doctor and nursing supply store in Dedham and stenciled on the back words to the effect that one of the Chicago Bears players sucked. The lab jacket would come in handy in protecting me from any stray vomit being spewed in my direction. We all talked about how the Pats were going to

372

surprise everyone. We had no metal goal post to carry down Route 1, but maybe we could carry the metal keg, the little tin man.

Someone quickly turned on the TV, and sure enough, all the retired jock straps were making their predictions. It was time for the national anthem, and we all stood up, proud of our country, and tried to sing the words. I could hear from my fellow patriotic men many different versions of the words for the song. Some were saying, "I pledge allegiance to the flag of…." Others, "My country tis of thee, sweet land of liberty ..." The only thing we all did correctly was have our right hands over our hearts. We were proud.

"The game" got underway, and for the first few minutes the Pats put up a fight. But then it became obvious that the Chicago Bears were the better team, even though they were probably cheating or had paid off the refs. The Pats were losing, and it was making *us* feel like losers. Once the game was embarrassingly out of hand, my friend OB made the medical decision to shut the TV off.

"Start fucking drinking, boys," he announced.

He was right, when things start to go wrong, it was time to, "start fucking drinking."

Drinks were poured, sandwiches disappeared, and the empty plastic barrel being used to collect vomit and urine was filling up fast. Once it reached halfway full, we would open the bulkhead door and muscle it out to empty it on the lawn. Time went on, and sure enough, a fight broke out. Fighting outside wasn't allowed, so two guys were rolling around on the basement floor. Once it had been broken up, I noticed that one of the combatants was River, the same guy that I called a commie for not standing up for the pledge of allegiance.

Hours went by and someone turned on the TV very briefly, not to ruin our alcohol-induced euphoria, but to see the final score.

Bears: 46

Patriots: 10

Ouch.

Now everyone yelled to shut it off. We needed more alcohol. The plastic vomit and urine barrel was full to the brim – with more vomit than urine. It was a sickening man-stew of foaming beer puke and small chunks of sandwiches. It was a real struggle to get it up and out the bulkhead stairs now. A few poor souls got splashed with its contents while trying to get it outdoors.

I awoke in my hallway, hugging the wall and inching my way into my room. I was still in full uniform: a lab jacket, Patriots hat, and work boots. The only thing I could recollect was the Pats losing, the fight, and the vomit and urine stew. Our team had lost. But they were paid a great deal of money. Here I was with very little money of my own, still drunk from the night before, lying on top of Star Wars sheets, wearing a lab jacket and a Patriots hat. Something wasn't right. I had to figure this out. It couldn't be the alcohol, for it had carried me this far. The few first hard drinks always provided me with the euphoria needed to get through the day; they turned on the pinball machine in my head, which triggered an awareness of all my life-graph goals and Docksider dreams.

I felt sick and needed the morning drink, which would shortly approach on a rumbling platter in the form of a mid-1970s LeMans. Simma never beeped, you could just hear the mumbling of the engine. I entered, and he handed me a beer, which I quickly slurped. I felt better. Why would I ever question queen alcohol and her magic? I figured I felt like crap because of something I was eating while I was drinking. That's what caused the blackout. I vowed to stay away from the bad food while drinking.

My Fellow Oceanographer

A temporary job opened up at the Recreation Dept. where I had worked as a lifeguard. It consisted of accompanying special needs students to certain places for day trips and then back to the pool in the afternoon for swimming. I would assist in all this, and I wouldn't have to drive. What was even better, even though it was temporary, was that it took place on Saturday, and that meant no electrical work or yard work for a couple months.

We were allotted a big blue van with numerous seats. I arrived at the high school parking lot, then all the special needs people began to arrive. One by one, they got out of their parent's vehicles and I helped them into the van. One guy that arrived and I recognized him right away. It was the kid from my marine biology class. He gave me a big high-five and threw his head back with laughter. Once all were on board, we headed off to Norwood and the bowling alley. The driver announced, "We're going bowling!" Everyone yelled with joy. I turned to my fellow marine biologist. He was taking his index finger, and pushing it in and out of a hole he made with the fingers on his other hand.

I turned and laughed. The driver saw what he was doing, and barked, "Young man, stop that now!" This made his finger go faster. I laughed harder. The driver barked again, even louder. The kid stopped, but it seemed to make him feel like he had succeeded, by getting someone upset. He threw his head back and cackled, looking up at the ceiling of the blue van, exposing all his molars. That was the only way to laugh, I thought: head tilted to the sky and mouth wide open.

The driver looked at me and snapped, "Don't encourage that behavior!" Then she asked, "Did *you* teach him that!?" She was giving me a *very* hairy eyeball.

"Heck no!" I said, as if it was the first time I had witnessed any behavior such as that.

Once my fellow marine biologist got a sense that someone was disturbed, or he was opening up a wound of annoyance, he would squeeze on the lemon juice. The lemon juice came in the form of his famous, "What's up doc!" He said it a few times, and the driver became even more annoyed and told him to stop.

That was all he wanted. I couldn't hold in the laugh, and I threw my head back in "the perfect" laugh. Head skyward, exposing all rear molars. The driver looked at me in disgust. She ceased barking "stop!"

And, shockingly, he stopped acting up. For the moment. We finally arrived and I yelled, "Let's go bowling!" Everyone shrieked and began unsnapping their seat belts, rushing to get out, pushing and shoving to go bowling. We got to the entrance and the driver tried to calm everyone down and attempted to get the kids in a single file so we could walk calmly into the Norwood bowling center. It worked until everyone was just inside the entrance.

Then they all ran to the alley. We had to corral everyone to get their bowling shoes. We got back to the shoe area, and the manager looked at us nervously. It looked like he owned the place and feared it would be destroyed. Everyone was fitted, and we were assigned two lanes, side by side.

"Let the games begin!" I announced.

The balls were lobbed, shot-put, and thrown like unwanted boulders in a garden. Shortly after, the manager came down and said, "Would you please show them the proper way to bowl?" I tried, but they went right back to what they were most comfortable with: shot putting, lobbing, and tossing the ball like a garden bolder.

The manager was yelling, "Hey, no lobbing!" Eventually, he stopped, knowing it was futile. One pin, five pins, or a strike, it didn't matter. Those kids were having the time of their lives. Jumping up and down, high fives, and even sliding on their knees with laughter and joy. It brought me back to my childhood, when I was free, living out of the margins that society put on us all. In the early seventies, it was common to go bowling for a birthday, followed by a trip to McDonald's. This scene brought me back to that feeling. Not being responsible for anything and getting three square meals a day.

The bowling ended, and the driver of the blue van held up the bowling records and brilliantly announced, "We *all* won!" Everyone jumped up and down on the beautiful wooden floor.

We returned the shoes to the glare of the manager He shot eye daggers at me. Being a professional eye reader, I could tell that his eyes said, "Don't you dare come back!" As if I had personally lobbed each and every ball. All the shoes were returned, and as we headed out I turned and whispered to the manager, "See you next week!" and winked.

We headed to our next stop and we didn't even have to announce where we were – we just pulled into the golden arches, the international symbol of every kid's favorite feedbag. I couldn't resist, so I yelled, "McDonald's!" All the passengers in the big blue van went into happy hysterics, yelling, waving their hands, pounding on the windows.

We entered and ordered sixteen Happy Meals. Nutrition aside, I appreciated McDonald's strictly for its speed. No fooling around, no waiter or waitress to tip, no long boring explanations of the daily soup. The boxes of Happy Meals were dispersed, and the room filled with eating noises. Every kid had a different way of eating. My fellow marine biology student ate fries one-by-one, like a snake eating its prey, one centimeter at a time. My boss initially told him to eat faster. She stopped saying that when she realized that, every time she did, he just looked at her and continued, devouring each fry one centimeter at a time, only *slower*. The eating, laughing, and joy finally ended, I'm sure to the happiness of the other patrons. We were now ready for swimming and piled back into the blue van. I announced, "swimming!" which brought on more cheering. The driver glared at me.

With these kids, there was no sticking a foot in the water to test the temperature, then making a shivering gesture, like "the floaters" did. It was pandemonium. Everyone ran into the pool from the locker room as if running from a fire. They cannon-balled, dove, and even pushed one another into the water. A few went to the diving board, performing some pretty spectacular moves, landing on their faces or flat on their backs.

You could see the panic in the other swimmers, as they grabbed their children and exited. Fine with me! We now had the pool to ourselves. None of these kids seemed to fear the water. Despite hairy eyeballs from the driver, she knew this was *my* turf, so she just hung back working on new ways to furrow her eyebrows and fold her arms. I just let it happen. I wouldn't give them margins. The lifeguards paced nervously, but there was no fear in the swimmers. One kid swum to the bottom of the deep end and just lay down, looking up. The lifeguard was about to go into rescue mode, when the kid surfaced, laughing. Before the driver could scold him, he dove back down and did it again.

The lifeguards couldn't wait to get us out and even prematurely started cleaning up the pool area to give us the hint. Like when you're the last couple at a fancy restaurant, not wanting the evening to end, and the waitress starts vacuuming a few inches from your table and giving you dirty looks. Or, when your wife is ready for your buddy to leave, and she starts to clank dishes and rearranges the plants while loudly sighing.

We cleared the pool and got out to the parking lot. All the parents were waiting. My fellow marine biology student turned to the driver of the blue van, smiled, and began poking his index finger through an imaginary finger-vagina (or, bunghole, I suppose; I had never really considered this quandary). She and his mother both looked at me as if it was my fault.

That was my best job *ever*.

Planet Tang

Spring had sprung. New buds appeared on the tree branches and new thoughts budded in my head. I thought about my drinking, especially the big black curtain that occasionally closed on me at a certain time in the night. I blamed it on the sandwiches or Cadbury Cream Eggs or whatever else I had eaten that night. I was now waking up looking at what I was wearing to see if they were still my clothes, or someone else's. I feared waking up in a black mini skirt or hospital scrubs.

I had committed several major sins: sleeping with my boots on, drinking alone before noon, sex before marriage. Oh, and the dastardly deed of eating meat on Friday. I was glad that – being a Catholic and all – I had the advantage of the confessional. No matter what sin I might commit, I could get it straightened out by ducking into the booth, saying what I did out loud, and then babbling 30 or 40 Hail Mary's. But a little whisper inside me worried that there must be some catch, some fine-print that I had missed.

Strictly due to the fact that my brother and sister were both distinguished graduates, along with Stew's homework, I had been accepted to the Massachusetts Maritime Academy. It was kind of shocking to me that they decided to let me attend. Even with Stew's help, I was a solid C-minus "student." Plus, there was that probation thing. MMA was actually a fairly prestigious educational institution, especially in New England. It had originally been established to train officers for the U.S. Merchant Marine.

If you wanted a career in shipping transportation, nautical engineering, or any other commercial shipping trade – and didn't feel like joining the Navy or Coast Guard – this was the school to go to. I hadn't thought about it much but knew I had to do *something* after High School. It wasn't Marine Biology or Oceanographer school – but it was close enough to the only two things that ever interested me academically or career-wise.

It was also a military school, and I figured it would straighten me out. I would go to college, study to be a merchant marine, sail to foreign lands, and then come home to dock in Massachusetts and be greeted by my lovely wife and kids. I guessed that's what would happen.

Due to the death of a cousin's cousin, my father had inherited a new car, a Ford Maverick. He also inherited the key to the cottage on Blue Fish Cove in the Irish Riviera. I was sorry about losing the cousin's cousin but was pretty excited about the cottage. It was time to take the Cro Mags to the place. Cashews was AWOL, but we had admitted a new member to our illustrious band, a kid named Jake from Cloverland. We were going to celebrate our impending graduation from high school. Most of us were near the bottom of our class, but we were graduating nonetheless.

There was always ample alcohol at this cottage, and there wouldn't be many people around. As we drove toward our destination, I began to smell the fresh, salty Atlantic breeze. It was the smell of freedom. The smell of cleansing. We entered the Blue Fish Cove area, passing by the trailer park, which was now empty, and toward the cottage. Like the other cottages there, it was raised up on cinder blocks, due to the marsh on one side and the Atlantic on the other, which made a bad combination during the monthly "full moon high tide."

There were only a few year-round residents, and one was the lobsterman next door. But he was out lobstering or at a bar talking about lobstering. There was also a cute girl a couple doors down in the other direction, a year or two younger than me. She threw me her usual big wave as we unloaded the car. The year-round residents got through the dark and cold season by drinking heavily. As we entered the cottage, I took a mental image of the place, so I could leave it as I found it. We sat down and realized we all needed a morning drink. It no longer mattered to me whether a morning drink could be classified as "hair of the dog" or actually *needing* a drink.

Every cottage in New England housed an enormous stash of liquor. It was like a state law or something. It seemed sensible to me. There was always the threat of some sort of invasion from outer space, or from the people whose countries were painted red on elementary school wall maps. Like the USSR. On every school map, globe and encyclopedia, it was depicted in RED, the same color as the school fire alarms: in case of emergency, break the glass and pull the lever. Cottage bars and liquor cabinets served the same type of purpose.

If we were being invaded by something out of *Creature Double Feature* or those bastard commies from Eastern Europe, we knew the drill: first, find the liquor cabinet; next, open the liquor cabinet; third, grab a bottle, unscrew the cap, and throw cap over shoulder; finally, and most important, start drinking. Once under the influence and feeling brave, the next step was to grab a garden tool, like a rake or hoe, raise said garden tool above one's head and, in a deep New England-accented holler, scream menacingly in the direction of the Reds or 40-foot spider: "You'se get ahtta he-ya you bas-tud!"

Ah, the New England cottage liquor cabinet. Behind its door was the medicine for all of life's ills and every cause to celebrate. It was now time to celebrate: we were climbing back up Mr. Simonon's life graph. My mother liked her wine, but she liked her vodka more. I suppose the acorn doesn't roll too far from the oak. There was ample cheap vodka, but I couldn't find any mixers.

I did, however, find the morning astronaut drink from the orange Planet Tang. Planet Tang people must be very friendly, providing us with all that ground up orange dirt so us 1970s kids could avoid drinking fresh, delicious, nutritious *actual* orange juice. I made the breakfast drinks for our celebration, a half-ass announcement was made in typically half-assed Cro Mag fashion, and we raised our glasses to all our accomplishments, and to our imminent exit from the brick beehive ... oh, and to the orange space dust from Planet Tang: "hula-boom!"

When the Tang hit my throat, it brought back a wave of childhood memories. My mother's arms swirling around like an octopus, making breakfast and prepping lunches. [Mental note ... I must remember to replace the vodka we drink with water.] By the time my mother tasted it in August, it could be written off as having gone bad. Jake had a few Cloverland green sticks. I wasn't a big fan of the reefer but was always told by "me ma," that when someone offers you food always say yes, and always devour the whole serving and always say thank you. This pleases the host and demonstrates good upbringing. When one does these three things, one's host will think to themselves, "That person must have an excellent mother."

Someone was now offering me something smoking and stinky, so it was my duty, in honor of "me ma," to say, "thank you" and indulge. I was told to smell it first. It gave the aroma of a hippie skunk. We passed around the large white cocoon, and soon there wasn't much talk in the room. A few laughs here and there for no reason, and lots of staring around at the walls. It was indeed very potent. Now I didn't feel like doing anything. I felt all the world's problems would eventually be solved by me laying there, zoning out, due to this most excellent combination of vodka, Tang, and marijuana.

I had already had a stiff drink, but I needed a few more. I noted the strange phenomenon. After eating a bag of chips, I was satiated and wanted no more chips. After drinking a large glass of water, I was no longer thirsty; I craved no more water. Yet, oddly, after drinking a glass of vodka (or pounding a heisted Foster's) I always wanted more. With booze, more was *always* better. Not just better, but somehow ... necessary. I did like the calming effect of marijuana, but it didn't give me the courage to explore or jump over buses like Evel Knievel. I poured more drinks and filled the empty bottle of vodka with water. I cracked open a new one.

The jazz of the sauce seemed to overpower the mellow of the marijuana, so we decided to take a swim. The ponds had melted back in our zip code, so it was time to plunge into the Atlantic. Jake and I walked down to my childhood swimming hole in the historic Blue Fish Cove. Simma and Sully followed. We left Wild Blumpkin at the house with the vodka and

Tang. He said he would be right behind us. We were fully courageous now, and it was time to cross the canal. On the other side was Burke's Beach, named after some guy who ... had the last name of Burke.

Sully and Simma dove in the canal and were immediately sucked under. The current was strong, and it tried to pull them out to sea. They made it to the other side but had drifted to the near end of the jetty. Jake and I went next, and I immediately felt the sting of the frigid water and the strong pull of the current. I was a lifeguard, however, and would be able to keep everybody safe. The cold seemed to freeze my muscles and the current did what it wanted to me. We were quickly carried out right to the mouth of the unforgiving Atlantic. I knew not to panic. I felt a hand grab my hair and pull. It was Jake, and he paddled me to the end of the jetty.

I thanked him as we climbed over to the other side, to an empty Burke's beach. I flushed out the radiator, and it was all orange liquid and salt water. We found Sully and Simma and walked around the beach. We mumbled and picked up strange natural souvenirs from the sea. We were all shaking and shivering, so it was time to go back and get some warmth.

We walked further down the canal this time, so the current wasn't so violent. I was torn to pieces trying to climb the barnacle-laden jetty. We made it back to the cottage and found Wild Blumpkin mired in an enormous forest of briar bushes in the backyard. Apparently, he had jumped in the Atlantic as well, was soaking wet, and fighting his way through the back-yard thorn forest. He emerged, cut and scraped, bleeding from head to toe.

We warmed up with a few more drinks. The vodka was getting low, and we needed more. Blumpkin sat on the couch, dazed. He made a hand gesture for another vodka and Tang. I poured him a stiff one and told him to stay put, that everything would be fine, that we were going to get more sauce. Being a lifeguard, I ordered him to stay out of the water.

We decided to walk the seawall. Simma knew the Irish Riviera like me; he had relatives there, so he knew there was a liquor store nearby, and that we could get there via the seawall. My muscles ached; they had been frozen and as they thawed out they only hurt more. I needed more alcohol.

We walked carefully along the seawall for what seemed like forever, and finally made it to the packy.

We gathered up our crumpled, wet currency and handed it to a patron who soon returned with vodka. We made it back to the cottage and found Wild Blumpkin sprawled out across the carpet. Lilly, the cute girl from two doors down, was waving a magazine on his face and attending to his multiple lacerations. It looked like he was vomiting as well as bleeding, as his face and chest were covered in regurgitated Tang, which matched his orange afro precisely.

We got him to the couch and, since his radiator was now flushed, immediately gave him a fresh drink. Lilly looked concerned, and asked, "Are you sure you should be giving him more?" We gave her a collective Cro Mag look of annoyance and experience, and she didn't speak anymore. We continued to drink, and so did Wild Blumpkin. Lilly applied a cold face cloth to this forehead, followed by a magazine wave. Time went on, and the room began to spin. Someone said, "Eh, time to go," and we piled into the Maverick.

Lilly assisted Wild Blumpkin to the car, and we were off. We pulled into a McDonalds. We had enough money for a couple of fries. I went in with Simma to acquire the salty sustenance. In true McDonald's fashion, they were delivered speedily and without any fuss. We exited the McDonald's and saw two police cruisers next to the Maverick. Apparently, Wild Blumpkin had miraculously sprung back to life upon spotting the liquor store next to the McDonald's. He had run in to get more vodka but apparently forgot to pay upon leaving.

The boys in blue just looked at me and said, "You'se look the best to drive. Now get ahtta our beach town!" I did as I was commanded, but quickly pulled over to let Simma take command of the Maverick. We reached home, and Simma said, "Hey, remember to get back and clean the cottage." I stumbled into the Star Wars sheets, shivering. We went to the Riviera a few days later, and the cottage was a disaster. It was covered with sand, Wild Blumpkin's blood, dried orange Tang vomit, and rather impressive little piles of beach stones placed randomly around. Lilly came over and asked if Wild Blumpkin was okay. I said he would be fine, and thanked her for taking care of him.

She seemed concerned for all of us.

"Drinking like that … that's not normal," she said.

I answered, "Eh, it's just a phase."

She gave me advice on the how to clean up, especially the dried orange Tang vomit. The little cottage raised on cinder blocks was soon cleaner than ever. The good news was that the Phantom wasn't with me, so I didn't have to worry about my parents finding a petrified turd or pyramid of used condoms smeared with peanut butter hidden somewhere.

I found out a week later that my mother and father had visited the cottage just a couple days after I cleaned. A drink was made, and they immediately noticed it tasted just like water. A summary investigation was conducted, but there were too many suspects to declare anybody conclusively guilty: there were too many keys floating around. Plus, my father said, it couldn't have been teenagers, because the place was too clean.

Final verdict? The vodka must have gone bad.

YOU ASKED SOMEONE ELSE?

As my senior year came to a close, drinking daily became mandatory. It didn't concern me, however, because it was just a phase. I pushed the thought of possibly having a drinking problem back to the recesses of my mind. Some days, I would take a couple morning belts from the bar downstairs, to stop the shakes. Now, the shakes, I attributed to a multitude of other causes. Perhaps the male body trembles for a few months between growth spurts?

I saw Leiko at the pool and she was lovelier than ever. A Lady Slipper. I was an ugly weed, a dandelion. Definitely not the kind of flower to be too near a Lady Slipper. One day at the pool, she waved me over. Her hair was down all the way to her waist. Her smile grew as I walked forward, which made me nervous. I walked closer, and I saw peace in those beautiful Japanese garden eyes as she looked into my bloodshot Anglo/Irish/Scot eyes.

"You know Andrew, it's prom season."

"It is?" I said.

"Yes, silly," she said. "It's spring."

I just stood there.

"Would you like to go to prom with me?" she asked. I looked behind, as she must have been talking to somebody else.

"Me?" I asked.

"Yes, silly, you," she said.

This threw me off and made me very nervous. I just said, "Can I tell you later?"

"Sure," she said.

I had to go to the locker room, I was so shaken. I rubbed my eyes together with both hands. The "floaters" emerged from the showers and looked at me with alarm. I got back to the pool, and she said, "Any answer?"

I said, "Eh, I'll call you later." She was still smiling, but I was shaking out of nervousness. I avoided the Lady Slipper up until I was picked up by my father with his cheek full of pistachios. I got home and quickly took a belt of vodka out of fear and happiness. I didn't like this good thing happening to me; it was an odd feeling.

My adorable Gerber baby days were long gone. As was the cute paper boy. And the charming kid who innocently applied suntan oil to the ladies with beehive hairstyles at Hale Reservation. Gone. I was now old enough to fight in a war and kill … but not old enough to legally have a drink.

A strange voice of thought came to my mind. It was the same voice I got when I was wearing plaid bell bottoms and platform shoes, and someone decided I was a freak that needed to be taught a lesson. I had fought the kid and won and went to kick him in the face … but an inner voice told me not to, so I walked away. Now, this gut feeling was telling me *not* to go to the prom with Leiko. I couldn't go with her: she worked too hard, she was too beautiful, and I didn't deserve to be with her, walking side by side. Besides, how would I drink around her?

I would call her that evening. I chickened out but saw her at the pool a few nights later. She was still beaming and looked great. I went into the locker room, looked at myself and saw a weed. I went back out to the deck, and said to the Lady Slipper, "I can't go." She slouched a little but didn't say anything. The night dragged on and we didn't speak to one another … she didn't even say goodbye. I had backed out of a situation that caused me anxiety, but I saved myself from any potential future damage.

I asked a young woman from Pigeon City to the prom, one that I could drink around. She said yes, so, mission accomplished: I would get the memorable prom picture that every parent wants. I saw Leiko a few days later in the hallway, and she looked at me with anger and hurt, and said, "You asked someone else?" She walked away.

THE BLUE LIMOUSINE

We gathered enough crumpled up dollars to get a limo and tuxes. Seanzo from Pigeon City was going to have a get together after the prom. His father was from Ireland and was back in the Emerald Isle visiting the old country, so there would be no parents around. There would be another get together down on Cape Cod the following day. It was at Pat's cottage, the guy that had the super bowl party.

It didn't matter if his parents were there or away because they allowed teen drinking. We picked up our tuxes and were instructed about the safety and care of these outfits. Right after the prom is over, we were told, we needed to put the tuxes in the carrying bag, so nothing would get dirty. I felt great looking at myself in the mirror wearing that penguin outfit. But I also felt uncomfortable.

It was tight and shiny. Most of my life I had worn comfortable pants, sneakers, or lifeguard shorts. I was always performing manual labor – on weekends in an attic running wires, or swinging an ax in the driveway, or performing some sort of removal: leaf removal, snow removal, grass removal. That was the cost of living in New England and enjoying its four seasons. So, I knew this scene in the mirror was very temporary. It wasn't me and wouldn't be me.

Prom night was upon us, and we all met at Seanzo's for a few drinks before heading to the big affair. Seanzo's was getting a reputation for "snapping," or "going ape," totally losing control under the influence of alcohol or, on rarer occasions, when he was completely straight. The out-bursts were okay at the Pigeon City drinking hole, or down at the bridge, but we would soon be in polite company. A fleet of limos showed up and we packed into ours. Arriving at the prom like celebrities (in our minds), we dispersed, ate, danced, were photographed ... and finally, it was over. I wanted a drink, and was anxious to get back to Seanzo's.

Seanzo had apparently pounded some booze at the prom without alert-ing us, and he entered the limo wild-eyed. We drove off, and I could see he was in a different dimension, twitchy and distracted. Out of the nowhere, he barked at the driver, "Hey man, this limo ain't black! I specifically ordered a black limo and this thing is dark blue!"

"I want my friggin' money back!" he snapped.

The limo driver yawned and said, "Eh, I'm just the driver."

"Well, drive me back to the lot man, I want a black one!"

The driver ignored him and kept driving.

We were finally back at Seanzo's in Pigeon City. We escorted him into the house, and he settled down, recognizing he was home. We cracked open the drinks and began to pour. In the backyard, Seanzo's older brother and his crew were circled around a keg. They were all blue-collar guys and mostly dressed in Dickies and work boots. They were known for causing trouble, but since they had their keg and area in the yard, we figured things would be okay. I went to the small front yard, and looked at the heavy traffic on Route 1 and chatted with Beanz about our future.

More cars pulled up, with beautiful dresses and tuxedos. Beanz and I stayed in the front, drinking and talking about our future. He was academ-ically brilliant and could have gone to any college and entered any career he wanted. But he was a natural craftsman and was going to go into the building trades. I was the opposite of a brilliant academic. I hated school and book learning. I liked manual labor. Yet, I was headed for the presti-gious Massachusetts Maritime Academy, which would straighten me out and get me out of this phase.

We then heard yelling and screaming coming from the backyard. Some girls ran around to the front as if being chased. Beanz and I ran around back and saw pushing and shoving between tuxedos and Dickies. Then two men separated. It was Seanzo and another guy. They exchanged punches and then it went to the ground. Seanzo was on the bottom getting pummeled. He had claimed that one of the Dickies guys stepped on his rented shiny shoe. Finally, they decided they'd rather drink than continue to scrap, so the Dickies guys went back to their corner of the backyard, and the tuxedos went to the inside of the house.

I went back to the front with Beanz to finish our big talk. It wasn't long before we heard the yelling again. There was another scrap between the tuxedos and Dickies. Seanzo's tux was ruined, and he was on the bottom again getting punched repeatedly. The brawl was stopped, and it was time to go.

We piled into the cars and headed to the Cape with plenty of alcohol. We got to Pat's cottage, and although his parents weren't there, we were told couldn't *actually* come in the house. We got directions to drive down the street and assemble on the beach. We piled into the cars again and found the beachhead. Some of us stripped down to our boxers, and some ran into the surf still wearing their tuxedos.

I sat back on a man-made wall and looked out on the Atlantic. The sun came up, and it was my first time seeing an entire sunrise. I was amazed at the perfection of everything. I felt God as I saw this. The beauty and perfection in the natural world *couldn't* be chance, there *had* to be a loving designer to give us all this beauty. I knew I had committed too many sins to feel close to Him, but I knew he was there and wanted me to be a better person.

Soon the early risers came out and were walking their dogs or taking a stroll. They looked at us with a bit of shock. Some of us were covered in sand, some were in boxers, some were still in their ruined tuxedos. I thought of this beautiful sunrise and wished I was with Leiko. But then I thought of last night's ugly, drunken, crazy scene, and was glad I never took the Lady Slipper. We headed back to the cottage for the morning drinks. The sauce stopped me from shivering and put me in my right state. The rest of the weekend was a blur, and I arose on Monday to the rumbling of the LeMans.

MUST BE FROM DOVER

I returned to my routine and even was assigned an additional night of lifeguarding. This took time out of my afternoon drinks, but it would provide more money for ... more drinks. I still had to save some for college. All the earnings from my years of paper route work, snow shoveling, snow blowing, lawn mowing, and weekend electrical work had been closely guarded by my father. As for the lifeguard money, I had to give a percentage for college but was allowed to keep a small amount for personal spending.

That meant, "hula-boom." The lifeguard on my new shift was very strict. I just paced the deck on the other side of the pool. I saw a friend of hers come in and talk; they looked at me, briefly, and then she left. The next week, the same girl came in, chatted with my shift mate, and left. As I was leaving, she said, "Would you like to go to a prom?"

I said I was busy. She said, "That girl that comes in once a week, she is my sister in law. You seem like a nice guy, and she goes to an all-girl school and needs a date."

"Nice guy, yeah," I said to myself.

Then there was the closing pitch.

"She is from a very wealthy family, and you won't have to pay for anything. Everything will be paid for, even your tux."

Free.

"Sound's great," I said.

Visions of free finger sandwiches and an open bar danced around in my head.

I had recently made a new discovery: the "nip," a palm-sized 50 ML bottle of booze that contained approximately two shots of the magical juice. I started carrying these bottles of mini-booze around with me, so I was never away from my sauce, not even for a moment. And this would be a time I would need some sauce. The date said we would be going to some downtown brownstone after the party and it would be a sleepover. Once there, no one could leave and there would be a keg. There were many pockets in the tux I rented, so I would stuff them all with nips.

The blue van days had ended, and I was again working every Saturday with my father. He asked about the prom, what school, where the dance was, etc. He knew everything about the area. It was all "high-brow," he said: the school, the hotel for the dance, and the sleepover at some brownstone in Back Bay.

"Eh, make you'se some friends while you'se high-browing it," he said. "Might get you out of crawling through attics the rest of you'se life."

I got home and prepped. I had purchased nips in advance and stuffed the secret pockets of my tux with them. I ran downstairs, poured some of the transparent Russian beverage, raised the glass, and hulla-boomed. I showered off the insulation from being in an attic. I put on the paid-for tux and looked in the mirror. I looked great, but it wasn't me, it was just a temporary outfit. The real me belonged in attics, in Dickies and work boots, and a t-shirt, yelling, "Got it!" back and forth for hours on end.

I could *look* different, like a respectable kid. But it didn't change the circuitry in my mind. I saw the big black metal snake pull up. I signaled to my father, an avid photographer who even developed his own pictures in the garage. My mother just stood there smiling, looking at us, the human trinkets. My father had us stand in a variety of locations and poses. Snap, move, snap, move … snap. As we were leaving, he was still snapping pictures.

We were off to pick up the next couple. They lived in Dover, one of my favorite towns to drive through in the fall. But that is all we did in Dover. Drive *through*. Their society is not of the LeMans, the Ford Maverick, the Olds 98 or the Country Squire. Those vehicles didn't fit in Dover, and neither did we. But you could drive *through* if you followed the speed limit. To us, Dover was a euphemism for a sign of any kind of weakness. If you were hit with a slap shot in the shin, you were told to skate around, to "skate it off." If you sat down on the ice and winced, somebody would lean over you and ask, "What?! Are you from Dover!" It applied to drinking, too. If someone vomited prematurely, he was accused of being from Dover.

Now we were picking up a couple and the female was from Dover. The vodka performed its initial work, so I was relaxed, in the state man was supposed to be in. I didn't have my fidgety leg syndrome. The sauce cured the "Fred Astaire" affliction. I wasn't squirmy yet, but wondered how long we would stay at this residence. I had my nips, and they were clanging in my jacket.

We entered this massive home in Dover, and we were warmly greeted. There were many "ooohs" and "aaaahs," from the mother of my date. I sat down and felt okay, but then, I noticed there were some very tiny snacks, and someone said we were still early, and we would be staying while. My leg started to twitch. The beautiful black rented shiny shoe seemed to move on its own.

What if they started to ask what grade I am in, and what I have been studying? What if they ask me some complicated calculus questions? Soon the left leg would be bobbing, and I would be in full-blown "Fred Astaire" mode. I sat on the couch, greeted everyone, and had some sort of tiny trinket snack. I tried to talk and sound sophisticated, but it just came out as blue collar public high school drivel.

Everyone was now seated and looking at me. I would soon be in the hot seat, fired trigonometry questions or history questions about who said what and when. My shiny rented shoe was moving faster, probably already making marks on their beautiful hardwood floors. I politely asked if I could use the bathroom. I closed and locked the door and grabbed a nip.

Ah, the nip: used and trusted by pilots, doctors, and other professionals in times of emergency, when a giant bottle of booze or silver flask wouldn't be appropriate.

I raised the nip, "hula-boomed," and emptied it. Dang, I thought, that seemed small. I needed one more. But two more would be better. They would ask some calculus questions, but I would give a funny answer, and say, "Well, ladies and gentlemen, I will answer like Henry Ford: I don't know the answer, but I can phone a friend that does and get back to you." That would create laughter, and the difficult questions would end.

I wrapped the empty nips in Kleenex to stop the clanging and went back out. I sat down and my legs slowly stopped moving as the sauce signaled the edgy nerves to settle down. A few moments later, the magic of alcohol was in effect and the fancy black shoes stopped moving altogether. No calculus questions were asked, rather, just where I lived, and what my father did. "Oh," was the only reaction. Then the mom appeared with fancy glasses. Then a fancy bottle was opened and made a popping sound. Everyone was handed a glass, and the father poured some of this fizzy, sour drink for everybody. I put on an act like I was scared of the drink, and as he poured, I said, "Whoa there, not too much."

"Good man! Not drinking too much!" he said.

There was a toast, but no hula-boom. I muttered it silently to myself, for I was representing the Cro Mags on this diplomatic mission in hostile territory, and it was the proper thing to do. We drank, and I made sure to drink slow. I managed to drink like them, keeping a close eye on their every move. I noticed they all did something with their pinkie finger. It looked like it was pointed to the future. It was pointed forward. That, I refused to do. I always had a death grip on my glass anyway, so it wouldn't fall or get taken away. A real wrap-around, monkey-like grip. The glass was emptied and put back on the round platter. It was time to go. I was grateful.

We piled in the limo after several photos, and we were off to downtown Boston. Not the Boston where I did electrical work on Saturdays. In the part of Boston where we headed, there didn't seem to be any of the "triple deckas," as my father would call them. These were all high rises and brown brick buildings. We pulled up to the front of a building; someone said 'Copley'-something. The place was all limos, and we entered into a beautiful ballroom. I could tell right away the differences between my high school prom and this one. Ours looked like it was some rod and reel club dressed up with a few balloons, with paper covering the same round tables where fisherman carved their initials.

I noticed a band dressed like penguins. The floor was immaculate and didn't creak like our floor did. The room was making me feel a bit nervous; like the tuxedo, I didn't belong in it. It was all temporary. I belonged in a dingy union hall, in work pants, work boots, and a t-shirt with a pocket containing a stubby pencil.

My date showed me a table that was prearranged. We sat down and more people followed suit. I was getting nervous. I took in everything electrical. The chandeliers, the sconce lights, the switches, and the receptacles. The chandelier alone looked as though it was hung with just the arms, and one by one, diamond-shaped pieces of glass were put on. The switch plate and receptacle covers looked like they were made out of gold.

I was lost for a moment as I looked at all the electrical work. I didn't notice the waiter in the penguin suit had put something down on my plate. Something very small and green. It resembled the same green that exited my grandfather's mouth in the 1970's, except it was solid. I watched closely to see how these high-brows ate this acorn-sized piece of solid green. A fork was used to slice it and put it in their mouths. They then made a "yum" sound. I did the same, and it was yummy.

This was nothing like our Patriots tailgates. No fist fights erupting over a small slab of meat or who had taken the last chip. The green acorn was now gone, and the waters came back to remove the plates. I again feared calculus questions and noticed my right leg had started its movement. I needed some drinks. I looked at everyone politely, and said, "pardon me." I headed to the bathroom, and there was even a guy in a tuxedo there. He had towels.

I figured he was standing guard to intercept my friend the Phantom. I got in a stall and pulled out to more safety valves. I looked up at the very fancy recessed fixtures that my father referred to as "high hats." I couldn't raise the nip too high. I managed one silent "hula-boom" and then another.

I wrapped these two bottles up, fake-flushed, then exited. I washed my hands and looked for the paper towel dispenser. The guy keeping watch for the Phantom pointed to a pile he had on the sink.

What was this, I thought. A towel? There was even a place to put the used towel. I walked over to the trash bin and emptied the nips. But it was a new trash bag, so the tiny bottles hit the bottom and made a clanky thud. I turned to the guy and just said, "candy." He seemed to be on the sauce himself and just grinned, and said, "Yes sir."

I exited the bathroom and was ready for history or calculus questions. I noticed more food on the table, but it still wasn't the main dish. When would they bring out the canned brown bread and hot dogs, I wondered? This was a salad-type of substance. I watched the others first and then ate the salad like they did. It was removed and then the main course came. This was good, for there wasn't much talk during eating time. I even worked the napkin like others just to fit in. Dabbing the napkin to the corner of my mouth, whether I needed to or not.

The nips kicked in and my leg stopped moving. There was some small talk, and non-alcoholic champagne was poured. I noticed even if they were drinking water, their pinky fingers pointed straight out ... to the future. This time, I did the same thing, with a twist. I pointed my pinky at the hair-do's of the females, as if taking apart all the knots and twists. This made me smile. It felt uncomfortable not grasping a glass like an orangutan with my hand wrapped completely around in a death-grip. But I needed to fit in.

I then aimed my pinky at the ladies' buttons and zippers, mentally removing just the top, exposing more shoulder. This made me smile more. Then there was the talk about the academies, and the fancy sports they played like lacrosse and field hockey and something called "sculling." Did that involve drinking out of some dead man's skull? Hmmm, the Cro Mags would like that. I wasn't asked too many questions. I threw out the fact that I was soon attending Massachusetts Maritime Academy, with an emphasis on "academy." Silent head-nods followed.

Their parents owned businesses, or were in some legal professions. My father could put pistachios in his cheek. He could roll his tongue under four or five pistachios, and slowly place them on his cavity-filled, cracked molars and chew them.

The penguin band started playing a song called Johnny B Goode. Out of nowhere, I was being beaten mercilessly by the invisible vodka bat. I felt like I should dance. I danced as if I had been "whacked" by electricity. Initially shaking from the jolt, jumping back, throwing my head up, waving my hands. I loved what booze was doing for me. I was headed up the life graph. Each time I did "the electrician" dance my date seemed to look more concerned. There was one more fast song, and then a slow dance. I was sweating profusely but didn't care due to the magic of the sauce. The date didn't seem to be as amused as I was. She just said, "You seem to be *enjoying* yourself."

"Why, yes I am!" I replied, gesticulating.

We slow danced and the vodka magically slid my shiny plastic shoes across the dance floor. I was a natural, under the influence. I looked in my date's eyes, and she seemed to relax. I wasn't looking at her. I was looking at my future behind her eyes. She came from money, and I would be all set. I wouldn't have to crawl around another old hag's attic ever again. I would be drunk most of the time, doing menial suburban work like mowing the lawn, raking leaves, or cutting hedges. Waving to my other suburban neighbors, perpetually smashed. We were both smiling now, me thinking of my future of never blowing a sober breath. Carving Thanksgiving turkeys. Pinky pointing forward whenever I drank.

The dancing ended, and I stumbled a bit. I got back to my table and looked at the "funny guy" who had been cracking jokes all night. He was telling more funny skulling stories. We were all friends now through the magic of alcohol. I did let out one laugh when there was no joke being made, and I noticed the others looked a bit concerned. This stage of the prom was over, and I felt like a movie star. We headed back into the limo and drove for the Beacon Hill area of Boston.

Everyone was smiling now. Why not, we were young, and headed on to big things. We pulled up to a brownstone, and there was even a doorman. He was very gracious, and I told him there was a lump in the rug after I stumbled a bit. He looked down and just smiled. The owner apparently had all three floors of this entire brownstone. We all entered, and the parents stood in front. A father said, "No one is to leave." A keg was rolled out. He said, "Now kids, enjoy yourselves and watch your consumption."

I was introduced to more people but only noticed the keg. Instinct kicked in, so I had to behave like I was at the Pat's game and guard this short stout tin man. I said to my date, "I have to go," and headed over to the keg. It wasn't long before I was actually pouring the drinks. I devised a plan: I would shut people off, to preserve the sauce in the tin man. I would lift it up periodically, and if I felt it was draining too fast, I would start telling people the spigot was broken.

There was one other guy there that had the same look as me. Like we had struck liquid gold. He said he was from a town next to mine, and we were the only ones there that didn't attend some private school. He muscled in, and I told him the plan. He agreed he would be my bouncer. The owner did a great job packing the keg, and the brew was ice cold. A small line formed and I poured half glasses for people. No one noticed too much. Mine, of course, was perpetually full to the brim. I had to drink fast before this thing ran out. I knew there was no beer bat, so I was okay. Beer did make me occasionally flush out the radiator. I would vomit beer foam, a sign that it was making room for more. I would get drunk, but not vodka-bat drunk.

There was always one of us guarding the tin man. If I went to the bathroom or to flush out the radiator, my bouncer took over. Nothing would go to waste. Time marched on, and once in a while, my date would pass by. I nodded my head to my future wife, indicating that all was well. The parents made their rounds, and we treated them kindly. The father decided to have "one," and I noticed he was one of those types that could have just "one."

I poured his drink and was a little more generous, seeing as how he paid for it and all. I poured it three-quarters full, just for him. I watched him sip it. For me, the first "one" turned on the circuitry in my head and lit up all sorts of thoughts, especially the thought to have one more, followed by *many* more. We were both human, this father and me, but alcohol certainly affected us differently. "One drink" meant something very different to each of us.

I kept an eye on the father, and when he was sipping and looking away, I would "galoop" my brew, after a silent hula-boom. The silent hulla-boom would be followed by a sucking sound, and the beer would disappear. He looked over at us now and then. The guy from the other public school was a real pro. He knew to put his brew down once the eye was on us. Finally, the father finished sipping and walked over to us. I tightened up like a mother bear guarding her cubs.

He came over and said, "You fellas are doing a great job! Not spilling anything and doing all the work." I addressed him like I did after getting a beat-down from police.

"Sir, thank you sir."

He smiled and made a request. "My wife and I are headed to bed, please be sure to watch your intake." I raised the keg hose and winked, "Oh, I'll make sure of it." The parents left, and I lifted the keg. It was still a good weight, but we had to start shutting people off to conserve what remained for ourselves. My bouncer/partner started shooing people away. He would say, "This is your last, I don't want anyone falling."

My date passed by; I smiled, but I was all business. I had to concentrate, after all. She motioned that she was going to bed. There were sleeping bags and many rooms. I just said to my future wife, "Nighty night," She looked disappointed ... and concerned.

One by one people began going off to the slumber part of this slumber party. We became less guarded around the keg. I stumbled to the bathroom, and dry heaved. I stumbled back and noticed a new kid. Upon closer inspection, I saw that he actually wasn't a kid, he was an adult. I was pie-eyed, but I sensed something wrong. True, I still had Star Wars sheets, but this adult was wearing Muppets pajamas.

He shook my hand and said he was the son, and that he couldn't sleep. He said he went to a special school for the learning disabled. He was one of us. He needed a drink, a full drink. He said it was his first time. That brought me back to *my* first time. I looked him in the eye, and said, "Never forget this," and handed him his first. This occasion needed a toast.

We filled ours and held up our cups and I yelled, "hula-boom!" He started to sip and then squinted. I then coached him and led by example. He did the same as me; he took a few swigs, and his beer was gone. He said, "Let's go to the study." No one was in this study, and I looked in the glass doors at all the books, beautiful red leather furniture, and even some special mugs. It was a very fancy room. It seemed like a trinket room: look, but don't touch. We entered, and I took the best chair, all thick leather with beautiful woodwork, and a matching Ottoman. The other two took the couch.

After finishing our drinks, we did the math and decided that the keg needed to be inside *this* room with *us*. We brought the tin man in. I looked in one of the glass cases and found some Ivy League-looking mug, with a gold seal and Latin words on it. I would use that to drink out of. There were more mugs, two of which looked like the white wigs probably drank out of them before writing the constitution. I handed them to my new friends. We poured and toasted in these special mugs. I announced "hula-boom" and then, in honor of the white wigs, stated, "Here, here." We drank and then slurred something about sports. The adult in children's pajamas lit up with information. He knew all my 1970s hockey heroes. They were guys who were heroes only to me, not the general public. The goons, the fighters. Stan Jonathan. Terry O'Reilly, Secord, Wensink.

He was no longer a "special ed" person in my eyes. I wondered if his folks knew all this. He just went on and on with sports trivia. I noticed my bouncer friend was nodding. He would soon be out. But me and this adult in children's pajamas kept talking. He went from sports into history, about the Revolutionary War that had taken place all around Massachusetts. The history that I was supposed to know.

Things were becoming brighter outside, and I stumbled out to see the new small green leaves that form on the trees during the prom season. I was then told what kind of tree was right outside the window. This guy literally knew everything. I finished my brew, and I felt my head begin to nod. I placed the mug on the coffee table then the black curtain fell. I was gone.

I was awakened by the repeated shouting of someone looking for someone else. It seemed rude to yell so early. I was able to open one eye, and noticed it was morning, and I was in a very nice book room. I figured I had made it in life and was very successful. Then memory came back as I looked at the two on the couch. One guy in a tux with vomit on the front of his tuxedo. An adult in Muppets pajamas with his head flopped back on the couch and snoring. I looked at these two, and the happy dreams they seemed to be having. Then memory slowly came back, and I heard more commotion from outside the study. It seemed many people were awake, and there was still shouting for someone.

Then an adult entered. It was the male owner of the house who only had "one" the night before. He then waved someone else in. It was his wife. She came in and put her hand over her mouth as she took in the scene. She then left. He looked at his special mug I had been drinking from, then at his son, then the chair, and then my shiny black shoes on this ottoman. Then he took the mug and, like a prosecutor, stated all the crimes we had committed at the top of his lungs.

"They broke into my study, drank from my mugs, sat in my chair, and fed my son beer!"

I figured it would be time to exit, and I stumbled out of the study. I saw all the high-brows in their high-brow pajamas. The mother was still covering her mouth in shock. Then I saw my date. Her eyes said, "We are never getting married." The father signaled to two guys, and they assisted their son into his bedroom. My bouncer friend and his now-crying date were ushered into their waiting limo. I held onto the rail. I was holding onto the banister, but everything was spinning. My date came over and assisted me outside. As soon as I felt the outdoor air, I vomited a huge stream of golden beer fluid, followed by foam. The dandies and posh folks stared in horror, gasping and covering their eyes.

I must have fallen asleep in the limo because before I knew it I was being nudged that I was home. I hugged my date, which helped me stand up to exit the limo.

"Get help," she whispered.

I wobbled into the house, to the bathroom and again vomited a large quantity of crappy beer and green foam. I still had my tux on; even the tie was still in place. I patted the trinket "show soap." I knew the sins of eating meat on Friday, sex before marriage, and not drinking (alone) before noon. But I wasn't going to commit the sin of sleeping with my shoes on. After a hockey goon-like tussle with those shiny bastards, I managed to pull them off, and slept in the tux. As I drifted off, I thought of how nice the shoes had looked resting on the red leather Ottoman.

"Someday, somehow," I thought.

I awoke to the rumbling of the LeMans. I peeled off the very ripe tux and crawled into my school clothes. Simma asked about the prom, and I told him about the "other" society that lived out there. He said, "Yeah, they probably all have the last name LeMans." He was right: they had it all. I was handed the morning brew, and we were off. All this would stop soon, once I got to college. There was no drinking allowed there. It would be all studying, marching, and pushups. It would be good for me. This "phase" of my life would be over.

THE HOW-AHYA BOWL

Graduation was upon us, and we weren't the only ones celebrating. The custodians were especially glad. They had narrowed down their list of suspects and were positive it was the Phantom, but just couldn't catch him in the act. We received a piece of paper saying that we had accomplished something. We had one more idiot fest at O.B.'s house, and we all shook hands. Simma, Beanz, and Seanzo were not bothering with college. They knew their place in this world and were going straight into the trades.

Sully was going to the University of Maine. Wild Blumpkin was headed to the University of Massachusetts. The Phantom and I would be at MMA getting "straightened out." We would all be going our own ways, only seeing each other at the annual How-Ahya Bowl. That was the Thanksgiving Day high school football game between our town and Holliston, the next town over. Everybody always came back to town to watch that game. You would see old acquaintances and friends, shake hands, and say, "How Ahya?"

We were officially out of the brick beehive, and aside from my lifeguard duty, I was free for a few weeks. I figured that I deserved to really go on a twister for the six weeks or so before going to college and being straightened out. Fourth of July was upon us, time to celebrate independence from those limey fuckers in Great Britain. I knew there was more to it but, having cheated my way through school the last few years, I didn't get all the details. I just knew we should celebrate.

The Phantom had some sort of cottage down in Marshfield. I never knew how the phantom acquired things or what was involved. However he managed to pull it off, he said he had this house, at the Brant Rock area of the Riviera, right on the water. It all seemed strange. Then there were the overly-specific directions: don't show up until a certain time, when it was dark, park at a certain place, then enter from one side of the seawall. We could drink in front of the house, but not go in. That was the Phantom. I imagined the homeowner went to bed at a certain time, was elderly, and deaf; the Phantom timed the guy's sleep patterns, then said he "had a cottage."

Simma drove Sully and me down. He had cousins there and announced that a blizzard was in the forecast. I gathered up my lifeguard money. We pulled over to drain our pickles, and Simma noticed a sign that said the Winslow House. I figured there must have been two Winslow brothers, one was very successful, and had a great deal of money. The other "snapped," and drank his money or business away. My family was clearly from that branch. We were left with little money, which explained why I had to wear out-of-style, plaid bell bottoms and knock-off Numbers Only jackets.

We got back on the road, and the fresh-smelling salt water of the Atlantic was on us. We ended up at a beautiful home; the parents were away. Simma knocked, and his cousin answered. It was obvious from his polite mannerisms that he had a coated enzyme. We stood nervously, and then got down to the money exchange, and were soon coating our enzymes. The vodka went down fast and easy. Eventually, I signaled to Sully and Simma, and we snorted one for the road and shook everyone's hand. We got back in Simma's car and drove down the main drag. It was dark now, and we looked to the left as we drove, scanning for the house number and reference points.

Simma noticed Blumpkin with his red afro. We skidded hard to a stop and tapped the bumper in front of us. The passenger got out, but he wasn't dressed in red, white, and blue for this great Independence Day. Instead, the blue lights went on. The driver got out. Undercover cops.

We rolled down the window, and they were now yelling and screaming at us. I had a fully coated enzyme, and as a result felt the need to talk eloquently to resolve the issue. I would return in a few days and pull the dent out, and then apply a nice chrome applicant, and buff out the scrapes … good as new!

I thought better of it, and just said, pointing, "Sir, that is where we are headed, we can park and walk over, and you won't have to do any paperwork, sir." He was obviously of British ancestry and still angry about the loss of this beautiful land, and said, "Another word, and I will smash your friggin' teeth out."

I was going to tell him my last name and that there was a house in town named after me, but held back. I feared singing "God Bless America," or the Star Spangled Banner with missing teeth. I said nothing. A crowd had formed, and they were on our side, telling the police to back off. Some even threw firecrackers our way. This did *not* calm the situation. Simma failed the sobriety test, was cuffed and put away. They shined the light on me next.

They told Sully to follow them. Sully got behind the wheel and did his usual left foot on the brake, right foot on the gas routine. We gas/braked all the way to the station; when Sully did one final break, I hopped out and vomited. We hung around the station until Simma finally emerged, and then Sully gas/braked us back to the Phantom's rendezvous. Simma said, "Fellas, don't say anything, I'll just go to court myself, and then it will be all over, and no one will know."

We found the cottage and followed the instructions. The place was packed and despite the questionable location, it was a true idiot fest. The good news was the tide was going out, which allowed us to stand on the beach, out of sight, and take in a massive bonfire. We were patriots and it was our duty to celebrate. There was all sorts of booze, and before long I was hit by the vodka bat.

Then the vodka bat whispered to me, "Climb on the top of the bonfire." I obeyed. I was wearing my lifeguard shorts, and after ascending to the top of the burning mass of wood, I pulled them down to the applause of the crowd. I shined a moon at England, our former colonial masters, and pulled my guard shorts back up.

As I ran down I noticed my sneakers were aflame, smoldering and melting. I sprinted into the Atlantic, and my feet emitted steam as the salt water enveloped them. I felt a twinge of pain, but the vodka kept it at bay so I could focus on fun. I made new friends that weren't from my town, and they said, "That was awesome man! Your feet were on fire!" Ah, success ... I would have a Winslow House, or at least a Winslow Cottage, built in my honor. It would likely feature a statue depicting a large man with his shorts pulled down to his ankles, and the date it happened. The "poor" Winslow's would be remembered after all. The major crowds left, and it was getting cold, so we sat next to the fire and made Cro Mag noises.

A massive orange and yellow ball rose out of the water and into the sky. It was a full sunrise, with not a cloud in the sky. There *was* a God, I thought; this *couldn't* happen by chance. Then I looked at all God's children: Simma, arrested for drunk driving; gas/break, and my friend Joe O., who had two fresh black eyes from the celebration. Now the sun was exposing the shiners. Joe O. looked at me, and said, "Dude, you are pitch black." I looked at my sneakers, and most of the rubber on the soles was missing. I felt a throbbing pain.

I needed vodka.

But first I had to take in this moment, of God's flashlight in the sky, shining on his creation at the Irish Riviera. The Phantom came down and gave us some news about a few of God's other children. Wild Blumpkin had been apprehended by the police. Seanzo had been taken away in an ambulance to have his stomach pumped. Yet, we were all ancestors of the Ark, the workers not mentioned in the bible. When the water had receded from the flood, our people had been dumped off in Massachusetts.

The sun was fully exposed, and I jumped into a car that was headed for Falmouth. There was a fireworks display scheduled for that evening. When we arrived, people looked at me funny. Apparently, more than my feet were singed. I looked quickly in the mirror, and I was indeed black, except for traces of fluorescent orange on my guard shorts. The pain was intense, and I needed a drink. Someone took pity on me, disappeared, and returned with a bottle. I dove in. The black curtain came early. I awoke to my father's, "It's hap passed." I had to go lifeguard. Looking down at my feet I realized that I had broken a cardinal rule: I had gone to sleep with my shoes on. However, I gave myself a pass, since they were literally melted to my feet.

Peeling them off, I saw scalded skin. I hobbled to the shower. I got to work and was told I had missed a day and didn't call.

"Yeah, well, listen," I began. "I was minding my own business at a party in Falmouth, roasting a marshmallow for my smore, when some drunk decided to climb a massive bonfire."

The manager said, "Yeah, I heard about those morons."

"The idiot climbed up, and couldn't get out, because he apparently had his foot stuck."

The manager looked at me, slightly side-eyed.

"It was just a natural instinct. I ran up and grabbed him, pulled him out, and dragged him into the Atlantic. We were both taken to a nearby cottage that had no phone service."

I then took one of my brother's borrowed sneakers off. The manager and assistant manager both grew wide-eyed and gazed in horror. Then they apologized. I figured it wasn't too much of a lie. Some drunk *was* on the bonfire. I applied ointment to my burnt feet and hobbled around for the next several days.

Harwich Swamp

Time seemed to whiz by as I got closer to straightening my life out at MMA. However, I had to get my ya-ya's out before becoming completely straight-edged at the military academy. After all, once college began, I would never again touch a drop of alcohol or a mood-altering substance.

There was going to be a little get together at my friend Pat's parent's cottage in Harwich. Since we were all going our separate ways, it called for a special celebration and a memorable meal of lysergic acid diethylamide. We made a call to our friend Dak. We met him in the parking lot. He was in his golf club/polo club/yacht club outfit. He had Docksiders, canary yellow pants, a belt with whales every few inches, an alligator shirt, and a canary yellow sweater tied around his neck.

Even though it was summer, there could be a stiff breeze rolling over the golf course or down the docks of the yacht club; when this happened, all the boat people simultaneously put down their drinks and pinkies and pulled on their sweaters. Dak wore his trademark grin and mirrored sunglasses. Dak informed us of the potency of this batch of lysergic acid diethylamide. It had a small rainbow printed on it; he said it was *guaranteed* crampless.

We jumped in the transport vehicle and were on our way. I reminded everybody of our vow to never go over the bridges to Cape Cod sober. We all carefully placed the paper slips on our tongues, and then washed it down with alcohol. We drove, and I took in the change of trees. It went from the hard-barked colorful, oak trees, to the soft green of the pines. By the time we got to the bridge that crossed the Cape Cod Canal, we were riding fast and hard on the A-train.

We still had about 40 minutes of driving to get to the Harwich cottage, but Simma decided to go real slow. He said he would, "let the gentle winds of Cape Cod carry us safely to Harwich." People whizzed by us; where were they going, so fast? The world was round, I thought. We were all going in circles, on a sphere, that was spinning, around God's eyeball, the sun. I noticed a car with a small child in back; her face, too, was pressed against the window. She saw me, smiled, and waved. She was maybe three years old. I remembered being three. You got three meals a day, snacks in-between, had no mid-term exams, people called you adorable, and then you got tucked in at night.

Where were they trying to get as soon as possible? Were they trying to squeeze as much as they could out of the weekend, so they could prepare for Monday, putting on a noose-like tie, and showing up at a scheduled time, and then sitting in a cubicle all day? That wouldn't happen to me. I would graduate from the Academy, sail the Seven Seas, and live in foreign lands. No cubicle for me.

The wind blew the old 70's model tank to the cottage. We got out, and instead of just heading to the door, we all did our own thing. I went to the closest Cape Cod tree and felt its bark. The rest of the guys took in the new scene. Pat came out, and he immediately got a sense that something was afoot.

He said, "Ah. I see. You guys are on something." As I was groping the thick bark of a tree, Simma was feeling the texture of the car he spent many cold New England weekends working on. The others were just walking around in small circles, looking at ants and gravel. Pat opened the door, and we went inside. Simma was a few weeks into being an apprentice carpenter and started looking at all the woodwork. Then he started caressing the molding around the windows.

I walked over to a fruit bowl and became transfixed. I held each piece of fruit up to the light. Where had this fruit come from? Why was each piece colored orange, red, or yellow? I decided that the bright orange fruit needed to remain with me.

It seems we weren't the only ones on the A-train that evening. There was another guy there from our school, a guy who rode the fence between the Cro Mags and the AP students. He seemed to be smiling for no reason on the couch, staring off into nothing. No one was telling a joke, but he seemed very happy. Joe O. was outside just walking around in figure eights, gazing at insects as if it was the first time he had ever seen, or noticed, them.

Pat had practically grown up in his parent's bar, so he had a certain radar for strangeness. He was looking annoyed as Simma continued to fondle the woodwork, and me walking around holding an orange up to the sky. He mentioned that we should go to an arcade, and get out of there. I remained focused on the fruit. I would take this beautiful round orange object with me. I held it softly in my hand; it matched my guard shorts, and that was exactly what I was going to do: guard this beautiful piece of fruit against anybody seeking to peel her orange skin; I had to defend her against any scumbag biting her with his crowned, capped, cavity-ridden teeth and then spitting out her reproducing seeds.

The lights, bells, and silver balls of an arcade sounded like a good idea. We would take two cars, one for those on the A-train, one for the others. As we walked out to the cars, Pat asked, "Winslow, what is wrong with you?" Seems I had developed a pigeon walk. The same type of walk as those pigeons I saw when my father would place onion rings on the hood of the station wagon.

One step, crane neck down, another step, whip head to the side, another step, whip head up. It took us a great deal of time to get to the car. We finally got to the car and sped off. There were many lights now. White, red, yellow, and green. They seemed not only to shine but to communicate with each other. Then there were the colors and shapes reflecting the light.

Pat's car pulled into a parking lot in front of us, and we followed. We got out and walked gingerly to the arcade. I was concentrating very hard on the pigeon walk and simultaneously holding my beautiful orange fruit, keeping her away from all evil, coffee-stained teeth. Simma and I went to one pinball machine, and we came up with a strategy. He would work one paddle, and I the other. I noticed Joe had made his way up to a pinball machine next to us. He didn't do anything but place his hands on it and look into it. Simma and I put the quarter in and the machine light up. I went to one side, and Simma to the other. The beautiful silver ball was automatically dropped onto the plunger. Simma pulled the lever, and the ball went all the way up, bounced on several objects, lit the screen up, and finally rolled down. I hit it with the paddle. It bounced several more times and we were gaining points.

I could see Joe at the other machine. He finally reached into his pocket and got out the one quarter Pat had given him. He turned on the machine and smiled. I kept one eye on my machine and hit the silver ball again. More bells and points. We were going to become rich, we would be boat people. I saw Joe as he apparently missed the ball with his paddle. For some reason, he did a handstand and then fell over, his feet landing on the top of the machine. The next thing I know, we were being escorted out, with the manager yelling, "I knew you'se were up to something the moment I saw you'se."

I still had my bright orange fruit tucked into my guard shorts. Simma was yelling about how high we had scored and demanded money. We got back into our vehicle and drove away. Mentally, I was now traveling at great speeds. Cars seemed to be time machines. The faster we went forward, the faster we would age. If we went in reverse, we would travel back in time. I thought of telling Simma to do this. To travel to the first time I took a drink. After that, I would quit, and end up with Leiko, maybe even having a great big textbook on my lap, laughing as I found out the answer to the question.

We pulled up to a familiar beach and got out. Pat said that he would check up on us, and to be careful, but we couldn't stay at his place. The beach was always a safe haven. Except for the occasional bonfire. We all got out and did our own thing. It was a cool night, and summer was ending. I built a small mound and placed the orange on top. I then covered myself with sand next to it. Sully was collecting shells. Joe seemed to be talking to someone that wasn't there. I looked at the orange piece of fruit.

She looked beautiful in the moonlight, taking in the small waves of the Atlantic. I told her I would keep her safe from some ugly human mouth. She just looked seaward, probably toward the journey she had to take. I was okay and had a bright future ahead of me. The moon seemed to make a path on the water that allowed one to walk out on the sea.

I looked up at all the stars. What was their purpose? Was it an explosion? Did God say, "I'm going to make so many of these so one night, the son of an electrician can gaze at them." I felt like crying, but still feared Cashews, the ostrich-like human being, coming out of nowhere, bending over with that long neck of his, seeing my bottom lip quivering or eyes welling up, and running around yelling, "Winslow is crying!"

I looked around; being a lifeguard, I had the instinct to count heads. Joe was still talking to an invisible person. Sully had a handful of shells. Simma and the other kid were looking intently at something in the sky. They kept saying, "There it goes" or, "It stopped," or, "It's looking at us." The AP student disappeared, and then returned. He said, "UFO."

I didn't see any UFO, just an enormous amount of stars. There were some formations I could see, like the Big Dipper. Probably named by some important king. It wasn't a working man's description, which would have been more like "The Adjustable Wrench" or "The Anvil." So, it had probably been named by a king. The Big Dipper, named after the thing servants used to wash his feet.

As I thought of the Dipper it seemed the UFO that Simma and the AP student saw was now landing right behind us. It had blue, red and white lights, whirling around. A white light approached us. I would welcome them to Earth with this round orange fruit that was next to me, with the instruction of not eating it like a savage animal; peel it gently, I would tell them, take each small piece and share it amongst your alien friends. Don't discard the seeds, but plant them and produce more orange round fruit.

The aliens were now behind us. I didn't move, as I did not want to scare them. I stayed covered in sand. They would come over the wall, and we would have an intelligent conversation. Then I would hand them the fruit as a sign of peace. One of the white lights was now shining on my head, then it illuminated the orange, then it moved back to my head.

"Hey you, get outta 'da sand."

My brain reeled as I considered the possibility that these might be hostile aliens.

"Don't make me drag you'se out!"

Crap, I thought. These weren't the friendly aliens I saw on the Tang commercials. I dug myself out of the sand and stood up. All my friends were there now. I noticed that these weren't aliens at all, but rather, police. What if they thought I was an alien? I had images of me, being put in some tank, forced to take all sorts of exams. They would announce to the public that, "He is indeed an alien, we suspect the planet he is from is intelligent, so we will use him to test household products."

I thought of my father looking through plexiglass at his son. Then trying to plead with the government laboratory people that I was human, showing them pictures of me at St. Margaret Mary's religious events, dressed as an altar boy. Then I imagined the government laboratory workers handing him the microphone to the plastic cage I stood in and him pressing his face against the plexiglass announcing, "Ya goose is cooked, pal! Ya mutha's back home ringing her hands, announcing that her reputation is ruined." I would plead with the lab workers not to leave, that they could even perform tests on me, free of charge ... just don't release me to my father.

They got to me and asked my name, and I gave the name of a guy we slugged-trained from elementary school. The cop went back into the cruiser; I imagined he had an alien expert in the back seat. The alien expert would look at us and try to match our names to the faces of other known aliens. I thought of the name I had given them. Some victims of the slug train became very studious and were headed to success. But I gave them the name of a kid who had dropped out of school and was living a life of crime. I saw the officer look up from his dashboard, directly at me.

He looked mad, stood up, and then he started approaching me. My orange fruit finally spoke. She said, "Run, Andrew, run!" I ran as fast as a human that is built like an octopus can run.

I ran up a massive mound of sand, which slowed me down. The two people that wanted to stick me in a plexiglass observation tank were fast on my trail. I rolled down the other side of the mound and felt water. I was a natural in the water. I turned over and backstroked. The light found me, so I paddled faster and hit a wooden object, then reeds. I ducked behind the reeds, and then dove down, holding my breath. The lights were on me now, and I put my hands up. I waited for the sting of a tranquilizer dart to hit my forehead, then a net being thrown over me. I had images of the guy from the *Planet of the Apes*, with a part of his head shaved and a scar where they took out a portion of his brain.

I kept my hands up as I crossed back over the mound. I was brought back to the swirling blue lights, covered with swamp muck. Probably frog vomit and goose dung. The police were laughing now, and said, "Why'd you'se run, kid?"

I had some sort of clarity, and told them that next week I would be attending Massachusetts Maritime Academy, and didn't want to be apprehended. They saw that I was a lifeguard, and I told them where I worked. Then I gave them my real name.

They said, "Everything's alright, kid." They told us to sleep it off, and don't make any more racket. I walked into the Atlantic to get the stench off of me. I then went back to the orange and covered myself with sand like a sea lion. I witnessed the sunrise but had no thoughts. That is the A-train, once it stops into the final station, you stop, and you stop thinking. We brushed ourselves off and headed back to Pat's. I put the orange back into its basket without a thought. She now seemed like me, lifeless. The black curtain fell over me. Next, I was being nudged to get out. I seemed to float through the darkness to my bedroom where I slipped under C3PO, Chewy, and R2D2.

THE ACADEMY

"What's your friggin' problem?!"

This guy with a shaved head was screaming at the guy in front of me.

"You were told to wear a collared shirt on your first day!"

Then he approached me.

"What's *your* problem!?"

Having been told to look people in the eye when they are talking to you, I politely turned to him and said, "What problem?"

"Don't look at me, you stupid bastuhd! You answer me beginning with sir and ending with sir and do it without looking at me!" I looked up at the ceiling and said, "Sir no problem sir!"

"You clowns give me 25!"

We blazed through 25 pushups. Panting, I got back up and looked forward.

It was my first day at Massachusetts Maritime Academy, located in Buzzard's Bay. I was being straightened out. No more drink, no more lysergic acid diethylamide, no more yea-yo. No more cheating. From now on it was, "Faster, Better, Stronger."

I finished my pushups and the line kept moving forward toward alphabetized tables. I walked up to the 'W' table and pointed to the paper with my name. The guy went ballistic. It was obvious that someone in his past with the last name Winslow had harmed him in some way. He came around the desk and tore into me. He was upset because there was a small piece of tape; I was supposed to have stood on the other side of that, and not walk over it toward his desk.

He was like me, I thought, he didn't like people too close to him. He respected the 2-foot distance. Anything closer registered as uncomfortable, as a possible threat. He screamed inches from my face. I was going to share with him that I had the same pet peeve. But he seemed really upset, so I figured he needed to cool down. We would talk later. I had to do another 25 pushups, then went into the gym and had new belongings given to me. I was then told to run onto this ship. As I did so, I was greeted at each entrance and every turn by angry guys just yelling at me, even though I made sure to stay two feet away from all of them.

Following others, I ran up a long portable staircase. At the top was another shaved head. He yelled, "You never asked permission to enter my ship!"

I then walked down a few levels, and I was surprised by the five-star service: my famous last name was taped to my bunk and my locker. Then out of nowhere, there was more yelling. Everyone was yelling to hurry up, get dressed, get back onto the parade field. Everyone seemed to be in a rush. I had to dress in these blue bellbottom pants, black boots, and shirt buttoned all the way to the top. It finally appeared everyone was present, and we were then told what was to go in our locker. The socks, the white t-shirts, and how they were supposed to be folded, etc.

We folded everything and placed them perfectly in our lockers. We were then rushed out to the parade field, and we did pushups, leg raises, and sit-ups. Then more yelling, and more being in a rush. I was dripping with sweat, then we ate. The way I grew up, meals should always be special, with no noise or commotion. But here were guys having to do special things because of not following some rule nobody told us about: some had their arms outstretched, some were flying around the room, others were doing deep knee bends. I just looked down at my meal.

We had to eat fast, it wasn't like eating at a restaurant with my father, and him sitting back after everything had been served, sipping his coffee.

We ate like crows eating a street pizza. We went to the belly of the ship and were given more instructions. We had a big day ahead of us, there would be classes and exercises.

I was sweating and shaking profusely. Even though I had ignored literally every science class I had ever been forced to attend, I knew this wasn't just from exercise; it was withdrawal. Or as Tuce would say, "It's the gah-bage exiting you'se systemz."

I tossed and turned all night, shaking. I saw flashes of dead relatives. I saw the Wicked Witch of the East flying by on a broom, pointing her long, crooked finger at me. The guy on the bottom bunk kept kicking my bed. Then I heard the banging of metal, and a trash barrel was thrown down the hallway. It was apparently time to get up. The lights came on. We had to make our beds, for something called "inspection," and get ready for the day. We showered, in cold water, and were yelled at about taking too much time.

We then went to our bunks and made them, and stood at attention. Then we had locker inspection. The first guy they inspected didn't pass, and they tossed his stuff all over the floor. The inspecting officer walked over to mine, looked at my stuff, and seemed impressed. My t-shirts were folded and crisp. They gave the impression of being neatly ironed and stored away, but only because I had yet to fully unwrap them; I had left the cardboard inside. He still looked impressed, and then he touched my neat stack of t-shirts … and felt the cardboard.

He tossed everything out of my locker and held up the cardboard in the shirts, and said, "Every once in a while some wise guy tries to pull the wool over our eyes!" He threw the shirt he was holding up in the air, and it landed on my head. I was then told to do 25 pushups and did them with the t-shirt still draped over my head.

I was told to rearrange my locker and then go out to the parade field. Everybody left. I did as I was told as quickly as possible and jogged outside. When I entered the parade field I was yelled at for being late. I had to do leg lifts all the while being yelled at by two people for being late. They didn't want to hear my excuses.

That whole day, I was singled out and running behind everyone else. Plus, due to exercise, the heat, and the "garbage leaving my systemz," I was sweating profusely, and seemed to be disorientated. I was glad to see the day end and stood in the shower letting the water fall over me for what seemed like hours. I still had the shakes, and my legs seemed to operate all by themselves, with occasional violent jerks, without my orders. We awoke to another trash can being thrown down the hall, and the guy below me, said, "You weren't as bad last night." He had a thick accent and said he was from New York.

I passed inspection and was even congratulated for my tidiness. It was back on the parade field, eating, and then classes. I was very fidgety and craved a few well-deserved hula-booms from the Russian mountains. It seemed every sound I heard was intensified. The chalk hitting the chalkboard made me cringe. I was perspiring constantly even when not exercising. I couldn't pay attention, and the room spun. I raised my hand, "Sir permission to use the head, sir!"

"Permission granted!" he barked.

I made it to the bathroom and unbuttoned my top button. I let out the garbage from my systemz, and it didn't stop flowing until the last few bits of glowing bile. Bile only comes out when you are violently upchucking. I went to the sink, and I was white as a ghost. I splashed my face with water and patted myself dry. I went back to class and soon felt a little better. The day ended, and I slept like a rock, with the occasional leg jerks.

I awoke feeling refreshed. Faster, better, stronger. I couldn't get the alcohol craving out of my head though. I deserved a drink for my performance these last few days, didn't I? Maybe even the expensive vodka, chilled. We ran out to the parade field, and an announcement was made: someone had missed the toilet by a mile, and defecated on the floor. They announced, "Now you will all pay the price."

I remembered that the Phantom was enrolled in the same school. He had obviously struck, and we were going to pay the price. We all were doing leg lifts. I pictured the Phantom, lifting his legs with that sick grin of his. He couldn't help it, it was like some sort of compulsion. Like someone washing their hands frequently or opening the refrigerator door constantly:

he couldn't stop. I knew this announcement and punishment would only cause it to continue. We did endless leg lifts. I was feeling better physically, but couldn't get the thought of that drink out of my head.

The two-week orientation/boot camp finally came to an end. We did some marching routine to the joy of our parents. Every Little Johnny there looked special. I looked special, and pictures were taken for me, this special looking person, in that special moment. Everyone was proud, and I was riding that red arrow on Mr. Simonon's life graph. I needed and deserved a drink now. I asked around, and it didn't take long to procure a small plastic bottle filled with clear liquid.

It wasn't Stolichnaya, but it didn't matter. "Hula-boom!" I drank it rather slowly, looking at the vodka. "I missed you," I said, staring lovingly at the bottle. Soon I was back in what felt like my normal state of mind and body. My thoughts eased, softened. I would graduate at the top of my class, wear a square hat and tassel, receive a plaque on a podium. It would have the fancy Latin words, "summa cum lately," and I would hear the cheers of my proud parents and friends. Shortly thereafter I would be captain of a ship. My household would be in some foreign country.

"Anchors away!"

"Yes, captain Winslow!"

"Full steam ahead!"

"Yes. captain Winslow."

"Steady as she goes!"

"Yes. captain Winslow."

"All ashore that are going ashore!"

"Yes. captain Winslow."

Ah, the magic of vodka. Dreams once hidden now popped out, from just a few drinks. Shortly before the drink, I was a jittery, shy, nervous person in my late teens, not knowing where I was going. Now, after a few hula-booms, I was the captain of a ship, spoke foreign languages, and had a beautiful wife that didn't annoy me, and a lovely family, somewhere near the Greek Isles. After that initial two-week boot camp, we got a few days off, and I spent that time staying in shape and working out. I saw some of the fellas. Simma was now working as a carpenter's apprentice. His massive hands were torn to shreds, but he said, "It's worth it, no exams or reports to worry about."

My few days off came to an end and I went back to the Academy. Freshmen were assigned to run back and forth to class. I liked the physical part of the school. But then there were the classes, which consisted of math, science, English, history, and pre-engineering classes. My head spun.

It seemed everything in life featured an initial two-week period. A two-week period where you can get away with being clueless without anyone knowing, whether it be in work, or in school. We all are given that two-week window of no one knowing who or what we are capable of. No one finding out about the *real* us.

I had a mild interest in some of the classes but had never practiced or learned how to study and retain information. I left chemistry class and was thinking about the table of the elements. But then I had to go to history class and focus on Machiavelli. By the time I was back at my dorm, my head was scrambled with all the information. Then it hit me: Who was going to do my homework?

I was getting the itch for a drink. But where? A week went by, and it was all confusion. I took a walk and saw upperclassman shooting the breeze in the hallway. I don't remember looking at anyone, but this guy with shaved hair said, "What the fuck are you looking at?"

I said, "I'm looking for a drink, to be honest, it's been ten days."

The guy smiled and said, "Well, come on in!"

I went into his room, and he just said, "I'm Shorty from Dorchester."

I sat down and he handed me a beer. He said if I told anyone, he would break my nose.

"Not a problem," I said.

It wasn't vodka, but I was grateful. I swilled the beer down in a couple gulps, and he handed me another one. He smiled, as I drank the next one down, and had another.

"Thirsty, huh?" he said.

"Yeah, it's been over a week."

I felt the calmness of a few beers take over. I was myself. Another guy entered, and Shorty gave him a hardy handshake and a brew. He came in and looked at me up and down. He stuck his hand out and said he was so-and-so from Charlestown. I just mentioned my name and not the zip code. He looked puzzled. I drank the beer and asked for another.

Shorty said, "He's all right, he lives next door, and he drinks like a fish."

This eased the guy from Charlestown, who smiled and exposed some chipped teeth. I was "in" because I drank like a fish. This guy had several scars on his face, and a crooked nose. I figured it wasn't from slipping on icy church steps. He went into stories of his summer and talked of fights, women, and other excursions. I noticed these two had their own language that consisted of swearing almost every other word.

I got my fill and decided to exit. I reached for my wallet, and Shorty said, "This one is on the house." I shook the hands of my two new friends. I went back to my dorm room and lay down. Thoughts of Captain Winslow came back to my head thanks to the alcohol. I was back on track in my mind. My roommate, the guy that was kicking my bed during boot camp, said he was itching for a drink. I told him I'd ask around.

I asked Shorty the next day, and he said he could get me anything. I came back with vodka, and we proceeded to drink. The guy from New York drank like me, but with a certain twist. I noticed his facial expressions started to change like that of Seanzo. This scared me and I became concerned. It meant trouble. I didn't like trouble and just liked the effect of the sauce, and the mental state I would be in by the first few, and then the complete oblivion after several. Well, we had several, and the vodka bat hit me.

Things got fuzzy. This guy was mumbling to himself, and then was taking his fist and hitting his open palm. Without notice, he started to destroy the room, tearing everything apart, and throwing stuff all over the place, all the while yelling. Two guys ran in and tried to subdue him, but he was attacking them. I jumped in and tried to break it all up. More people came in, people that looked important.

The black curtain was dropped, and I woke up. The room was a mess, and I had committed the cardinal sin of sleeping in my shoes. Some high-ranking upperclassman came in and said we had to go downstairs. We went in front of older men, faculty. They read off all these falsehoods: drinking, fighting, destruction of property. My head was spinning. Then we were dismissed.

I figured they would forgive us, and all would be well. I gathered up my belongings and ran to classes. The rooms spun. I ate, and then got back to my dorm, and there were slips on my door. They were for both of us. Each pink slip listed a charge and a punishment. Drinking. Drunkenness. Destruction of Property. Then someone came in and announced we had to get into our work clothes. These were the bellbottom denim jeans, the steel-toed boots, long sleeve blue shirt, and our black baseball hats. We changed and were told to wear the hat backward.

We were told that each demerit was one hour of work. Each pink slip had something like 50 demerits. This guy smiled and added up the slips, and said, "Looks like you guys are the new custodians for this place."

We were introduced to another group that had done something wrong as well. These would be our new friends. We went to work cleaning, mopping, applying floor stripper, cleaning that and then applying a wax. The floor looked new. By the time I got out of that outfit and showered, it was getting late. I was doing this every night now. My grades were slipping, but I figured next year would be a better year. Most nights we were assigned our cleaning jobs, and then the officer in charge would leave and go do his own thing.

On weekends I could work more hours to get through the demerits quicker. Most of the times the person assigned to watch us would leave, and then return many hours later to inspect our work. That was when the alcohol and marijuana would show up. I realized that through my drunken escapades I had inadvertently joined the drinking-and-getting-high club. Funny, we were all there for alcohol or drug offenses, but once the back of authority was turned, we were right back on the sauce. It was natural for us.

I peered out several times, with my cleaning outfit and hat on backwards, and broom, mop, electric buffer, looking out to the canal at the passing boats and ships. It was a nice sight, and I knew I would be out there someday. This was just a hiccup, just a rough phase I was going through.

The year wore on like that, and I looked forward to the "end of the year cruise." Each year, we were scheduled to go on a cruise and work on a real ship out at sea. Before graduating and taking the coast guard exams senior year, you needed so many weeks and hours on the training ship. As our time approached, we got word that there were mechanical issues on our ship, so we would not be setting sail to get our training. We would have an additional month of free time, or to work, for the summer. This would allow me to straighten out, and come back a new man: faster, better, stronger.

OH, DO YOU LIKE
THE SILVERWARE?

Well, now there were two causes to celebrate, the mechanical failures on the ship, and the fact we were going to have an extended summer. Plus, St. Patrick's Day was right around the corner. I had a plan: I would hook up with my friend Dak, and pick up some lysergic acid diethylamide (enough to bring some back to the Academy). But first, there was a gathering scheduled in Providence. I managed to find a green sweatshirt that looked acceptable for the swanky private club, along with my black school pants, shoes, and long black pea coat.

Me and my new bunk-mate would be meeting up at his mom's where she would have a traditional Irish meal of boiled vegetables and boiled meat, then we would be off to the club for a couple beers, then back to the Academy. He wasn't in on the plan to take the A-train. He was a drinker, but that was it.

We headed out, and there was just that quick pit-stop at Dak's. He now lived in Brighton, an area with two major schools, Boston College and Boston University. The whole area looked like carbon copies of itself, an endless sea of brick buildings, each 3 to 4 stories. Dak's place was different, however. There was a smokestack and on it was painted, "The House of Pain." Once we were on the right of the road, I would just look up to the smokestacks, and see those words and tell whoever was driving that this was the place.

We found it and headed upstairs. I knocked, and a young lady answered and let me in. I entered and saw Dak surrounded by a mesmerized crowd. He pointed his finger to not interrupt, and he continued his historical speech on St. Patrick. He was dressed in shiny loafers, chinos, and a nice green sweater, in celebration of his Irish heritage. He finished his speech. He shook my hand and we walked into his room. It was obvious that the small gathering that just heard his speech had no idea that he lived another life, as a drug dealer. But that was Dak, the chameleon. One day he could be at a biker rally, the next, dressed impeccably at some $300 dollar a plate gathering drinking with his pinkie finger pointed forward to the future.

He spoke softly and asked how much I needed. I ordered six. He reached into a mini fridge, pulled out some aluminum foil, and then with tweezers pulled off six bits of paper and placed them in a circular, empty film case. Then he pulled another one off, and said, "Happy St. Pat's day." I tilted my head back, opened my mouth, and he placed it on my tongue. Dak went back to his historical discussions and smiled as we left.

We drove to the dinner house, in a town called Seekonk, close to the Rhode Island border. As we drove I was astrally projected from the front passenger side seat of this pickup truck and onto the smooth tracks of the A-train. My bunk-mate didn't see anything happen, as it all took place in the spongy thing between my ears. The drive seemed slow; perhaps only I was aware that we were in a vehicle that could control time. Hit the pedal, and we would arrive in the future. If we veered into the right lane, where the Q-tips drove, time would crawl backwards. But here we were, going the speed limit. A mark set by white wigs many years before, when men traveled in horse and buggy.

We arrived at his folk's house, and they were glad to see their boy. Perhaps I was the only one who noticed that everyone was operating in slow motion. They were kind to me, and said, "Glad to finally meet you." His father had some sort of hunting cap on. He wasn't verbally expressive, but also didn't have that parental, investigative look in his eyes. Right away I could tell this wasn't like the homes in my neighborhood, where a crucifix and a picture of the pope were standard-issue. This appeared like an Elk's Club or VFW hall. We sat down, and I tried to relax. There were all sorts of weapons and other memorabilia all over the place. The memorabilia looked like plush animal toys protruding from the walls.

All the stuffed animals were gathered around this room, and now, thanks to acid, they all were looking at me. They didn't look happy. The ones on the wall gave the impression they were swooped up in a storm, and had been thrown through the wall and just became suspended. Then there was the deer head. He must have been thrown through the wall in a great storm, but the gust of wind wasn't strong enough to smash him all the way through, so just his head made it through. The other side of his body must have been hanging out back.

I whispered to my friend, "What is this? Why didn't you tell me about this?"

He said, "Oh, my father is an avid hunter, and his best friend is a taxidermist. He hunts, and then brings the remains of his kills to his friend the taxidermist, then his friend fixes them up like this. Cool, huh?"

Thoughts raced through my head. These animals were alive at one time, shot, then stuffed, and were now looking directly at me. My brain started to send a nervous signal to my leg, which gave a signal to my feet, which started the twitchy forward and backward movement. Slowly at first, then more rapidly.

I should have just looked straight ahead, but I took in the entire room. I noticed something, an old familiar friend. It was the crow. The garbage man of planet earth. Taking care of all our waste, without a complaint. The crow I saw out my bedroom window as a kid. The crow that followed me on my morning paper route. The crow that watched over me as I clung to the boob rock in the forest. Now here he was, looking straight at me, with those pitch-black eyes. Only, they weren't blinking. He was pissed, looking directly at me. Being an experienced eye reader, I could tell that his eyes said, "You could have prevented this."

This sight made my feet in the institutional shoes slide faster and faster across the floor. My friend took notice. He asked if I was ok. I simply said, "Can I take a shower?" The shower would stop the speed of my thoughts. We were excused, and I was handed a towel and loped toward the bathroom. I needed to clean these thoughts, and wash the acid out of my system. It was too powerful. I would even open my mouth to the shower head, and let the water drain onto my tongue, washing the chemicals off.

The shower would fix things. I would step out and off the A-train, and back into reality. We would have a traditional Irish meal as planned, and I would even be cutting the corned beef, as the guest. I got into the shower but felt caged in. Maybe this was *all* a cage? Maybe it was *all* a trap? I kept fidgeting with the door, to see if it would still open. I turned the shower on and cracked the window. If I saw his father enter with his camo hunting hat, I would have to escape.

The water sprayed onto my skin, but seemed to just bounce off like I had been water-proofed. I opened my mouth to let the water hit my tongue. I kept playing with the valve, indecisive as to what temperature was needed to slow down the A-train. I decided first I would freeze the acid out of me. I would get it into a shivering little speck, and then I would burn it. I shook as I entered the freezing acid phase of my plan. After a few moments, I turned the valve to its other extreme and went from shivering to "fighting the pain" … the pain of the New England winters, snow crashing horizontally into one's face, trudging forward with a shovel, a snow-blower, or the *Boston Globe*. Fighting the pain.

The water was now scalding hot, and I gritted my teeth like the good paper boy, fighting the horizontal snow. Water, I thought, kills many every year, cleans people, and scalds people, boils things, and most importantly, saves people. Now, it would save me. I emerged from the shower in a great deal of pain but figured I had scalded the tiny LSD creature that was in my head. I toweled off and went into another room. It was obvious from my pigeon walk that the shower method didn't work. I was still on the A-train. I dressed, but didn't know where I was headed, or where I was. Then I heard, "Andrew, time for dinner." Whose dinner? What dinner? Then as I went to go downstairs, I noticed the suspended animals and birds protruding through the walls.

I freaked between my ears. I would be next. They had a plan. They would pretend it was a meal, but then as I was eating I would be bludgeoned from behind, and sent to the taxidermist. My head would be mounted next to the basement electrical panel as "son of an electrician." I pigeon-walked down the stairs, taking in all the animals. Then I made my way to the kitchen. There, everyone was sitting. I sat down, feeling the pain of the boiling shower as my back leaned against the chair.

I noticed the food of boiled vegetables and corned beef. It was St. Patrick's Day. Now I remembered. His mother even gave me a big grin and said, "Happy St. Patrick's Day."

"To you too," I said, with a smile and massive acid eyes.

The moment of levity left, and my mind went back to what was really about to happen. They wanted to mount my head, the son of an electrician, next to the electrical panel. I kept my wide acid eyes open for any quick movements. His father's eyes were very shifty, yet he never looked directly at me. He kept his hunter's cap on and concentrated on his food. He made the same noises my father made when he ate.

"Yum sum, lum yum."

I would have made Mrs. Mooncai very proud, as I sat totally upright. I put one eye on the food on my plate, put my fork in it, and raised it to face level, and then opened my mouth.

This upright posture allowed me to keep an eye on everyone. I wouldn't lean over the plate, leaving me susceptible to being bludgeoned, or missing the signal from someone at the table for the taxidermist to enter from the basement behind me and administer the blows of a ball peen hammer. I then got a great idea. I held the spoon up and turned the convex side toward me. This allowed me to take in any activity behind me. I didn't see anything and put the spoon down. I put some food in my mouth and then again held the spoon up.

The mother of the house saw me and smiled. She said, "Oh, do you like the silverware?"

"Yes, it's beautiful," I said.

She mentioned its history, and that it was only used for *special occasions*.

Yeah, "special occasions," I thought. Like, just before someone is bludgeoned. She was onto me. The spoon technique for catching the sneaky taxidermist behind me had to be changed. I switched to rotating between the glass and the knife, and once in a while I would politely turn my head around and say, "Such a nice home." We finished our meal, and then dessert was served. It looked like I might make it out alive ... but figured I would have a net thrown over me on the way out.

We ate the dessert, and I took a few last looks into the silverware to see any movements behind me. I was sure I would walk out of the kitchen into the living room, and a net would be dropped on top of me from the second floor. There would be wrestling, me trying to fight the net, and then I would feel the sting of a tranquilizer dart. That would be my last memory. My body would be cut up and my head saved and mounted next to the electrical panel in the basement.

Bars

If there was a heaven, I figured, I wasn't going there anyway. I had committed too many of the unpardonable sins: eating meat on Fridays, sex before marriage, getting pleasure out of seeing a fresh fecal deposit by the Phantom. Alas, before I knew it, my host stood up and rushed us out of there. I politely thanked the mother and father for the meal, and we quickly exited. We were now headed for Providence. Everything seemed in slow motion, except my mind, as we drove.

It seemed that universal powers greater than us didn't want any of us going anywhere fast. There were limitations put on everything. There was a speed limit. If you went above this limit, you were outside the limit, and you were a threat. You went from a law-abiding citizen to someone that needed to be apprehended.

Things needed to be reversed, I thought. We needed to drive a minimum of 100 mph. The driver's exam should consist of performing three-point turns as fast as possible. There should be obstacle courses performed at high speeds. And a track with a patch of one hundred yards of snow, where the driver would have to maneuver through, slam on the brakes, and pull the wheel into a skid.

Based on this grueling exam, and how well you did, your insurance rates would go up or down. I thought of this new minimum speed limit, and how many people would fear going so fast, feared getting behind the wheel. But no, the car companies wanted sales, and that meant making it easy and safe, not scaring anyone. Hence, speed limits were set.

Now here I was traveling a hundred miles an hour on the A-train, watching my friend drive 55 miles an hour, with his green camouflaged hunter's cap. Providence seemed half the size of Boston, which was good: less traffic. We got to the club, and I noticed we were the only ones driving a pickup. Everyone was dressed in shiny new clothes. The only thing that shined on *me* was my bright green sweatshirt and freshly polished shoes. My bunk-mate didn't shine at all. I noticed too that he didn't breathe through his nose; he was always breathing through his mouth. What did the doctor say when he was born?

"Congratulations Mr. And Mrs. Bailey. It's a boy, 7 pounds 6 ounces. Healthy, but he breathes through his mouth."

We entered the club, and there were a few very large men at the door checking IDs and collecting money. Bouncers: A term for bouncing the heads of unruly drunks against walls or down a flight of stairs. I greeted them like I did the officers at my military college.

"Sir, good evening sir."

They seemed to like this.

We entered the club, and I grabbed a seat at the bar. I needed booze badly. The cold/hot extreme didn't burn the acid out of my system. Maybe vodka would. I ordered a stiff vodka and tonic. It came back, and I remembered why I hated bars. It was like the highway with its limits. It seemed I could only taste the tonic water. I raised the glass and said "hula-boom" to St. Patrick. I ordered another one, and the bartender gave me a hairy eyeball. His eyes said, "I'll be watching you." I felt uncomfortable. The drink came back and I took another whiff. I could barely *smell* the vodka. No tip for this guy.

I missed the days of a nice fire in the woods, drinking as much as we wanted, and not having to reach into our pockets all night. There were no bouncers, and if you over-indulged, you were carried out of the trees with a fellow Cro Mag on each side of you, your arms around their shoulders, feet dragging on the ground, placed gingerly on your parent's front lawn. This place wouldn't treat me the same way.

Bars.

I looked at the patrons coming in, and they were all shiny. Then there was a very large man, large not from weightlifting, but from overeating. I noticed he didn't have to flash *his* ID or reach into *his* pocket to pay an entrance fee. I noticed this fat bastard had his own table. He didn't even look Irish and wore no green. His only green was in his wallet. He signaled to the bartender, a drink was made, and a barmaid brought it over. The bartender looked at me as I swilled my lame drink.

He said, "You better watch yourself, with that guy around."

I ordered another, but it was lame, too. These drinks weren't slowing down the A-train. I thought of the creatures that were mounted on the wall of the last house I was at. All their eyes looking at me. I looked at the bouncers, the fat guy, the bartender, and my friend with his hunter's cap, mouth wide open, breathing in and out like some sort of a machine. I had to get out of there.

It wasn't a good environment for a Cro Mag. I signaled to my open-mouthed friend, and said, "We got to go." He didn't argue. People with open-mouth syndrome seem to be agreeable. We left and started to drive north again. He said, "Why don't we just have a few at my mother's and drive back to school before the morning assembly on the parade field?"

But, nope. I couldn't go back into the dead animal carnival. I asked how to get back to beautiful Buzzard's Bay. He said, "take thus and such highway." Fine. I would hitch-hike back. He dropped me off on the highway and mentioned that there was a fork in the road. My life story, I thought. Always a fork, always a bent path. It was sleeting now. I headed off with my pitch-black pea coat, black pants, shiny shoes, and green sweatshirt. I was now on foot, but still being transported by the A-train.

"This acid is only getting stronger," I thought to myself. Nothing had worked. Not the hot and cold shower. Not the weak drinks. Not the freezing sleet. There I was, loping along in my acid pigeon walk. Take one step, crane neck down, take another step, crane neck upward, take another step, look left onto the highway, take another step, look right into the woods. Pause. Take a step, look up, stick tongue out in an effort to catch sleet. Crane neck left. Put thumb out. Take step. Hitch-hike. Get to Buzzard's Bay. That's what my brain and body were capable of.

A car pulled up, and a black guy yelled, "Hey chief, need a ride?!" I pigeon-walked over to the car and got in. I put both hands on the dashboard. He drove and said, "I'm heading to Beantown, where are you headed?"

"Buzzard's Bay," I said, "Near the cape."

He questioned my all black outfit, and said, "You're gonna get killed out here in the dark dressed like that." I said I had a green sweatshirt on underneath and he said, "Oh, happy St. Patrick's Day." We shook hands, and he said I was cold as ice. I kept my hands on the dashboard of his time machine. We were driving slow in the right-hand lane. Then I saw the fork. He pulled over and said, "Here you go. The Cape is that way."

It took me awhile to get out of his car. The pigeon walk apparently didn't translate well to sitting down and getting up. He looked at me.

"Brother, you got to lay off whatever stuff it is you're on."

"Sir, yes sir!" I said.

I walked, pigeon-like, with thumb out, and was shortly picked up again. This guy had obviously been celebrating. He said, "Hey, need a ride?"

I said, "Yeah, Buzzard's Bay?"

He said he wasn't going that far, but would drop me off at his exit. His time machine had muffler problems, and he couldn't control the wheel too good, either. He was drunk … and I was jealous. Instead, I was on the A-train. Being transported to its destination rather than mine. He said he was Portuguese, but Catholic, and always tied one on for St. Patrick's Day.

He recognized his exit and jerked to the side of the road. I performed my awkward pigeon-like car extraction. His time machine swerved away, and he disappeared into the darkness. I put my thumb out and pigeon-walked. It was cold, and sleet started to accumulate as ice onto the shoulders of my pea coat. It formed ice epaulets, giving the impression that I was some important figure from the military. I saw what looked like a

Massachusetts state police time machine on the opposite side of the highway. He slowed down briefly and shined a round light my way. Then sped off. I thought of the police motto, "To serve and protect."

I had good thoughts now, thinking of this motto. He would pick me up, wrap one of those warm and fuzzy gray police blankets around me, and then serve me a donut, some warm soup, and better yet, some warm Swiss Miss cocoa. Then he would drive me to the front door of the Massachusetts Maritime Academy. The police time machine pulled up and his lights were flashing. These blue lights didn't freak me out as they normally did, because I would be served and protected. I smiled and started to walk toward the blue lights to get my gray blanket and snack and then front door service to the academy.

There was an announcement made by the vehicle.

"Stay where you are. Don't move. Put your hands up."

I did what this colorful time machine said to do. Maybe there wasn't anyone in this machine? Perhaps it was fully automated, and just cruised the highways, serving and protecting. Maybe with my arms outstretched to the sky, it would be easier to wrap me up in the warm and fuzzy blanket. I smiled at this thought and decided to walk closer. Alas, the time machine was not fully automated, and its captain opened the door. He seemed to be pointing something at me. Maybe it was the blanket wrapping device?

"Now! On your knees!"

My mind was racing. The white lights of the machine were on me. My knees were in a couple inches of slush. The blue lights seemed to spin all around. The guy that was going to serve and protect me walked almost pigeon-like himself, like he was involved in some sort of a duel. He yelled, "No funny business or I *will* put a hole in you!" I had images of Swiss Miss pouring out of this hole. He then walked behind me, grabbed me by my collar, and flopped me to the hood of the car. He kicked my feet out from under me. I waited to be wrapped in the blanket. He rifled through my pockets. He removed my wallet, and then the film case. I would have to come up with excuses.

I thought of James Bond movies. He would question the little pieces of paper in the film case. I would say I was a secret agent, my laboratory was in Buzzard's Bay, and I needed to bring those back to the lab and place them under a high-powered microscope. There was writing on them, and we were going to interpret it, to prevent a nuclear catastrophe.

He opened my wallet. I forgot I was carrying a fake ID along with my read ID. The guy on my fake ID was from Jersey and had brown eyes. He took the long black flashlight and shined the light into the film case. There was no film. All he could see was tiny pieces of paper. I had to think fast. Easter was around the corner, those six pieces of paper were the final touches to a papier-mâché Easter bunny we were making in art class. The tiny pieces of paper would make up the eyes, nose, and mouth of the Easter bunny. We would then donate the bunny to a local orphanage. My mind raced … should I say I'm a secret agent, or an artist whose work goes to local charities?

He held the two ID's up and screamed, "It's time to get straight!"

For some reason, I told him (mostly) the truth. The container held LSD. I went to Massachusetts Maritime Academy. I had a fake id. He asked me if I was on acid, and I lied about that. He went back into the well-lit time machine, and I could see him communicate with the mother ship. I feared being apprehended. I feared being strapped down and my mother, father, and an important Catholic figure looking through plexiglass at me, my mother, saying, "I'm so embarrassed!" My father, mouthing, "You bum!" and then finally the religious figure in his red pointed hat and red robe announcing, "You committed a cardinal sin!"

The police officer emerged from his vehicle.

"You were straight with me."

He shined the powerful light in my eyes, and then dumped the eyes, nose, and mouth of my Easter bunny project onto the ground, stepping on it.

"Now, there is no evidence against you, and no paperwork for me!"

He said he would hold onto the ID. He then shined the big flashlight in my eyes again, and said, "Are you sure you didn't take none of that stuff!" I said, "Sir, no sir."

"Then get off my highway!" he yelled, pointing to the now snow-covered woods.

I went over the guardrail, and into the woods. Without a gray blanket, without a donut, without soup or a hot cup of cocoa. I rolled down the embankment, and the time machine with blue lights sped off. I was in the woods, it was swampy, sleeting, and I had just rolled down an embankment. This would be where I would spend the bulk of my St. Patrick's Day. I had to find a dry spot. I noticed a collection of trees. I found a small patch of dry land and laid down. My mind spun one image after another. I feared living like this the rest of my life. Eating the swamp vegetation that surrounded me. Or some half-eaten burger a motorist tossed out the window. I would be the "guy down by the highway."

Once in a while, a kind elderly woman would come by wearing long rubber boots, carrying a real spread. She would say, "Oh, you poor thing," and watch me growl as I ate my food. I lay on my back and just tried to stay calm. I would be safe if I could avoid being discovered. I looked up at a massive oak tree.

The sleet had accumulated and gave old man oak the impression of having gray hair. I had thoughts of the *Wizard of Oz* and the Scarecrow being attacked by the branches of a tree. While lying on my back, I pushed with my feet to get out of the reach of the oak trees branches. I was now closer to a pine tree. Ah, the lady pine. She seemed friendly. The sleet seemed to cover her pines boughs with lovely white necklaces.

I then noticed the branches of both trees swinging. The trees were talking. This special event of tree talk could only be witnessed while riding the A-train. The oak tree was very judgmental. His branch waved and said that I was no good. Lady pine waved back and said I was still young, there was still time to straighten out. I pushed with my now muddy black military dress shoes. I noticed a small birch tree. I imagined it was the offspring of the pine and oak. I felt safe near this birch, and while lying on my back, extended my arms behind me, as if practicing the backstroke.

I watched as the branches slowly waved up and down between lady pine and old man oak, clinging to their offspring, little birch. I didn't fall asleep, I just closed my eyes. I opened them, and it was getting clearer outside. I had to get closer to a town. I scaled a fence and just walked. I noticed a familiar orange and blue building. The Dunkin Donuts building. I felt safer. I had no money, so I just sat at a booth, close to the plexiglass. Here I was, an adult, watching the donut guy making the donuts. I was able to see my reflection: white as a ghost, covered in dirt and scrapes.

The waitress gave me another glass of water. I feared coffee, remembering the effects it had on my father. He would drink a cup and either want to hike Mount Everest and make it home by dinner or lose his cool over nothing. Coffee scared me. People filed in as time went on, and I noticed one guy had on an MMA jacket.

I recognized him as the maintenance man. I went over to his booth. I recognized his "Budweiser blush," a flush one gets after tying one on the night before. He had the shakes too; drunks have a bond. We looked into each other's eyes as only fellow drunks can, and just grunted. He looked me up and down, and said, "Rough night?" He noticed my outfit and said, "You'se probably need a ride."

We waited for the rest of his crew, then got in the car and headed out. The whole vehicle stunk of alcohol and sweat escaping everyone's pores. There wasn't much talk. We finally made it to the campus, just as everyone was marching out to raise the United States flag. I ran into my company and acted like nothing happened.

It was time for classes. I was suffering post-LSD "mind wipe." I sat upright and just looked at the chalkboard, not collecting any knowledge. I came back to the dorm and there were slips on my door, mentioning the uniform, the tardiness. I was assigned more demerits and would spend the rest of the year cleaning. The good news was, the year was almost over.

I mopped, stripped, and waxed floors for the remaining 4 weeks. The bad news was, I would have more demerits waiting for me when I returned my sophomore year. I was looking at close to 5 months of either playing catch up with school – spending time at work, and then going directly to the library preparing for sophomore year – or going off the deep end, and bending my elbow for twenty weeks. Hmmmm.

ALL A MAN NEEDS

After the last day of class that freshman year, I got home and immediately made a stiff one. I had completed my first year of college by the skin of my teeth, somehow, even without Stew to do my homework. I finished the year with a solid C- average. I now had four months to read as much as possible and really get prepared and serious about my sophomore year. I could do it! After this one drink, I would get on track. I would turn it around, be voted, "Most Improved," get a gold tassel, and soon be in charge of my own ship. Captain Winslow.

"Hula-boom," I said, as I downed my last, big, stiff drink.

I noticed that most of the people from my old crew who had gone to college had already quit school or, as they explained to their parents, were "taking some time off." Then there were the guys that went straight into the trades. They seemed fine and like they were enjoying their jobs. It was still early in the season, so my lifeguarding job at Houghton's Pond hadn't started yet. I got word from my friend O.B. that there was a position at the liquor distributor from which the Foster's were regularly heisted. O.B. was tipped off by Skinny – the same guy that bowled the pig fetus across the mezzanine onto the cafeteria floor. I called Skinny and got the job.

He said, "You'se will fit right in."

I was to start immediately. The liquor distributor needed three highly qualified men, and *we* were those men. O.B. would pick me up in the morning, and we would head off to work together. So, the plan, in my head, was go to work, go to the public library, gain a ton of knowledge, excel the next year in school, and eventually become Captain Winslow. I got a good night's sleep and was ready for my new life.

O.B. beeped, and I headed out to his yellow Zephyr. It already had a reputation for the rearview mirror being taken off repeatedly, having powdery substances dumped on it, inhaled, licked, and then put back onto its designated location.

O.B., although clean-cut and never wearing the leatherhead attire, was a heavy marijuana user. When I got in the car, his wooden bowl was already smoking. I put on my seatbelt and was handed the bowl. We drove and shortly arrived at a massive warehouse. I was now stoned, and slow-moving. We met Skinny, and he was all smiles. He said he wanted to show us something. He told us to wait in front of a bay door where the big trucks back up.

We stood at this loading dock, just staring at the metal door. Then the sound of a motor was heard, and the metal door started to rise. At first, I only saw Skinny's shoes, then his pants, then all sorts of colors. Then it was Skinny's wide grin, probably the same smile he exhibited just after he bowled the slippery pig fetus a few years earlier.

I then saw what looked like perfectly wrapped presents stacked all the way to the ceiling. Skinny announced, "Welcome to heaven men, it's *all* alcohol." We were all smiling know. We were indeed in heaven. Skinny then brought us to an office. There we met his uncle who introduced us to our supervisor. The supervisor had a mustache where the hairs seemed to protrude vertically. His hair was unkempt, and a chunk of it covered one eye.

He constantly flipped his head back so he could see out of both eyes. I wondered if he liked this, or if it was to make a point. He had a thick Boston accent. He said, "Eyez am ya supah visah an eyez will show you'se around, and what you'se got to do's." He must have noticed our awe at the sky-high pallets containing alcohol. He smiled at our turkey like heads bobbing up and down and left and right. He went over our job description. The entire warehouse was imported beer; some trucks would deliver the beer to the warehouse; other trucks would be filled with this beer; then they would deliver the beer to stores and bars.

During this process, the canned imported beer could sometimes end up damaged. Our job was to take the damaged cases, inspect all the cans from the case, and dispose of the dented cans into a certain barrel. O.B. repeated, "Dispose of the dented ones?" The supervisor looked at us and smiled.

"Yeah, *'dispose.'* In 'dis heya barrel."

We were all on the same page as we looked at each other.

"Dispose."

Then we would take a fresh case package, and repackage a new case with undamaged beers from the case that had contained the dented ones. When we were done with that, there were pallets outside in a massive heap. We had to organize them, according to the brand stamped on the side. The trucks would empty the pallets and we would re-palletize according to the brand, once the repackaging of cases was done. We had our own work area containing tables, massive plastic barrels, big rolls of clear tape, and a section of flattened, empty cases.

We found a pile of dented cases and got to work. I was moving very slow, not blinking, and not worried. I was stoned from inhaling the contents of O.B.'s wooden bowl. We emptied a dented case and separated the good cans from the bad. Skinny opened a dented can and poured it into a massive barrel and then threw the can into another empty barrel. O.B. and I looked at each other in disgust. Skinny had just committed a terrible act. Like someone blowing their nose onto an expensive cloth napkin.

Skinny looked at us, and he knew he had just committed a serious offense for our zip code. We had to think quick. We looked for cameras; there were none that we could see. We thought fast. If it was a busy day, and there were many dented cans, we would pound some, and bring others out to the pallet area. Then we would carefully place them in the trunk of the Zephyr. It was a Monday, and it wasn't that busy. So ... we disposed of the dented cans via gullet exercises.

We had to fake emptying the other plastic container that was supposed to contain the liquid from the dented cans. Our own assembly line was working perfectly. We had devised a plan, and within a few minutes, we had our lab, our own mini-factory, and our own procedures. The guy whose hair was parted to one side walked over to us, threw his head back exposing his covered eye, and said, "You'se can take a coffee break now." Then he disappeared.

We punched out for coffee break and saw the other fellas in the office. We all just gave each other a cold New England head gesture, and said: "what's up." None of those long, drawn-out salutations or chit-chat. We headed to O.B.'s Zephyr, and he prepped his wooden bowl. I had an alcohol buzz going, and it was only nine o'clock in the morning. Now, with the bowl being passed, I was in the marijuana dimension. O.B. muttered, "We'll be drinking for free."

"Drinking ... for *free*..." I said.

We looked at the clock, and it was time to punch back in. We headed back to our mini-assembly line. More trucks arrived, unloaded, and exited. More damaged cases for us. Beer from all over the world ... even from Japan. Now we were tasting worldwide flavors. My head was spinning from all the imported beer and the strong marijuana. Soon it was lunch break and we punched out. We got to the Zephyr and O.B. took us for a ride. The bowl was packed, and we headed for his drinking spot. There was more chatter of our perfect job.

Stoned again, we headed back to "work." We finished what was left of the damaged cans, and headed out back for the final hour to repalletize the pallets. I was stumbling now, and tried to get the lead out and be a good worker. The day ended, and I was literally shuffling on my way to punch out. We piled into the Zephyr, and O.B. lit up the bowl. I was never a big marijuana smoker, and could never understand how much you were supposed to smoke, or if there was a chance of going overboard, like with alcohol ... having your lungs pumped out due to too much weed smoke?

Apparently, a reefer overdose was uncommon, or non-existent ... or at least of no concern to O.B. My mother always taught me to accept invitations for food, and then say thanks shortly after, so I wasn't going to say no. I didn't talk during the ride home. When we arrived I walked into the house and greeted the cocker spaniel and the Boston terrier at the top of the stairs. I stumbled downstairs and lay on my back looking at the plaster.

I observed that while under the influence of marijuana, I tended to be more *observant*. I observed the tongue of the terrier now, in and out, while the tongue and mouth of the cocker just stayed open, panting. Time drifted toward dinner. My father made his loud appearance, and we all headed for the table. We said grace, and I was asked how the new job was. I muttered that it was challenging. My father gave me a funny look.

My head was spinning, but the marijuana and its aftermath gave me the desire to eat large quantities of food. This pleased my mother, but threw my father off, because he knew that heavy drinkers don't usually eat much. I finished and went to my room, to do some "reading," and crashed. I was woken up by O.B. and his yellow Zephyr beeping. The routine was the same, and time passed; it *was* the perfect job.

A couple weeks went by, and there was a new guy. I could tell right away, he was educated. But I took a liking to him, for he was a worker, and things weren't handed to him. After he was taught "the" rules, we taught him "our" rules. He followed along with ease. He was a heavy drinker, and once in a while would even get fried with us at lunch break.

He went to Columbia University, and told me about some of the books he was reading, and the authors, and some of their bad drinking habits. I wished I could hold a book and not be distracted by a fly entering the room, and lose focus. How did he do it?

That summer turned into one long drunken episode, seemingly with no interruption. My father was wise to it, and one day said, "Getting' close to the last straw, Joe." I didn't know what that meant, but a few days later I was woken up by him yelling, "Last straw! Screw!" He threw a pile of clothes at me and pointed to the door. I grabbed the clothes, but they were clothes I would never wear. These were leftovers from my brothers from the previous decade. I gathered them up with a few other things and stumbled out, and walked away from Crystal Hill.

School was out for most people, or they had flunked out or quit. Dak's school was out, and his mother was a flower child of the sixties, so I knew it would be cool to crash there for a period of time. I told him my dilemma, and he said I was welcome. He had a spare room, with a pool table, and couch behind the pool table. I even had a separate entrance. This was true freedom. No scheduled dinner and curfew. So, I would turn it up a notch for a few weeks; but just a *few* weeks. Then I would close the valve and educate myself the remainder of the summer.

Dak introduced me to two brothers that were twins. They drank like me, and we became trusted friends. I had a routine, working at the beer distributor, crashing for an hour on the pull-out sofa, then heading out again for the evening. One day, we were toking on O.B.'s bowl, in an abandoned Monte Carlo where the pallets were. Our supervisor, with his trademark chunk of hair covering one of his eyes, knocked on the window out of nowhere and said, "Once you'se guys gets ya heads cleared, weez got to talk."

We slowly got out of the smoke-filled Monte Carlo, and the boss flipped his head back and gave us the news: the company knew it was inevitable that we were going to drink, but not to the excess that we did. There were cameras all over the warehouse, he said, and our well-thought-out plan had been caught on tape. We had to leave.

The good news was, I was starting my lifeguard job soon, and that was where I could "get my act together." I got back to Dak's and thought things over, with the help of vodka. It was still late spring, and I had plenty of time to educate myself at the local library. I just needed to cut back dramatically on my alcohol intake ... or stop completely. Well, I spent the week drinking as much as possible. After all, I deserved it, and had to get it out of my system before starting my lifeguarding job.

Houghton's Pond wasn't too far from Dak's house, and the twins allowed me to use a late model girls Schwinn bike for transport. It was powered blue, but I had plans to pedal fast to and from work; I would be just a flash and nobody would recognize me on the girl's bike. The big day arrived. The lifeguarding job would pay a great deal more than the beer sorting job, but it didn't have the perks of free imported brew all day. I paced the beach. It was a stressful job, and now I had these experiences of shaking and sweating for the first few hours of every day. I recognized a laborer that liked to bend his elbow, and headed out with him at lunch for a "cold one." There was a bar down the street, and he knew everyone, so my underage status was not of concern.

It was nice to get that first drink down. It seemed to stop the shakes and put me in my right mind. I never liked bars and their restrictions. The other thing I didn't like about bars: you had to keep your wits about you. I was a Cro Mag and liked being outdoors, by a fire, the bathroom ten feet away in every direction. Being as loud and obnoxious as I wanted to be. This bar was okay; the vodka and tonics were stiff. The bartender had a crooked nose and massive hands and poured a fresh drink as soon as I finished the last one. It wasn't free, however, so I had to be careful and tip decently.

"Lunch" had worked … I was now in a different dimension, not drunk but "right." I came back smiling from ear to ear, talking to people on the beach, pacing back and forth proudly, just like I would as captain of my own vessel in a few years. The first day ended but, being an eye reader, I could tell that management suspected something. I would have to come up with a plan. I found an old mini cooler at Dak's house, and he allowed me to use it. My possessions now were a 50's style powdered blue girls bike, a mini cooler, lifeguard shorts, a whistle, a couple of t-shirts, and big blue baggy pants.

The cooler even acted as a portable locker, and I was able to fit the blue baggy pants in it.

"All a man needs," I thought.

Mornings were tough, riding the bike into work, either still drunk or with the pounding after-effect of drinking. Plus, it was difficult to maneuver the girl's bike. Especially with the cooler in one hand, draped over the handlebars. It seemed that the slower I went, the more the girl's bike wobbled, so I had to maintain a certain speed. I was wobbling down the dirt path to work and saw the managers standing there at the entrance to the bathhouse. They didn't seem amused. They just looked at me, the girls bike, the cooler, and shook their heads.

I nodded at them and gave them a warm Massachusetts greeting of, "What's up." They weren't overly-friendly and just looked at each other. I put my bike in the bathhouse and put on my lifeguard outfit. I headed out to my spot. The good news was, I was still drunk from the night before, so that would last almost till lunch break with my new bartender friend with the crooked nose. That guy was a Cro Mag at heart; he served stiff drinks, understood my grunted signals for refills, and appreciated my giving him good tips. But it all had to be monitored, for I still needed money for the cheap bottles at night.

This went on for a couple of weeks, and then one day I came wobbling down the dirt path of Houghton's Pond leading to the bathhouse when I saw the lead manager. She was a female bodybuilder. She grabbed my handlebars, came inches from my face, and said I was fired.

The good news was, all my belongings were right there in my mini cooler. I thought I had kept things under the radar. But she went into a litany about me sleeping in the first aid room, sounds of me vomiting in the bathhouse, my stumbling around on the beach. All things I didn't really remember. I turned the bike around and headed back to Dak's. It was a weekday, and the twins were just getting up. It was summer, so we would have a few morning drinks. Perfect!

I went back to Dak's, sat on the couch, and thought about things. Dak came home from his summer painting job, walked up to the pool table, and didn't look happy. He, too, gave me a list of things I had been doing that I wasn't aware of. Apparently, I had lady friends up on the pull-out sofa. His mother, being a big real estate agent, had clients over, and they heard noises from my area. I would even make noises when I was sleeping, he said.

All of this meant the same thing: I had to go. He put it in Dak fashion: I was still well-liked, I just couldn't stay there. I worried a bit about these parts of my life that I was forgetting or missing, things that bothered other people. I didn't remember sleeping in the first aid room of Houghton's Pond, or bringing lady friends up to the pool room at Dak's. It made me a bit concerned, but a few drinks behind the twin's house around a fire would help me figure things out. Soon I was there, drinking.

I stared at the fire. This would be my resting place for the night. I peered into the flames and got some ideas about where to live. There was an old friend, NM, who had moved out of town. He came from a family of eight, was an athlete, and a good student. But he had enough of school, so he, too, was now enjoying the summer of '87 – and going off the deep end a bit as well. I would call him in the morning. I had seen his father on TV once in handcuffs, but he was still always friendly.

It got late. The twins left the fire, and left me behind. I looked out over this part of our town, down onto University Avenue and Route 128. I wondered if people could see me, sitting Indian style, looking at them. What did I look like to them? Some great wise man, probably, I thought. Maybe a guardian angel of this particular neighborhood.

A Few Dents and Dings,
But the Engine is Sound

The good news was, when I passed out by the fire, I had fallen on my back, and not forward, thus avoiding being burnt. I was woken up by one of the twins and headed back to their house. I was able to shower, and even wash my clothes with their hose. Being summer, they dried quick. I made the call to NM and told him of my circumstances. No job, no home. He said I had a place. I left the powder blue girl's bike in the garage, and the twins dropped me off.

I entered NM's, and everyone was kind. I had just showered and looked okay. His father had a chat with me: I would start work the next day, cleaning his cars, then transporting them. For now, he said, I should eat one of the sandwiches on the counter and then go lay down.

"You look beat up, kid," he said. "But nothing some rest and honest work won't fix."

I ate a sandwich, then lay down in the spare bed, and immediately fell asleep. I woke up, and we were off to work. His father owned some sort of "used car" operation. We drove to the lot near the Rhode Island border, not far from the massacred animal carnival house. Yeesh. My job was to wash the vehicles inside and out, and then transport them if necessary. I got right into it. Washing just about anything gives one a sense of accomplishment. It seemed to always make me feel better and lift my spirits.

One particular car appeared to have come from some sort of jigsaw puzzle. It had mismatching tires, seats, etc. But when I was done washing it, it glowed. NM's father called me over and said I would be transporting the vehicle to a certain location in Boston. If pulled over, I was to say, "I'm just the driver," and take whatever rap I was assigned. The location was an area of Boston called the South End. I was to go to a certain diner, and just take a seat. There would be a guy that would meet me there with a thick German accent. I got the directions and headed off.

I took in the whole car. It didn't look like it came from a factory floor. The faster I drove the more this puzzle-car I was driving shook. I made it to the diner and walked in. I looked around and a waitress said, "Are you the driver for Mr. so-and-so?"

"Eh, yeah," I muttered.

I was given the menu and figured I would wait. Then a guy came in with a very intense look. He said hello to the waitress in a thick accent, similar to the Phantom's father. I guessed it was German. He approached me and said, "Give me dah keys to dah vehicle." He was wearing a leather jacket, which was strange for that time of year.

I gave him the keys, and he disappeared. He shortly returned, and then said, "Vee order breakfast."

We ordered and the food soon arrived. We ate. He looked at his food as his fork mechanically entered his mouth. He had good eating habits, which made me appreciate the man even more. He waited for me to finish and then said, "Okay. Vee exit dee premises." It was not so much a suggestion, as an order, like if we didn't leave immediately, the whole block was going to blow up.

The car I drove had vanished, and I was now in a nice new BMW. This guy said, "Vaht train station?"

"What?" I said.

"Vaht train station are you being dropped off at?"

"South station," I fumbled. It was the only one I was familiar with.

He went very fast, with both hands on the wheel, and seemed to be in a rush. I asked where he was from, and he said, "Originally from Germany, temporarily in Somerville."

"Somerville is a nice town," I said.

"It should be a nuclear test site," he replied.

Then we arrived at South Station.

He said, "You're done," and handed me seventy dollars. I got out, and got on the next train to Attleboro and called NM. He picked me up and said the day was over. It all felt strange, but seemed like easy money. I had a job, and it paid well. I had a place to sleep. I behaved myself that night and didn't leave the premises. I felt bad eating the food that was served, for I seemed like an outsider. It was one thing if it was a religious occasion, but I didn't want to be a mooch or free-loader.

The next day arrived, and there was a car on the lot that I didn't recognize. I was assigned to wash it, and then it would be driven and dropped off at a certain location. It was a Jaguar and seemed to have everything intact. Everything looked as though it matched and was original. I went into NM's father's office and told him I was done cleaning the vehicle. He said, "Good," and then got on the phone.

"The Jag is ready, it has a few dents and dings, but the engine is sound."

I was told I would go with his son, drop this car off, pick up another one, and bring it back to the lot. NM and I were handed the keys to this now shiny Jaguar, and we were off. I felt a sense of importance, as we drove off to a town located in the North Shore area of Massachusetts. I was in a Jaguar; I was important. This would be the type of car I would drive shortly after graduating from college and becoming a Captain. People seemed to pass me by and look at me with a little more respect.

We drove for about 45 minutes and were approaching a town called Woburn. Then something started to happen to that "sound" engine. The dashboard lights were giving us all sorts of signals. NM had a look of concern as the warning lights came on, and the car started to cough. I noticed there was a small trail of smoke following us. NM was never one for lengthy conversations and just stated that we had to pull over. We pulled off at an exit and drove a mile or so to some sort of war veterans meeting house or bar.

NM went in and made a call to his father, who then made a call to the person we were supposed to deliver the car to. NM just looked at me, and said, "Now, we wait." One moment I was driving in the Jaguar feeling impressive, and important. Now, we were stuck. At a standstill. A nice-looking Monte Carlo pulled into the lot and the driver said, "You two's jump in." He was a well-dressed man in a sleazy kind of way and said a Mr. so-and-so was very upset. That was the only thing he said for the 20-minute ride we had back to the car dealership. I thought of a mob movie like the *Godfather* and this guy driving to a toll booth, and then leaping out, right before we got gunned down.

We finally arrived at a lot, and were told to follow "that guy." We walked through the lot, then through the showroom, and into the guy's office.

"Here's the drivers."

It was NM and me on one side of the desk. On the other side of the desk was a man with a very expensive suit and a shiny watch. He had two guys with him who were dressed in suits as well. NM was wearing black shoes, black socks, shorts, and a t-shirt; I had on sneakers, oversized blue pants, and a t-shirt. We looked like bums. No one on the other side of the desk looked happy. The guy at the desk looked at NM from his shoes up and then to me from my converse sneakers to baggy pants, t-shirt, to size nine octopus-like head. He oozed condescension.

He pounded the desk.

"You'se clowns tried to drop me off a lemon."

I figured those were the last words I would hear in my earthly existence: "clowns" and "lemon," as my feet were placed into a flower pot, cement poured in, and I was thrown over the side of a lobster boat, never to be seen again. We said nothing. He just gave us a set of keys, and one of the large men standing behind him escorted us out. We were given a car to get home in. The large man said nothing. I figured the car we were given had been pre-loaded with dynamite, and that was the way we were going to go. So be it. It would be a closed casket funeral, with a picture of me on top of the pine box.

The whole scene worried me, and I told NM that my driving career was over. I got all my belongings, which consisted of a lifeguard uniform (i.e., a pair of orange swim trunks) stuffed into an Igloo cooler. I was then dropped off at the twins' house. Both their parents worked, so I was able to openly discuss my situation. They said their cousin down the street had a room above the garage, and the parents were away for the summer. One of the twins went off to make a call and soon came back with the good news: I was in.

MIGHT NOT

I knew the cousin as an acquaintance from the neighborhood. He wore an Alligator shirt but his wild hair and insane smile suggested that he had a wild side. His father was a successful businessman and had risen up the ranks from Columbia Point in South Boston, a really tough neighborhood, to our zip code, which was now considered cushy. I had seen his father around, and noticed he always had a menacing look; I feared him. But I was assured he wouldn't be around.

I grabbed my belongings and walked a couple hundred yards down the street to the house. I knocked on the door, and this guy 'T' answered. He was wearing summer attire of a polo shirt, matching shorts, and fancy loafers. I would find out very soon that this outfit was just facade. He could be pulled over by the police, and they would see his polo shirt, and say, "Eh, he doesn't look like a troublemaker," and let him go. However, I would soon see behind the polo shirts as I glimpsed his daily activities.

He said, "Come on in," and snapped his head back in the direction of the living room.

"So, you need to crash somewhere? Follow me."

I stepped in with my massive blue baggy pants, t-shirt, and all my belongings in a mini-cooler. We walked up a semi-circular staircase. Then to the room above the garage. Before he opened the door, he turned to me with a smile and said, "Welcome to the pit." The door opened, and we walked in. There was barely any room to walk in this place. It was all soft

454

brown furniture and matching square Ottomans. It looked like one giant brown bed.

He told me to relax so I put my Igloo cooler down and gazed at the sea of couches. There was a massive collection of albums, two very big speakers, and a stereo system. I immediately felt comfortable. I inquired about possible surprise visits from his father. He assured me that, once he left for the summer, he would not return. He had a cottage somewhere. Okay, so I relaxed. It was a strange feeling, not owning anything, and living out of an Igloo cooler. There was the freedom of being very mobile, but there was also the feeling of never being anchored, of being told to screw and get on your way at any moment. Here today, gone tomorrow.

But, like with all feelings, a good stiff drink would abolish any negativity. T came and went. He walked downstairs and made some racket. Then I heard a car pull up, its radio blaring. It was a convertible and very small. I looked out and saw a tall, skinny guy with wild looking strawberry blonde hair. He entered the house like a relative: he just walked in. I heard him talking to T about the fact that there was a guest in the house.

I heard a loud, "What's his last name?" Then someone ascended the semi-spiral staircase very rapidly. Then the door opened. He said with a demented smile, "Your last name is Winslow?!"

I nodded.

He said, "Your brothers are Jeff and E.J."

I nodded.

"I played in the band with Winnie and Squeege," he said, referring to my brothers' nicknames. He said, "Relax, dude," and then two words I would hear at the start of nearly all his sentences for several weeks: "might not."

He said, "Might not make you a nice booze drink."

He disappeared, and I figured he would be gone for a while and return with some fancy drink with an umbrella in it. Instead, he returned very quickly, bouncing up the stairs. He handed me a big glass with a brown liquid and some ice. Then he said, "Might not do gullet exercises." He then drank his entire drink down in one gulp. He looked at me like, "What are you waiting for?"

I then performed the "gullet exercise." I said, "hula-boom" and drank it down. I immediately knew it was some sort of whiskey. It had been foreign to me for a long time. It wasn't my drink of choice, and I knew why. It burnt and tasted awful. I made no face and even said, "Eh, thanks," and he smiled. He took my glass and said, "Might not make you another one." He shortly came bounding back up the stairs, and it was the same routine.

Ah, the feeling of the first few drinks came over me. No worries. No worries about being a transient or nomad. People would actually want me to be around their property. I would be welcome wherever I went. Then he yelled down to his brother, my friend T. "Hey get up, and bring your satchel." Then he said, "Might not roll one."

T entered with a massive bag of reefer. A joint was rolled with real professional style. It was lit and passed, and then the feeling of weed haze came over me. I was more imaginative and very slow in my movements. A great combination. The way life should be. Now the whole pit was engulfed in smoke. Then T's brother got up and came back with two more large glasses. We did our gullet exercises and he disappeared. I heard the roar of an engine and turned my face to the window and the guy with strawberry blonde, wild, hair drove off in an old British convertible.

I was amazed, especially with the potency of the marijuana ... how could anyone drive on this, I wondered? T said, "My brother's name is Ricky." He was known as "Sick Ricky." T left shortly after. I seemed to dribble into the couch cushions like a spilled drink. I thought of my religious upbringing. I thought of Jesus and the Last Supper. I thought maybe before the Last Supper, he had a "last night at The Depths," where he would relax with me and take it easy.

He would say, "I will be crucified, die, and then rise again. But, I will put a good word in for you." We would both do gullet exercises, and say "hulla-boom" before drinking. "I love you, Jesus," I would say, as he sped away in an old British convertible.

FOR WHAT I AM
ABOUT TO RECEIVE

The black curtain raised itself and I felt numb. A doctor with strawberry blonde hair standing on end and a cigarette dangling from his mouth said, "Might not hand you a hair of the dog." I was in a fog. Why would a doctor be handing me a glass cup with brown liquid and ice cubes?

I looked around and was surrounded by furniture. I was in The Pit. A safe place. I propped myself up and decided to gather more clarity. I welcomed the drink, the hair of the dog. I wasn't a big whiskey drinker, but got it down. Sick Ricky had the bottle with him. It said Wild Turkey, and had the image of an ugly turkey on the bottle. He immediately poured another one. I forgot to raise my glass for a toast on the first one, so on the second one I said an extra loud, "hula-boom."

Almost immediately, all was well. I had to make plans – grand plans – which the first few drinks always gave to me. I didn't know what day it was, but I should go to the library. The drinks would help me concentrate and quell my normal state of mind, which was a thousand thoughts at once. We sat there on the couch, and he kept pouring. My attending physician reached into his pocket and pulled out an envelope. I figured I would soon be coating my enzymes. Instead, he said, "Ever been on the E-train?"

I didn't know what that term meant and replied no.

He said, "It's ecstasy man."

I said, "What will it do?"

He just stuck out his tongue and made the noise a balloon makes when you let air out.

"Blluuush."

The noise sounded positive.

"I'm game," I said.

He poured some powder into the wild turkey, and I drank it up. I sat back and relaxed with my head on the couch. It didn't know what to expect. The only information I had been given about ecstasy was a half farting noise. Who would make this noise first? I don't know how long it took, but I began to feel at peace. Colors that were once unrecognizable, were now seen. I touched the texture of the couch, and it was soft and comfortable. I seemed to sink deeper into this sea of couches and Ottomans.

He had apparently done this E-train before and knew what the feeling was. It seemed to me like a peaceful A-train. There was still the intense colors, but there wasn't the fear one feels on acid. I didn't have grand thoughts that I normally did on the A-train. But it seemed to advance my senses of taste, touch, and sight. I made another booze drink, and it tasted different, like there was a great deal of thought put into the harvesting and cooking of the ingredients of this whiskey, and of course the well-thought-out name of Wild Turkey.

It didn't even announce "hula-boom" in my normal fashion. I actually tasted the drink and its contents from mother earth. I swished them around in my mouth and then swallowed. This would be how I drank and ate from now on. Slowly enjoying every bite and swallow, savoring the moment. Instead of announcing "hula-boom," I would hold up the drink or food like a priest and announce, "Thank you Lord for what I'm about to receive."

My surroundings exploded into me ... all the shapes, colors, and sounds of The Pit sank into me. Like a child, I had to touch everything. Sick Ricky said he, "had to go to Connecticut and pick up Hondo."

"Might not do one more gullet exercise."

He then poured a drink and snapped his head back.

I slowly followed him down the staircase. He grabbed the keys and stepped into his car. I was amazed that he could do this. It appeared to me, everything needed to be touched or looked at from inches away. His tires spun and he was off to pick up a guy named Hondo in Connecticut. I was alone and barefoot in The Pit. I felt the rug under my feet. I then looked at all the trinkets.

Everyone seemed to have trinkets. Little porcelain animals, bells, special soap, gourds, pictures of "Fred's carefree years." I was touching everything, craning my neck down just like a wild turkey in a gentle field. It seemed to take me forever to reach the bathroom because everything needed to be discovered.

I figured I would shower while in the bathroom. There were more trinkets there as well. What is a bathroom without trinkets? I took a shower and cleaned the smudges of grass and dirt from my body. I noticed the water didn't enter my skin; it just bounced off. I felt clean.

I dried off and although I felt cleaner, I was still very much drunk now, and this chemical that I drank was doing what it was supposed to do, make me real childlike, explorative, taking in my surroundings. I felt like jumping into a laundry basket and sliding down the stairwell like I did as a kid. I made it back to The Pit, and let the furniture envelop me. I felt like an infant in a crib. Like show soap in a porcelain manger. All was well, I was warm, protected, and cared for. My bottle was right near me, and it was called Wild Turkey.

Wild-eyed Sick Ricky entered with another guy, and said, "This is Hondo." This guy looked nothing like John Wayne. He had a mushroom-shaped hair that covered his ears and a reddish face. Ricky told this guy to sit down, and said, "Might not make you a booze drink." I handed him the bottle, but it was getting low. He smiled, and said, "Winslow might not be on planet X right now."

Sick Ricky grabbed a glass and poured the liquid into the glass. Then he poured some more white powder into the drink. Hondo seemed to be concerned and said, "Hey, man, what is that?"

"Bluush," said Ricky.

Hondo looked at me, and I just nodded in approval.

He started to drink.

"Might not get refills," said Ricky.

He ran downstairs, jumped in his car, and was off. He returned some time later with more alcohol.

This went on for a few days, drinks, e-train, using the bathroom, and taking a shower.

Gorilla Biscuits

My old friend Beanz from Pigeon City got tipped off to where I was hiding. He called and said he was heading over in a few hours for a get-together at his sister's boyfriend's house in Roslindale, also known as Rozzie. I knew the boyfriend from a few festivals at Pigeon City. He had a rough exterior, but we had a common bond, our love for hardcore music and alcohol. This wasn't a potluck, rather, just a "show up." T showed up.

He seemed to always have reefer on him, like a 1950's guy always had a handkerchief or a pair of galoshes nearby. T just rolled a white snake and lit it on fire. This soon cured my throbbing headache and physical restlessness. I was awakened by a beep and went downstairs to see Beanz' pickup. I remembered the engagement we had. I got on my blue baggy pants and my reggae t-shirt. I felt awkward, and wanted to be alone, but went anyway.

Roslindale was a few miles away and, although not far away by distance, the scenery changed dramatically. Even the wildlife changed. It seemed the only wildlife was the pigeons, and they seemed tougher here. Then there was the condescension of Rozzie people toward people from the cushy suburbs.

We got to Roslindale Square and took a right at the library. I remembered that I still had to make it to a library, and cram as much knowledge as I could into what remained of the summer. I turned away and was surrounded by triple deckers. We snaked around and pulled into a yellow triple decker. Beanz rung the bell. A woman with a snappy voice answered the door and said, "What do you'se want?"

Beanz just said, "Paul."

The door cracked open, and a female with 1950's-style glasses looked at our feet, then up to our eyes, obviously disturbed by our presence, and then unhooked the door. We entered and she just glared with arms crossed and said, "He's in the basement." There was no talk of, "How are you guys doing in college?" or "What's your grade point average?" Beanz walked over to a door and turned the knob.

The door opened and I could hear music. Hardcore music. We descended below ground, into the basement. Beneath the foundation of the house, where one goes in case of a hurricane or tornado. Supposedly, the safest place. The music got louder and louder. The walls were all artwork. It was immaculate. He was obviously an artist, but had probably been told after a certain age to "grow up," and now was confined to drawing artwork on his basement walls.

I hadn't yet had my first few drinks and was very fidgety. I waited for Beanz to be seated and then took a look around. I didn't see much alcohol. There was one guy that looked like either a terrible painter or had difficulty operating caulking guns. He had white smudges all over the blue windbreaker he was wearing. Paul, the host, politely introduced me to everyone. The guy wearing white painting pants and a windbreaker put his arm up as if they were very heavy.

There was a guy on the floor, who seemed to be trying to sing the lyrics to the band I now recognized as the Clash.

"London calling till the zombies are dead," he droned.

Paul just said, "That's Rat."

Rat made no sign of recognition.

Paul told me to sit down and pointed to a couch. There was a beautiful girl sitting there. I became very fidgety, and my leg went into its bobbing routine. I needed a friggin' drink, and bad. Even though I was surrounded by great music and non-threating people, I felt panic. I was having difficulty breathing. The walls seemed to get closer. I thought of the door upstairs being locked, and I felt an urge to run outside just to breathe.

The girl next to me said, in a very heavy accent, "Relax, eye'z don't bite."

Beanz must have seen my fear, and said, "Hey, Paul, he needs a drink." Paul opened a mini fridge and threw me a beer. I got a brief glimpse of the inside of the fridge and only saw a few beers. This made me nervous. I swilled the beer without the salutation of hula-boom. The girl next to me said, "Hey Paul, he needs another one." Paul went to another area and reached for what looked like a prescription bottle. He came back with a blue pill, and said, "Open up."

I opened my mouth and he threw in a tiny blue pill.

I asked nervously, "what is it?" After all, I couldn't take anything that would accelerate my claustrophobia. Paul just went about his business.

"It's a gorilla biscuit," he said, and put on an album from a band called the Cramps.

My mind raced again, considering all the information it could gather on Gorillas. I remembered them from *Mutual of Omaha's Wild Kingdom*. I remembered the gorillas acting one of two ways. Either they were pissed off that an outsider was on their turf, running at great speeds, sometimes even carrying a big branch, or they were very tranquil, with the female picking tiny insects off of the male and eating them.

Then the fearful thought of King Kong came into my mind. A "gorilla biscuit?"

It was too late, it was already swallowed.

I tried to breathe. The beer didn't do anything, and I needed one more. Paul smiled and said, "You'se is a drinker, huh?"

I nodded.

I was working on my third brew and had a feeling of sinking into the couch. It wasn't the brew. My foot slowly stopped moving forward and back. Now, it was just a few inches forward and a few inches back, and then stopped altogether. The claustrophobia subsided, and I had a feeling that I belonged. The beautiful girl sitting next to me didn't make me as nervous. Everything was okay. I even looked into her eyes. She smiled. She was attractive but had a rough edge, a city edge. I felt she could blurt out, "What the fuck are you'se looking at?" and put a cigarette out on my forehead.

But she didn't. She just smiled back, and said, "The pill is workin' huh?"

This gorilla biscuit *was* working. Soon I would have my oversized head resting against the back of the couch, and she, being the female gorilla, would start picking microscopic bugs off of my body and placing them in her mouth. Oh, man. I loved these gorilla biscuits. Paul, although into hardcore music, still kept the place clean, and would occasionally pick up an ashtray.

The guy with the blue windbreaker covered in splotches of white caulking must have forgot he lit a cigarette; Paul removed it from his hand before it burnt his fingers. The guy Rat was still trying to sing a song from the Cramps. Beanz now looked sedated as well, and being a natural carpenter, seemed to be taking in the surrounding woodwork.

I mumbled to the girl next to me, "What was this thing I took?"

She said, "It's a benzo ... you know, a downer."

Ah, I thought, the half-closed eye. I sat with my head back on the couch and remembered my first half-closed eye and the record I set on my bike for my 12-foot jump. The feeling came back to me, and it was a joyous feeling. Paul lit something that stunk like fuel. It was passed to me, and I looked over at him and asked what it was. He just said, "It's a moon-bar, you know, dust." I inhaled and held it in the smoke like a good guest.

I mumbled, "Eh, what does it do?"

"You'se are going to feel like you'se are walking on a giant marshmallow."

This moonbar had a numbing effect. Time wasn't being recorded, but Beanz announced that it was time to go. I hated hearing the word "time," but by then I didn't care much. Paul came over to me and handed me a few of the gorilla biscuits.

"For the road," he said.

I stood up and indeed I did feel like I was walking on giant marshmallows. The stairwell going up to the first floor seemed to be wavy, and I needed the assistance of the railing. We made it to the first floor, and I did a lunar walk across the room. I felt my hip was displaced and I was tilted forward. Beanz, who was in front of me, seemed to have this limbo-walk, as he was tilted backward.

My legs seemed to extend really high, then slowly come down. I thought of the crew downstairs and the guy with the windbreaker covered in white stains, and Rat with his Mohawk. We got in the car, and the road seemed very wavy, like a black blanket blowing slowly on a clothesline in a breeze. Moments later I was at the entrance to the house that contained The Pit. I got up the stairs and into The Pit. I laid down, and the black curtain dropped.

Yellow Soap

I was awakened by twin aliens. They were thin, had blonde hair, and were both about 6 feet tall. They were cousins with the sons of The Pit. They mentioned their father had a position open at his truck washing business. Even better news, the job was on weekends and it was 12 to 15 hours a day. So, you could almost get a full work week done in two days. These guys had a funny way about them. One of the twins would do most of the talking, then the other would finish the last few words of the sentence. They both chained smoked Newports. As I lay down on the soft furniture of The Pit, they sold me on the position.

"All you will be doing is working the soap wand, just raising your arm up and then bringing it down."

"Just up and down," said the other twin.

I wondered if I was seeing double from my first experience with the moonbar and gorilla biscuits. But I looked between them and said, "I will take the job."

They both said in unison, "Good."

Then I was told I would be starting in two days.

Two days later, I walked down to the twins' house. The side of a van door opened. I was showed valves, and where to enter this bright yellow soap. Then the back door was opened, and there were two coiled up hoses, one was the rinsing wand, and the other was the soap wand. The doors were closed, and we were off to a truck lot. It was a parking lot full of trucks. We pulled in.

A hose was attached to the water supply of the building. The van remained running, which kept this mini factory in the back of the van going, maintaining pressure to the rinsing wand, and a steady supply of soap through the soap wand. There was a brief demonstration: stand a few feet away from a truck with the soap wand, press the nozzle, aim, start high and bring the wand down, then move up, and then down again.

I noticed right away this bright yellow soap started to penetrate the built-up debris on the truck. Right behind me, one of the twins would follow with the rinse wand. That blew most of the soap and muck back onto me. It didn't bother me so much, and as time went by, I knew I was going to like this job. There was little stress, unlike lifeguarding. My face and hands burned from the bright yellow soap. But the day flew by, and I made money. The job involved almost zero stress and enabled me to accumulate many hours of work in a short period of time. I came back to The Pit with a red complexion from the heavy yellow chemical "soap," but after a shower and a few stiff "booze drinks," the pain of the chemicals went away.

I woke up to a beep and headed out to the van. I was sick from drinking heavily the night before, but all I needed to do was stay on my feet, and raise my hands up and down. The sun was glaring at me. Being covered in yellow soap, surrounded by tractor trailers and noisy traffic, combined with my drinking the night before, made my head spin. But all I had to focus on was applying one even sheet of yellow chemical after another.

The good news was, unlike lifeguarding, I didn't have to run into the first aid room and vomit in that toilet. I could vomit *anywhere*. We had big rubber boots, and we were in a truck lot. I coughed up a foamy mess, and then hit it with the soap wand and kicked it with my rubber boots. I stayed on my feet and, slowly, the hangover was leaving. It was the perfect remedy for drinking heavy. Sunday ended, and in two days we averaged almost 30 hours of work. I was dropped off at The Pit and fixed a well-deserved drink.

Don't Trash the Place

I learned that we were paying an old friend a visit in Washington D.C. It was a week away, and Skinny was organizing the whole thing. I just had to come up with some money. I tightened my belt buckle and drank cheap vodka. After a few belts, it numbed the tongue and it went down like water. I was able to save money this way; the plastic bottles only cost me five dollars each. The week went by, and I liked this manual labor. Produce, and get paid. No impending doom with school work, term papers, etc. Drink, go to work, drink, crash, work, drink, make money.

Perfect.

Maybe I wouldn't be the captain of a ship after all. Maybe I would eventually own a fleet of these truck washing vehicles, and have my own office overlooking the workers as they came and went on their truck routes. Skinny showed up, and I was told we were going to leave in the morning to visit our friend Danny who attended Georgetown University. I had attended his bar mitzvah years before, and he was always good to me, providing frequent small bashes with ample liquor. I always noticed, though, he had a handicap or some sort of strange habit: He would only have a few drinks and then … stop. This still made him a friend, but not in the inner circle of heavy drinkers, the inner circle that got the last drop of alcohol out of a bottle or keg.

What was this strange mind malfunction of having a few drinks, and then shaking hands, stating you had to study the next day? Some sort of bizarre "shut off" mechanism in his head, just closing it down after a few drinks. Whereas, in my mind, it awakened the circuitry of wanting to drink more, and be adventurous. I remembered throwing a bash while my parents were away. It didn't bother me that people had urinated in certain corners of the house, or broken expenses vases. But I wanted to track down and question those that left remains of alcohol behind in their glasses.

I dozed off and was awakened by a horn. I put on my baggy blue pants and white t-shirt and jumped in the car. All was arranged. We headed for Logan Airport. We parked and headed to the terminal. We landed a short time later. The good news was, the drinking age was 18 in D.C. We got out of the airport, and I was hit with an immediate wave of heat. Not just heat, but humidity. It seemed much more intense than Boston, and I started to sweat. We went to a fancy restaurant, and Pat made us stay outside until he spoke to Danny, who was working as a waiter. Then he signaled for us to come in. Danny's eyes widened.

The six of us marched into the restaurant and sat down. Danny counted us with his eyes. He was not only a whiz in school, but he had a great deal of common sense. I could see that common sense come out as he counted us and considered the potential consequences as we walked by. His eyes took in the fact the drinking age was 18, took in the fact that he worked in a restaurant that served alcohol … and the final blow … that he would be picking up or trying to lose our bar tab.

We became louder and louder as the drinks were ordered, delivered, and consumed. We eventually had the place to ourselves. It was as if we had waited all our lives to drink like this, like free men, able to pound on the table and yell, "Notha round!" I felt total freedom as the vodka was cutting off the nervous signals to a part of my brain that made me look and feel fidgety and agitated in most of my comings and goings.

Danny's shoulders were becoming more and more slumped as he continued to bring back drinks, nachos, and cheese sticks. I watched the "eye language" from the other staff: the waitresses would stop before going through the swinging door, and our eyes would meet.

"Would you please leave?" the eyes said, and then they would disappear, into the kitchen.

Danny stepped forward and said, "You guys have to go. I'm leaving early and will bring you to my place." A check was dropped on the table, and we looked at each other. It was outrageous, and we didn't even bother pulling out crumpled up dollars from our pockets. Danny needed this gig, he couldn't be fired. It was part of this "goal" thing people talked about. Work at school, work at a restaurant, do good, be successful. He backed away again and took in our puzzled faces now covered in yellow cheese and glowing nacho grease. He did the math; he was going to have to take care of the bill.

Dan was now out of his apron and just said, "Follow me." His shoulders were as slumped as they could physically go. We walked great lengths and took in the surroundings of D.C. We finally arrived at his brownstone. He pointed to the floor, and said, "You guys can crash here." He walked around like he was the concierge to hell and had no soul left. He seemed to just shuffle around as we wallowed in purgatory. The real hell was still to come: we were going to make his once routine life five straight days of debauchery.

He shuffled back and said, "Just don't go upstairs. I have two female roommates." Simma and I looked at each other. To us, "Don't go," definitely meant, "Go!"

We needed refills. Danny told us where the liquor store was, and the good news was, it was just a couple of blocks away. We gathered up the crumpled dollars. We marched proudly to the liquor store. We had finally graduated, achieving our goal of being able to purchase alcohol and walking with our achievements in brown bags, not looking over our shoulders or worried about being jumped or chased by the local authorities. Although Simma and I graduated together, he was put in school early in life, and I late. So, I would make the purchase. It was an emotional moment. I almost cried, but feared Cashews coming out from under an aisle and screaming, "He's crying!"

We bought what we could with the crumpled-up dollars: a couple of plastic half gallons of vodka. The plastic bottle idea was great, it kept people safe. I imagined myself rolling down the stairs of the Lincoln Monument, and the bottle in my hand never broke; then old Abe gave me a wink, and all was well. I noticed a box of something called No-Doz as we were about to check out. It said, "stay alert" and it was cheap. We *needed* to stay alert. The cashier was very polite but spoke funny. He said, "Ha ya'll doon?" We said, "Good." It wasn't, "Hows you'se doin'?" or "What's up?" or a simple head-nod, like up North.

We headed back and started pouring. The good thing about vodka is, as it wears off you are hit again with the bat. One minute coherent, the next slurring your speech. It grew dark. Simma and I looked at each other. It was time to check out the area. I was stumbling now, so Simma assisted me. We quickly noticed that we were the only white guys as far as the eye could see.

We entered an arcade and started playing. Not long thereafter someone mentioned that the game we were playing that was *their* game. Well, we needed to finish what we started. I tried to tell him that, but he said, "No, this whole *place* is mine." He didn't look like he would give me a return on my quarter, so we left. The several No-Doz pills I had taken at least kept my eyes open for the long walk back.

We got back and our crew was all in the fetal position, sleeping like babies. I went upstairs – to the forbidden area. There were indeed two girls in one room. I asked to lie down by one of them. She seemed nervous at first, but then said okay, "but keep your pants on, and take off your shoes." Well, I knew to take off my shoes anyway. If you slept with your shoes on, it was a sign of being a bum, like drinking (alone) before noon. I stumbled a bit taking off my shoes, and then fell into bed.

I noticed this girl had a heavy accent. I stared up at the ceiling, and said, "I'm from Massachusetts." She said, "Good for you. I'm from Baton Rouge, Louisiana."

She had noticed that I was sweating profusely, and put her hand on my chest. I told her it may be the No-Doz. She looked concerned and said, "Sugar, ya'll got to be careful with that." She got up, and I noticed she was very fit. The vodka wanted to make me say, "Sum lum yum," or some other phrase only understood by another drunk. But the No-Doz allowed me to hold somewhat of a conversation. She came back with a face cloth and stood over me and patted my sweat-covered body. She patted me some more, and once in a while would put her hand on my heart.

"Ya'll's will be fine," she said.

We talked about our upbringing and environments. I told her about the Academy and how I was going into my sophomore year. I was studying to be a Captain. I told her I would steer the ship someday to Louisiana. She laughed. I didn't sleep that night; my dime-slot eyes darted back and forth between the plaster ceiling and this sleeping beauty next to me. Maybe this was my future wife, I thought.

The alarm went off, and I jumped up. My future wife from Baton Rouge laughed and said she had to go to work. She told me not to look as she got out of her nighty and put on her clothes. She caught me looking and said, "Naughty boy." I said, "What's up doc?" She giggled. She felt my heart again, and said, "Ya'll are gonna make it." She kissed my fore-head and then I giggled. I heard her go downstairs and talk to Danny. She told him not to worry, that I behaved.

I heard the guys start to stir and begin muttering. It was time to go downstairs. Someone had purchased more vodka, and since I was on vaca-tion, and not alone, it was time to start drinking. They were all moaning and groaning now. I felt like a child emerging down a flight of stairs on Christmas to see all the presents. I saw the new, full plastic bottle. Ah, I was just a few drinks away from no longer being moody or irritable. Danny was dressed as a waiter and he walked toward the door, heading to work. His shoulders were slumped.

"Don't trash the place," he mumbled.

THE INSECT

We downed a couple more drinks and packed our tourist gear of vodka, tonic water, and a half a box of No-Doz. I didn't want to miss anything, so I swallowed a couple on the way out the door. A wall of humidity blasted me in the face. By the time we made it to the Lincoln Memorial, I was soaking wet. Lincoln looked calm. He didn't have the fidgetiness that I possessed. There was a 1950's guy that seemed to follow us around.

We had brown bags and were being kind of boisterous. I had been raised by a guy like that, as had all my friends. Here was a guy that shaved, showered, and ate at the same time every day. He needed uniformity and rigidity. So, us showing up, swilling out of brown bags in front of Lincoln, upset his sense of calm and order. It was outside of his handbook. He didn't know how to react. He just said, "What you fellas up to?"

"We're looking at friggin' Lincoln," O.B. said. He respected the guy's age, which he demonstrated by not coming out with a real f-bomb.

There were facts and figures inside the monument that you could read to learn more about Lincoln, but all that bored me. After all, what do you do with that information? Who do you recite it to? The next place we headed was the zoo. Now, this was a place I was interested in. The zoo would have attractions that reminded me of my friends and the way we lived. But, when we got to the zoo, I was immediately hit with the vodka bat.

The baboons reminded me of us when we first developed the slug train. Running around making scary noises, and chasing other baboons.

We next arrived at the gorilla section, and I was having difficulty walking. The good news was there was an observation bench. The others kept walking and said they would come back later. The largest gorilla, who was probably named something warm and fuzzy like "Mittens," made his way over to the glass.

He glared at me. Being an expert eye-reader, I knew what he was thinking. *He* knew that I knew that his real Gorilla name was "Back Crusher." We got into a staring contest; his eyes were like big black marbles. I was grateful for the plexiglass that separated us. I had images of me entering the cage, where he would either rip my arm off and beat me with it, throw me around like a tire, or pluck off body lice and place it in his mouth. One thing was for certain: he won the staring match.

My buddies came back. We were all good and drunk and it was oppressively hot and humid out. The sun was slamming down on us. We decided to go back to Danny's. My future wife from Baton Rouge came in and said, "How ya'll doin?" She then went upstairs. We drank the rest of the evening, discussing our favorite zoo animals until the sky was dark and it was time to hit the rack. The rest of my crew had to sleep on a hardwood floor. But I got to creep upstairs to see my future bride. I took my sneakers off, proving that I was not a bum and did not have a drinking problem, and lay down.

I spoke to my future wife about the zoo, Lincoln, and the 1950s guy. She put a wet face cloth on my head. The alarm went off, and she warned me not to look but I snuck a peek anyway. Someone had the wits to buy vodka first thing in the morning. We had no money for food, but always had enough crumpled up dollar bills for another plastic bottle of vodka. We had our morning drinks and packed our tourist gear – red plastic cups, plastic half gallons of vodka, and tonic water. We were off to the Washington Memorial and the Vietnam Memorial. We opened the door and were again hit with a tsunami of heat and humidity.

We walked about a mile and needed to take a break. It seemed the heat was rapidly evaporating the vodka from us. We needed a resupply. I thought of the British, and our battle with them, and how hot they must have been walking around in those red sports coats, sweatpants, and funny wool hats. No wonder they eventually dropped like flies and scurried back to crappy Old England. We arrived at the Vietnam memorial. I wasn't big on history or memorizing facts for the sake of being able to recall them later, but war talk was one of the few things I would listen to with some intent.

For guys of my era, our fathers, grandfathers, uncles, and even older brothers had all served in World War II, Korea, and/or Viet Nam. My generation had gotten lucky, no wars to fight and no draft. But we all grew up hearing stories from the men in our families about war. Plus, we were kids when televisions went color and the Vietnam war was the story of the day from the time we were toddlers right up through the end of elementary school. It was burned into us.

I developed a bitterness early on about those that were exempt from the wars. None of our families got anybody exempted. Our families generally couldn't afford college, which was the privileged coward's easy way out. Our brothers and uncles just got drafted, and they served, proudly, without hesitation. Our drunkenness and laughter stopped as we looked at the Vietnam Memorial.

People were crying, touching the names of those now gone, memories flashing through their minds … memories of them as children, or what their father had been like. All they had now was a name etched on a wall. We walked past, not saying a word. We finally got out of there. We walked further and took a break, none of us saying a word. It was time to drink, especially after that experience. I looked at my crew, the Cro Mags. If there was another war, we would be plucked first.

Who were we? The sons of a maintenance man, an electrician, a bartender. Guys that spent their Saturdays cleaning up whatever the New England season has dumped: overgrown grass, fallen leaves, or snow. All of that was a training ground to enable a person to "hack it" in life, whether that be war or blue-collar work.

We drank and soon loosened up a bit. I felt a little less bitter as we headed over to the Washington Monument. To me, it was just another piece of stone. We found a nice place to lay down and drank some more. We looked up at the monument. I thought of the one guy on every job that always seemed to get hurt. Surely there was that one guy that fell from the top of this thing before it was finished. His body was carted away, and it was announced, "Fred was a good man," at his service – but they wouldn't place *his* name on the monument.

I was soon myself again, in the vodka dimension. Acrimony was completely gone. It was time to get off the beaten path. Let the vodka and its magic direct me left or right. We broke up; me O.B. and Skinny grabbed our brown bags and Simma, Joe, and Nades went their own way. D.C. appeared to be a very busy place. Many people wore ties. To me, a tie was a symbol of being owned, another form of a dog leash.

I never understood the tie. A three-foot piece of cloth, wrapped around the neck, tied in a fruity knot, sometimes with a gold clip on it. Tie-people seemed to only talk to other tie-people, like they had a bond. I decided *never* to wear a tie. Tie-people were like the college students: they don't go to war. They were the ones who ended up being in politics and figuring out how to modify a sub sandwich while charging more but adding less meat. I vowed never to be a tie.

People seemed to rub and touch the monuments all around us and take lots of pictures. Random 1950s guys seemed to pop up everywhere, explaining the statues' significance to strangers. What we were walking to or away from I had no idea, but we just walked, stumbled, around D.C. for who knows how long. We walked by an outdoor café and I noticed a strange bird, one I had never seen in New England. I became transfixed and just stared at it. Apparently, the bird was right next to two men that I hadn't noticed. These two fellas thought I was giving them the hairy eyeball. They stood up and were very large. One of them said, "What the fuck are you looking at?" The crowd at this outdoor cafe began to look.

I couldn't say I was looking at a bird. The two giant men would have thought I made that comment to them like I took them to be birds, the English slang for females. The No-Doz was edging me on to get into a beef. I had been hit by the vodka bat, so I wouldn't feel the blows. The No-Doz would give me the agility and speed of Muhammed Ali. I would circle around them so fast they would feel they were surrounded by ten of me. A beef was on.

The good thing about public beefs is, they usually don't last long. An elderly woman, a man of the cloth, cops, bouncers, or friends would step in and stop the commotion before *too* much damage could be done. So, worst case, even if you're losing, it will likely be broken up quickly. I walked toward the big guys, and they put their beers down. I noticed some of the ties in the audience, and how they tilted their bodies backwards in fear of getting their pressed shirts and vests covered in snot, blood, and beer.

As I made my way down the stairs I pointed to my chest and said, "You talking to me?" Then I looked over my shoulder and said, "I don't see anyone else here, you must be talking to me." This didn't scare them … the beef was on.

"You were eye-balling us," one of the guys said. As he brought his head down to my level, and as I eyed his chin, the No-Doz was telling me to throw the uppercut. Before I could, a massive black-winged insect landed on his shoulder. It was the size of a small rodent. I grabbed the massive black bug and ate it like my father ate his pistachios, slowly, menacingly, deliberately. The two guys smiled and backed away. By now O.B. and Skinny had shown up and looked concerned. They saw me chewing on a bug and started laughing. We all sat down at a table and, within minutes, the waitress brought us three beers.

"Those two big guys over there bought you a round," she said, chuckling.

We put the paper bags down, and relaxed. All was well. I realized, judging from the horse-like size of the guy's neck, that I may have lost the beef had it actually gone down. I took a sigh of relief, and we had a toast. "Hula-boom," I said, to the big black flying insect. We relaxed and drank our cold beers. Two local guys approached and asked if they could sit down. "Pull up chairs," we said.

They did, and asked, "You guys want in on dust?"

I thought it was a kind offer and the price was right, only a few dollars. We were outside, in the back of this cafe, with nobody else around. I knew the last time I smoked dust, or moon-bar, I felt as if I was walking on marshmallows, and I didn't feel like walking on marshmallows in this heat. Skinny and O.B. smoked the stuff while I watched, but they were gracious and exhaled the smoke into my face. I noticed Skinny and O.B. immediately become less responsive.

I had no watch. Watches were like turtleneck sweaters, constricting. I hated hearing, "time to go" from someone like an elementary school teacher or state trooper. But it *was* time to go. The guys needed assistance standing up, but once upright they were steady. Skinny, who usually kept his bearings, had been smart enough to write down Danny's address.

I'M FROM GEORGIA

As we tried to make our way down the sidewalks, I would walk ahead and ask where the address was. People kept saying we were close, but it was taking us forever just to go one block. Finally, I recognized the area and we found Danny's place. There were two girls that lived below him, and they asked us who we were. Skinny did his walking on marshmallow routine and gingerly slid by us. O.B. engaged in conversation as best he could.

I pointed to the door and stumbled up into Danny's pad. I went to the bathroom and noticed I was white as a ghost. I remembered a saying in first aid class: "head pale, raise the tail." I grabbed a glass of water and lay on the floor with my feet up on the wall. O.B. came in shortly after and announced, "We got a date."

I finished my water, and O.B. ripped the glass out of my hand.

"Get ready," he said, and poured me a glass of vodka.

I drank as I lay with my feet against the wall. I was feeling better … or, at least, the blood that was stuck in my feet from walking all over D.C. was now making its way down to my head. I was feeling less dizzy. "A fresh glass of vodka always does the trick," I thought. I tried to relax but the No-Doz kept poking at me. O.B. came running down the stairs after taking a shower, and said, "Man-up … let's go."

I needed assistance getting up off the floor and to the door. The door opened, and that oppressive heat was still there. I grabbed onto the railing. I was grateful for railings and the assistance they provided. I followed O.B., and we went downstairs and knocked on the door. One girl answered and O.B. said, "She's with me." She looked great and said, "Come on in." We entered, and she sat us down. She said they would be a few more minutes and asked, "Do you want a drink?" Like twin ventriloquist dummies we looked at each other simultaneously.

"Pop, water, or wine?"

Pop must have been the Southern expression for soda; water, I just had. O.B. and I turned to each other, then faced forward and announced, "Eh, wine."

It wasn't vodka, but it would probably defend against the next phase of this progressive heat stroke I was experiencing. Plus, the crushed grapes would provide some form of nutrition. The only thing I had eaten all day had been a three-inch flying insect sent by God. She came back from the kitchen with four glasses and a bottle of wine. She poured; we yelled, "hula-boom."

There was no fancy announcement about the vintage or bouquet, and we didn't hold our glasses like newborns and raise our pinkies skyward. It tasted great. I knew by watching people on TV that there were certain ways to drink wine. You sniff it, swish it around, extend a pinky finger and sip. We weren't *those* people though. We just chugged. It tasted different, but there was no wincing like you do with the first vodka drink in the morning.

The girls left to "finish getting ready," and we worked on the wine. I thought about it: I sure was grateful for curling irons, makeup, and all the other devices and practices women needed to prepare before stepping out into public. It gives us men our own "prepping" time. The wine flowed like water. By the time the ladies emerged, the bottle was empty. They finally walked out, and the girl I was paired up with looked stunning. She was very polite. She seemed happy to see me. Why, I didn't know. In my mind, I was a tall, long-armed creature with a fat head that belonged in the water. But with the magic of the sauce, I felt like I belonged.

She put her hand out, and I made my "thanksgiving gesture." The one you do when the meal ends and you move your chair back and announce, "I will get the dishes." But this time I couldn't get up. Fortunately, she said, "Oh, don't get up," and I shook her hand.

"I'm from Georgia," she said.

The No-Doz must have kicked in, since I was able to produce words.

"I'm from Massachusetts," I said.

The other room-mate came out and sat down. She grabbed the bottle and noticed it was empty. She said, "Wow, ya'll was thirsty, huh?" O.B. reminded her that we were Northerners and not used to "the heat." She left and came back with another bottle. We watched intently at what they did with the wine. She held it up to her friend and announced the vineyard and vintage. Her friend smiled and leaned back. She carefully unpeeled the wax from the top and then tenderly inserted the corkscrew. She smoothly started to untwist the cork.

I was becoming annoyed. O.B. and I looked at each with the same thought: "Hurry the fuck up." She then gently pulled the cork, and the bottle made a slight hiss, which made the two girls smile knowingly at one another. Then the wine was sniffed from the bottle, and the bottle was held aloft before the light as they peered into it and commented on its color.

"Hurry the fuck up," O.B. and I telegraphed to one another.

Finally, she poured, but only about an inch into each glass. So, we all had an inch of red wine in our glasses, and their pinkies went out. Before I could take a sip, they started the glass-swirling and sniffing routine. I tried to put my pinkie out but feared this would decrease the torque of my grip on the glass, thus increasing the chances of a spill, which would mean less alcohol to actually drink.

Finally … they raised their glasses, and said, "A toast to our dates!" The glasses clinked together. O.B. and I muttered, "hula-boom" and snapped our heads back. We put away the inch of wine in our glasses in a gulp. Our heads snapped back and we were greeted with looks of surprise. They had just *sipped* their inch of wine. What was all this waiting and ritual stuff? My life was go, go, go. Drink fast, then go somewhere. Race late to work, "hurry up will ya?" ... and race home from work.

She then poured another inch of wine into my glass, and ... put the cork back in the bottle.

What was that? My brain seized up like an oil-deprived Hemi. "Does not compute," I thought. You never take a few drinks and put the bottle away. You drink until the bottle is empty, and then you go somewhere and do something. We snapped our heads back. We couldn't control it. Our glasses were taken away. How rude, I thought. I noticed the girl from Georgia sniff her wine and then smile. You don't sniff drinks, I thought. You *drink* drinks and then you "go."

Finally ... they finished sniffing and sipping their one-inch of wine, and I tried to get out of the couch. The glass of vodka had put me into the zone and the bottle of wine was now assisting. She thought maybe I wasn't used to the deep plush of the soft couch and reached out her hand.

Finally ... We were off. Everything was "blocks" down here, and we were only five blocks away from the restaurant. My head was spinning. The No-Doz wanted to walk fast, but the vodka and now wine wanted to wobble slow. I feared falling so I reached for this girl's hand, and she accepted. She even smiled. It acted as a cane for me and stabilized my walk. We finally made it to the restaurant and there was a line. Then every-thing hit me all at once. The humidity, the No-Doz, the lack of nutrition, the vodka, the tonic water – and most recently, wine.

My alky radar went up and intuitively noticed there was a small alley next to the restaurant. I excused myself from this beautiful south-ern woman, and walked closer to the entrance of the restaurant and then ducked into the alley. I bent at the waist just like my grandfather and ... it began.

The first splat was the red wine. I was happy to have that swill out of me. I bent back up at 45 degrees, then back down. Next, it was a clear liquid, the vodka and tonic water, and a great volume of it. My feet went backward and my body curved and out it came – the glowing green foamy bile. Splat! It hit the pavement like a fat kid doing his first belly-flop. I wiped my mouth and staggered from the alley. Everyone looked at me in disgust, except O.B., who looked at me proudly.

I announced, "Sorry ladies, just flushing out the radiator!"

The girl from Georgia now looked like *she* was going to vomit. I used O.B.'s excuse, "Eh, the sun, the heat." She glared straight ahead. The line moved and we finally passed the alley where I had vomited. There it was, for all to see. The remains of the "flush," a foamy green puddle of shame. My date didn't seem sufficiently appreciative of the sacrifice I had made to make room for dinner.

We *finally* entered the establishment and, boy, I was glad to sit down. This would be the first real meal I had eaten in days. The waiter came over and asked if we wanted "drinks," the magic word. O.B. and I once again swiveled our heads and looked at each other. The girls ordered wine, but it took them an annoyingly long time to discuss the vineyard and vintage and bouquet with the waiter.

Finally, we ordered our vodka and tonics, along with appetizers. Drinks came. We immediately drained ours and ordered "another" while the ladies went through their whole sniffing and swirling and pinkie routine. While they were doing that, the appetizers arrived. By the time the ladies had finished their foofy wine rituals and had taken the smallest of sips from their glasses, O.B. and I had obliterated the appetizers. The ladies looked at one another with a growing sense of alarm.

Next, there was salad, and its nutritional value. I was inherently suspicious of any vegetable that hadn't been first frozen for months in a warehouse and then boiled in a pot for at least an hour, but I chewed it down. I had ordered a massive steak. When it arrived it even caught the eyes of other patrons, it was so big. The waiter must have realized we had walked there and were famished and thirsty because the vodkas kept coming out, one after another, as quick as we could drink them ... which was pretty quick.

O.B. wore a dummy grin as the sides of his mouth were covered with salad dressing; his teeth had slivers of meat hanging from them. I looked up briefly, between hearty chews on my steak, and saw that the dates looked deflated. My date took a napkin and wiped off the chunks of half-masti-cated cow and creamy dressing from around my mouth. I ignored her and took large gulps of the vodka and then went back to the massive piece of seared bovine before me.

"Argh ... mumf ... growl ... roah."

I attacked the meat all the way down to the bone. I held the bone up and continued to make caveman-eating noises, "argh ... flump ... gah ... goot." The bone was finally without meat. So, I gnawed on it a bit. The girls looked disturbed and didn't seem to take even one bite out of *their* food. I signaled to the waiter for more drinks by pointing at him and then my empty drink. He nodded.

Ah, a fellow heavy drinker. He knew. I started attacking the chicken that my date had ordered, with the same ferociousness. I looked up between gnawing and swallowing and saw a flash of growing disgust. Faces were red. We polished off the meals our dates wouldn't eat. The waiter looked impressed, as there was absolutely nothing left over on our table. Even the basket of bread and butter was eliminated. The only thing not devoured was the salt and pepper.

The waiter came over and said, "Delicious?" O.B. and I were suffer-ing the initial stages of the meat-sweats and just stared blankly. He then presented a dessert menu. The girls got fidgety, making those Sunday foot-ball female signals that it was time to go, but the meat sweats prevented us from picking up on those signals. Besides, of course, we needed des-sert. There were fancy names for these desserts, and I only recognized one: chocolate mousse something. They must have misspelled "mouse" or "moose" on their fancy menu, I thought. But hey, chocolate was always good, and mouse or moose seemed nice as well.

The deserts came out with our final drinks. O.B. and I raised our glasses, but the two girls just glared silently. We said "hula-boom" and threw the last one back. Desert went down at about the same rate as the appetizers, salads, bread, steaks, and chicken. Our mouths were now slath-ered with creamy brown slime. We sat back in our chairs and exhaled. Ahhhh. What a great meal – and with two beautiful women, mine with a lovely southern accent.

She seemed disturbed, angry even, so I looked behind me. Maybe an old boyfriend was sitting behind us. Her stare went right through my forehead.

"Great city," O.B. exclaimed. The two girls gave no response.

The bill came out and O.B. grabbed it. I always seemed to have a few crumpled-up dollars in my blue baggy pants. I pulled one out and flattened it out on the table. I felt metal things as well. I put those on top of the now flat bill. O.B. patted the front pocket on his shirt, and then his two pockets on his shorts.

He gave me a look. He had no money. One of the girls grabbed the folder that contained the bill, and they both said, "Oh, my, gosh!" Apparently, the tab was more than the crumpled up dollar and change I had placed on the table. She reached into her purse and grabbed a plastic card. Then she looked at us with something that resembled the vermin offspring of contempt and disgust. The waiter came back again and she signed something. The waiter smiled at us, and said, "Glad you liked your meal."

I said, "Hey, thanks!"

I even thanked our dates. My mother hadn't raised a boor, after all.

"Wonderful time," I said.

They said nothing. I got up and we exited the restaurant. Once on the sidewalk, the vodka bat hit me and I had difficulty walking. I put my long octopus arms over the head of my date and held on to her. She assisted in getting me home. I whispered in her ear, about her beautiful southern accent … the great time I had … how much I loved that steak … and her chicken … how beautiful she was. We finally made it home. She flicked my arm from around her shoulder, took a step back, looked at me with something that resembled the malformed offspring of pity and revulsion.

"Get help," she said.

"Help for what?" I thought?

Well, O.B. helped me into the house and I crawled up the stairs and was able to take my shoes off, proving again that I didn't have a drinking problem. I slid into bed, next to my future wife from Louisiana. I told her about my day and ended with saying something about a chocolate mouse. Then she woke me up and said, "This is your last day," and kissed me on the forehead.

"You really need to get help for your drinking," she said, gently, and left the room.

A Hundred Here, Fifty There

I heard someone yell to me that we had to leave. I made my way downstairs, and everyone was packed. We got to the airport and waited around. Someone had purchased some beers, or more likely, had taken them from Danny's fridge. Beers were thrown around and swilled, there was a small ruckus, and then it was time to board the plane. We went to the gate and the woman taking tickets looked nervous. She picked up the phone, and a very large police officer came over. We were escorted out and told to leave. "Come back sober," he said. We got a cab and headed back to Danny's.

The cab stopped and everyone looked at each other. The no money look. We fell out of the taxi and ran around the block as the cab whizzed after us. We scattered, which confused him, and we soon all made our way back to the brownstone. My buddies were there and Danny didn't seem happy. He said he would get us on the next plane. He would give us one more night, but we had a flight the next day, very early.

Danny woke us all up, and there was a cab waiting outside. He said nothing and just made sure we got in the cab. The cab stunk of body odor and stale booze with all of us in it. We arrived at the airport, and shortly after, boarded the plane. Somehow, I made it back to The Pit and passed out. I had dreams of faces. The face of Lincoln, the gorilla, and the two girls telling me to get help. I was awakened by one of the twins. It was a Saturday so, time to wash trucks.

I had barely enough mental faculties and physical energy to raise a soap wand up and down the side of a tractor-trailer. The rinsing wand and its spray felt great against my boiling skin. I was covered in canary yellow industrial soap. After 14 hours of that, I stumbled back to The Pit and didn't even have the energy for a shower. The layers of yellow soap caked on my skin burned. I was too tired to scrape it off in the shower, so I just crashed. There is sleeping, and then there is crashing. Crashing is your whole body hitting a wall. The Pit was a great place to crash. I fell into the wall of furniture. I was then awakened by T who said his parents were coming home in a week.

What happened? I thought. What happened to the summer? I didn't make it to the library, but I would study harder this following year. I would curb or completely eliminate any "gah-bage" from entering my body. For now, I had to move, and that made me a little nervous. One of the twins beeped, and I went outside. I needed my own car, that would allow me to look for jobs, and travel if need be. He hooked me up with an old pal that was a mechanic. We talked and made payment arrangements on an old Datsun. A hundred here, fifty there, until it added up to $400.

My father would have objected to the purchase of a foreign vehicle. He didn't even like foreign cars parked in his driveway. But it was a rock bottom price, and I needed transport. I was deathly afraid of the police, and their power to beat my head in, so I rarely saw the Datsun. I usually threw the keys to someone and was picked up the next day at the place where the gig happened.

It was time to register for classes again, and I would be able to spend a night at the Academy. I went into the gymnasium and walked over to the assigned table for those with the last names starting with O through Z. There was a retired Navy guy that was in charge of our company who proceeded to bang on the table. He commented on my appearance, unfavorably. I was someone that wouldn't frequent a mirror. I thought mirrors should be looked into every ten years.

How does one answer three people with three different questions, all yelling at the same time? I did hear that I would be mopping all year. A repeat of the previous year. But I would pull it off and behave, be rewarded with little pins on my chest for having the cleanest room at all times, and the most improved grade point average. I went to my room and sat down. The next few days would be registering and making payments, getting new sheets etc. I stared up at the ceiling and looked around at the masonry blocks. It scared me, this brick beehive.

I realized then and there that I couldn't spend my father's check on this college that I hated. I drove home in my Datsun and returned the tuition check to him. He said, "Well, I can put you'se to work as a union laborer." I said I would get back to him on that. I went back to my truck-washing job. Most of the old crew who had gone off to college had also washed up by now, which provided ample opportunity for fall entertainment.

We were still young enough to enjoy being surrounded by woods and a nice warm fire. But we were now also frequenting the Boston Commons. We would buy a half gallon, and some mixers, and red cups and have at it. The Boston Police would just give us a head nod. They recognized us, knew what we were up to, but at the same time, were nodding that they were in charge. They were cautioning us to "keep it cool," as they were too busy with people committing more serious offenses.

We sat at a statue and watched the people go by. They all seemed to have a purpose. Some strolled, some jogged, and as it became darker and darker and later into the night, the people with purpose seemed to disappear, and then another shift came on the clock. This was a set of people looking for something, or escaping from something. My crew would frequently leave to go home before I was done watching and drinking and pondering. They would take my car, and I would find a place to sleep. I enjoyed the outside, and would always make sure there was a couple of inches of clear liquid left in the bottom of the vodka bottle for the morning drink. I liked the excitement of seeing the shifts of different people come and go.

The wealthy couples of Beacon Hill strolling around the commons, probably having enough dough to not worry too much. They would point to the statues and throw me a hairy eyeball like I was ruining their view. He looked as if he even knew the Latin names for the trees. "Lovey, this is the oak tree, the Latin name is *oakus giganticus*."

He would give me one last look of disapproval for preventing him from comfortably walking up to the statue and putting on some presentation as to its history and significance. They were finally gone along with the others from their shift, and then it was the night shift's turn. This was the shift you had to keep your eyes open for.

I laid back on this historic monument and took in the night shift as it came on duty. They scampered, looking left, and then right, then moved by and disappeared into the darkness. Then would come dusk and the bitterness of the New England fall you had to endure for a few hours. The vodka kept the Russians warm in winter, and it did the same for me. I loved the one time I got to be truly alone, between 3:30 and 5:00 a.m. There was silence on the stage.

Then the show was back on, and the next character up was the guy that truly lived by the clock. He had to be in a suit and out the door, sitting in the office at a specific time. He would check his watch while walking briskly through the commons because he couldn't be one minute late: it would throw his whole day off. He didn't even have time to shake his head at me, that would disrupt his schedule. He lived in fear. His cubicle was his second home. If he was told they were remodeling his floor, and he had to face west, and no longer have the view of Boston harbor, he would become infuriated. But, it wasn't losing the view he was angry about, because he had lost his ability to simply "gaze" many years ago.

He could "see" the same things I did, but he didn't really *see* them. The fishermen returning to port, the planes descending and ascending at Logan airport, the seagulls circling the docks for a scrap of meat. The sun and its positions. The approaching storm. He was aware that these things happened, but it might as well have been a TV show in the other room, or a radio program he heard but wasn't paying attention to. He now lived in fear, fear of his job, fear of cubicle relocation, fear of being replaced by machinery, or foreigners. His job was his identity. He looked at me and scurried away.

Next came more and more office workers, the "sheeple" that herded along into their high-rise pens. I had no dream of what I wanted to be now, but I knew what I *didn't* want to be, and that was part of the crowd that was passing by in front of me. I took my morning drink, to quell the uneasiness of my own reality. I stayed there a little longer, but left for home before the teachers arrived with their field trips.

I walked into the split-level on Crystal Hill and heard, "Ah, the prodigal!"

"Ya hair's all over da place!"

"I just need some clothes," I said.

He lightened up and said, "You'se can stay here until you got enough money for rent somewherez else."

I agreed, and he went on and on about construction being pretty busy at the time, and how he could get me a job in the laborers union working on the orange line at Jamaica Plain. I sighed. I agreed. I asked for a sawbuck to get cleaned up at Angry Tony's. I tracked my car down and headed off. Angry Tony hadn't seen me in about six months. My hair was all over the place. It was the happiest I had ever seen him. He looked even happier than my father. He shook his head at the mop on top of my head. I got the works, and he even shaved me with the old school razor. I returned home and my father had made his "few phone calls." I was starting as a laborer first thing in the morning. Life was looking up.

I was to report to the Orange Line in Jamaica Plain bright and early. I found the location and approached a group of guys that looked like they were ready to work. I had to meet a guy named DiFranco. He emerged and showed me what we had to do. There were rocks beside the third rail, the rail that has a high number of volts running through it. We had to shovel out the newly poured rocks that were there, so the electricians could run their PVC into the ground. I was told how deep to dig and got underway, shoveling as fast and hard as I could. After, a couple hours it was time for a coffee break.

I drank out of a water jug and was further instructed on how to work. I was going too fast, he said, and would burn out either today or within a couple of days. DiFranco showed me how to do it. Just move the shovel into the small rocks, and push the shovel down with your foot. Lift it up carefully, not spilling any rocks, and dump the rocks to the side. That way, nothing caves in. I did as I was told. A few more hours passed, and he was right. I would have expended most of my energy and been shot. I liked the physical labor, but looked around at some of the guys, and noticed they weren't young. I couldn't imagine how they did this day in and day out. After lunch, it was back to digging for a few more hours.

I slept like never before and didn't wake to "might not" or twins starting and finishing each other's sentences. Or someone telling me to leave their premises. I drove to Jamaica Plain. I got to the supply truck, picked up a shovel and got into the ditch. I did what I was instructed to do and pushed the back of the shovel and dug it in. The rocks were collected and piled to the side, nothing was spilled, and I operated like a machine. I was making it. The week went on like this, and surprisingly I didn't pick up a drink.

I felt new muscles, and now it was Friday. The next day I would be truck-washing for 12 hours or more. That was less of a strain, just raising my arms up and down with the soap wand. When I finished the workday I felt that familiar whisper in my mind ... I needed a drink. My anxiety was coming back, and I owed it to myself, after all. I held the glass up to plaster announced, "hula-boom," and drank it down like a fiend. It brought a smile to my face. I knew I would feel good in a few moments. I drank a few more tall glasses and sat down. I would soon have to replace the bottle I was drinking out of.

I made it up to my room and thought about things. Maybe I would return to the Academy and eventually become a captain ... but for now, I needed a year off. Just physical labor. I woke the next day, still somewhat drunk. The good news was, I wasn't driving in, and didn't have to think too much: just raise my arms up and down. The day was a blur, but the next day I felt fine. I was proud of myself for only hitting the sauce on Saturday nights now.

THE BULB CHANGER

I got word that I could have a better job in a couple of weeks: simply changing light bulbs at a high-rise building my brother worked at. I was moving up in the world. I thought of this as I dug a trench next to a 600-volt rail line. Eventually, I would own the top floor of that high rise. I would evolve from bulb changer to an executive of lightbulbs up on the top floor, wearing a fancy suit with my feet up on the desk. I would wear the suit, but I wouldn't wear a tie ... and I wouldn't have a cubicle.

The day came when I would be moving amongst the crowd of sheeple. My father gave me directions, and as usual, with pinpoint accuracy.

"Ya best bet is to ... from there you exit the train ... take a shahp right ... aftah the toll collector with the double chin ... head out of the subway and take a left. You'se will be at downtown crossing ... just keep walking down Tremont Street ... you'se will pass by a joint that sells the best bagels in town ..."

I noted the directions and got on and off subways. I noticed that people on these trains could tell that I was new and wasn't fully a sheeple just yet. I didn't have the look of having the life drained out of me, of a blank stare, of rising and sitting from certain noises of the train. I finally reached my destination and got out. It was strange being surrounded by these people, and tall buildings. I felt if I happened to fall, I would be trampled by the zombified sheeple.

I made it to the high rise and reported to the front desk as I had been instructed. My brother scored me the job, and I couldn't let him down. He wore a tie. I looked clean cut, from the recent visit to Angry Tony's. This was a new me. That day was all introductions. I took the elevator up with my brother to the mechanical floor, to meet the supervisor. My brother told me his first name was "Dick" but to call him Mr. So and So. We entered the room and there were a few men dressed in brown Dickie's head to toe. I shook hands with everyone. They gave me a warm Boston greeting by throwing their heads back and just saying, "What's up."

There was one massive guy at the end that had his own desk, and his own uniform. It was a full-length white shirt with brown pants. He was "Dick." Dick was massive, not to be teased about being named after a penis. He stood up and his back seemed to take up the whole room. He smiled and stuck out his hands. It was like shaking a bunch of bananas. My long chopstick-like fingers seemed to disappear in his catcher mitt hands. He didn't let go of my hand in the normal timeframe. As he squeezed my clown shoe-sized hand he looked me up and down. He smiled a bit and said, "I like the flat top," and then looked over my shoulder and said, "He looks clean cut." But he still wouldn't let go.

"Wee'ze aren't gonna have any problems wit you."

I didn't know if it was a question or a statement. I simply said, "Sir, no sir."

I then went to another department and had measurements taken for my brown outfit. I went to another office and had more intros. It was payroll. They asked for bank info. I didn't have one. Checks were always cashed immediately and spent immediately. Was there another way to live? I would have to open a bank account and get back to them. I would have health insurance. Oh, my.

A bank account, an outfit. Health insurance. I was then reintroduced to some of the guys. The last bulb changer had quit. They introduced me to his cart and basically told me what he did. He would get a call on his radio, and then report to the tenant's floor, then report to the person who made the call. The bulb was changed. I was getting a walkie-talkie. That was a big deal for me. Oh, my. I would be getting a walkie-talkie, four sets of brown Dickies pants, and matching brown shirts with my name sewn above the left pocket.

The day ended, and I followed the sheeple out of the building. They seemed to be happier walking out than walking in. I thought of walking around the city and taking a later train. I now saw a different scene than the many nights I sat at the statue and watched the shift changes. Here it was, after 4 p.m., and I saw people proud of themselves for doing a good day's work. The week ended, and my brown Dickies would be arriving on Monday. It would be a big ceremony. I got home and attacked the vodka hard.

DICKIE DAY

The weekend ended. There was a call over the radio.

"Andrew, report to the 14th floor."

I got to the corporate headquarters floor, and people were smiling. It was "Dickie Day," my graduation. You didn't get your embroidered Dickies until you had passed your probationary period, not missed any days or come in late, and gotten a good report from your supervisor. I was proud. The duds were not only brand new but had been washed and ironed. I would also get my own locker. The Dickies would stay in there. I could come in however I liked, and then change into the Dickies.

A few weeks passed, and I was doing fine. I was getting to know people, my bulb changing cart was neatly packed with every type of bulb known to man. Everything was orderly, I always had a clean-shaven face, a fresh flat-top haircut, and kept a notepad describing when I changed the bulb, what tenant, and what type of bulb, etc.

I met two guys that seemed to be like brothers. They both had dark black hair and talked with their hands a lot. In passing, we had introduced ourselves. The tall guy knew everyone and said he was from Chelsea. The short guy said he was from Everett. These were areas that fell into the "North Shore" section of Massachusetts.

I got a call and had a bulb to change in the garage. That area was for the big wheels, it was VIP parking. The two North Shore guys walked by as I was finishing up and rolling my bulb cart away. They looked at their watches simultaneously, and said: "Wrap it up." They walked over to a massive car, and I took notice. The big guy said, "You'se like it? It's a Cadillac bro-ham." He then opened the doors and showed off the leather seats, then the size of the trunk. It was stunning.

"Tomorrow wez'll go out for a cold one," said the big guy.

We all smiled and shook hands. It amazed me that these two maintenance men could park their bro-ham in the VIP section of the parking garage. I looked up from pushing my cart and nearly rolled it into my boss. He looked in the direction of my two new buddies in the bro-ham, and said, "Stay away from dem two's, dey'z bad news."

I got to the maintenance floor and neatly packed everything away. I was feeling like Mr. Rogers, everything going in its proper place. I feared being too straight-edge, too straight-laced. The North Shore guys came in and seemed happy to be leaving for the day. They told me where to rendezvous across the street the next day. I got a pat on the back. I left the forty-story beehive and gazed at the pub where I would have a cold one the next day with my new friends.

The thoughts of being a captain of a ship were gone. Who, after all, wanted to be out at sea? I had read stories of mutinies and pirates ... there was danger out there. I would stay on land, and see my family every day. I would have a chauffeur, like the VIPs in the parking garage. Top floor for me, and soon. The next day arrived and I was very eager for the cold one. I answered all the morning calls and changed all the bulbs. I exited the building carefully, so my boss didn't see me, and walked to the bar.

I took a seat and pretended to look at the window. Then a great deal of noise came from the entry and it was my two new Italian friends from the North Shore. The short guy was quieter than the tall guy, who again seemed to know everyone. He was patting people on the back, shaking hands, like he just won an election. He saw me, and said, "Hey, my man!" Then he headed over to me. The short guy was at the bar, and yelled to us, "What do you'se wants?"

I didn't know what would be appropriate, and looked up at the big guy and said, "Can I get a vodka?"

"Anything you want, my man!"

I ordered a vodka and tonic. The short guy returned with a tray of drinks, and I reached for my wallet, and the tall guy said, "Wee'ze gots you covered." Losing the thought of where I was, I raised the glass and said, "hula-boom." The two guys looked at me quizzically and said, "what?"

I said, "hula-boom".

They smiled and said, "Oh … we say 'salu." They raised their glasses and took sips, while I pounded mine back. It tasted great, and I knew shortly after the results of the first one would take effect, and I would start to feel less anxious. They both looked a bit astonished, and the big one made hand gestures, for a refill. I reached into my wallet again, but the big guy said, "We got something worked out."

We sat down, and everything seemed to be going well. We began talking and the small guy said what he did, and talked a little bit about his girlfriend. She was a stripper in the Combat Zone. I thought of this guy's house having a stripping pole in the living room, and the short guy getting the first dance before she headed to work. The drinks kept arriving, and the two guys were impressed at first, but eventually had a little concern – not about the cost, but my safety, going back and changing bulbs.

"Be careful. You don't wanna stick you'se hand in a socket."

I pointed to my drink, and said, "This is the last one." They seemed to relax. Lunch was ending, and I was in the state of mind only attainable with adult drinks. Why had God not designed me to feel like this naturally? Why had he designed my natural state to be anxious, fidgety, constantly worried? Now I was relaxed, not afraid to face the world outside. I looked at the base of this forty-story highrise and was proud of my position. I provided illumination for this high rise, so the worker bees could get their jobs done. It was something to be proud of.

We exited the bar and were all very happy. I thanked the guys and reached for my wallet, but the big guy insisted that it was "all set." I had new friends, and that was a good feeling. We went our separate ways, and

I went to get my bulb cart. In the corner of my eye, I saw a white rectangular object the size of a basement meat freezer peering out the window. It was the shirt of my boss, the man I had started calling "the chalkboard," because of his size and white shirt. He didn't look happy.

Maybe he was looking outside, on a life he wasted? Maybe he saw his reflection, and thought he should lose a few pounds here and there? I returned to my bulb cart and got back to work. I didn't receive any calls initially, so I decided to take my cart to the top floor, park it, and climb the stairs to the roof. I noticed the freight elevator operator must have had a few drinks under his belt as well. I was always friendlier to people after a few drinks and shook his hand for picking me up.

As the elevator door closed and we ascended up 40 stories, I looked down at the neatly packed cart full of bulbs. That would be a great place to hide a pint of vodka, I thought. It would almost look like a bulb. The elevator stopped, and the operator said, "All right chief, fortieth floor." I got out and hid the cart in a closet. I looked left and right and headed up to a stairwell. I noticed a sign that said only "certain personnel" were allowed beyond it. Well, I was that "certain" guy, and pushed the door to my future wide open.

I stepped out, and the crisp New England air hit my face. I was normally afraid of heights, but not now, with alcohol. I belonged on this roof. I looked in each direction. Out to the Atlantic, I noticed a few massive ships, and planes landing and taking off at Logan. I didn't want to be a captain anymore, but rather, the "cat's ass," as my father would say. A "big shot," on the top floor of this building. Having my own plane leaving Logan, and of course, a yacht named after my wife heading out to the Atlantic to see foreign ports.

I headed downstairs and pressed the button, and the elevator guy took me to my destination. I went to the front desk and was given a name and unit number that needed a bulb changed right away. I zipped up there, was let inside and quickly changed the bulb. The occupant, a tie-guy, just watched as I did my work. I shook his hand, and was on my way. He then said, "By the way, there is a Christmas party in a few weeks, for our office, and you are welcome to attend."

"There will be drinks served," he said. This made the handshake last longer and we were both now smiling. I cocked my head downward and repeated, "drinks served?"

"Yes, drinks," he said.

We spoke the same language. We had that drinkers trust and bond. He was a drinker like me, he knew the magic in the alcohol, and he used it like me as a physical painkiller as well as an emotional fixer. "I will be there, sir," I said, and pushed my cart away.

All the mechanics were having our own Christmas party, so I would attend that and then head down to the suit and tie party. It dawned on me that no matter what the outfit, drinkers were all the same. I had images of the tie-guy, and how he drank. He put on a show on weekdays. But it killed him, I thought.

He pretended to be Mr. Rogers in front of the other tie-people and female office workers. He would even keep it under wraps during the weekdays, but once Friday arrived, and he put his tie away, he was just like me, pounding away, yelling "hulla-boom" as he raised the glass to the sky, throwing the drinks down.

He couldn't stop there, however. He would then break out costumes, like his gorilla suit, and call the same escort he had been calling for years. He would play King Kong, and chase the escort around the room, even jumping up on the furniture pounding his chest. Come Sunday morning, the escort was gone, and he would go into the "hair of the dog" mode, and reach for that wonderful morning drink.

That forbidden drink, the drink society tells you not to take before noon. That would be a sure sign of being an alcoholic. But it seems many things forbidden by society are more enjoyable. The tie-guy, although drunk all day, managed to pack his lunch, iron his clothes, and shine his shoes ... to keep up the façade. He crashed early on his bed, waking to put on the shiny shoes and get on the same commuter rail, to go see the same office workers. But I knew better. He had the look. Just like me. But no one would suspect him. Because he wore a tie.

I finished the day and felt great with those drinks under my belt. I felt normal, not irritable, not discontented. I undressed and headed home. I brought that thought home with me, about slipping a small bottle between the bulbs, or in other areas of the building. That would allow me to perform better and interact better with people, which was always the case with alcohol. I wouldn't be seen walking into a bar by anyone, either. I would be in my own world. I still wasn't quite the age to buy alcohol but was close, and I was able to buy in a few local packies. It was best to go to a liquor store right after work. That way, there would be a rush of tradesmen and office workers eager to get their sauce and head home. The clerk wouldn't have time to inquire about whether I was 20 or 29 with a long line of twitchy alkies behind me, impatient for their sauce.

I looked at some of the folks in line and feared not so much the amount they may consume, but what their lives may be like after hours. Was it a simple meal, then sitting on the couch and drinking away while watching television? That was no way to drink, I thought. One needed to be adventurous after a few drinks. But it seemed to be all over for some of these people in line at the liquor store. The excitement of alcohol was gone, and they now just had the tranquilizing effects that enabled them to endure their soul-crushing routines. They were in a zone, a zone that encompassed their entire lives: commute, work, commute, liquor store, dinner, couch, TV, drinks, then bed. Then repeat. Endlessly.

I wouldn't be like that. I had to avoid routine. I wanted a gallon of vodka, but it was too big and would be difficult to hide. So, I bought a few pints. I would spread them throughout the high rise. The cashier operated like a machine, and as predicted, was too busy to check IDs or look at people. He was in New England mode, not looking up, not caring who was in front of him, and not giving eye contact. I was rung up, and there were no salutations. I had my magic elixir for my new job. I would start bringing a mini cooler to work disguised as a lunch box, like some of the other guys. After all, no one searches a man's lunch pail. I threw some fruit in, just to separate the bottles and prevent clanging.

I was all set, and the next day arrived. We had our morning meeting. It ended, and as I was walking away I heard the Chalkboard say, "You'se. Stay behind."

I turned and said, "Me?"

"Yeah. You'se."

I put my lunch pail down, away from his reach. He told me to pull up a chair, so I pulled up a chair. He rolled his massive swivel chair around his desk over to my stationary chair. He rolled in circles with his chair around me. He started out saying, "I saw you'se leaving the bar yesterday with those two clowns. What were you'se doing at a bar?"

I was about to answer, but it was as if they weren't questions, rather, thoughts. When he circled around front, our eyes locked. It was there that I saw a close-up of his face. He had several mini scars, and his nose was astonishingly crooked, in like three different places. His nose made noises that a normal uncrooked nose doesn't make. Like a broken vacuum cleaner. It seemed difficult for him to pass air through this nose. Then he swiveled around again, and said, "Ya brudda, he is a good kid. Don't you'se m-barrass 'im."

He circled again, and he stared at me. It seemed his eyes were controlled by something else in the room. He must have had a rough childhood. The scars weren't from tripping on his way to mass. They were the result of acts of force. He was from the South End, and I now recalled that he was an ex-boxer. He circled again, and told me about the two guys, and why he didn't like them. They were frequently late, they frequently left early, and they played all sorts of "games."

He said, "I'm only warning you'se cause eye'z like ya brudda."

Then, using his feet like paddles, he drove his chair over toward his desk.

"Now, get outta here."

I grabbed my lunch pail and left.

THE HOLIDAY SPIRIT

I had to stay tight that day, and not drink. The high rise had many hiding places, and I had many keys to hide the bottles. I just did my job, real Mooncai-ish, not looking at anyone or anything, just doing my gig. The bar was too obvious, wearing brown Dickies and my name on the front. But I had a high rise to play with, and soon I would be able to drink on the job and be my real self. Relaxed and friendly, the way a bulb changer should be. I found some nice spots to hide the bottles, where I could open a door, step in for a momentary swill, and not worry about anyone. Broom closets, telephone closets, fire pump rooms, crawl spaces, electrical closets. I would hula-boom real quick and head back out and do my job. But in a different mental state.

I got word that my old friend Glenn would be visiting around Christmas-time, so I scheduled a rendezvous at "the statue," on the Boston Commons. He knew the place. Life had become work and drink. It was fine with me, I was making the most money of my life, the sauce was working, and I had many friends.

Now all the Christmas parties were coming around. It seemed I knew someone on each floor of the building and had many invites in-hand. I especially looked forward to the two big ones. There was the mechanic's Christmas party, and then the party tie-man had invited me to. The big day arrived, and the fun started at noon. First, our party, then, the office party. Then it would be off to the Boston Commons, to see Glenn. The last time

I saw him he was driving a pontoon boat on a lake in cape cod, wearing rubber penis glasses. I headed up to the property management firm for "our" office party. There were many ties there, and after a few moments, it seemed everyone was in attendance. Then one of the head ties made an announcement about our service.

"I'm proud of … blah blah blah …"

I was eyeing the finger sandwiches and the drinks that were being lined up. Then I saw a massive object sitting with some ties. Oh. It was the Chalkboard. The sight of him made me a bit nervous. The announcement ended, and I made my move, first to the finger sandwiches, and then to the vodka. I had to wait to let the other suits and mechanics have their drink first, and I was getting impatient. Finally, it was my turn. I looked at the bottle of vodka, and could tell two things right away: it wasn't made of plastic, and it said Stolichnaya.

"Vodka and tonic," I said.

"Yes sir," the well-dressed man said, as he prepped the drink with ice. I hated ice in my drink. He handed me my drink and even said, "Merry Christmas." Indeed, it was the time to be merry. I tried to control my intake, and drink like the others, but it was very difficult. I could feel the Chalkboard's eyes on me, so I turned my back and muttered, "hula-boom", and took a blue-collar swig. I mingled with the other mechanics. I devised a plan: when one of them went up to the bar, I asked them to refill my drink. This would keep me from going back and forth to the bar. I was dipping into everything at the snack bar. Deviled eggs, shrimp, finger sandwiches. There were no restrictions.

Someone was heading to the bar, and I asked politely for a refill while they were there. I soon had my next drink and was feeling the magic of the river vodka coursing through my veins. Soon, the next drink came, and my brain signaled that it was time to drink faster … and faster. I noticed some of the other mechanics were stepping it up a notch as well, due to the effects of the sauce. Their smiles became broader, they were amused more easily. Guys that were once quiet, and who normally kept to themselves, were now happy and even shared entertaining stories. The sauce brought out their true selves. I had to keep an eye on the clock because, in a couple hours, I had an invite to the other office party.

We took turns heading up to the bar, and this kept me out of the vision of the Chalkboard and prevented him from keeping count of the number of vodkas I was consuming. I had him fooled. I was now past the giggly feeling of a few drinks. I knew my depth perception was off as was my general sense of self-perception. I was throwing my head back while I laughed. It was now apparent that the circle of men in brown Dickies was the loudest. A few people were checking watches, and some signaled they had to go. I still had time before the next party. The ones leaving were mostly the suits. Then the Chalkboard stood up and said he was leaving. He came over to our circle of brown, and said, "I wish you'se all a Merry Christmas," but he threw us a look, like, "I am watching you'se all."

Soon, the room was mostly brown Dickies. The head of the property was still there, but he seemed to be catching up on work in his office. It was finally time now to drink like I was trained to in the woods of Crystal Hill. I went up to the bar and ordered a drink. I went back to the circle and looked up to the fluorescent lights and yelled, "hula-boom!" I threw the drink back like a free man. This made the others look at me funny. One of them asked what I just said. The North Shore guy explained that it was my version of "salu." Soon, they all raised their glasses and said "hula-boom!" At one time we all scurried around the building barely saying a word, moaning to each other, or just giving a head nod. Now we were all speaking the same language.

The office was pretty much ours now. The last remaining tie seemed to be busy and distracted. Once in a while, he took a look up. I tried to devour as much free food as I could and was now drinking and talking with a mouthful in my cheek. I was in my element. People were swearing. The clock whizzed by, and I figured I would show up an hour late to the other party I had been invited to. The vodka bottle was running low, and I felt the urge to grab it and claim it as my own. I felt a sense of panic. What if next office party was … dry?

I ordered one last drink and sure enough, the bottle was empty. The bartender noticed and removed the bottle. I felt panic. I drank and wished everyone a Merry Christmas, and headed downstairs. As I got off the elevator, I heard the noise and turned the corner and there it was: a slice of heaven. One table loaded with food, another table loaded with alcohol. There was the guy I met roughly a month ago. He had a sauce-induced grin and an even heftier handshake. He introduced me to the suits, and due to my intoxication, I felt no fear.

I even said, "I keep your lights on." Most laughed. I noticed I was the only one in Dickies and felt important. I was telling people about my big plans. It was hard to switch out of my Cro Mag mind and into the office space hive-mind. I noticed that the office employees were holding their drinks with their pinkies pointing out to the future. This was different than the men in brown Dickies I was just with moments before. Those guys held their drinks like, if they let go, they would burst into a ball of flames.

The guy that appeared high in command, the one that invited me to the party, had loosened his tie and was making the rounds. He introduced me to the tender of the bar. I noticed that, unlike the mechanic's party, these office workers weren't crowded around the bar. They seemed to take their drinks, and scatter into small circles. I told the tender what I wanted, and he made the vodka and tonic. My new office manager friend's smile broadened as he said, "Ah, you are a vodka drinker."

I emerged from the bar, and he introduced me to some more folks, happy young office workers. They were in their early twenties, like me, and the world was still open for them. Life was still new. We began to talk, and I came up with the idea that I was just taking a year off, and then would go back to college for finance, and joked that I would soon be on the top floor. I finished my drink, quickly, and went back to the bar for refills.

As I turned, I was hit by the vodka bat. I stumbled over to the small group of people I was talking to. I put my arm against the wall to hold myself up. They all looked concerned, but I pretended like nothing happened, and tried to pay attention. But now they were all looking at me. I was the center of attention, the disturbance. All I could do was smile and hang onto the wall. I kept my balance and just grinned like a monkey while the small circle kept talking and looking at me. I drank the vodka like I was in the woods, but I had enough sense not to pull my Johnson out and start urinating.

I was grateful for the wall but felt like the sheetrock was softer than usual. I thought of sheetrock briefly. Those that install it, those that then apply joint compound, or plaster to it, and then those that paint it. Then the trinkets, pictures, posters, flags, that are tacked up against that wall. Of course, there are the times when sheetrock is not your friend. Say, you owe someone money, and he grabs you by the collar, and throws you up against the sheetrock and says, "Where's the dough you owe me?"

My small circle of friends now asked if I was okay. I held my glass out. I was indeed "okay," but I needed another drink.

"You want *another* one?" somebody asked, looking concerned. My eyebrows came together in anger and I threw a hairy eyeball. My glass was taken, and a new refill soon came back. I took a long draft of it and looked around. A Cro Mag thought came to mind. I had to find the woods. I was spending too much time in this artificial world of brick, sheetrock, and fluorescent lights. I needed to be surrounded by trees, and blades of grass. I drank my drink down, stumbled over to the bar, and put the empty glass down. I yelled "Merry Christmas!" and stumbled away. I got on an elevator. It was full, and people that seemed to back away from me. The door opened, and I headed in the direction of the Commons. I found a patch of grass and urinated for what seemed like forever. I then had to find the statue.

I never knew what it was, or who it was for, but I knew its shape. I spotted it and went over to it. There was no texting or cell phones back then. It was the late 1980's. If someone said "meet," you met. No second guessing, and if that person was late, it was a sign of disrespect; if they were a no-show, it could result in the loss of a friend. We had agreed to meet "around 6ish," which meant between 6 and 7. Not a minute later.

I was alone and leaned up against the statue, watching the people go by. Everyone seemed to be happy. T'was the season to be jolly. I saw three men walking towards me. Three buddies of mine. It was Who Man, Nades, and Glenn. There he was, a product of the United States Military. He was a few inches taller and had obviously been lifting weights. He stopped and reached around and pulled out a big brown bag, yanking out two plastic half gallons of vodka. He looked up to the sky and said, "Merry Christmas!"

Indeed, things were merry. It was the Christmas season, we were surrounded by the festive lights in the historic Boston Commons, amongst friends, and now about to crack open some new vodka. We got down to business, and pulled the Christmas supplies out: red plastic cups, then the tonic water and, lastly, the vodka. We made our drinks and raised our glasses. I was drunk already, so I didn't taste much as it went down like water. Those guys were just starting out, and they were still tense from the chill in the air. But it only took a few drinks before their shoulders seemed to droop a little, and they relaxed. We started to talk about our past, our goals, and our future.

The vodka bat had hit me again, hard, and I felt no cold. I probably wasn't making much sense. Then, the black curtain dropped. This was happening more and more of late. The last thing I remember, I was going through a turnstile, falling, and looking up. People in suits and shiny shoes were looking down on me. I collected my wits as best I could and made my way home. My father must have heard the door. He stood at the top of the stairwell and just shouted. About work. About embarrassing my brother. About having no regard for anyone. Why was he so angry during this holiday season, I wondered?

Then, it made sense. Apparently, I had blacked out for an entire 36 hours and had missed a day of work. He disappeared and slammed the door to his room. I went downstairs and made myself a strong one. I hula-boomed it down and waited for its effects. It took the dizziness away, and I went to my room.

I had to think. There were two more people that would be upset: my brother for getting me the job, and the Chalkboard. I took my boots off and laid down. I slept through the rest of the day and night, arose, and headed to work. When I arrived, we had the meeting of all the mechanics, and afterward, the Chalkboard again had me stay behind.

"You'se on real thin ice," he said.

"You'se embarrassed ya brudda," he said.

He just stared at me.

I told him it was the last time it would happen, and he let it go at that. I bumped into my brother, and he looked like he feared for his job. I told him the circumstances, and he accepted the Christmas season excuse, but I could tell he was mighty disappointed. I went about my duties and stayed away from the drink for that day. I came up with a plan: I would still hide nips and pints in this 40-story fun park, and in between the bulbs on my cart. But I would keep tight at night, and I wouldn't miss work again.

SAVED

Things were okay for a while, except for the fact that I was becoming more and more fidgety between drinks. Shaking in the hands, fumbling my words. Some people would ask if I was okay. I needed to hide more bottles around the beehive. My favorite spot was an area above a bank. There was an entrance that few had access to except the "bulb changer," where I could place a pint anywhere. Then there was the occasional run over to the bar across the street. I noticed the Chalkboard was back on my case.

"Eye'ze been watching you'se, and you'se been back up to your old tricks."

I was getting annoyed with being watched and felt I needed more freedom. I got myself into a nice stupor and headed up to the roof. There, the cold air of the Atlantic blew through me. I looked north, south, east … and west. I would go west. Ah, that still voice, the one you only hear while under the influence of the sauce. I felt bad for those that didn't have the assistance of alcohol and the ability to hear these inspired directions to guide them in life. I couldn't wait to lean over to the Chalkboard and announce that I was going west. He would soon see me on TV, rich and famous. I felt bad having to announce to the twins and their father that I would be leaving the truck washing company. But, so be it.

I went home and had a few more belts. I tried to reach the still small voice. I thought of going to California. My sister had lived there, and I could look up her old boyfriend. It didn't matter who broke up with who.

He would be over it by now. He would set me up with a place to stay, a job, and even a nice girl. Tomorrow, I would start giving announcements of my departure. First, to the employers, then to the family. In two weeks' time, I would be flying away. I gave the chalkboard the news first, inches from his face, like he did me. He didn't seem intimidated. He just shook his head but thanked me for the courtesy of a two-week notice.

I told the travel agent I only needed a one-way ticket. I was never coming back, I explained. Now that I think of it, she may have sensed something and lied to me, but she explained that the cost was the same for a one-way ticket as for a round-trip ticket. Well, she was the professional. The two weeks sailed by via a pretty constant alcohol stupor, and before I knew it, I was boarding a plane. The travel agent did as I said, and booked me a window seat. I was a watcher, and wanted to watch as I flew away from the cold, dark, fast-paced northeast to the warm, sunny, free-spirited west coast. I pressed my face against the window and watched as the guys prepped the plane. They looked like the surroundings: pale and cold and rigid.

Me? I was going to kick the door down on the west coast. I would no longer be involved in New England chores. Raking leaves, shoveling snow, mowing lawns, pulling weeds for my mother, cutting wood for my father's potbelly stove, cleaning gutters, installing screens for the windows in the spring, removing the screens in the fall. My new life would be multiple streams of income, playing volleyball, roasting marshmallows with friendly people on the beach, and a nice girl leaning on the "Andrew" emblem of my shirt. I would be drunk most of the time, directed by the inner voice of alcohol.

The plane took off, and I felt some anxiety about being trapped. Fortunately, I packed a pint, just in case. I pulled it out of my sock, turned to my side, hula-boomed, and that pesky anxiety soon vanished. The guy in the aisle seat gave me a grin; he was like me, and shortly he was ordering a drink as the stewardess came rolling down the aisle. I discreetly watched him and his reaction as he swilled his drink. He didn't say "hula-boom," but muttered his own local saying of, "ahhh." He had three tiny nips in front of him. He put his head back and finished one after another. I felt bad for the guy in the middle row. He looked like he wasn't having fun reading his book. He wasn't going to hear that inner voice.

I looked out the window, and not long after takeoff, the congestion of eastern Massachusetts was fading behind me. My life seemed congested, I grew up on a bunk bed, surrounded by busy-body neighbors, meddling teachers at school, up-my-ass bosses and co-workers, in-my-face parents … always surrounded by people. Now, as I looked out the window, I just saw open land. I had to switch planes in Utah, and then re-board to San Jose, where my sister's old boyfriend would be waiting in his Corvette. He would drive me to my new place, with a new job that entailed doing very little work while getting paid a great deal of money. He probably had a couple gorgeous beach babes lined up for me already.

We finally landed in Utah, and I was amazed at the mountains surrounding the city. I had to leave the plane I was on and go to another terminal to board a different plane. I heard the familiar laughter coming from a bar. I had just finished one pint of vodka. Now, I would get myself a fancy new one, to toast my new life. I needed a quick visit with my people. Drinkers. After all, I had just spent 5 hours next to a guy that read a book for excitement.

I bought several pints, in case of flight delays, or, God forbid, a plane crash where I was the only survivor. How would I get by without vodka? I still wasn't 21, but I had the look and knew the lingo. I reached into the pocket of my leather jacket and pulled out a fin and said, "Vodka and tonic." The bartender said, "Sure thing pal." I watched him pour. He made it strong, and I sat down. My name emblem was exposed on my shirt, and he said, "Here you go, Andrew." I felt welcomed. I said, "hula-boom" a little too loud in excitement, and the people around me looked and giggled.

I finished my drinks and tipped the bartender. I made it over to the terminal, boarded my plane, and pressed my face against the glass. A beautiful woman approached me, with a man. My suspect-detector went off. Then they asked something about God, and me, and being saved.

"Of course I'm saved," I said. "I'm Catholic, I was named after a priest."

We all smiled. I was saved, thank God. They smiled a bit nervously. I explained the Catholic process, and they looked disappointed for me and walked away. But, I sincerely hoped they got my message of salvation. I was off to California.

The plane landed. My new life had begun. It would be a life of fame. Plus, I was saved. I got off the plane, but didn't see my sister's ex-boy-friend. Maybe he would surprise me at the luggage terminal. I got down to the luggage and eventually got my bags. I came back up and made a call. There was no answer; he must be on his way, I thought. He had cherry red Corvette that was a convertible. I couldn't wait to hop in and absorb the sunshine while being escorted to my new pad. I would drop my luggage off there and soon meet my new girlfriend and start my new job.

Time went by and I began to get worried about him. I hoped he was okay. I had left all the information about my flight arrival on his answering machine, so I didn't see what the problem was. About ninety minutes went by, and he was still absent. I placed another call, and he answered. I asked if he was all right.

"Yeah, but your sister and I had a bad breakup."

"That's awful. Let's talk about it when you pick me up."

"Uh, I won't be picking you up. Sorry."

Click.

I went to the information booth and told the lady my situation. No car. Needed someplace to stay for a few weeks, for employment and enjoyment. She explained that if I didn't have a car, San Jose would be difficult, as it was not a "walking city."

"But, just up north is San Francisco," she said. "And it's a walk-ing city."

Ah, okay. San Francisco! Within a few days, I would have a car, a job, and my own pad. All found by foot. I took a cab, and we were off. I noticed some fidgetiness, in my legs, with my red wing boots sliding forward and backward. I needed a drink. I couldn't wait to have a drink and get my mind working properly again. I told the cabbie about my new life, and he wished me well. He said there were lots of opportunities out here in the west. We were approaching San Francisco and I looked at our surroundings. Rolling hills. Colorful houses. Smiling people. I just needed a hotel. As we drove, I noticed a man with green hair, then another in a woman's bathing suit, twirling a baton. This *wasn't* Boston. We found a pretty fancy hotel, and I tipped the cabbie. We shook hands, and I told him that once I made it big, he would be my driver. He smiled and said, "Yeah, uh, good luck."

I got to the front desk, filled out the paperwork, and opened my leather jacket, exposing my name tag. She called me Mr. Winslow. We both smiled. Soon the phone to my room would be ringing off the hook with job prospects. I grabbed a paper and headed to my room. It was nice. Everything was clean and ready to go. I would start job hunting immediately ... but needed a bottle first. I headed outside to grab another newspaper and a bottle. I spotted a liquor store. I would drink the fancy stuff, in honor of me being a new arrival. I deserved it. I picked up my vodka, grabbed a newspaper and headed back to my room. The nice girl at the front desk smiled and said, "Hi Andrew." I smiled back.

I got to my fancy room. I opened my Stoli. There were even glasses in my room. I planned on sticking out my pinkie finger for this drink, like the wealthy did. I took a nice clean glass from the bar area and poured a tall drink.

"Aahhhhhh."

I put the bottle in the mini fridge so it could chill. I looked up at the plaster ceiling in this hotel room. I grabbed the paper and began to look for "bulb changer" or "truck washer" jobs. I would work my way up from those jobs, and in a few weeks, be manufacturing my own bulbs, and running a trucking business. I didn't see anything in the paper for these kinds of jobs. Hmmmm. I just needed to drink more, so I could think more clearly. I needed to think of bulbs, how could I make them last a lifetime. I now noticed that inside of the mini fridge there were all sorts of liquor nips, crackers, and peanuts – all for me. It was a nice compliment of the hotel, and I began to devour all the free stuff. How often would they replenish this? It was a great idea, this stocked fridge, it would provide at least one meal a day, and drinks to get me started. I awoke to sunlight, covered in peanut wrappers, empty nip bottles standing at attention, looking at me. I heard my father's voice: "Get the lead out!" I got ready to hit the pavement and look for work.

I would walk the streets and look for other mechanics dressed in Dickies, find a job, change bulbs for a few weeks, learn finance, and … boom … I would soon be in my own office on the top floor. Just after walking a few blocks, it was obvious how different California was from New England. It was so clean, for one thing. Even the street gutters were immaculate. Back home they were all disgusting, but I had never noticed … in winter slush, in summer filled with papers and trash, in fall rotting brown leaves, decomposing. These curbs even had what looked like freshly laid paint. Strangers on the street said "Hi" to me. That type of behavior was asking for an ass-kicking in Boston.

I turned around to see if I recognized them. How could someone just say, "Hi"?

The sun seemed to loosen my ligaments and soften my bones, and automatically pull my shoulders back. The tight muscles, the stiff skeleton, and the hunched shoulders seemed to be an automatic reaction in New England, a phenomenon that happened shortly after Halloween. The body senses colder weather, and it tightens and curls. I decided just to walk, and think, and that is what I did. The streets were perfect for a drunk. You struggle up one hill, and then gravity pulls you down the other side.

It wasn't humid like in D.C., but it was hot, and the walk and hills seemed to open up all the pores in my body; soon I was soaked. I kept walking, to get to the dry period, where you can't sweat anymore, and you start to evaporate. The whole city appeared to be decorated in fresh paint, all sorts of colors. The combination of sun, exercise, and colors seemed to lighten my mood. I was happy. For no other reason than having walked all day, loosening up, sweating, drying out, being surrounded by happy people and fun colors.

I couldn't wait to see my friends at the front desk. I came back to the hotel and was eager to start pounding down the complimentary nips, followed by the free snacks. The front desk girls were smiling as I bounced in, still walking with joy in my leather jacket, Red Wing boots, and Dickies.

We were all smiling. As I headed for the elevator, one of the smiling front desk girls called me over. They would be inquiring about how my day was, I was certain. They were so nice. Her eyes were glistening as she showed me a nice envelope with my name on it. Maybe there was a relative of mine on his deathbed, and he had left an inheritance for me?

I opened the envelope … and it was the bill. I was being charged for 2 days, even though I hadn't even been there a full 24 hours yet. Then there was the snacks and nips, which apparently were *not* free after all. They charged me movie theater prices. The smiles left both of our faces until I paid up.

I had to leave before I got swindled into paying for 5 days but only sleeping there 3 days. I told them my situation, that I needed a place I could rent for a week at a time. They said there was a YMCA, not too far away. They sort of giggled when they said it. They especially eyed my shiny leather jacket and work boots. I ran upstairs and packed everything, and checked out so I didn't get pinched for anything else. I grabbed a mint and held it up, and asked if it was complimentary. They called someone up to see that I left the room in order and hadn't spent the last five minutes tearing things up with a razor knife and pocketing nips and crackers.

I wheeled my luggage down the street. I finally made it to the YMCA. As I approached, I got an eerie feeling. Outside seemed to be my type of people, birds of a feather. Drunks. But these guys were on the tail end of their journey. Their faces were red and yellow and cracked. I got to the front desk, and the guy wasn't smiling. There was no, "Hello, Mr. Winslow." It was just, how many nights, pay by the day. Okay, I would pay by the day. I was handed a key, went to my room, and laid down. I needed a drink. My legs started to become fidgety. I went outside. It was like a chorus of missing teeth and cracked skin. They gave me directions to the liquor store. I had enough money to buy a couple half gallons of vodka. With my purchase, I came around the corner as if scoring the winning touchdown.

I passed by the front desk. He glared at me like I was just another guy with a brown paper bag. I got to my room, and couldn't wait to do some old school drinking. Twist the cap off, throw it over my shoulder, not to be put back on again. This was my bottle, and my type of scene, nothing fancy. I did remember to mutter "hula-boom" and started to swig the clear liquid from Russia. I was shortly thereafter in my comfort zone. That bad spirits of anxiety and fear had left. I looked out my window and took in the streets.

I needed to walk and maybe look for jobs, so I walked ... and walked. I soon found myself in a neighborhood filled with dragon statues. All of a sudden, I seemed to be in a foreign land. I was the only non-Asian there. Everyone seemed to walk with purpose. I also noticed that this place was a lot cleaner than the Chinatown in Boston, which locals called the Combat Zone.

I stopped into a small diner and sat on a stool. I ordered a soup and without even requesting it, I was given tea. Fancy joint, I thought. I grabbed a paper and searched the want ads for "bulb changer" or "truck washer." I didn't see any today, but I knew such ads would surely be appearing soon. After all, it was a highly specialized craft.

The Chinese waitress was filling up my second cup of tea. Back home it would be, "Get a job, you bum." But here, the weather and people seemed sympathetic, and optimistic. I was enjoying myself ... until I opened my wallet. Funds were running low. I didn't like that feeling. The tea made me a bit edgy, sort of like the No-Doz, and I needed a drink. The drink would make me feel as if I did have money.

My thoughts raced. I had quit the bulb-changing job back home. Even if I wanted to go back, I would be harassed and called "Hollywood" or "Movie Star" for at least a few weeks, just for going to California. But the truck washing job ... that could still be mine. Something in those cups of tea made me panic. It made me think too much. What if there were no bulb-changing jobs here? I headed back to the Y and stared at the ceiling. I didn't take a drink ... and attributed the inevitable shakes, nervousness, and racing thoughts to the weird Asian tea.

For the next few days, I followed the same pattern. I would get up, grab the paper, look for bulb-changer or trucker-washer jobs, not see any, then walk the streets hoping to run into a fellow mechanic who would see my name embroidered on my Dickies jacket and offer me a job; each day, this failed to happen, and I would slink back to the YMCA, grabbing a plastic bottle of vodka on the way. Once there, I would guzzle, stare at the ceiling. As the alcohol took effect, my confidence would be restored that tomorrow my luck would change. But it didn't.

I woke up with a pounding head and a half-eaten sub sandwich sleeping on my chest, and decided I would start the day with vodka. I opened my wallet, and my stomach sunk. That was it ... I made a decision ... to head home. I had only been there in California for six days. I brushed my arms as if there were tiny insects playing on them. My legs were racing to the metronome of my mind. Or was it the other way around? I was soaking wet with sweat. I swilled and slept, but it was all nightmares. I was chased by massive swamp life: snakes, frogs, dragonflies. I seemed to be running in molasses. I awoke now and then to take another swig until finally, there was nothing to swig. The plastic bottle was empty.

I looked in my wallet and took out my open-ended, return ticket and my last $20 bill and called the taxi company. I headed to the airport, boarded the plane, and left the warmth of California. I would save face back in Boston by simply saying, "Well, I was just scoping it out."

The good news was, after paying my fare and tipping the cabbie back in California, I had just enough change left to take two trains and three buses from Logan back to my zip code. We took off, and the clatter of the Stewardesses cart was soon heard. I was getting wiggly and knew I needed a drink, but the $5.47 in my pocket would only get me one, and that would just make me angry ... plus then I wouldn't have bus fare back to Crystal Hill.

A guy with a red face and a suit sat next to me and eye-balled me. He kept looking at me as I twisted and fidgeted and played the Fred Astaire game with my feet. The plane took off, and soon the stewardesses were rolling by with the drink cart. I was about to excuse my self to the bathroom, where I could maybe ride out the flight in painful solitude, when the guy next to me ordered two vodkas. The stewardess handed then to him, and he said, "keep 'em coming." When she rolled her cart away, he handed one to me.

"You'se looks like you'se could use a nip, my friend," he said. "I'se been there myself. On me …"

Thanks to that good Samaritan, I drank nips of Vodka all the back to Massachusetts. Maybe this was my consolation prize for swinging and missing on my California dreams, I thought.

OH, GREAT, A PERVERT

"We are arriving at Logan airport," I heard the pilot say. It was still winter there. I exited the airport and found the pay phone. I had to collect my thoughts. I called me Ma. I didn't let on that I was in Massachusetts. Instead, I said I was doing great, and staying at the River Edge Hotel in San Francisco. Clean sheets and a continental breakfast every day. She sounded happy that I was making it, and that I had clean sheets. She mentioned that I got a letter from the electrical union and that she had accidentally opened it; it said that I had passed the exam and that the electrician apprenticeship classes were starting in September, but there were many meetings and interviews required before-hand.

Ahh, I thought. There's my break.

"Well, Ma, that's actually what I was calling about," I stammered. "I mean, things are going great out here in California. But I remembered that I had applied to the union apprentice program and thought I'd call to see if I got in."

"Well," she said, "you'll have to talk to your father before coming home. He was pretty disappointed with how you left the job your brother got you."

"Tell you what, Ma," I said. "I'll fly home tomorrow and come by the house for dinner. Tell pops I'll be there, and want to talk about it. I think being an electrician is what I'm supposed to do. Tell him that being in California cleared my head, and I'm ready to get serious."

I could hear her wringing her hands over the phone.

With my last few coins, I called everybody I knew to try and find a place to crash that night. Everybody answered the phone, but each of them came up with some excuse or another. They were busy, going out with a girl, or working, and couldn't be bothered. Fuck it, I thought. I'll go sleep under my old statue on Boston Commons. It would be cold, but what else could I do? I lurked around the bus stop until I saw somebody get off and toss their transfer ticket on the ground. I pounced on it like a ravenous sea lion and quickly boarded the bus from Logan to downtown Boston.

I got off the bus and began walking toward my statue. It was getting colder by the minute, but I was getting sweaty and agitated. The airplane drinks were wearing off, fast. What would I do? I thought about trying to pull off a five-finger discount from the packy by the Commons, but thought better of it. That was a sure way to get a back-alley beat-down, and I also couldn't afford any criminal record, now that I was an adult … that would make me ineligible for the union apprentice program. My mind was racing. It was getting dark, and the shifts had just changed. The day people were gone, and the night crew of rummies and addicts and petty criminals and the mentally ill were coming on duty.

I approached my statue and saw that a figure had already claimed it. Screw it, I thought, he's gonna have to share the statue tonight. That was *my* statue. I shuffled up and sat down next to a guy that looked like a scraggly, dirty, anorexic Santa Claus. He wore a mangy, faded red stocking cap and his unkempt beard was littered with detritus, old leaves, crumbs, dust. He was covered with one of those grey police blankets, and it was covered with stains – I didn't want to know what they were from. I plopped down and sighed. He looked at me and began to pull his blanket off him.

Oh great, I thought, a pervert.

Rather than pull out his Johnson, he pulled out a nearly-full plastic half-gallon bottle of vodka, looked at me, nodded, said, "What's up," and handed it to me.

I drank vodka with creepy Santa until consciousness faded away, and woke up under my Star Wars sheets.

Dismissed

I had to have a talk with my father in the closed-in porch regarding getting into the electrical union. There was no hug, no, "Welcome home, son." He sat in his usual chair and held up the acceptance letter.

He pointed to another chair. I sat down. "Congrat-chuh-layshuns on getting' in," he said, emotionless. "If you make it, you'se will be a third-generation electrician. 'Dat's not nothin'. Just don't embarrass me. My ass is on the line here, so no shenanigans. As long as you show up every day and do what they tell you to do, you'se can stay here." He handed me a $20 bill. "Get you'se self cleaned up," he said, eyeballing me with a derision and pity. "You'se smell."

I was dismissed.

We then had our traditional meal. After, I read some of the instructions from the electrical union. There were lots of interviews and orientation meetings coming up. I crept downstars and took a couple slugs from the vodka bottle just to help me sleep. I headed to Angry Tony's in the morning and got cleaned up. I mentally prepared myself for the ordeal ahead. This would be a major career change, but I had to do it. And I had to go straight-edge. "Straight edge," was just what it sounded like. Staying between the margins. In bed early, rising early, shoes and clothing laid out the night before. Lunch made and ready to be packed into a metal pail. Walk onto the job, work diligently. Come home, exercise, shower, eat a hot, nutritious meal, brush teeth, say prayers, and off to sleep, arms by my side.

I weaseled my way back into weekend truck washing and staying relatively straight-edge for about two weeks. This allowed me to put some money in the bank. My father announced that since I was now accepted into the electrical union, it was time to get my own car, an American made one. We found a Ford Escort. My father knew automobile basics and he said he would take me over so we could look at the car. We headed out and stopped at Dunkin Donuts so he could get his chocolate cruller and coffee with 10 sugar substitutes and cream. He slugged his coffee back and devoured his donut. Then he took a couple belts of Maalox. When we arrived in Cambridge to look at the car, he had bits of chocolate and traces of white Maalox on his lips.

He said, "Can I take it for a spin?" He drove around the block while the owner and I stood on the sidewalk. He sped off and we saw him accelerating around the corner. He rounded the block and then slammed on the brakes in front of us, and then speed off again. He came around the corner again and slammed on the brakes again. With a red face accented by traces of Maalox and chocolate donut, he yelled so all the beautiful people of Cambridge could hear: "It needs a brake job!" He then did a three-point turn and parked the car. They discussed the price and he made a low-ball offer, on account of the brakes. We left, and he said, "We'll see if she goes for the offer." A couple days later, she called and accepted and we went over and picked up the Escort. I finally had my own American made car.

I needed a drink for this occasion. It had been 14 days since my last one, the longest I had gone in many years. I swilled the much-deserved drink to my first American car, my new occupation, and the new me. The next day, I washed and waxed the Escort. It was yellow with brown trim. It appeared as some sort of tropical canary bird. I had an interview for the union shortly, and I was feeling ready. I arrived for the interview.

"What type of cah do you drive?"

"Ford Escort," I said.

"Good. American-made."

I was dismissed.

Having passed the interview, I was to report to the apprenticeship hall in Newton. I arrived and was greeted by two angry looking men, the apprentice directors. They were both in ties and told us to go downstairs. We went downstairs and were assembled in our seats. The two ties came in and the older one screamed, "Silence!" The younger one just stood there with his arms crossed and stared at us. The older one paced around and went into some sort of tirade as if someone had slashed all his tires.

"Welcome to the electrical apprenticeship union, we train you here to become skilled electrical craftsman! My job here as apprentice director is to wean out the bums. From now on, you will not wear any type of jewelry, especially earrings ... only women wear earrings! Jewelry is a hazard in the electrical industry, and besides, it is for old ladies! Are there any questions? Remember, there are no dumb questions!"

One guy up front raised his hand and asked if a watch was considered jewelry.

"That's the dumbest question I ever heard!" the apprentice director yelled.

We then filed into lines based on our last name. I was handed an envelope, and it gave me my assigned electrical company I was to go to, and listed the nights I had classes.

"Dismissed ladies!"

THE SIXTH FINGER

The first day arrived, and my father had directions out for me on the table. I was ready to go. I drove proudly in my newly polished Ford Escort. I thought of my future, getting out of my electrician's van, putting on a tool belt, with a bounce in my step, knocking on the door and announcing, "Electrician!" I made it to the location, and it was a normal house, and what seemed like a garage almost as big as the house. I saw a man in the garage moving around.

"Come in!"

I entered a room full of cigar smoke.

"What kinda cah is dat?"

"Ford."

"Good. American-made. All right, kid, I'm gonna have you'se drive and learn the streets, our stock, and where all our jobs are. If you'se behave, after a few months I will put you'se out on 'da job sites. Remember, no games, kid."

He pointed to a flatbed truck, and said, "There she is, take care of her."

He explained that there was a map in the truck and my job would be to organize the stock, maintain the inventory, pick up and deliver stock to and from suppliers and job sites.

"Good luck kid!" was all he said.

I piled the stock onto the back of the flatbed and headed out. There were about six or seven different job locations, mostly in Boston. I went to electrical supply houses and to the job sites. As I delivered the stock, everyone called me "kid," and had a rough look. These guys bore a lot of wear and tear from the elements of construction sites and the New England weather. I learned not to show up at coffee break or lunch break. I followed this routine for weeks and liked the time alone in the flatbed. I kept the sauce down to one night a week, on Saturdays. I was now working seven days a week, and doing well. After 4 months I got the word: I would now be working with the tools. I was given an address, in Chinatown.

I had the weekend to prep for my first day on the job, on Monday. I came home and announced my "promotion" to the family. My father grinned, and said, "We'll talk about things after dinner."

Dinner ended, and my father had me wait in the porch. He came back with a pair of blue handled electrician pliers, new, right out of the box. Of course, I had years of experience handling these pliers while working with him on weekends throughout my youth. But now, I had my own brand-new pair. He pulled them out of the box, and held them in his hands, like they were the Hope Diamond. He opened and closed them repeatedly. He grinned and said, "These here will be you'se sixth finger." He opened and closed them some more, as if cutting some imaginary wire. Then put them back into the box. He would never say, "I'm proud of you son," followed by a hug. But, anyway, I could tell he was proud of me by the thoughtfulness of the gift, the amount of pistachios he threw in his mouth, and the speed at which he chewed them.

He told me the most important thing was to always, always, get to the job site earlier than anybody else. Next most important: always be clean cut and freshly shaved. After that, always carry the proper tools of the journeyman electrician. Next, don't be a wise-guy. Then he told me about all the other trades – carpenters, plumbers, masons – and how to work with them. He mentioned that ironworkers have "a sized 46 shirt and a size 5 hat."

The directions were simple: board the commuter train at the 128 station, and take it to South Station. I boarded the train with lunch box and metal toolbox. I liked the idea of the train: no traffic. The train arrived blowing cold and bits of snow at us as we stood there. We arrived after about six stops and I disembarked. People were pushing and shoving to get off and out into the cold again. I was early so I stopped at a coffee joint. No welcoming party, just cold, hard New England stares. I looked outside and watched as the construction workers filed into the building.

There were some with all white hair, clean shaven, and probably a year away or so from retiring. Then there were those with long hair, probably from the 1960s, biker types. Then guys around my age with flat tops. The clock moved, and I decided to head over. I walked into the ground floor and up a ramp, and there was a guy looking at blueprints. I asked him where the electricians were. He simply pointed to a stairwell, and said, "basement." I went to the basement. I headed over to what looked like the electrical crowd. There were small groups gathered within the crowd. I was pointed in the direction of the lead man.

"Welcome, kid," he said. "Hang around with the other apprentice. He will show you the ropes. But, basically, all you will be doing is humping stock up and down the stairs."

He chuckled.

"Basically," he said, "You'se will be our elevator."

Big metal boxes clanged as they opened. The oldest guy, said, "Hey kid, take this up to the top floor electrical room."

He didn't introduce himself, he just gave me the order. I grabbed his toolbox and headed up the six floors. I dropped them off, and headed back down, gingerly descending a partially built stairwell. I made it down to the basement and found the other apprentice. He was gathering stock, and putting it into small boxes, marking who each was for and what floor it went to. He handed me one at a time, and I went off to deliver each box. I ran up and down the floors, dropping off pipe, couplings, wire etc. I was breathing heavy, but time was flying by. I made it back down to the basement and was told we would be making the coffee rounds. The other apprentice had a long piece of cardboard and a black sharpie.

We then proceeded to take the orders. We went all over the building, wrote down orders, and headed out to the coffee shop.

My fellow apprentice drove us to a local diner. The girl that took our order seemed rough, but then again, she served rough men all day long. She took the order and yelled it out to a guy on the grill.

"You'se new?" She asked me. I said I was. Her reply was, "Well, good luck."

Our order soon came back, food in one box and coffees in another. We returned to happier faces in the basement, but there was still no warm, fuzzy reception for the new guy. Just blank stares. Little groups formed by what seemed to be age or war experience. I was with the flat tops, the other apprentices or new journeymen electricians.

That coffee break ended, and I was told to clean up the mess. Then it was back to running up and down the stairs, dropping off stock until lunch time. Lunch was different: a few guys stayed in the basement with their lunch pails, while others went off to their cars or to restaurants. When everybody came back, it was obvious that some had a few drinks for lunch. Now, they were kinder to me. The day ended without injury, and without fulfilling my nightmare of cutting the power off to the entire city, followed by a gang chasing me home with pitch-forks and torches.

I made my way back to the commuter rail, and couldn't tell if it was the bitter cold or not having had a drink in twenty-four hours, but I was shaking. I needed a drink, to celebrate my first day, but I couldn't blow it either. I had to curb it. Shortly after dinner and a shower, I crashed. I didn't even need alcohol. My body just shut down. I awoke to, "Up and at 'em!" and headed out. It was the same routine all week. On Friday, about an hour before lunch, one of the guys from the older generation said to me, "Hey kid, you'se come with me for lunch today."

I thought it was nice of him to be buying me lunch. No one up to this point had said, "Hey kid, you are doing a great job." But now I was going to get a hot sandwich and soup in appreciation of my hard work. About five minutes before lunch, I headed outside. There was a small group of us, and even a few from the other trades. We marched down the street to a large Chinese restaurant called the Moon Villa. We entered and the lead guy seemed to know everyone. The hostess seemed happy to see us and marched us off to a corner away from the other patrons.

We sat at a long table, and I looked at the menu. How would I get my egg foo young ordered, cooked, delivered and eaten, in 30 minutes? I asked, "They must cook fast here. Will be able to order and eat it in time?" The guy said, "This is a liquid lunch kid." He ordered some sort of platter for us, and then the drinks. I raised my hand to order, but he said, "I'll order ya' drink." He raised his hand to the waiter and then pointed down to our table. The waiter emerged moments later with a tray of drinks, all with umbrellas.

We were all smiling now, and then a platter with a flame in the middle arrived, and we appeared as kids around a fire with marshmallows. I took the umbrella out of my drink and spun it. The drink had the smell of strong alcohol and I muttered "hulla-boom" and threw it back. This made the others grin. The lead guy got the attention of the waiter again and ordered more drinks. I wanted at least three or four before the end of lunch. Then the guy said, "Take it easy, kid, we have a little extra time today. It's Friday." He must have seen me repeatedly checking my watch.

My drink arrived, and I gulped it down. I scanned this big table we were at and took everyone in, all sorts of generations, and even a couple different trades. I glanced briefly at the ironworker next to me. I was 6'2" and he seemed to be much larger. I took a look at his head, and indeed, it was smaller than mine. My father was right: the ironworker had a size 48 shirt and size 5 head. He had a piece of meat on a stick and seemed to be biting the stick as well. He grabbed for another one and handed it to me. I noticed some of his fingers were touching the meat, but I didn't feel I should decline. We all got another round, so I was working on my third drink and was feeling better.

Everyone seemed to relax a bit, and the other apprentice said something about a nightmare he had about spiders crawling up his legs. The guy said, "You want to talk about nightmares? I was in friggin' Normandy." This silenced everyone for a moment. The other kid stopped talking and we went on about sports, the job, etc. Cigarettes were lit, and the rounds of drinks kept coming. Our faces changed from tight and frozen in-place to giggly kids after s'mores. Almost 50 minutes went by, and the guy looked at his watch. "Time," he said.

We all patted our pockets and reached in. Crumpled up dollars piled up and the eldest counted it. He smiled and said we had enough. I rose up but was hit hard by the alcohol bat – and felt great. As we exited the guy put his hand on my back and said, "What do you think of your first liquid lunch?' I just smiled. He said, "Ya' gonna make it in this trade. You'se aren't afraid to hump up and down the stairs, and you'se ain't a punk." Hearing those words felt like receiving the Congressional Medal of Honor.

JINGHUA

The next week was exactly the same, except for the liquid lunch on Friday. After the order was placed, and before the flaming meat and umbrella drinks arrived, I excused myself to the bathroom. It was one of those one-at-a-time men's rooms, so I had to loiter outside the door while the current occupant finished his business. While I was loitering, a beautiful Asian girl walked up, tried the door to the ladies room, and finding it occupied and locked, began loitering next to me.

"Hi, I'm Jinghua," she said.

I just stared at her. She was gorgeous.

"My aunt and uncle own this place. I'm a college student. Are you with the electricians out there?"

"Yeah," I said, "I'm a new apprentice."

"Want to grab a drink sometime?" she asked.

"Er ..."

While I was fumbling, she wrote her number on a piece of paper and handed it to me. She then handed me a pen and a piece of paper and said, "Give me your number, I'll call you."

Still stunned, I complied. The ladies room door opened, she winked at me and went in. I was so flustered, I forgot all about needing to use the bathroom, and returned to my table, shoving her number into my pocket.

As I left for work the next Monday, I heard my father yell, "Some broad named Jinghua called!"

I noticed there was very little chatter at the job site on Mondays. One of the old timers said, "Monday's the hardest day, but if you can make it past coffee break on a Monday, the rest of the weak is gravy."

I made it past coffee break on Monday, and the rest of the week was gravy. Things were going well. I needed a drink. I remembered that the Jinghua broad had invited me out for drinks. I was trying to keep a straight-edge, but it was Friday, and it would be a date, not like me slugging vodka out of a plastic bottle with a homeless, anorexic Santa at the base of a statue on Boston Commons, so I figured it would be okay.

I had no idea why she would have any interest in me; I was more intrigued by her invitation that involved alcohol. I went home and made a few stiff ones to keep the spirit of fear away and wake up the spirit of bravery. I would just let her do all the talking.

"This is Jinghua, she said," answering the phone.

"Hi, my name is Andrew and we met at the restaurant."

"Hey! Thanks for calling!" she said. "Want to get together?"

She gave me the address and plans were set. I took a few more belts, went upstairs, and let the magic of alcohol take effect. I laid on the bed and thought of my new future with Jinghua: giggling together, sharing drinks with one straw.

I made it to her apartment complex and rung the bell to her unit. A pleasant voice said, "I'll be right down." I waited in the lobby and tried to remember what she looked like. She came down, and she too seemed to bounce. She looked stunning. I grew more anxious. We made it to the restaurant. We were seated, and a dim light illuminated her face. She was so pretty. What could she possibly want with me?

"So, you want to order drinks?" I asked.

"Oh," she replied. "I was just kidding about getting together for drinks! That just seems like a normal way to ask somebody out." She giggled.

"I mean, who wants to get drunk on a first date?"

Then I started to lose concentration. In the horizon, just over the top of her head, was the bar!

Then the people around us began to get drinks, colorful drinks, drinks with little umbrellas. I was losing focus, as the drinks were placed on the surrounding tables. She still seemed happy, but noticed I was looking at the drinks.

"Get one if you want," she said, eye-balling me. This was a test.

"Oh no," I said, "I don't drink much."

I tried to keep my eyes on her. Jinghua talked about her goals, dreams, family. Her family owned a couple of Chinese restaurants, and eventually, she would learn the ropes and take control of one of them. Her goals even had deadlines, and dates. My immediate goal was to get a soothing booze drink in me, to calm me down. The room seemed to spin, with sounds of laughter, the color of the drinks. Our food came and I ate, but it could have been an old shoe, I was so jittery and distracted.

I just kept my gaze on her eyes, as best I could, and did a lot of "listening," since I read somewhere that girls liked that. It made it easier. We left and drove around a bit, but I decided I couldn't take it and dropped her off early. She thought that was strange ... but polite. We planned another date. I sped home. I was desperate for a drink. It wasn't fair, to be tempted like that at a bar. I took a few belts, laid on my rack and thought of Jinghua, her beauty, and her goals.

We kept meeting on Fridays for a while, and, as astonishing as it seemed, we really hit it off great. I had devised a plan whereby I took a few stiff belts right before leaving to meet her each week and planted 4 nips on my person, two on each ankle, inside my socks. I still had a mortal fear of driving drunk, so I explained to her that my sister had borrowed my car for a couple months, so we'd have to meet someplace on the commuter line. We'd meet, and I'd excuse myself exactly twice: once right after ordering, and once right after paying the bill. Each time, I would go to the bathroom and down two nips. It wasn't ideal, but it got me through.

I wasn't drinking much during the week, which was extremely uncomfortable. Just a couple belts upon getting home from work and the Friday liquid lunch with the boys. Jinghua made plans for me to meet her family. Things were getting serious with us. She had even muttered the "L" word once. I was shaking like a whore in church and could barely hold my pliers. The day arrived and I could hardly shave correctly, I needed two hands. I decided that I wasn't going to do my nip routine, on account of meeting her parents, so I took my car for the voyage.

As I drove toward my future wife, I was growing impatient. I could make it to Jinghua's 20 or 30 seconds earlier if I could only pass the car in front of me. My Red Wing boot pressed as hard as it could on the accelerator and passed to the left of the car, but apparently, the light on the other side had turned green.

I got a glimpse of the woman in the car in the oncoming traffic. She was young and attractive, and looked like she was shouting the same thing I was: "What the?!" I woke up in a meat wagon, with a guy sitting over me.

"We are taking you to the hospital, sir, you've been in an accident."

"Does it hurt anywhere else?" he asked.

I knew I felt pain in my right hip and announced, "right hip." We got to the hospital and I was wheeled away. Everyone seemed to have consumed that dangerous drug, coffee, as they were very hyper. The guy in a lab jacket spoke to a woman and I was put into some high-tech machinery. I had to get to Jinghua's, so I was glad they were rushing. I was then placed somewhere else. I looked up at the tile and lighting. The only thing I could do was count the dots on the tile. Pain throbbed all over me. Another lab jacket came back and said the x-rays looked okay for my head, but my hip seemed to have some abnormality.

I looked up at the ceiling some more. When I made it big, I decided, and constructed my own hospital, the ceiling tiles would have beach images, or slogans like, "You'll be fine."

I had to get to Jinghua's. I looked to the left and right. There were no lab jackets in sight. I made a break for it. My right leg was dragging. I made it to the red sign that stated "exit" and I passed by a green dumpster. It most likely contained body parts, I figured. Well, they wouldn't cut my leg off and discard it in a dumpster!

I noticed people backing away from me as I limped and ran, my leg dragging. Some looked at my forehead. I saw a liquor store and limped inside. I shuffled my way to the plastic vodka bottle aisle. The cashier noticed my forehead, pointed, and said, "Got an egg? In a beef?" I smiled and said, "You should see the other guy." He wrapped my bottle in a brown bag, and I limped away. I needed to find a dimly lit place. I was woozy and in pain, but a few belts would have me right as rain, and I could pull off this "meet the family" date with my future bride, Jinghua.

I found an alley and unscrewed the bottle. I forgot to bless myself with "hula-boom," but the pain was excruciating. Soon I would be walking upright for my introduction to Jinghua's parents. I drank and drank until the pain subsided and confidence rose within me. I limped around as fast as I could until I found her high-end condo. I buzzed the buzzer and was buzzed inside. He mother opened the door.

I smiled and put the brown bag down. Jinghua came around the corner smiling, then her face changed to a look of horror. I handed her the brown bag. She went from a look of horror to a look of sadness. There was a lot of very louder chatter in Chinese, pointing to my head, the blood on my shirt, and the brown bag. Jinghua then escorted me to her room. I sat down on her bed, and then she asked, "What happened."

"Someone ran a red light," I said.

I needed more vodka, so I grabbed the brown bag and took some swigs. Her mother was then in the doorway to her room, and there was more yelling in Chinese as I took another swig. They argued, and it appeared Jinghua won, for her mother shortly appeared with a bag of ice. Jinghua applied the ice, and tears came out of her face. She said something about "goals" and "drinking" and "us."

I needed to defend lady vodka, so I told her the whole picture. I had no insurance, so the longer I stayed in the hospital, the longer the bill would be. Plus, they were about to amputate my leg and throw it in a dumpster. Vodka was the only medicine I could afford. Her eyes stopped leaking, and as I wiped away her tears, we smiled.

It was a close call.

My Mother Was Right About You

I was getting woozy, and called home to get a ride. Me ma answered, and I heard the king of the house yelling in the background. He grabbed the phone and barked:

"Goose cooked…"

"Hospital called…"

"Escort totaled…"

"Last straw…"

I couch hopped for a month. Jinghua and I were doing great. I had managed to make the nip routine work for me. She and I were going out almost every night of the week that I didn't have a class. However, she was now extremely cautious and paranoid about me drinking. In her culture, heavy drinking was a shameful moral failure. She didn't exactly nag me, but she routinely managed to bring up the subject, and remind me that, while we did have some "goals" together, those "goals" would not be possible if I was a drinker.

Jinghua figured out that I was couch-hopping.

"Andrew, I just moved into my own apartment. I know your parents kicked you out. Why don't you leave a bag of your stuff at my place, and you can crash with me until you get things figured out?"

After a quiet period, my father started speaking to me again. He said he would help me find a new car. After some research and a few embarrassing test drives, we found a 1966 Galaxy 500, a real "boat." I decided I would treat Miss Galaxy like a queen and would continue to commute to work via train and bus. She would only be driven on special occasions.

Sunday was a mellow day to drive, so I decided to take a ride to Jinghua's, and really test her eye for beauty. I was sober as a judge, and the shakes I normally had from being off the sauce for more than 24 hours seemed to be absent, probably due to the rigorous washing and waxing of the Galaxy. Jinghua hugged me, but it was a two-part hug – one for affection, the other, to check me for the scent of alcohol, and look in my eyes. By now, she could tell when I had a few drinks; my right eye would slim to the shape of a dime slot. I passed the test and said I had a surprise. We walked a couple blocks and I pointed to the Galaxy. She smiled, and it was genuine.

We then went for a spin. Jinghua liked the dashboard and its instruments. I looked at Jinghua and the Galaxy. She would reach her goals, I would become an electrician, and we would have children together. It would be the same scene we were in now, but with three children in the back, singing family songs.

A long weekend was about to come upon us. Jinghua had said after all her exams, it would be nice to get away. She showed me the brochure and talked about fireplaces, cozy rooms, and being together for a romantic weekend. I had brief images of poking a fire, and Jinghua and me under a blanket. The Galaxy was parked in the suburbs at my parents, and I picked it up for the long weekend cruise. My folks were prepping a Friday night meal, no meat, but fish and macaroni. I stayed for the meal and told them of my plans. Since it was a religious meal, I mentioned that we had separate rooms.

I packed some swimming trunks, fireplace slippers, and a nice shirt that could be worn for a candlelight dinner. Then I stuffed it all in a brown grocery bag and placed it in the trunk. I thought of myself with my feet propped up on an Ottoman, being warmed up by the fire, cuddled up with Jinghua, drinking responsibly, my pinkie pointed to the fire, talking about our future. I started the Galaxy and headed out.

I reached Route 109 and took a left. I passed by Simma's house. Then a quick left into Mike's Sunoco. I thought of Simma's house. I had noticed a few extra cars there, and one shiny one in particular. That most likely meant the car salesman was there. I should stop by, and stick my head in to say hello. Mike finished filling the car with gas. I pulled up to Simma's, walked to the side door and noticed the shades were down. I then saw the candy on the little table to the left of the door. I could hear Simma's size 14 feet walking down the hallway. He opened the door, and he had an extra strong handshake. His eyes were wider than usual. It was obvious that his enzymes were coated. I went in, and the door was locked behind me. The lights were dimmed, and the car salesman passed me by and gave a head nod.

"I was just driving by and thought I'd stop to say hello," I said.

They had some 3-inch white powdery snakes lined up, and they pointed to one. One would help me get to my destination, I thought. Just one would get me there safely and keep me awake at the wheel. Just one wouldn't make me drive recklessly. I announced my intentions of heading north, and talked about the brochure Jinghua had obtained. Fireplaces, beautiful surroundings, warm quilts, historical covered bridges.

The car salesman pointed to one of the 3-inch powdery snakes and said, "One for the road!" Indeed, one for the road. I would be focused after one of these powdery snakes worked its magic. It would allow me to have intelligent conversations, making Jinghua even more interested in me. I inhaled, snapped my neck back … within a few moments, I would be entering the zone of love and knowledge.

The salesman left and soon returned with a drink.

"Stoli's, he said."

I was a guest, and it would be impolite to decline hospitality. And, it was only one. Just "one for the road." I kept one eye on the clock and one ear on the scattered conversations. A few more drinks were poured. I reached into my pocket and pulled out some money. It was the polite thing to do. The gesture was appreciated. I mentioned how I was running out of time and had to leave.

Then one of the other salesmen mentioned the dangers of driving up north. I had images of hitting black ice, Miss Galaxy spinning out of control, Jinghua on the verge of crying with her bottom lip quivering, and the Galaxy being pulled away on top of a wrecker. The other salesman suggested I call her, and tell her we would leave first thing in the morning. That sounded like a smart idea.

I did just that, and she sounded disappointed but said, "Okay, but promise, first thing in the morning." I agreed and let out a sigh of relief. I could relax now, and no longer watch the clock. When I felt the sunlight trying to pry through the shades, I would split. Vodka was poured and lines were sniffed and before I knew it, the black curtain fell over me. I awoke and found my head beating. I noticed it was very bright out, and peaked through the shades.

There were people in the kitchen, and it started to smell like food. I nodded to a couple guys on the couch. Somebody suggested we have all have a nip of the hair of the dog that bit us. The mirror came out and lines were cut. There were many birds out, but I felt it was still early enough to drive up north. Simma poured me another drink. I looked at the clock and it was 12:45 p.m. What happened to the clock, I thought? I asked about the clock and said it must be broken. Simma looked at his watch, and said, "No, it's the afternoon." I said I needed to leave right away for my perfect getaway weekend with my perfect girlfriend.

"Yeah, but consider this," somebody said. "If you get up north too early, and you spend too much time with her, eventually you'll get bored, and even argue. Then the whole weekend will be ruined anyway."

He was right. That was great advice.

The day went on, and soon it was dark again. I figured rather than call Jinghua to tell her of our new schedule, I would surprise her. Wouldn't she be happy! I was whacked by the vodka bat as I got up, and stumbled a few steps backward. I came up with a plan: Take the train into Allston, surprise Jinghua, crash there, take the train back in the morning, pick up the Galaxy and spend a one-night weekend getaway with Jinghua.

The car salesman gave me a ride to the train station, and I told him I would call in the morning. He just nodded. I got on the train and everything was somewhat of a blur. I got out somewhere in Brighton. I recognized a few landmarks. I stumbled my way to Jinghua's. Just before reaching her door, I felt round objects in my pockets. I pulled them out and they were Cadbury Cream Eggs. What a way to say sorry, I thought, by pulling out a handful of Cadbury Cream Eggs. I knocked on her window, and she opened the blind. She looked at me, and then at my handful of Cadbury cream eggs. Her bottom lip started to quiver, and then she looked at me again. Then she started to cry.

I smiled and said, "Buzz me in." I went over to the door, and the buzzer sounded. I entered and walked in as if carrying very delicate eggs. I knelt down beside her. The Cadbury cream eggs had obviously brought back many happy childhood memories to Jinghua. That explained why she was so emotional. She didn't look at the eggs, but at me.

"My mother was right about you!"

I told her I only had a couple. I needed to lie down. I mumbled a few things and as I figured I was finishing a very eloquent and romantic sentence. The black curtain fell. I came to. Jinghua was standing over me. I smiled. She didn't.

"You need help."

All I heard was, "Help ... blah blah blah."

I needed a *drink*, not help. I shook her hand, said goodbye, and focused on getting a drink. I stumbled to the station and boarded the train. For some reason, people looked at me oddly. I headed to Riverside and placed a call at the pay phone. The salesman picked me up, and just said, "You look like you need a drink."

I explained to him how the romantic weekend never sort of worked out, and how my future bride was angry with me.

"Just give her two weeks, then go give her flowers," said the salesman.

My Only Job

I gave Jinghua two weeks. Surely she would forget my shenanigans after a grace period, which was very considerate of me, after all. So, once two weeks passed, after work, being sober as a judge, I knocked on her window. But there was no answer. I buzzed the door, and her room-mate let me in. She seemed to be very upset. She told me that Jinghua moved out, and didn't want me to know where she was. Then her room-mate said her old boyfriend had passed away from excessive drinking.

"You need help," she said. "Or, you will end up in the same predicament."

I apologized for her loss and left. I jumped into the Galaxy and drove off. I figured Jinghua just needed some time to reach her goals. I'd give her some more time. One day soon I would go to me Ma's, and there would be a note there that Jinghua had called. I was sure of it. Time marched on, but there was no call from Jinghua.

At work, I was learning more and more as an apprentice and wasn't being called "kid" as much. At the bar after work there was some chatter about construction slowing down, and there were even some layoffs. When I got to work the next Monday, I was handed a pink slip. The job was over. No girlfriend. No job.

A drink would fix all that and give me the brilliance I needed to come up with a plan. I left the job site with my final check. I walked to the packy, cashed my check, and bought two plastic half gallons of vodka. I walked to the statue in Boston Commons and sat down next to the bum who was already there. I opened the bottle, tossed the cap, took a long swig, and handed it to him. I woke up the next day under Star Wars sheets.

My only job now was keeping just sober enough once per month to show up at the unemployment office, state some facts, or show an ID. No work, no car, no girl. Just drink. I put the shades down. I pulled out a bottle from under my bed. I took a big swig. I took another. I stared at the ceiling.

I awoke in a hospital in Jamaica Plain, with a doctor checking my vital signs. There were two guys with me that I didn't recognize. They both looked rough around the edges, and one had a Scally cap with red hair protruding out the sides. I asked them what was going on. The guy in the cap said they belonged to a club where nobody drank alcohol.

"We found you'se wandering outside a church in Dedham," said the guy.

"You didn't look too steady and didn't seem to know where you'se was or what you'se was doing," said the other guy.

"Yeah, we hold our club meetings in that church, so it was a good thing you picked that place to be wandering around mumbling," said the guy in the cap.

"We'se just wanted to have you checked out, since we can't be having anybody die or whatnot where we meet," he said. "If the doc gives his okay, we got a nice place for you to go and rest and relax for a few days … we asked you on the way over and you said that sounded great, so we made all the arrangements."

The doctor gave his okay. I was suffering from almost complete mind-wipe. I couldn't really formulate any thoughts beyond blankness and numbness. I certainly couldn't engage in a conversation. I was tired, totally wiped out, so going to rest someplace for a few days sounded like a great idea. They drove me to a creepy-looking brick building in Mattapan. The sign above the door said, "detox." My debilitated mind merely thought of some sort of fancy European juice clinic where nice ladies would feed me fruit and juice and vitamins while I got my strength back.

A kind lady in white and a man in a tie greeted me inside. The two guys from the church club stepped around the hallway corner with them and they all spoke for a few minutes.

"Looks like you're in!" said the man in the tie.

"Welcome to the first day of the rest of your life, Mr. Winslow," said the nice lady in white.

Cool, I thought, I was admitted. I was grateful to hear that these people finally realized that a part of my ancestry was Pilgrim and had come over on the Mayflower and were calling me "Mr. Winslow," as a sign of respect. Finally, I thought, after all these years, I was getting the royal treatment. They must have gone into some sort of ancestral archive and figured out who they were dealing with.

"Relax, Mr. Winslow."

"Hold still, Mr. Still Winslow."

"Take this, Mr. Winslow."

"That's it, Mr. Winslow."

I was taken to an examination room and given slippers, hospital pants, and a clean shirt, and told to take a shower. I showered and dressed and then the nice lady in white escorted me to a room full of beds and said, "Now lie down and rest, Mr. Winslow."

I looked around there were lots of other men lying down as well. They looked like corpses, completely lifeless, except for their snores or moaning. I wondered if, when they woke, would they realize or be told that they were rooming with one of the descendants of the Mayflower, "Mr. Winslow"? I lay my head on the pillow and looked at the ceiling for shapes resembling dead relatives, but before I could locate any, I was out.

I didn't have dreams, but was awakened by thick black snakes at the base of my feet. They were shiny and had their mouths open. The insides of their mouths were bright red. They twisted themselves around my ankles and as I tried to kick them off, their grip on me got tighter. I looked to see if their tongues were red or black. A black tongue meant they were poisonous, I seemed to remember. As I was fighting off these snakes, I woke the guys sleeping around me. They looked horrified that snakes had crawled into the base of my bed and were wrapping themselves around my ankles in a death grip. A different lady in white came in with a very large man and offered me snake assistance.

I told them I couldn't see the color of the snakes' tongues so I didn't know if they were poisonous or not. She just said, "I understand, Mr. Winslow." The big guy held me while the woman called me Mr. Winslow, and she gave me some sort of snake repellent pills. It took some time, the snakes uncoiled and I was asleep again. I awoke again and was glad to see the snakes gone, but I immediately vomited. I seemed to vomit everything I had ever eaten, and it was green and glowing.

I ran to the bathroom and wiped my face, and looking in the mirror I saw bugs crawling all over me. I ran out of the bathroom furiously wiping my arms off to get those bugs off me, and I was greeted by the large man and the nice lady in white. He helped me sit down on my bed and gave me a drink of juice and anti-bug pills. When I woke up, a nice man told me that breakfast was ready. I was escorted downstairs, and given a baloney sandwich, and a Dixie cup containing some sweet, brightly colored drink. I looked around to other people in hospital pants and shirts. Some smiled. Others had no expression. Some just looked at the wall.

We sat for awhile, and then the same lady in white, who I now realized was a nurse, asked me to come to her office. She sat me down, took my vital signs, and gave me more pills. Then she sent me off to bed again. Wasn't this my life before, I thought? Pills and sleeping? Now I had hospital pants and shirts, slippers, and baloney sandwiches. I fell into blackness as soon as I lay down, and was awakened by someone telling me there was a meeting I should go to. Okay, I thought, I was kind of tired of laying in that bed, anyway. My new friend assisted me downstairs. His walk was steady. I was a bit wobbly.

I took a seat and just sat there. I still didn't feel capable of doing much more than that. Sitting. Then, clean, shiny people entered the room from the outside. They started to talk. I began to feel bad for them, listening to their stories. They all talked about how they had drinking problems but didn't drink anymore. Wow, I thought, that's two bad things you all have to deal with: One, you had a drinking problem which ruined your life, and two, now you can't even take a drink to take the edge off. They looked bright and clean, however, and seemed happy. I wondered why they would be happy if they had a drinking problem and couldn't drink. That sounded awful to me.

The meeting with these outside clean people ended, and one guy tapped me on the shoulder and just said, "Don't worry, pal, it will get better."

What "it," I thought?

I went into the hallway and the smiling nurse greeted me with a small cup. I had regained my pill popper reflexes so I snapped my neck back and swallowed. Her smile grew and she said, "Ah, I see you have taken pills before." I laughed a sinister laugh, a laugh that exposed all my rear molars. I was making my come-back. A few more days in this place and I'd be all refreshed and ready to go get a plastic bottle of vodka.

I awoke and for the first time after checking in with the nurse, I didn't have to take the pills. The nurse said she had counselors for me. I pointed at myself.

"Me?"

I told her I was okay. I just needed a rest due to the rough patch I was in. I pointed out how I had been unfairly laid off from my job, and how my future bride Jinghua had dumped me, very unfairly, and how I was waiting for her to leave a message with me Ma.

"That's why you need counseling, to sort it through," she said. "Maybe it wasn't her fault? You never know. Perhaps we can get her in here and she can apologize for hurting you?"

"Well, *maybe* …" she said, followed by a laugh.

I went to the second floor for my appointment with the counselor. She was nice enough, but kept inquiring about my drinking. I tried to explain about all the outside issues and circumstances and people that had landed me in this predicament. Why was she harping on my drinking? I didn't see the connection at *all*. She just nodded, like she had heard it all before. She said she had a place for me after I was done with detox, a place where I could live with people that don't drink or take drugs.

"That's nuts," I said. "I'm not one of *those* people. In fact, I feel bad for those people, the ones that can't handle the phases of drinking. That's all it is, phases," I said. "You know, you go through a phase, then stop. I can turn it on and off at will. It's just a phase."

She just nodded.

"Okay, Mr. Winslow," she said. "We'll see."

I sat down in the dining area and looked around. The room started to fill with the clean, shiny people and I realized it was time for another one of their meetings. Once again, they seemed happy, but all they did was talk about how long it had been since they had a drink and what happened when they did. I just felt bad that they couldn't control their phases.

I had to think deep, so I brought my eyebrows together, to make contact with the relay in my brain. After a few minutes of this deep thinking, it struck me. I had to get out of Massachusetts. All my problems stemmed from Massachusetts. I thought of the west coast and San Francisco. My old friend Glenn was out there living with a woman, and that could be my head start. I thought of the beautiful fog of the bay and the city, the warm weather, the clean gutters. I would need to work for about a month to gather money, and then I would head west. I would tell the counselor at our next appointment.

I kept quiet in detox, attended the meetings and sat out on the balcony and ate my baloney sandwiches. I made friends with one guy, from Roxbury. I told him about how I could handle the phases of drinking and my plans to fix my problems by going to San Francisco.

"Yeah, you might want to think that one over again," he said, looking unimpressed. "No matter where I go, I always end up in the same problems. I'm starting to think my problems have nothing to do with *where* I am."

"Yeah," I said. "But you're a heroin addict."

"Yeah," he said. "Well, booze is *your* heroin. Look at us, we're both sitting in the same detox eating the same crappy bologna sandwiches. What's the difference?"

My day to see the counselor arrived, and I gave her the good news. She didn't seem impressed or happy for me.

"You're just trying to run away from your problems," she said. "Your problem isn't 'Massachusetts,' your problem is *you*, and you're going to have to deal with yourself wherever you are."

I disagreed and went over my track record with her. My awesome job, washing trucks. My even more awesome job, changing light bulbs. My acceptance to an elite military college, the Massachusetts Maritime Academy. My acceptance to the electrical union as an apprentice. All the cool girls I had dated.

"And, where are all those things now?" she asked. "And what do all of those things have in common?"

I squeezed my eyebrows together to think of the answer to her question. What did all those things have in common? I was struggling to come up with an answer that made sense, when the counselor spoke up.

"You, Mr. Winslow," she said.

Now, she was just getting annoying and on my nerves. I used her phone and scheduled to have my folks pick me up in a couple days. When they arrived, they didn't seem very happy to see me. Mattapan was my father's old stomping grounds, and it was now run down and seedy, just like this detox place, and just like me.

SOMETHING DIFFERENT

They picked me up the following day, and we drove home in silence, my father violently chewing pistachios, and my mother wringing her hands. When we parked in the driveway on Crystal Hill, I bolted out of the car and to my room before my father could say anything. I crawled under the Star Wars sheets and fell asleep.

My eyes cracked open. There were two sets of eyes looking down at me. They were my parents. They looked concerned. I propped myself up for the tsunami of a lecture that was about to ensue. They went on and on, about chances, about alcohol. About their relatives and booze. I felt bad that they had relatives that were alcoholics. My father spoke of his battles with the bottle. They said I had to do something. Because this was the last time they would bail me out. Ever. No more calling from jail, or a hospital, or a detox, or the airport, needing "one more chance."

It was over.

I said I had a plan and would soon be a new me, with exercise and work.

"Yeah, well, we'ze have heard 'dat before," my father said. "No more of your same old 'plans. I wanna hear something different from you'se. You gotta try something new."

They had me cornered. My mind raced to come up with something.

"Okay, I'll try some of those 12 Step meetings they had at the detox," I said.

"Okay," said my father. "But you're going tonight."

That seemed to pacify them, and I went back to sleep.

"Get the lead out," my father yelled, as I rubbed my eyes.

"Time for you'se meeting."

He drove me to a building and I walked into a church. People were trying to be friendly, trying to hug me, and talk about God. I kept to myself and stared at the ceiling. Not much else penetrated my wounded mind. The meeting ended and I was picked up. I got home and went to my room to think. I needed to think. I couldn't stop drinking forever, that was *crazy* talk. Maybe I would quit for the summer, and then when football season started, I would start drinking again?

Every day my father appeared at my room and said, "Get the lead out, it's time for you'se meeting," and he would drive me to some new location. He had some buddies who were in the twelve-step program, so he had put together a detailed schedule of where each meeting was every day.

As my mind cleared, I started to like the meetings ... a little. I said nothing and just took it in. I noticed that I seemed to have a lot in common with the people. Still, I knew I wouldn't ever stop drinking forever. I just needed a break. I soon figured out where more meetings were, and began going to one at noon every day by myself and then another at night that my father would take me to.

I exercised and paced the house in between meetings. The weeks flew by, and before I knew it, it was time to re-start my electrical apprenticeship training, which was two nights a week. My father saw I was putting in the effort and not causing trouble, so he made some calls and found me a fill-in job stripping and waxing floors. It was hard work. I was on my hands and knees stripping the floors and then cleaning them, and then applying the wax and buffing. They looked like mirrors by the time I was done. I felt a sense of accomplishment. I liked the work and it paid pretty well. I just let myself be absorbed by this new busy schedule, twelve-step meetings, electrical training, work. Repeat.

My father made some more calls and found a friend who had an empty apartment on the Dedham and West Roxbury line. It overlooked a place called Molly's and the Irish Ale House. I made one friend at the meetings, a guy named Paul that lost his toes and half his foot due to drinking too much and passing out in a snowbank. I liked the guy, because from what he told me, he drank just like me. My father called me up one day and said he was going to pick me up, that they wanted me over for dinner. He knew people everywhere, from all walks of life, and he knew that I had been keeping things on the up and up, working hard, going to meetings, going to school. He picked me up and as we drove up Crystal Hill and towards our drive-way, I saw a "new" old car parked there.

"Hey, I know you'se been working hard and keeping ya nose straight and are busy," he said. "A friend of mine needed to get rid of this heap. It doesn't look like much, but I checked it out and it's solid as a rock. I know you'se got some money saved, so give me five bones next time I see you'se and we'll be square."

We went into the house for a traditional meal of beans and brown bread from a can, and when we finished, he slid me the keys across the table. I didn't say much, but thank you. I kissed my mother on the cheek on my way out and drove home in my "new" car. As I drove, strange thoughts came into my head.

I now had my own car, my own apartment, and a job. I felt better due to all the hard work and exercise. Maybe it was time to drink and celebrate my achievements? I told my new friend Paul about my plans when I saw him. I figured he would agree with me that I deserved a drink. He just looked at me and shook his head. He told me about his former success as a stockbroker, constantly getting in trouble due to drinking, losing job after job and getting bailed out time and again by family and friends. But, he said, there came a day when he had gotten into trouble, and there was nobody left to help him. He knew they still loved him, but he had broken too many promises.

Then he ended up living in the woods, where his life consisted of scrounging up enough money every day to buy a few little plastic bottles of vodka, and drinking himself into a blackout. He only got help when he passed out one night during a cold snap, and for some reason had taken his shoes off. He woke up with frostbite and hobbled to the emergency room, where, after his foot was amputated, a social worker had gotten him into the same detox I had gone to. That's where he found the twelve-step meetings, and he'd been going ever since.

"Andrew," he said. "You drink just like me from what you've said. You're a good guy and have a lot of things going for you now. I can guarantee you that if you go celebrate your accomplishments with vodka, you'll lose it all. I guarantee it. I *promise* you."

"You take that drink," he said, "and within a few weeks or months you'll be calling your parents up to pick you up and give you a place to stay, and they'll say 'no.' You'll call all those friends who already let you crash at their place 'temporality ...' how many times? And they'll say, 'sorry, can't this time.' Then you'll be back to sleeping under a statue. Don't do it, Andrew."

I was kind of annoyed with him speaking to me this way. After all, that wasn't how one man talked to another man in Catholic, blue-collar, New England. However, in a way, he spoke a language I understood. It was a new language, and I barely understood it, but it was starting to make sense.

I would hold off on drinking for now. I went about my life, work, school, and meetings. Every evening I would pick Paul up and we would go to a meeting together. I would help him and his half-missing foot into my "new" old car. Every time I saw his foot, I felt a sting go through me, like a warning.

I went home to my place after work one day and there was a message from Paul that he didn't need a ride to the meeting that night. So, I went to the meeting myself. I didn't see him around for the next few days, so I figured I would check on him. I would sometimes pick him up for meetings at his mother's so I had her phone number. I called his mom. She answered and sounded tired.

"Hi, this is Andrew," I said. "The guy who has been picking Paul up for meetings."

"Hello, Andrew," she said, in a whispery voice.

"I haven't seen him around and was just wondering if you knew where I could get a hold of him, or if you could pass along a message for him to call me."

There was a long pause on the phone.

"Paul didn't make it through the weekend," she said. I heard a whimper and she hung up.

What did *that* mean? Not make it through the weekend? I called another of our twelve-step acquaintances, a guy who seemed to have been around a long time.

"Hey, it's Andrew. I'm the new guy that has been giving Paul rides to meetings. I just talked to his mother and she said he didn't make it through the weekend ..."

"Paul is dead," said the man.

The result of alcohol. Paul had gone out on a bender, nobody knew why, and was found dead in his bed. Just like that. His body finally gave out.

For the first time in my life, it occurred to me that maybe I wasn't different. Paul and I were exactly alike in our drinking and our thinking. Maybe I did have this thing, alcoholism. Maybe it couldn't be fixed by toast and ginger ale and cracking the window. Maybe it couldn't be fixed by taking gorilla biscuits, or moon bars, or half-eye pills, or smoking crack, or sniffing yea-yo, or lysergic acid diethylamide ... or another drink.

A service was held and I saw his mom. We looked at each other. She touched my face with both hands.

"Don't let it happen to you," she said. "If you drink even one more time, you could die, Andrew. You know it in your heart, I can see. Just promise me, don't let it happen to you."

THE REST OF MY LIFE

I didn't feel like being alone, so I drove to Crystal Hill for a traditional Catholic meal of boiled potatoes, soup and brown bread from a can. My father tried to be sympathetic, in his own way.

"I'se seen a thousand guys go like that," he said. "In our neck of the woods, dying by drink is more common than getting' the flu. Remember's 'dat."

I chewed my potatoes listlessly. I watched my mother chew hers, with even less enthusiasm than me. I could tell that she was mentally wringing her hands.

"So, Joe," my father said.

I braced myself for the inevitable annoying anecdote.

"Eye'z heard construction is picking up," he said. "if ya'z can pass your test, 'ya number at the apprenticeship hall should be moving up. You'se'll be working soon."

I almost couldn't believe my ears. I didn't mind the floor waxing job, but it was getting boring, and I had been wracking my brain trying to decide what was next for me – seek fame and fortune in California or try and complete my apprenticeship and become a journeyman electrician. Now, something about being an electrician felt right; it was in my bones. Only, I didn't know if it would put me forever in my father's shadow, or actually take me out of it, in his eyes.

"You'se will still be an apprentice, and will still be called 'kid,' but yah no longer a green horn or a cub. You won't be schlepping coffee for the work crews, or humping tools and materials for the journeymen. You'se will be trusted to do more work."

Hmmmm.

"You'se an' me are gonna starts getting' togedder like we did with the drivers test," he said. "And we's'll meet every Sunday after mass. I's'll learn you about electricity, A to Z. What 'ya really need 'ta know."

I finished chewing my potatoes, now with a little more enthusiasm. I thanked my father and kissed my mother on the forehead and drove home.

Indeed, my number came up, and I went to work. I had some anxiety, but with rigorous exercise it subsided, even without the sauce running through my veins. I stayed on course and focused on becoming a journeyman electrician. I had difficulties in school and it was after work so my body and mind wanted to collapse. But Sundays with my dad studying after brunch, with his stories and drawings, made the study of electricity a little easier. It seemed he always had a good way to explain the topics so that I could actually understand (unlike the books, which only brought on the blue-assed fly syndrome) whether the topics be it motors, transformers, or Eddy Currents.

"'Doze was named aftah me," he said, finding himself hilarious.

I was amazed at his love for and knowledge of the electrical industry. He was able to not only explain things verbally, but he could draw it all out as well, which is what I really needed to fully grasp things. I finally made it through school and passed the state electrical exam on my first try. Those weeks were nothing but work, school and twelve-step meetings, and my head was reeling. I thought about cutting back on the meetings to free up my time, but in my heart, I knew it as the meetings and the influence of "the program" that was getting me through it all.

It seemed my father and I had been apart for many years, but now there was a bond again that emerged on those Sunday meetings of studying electricity and all its works. It was one of the gifts of sobriety. Thanks to those Sunday meetings with my old man (and my own blue-assed diligence) I was now a journeyman electrician. The third generation of Winslow to attain the title.

Following his advice, I showed up early at the hall every day and within a couple weeks, I got a call and had my first assignment – working as a fill-in at South Station, the commuter train hub. It was eerily similar to the MBTA, the place my father had worked for going on 30 years.

That seemed fitting ... and ominous ... and interesting. I definitely did not want to be an Amtrak or MBTA electrician for the rest of my life. But the thing about being a journeyman is, you can go to any electrician's union hall in the country, put your name on the list and, based on seniority, you'll pull a job sooner or later – depending on the size of the hall and the local economy. All I needed to do was finish this first assignment, get some hours logged as a licensed electrician, and then I could figure out what and where I wanted to be.

It was a good thing this happened when it did because I had been facing what was to become the third major demon in my life – boredom. The first was, obviously, anxiety. That inevitably lead to the second: booze (or drugs). Now that I was no longer drinking, I had less anxiety, but it wasn't gone altogether. I was just learning that, when anxiety hit, or even better, before it hit, I needed to stay busy. And even though I was starting to get the hang of this sobriety thing, and was appreciating more and more the benefits of not being a drunken slob, but it did come with a lot of boredom.

I realized that boredom and anxiety go hand-in-hand. I couldn't stand doing nothing, because it caused my ears to ring with, "Get the lead out!" I was glad for the work ethic my father had instilled in me, but it was like a ghost that never let me rest. I would get bored, and it would immediately turn into anxiety, which always lead to booze. Now that I wasn't drinking, I was bored a lot more.

My first day on the South Station job was about what I expected ... getting called "kid" a lot and pulling all the menial tasks. I looked at the crews I was working around, and it occurred to me that every electrical job I'd ever been on basically had the exact same cast of characters, just with different names. There were always the gruff old-timers from the 1950s and 1960s, all business; they had the world figured out in their own minds and weren't interested in anything changing. They grumbled about life but had reckoned out a way to live it, and that was good enough for them.

Then there were the Viet Nam-era guys, from the 1970s. They were just as cynical as the older fellows, in their own ways, but their minds didn't seem as tight. It was like they knew they had escaped something terrible and were at least glad to be living free. Lastly, there were the "kids" like me ... the children of the 1970s. For some reason, we all seemed to lack that certainty about life these other cats had; we all seemed to float around with an air of unsureness and ... anxiety.

One thing every group shared was a love of the sauce. The first few days on the job, the guys all went their own ways after work, without inviting me. Friday, at the end of my first week, I was finally let into "the club." I knew it would happen eventually, but I was still dreading it. That day, everybody kicked me around from dawn till dusk; nothing I did was right, and I was sick of being called "Junior Journeyman," a name given to those that just received their license. What made it worse was, I was bored and, as I thought about the night and weekend ahead, I was drawing a blank. I could only go to so many twelve-step meetings to fill up my time. I was deathly afraid of just sitting around my apartment by myself, though.

"Hey, kid, you made it through 'ya first week ... I guess Murph wins the bet, none of the rest of us thought's you'd cut it," said Fitzie, the dean of the 1950s guys.

I assumed they were kidding about the bet, when they all started passing bills around. One of them handed Murph a wad of cash. He smiled at me.

"Hey, kid, drinks are on me," said Murph. "I figure I should cut you'se in on my winnings."

I didn't really want to drink, but I couldn't exactly turn down the invitation. Directions were given and we all met at a place called The Grog Shop frequented by fisherman, lobsterman, and tradesmen. My mind was spinning, trying to come up with a plan. Should I find a payphone and call somebody from my twelve-step program? Should I just duck out the back? Pretend to have a seizure? We took our seats and without even ordering, the waitress brought over two pitchers of beer and glasses. Sully started to pour, and the filled glasses were being passed around.

I looked around the room and saw everybody having fun. Laughing. Joking. Slapping one another on the back. Smiling. They seemed at ease. I was *not* at ease, and I wanted to be. Didn't I deserve a drink? How bad could it really be? I wouldn't even have to tell anybody from my twelve-step program. I could just have a couple beers and then never have another, and nobody would know.

Once I had mentally decided to have "just a couple," I noticed the bottles on the back of the bar. There she was – lady Vodka. Well, heck, if I was going to drink, I might as well drink what I liked. My feet were going a million miles an hour under the table. Murph slid a beer my way and looked at me. Then, it was as if some other person inside of me took over my body, and I was just passively listening and watching.

"Eh, thanks, Murph. Thanks, guys for inviting me here," I said.

They all stared at me.

"But, uh, I'm not a drinker…"

Their stares grew colder.

"I mean, I am a drinker," I stammered. "But I don't drink anymore. I love the sauce, but my doctor said it wasn't good for me."

I waited for the inevitable, merciless ribbing. I was just about to wince.

"Good, kid," said Murph. "You'se faddah told us you'se was on the wagon. We'se was just testing ya to see what kind of guy you'se was."

"Yeah," said Fitzie. "No shame in not drinking. I watched me faddah go down the tubes with drink. My favorite uncle and middle boy are both on the wagon. It takes real stones to do 'dat."

I was actually stunned. Speechless. The waitress walked over and handed me a Coca-Cola. With a tiny umbrella in it.

THE CLUB

I told this story at my next twelve-step meeting and it gave me a lot of enthusiasm. That was the first "magic" type thing that had ever happened to me ... the first time I felt God's presence ... when I wasn't high or drunk. It gave me some added motivation to keep up with the meetings, which was good, because I had been getting awful bored. The people were great, some of the meetings were fun, and we usually went out for coffee or food after, but ... after a while it just became so routine. It seemed like I heard the same stories over and over and over and over.

My third week on the South Station job was especially mind-numbing. My work days were so tedious, in fact, that after work I just couldn't bring myself to go out to a dry-as-toast recovery meeting to complete my dull day. I watched television, which was also uninteresting. I noticed that as I would try to fall asleep at night, some little voice in there started whispering that some nips of vodka would help me sleep, and maybe make this boredom more tolerable. I knew the voice was just trying to ruin my life, that it wasn't really "me." People at meetings talked about how "their disease" lived inside them, how it wasn't really them; it was always trying to kill them and would never go away. Saturday morning I was laying on my couch, swimming in nothingness, when my phone rang.

"Hey, you'se ain't been to the meetings 'dis week, just wondering if you'se are okay?"

It was Mickey, a guy maybe 10 years older than me, also an electrician. He had kind of gone out of his way to look after me at meetings.

"Eh, I'm okay," I said. "I'm just tired."

I was going to tell him some bullshit story about having had a busy week when he cut in.

"You'se ah bored, ain't ya?" he asked.

My ears pricked up.

"I'se know the feeling," he said. "You'se are at 'dat place."

"No, I'm not at the bar!" I protested.

"Not 'dat place," said Mickey. "You'se are at 'dat in-between place, and there's a reason, and there's a solution."

I was listening.

"You been doing good, going to the meetings, getting to know the guys, helping make coffee and clean ashtrays … that's all good," he said. "But now you'se are at that point where you gotta start working the program … you know, the steps."

Honestly, I had heard about these "steps" at the meetings and wasn't too interested. They were listed on a big poster on the wall at every meeting, and usually, one especially annoying man or woman would spout off like some new age guru about "the steps." They looked like religious mumbo jumbo to me. I was just going to the meetings to stay sober. I was Catholic, after all, saved.

"Hey, I'm Catholic, too," said Mickey, as if reading my mind. "That's all good and well, but if being Catholic was enough, we wouldn't have gotten in trouble with our drinking, now would we?"

Hmmm. He had me there.

"Just quit skipping meetings, okay?" he asked. "Just start going back to all you'se regular meetings. We's'll go out for coffee anyways after, like normal. I'll bring the book and take you through the steps. You'se ain't really a member of the club until you do the steps … and in my experience, guys that just hang around, almost always get drunk sooner or later."

Well, I was bored with being bored, so what the hell?

It really wasn't as bad as I thought it would be. Mickey didn't try to get me to do any secret handshakes or take any solemn oaths. Each night, for two weeks straight, he and I met at my usual meeting, and afterwards went out to the local greasy spoon. The waitress knew him and always gave us the booth in the far corner of the back room, where nobody else was within earshot. Each night, he had me read the chapter from the book on a step, starting with Step One. After I read it, he asked me if I had any questions, had any issues with any of it, if there was anything it was asking me to do that seemed disagreeable or violated my principles. Then he said, "Okay, so do it."

Each step was basically a principle of living, and all "taking the step" involved was saying a specific prayer with sincerity, or making a commitment to myself and God to do a certain thing. Like, Step One just asked me to "admit" that I was powerless over alcohol, and that my life had become unmanageable. That was an easy ask. Step Two just asked me to "believe" that a power greater than myself could restore me to sanity. That was an easy ask, too. I knew I was a certified nutjob and my best solution so far in life for dealing with my anxiety was hulla-booming and riding the A-Train, which had landed me in a loony bin.

The toughest step for me was Step Nine, which involved "making amends" to all the people I had harmed in my life. I was actually kind of crushed when we read that one, because it felt impossible. But then Mickey explained that I just had to be *willing* to do it, and I just had to do my best, and that I didn't have to do it all at once. I just had to start. Okay, I could do that. I started with me Ma and Pa the next day.

After the two weeks, I had gone through and taken – or started – every step. The last one just asked that I try to help other people with their drinking problems, now that I had found my own way out. I didn't know how I felt about that, but Mickey explained that I just had to be willing to do it. I couldn't stay sober by just going to meetings, or just worrying about myself.

"From here on out, kid, you gotta get outta yourself. You'll like it," he said. "I bet if you try, you's'll find that you ain't hardly never bored." Damned if he wasn't right.

THE ITCH

I had gotten into a good routine with the South Station job. It wasn't the most fun thing in the world, but as my father said, "If it was fun, they wouldn't call it work."

The twelve-step stuff was going good, and I actually looked forward to going to meetings now. I was no longer focused on whether or not I would hear the same boring stories or see the same boring people. Because now, when I went, I was looking for the new guy, the guy I could help. Mickey said all I had to do was just be friendly.

Still and all, I was starting to get that itch. I started to notice the pretty girls as much as the new guys. I was terrified of dating, always was, but I was a young man, and nature seemed to be pawing at me. I talked about it with Mickey.

"Yeah, well, standard rule is, you 'prolly shouldn't date or get involved with broads until you been sober a year. And You been sober, what? 6 months? In your case, you might wanna wait three years!"

He was correct.

"Still and all," he said. "It's not really a rule so much as a guideline. I mean, I wouldn't recommend it. But the main thing is, don't get involved in anything too intense, and leave the girls around the meetings alone. But, hey, if you'se meets a nice broad out there in the real world, and you'se wanta take her outs to dinner, that's just normal. Do it, just don't go crazy.

I seen it a million times. Broads is maybe the number one reason for guys getting back on the sauce, but it's usually the guys who ain't woyk'd the program ... and you'se is woykin' the program."

I filed that wise advice away and carried on with my routine. I was becoming aware that it was good to have routines, but that they could quickly turn into boredom. I was still edgy about the whole, "between the margins," thing. But I was seeing that there was a middle place. During my entire childhood and teenage years, I had been mortified by this idea I had of becoming a Sheeple. Doing the same thing every day until I died. But I started to see that this was an unrealistic picture of being an adult ... it was an "extreme." Just like my antidote to it had always been, being a wild man, stumbling through the woods on acid, or climbing a bonfire while in a blackout. Sure, living like that made me feel like I wasn't a Sheeple, but was it any better, really? It was an "extreme," too.

Now I was seeing that I could have healthy routines that kept me on track, and that both the Sheeple and the Wild Man were themselves the margins that I had wanted to avoid my whole life... I just had to stay between those, and not get too close to either.

Time went on, as it tends to do, and as I approached my one-year anniversary of sobriety, I began thinking about what to do next. Every chance I got, I chatted up the guys from the union who were in town as journeymen. I grilled them about where the jobs were, what the different cities were like, which union halls liked to work with journeymen, and which guarded their local jobs like a lonely cat lady guards her pint of ice cream. I still went out with the crew on Fridays, and the waitress always brought me my Coca-Cola. I asked Mickey if this was weird, but he explained to me that as a sober man who had done the steps, I didn't need to be afraid of being around alcohol, as long as I had a reason to be there, and wasn't just tempting fate or trying to get a contact high. Fair enough.

But I knew deep down that I had no real business to justify frequenting a dive bar. So after that next Friday, it would be goodbye to the Grog Shop and its clientele of lobstermen and fisherman in their rubber boots and tradesmen with gnarled hands and worn looks.

Walking back to my car from my last appearance at the Grog Shop that Friday, I spotted a very attractive Asian lady walking my way. She looked familiar. Was it Jinghua? As the wheels were turning, she said, "Andrew?!"

It was Jinghua's sister. We stood there chatting and I told her about all that I'd been through.

"That sounds great, Andrew. I'm really happy for you," she said. "I know Jinghua will be happy to hear it."

"Yeah, uh, well," I said. "Actually, I need to talk to her, if you can put us in touch."

"Well, she'll be happy to hear you're doing well, but I don't know that she wants to actually see you. You hurt her pretty bad."

"Yeah, that's the thing," I said. "Really, I just want to apologize to her in person. That's all."

Her sister seemed impressed and said she would give Jinghua my number. Mickey had told me that when it came to apologizing to people, some of them might not be in the forgiving spirit, and some might refuse to see me, but that all I could do was give it my best effort. So, I wasn't holding my breath with Jinghua.

To my surprise, when I got home later that evening, the red light on my answering machine was blinking, and there was a message on there from Jinghua. She said she'd be happy to see me, and gave a date, time and address ... the next day, Saturday, at some place on Route 1 in Walpole. She didn't give the name, just the address.

I was nervous all day on Saturday and rehearsed over and over in my mind what I was going to say. I had been told to just keep it simple, state what I had done that hurt the person, say I was sorry, and ask if there was anything I could do to "make amends." I hit two meetings that day, went home and cleaned myself up, and got in the car to drive over to Walpole. I wondered if there was some new restaurant there that Jinghua wanted to try. As I drove down the appointed street, scanning the building numbers, it hit me. We were meeting at the Kahana, the place with the bar and the fish tanks. Oh boy.

I walked in, and there she was, sitting at my old booth. Right behind her was the bar, and the bottles of vodka seemed to be laughing at me. I sat down in the seat across from her, and she just looked at me. I looked at the fish. The waitress walked by us with a huge tray full of happy umbrella drinks and passed them out to the patrons. They all looked joyful. I scanned the room, and every single person in there was drinking, buzzed, and seemed to be loving life. And here I was, tight as a drum. My feet swung furiously.

"So," she said. "My sister says you finally got your act together? You look ... good."

Her face softened. I looked at her and exhaled. She started telling me about what she'd been up to. She had finished her business degree and was now managing one of her family's Chinese restaurants. My head was swimming with the fish. Maybe I could excuse myself, go to the bathroom, and grab a couple quick shots of vodka on the way. That would only make sense. After all, I was here to apologize for being a drunken idiot. I was doing something for the program. Surely that got me some sort of "drinking credit" I could cash in. It was all for a good cause, right?

"So, what do you have to say for yourself?" she asked.

Once again, some voice inside of me took over, and I seemed to be merely a spectator.

"Jinghua, listen. Thanks for meeting with me. I just want to apologize for how I treated you. Missing our weekend getaway because I was drinking and doing coke at Simma's. Showing up the next day drunk and bleeding, embarrassing you in front of your family. I'm truly sorry. I've learned that I'm one of those people who can't drink. I got help, like you suggested. It's been almost a year without a drink. Is there anything I can do to make things right? Would you like me to apologize to your parents?"

I was kind of stunned by what I just heard myself say. All of a sudden, the notion of taking a couple of shots of vodka seemed utterly absurd. My legs were no longer shaking.

"That's sweet of you, Andrew," she said. "It means a lot to me. No, you don't need to apologize to my parents. It took a lot of courage to apologize to me. It's funny," she said. "My cousin is in recovery and he told me that after a year you can start dating again … so, are you dating anybody?"

Now her gaze was much softer, and her hand crept across the table and rested on mine.

"Eh, yeah, that's correct," I said. Her gaze hardened.

"I mean, about the one-year thing," I said. "No, I haven't dated anybody."

"Well, when is your one-year anniversary?" she asked.

"Actually, it's next week."

"Well, why don't we celebrate it with a … date?" she squeezed my hand.

"Just think about it," she said. "I don't want to put any pressure on you. Tell you what. I'll be here, in this same booth, the same time next week. If you want to try another date with me as sober Andrew, just show up. If not, no hard feelings."

Fair enough, I thought. We ate our appetizer sampler platter, chit chatted about the electrical business and the restaurant business and went our separate ways.

As the week wore on, I grew more and more nervous about seeing Jinghua. Was it the right thing to do? Was she seeing me out of sympathy? Was I setting myself up? Could I even date without drinking? It was kind of terrifying. I still just didn't feel "good enough" for a person like Jinghua. But, who was I to tell her who was good enough for her? I hit a few extra meetings that week, screwed up my courage, and walked into the Kahana the next Saturday at the appointed time. There was Jinghua, looking stunning. I went to sit down across from her in our booth, but she grabbed my hand and it pulled over next to her.

Funny thing, sitting there on her side of the booth, I didn't have to look at the bar. And I didn't notice the waitress bringing drinks. I did notice a couple a few tables away, and the broad didn't look too happy. I glanced at the guy she was with, and he was swilling a big glass of booze. Jinghua and I talked about nothing and everything. And it was me talking, not the voice in my head. After we had finished our appetizers and meal, she turned to me.

"I like sober Andrew," she said. "I want to see more of sober Andrew. Does sober Andrew want to see more of me?"

"Well, yeah," I said.

"Good," she continued, leaning in to kiss me. "Let's just take it slow and keep doing this. It's fun."

GHOSTS

We'd been dating a couple of months when I told Jinghua about my plan to travel around a bit as a journeyman electrician. She didn't seem upset, like I thought she might be. She said she was happy with her job in Boston and wasn't going anywhere. She was happy with me, but she wasn't looking to get married or anything. She just enjoyed my company. It was funny ... every time I had ever had a crush on a woman, for my entire life, I always skipped right to the end, us married with kids.

But now, I kind of felt the same way Jinghua did. I didn't care about the future that far off, I was just enjoying her company. I seemed to have this weird balance in my life. Staying sober was #1 ... building my electrical career and seeing the world was #2 ... and enjoying life would come as a result of doing those two things, so it had to come #3. And I was fine with that.

I had done my research and decided that Nashville, Tennessee, would be the first place I went to try life as a real "journeyman" electrician. Things were booming there, I had a few contacts from guys on the job site, and they told me that if they called ahead for me to the union hall business agent, I'd have work waiting for me when I got there. I even had numbers to call for places to stay while I got set up. One of the guys was in "the program" and gave me a schedule of the "good" meetings to hit when I got there. I put my plans in place and was looking forward to telling Jinghua about it.

I was just adjusting the hair gel on my dome, getting ready to drive over to Kahana to see her, when my phone rang.

"Hi Andrew, it's Jinghua."

"Hey gorgeous, you ready for some dinnah?" I asked.

"Uh. Look, Andrew. It's been fun. I'm glad you're sober and doing well. But I don't want to see you anymore. It's nothing personal. It's just that you seem to be focused on life outside of Boston, and I know this is where I'll live the rest of my life. Be well, Andrew. I'll always hope the best for you."

Click.

I tried calling her back, but the phone was off the hook. Well, what the heck? Here I was, doing everything right, everything I was being asked to do, not freaking out or anything, and now this. Why? I thought if I "did the right thing," then everything would go my way? Well, I was all dressed up and hungry. Should I go to a meeting? That would be the sensible thing to do, I thought. But, nah. I was going to go out to dinner, and mentally say my goodbyes to Jinghua.

I walked into the Kahana and was taken to my usual seat, in "our" booth. I thought about sitting on Jinghua's side, so I didn't have to look at the bar, but something in me said, "Fuck it," and I took my side. Immediately, the bottles of vodka started staring at me.

"Get you a drink?" a new waitress asked me.

Just as I was considering this, my normal waitress walked up and said, "I got this, hun, he's my regular."

She took my order for the appetizer sampler platter and a Coca-Cola, and I stared at the fish. I felt dead inside. My feet began to twitch. I was scared about moving to Tennessee, even though it was what I wanted to do. My food and beverage came, and I attacked it like a crow on a road pizza. Just as I was finishing, the new waitress walked over and placed a large vodka and tonic right in front of me. I immediately smelled it, and it smelled good.

Maybe this was fate? Maybe this was God giving me a free pass? I could take this one drink and be on my way. My arm stirred. My hand moved toward the glass.

"I'se told you, stay outta my section!" the usual waitress yelled at the new one. She grabbed the drink out from in front of me. "This is for table eight, you ditz," she said as she handed it to her co-worker.

I dropped a $20 bill on the table and left as fast as I could.

What now? Maybe I would grab some pizza and go home and watch a movie? I knew I should probably have gone to a meeting, but I just felt like being alone and ... pounding pizza. I snaked through the streets as it grew dark and made my way to the convenient store for a few slices of counter-top pie. As I pulled up, I noticed a familiar car.

It was Simma's. He had become something of a legend in the local building trades. He was only a couple years into his work, but he was already known as the finest framing carpenter around. He did beautiful work and could perform the output of three guys, only better. But he was also known as a very hard partier. He missed a lot of work and had been arrested several times on minor beefs. But his reputation as a carpenter was so good that people let him slide. I pulled into a parking spot and was considering backing right out again to avoid Simma when I heard a knock on the passenger window.

"Winslow!"

I rolled my eyes, put it in park, and hit the button to unlock his door. He slid in with an evil grin. He was holding several bottles of tonic water. He looked thin.

"Long time, Winslow," he said. "I hear you went soft on us ..."

Simma was one of my oldest friends. We'd been through the trenches together, from the time we were little kids. Mickey had warned me about hanging around with the old crew.

"When you go to a place that serves booze for a legitimate reason, that's one thing," he said. "But old drinking buddies, unless you'se seeing them for work, that's asking for trouble."

So, I had kept an extremely low profile in the old neighborhood for the last year. The old crowd was all busy doing their own thing, anyway, mostly getting drunk, sleeping in their mother's basements, and getting arrested.

"Having a blizzard tonight in the historic homestead," he said. "Why not come by for old time's sake? I just finished a big job on a mansion for some yuppie scumbag and made a mint on it. It'll be on me, my treat ... plus we got a freezer full of Stoli."

What the fuck, I thought. It seemed like lady vodka was actually chasing me. First the restaurant, now this. But, what if I just did a few lines of coke? That would be okay, surely. It would pep me up and take my mind off Jinghua. It would give me some enthusiasm for my trip to Tennessee. Plus, I could still go to my twelve-step meetings and say that I "hadn't had a drink." And, technically, it would be true. Fuck it. Fine.

I told Simma I would follow him back to his place. He flashed me an evil grin, got in his car and burned rubber out of the parking lot. I followed him, block by block, turn by turn, into the old neighborhood. We approached his house and all of a sudden I remembered the last blizzard ... that was the time I was supposed to take Jinghua away for a romantic weekend, and what did I do instead? Spent the weekend talking nonsense to cheesy car salesmen, ended up in a blackout, looking up from the cement floor of a train station.

He beeped his horn as he pulled into his driveway. I beeped my horn and hit the gas. I pulled off Route 109, onto Mill Street, and beeped as I went by Crystal Hill and kept driving. It seemed like some other person took over. I just drove around for what seemed like hours, not paying attention to where I was going. It was like I was in a trance. For a brief moment, some voice surfaced in me and whispered to go to a meeting, or stop at a pay phone and call Mickey, or to just go home and go to sleep. But that voice faded away. I felt absent from myself, like I was just watching myself from above, distant, cold.

RESPECT IT

My mind became a blur of a thousand thoughts, all chattering and babbling at me at once. It got louder and louder and I sort of faded into myself to get away from it. Finally, the voices stopped. Where was I? Oh, my … I was walking out of the packy with a brown bag in my hand. It was a half-gallon of vodka, in a plastic bottle. I was headed toward Boston Commons.

Fuck it, I thought. After a night like this, why NOT drink? I did everything I was supposed to, and my girl left me, some new phantom waitress tried to serve me vodka, Simma came out of nowhere and pushed coke on me. It felt like no matter what I did, it was after me. So, fuck it. I walked toward my old statue. I was defeated. If working this hard at being sober only got me lonely and in a constant struggle against the drink, then I might as well drink. Because, at that rate, it was only a matter of time.

I was looking forward to just sitting at the base of my old statue, swilling lady vodka until the sun came up, watching the shift change from night people to office Sheeple. I didn't even care about Tennessee, or Jinghua, or Mickey, or anything. I just wanted it to go away. All of it. And I knew the clear sting of a few hulla-booms would do it. I approached my statue and saw a figure slumped over. I sat down next to him and pulled the bottle out of the bag.

"You look mighty clean cut to be sitting here this time of night with a plastic half gallon of vodka," he said.

"Yeah, well, I've been on the wagon for a year – but it doesn't seem to be working out."

"On the wagon, huh?" he asked. He looked like Alice Cooper, if Alice Cooper had been living rough in an alley with a pack of stray cats for ten years. And, he smelled.

"I'se was on the wagon once," he said. "For ten years, as a matter of fact. Was a journeyman electrician. Had a great life. Traveled everywhere. Made good money. Had a wife and kids. But I stopped going to meetings, stopped trying to help people, and eventually, the bottle chased me down. Now I been drinking again for two years and it looks like … this is it."

I stared at him. Was he real? Or was I being chased by ghosts on this day? The ghost of Jinghua. The ghost of Simma. The ghost of vodka. The ghost of my father. I set my bottle down.

"Let me tell's ya something, kid," he said. "If you'se haven't actually taken a drink yet – and it looks like you'se ain't – 'den, don't friggin' do it."

I looked at him. My heart started to pound, and something in me started to soften.

"I'se'll share a secret with you. An electrician secret. Dat 'dere booze is just like life. If you don't take it seriously, it will kill you. But here's something my old man told me about electricity… and he was an electrician, too. He said, 'Don't be scared of it, just respect it.' That means, don't play footsie with it. Don't ignore it. Treat it like a live wire. Take it from me. Just walk away from 'dat bottle. Go home. Go to a meeting. Call you'se sponsah. Just get outta here. You'se'll thank me. Go on, get!"

I trotted back to my car. I drove home. I was kind of dazed. I went to unlock my door, and my key broke off in the keyhole. Could this night get any worse? I walked back to my car. There, sitting on the dash, was a pair of blue handled electrician pliers, the ones my father had given me.

"You'se sixth fingah," he had said.

I grabbed them and walked back to the door. I used the pliers to grab the broken key, still in the lock. I gently held the doorknob and twisted. The door opened.

I walked to my bed, took off my shoes and laid down. I grabbed the phone and called Mickey. His machine picked up.

"Yeah, uh Mickey, it's Andrew. Had a rough night, but I'm okay – still sober. Look, let's meet tomorrow morning at the usual place. I'll be there."

I hung up and pulled my sheets over me. I stared at the plaster ceiling. There, in the shapes, was my grandfather, puking green bile. In another shape, was my grandmother, reaching out to me with both hands. I could hear her saying, "Hello, pumpkin!"

I knew exactly where I was, and where I was headed. I was sober. I was an electrician. I took a deep breath, and the soft black curtain of sober slumber fell over me.

Afterword

This book is what Felix "Fookin" Finch, the literary critic in David Mitchell's *Cloud Atlas*, would call a "bloated autobio novel." It is largely based on my own life and the lives of the people I grew up around. However, I have changed some names and streamlined some events for the purposes of telling this story. After getting through those rough days described at the end of the book, and realizing I was supposed to be sober and an electrician, I began a long and rewarding, though challenging, career that has taken me all over the world.

My most recent work has had me in war zones throughout the Middle East. I returned from Afghanistan in 2015 after working there for four straight years. It was winter and Massachusetts was about to get hit with another record snowfall; the perfect time to skate. The weather was cold enough to freeze ice but there was no snow yet. I arose early and went to my favorite childhood place, Hale Reservation. The gate was closed, so I walked the long path down to the pond. The leaves had fallen, but it was still nice to see so many trees again. Afghanistan was like a moonscape, the earth there was powdery. I was carrying for the first time in my life hockey skates that were mine, brand new and sharpened.

I looked at the empty parking lot at Hale and got a flashback to the 1970's while remembering all the colorful American-made cars that used to fill the lot. In a wave, the sounds of the 1970's, the smells of the food and the images of women with their beehive hairstyles flashed through my mind. I walked down the path to the beach itself. This was the same path I once saw my father walk down with a bag of Kentucky Fried Chicken. I found a picnic table and laced up my skates.

It had been many years since I skated, so I was a bit wobbly. It didn't take long to get back into the groove, though, and I started skating in massive circles. I felt free. The cool New England air was blowing against my face. I would have given almost anything to feel that cold breeze over in Afghanistan. I looked to the woods as I circled, and in a whiff, the sights and sounds of the 1970's left me. I wondered if I would hear the dreaded rocket alarm that I heard in Afghanistan every other day.

"Incoming, incoming, incoming!"

I realized that I was totally exposed out on the pond, and I needed to take cover immediately. Fear of a rocket landing and shards of ice slamming into my body made me skate as fast as I could to a secluded edge of the pond. I looked around and waited to hear the thud of a rocket landing, but nothing happened. It took me a few minutes to realize I wasn't in Afghanistan, and I wasn't in the early 1970's either. I was in my mid 40's trying to enjoy a morning skate. It took some time to come back and and realize where I was. I gingerly resumed skating in massive circles, nervously looking around with each pass. "I am at Hale Reservation in Westwood Massachusetts," I told myself.

Then came the bad memories. Memories of those I hurt, those that ended up "gone." And some good memories … of the births of my two sons and the adoption of a two-year-old. All the ups and downs of life swirled through my mind.

"Life on life's terms," as they would say in "the program." I counted my blessings and reminded myself to live life just one hour, even one moment, at a time. I had witnessed people in a military hospital, people who would never walk again, people who were blinded, or missing a limb. I thought of all my fellow military contractors that had perished or were maimed in Afghanistan. They never got in the news, but there were so many from the building and construction trades that risked their lives doing support work for the military. I took a deep breath. I had my faith, I was sober, and I had all the tools of the Twelve-Step program.

I am writing this from Saudi Arabia, going on 30 years in the electrical construction industry. Close to 15 years of that has been as a journeyman, constantly "hitting the road," performing electrical work in a different city, town, or country every few months. I've been sober for over 26 years. No matter where I am, if I cannot find a Twelve Sep meeting or a church nearby, there is always someone less fortunate that I can help.

I wrote this book with mixed feelings. I confess to being a non-denominational Christian. Many times, while writing this, I was sure that the stories recounted here would get me thrown out of church services and bake sales. I worry that the contents of this book may even embolden those that hate the mention of God. It's not popular to be a Christian in today's world. But how could I not be attracted to Christ? He turned water into wine. He was a carpenter. He had a temper. He hated hypocrisy. Now there is a guy that an alky electrician can relate to.

I wrote the book specifically for those in the trades and those who grew up in the 1970s like me. We remember a time when people didn't lock their doors; when people helped their elderly neighbors by shoveling their driveway after a snowstorm. I wrote this book for the man or woman shaking on the edge of their bed or chair, for those at extreme heights, looking down, frightened; for those ready to end it all, thinking there is no hope. I know the hourly and daily struggles the working man and woman endure just trying to make ends meet. I know about being violently ill from the use and abuse of drugs and alcohol.

But, I also know there is hope. You may not feel it now, but just reach out and mutter any prayer you can think of for the obsession or pain to be removed. It works. We live in a time where the world can appear to grow more evil every day. I have to constantly remind myself that there is still goodness in the world, that all is not lost. There are those that are willing to lend a helping hand.

I have been blessed to see several generations of men and women come and go. Strong men and women, men and women that endured wars, the Great Depression, illnesses. Men and women who went through it with dignity, and maybe a few stiff drinks, but still got through life's hardships. There was no self-help program for those people, but they had their religious beliefs, and faith, and families and friends, and they got through it. Those generations offer us the power of their example. It has been a blessing to work with the true craftsmen of my father's generation, men who took pride in their trade. Their concern was quality, not quantity. They taught me well.

I have plenty of good days and plenty of learning days. I'm divorced. I live out of a suitcase. I work in the desert in Saudi Arabia. I possess a few sets of Dickies, a pair of Red Wing boots, a couple dressy outfits, and luggage with wheels.

I have carried with me tremendous guilt for many of the things I did while drinking. And for many things I did in elementary school before I ever took a drink. I'm truly sorry to those that I hurt, but fortunately, I have been able to make amends to most of them.

I count my blessings and am grateful that I don't get what I deserve. If my story can help just one person suffering from the insanity of alcoholism, then this book is a success. You are not alone.

- Andy Winslow
August, 2018

Me and my work crew in our "safe space" in Afghanistan.

Skaing at Hale Reservation in Westwood.

Thanks to the gift of sobriety, my employer even trusts me with a company car.

*Red Wing boots and a suitcase with wheels:
the journeyman electrician's traveling kit.*

A rare day off on the beach in Dubai.

With some friends in the Phillipines.

From the Collaborator

I've known Andy Winslow for a long time. What struck me when I first read his rough manuscript was how similar our childhoods had been, even though I grew up outside Detroit and he grew up outside Boston. *Mutual of Omaha's Wild Kingdom*, the *Wonderful World of Disney*, horrific crashes on BMX bikes, chores, paper routes, omnipresent religions. We came of age during the tail-end of Viet Nam. We were living and breathing during an era when the Depression and World War II were still very much in "the air" and on the minds of our older relatives.

Today, most parents want their kids "safe at home," but Andy and I grew up in a time when our mothers would kick us out of the house promptly after breakfast, "allowed" us home for a quick lunch, and then promptly booted us out of the house again until the streets filled with the call of "dinner time" – yet after dinner we were told once again to "go out and play until the streetlights come on."

It was an era when we literally practiced in school how to "survive" the world-ending nuclear war we were told was imminent. Nobody's mother was giving out naturopathic remedies; for us, it was "eat your vegetables and go get some fresh air" or simply, "walk it off." We came into adolescence when divorce was, for the first time, *not* considered shameful; many of us had to find our way in the world as our parents drifted off on "self-actualization" journeys that didn't involve us at all. Because of that, concern about teen sex and even teen substance abuse was minimal. Many kids of our era didn't survive.

Here we have a coming of age tale set amidst all these forces, about battling inner demons so common to our generation, and ultimately finding our way through it all. Most of us who did find our way through did so by eventually seeing the wisdom in some of those boring and annoying "values" our parents actually did try to teach us: be honest, help others, work hard, show up on time.

I thank Andy for involving me in this project and am grateful to H.D. for her encouragement and support throughout the whole ordeal. We want this book to give hope to members of our generation that are still struggling. We hope it gives some solace and satisfaction to our parents. We'd love it if this inspires the younger generations behind us to put down their smartphones and video games and VR helmets and go get their hands dirty … go get lost in the woods for the better part of a day once in a while. It'll do you'se good!

- Jeff Muir
August, 2018